Harry Potter
AND THE PRISONER OF AZKABAN

J.K. ROWLING

3

英汉对照版

Harry Potter

哈利·波特
与阿兹卡班囚徒

〔英〕J.K. 罗琳 / 著
马爱农 马爱新 / 译

著作权合同登记号　图字　01-2024-1019

Harry Potter and the Prisoner of Azkaban
First published in Great Britain in 1999 by Bloomsbury Publishing Plc.
Text © 1999 by J.K. Rowling
Interior illustrations by Mary GrandPré © 1999 by Warner Bros.
Wizarding World, Publishing and Theatrical Rights © J.K.Rowling
Wizarding World characters, names and related indicia are TM and © Warner Bros.Entertainment Inc.
Wizarding World TM & © Warner Bros.Entertainment Inc.
Cover illustrations by Mary GrandPré © 1999 by Warner Bros.

图书在版编目（CIP）数据

哈利·波特与阿兹卡班囚徒：英汉对照版/（英）J.K.罗琳著；马爱农，马爱新译．—北京：人民文学出版社，2018（2025.9重印）
ISBN 978-7-02-014183-8

Ⅰ.①哈… Ⅱ.①J…②马…③马… Ⅲ.①儿童小说—长篇小说—英国—现代—英、汉 Ⅳ.①I561.84

中国版本图书馆CIP数据核字（2018）第246406号

责任编辑　翟　灿
美术编辑　刘　静
责任印制　苏文强

出版发行　人民文学出版社
社　　址　北京市朝内大街166号
邮政编码　100705

印　　刷　三河市龙林印务有限公司
经　　销　全国新华书店等

字　　数　916千字
开　　本　640毫米×960毫米　1/16
印　　张　39.5　插页3
印　　数　198001—208000
版　　次　2019年4月北京第1版
印　　次　2025年9月第16次印刷

书　　号　978-7-02-014183-8
定　　价　78.00元

如有印装质量问题，请与本社图书销售中心调换。电话：010-59905336

To Jill Prewett and Aine Kiely,
the Godmothers of Swing

献　给
斯汶的教母
吉尔·普威特和艾妮·基利

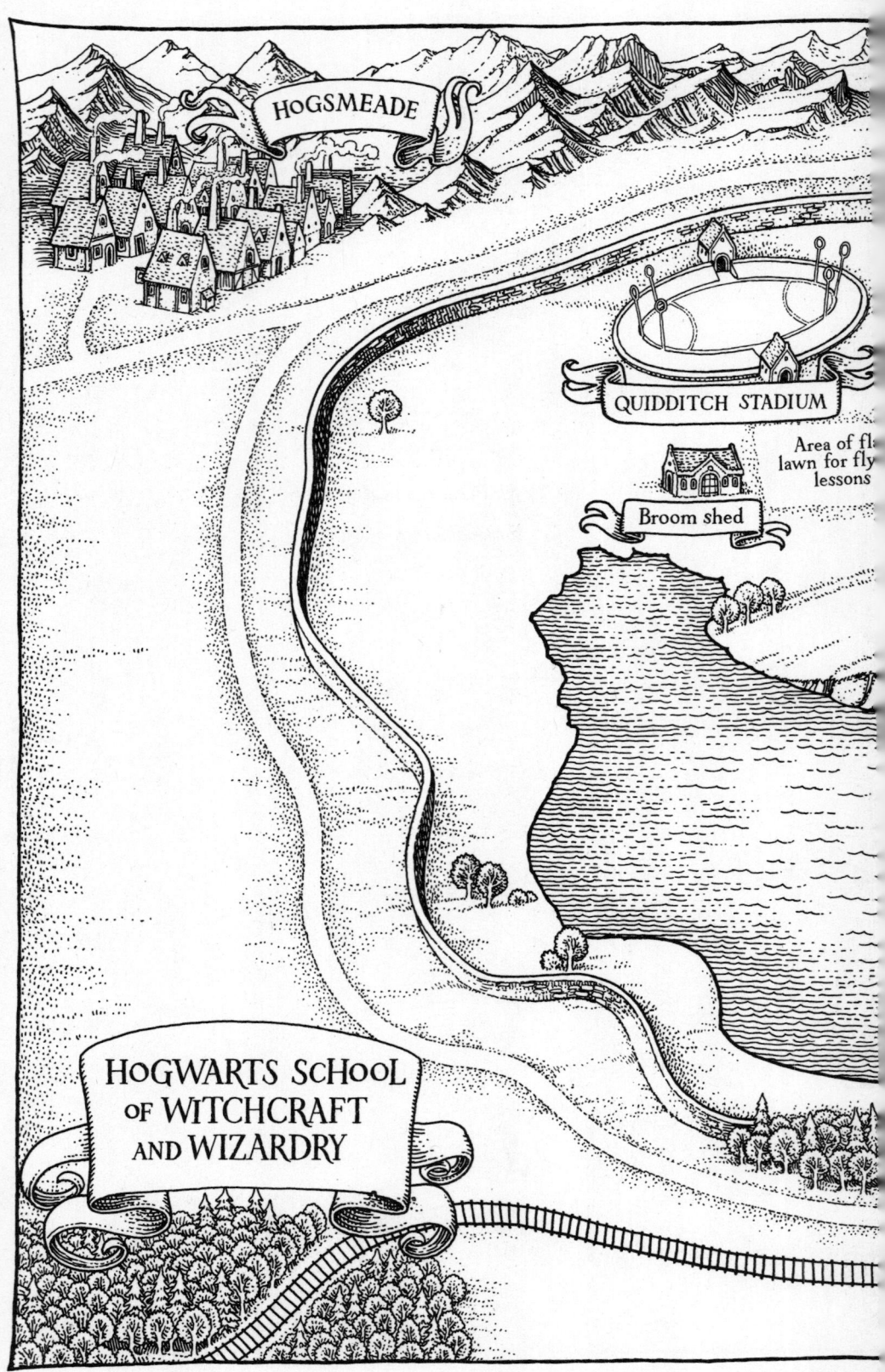

CONTENTS

CHAPTER ONE	Owl Post	006
CHAPTER TWO	Aunt Marge's Big Mistake	028
CHAPTER THREE	The Knight Bus	050
CHAPTER FOUR	The Leaky Cauldron	076
CHAPTER FIVE	The Dementor	106
CHAPTER SIX	Talons and Tea Leaves	144
CHAPTER SEVEN	The Boggart in the Wardrobe	182
CHAPTER EIGHT	Flight of the Fat Lady	208
CHAPTER NINE	Grim Defeat	238
CHAPTER TEN	The Marauder's Map	268
CHAPTER ELEVEN	The Firebolt	308
CHAPTER TWELVE	The Patronus	340
CHAPTER THIRTEEN	Gryffindor versus Ravenclaw	368
CHAPTER FOURTEEN	Snape's Grudge	392
CHAPTER FIFTEEN	The Quidditch Final	424
CHAPTER SIXTEEN	Professor Trelawney's Prediction	456
CHAPTER SEVENTEEN	Cat, Rat and Dog	482
CHAPTER EIGHTEEN	Moony, Wormtail, Padfoot and Prongs	506
CHAPTER NINETEEN	The Servant of Lord Voldemort	518
CHAPTER TWENTY	The Dementor's Kiss	548
CHAPTER TWENTY-ONE	Hermione's Secret	560
CHAPTER TWENTY-TWO	Owl Post Again	602

目　录

第 1 章　猫头鹰传书　　　　　　　　　　　007
第 2 章　玛姬姑妈的大错误　　　　　　　　029
第 3 章　骑士公共汽车　　　　　　　　　　051
第 4 章　破釜酒吧　　　　　　　　　　　　077
第 5 章　摄魂怪　　　　　　　　　　　　　107
第 6 章　鹰爪和茶叶　　　　　　　　　　　145
第 7 章　衣柜里的博格特　　　　　　　　　183
第 8 章　胖夫人逃跑　　　　　　　　　　　209
第 9 章　不祥的失败　　　　　　　　　　　239
第 10 章　活点地图　　　　　　　　　　　　269
第 11 章　火弩箭　　　　　　　　　　　　　309
第 12 章　守护神　　　　　　　　　　　　　341
第 13 章　格兰芬多对拉文克劳　　　　　　　369
第 14 章　斯内普怀恨在心　　　　　　　　　393
第 15 章　魁地奇决赛　　　　　　　　　　　425
第 16 章　特里劳尼教授的预言　　　　　　　457
第 17 章　猫、老鼠和狗　　　　　　　　　　483
第 18 章　月亮脸、虫尾巴、大脚板和尖头叉子　507
第 19 章　伏地魔的仆人　　　　　　　　　　519
第 20 章　摄魂怪的吻　　　　　　　　　　　549
第 21 章　赫敏的秘密　　　　　　　　　　　561
第 22 章　又见猫头鹰传书　　　　　　　　　603

CHAPTER ONE

Owl Post

Harry Potter was a highly unusual boy in many ways. For one thing, he hated the summer holidays more than any other time of year. For another, he really wanted to do his homework, but was forced to do it in secret, in the dead of night. And he also happened to be a wizard.

It was nearly midnight, and he was lying on his front in bed, the blankets drawn right over his head like a tent, a torch in one hand and a large leather-bound book (*A History of Magic*, by Bathilda Bagshot) propped open against the pillow. Harry moved the tip of his eagle-feather quill down the page, frowning as he looked for something that would help him write his essay, 'Witch-Burning in the Fourteenth Century Was Completely Pointless – discuss'.

The quill paused at the top of a likely-looking paragraph. Harry pushed his round glasses up his nose, moved his torch closer to the book and read:

> *Non-magic people (more commonly known as Muggles) were particularly afraid of magic in medieval times, but not very good at recognising it. On the rare occasion that they did catch a real witch or wizard, burning had no effect whatsoever. The witch or wizard would perform a basic Flame-Freezing Charm and then pretend to shriek with pain while enjoying a gentle, tickling sensation. Indeed, Wendelin the Weird enjoyed being burnt so much that she allowed herself to be caught no fewer than forty-seven times in various disguises.*

Harry put his quill between his teeth and reached underneath his pillow for his ink bottle and a roll of parchment. Slowly and very carefully he unscrewed the ink bottle, dipped his quill into it and began to write, pausing

第 1 章

猫头鹰传书

哈利·波特在许多方面都是个很不寻常的男孩。比如，他在一年里最讨厌暑假。再比如，他其实很想做家庭作业，却不得不在半夜三更偷偷地做。还有，他碰巧是一名巫师。

差不多午夜了，他俯身躺在床上，毯子拉上来盖过头顶，像支起一顶帐篷，一只手拿着手电筒，一本皮封面的大部头书（巴希达·巴沙特的《魔法史》）摊开了靠在枕头上。鹰羽毛笔在纸上移动，哈利皱着眉头，查找对他写论文有帮助的东西，论文题目是"十四世纪烧死女巫的做法完全是无稽之谈"。

羽毛笔停在一段看上去有点价值的内容上。哈利把圆框眼镜往鼻梁上推了推，让手电筒凑近书页，读道：

在中世纪，不会魔法的人（一般被称为麻瓜）特别害怕魔法，却对魔法缺乏足够的认识。偶尔，他们抓住一个真正的女巫或男巫，焚烧是根本没有用的。巫师只要施一个最基本的凝火咒，就可以一边假装痛苦地尖叫，一边美美地享受那麻酥酥的快感。怪人温德林太喜欢被焚烧的感觉了，她故意化装成各种样子，让人家把她抓住了至少四十七次。

哈利用牙齿咬住羽毛笔，伸手到枕头底下掏出墨水瓶和一卷羊皮纸。他慢慢地、小心翼翼地扭开墨水瓶盖，把羽毛笔放进去蘸了蘸，开始写了起来，并不时地停下来侧耳细听，因为如果德思礼家的谁起

CHAPTER ONE — Owl Post

every now and then to listen, because if any of the Dursleys heard the scratching of his quill on their way to the bathroom, he'd probably find himself locked in the cupboard under the stairs for the rest of the summer.

The Dursley family of number four, Privet Drive, was the reason that Harry never enjoyed his summer holidays. Uncle Vernon, Aunt Petunia and their son, Dudley, were Harry's only living relatives. They were Muggles, and they had a very medieval attitude towards magic. Harry's dead parents, who had been a witch and wizard themselves, were never mentioned under the Dursleys' roof. For years, Aunt Petunia and Uncle Vernon had hoped that if they kept Harry as downtrodden as possible, they would be able to squash the magic out of him. To their fury, they had been unsuccessful, and now lived in terror of anyone finding out that Harry had spent most of the last two years at Hogwarts School of Witchcraft and Wizardry. The most the Dursleys could do these days was to lock away Harry's spellbooks, wand, cauldron and broomstick at the start of the summer holidays, and forbid him to talk to the neighbours.

This separation from his spellbooks had been a real problem for Harry, because his teachers at Hogwarts had given him a lot of holiday work. One of the essays, a particularly nasty one about Shrinking Potions, was for Harry's least favourite teacher, Professor Snape, who would be delighted to have an excuse to give Harry detention for a month. Harry had therefore seized his chance in the first week of the holidays. While Uncle Vernon, Aunt Petunia and Dudley had gone out into the front garden to admire Uncle Vernon's new company car (in very loud voices, so that the rest of the street would notice it too), Harry had crept downstairs, picked the lock on the cupboard under the stairs, grabbed some of his books and hidden them in his bedroom. As long as he didn't leave spots of ink on the sheets, the Dursleys need never know that he was studying magic by night.

Harry was keen to avoid trouble with his aunt and uncle at the moment, as they were already in a bad mood with him, all because he'd received a telephone call from a fellow wizard one week into the school holidays.

Ron Weasley, who was one of Harry's best friends at Hogwarts, came from a whole family of wizards. This meant that he knew a lot of things Harry didn't, but had never used a telephone before. Most unluckily, it had been Uncle Vernon who had answered the call.

'Vernon Dursley speaking.'

第1章 猫头鹰传书

来上厕所时听见了他羽毛笔的沙沙声,恐怕他整个暑假都会被关在楼梯底下的储物间里了。

就是因为女贞路4号的德思礼一家,哈利从来没有好好享受过暑假的日子。弗农姨父、佩妮姨妈,还有他们的儿子达力,是哈利在世界上仅有的亲人。作为麻瓜,他们对魔法的态度很像中世纪的人。哈利已故的父母都是巫师,多少年来,从没有人在德思礼家提起过他们的名字。佩妮姨妈和弗农姨父曾经希望,只要尽量对哈利严加控制,就能把他身上的魔法挤压掉。然而他们没有成功,这使他们十分恼怒。这些日子,他们整天提心吊胆,生怕有人发现哈利最近两年是在霍格沃茨魔法学校读书。但他们所能做的,也就是在暑假一开始就把哈利的魔法书、魔杖、坩埚和飞天扫帚锁起来,并且不准哈利跟邻居说话。

对哈利来说,拿不到魔法书确实很成问题,因为霍格沃茨的老师们布置了一大堆假期作业。其中有一篇论文特别令人头疼,是关于缩身药水的,那是哈利最不喜欢的老师斯内普教授布置的。斯内普教授肯定巴不得哈利完不成,好有个借口来关他一个月的禁闭。因此,在暑假的第一个星期里,哈利抓住机会,趁弗农姨父、佩妮姨妈和达力到房子前面的花园里欣赏弗农姨父的公司给他新买的汽车(他们嚷嚷的声音很大,好让街上的人都能听到),哈利偷偷溜到楼下,撬开楼梯底下储物间的锁,抓出几本教科书,藏在了自己的卧室里。只要他不把墨水滴在床单上,德思礼一家就不会知道他在夜里偷学魔法。

眼下,哈利特别当心避免跟姨妈、姨父闹矛盾,他们已经对他的态度特别恶劣了,这都是因为在暑假的第一个星期他们接到了哈利巫师同伴的一个电话。

罗恩·韦斯莱是哈利在霍格沃茨最好的朋友之一,他家里的人全是巫师。也就是说,他知道许多哈利不知道的事情,但他以前从来没打过电话。最倒霉的是,那个电话偏偏是弗农姨父接的。

"我是弗农·德思礼。"

CHAPTER ONE Owl Post

Harry, who happened to be in the room at the time, froze as he heard Ron's voice answer.

'HELLO? HELLO? CAN YOU HEAR ME? I – WANT – TO – TALK – TO – HARRY – POTTER!'

Ron was yelling so loudly that Uncle Vernon jumped and held the receiver a foot away from his ear, staring at it with an expression of mingled fury and alarm.

'WHO IS THIS?' he roared in the direction of the mouthpiece. 'WHO ARE YOU?'

'RON – WEASLEY!' Ron bellowed back, as though he and Uncle Vernon were speaking from opposite ends of a football pitch. 'I'M – A – FRIEND – OF – HARRY'S – FROM – SCHOOL –'

Uncle Vernon's small eyes swivelled around to Harry, who was rooted to the spot.

'THERE IS NO HARRY POTTER HERE!' he roared, now holding the receiver at arm's length, as though frightened it might explode. 'I DON'T KNOW WHAT SCHOOL YOU'RE TALKING ABOUT! NEVER CONTACT ME AGAIN! DON'T YOU COME NEAR MY FAMILY!'

And he threw the receiver back onto the telephone as if dropping a poisonous spider.

The row that had followed had been one of the worst ever.

'HOW DARE YOU GIVE THIS NUMBER TO PEOPLE LIKE – PEOPLE LIKE *YOU*!' Uncle Vernon had roared, spraying Harry with spit.

Ron obviously realised that he'd got Harry into trouble, because he hadn't called again. Harry's other best friend from Hogwarts, Hermione Granger, hadn't been in touch either. Harry suspected that Ron had warned Hermione not to call, which was a pity, because Hermione, the cleverest witch in Harry's year, had Muggle parents, knew perfectly well how to use a telephone, and would probably have had enough sense not to say that she went to Hogwarts.

So Harry had had no word from any of his wizarding friends for five long weeks, and this summer was turning out to be almost as bad as the last one. There was just one, very small improvement: after swearing that he wouldn't use her to send letters to any of his friends, Harry had been allowed to let his owl, Hedwig, out at night. Uncle Vernon had given in because of the racket Hedwig made if she was locked in her cage all the time.

Harry finished writing about Wendelin the Weird and paused to listen

第1章 猫头鹰传书

哈利当时正好在房间里,听见电话那头传来罗恩的声音,顿时呆住了。

"喂?喂?你听得见吗?我——要——找——哈利——波特!"

罗恩嚷嚷的声音太响了,弗农姨父吓了一跳,把听筒举得离耳朵一尺远,又愤怒又惊恐地瞪着它。

"是谁?"他冲着话筒吼道,"你是谁?"

"罗恩——韦斯莱!"罗恩大声嚷着回答,就好像他和弗农姨父是隔着一整个足球场在喊话,"我是——哈利——学校里的——朋友——"

弗农姨父的小眼睛转过来瞪着僵在原地的哈利。

"这里没有哈利·波特!"他咆哮道,伸直手臂举着话筒,好像生怕它会爆炸,"我不知道你说的是什么学校!别再跟我联系!不许接近我的家人!"

他把听筒扔回电话上,好像甩掉了一只有毒的蜘蛛。

随之而来的争吵空前激烈。

"你竟敢把这个号码告诉——告诉跟你一样的人!"弗农姨父吼道,喷了哈利一脸唾沫。

罗恩显然意识到自己给哈利惹了祸,没再打过电话来。哈利在霍格沃茨的另一个好朋友赫敏·格兰杰也没有跟他联系。哈利怀疑是罗恩警告过赫敏别打电话,这真可惜,因为赫敏是哈利这个年级最聪明的女巫,父母都是麻瓜,她完全知道怎么打电话,而且大概也不会糊涂到说自己是霍格沃茨的学生。

所以,漫长的五个星期过去了,哈利没有得到巫师朋友的一丁点消息,看来这个暑假差不多跟去年暑假一样糟糕了,只有一点小小的改善——在哈利发誓不给朋友送信之后,弗农姨父总算允许他在夜里把猫头鹰海德薇放出去了。弗农姨父之所以让步,是因为海德薇一直被关在笼子里就会吵闹不休。

哈利写完怪人温德林的内容,又停下来听了听。漆黑的房子里静

CHAPTER ONE — Owl Post

again. The silence in the dark house was broken only by the distant, grunting snores of his enormous cousin, Dudley. It must be very late. Harry's eyes were itching with tiredness. Perhaps he'd finish this essay tomorrow night ...

He replaced the top of the ink bottle, pulled an old pillowcase from under his bed, put the torch, *A History of Magic*, his essay, quill and ink inside it, got out of bed and hid the lot under a loose floorboard under his bed. Then he stood up, stretched, and checked the time on the luminous alarm clock on his bedside table.

It was one o'clock in the morning. Harry's stomach gave a funny jolt. He had been thirteen years old, without realising it, for a whole hour.

Yet another unusual thing about Harry was how little he looked forward to his birthdays. He had never received a birthday card in his life. The Dursleys had completely ignored his last two birthdays, and he had no reason to suppose they would remember this one.

Harry walked across the dark room, past Hedwig's large, empty cage, to the open window. He leant on the sill, the cool night air pleasant on his face after a long time under the blankets. Hedwig had been absent for two nights now. Harry wasn't worried about her – she'd been gone this long before – but he hoped she'd be back soon. She was the only living creature in this house who didn't flinch at the sight of him.

Harry, though still rather small and skinny for his age, had grown a few inches over the last year. His jet-black hair, however, was just as it always had been: stubbornly untidy, whatever he did to it. The eyes behind his glasses were bright green, and on his forehead, clearly visible through his hair, was a thin scar, shaped like a bolt of lightning.

Of all the unusual things about Harry, this scar was the most extraordinary of all. It was not, as the Dursleys had pretended for ten years, a souvenir of the car crash that had killed Harry's parents, because Lily and James Potter had not died in a car crash. They had been murdered, murdered by the most feared Dark wizard for a hundred years, Lord Voldemort. Harry had escaped from the same attack with nothing more than a scar on his forehead, when Voldemort's curse, instead of killing him, had rebounded upon its originator. Barely alive, Voldemort had fled ...

But Harry had come face to face with him since at Hogwarts. Remembering their last meeting as he stood at the dark window, Harry had to admit he was lucky even to have reached his thirteenth birthday.

悄悄的,只有远处传来大块头表哥达力粗重的呼噜声。时间一定很晚了,哈利想。他的眼睛累得发痒。要不,还是明天夜里再把论文写完吧……

他把墨水瓶盖上,从床底下拖出一个旧枕头套,把手电筒、《魔法史》、他的论文、羽毛笔和墨水放了进去。他从床上下来,把那些东西藏在床底下一块松动的地板下。然后起身伸了个懒腰,看了看床头柜上的夜光闹钟。

深夜一点。哈利的心异样地跳了一下。不知不觉,他满十三岁已经整整一个小时了。

哈利还有一个与别的孩子不一样的地方,就是他不太盼着自己的生日。他从生下来到现在没有收到过一张生日贺卡。前两年他过生日的时候,德思礼一家根本不闻不问,他没有理由指望他们能记得今年的生日。

哈利穿过黑乎乎的屋子,经过海德薇空空的大鸟笼,来到敞开的窗口。他靠在窗台上,刚才在被子下待了那么久,此刻清凉的晚风拂在脸上真是舒服。海德薇已经两个晚上没有回来了。哈利并不为它担心。它以前也曾出去过这么久。但是哈利希望它能很快回来,这个家里的所有活物,只有海德薇看见哈利不会皱眉头。

相对同龄人来说,哈利长得又瘦又小,但这一年里他也长高了几英寸。不过,漆黑的头发还和以前一样——不管他怎么鼓捣,都乱糟糟的不肯服帖;镜片后面的眼睛绿莹莹的,额头上的头发间,一道细细的伤疤清晰可见,形状像一道闪电。

在哈利所有的不寻常中,这道伤疤是最不同凡响的。它不像德思礼一家十年来所声称的那样,是那场导致哈利父母丧生的车祸留下的纪念,因为莉莉和詹姆·波特并不是死于车祸。他们是被杀害的,是被一百年来最可怕的黑巫师伏地魔杀害的。哈利从那次袭击中死里逃生,只在额头上留下一道伤疤。伏地魔的咒语没有杀死哈利,而是反弹到自己身上。伏地魔不死不活,逃跑了……

可是,哈利在霍格沃茨又跟伏地魔碰上了。哈利站在黑黢黢的窗口,回忆着他们的上一次交锋,不得不承认他能活到十三岁生日真算是幸运了。

CHAPTER ONE Owl Post

He scanned the starry sky for a sign of Hedwig, perhaps soaring back to him with a dead mouse dangling from her beak, expecting praise. Gazing absently over the rooftops, it was a few seconds before Harry realised what he was seeing.

Silhouetted against the golden moon, and growing larger every moment, was a large, strangely lop-sided creature, and it was flapping in Harry's direction. He stood quite still, watching it sink lower and lower. For a split second, he hesitated, his hand on the window-latch, wondering whether to slam it shut, but then the bizarre creature soared over one of the street lamps of Privet Drive, and Harry, realising what it was, leapt aside.

Through the window soared three owls, two of them holding up the third, which appeared to be unconscious. They landed with a soft *flump* on Harry's bed, and the middle owl, which was large and grey, keeled right over and lay motionless. There was a large package tied to its legs.

Harry recognised the unconscious owl at once – his name was Errol, and he belonged to the Weasley family. Harry dashed to the bed at once, untied the cords around Errol's legs, took off the parcel and then carried Errol to Hedwig's cage. Errol opened one bleary eye, gave a feeble hoot of thanks, and began to gulp some water.

Harry turned back to the remaining owls. One of them, the large snowy female, was his own Hedwig. She, too, was carrying a parcel, and looked extremely pleased with herself. She gave Harry an affectionate nip with her beak as he removed her burden, then flew across the room to join Errol.

Harry didn't recognise the third owl, a handsome tawny one, but he knew at once where it had come from, because in addition to a third parcel, it was carrying a letter bearing the Hogwarts crest. When Harry relieved this owl of its post it ruffled its feathers importantly, stretched its wings and took off through the window into the night.

Harry sat down on his bed, grabbed Errol's package, ripped off the brown paper and discovered a present wrapped in gold, and his first ever birthday card. Fingers trembling slightly, he opened the envelope. Two pieces of paper fell out – a letter and a newspaper cutting.

The cutting had clearly come out of the wizarding newspaper, the *Daily Prophet*, because the people in the black and white picture were moving. Harry picked up the cutting, smoothed it out and read:

第1章　猫头鹰传书

　　他扫视着群星璀璨的天空，寻找海德薇的身影，也许海德薇会嘴里叼着一只死老鼠朝他飞来，期待他的表扬。哈利漫不经心地扫视着那些屋顶，过了几秒钟才意识到自己看见了什么。

　　在金黄色月亮的衬托下，有个大活物奇怪地歪着身子、扇动着翅膀朝哈利这边飞来，越来越大。哈利一动不动地站着，注视着它渐渐降落。哈利的手放在窗户插销上，有过片刻的迟疑，不知道是否要把窗户关上。接着，那个怪家伙从女贞路的一盏路灯上方掠过。哈利认出来了，赶紧闪到一旁。

　　三只猫头鹰从窗口飞了进来，其中两只托着第三只，它看上去已经失去了知觉。它们扑嗒一声落在哈利床上，中间那只灰色的大猫头鹰立刻倒了下去，一动不动，它的腿上绑着一个大包裹。

　　哈利一眼认出了那只昏迷不醒的猫头鹰——它名叫埃罗尔，是韦斯莱家的。哈利冲到床边，解开埃罗尔腿上的绳子，拿下包裹，把埃罗尔抱到了海德薇的笼子里。埃罗尔睁开一只视线模糊的眼睛，无力地叫了一声表示感谢，便大口喝起水来。

　　哈利转向另外两只猫头鹰。那只又大又白的母猫头鹰正是他的海德薇。它也带着一个包裹，露出一副扬扬自得的神情。哈利去解包裹的时候，海德薇亲热地用嘴啄了他一下，然后就飞到屋子那头找埃罗尔去了。

　　哈利没有认出第三只猫头鹰，这是一只挺漂亮的棕褐色猫头鹰，不过哈利立刻就知道它是从哪儿来的了。除了第三个包裹外，它还带着一封盖有霍格沃茨饰章的信。哈利取下这只猫头鹰身上的东西，它煞有介事地抖抖羽毛，展开翅膀，从窗口飞到了外面的夜色中。

　　哈利坐在床边，抓起埃罗尔的那个包裹，撕开包装纸，发现里面是一个金纸包着的礼物，还有他平生收到的第一张生日贺卡。他手指微微颤抖着打开信封，从里面掉出两张纸——一封信和一张剪报。

　　剪报显然来自巫师报纸《预言家日报》，因为黑白照片上的人都在动。哈利拿起剪报，展开来读道：

CHAPTER ONE   Owl Post

MINISTRY OF MAGIC EMPLOYEE
SCOOPS GRAND PRIZE

Arthur Weasley, Head of the Misuse of Muggle Artefacts Office at the Ministry of Magic, has won the annual *Daily Prophet* Grand Prize Galleon Draw.

A delighted Mr Weasley told the *Daily Prophet,* 'We will be spending the gold on a summer holiday in Egypt, where our eldest son, Bill, works as a curse breaker for Gringotts Wizarding Bank.'

The Weasley family will be spending a month in Egypt, returning for the start of the new school year at Hogwarts, which five of the Weasley children currently attend.

Harry scanned the moving photograph, and a grin spread across his face as he saw all nine of the Weasleys waving furiously at him, standing in front of a large pyramid. Plump little Mrs Weasley, tall, balding Mr Weasley, six sons and one daughter, all (though the black and white picture didn't show it) with flaming red hair. Right in the middle of the picture was Ron, tall and gangling, with his pet rat Scabbers on his shoulder and his arm around his little sister, Ginny.

Harry couldn't think of anyone who deserved to win a large pile of gold more than the Weasleys, who were very nice and extremely poor. He picked up Ron's letter and unfolded it.

> Dear Harry,
> Happy birthday!
> Look, I'm really sorry about that telephone call. I hope the Muggles didn't give you a hard time. I asked Dad, and he reckons I shouldn't have shouted.
> It's brilliant here in Egypt. Bill's taken us round all the tombs and you wouldn't believe the curses those old Egyptian wizards put on them. Mum wouldn't let Ginny come in the last one. There were all these mutant skeletons in there, of Muggles who'd broken in and grown extra heads and stuff.
> I couldn't believe it when Dad won the Daily Prophet Draw. Seven hundred galleons! Most of it's gone on this holiday, but they're going to buy me a new wand for next year.

第1章 猫头鹰传书

魔法部职员赢得巨奖

魔法部禁止滥用麻瓜物品办公室主任亚瑟·韦斯莱赢得了一年一度的《预言家日报》大奖金加隆奖。

韦斯莱先生高兴地对《预言家日报》说:"我们准备用这笔钱到埃及去过暑假,我们的大儿子比尔在那里的古灵阁巫师银行当解咒员。"

韦斯莱一家将在埃及待一个月,于霍格沃茨新学年开始时返回,韦斯莱家的五个孩子目前正在该校就读。

哈利看了一眼活动照片,看见韦斯莱一家九个人站在一座巨大的金字塔前,正使劲地朝他挥手,他脸上不禁绽开了笑容。矮矮胖胖的韦斯莱夫人,高大、秃顶的韦斯莱先生,六个儿子和一个女儿,全都是(虽然黑白照片上显示不出来)一头火红的头发。瘦瘦高高、笨手笨脚的罗恩站在正中间,肩膀上趴着他的宠物老鼠斑斑,一只胳膊搂着他的妹妹金妮。

哈利觉得,没有谁比韦斯莱一家更有资格赢得一大堆金币了,他们非常善良,又十分贫穷。哈利捡起罗恩的信打开。

亲爱的哈利:

生日快乐!

唉,真对不起我打了那个电话。希望那些麻瓜没有为难你。我问过爸爸了,他认为我不应该大喊大叫。

埃及真是太神奇了。比尔带我们看了所有的古墓,古埃及巫师给古墓施的那些魔法,我说出来你也不会相信。妈妈不愿意让金妮进最后一个古墓。那里面许多奇形怪状的尸骨,都是闯进来的麻瓜,还长出了好几个脑袋什么的。

我真不敢相信爸爸赢得了《预言家日报》的大奖。七百个金加隆啊!大都花在这趟旅行上了,不过他们要给我买一根新魔杖开学用。

CHAPTER ONE Owl Post

Harry remembered only too well the occasion when Ron's old wand had snapped. It had happened when the car the two of them had been flying to Hogwarts had crashed into a tree in the school grounds.

> We'll be back about a week before term starts and we'll be going up to London to get my wand and our new books. Any chance of meeting you there?
> Don't let the Muggles get you down!
> Try and come to London,
> Ron
> PS: Percy's Head Boy. He got the letter last week.

Hary glanced back at the photograph. Percy, who was in his seventh and final year at Hogwarts, was looking particularly smug. He had pinned his Head Boy badge to the fez perched jauntily on top of his neat hair, his horn-rimmed glasses flashing in the Egyptian sun.

Harry now turned to his present and unwrapped it. Inside was what looked like a miniature glass spinning top. There was another note from Ron beneath it.

> Harry – this is a Pocket Sneakoscope. If there's someone untrustworthy around, it's supposed to light up and spin. Bill says it's rubbish sold for wizard tourists and isn't reliable, because it kept lighting up at dinner last night. But he didn't realise Fred and George had put beetles in his soup.
> Bye – Ron

Harry put the Pocket Sneakoscope on his bedside table, where it stood quite still, balanced on its point, reflecting the luminous hands of his clock. He looked at it happily for a few seconds, then picked up the parcel Hedwig had brought.

Inside this, too, there was a wrapped present, a card and a letter, this time from Hermione.

第1章 猫头鹰传书

哈利清楚地记得罗恩那根旧魔杖折断的情景。当时他们俩开着汽车飞向霍格沃茨,结果撞到了学校场地的一棵树上。

我们将在开学前大概一星期回来,然后去伦敦买我的新魔杖和我们的新课本。有希望在那里碰到你吗?

别让那些麻瓜弄得你不开心!

争取到伦敦来。

罗 恩

又及:珀西当上男生学生会主席了。他上星期接到了信。

哈利又看了一眼照片。在霍格沃茨七年级毕业班就读的珀西看上去特别踌躇满志。他一丝不乱的头发上戴着一顶漂亮的土耳其帽,学生会主席的徽章就别在帽子上,角质镜架的眼镜在埃及的阳光下闪闪发亮。

哈利转向他的礼物。他把礼物打开,里面是一个类似小玻璃陀螺的东西。它的下面又是一张罗恩的字条。

哈利——这是一个袖珍窥镜。如果周围有可疑的人,它就会发亮、旋转。比尔说这是卖给巫师游客的伪劣商品,不可靠,因为昨天吃晚饭的时候它一直亮个不停。比尔竟然没有发现弗雷德和乔治在他的汤里放了甲虫。

再见——

罗 恩

哈利把袖珍窥镜放在床头柜上,它安安静静地倒立着,映出闹钟上的夜光指针。哈利喜滋滋地看了几秒钟,又拿起海德薇带来的那个包裹。

里面也是一份包好的礼物,一张贺卡和一封信,是赫敏寄来的。

CHAPTER ONE Owl Post

Dear Harry,

Ron wrote to me and told me about his phone call to your Uncle Vernon. I do hope you're all right.

I'm on holiday in France at the moment and I didn't know how I was going to send this to you - what if they'd opened it at Customs? - but then Hedwig turned up! I think she wanted to make sure you got something for your birthday for a change. I bought your present by owl-order; there was an advertisement in the Daily Prophet (I've been getting it delivered, it's so good to keep up with what's going on in the wizarding world). Did you see that picture of Ron and his family a week ago? I bet he's learning loads, I'm really jealous -the ancient Egyptian wizards were fascinating.

There's some interesting local history of witchcraft here, too. I've rewritten my whole History of Magic essay to include some of the things I've found out. I hope it's not too long, it's two rolls of parchment more than Professor Binns asked for.

Ron says he's going to be in London in the last week of the holidays. Can you make it? Will your aunt and uncle let you come? I really hope you can. If not, I'll see you on the Hogwarts Express on September the first!

Love from

Hermione

P.S. Ron says Percy's Head Boy. I'll bet Percy's really pleased. Ron doesn't seem too happy about it.

Harry laughed again as he put Hermione's letter aside and picked up her present. It was very heavy. Knowing Hermione, he was sure it would be a large book full of very difficult spells – but it wasn't. His heart gave a huge bound as he ripped back the paper and saw a sleek black leather case with silver words stamped across it: *Broomstick Servicing Kit.*

'Wow, Hermione!' Harry whispered, unzipping the case to look inside.

There was a large jar of Fleetwood's High-Finish Handle Polish, a pair of gleaming silver Tail-Twig Clippers, a tiny brass compass to clip onto your broom for long journeys, and a *Handbook of Do-it-Yourself Broomcare.*

第1章 猫头鹰传书

亲爱的哈利：

　　罗恩写信跟我说了他给你弗农姨父打电话的事。希望你一切都好。

　　目前我在法国度假，正发愁怎么把这东西寄给你——如果海关打开检查怎么办呢？——没想到海德薇出现了！我认为它是为了确保你生日能收到点东西换换心情才来的。我是通过猫头鹰邮购给你买的礼物，《预言家日报》上登了广告（报纸每天都送来，能了解巫师界的最新情况真是太好了）。你看见一星期前罗恩和他家人的照片了吗？我猜他肯定学到了不少东西。我真嫉妒他啊——古埃及巫师是非常神奇的。

　　这里也有一些有趣的巫术地方史。我已经完成了魔法史的论文，把我在这里发现的东西都写了进去，希望不是太长——比宾斯教授要求的多了两卷羊皮纸。

　　罗恩说暑假最后一星期要去伦敦。你能去吗？你的姨妈和姨父会让你去吗？真希望你能去。如果不能，我们就九月一日在霍格沃茨特快列车上见吧！

赫敏致以问候

　　又及：罗恩说珀西当上了男生学生会主席。我猜珀西肯定特别开心。罗恩好像对此不太高兴。

　　哈利笑着把赫敏的信放到一旁，拿起她的礼物。很重。以他对赫敏的了解，他以为肯定是一本大厚书，里面全是艰深的咒语——没想到竟然不是。他撕开包装纸，心猛地跳了一下，看见了一个漂亮的黑皮匣子，上面印着银色的字：飞天扫帚护理工具箱。

　　"哇，赫敏！"哈利小声说，拉开匣子的拉链往里面看。

　　一大罐弗利特伍德速洁把手增光剂，一把亮闪闪的银质扫帚尾枝修剪刀，一个长途旅行时挂在扫帚上的黄铜小指南针，还有一本《飞天扫帚护理手册》。

CHAPTER ONE Owl Post

Apart from his friends, the thing that Harry missed most about Hogwarts was Quidditch, the most popular sport in the magical world – highly dangerous, very exciting and played on broomsticks. Harry happened to be a very good Quidditch player; he had been the youngest person in a century to be picked for one of the Hogwarts house teams. One of Harry's most prized possessions was his Nimbus Two Thousand racing broom.

Harry put the leather case aside and picked up his last parcel. He recognised the untidy scrawl on the brown paper at once: this was from Hagrid, the Hogwarts gamekeeper. He tore off the top layer of paper and glimpsed something green and leathery, but before he could unwrap it properly, the parcel gave a strange quiver, and whatever was inside it snapped loudly – as though it had jaws.

Harry froze. He knew that Hagrid would never send him anything dangerous on purpose, but then, Hagrid didn't have a normal person's view of what was dangerous. Hagrid had been known to befriend giant spiders, buy vicious, three-headed dogs from men in pubs and sneak illegal dragon eggs into his cabin.

Harry poked the parcel nervously. It snapped loudly again. Harry reached for the lamp on his bedside table, gripped it firmly in one hand and raised it over his head, ready to strike. Then he seized the rest of the wrapping paper in his other hand and pulled.

And out fell – a book. Harry just had time to register its handsome green cover, emblazoned with the golden title, *The Monster Book of Monsters*, before it flipped onto its edge and scuttled sideways along the bed like some weird crab.

'Uh oh,' Harry muttered.

The book toppled off the bed with a loud clunk and shuffled rapidly across the room. Harry followed it stealthily. The book was hiding in the dark space under his desk. Praying that the Dursleys were still fast asleep, Harry got down on his hands and knees and reached towards it.

'Ouch!'

The book snapped shut on his hand and then flapped past him, still scuttling on its covers. Harry scrambled around, threw himself forward and managed to flatten it. Uncle Vernon gave a loud, sleepy grunt in the room next door.

Hedwig and Errol watched interestedly as Harry clamped the struggling

第1章 猫头鹰传书

除了几位朋友,霍格沃茨最让哈利牵肠挂肚的就是魁地奇,这是魔法界最受人喜爱的一项运动——高度危险,极为刺激,是骑在飞天扫帚上的运动。哈利碰巧是个非常优秀的魁地奇球员;他是一个世纪以来被选入霍格沃茨学院队的年龄最小的队员。哈利最珍爱的东西之一就是他那把光轮2000飞天扫帚。

哈利把皮匣子放到一边,拿起最后一个包裹。他一眼就认出了包装纸上歪歪斜斜的笔迹,是霍格沃茨猎场看守海格写的。哈利撕开最上面一层纸,看见了一个绿莹莹的、类似皮革的东西。没等他完全拆开,包裹就开始异样地颤抖起来,且不管里面是什么,反正发出了响亮的咬东西的声音——就好像它有嘴巴似的。

哈利呆住了。他知道海格绝不会故意把危险的东西寄给他,但是,在什么东西危险的问题上,海格的看法同一般人不一样。大家都知道海格跟巨大的毒蜘蛛交朋友,在酒吧里从别人手里买下三个脑袋的恶狗,还把非法的火龙蛋偷偷弄进了他的小屋。

哈利战战兢兢地捅了捅包裹。它又发出咔咔咬东西的声音。哈利伸手拿过床头柜上的台灯,用一只手紧紧攥住,举过头顶,做好进攻的准备,然后用另一只手抓住剩下的包装纸,用力一扯。

掉出来了——是一本书。哈利刚来得及看清漂亮的绿封面上印着的金灿灿的书名:妖怪们的妖怪书,书就腾的一下立了起来,像某种古怪的螃蟹一样,横着身子在床上快速地爬行。

"啊呀。"哈利轻叫了一声。

砰!书重重地从床上摔下,又匆匆地朝房间那头爬去。哈利轻轻跟了过去。书躲在黑洞洞的书桌底下。哈利一边祈祷德思礼一家仍然睡得死死的,一边趴在地上,伸手去够书。

"哎哟!"

书猛地合在哈利手上,然后扑啦啦从他身旁飞过,仍然靠着封皮在地上匆匆走来走去。哈利赶紧转身,向前一扑,总算把它压住了。弗农姨父在隔壁房间里睡意蒙眬地大声咕哝了一句什么。

海德薇和埃罗尔饶有兴趣地看着哈利把拼命挣扎的书紧紧夹在怀

CHAPTER ONE Owl Post

book tightly in his arms, hurried to his chest of drawers and pulled out a belt, which he buckled tightly around it. *The Monster Book* shuddered angrily, but could no longer flap and snap, so Harry threw it down on the bed and reached for Hagrid's card.

> DEAR HARRY,
> HAPPY BIRTHDAY!
> THINK YOU MIGHT FIND THIS USEFUL FOR NEXT YEAR.
> WON'T SAY NO MORE HERE. TELL YOU WHEN I SEE YOU.
> HOPE THE MUGGLES ARE TREATING YOU RIGHT.
> ALL THE BEST,
> HAGRID

It struck Harry as ominous that Hagrid thought a biting book would come in useful, but he put up Hagrid's card next to Ron and Hermione's, grinning more broadly than ever. Now there was only the letter from Hogwarts left.

Noticing that it was rather thicker than usual, Harry slit open the envelope, pulled out the first page of parchment within and read:

> Dear Mr Potter,
>
> Please note that the new school year will begin on September the first. The Hogwarts Express will leave from King's Cross Station, platform nine and three-quarters, at eleven o'clock.
>
> Third-years are permitted to visit the village of Hogsmeade at certain weekends. Please give the enclosed permission form to your parent or guardian to sign.
>
> A list of books for next year is enclosed.
>
> Yours sincerely,
>
> *Professor M. Mcgonagall*
> Deputy Headmistress

Harry pulled out the Hogsmeade permission form and looked at it, no longer grinning. It would be wonderful to visit Hogsmeade at weekends; he knew it was an entirely wizarding village, and he had never set foot there. But how on earth was he going to persuade Uncle Vernon or Aunt Petunia to sign the form?

里，快步走到五斗橱前，抽出一条皮带，把书牢牢地捆住了。《妖怪书》愤怒地颤抖着，却再也不能扑闪和咬人了。哈利把它扔在床上，去拿海格的贺卡。

亲爱的哈利：

　　生日快乐！

　　我想你会发现下学期要用到这本书。这里不多说了，见面再谈。希望那些麻瓜待你不错。

　　祝一切好。

海　格

海格居然认为要用到一本会咬人的书，这使哈利有一种不祥的预感，他把海格的贺卡放在罗恩和赫敏的贺卡旁边，脸上的笑意更浓了。现在只剩下霍格沃茨的来信了。

哈利发现这封信比平常厚得多，他撕开信封，从里面抽出第一张羊皮纸，读道：

亲爱的波特先生：

　　请注意新学期是九月一日开学。霍格沃茨特快列车将于十一点钟从国王十字车站 $9\frac{3}{4}$ 站台出发。

　　三年级学生可允许在某些周末前往霍格莫德村。请把随信所附的许可表交给你的父母或监护人签字。

　　随信附上下学期的书单。

你忠实的
副校长麦格教授

哈利抽出霍格莫德许可表看着，脸上的笑容消失了。周末去霍格莫德多奇妙啊，他知道那个村子里全都是巫师，他还从来没有去过呢。但怎么可能说服弗农姨父或佩妮姨妈在表上签字呢？

CHAPTER ONE   Owl Post

He looked over at the alarm clock. It was now two o'clock in the morning.

Deciding that he'd worry about the Hogsmeade form when he woke up, Harry got back into bed and reached up to cross off another day on the chart he'd made for himself, counting down the days left until his return to Hogwarts. Then he took off his glasses and lay down, eyes open, facing his three birthday cards.

Extremely unusual though he was, at that moment Harry Potter felt just like everyone else: glad, for the first time in his life, that it was his birthday.

他看了看闹钟。已经是深夜两点了。

哈利决定等睡醒了再为霍格莫德许可表发愁,他回到床上,伸手在图表上又划掉了一天——这个图表是他自己做的,一天天倒数着回霍格沃茨的日子。然后,他摘掉眼镜,躺了下来,眼睛却还睁着,看着他的三张生日贺卡。

哈利·波特虽然十分不寻常,但这个时候,他的感觉跟别人一样——他平生第一次为自己的生日而高兴。

CHAPTER TWO

Aunt Marge's Big Mistake

Harry went down to breakfast next morning to find the three Dursleys already sitting around the kitchen table. They were watching a brand-new television, a welcome-home-for-the-summer present for Dudley, who had been complaining loudly about the long walk between the fridge and the television in the living room. Dudley had spent most of the summer in the kitchen, his piggy little eyes fixed on the screen and his five chins wobbling as he ate continually.

Harry sat down between Dudley and Uncle Vernon, a large, beefy man with very little neck and a lot of moustache. Far from wishing Harry a happy birthday, none of the Dursleys gave any sign that they had noticed Harry enter the room, but Harry was far too used to this to care. He helped himself to a piece of toast and then looked up at the newsreader on the television, who was halfway through a report on an escaped convict.

'... the public is warned that Black is armed and extremely dangerous. A special hotline has been set up, and any sighting of Black should be reported immediately.'

'No need to tell us *he's* no good,' snorted Uncle Vernon, staring over the top of his newspaper at the prisoner. 'Look at the state of him, the filthy layabout! Look at his hair!'

He shot a nasty look sideways at Harry, whose untidy hair had always been a source of great annoyance to Uncle Vernon. Compared to the man on the television, however, whose gaunt face was surrounded by a matted, elbow-length tangle, Harry felt very well groomed indeed.

The newsreader had reappeared.

'The Ministry of Agriculture and Fisheries will announce today –'

'Hang on!' barked Uncle Vernon, staring furiously at the newsreader. 'You

第 2 章

玛姬姑妈的大错误

第二天早晨,哈利下楼去吃早饭,发现德思礼一家三口已经围坐在厨房的餐桌旁。他们在看电视。这台崭新的电视机是欢迎达力回来过暑假送给他的礼物,因为他一直抱怨从冰箱走到客厅电视机前的距离太远。暑假里,达力大部分时间都待在厨房,一双小眼睛一动不动地盯着电视屏幕,嘴里吃个不停,五层厚的下巴一直在颤动。

哈利在达力和弗农姨父中间坐了下来。弗农姨父是个身材高大、粗壮的男人,脖子很短,留着一撮浓密的小胡子。德思礼家的人谁也没有祝哈利生日快乐,像是根本没有看见哈利进屋似的,好在哈利对此早已习惯,不在乎了。他自己动手拿了一片面包,抬头看着电视上的新闻广播员,那人正在念一篇报道,是关于某个在逃罪犯的。

"……提醒公众,布莱克持有武器,极端危险。现已开通一条专用热线,不管有谁看见布莱克都应立即报告。"

"不用说,他肯定是个坏蛋,"弗农姨父从报纸上方盯着那个罪犯,粗声粗气地说,"你看看他那副样子,十足一个下三烂!看看他的头发!"

他恶狠狠地扫了哈利一眼,哈利乱糟糟的头发一向令弗农姨父很恼火。电视上那个男人枯瘦憔悴的面孔周围是又脏又乱、纠结在一起的长发,哈利跟那个男人一比,觉得自己还算蛮整洁的。

新闻广播员又出现了。

"农业渔业部今天宣布——"

"慢着!"弗农姨父气愤地盯着新闻广播员,咆哮起来,"你还没

CHAPTER TWO   Aunt Marge's Big Mistake

didn't tell us where that maniac's escaped from! What use is that? Lunatic could be coming up the street right now!'

Aunt Petunia, who was bony and horse-faced, whipped around and peered intently out of the kitchen window. Harry knew Aunt Petunia would simply love to be the one to call the hotline number. She was the nosiest woman in the world and spent most of her life spying on her boring, law-abiding neighbours.

'When will they *learn*,' said Uncle Vernon, pounding the table with his large purple fist, 'that hanging's the only way to deal with these people?'

'Very true,' said Aunt Petunia, who was still squinting into next door's runner-beans.

Uncle Vernon drained his teacup, glanced at his watch and added, 'I'd better be off in a minute, Petunia, Marge's train gets in at ten.'

Harry, whose thoughts had been upstairs with the Broomstick Servicing Kit, was brought back to earth with an unpleasant bump.

'Aunt Marge?' he blurted out. 'Sh-*she*'s not coming here, is she?'

Aunt Marge was Uncle Vernon's sister. Even though she was not a blood relative of Harry's (whose mother had been Aunt Petunia's sister), he had been forced to call her 'Aunt' all his life. Aunt Marge lived in the country, in a house with a large garden, where she bred bulldogs. She didn't often stay in Privet Drive, because she couldn't bear to leave her precious dogs, but each of her visits stood out horribly vividly in Harry's mind.

At Dudley's fifth birthday party, Aunt Marge had whacked Harry around the shins with her walking stick to stop him beating Dudley at musical statues. A few years later, she had turned up at Christmas with a computerised robot for Dudley and a box of dog biscuits for Harry. On her last visit, the year before Harry had started at Hogwarts, Harry had accidentally trodden on the paw of her favourite dog. Ripper had chased Harry out into the garden and up a tree, and Aunt Marge had refused to call him off until past midnight. The memory of this incident still brought tears of laughter to Dudley's eyes.

'Marge'll be here for a week,' Uncle Vernon snarled, 'and while we're on the subject,' he pointed a fat finger threateningly at Harry, 'we need to get a few things straight before I go and collect her.'

Dudley smirked and withdrew his gaze from the television. Watching Harry

第2章 玛姬姑妈的大错误

告诉我们那个疯子是从哪儿逃出来的！那有什么用？如今疯子随时都会跑到大街上来！"

佩妮姨妈骨瘦如柴，长着一张马脸。这时她快步走来，热切地盯着厨房的窗户外面。哈利知道佩妮姨妈巴不得成为那个打热线电话的人。她是世界上最爱管闲事的女人，一辈子大部分时间都在刺探那些乏味的、遵纪守法的邻居们。

"他们什么时候才会懂得，"弗农姨父用紫色的大拳头捶着桌子，说道，"对付那些人的唯一办法就是把他们吊死！"

"太对了。"佩妮姨妈说，仍然眯着眼睛打量着隔壁家的红花四季豆。

弗农姨父一口喝干杯里的茶，看了看表，又说："佩妮，我最好马上动身，玛姬的火车十点钟进站。"

哈利一直想着楼上的飞天扫帚护理工具箱，这时像是被猛击了一下，突然回到了现实中。

"玛姬姑妈？"他脱口而出，"她——她该不是要来这儿吧？"

玛姬姑妈是弗农姨父的姐姐。尽管她跟哈利没有血缘关系（哈利的妈妈是佩妮姨妈的妹妹），但哈利一直被迫叫她"姑妈"。玛姬姑妈住在乡下一座带大花园的房子里，养了许多条牛头犬。她并不经常住在女贞路，因为舍不得离开她那些宝贝狗，但每次来访都给哈利留下了恐怖的印象，至今记忆犹新。

在达力五岁生日的宴会上，玛姬姑妈用拐杖狠敲哈利的小腿，不让他在音乐定格游戏中胜过达力。几年后，她在圣诞节时出现，给达力带来一个电脑控制的机器人，送给哈利的却是一盒狗粮饼干。最后一次是哈利去霍格沃茨的前一年，哈利不小心踩了她那条宝贝狗利皮的爪子，被那狗追得跑到外面的花园里，爬上了一棵树，玛姬姑妈过了半夜才把狗叫回去。直到今天，达力一想起这件事，仍然笑得眼泪都要流出来。

"玛姬要在这里待一个星期。"弗农姨父咆哮着说，"既然我们谈到这个话题，"他恶狠狠地用一根肥胖的手指戳着哈利，"在我去接她之前，有几件事我们需要先说清楚。"

达力得意地傻笑起来，把目光从电视机上收了回来。看着爸爸教

CHAPTER TWO   Aunt Marge's Big Mistake

being bullied by Uncle Vernon was Dudley's favourite form of entertainment.

'Firstly,' growled Uncle Vernon, 'you'll keep a civil tongue in your head when you're talking to Marge.'

'All right,' said Harry bitterly, 'if she does when she's talking to me.'

'Secondly,' said Uncle Vernon, acting as though he had not heard Harry's reply, 'as Marge doesn't know anything about your *abnormality*, I don't want any – any *funny* stuff while she's here. You behave yourself, got me?'

'I will if she does,' said Harry through gritted teeth.

'And thirdly,' said Uncle Vernon, his mean little eyes now slits in his great purple face, 'we've told Marge you attend St Brutus's Secure Centre for Incurably Criminal Boys.'

'*What?*' Harry yelled.

'And you'll be sticking to that story, boy, or there'll be trouble,' spat Uncle Vernon.

Harry sat there, white-faced and furious, staring at Uncle Vernon, hardly able to believe it. Aunt Marge coming for a week-long visit – it was the worst birthday present the Dursleys had ever given him, including that pair of Uncle Vernon's old socks.

'Well, Petunia,' said Uncle Vernon, getting heavily to his feet, 'I'll be off to the station, then. Want to come along for the ride, Dudders?'

'No,' said Dudley, whose attention had returned to the television now that Uncle Vernon had finished threatening Harry.

'Duddy's got to make himself smart for his auntie,' said Aunt Petunia, smoothing Dudley's thick blond hair. 'Mummy's bought him a lovely new bow-tie.'

Uncle Vernon clapped Dudley on his porky shoulder.

'See you in a bit, then,' he said, and he left the kitchen.

Harry, who had been sitting in a kind of horrified trance, had a sudden idea. Abandoning his toast, he got quickly to his feet and followed Uncle Vernon to the front door.

Uncle Vernon was pulling on his car coat.

'I'm not taking *you*,' he snarled, as he turned to see Harry watching him.

'Like I wanted to come,' said Harry coldly. 'I want to ask you something.'

Uncle Vernon eyed him suspiciously.

'Third-years at Hog– at my school are allowed to visit the village

第2章 玛姬姑妈的大错误

训哈利,是达力最喜欢的一项娱乐。

"第一,"弗农姨父吼道,"你对玛姬说话时,必须记住使用礼貌用语。"

"没问题,"哈利没好气地说,"只要她对我说话能做到这点。"

"第二,"弗农姨父就像没听见哈利的回答似的,继续说道,"玛姬对你的那些怪异之处一无所知,我不希望她在这里时出现任何——任何奇怪的事情。你必须规规矩矩,明白吗?"

"只要她能做到,我就能。"哈利从紧咬的牙缝里说。

"第三,"弗农姨父难看的小眼睛在紫色大脸膛上眯成了一道缝,"我们已经告诉玛姬,你进了圣布鲁斯安全中心少年犯学校。"

"什么?"哈利嚷了起来。

"小子,你也要咬住这种说法,不然有你好看。"弗农姨父厉声吼道。

哈利坐在那里,脸色煞白,怒火中烧。他盯着弗农姨父,简直不敢相信他说的话。玛姬姑妈要来住一个星期——这是德思礼一家送给他的最糟糕的生日礼物,就连弗农姨父的那双旧袜子也没这么糟糕。

"好了,佩妮,"弗农姨父说着,笨重地站了起来,"我去车站了。达达,想不想跟我一起出去兜兜风?"

"不想。"达力说,看到爸爸已经教训完哈利,他的注意力又转回到电视上。

"达达要把自己打扮得漂亮些,迎接他的姑妈呢。"佩妮姨妈用手梳理着达力浓密的金黄色头发,说道,"妈妈给你新买了一个漂亮的领结。"

弗农姨父拍了拍达力肉乎乎的肩膀。

"那就过会儿见。"他说完就离开了厨房。

哈利像是被吓傻了似的,呆呆地坐在那里。突然他灵机一动,想出了一个主意。他扔下面包,迅速站起来,跟着弗农姨父走到前门。

弗农姨父正在穿便装短大衣。

"我不带你去。"他一转身,看见哈利正注视着他,便没好气地吼道。

"我才不想去呢。"哈利冷冷地说,"我想问你点事。"

弗农姨父怀疑地打量着他。

"在霍格……在我们学校,三年级学生可以偶尔到村子里去。"哈

CHAPTER TWO   Aunt Marge's Big Mistake

sometimes,' said Harry.

'So?' snapped Uncle Vernon, taking his car keys from a hook next to the door.

'I need you to sign the permission form,' said Harry in a rush.

'And why should I do that?' sneered Uncle Vernon.

'Well,' said Harry, choosing his words carefully, 'it'll be hard work, pretending to Aunt Marge I go to that St Whatsits ...'

'St Brutus's Secure Centre for Incurably Criminal Boys!' bellowed Uncle Vernon, and Harry was pleased to hear a definite note of panic in Uncle Vernon's voice.

'Exactly,' said Harry, looking calmly up into Uncle Vernon's large, purple face. 'It's a lot to remember. I'll have to make it sound convincing, won't I? What if I accidentally let something slip?'

'*You'll get the stuffing knocked out of you, won't you?*' roared Uncle Vernon, advancing on Harry with his fist raised. But Harry stood his ground.

'Knocking the stuffing out of me won't make Aunt Marge forget what I could tell her,' he said grimly.

Uncle Vernon stopped, his fist still raised, his face an ugly puce.

'But if you sign my permission form,' Harry went on quickly, 'I swear I'll remember where I'm supposed to go to school, and I'll act like a Mug— like I'm normal and everything.'

Harry could tell that Uncle Vernon was thinking it over, even if his teeth were bared and a vein was throbbing in his temple.

'Right,' he snapped finally. 'I shall monitor your behaviour carefully during Marge's visit. If, at the end of it, you've toed the line and kept to the story, I'll sign your ruddy form.'

He wheeled around, pulled open the front door and slammed it so hard that one of the little panes of glass at the top fell out.

Harry didn't return to the kitchen. He went back upstairs to his bedroom. If he was going to act like a real Muggle, he'd better start now. Slowly and sadly he gathered up all his presents and his birthday cards and hid them under the loose floorboard with his homework. Then he went to Hedwig's cage. Errol seemed to have recovered; he and Hedwig were both asleep, heads under their wings. Harry sighed, then poked them

第 2 章　玛姬姑妈的大错误

利说。

"那又怎么样？"弗农姨父厉声问，从门边的挂钩上取下汽车钥匙。

"我需要你在许可表上签字。"哈利一口气说道。

"我凭什么那么做？"弗农姨父冷笑着说。

"这样的话，"哈利小心地斟词酌句，"那就难了，我是说骗玛姬姑妈我上的是那所圣什么什么……"

"圣布鲁斯安全中心少年犯学校！"弗农姨父吼道，哈利高兴地听见弗农姨父语气里透出明显的紧张。

"对极了，"哈利平静地抬头望着弗农姨父那张酱紫色的大脸，"记起来挺费劲儿的。我还要让它听起来真像那么回事儿似的，对吗？万一我不小心说漏了嘴呢？"

"我会把你的肠子都揍出来，知道吗？"弗农姨父吼道，举起拳头朝哈利逼来。但是哈利没有退缩。

"把我的肠子揍出来，玛姬姑妈也不会忘记我想告诉她的话。"他一字一顿地说。

弗农姨父怔住了，拳头仍然举着，脸变成了一种难堪的紫褐色。

"不过，如果你肯在我的许可表上签字的话，"哈利一口气接着往下说，"我发誓我会记住我应该在哪里上学，我会表现得像个麻……像个正常人一样。"

哈利看得出来，弗农姨父脑子里在盘算，尽管他龇着牙，太阳穴上的血管在突突跳动。

"好吧，"最后他气冲冲地说，"在玛姬来访期间，我要好好监视你的一举一动。如果最后证明你一直循规蹈矩，没有把话说漏，我就给你签那张该死的许可表。"

他一转身，拉开前门走了出去，重重地把门关上。他使的劲儿太大，门顶上的一小块玻璃被震得掉了下来。

哈利没有再回厨房。他上楼走进自己的卧室。既然要装成一个真正的麻瓜，最好现在就开始行动。他闷闷不乐地把所有的礼物和生日贺卡慢慢收拢起来，跟他的家庭作业一起，藏在那块松动的地板下。然后走向海德薇的笼子。埃罗尔看上去已经恢复了，和海德薇一起睡

CHAPTER TWO   Aunt Marge's Big Mistake

both awake.

'Hedwig,' he said gloomily, 'you're going to have to clear off for a week. Go with Errol, Ron'll look after you. I'll write him a note, explaining. And don't look at me like that' – Hedwig's large amber eyes were reproachful, 'it's not my fault. It's the only way I'll be allowed to visit Hogsmeade with Ron and Hermione.'

Ten minutes later, Errol and Hedwig (who had a note to Ron bound to her leg) soared out of the window and out of sight. Harry, now feeling thoroughly miserable, put the empty cage away inside the wardrobe.

But Harry didn't have long to brood. In next to no time, Aunt Petunia was shrieking up the stairs for Harry to come down and get ready to welcome their guest.

'Do something about your hair!' Aunt Petunia snapped as he reached the hall.

Harry couldn't see the point of trying to make his hair lie flat. Aunt Marge loved criticising him, so the untidier he looked, the happier she would be.

All too soon, there was a crunch of gravel outside as Uncle Vernon's car pulled back into the driveway, then the clunk of the car doors, and footsteps on the garden path.

'Get the door!' Aunt Petunia hissed at Harry.

A feeling of great gloom in his stomach, Harry pulled the door open.

On the threshold stood Aunt Marge. She was very like Uncle Vernon; large, beefy and purple-faced, she even had a moustache, though not as bushy as his. In one hand she held an enormous suitcase, and tucked under the other was an old and evil-tempered bulldog.

'Where's my Dudders?' roared Aunt Marge. 'Where's my neffy poo?'

Dudley came waddling down the hall, his blond hair plastered flat to his fat head, a bow-tie just visible under his many chins. Aunt Marge thrust the suitcase into Harry's stomach, knocking the wind out of him, seized Dudley in a tight one-armed hug and planted a large kiss on his cheek.

Harry knew perfectly well that Dudley only put up with Aunt Marge's hugs because he was well paid for it, and sure enough, when they broke apart, Dudley had a crisp twenty-pound note clutched in his fat fist.

'Petunia!' shouted Aunt Marge, striding past Harry as though he was

第 2 章　玛姬姑妈的大错误

得正香,脑袋埋在翅膀里。哈利叹了口气,用指头把它们俩都捅醒了。

"海德薇,"他愁眉苦脸地说,"你必须出去避一个星期。跟埃罗尔一起去,罗恩会照顾你的。我给罗恩写一封短信,把事情跟他说清楚。别用那种眼光看着我,"——海德薇那双大大的琥珀色眼睛里满是责怪,"这不能怪我。只有这样,我才能跟罗恩和赫敏一起去霍格莫德村。"

十分钟后,埃罗尔和海德薇(腿上绑着一封给罗恩的短信)飞出窗外,消失不见了。哈利觉得心情低落到了极点,把空鸟笼藏在了衣柜里。

不过哈利并没有多少时间独自郁闷,很快,佩妮姨妈就朝楼上尖声嚷嚷起来,叫哈利下楼做好准备,迎接他们的客人。

"想办法收拾一下你的头发!"佩妮姨妈看见哈利走进大厅,气冲冲地说。

哈利看不出把头发弄平整有什么好处。玛姬姑妈最喜欢对他评头论足,他的模样越邋遢,玛姬姑妈就越高兴。

一眨眼工夫,外面就传来砾石被碾轧的嘎吱声,弗农姨父的汽车慢慢拐进了车道,然后车门砰砰关上,脚步踏着花园的小径走来。

"快到门口去!"佩妮姨妈压低声音对哈利说。

哈利垂头丧气地过去把门打开。

门口站着玛姬姑妈。她长得很像弗农姨父,身材高大、粗壮,酱紫色的脸膛,甚至也有一撮小胡子,只是不如弗农姨父的那么浓密。她一只手提着一个巨大的箱子,另一只手搂着一条坏脾气的老牛头犬。

"我的达达呢?"玛姬姑妈粗声大气地问,"我的乖侄儿呢?"

达力摇摇摆摆地走进门厅,金黄色的头发平塌塌地贴在胖脑袋上,一个蝴蝶形领结几乎被他那么多层下巴遮得看不见了。玛姬姑妈一把将箱子杵到哈利的肚子上,杵得哈利喘不过气来。然后她伸出一只胳膊紧紧搂住达力,在他面颊上使劲亲了一口。

哈利知道得很清楚,达力能够忍受玛姬姑妈的搂抱,只是因为他能得到丰厚的报偿。果然,他们分开时,达力的胖拳头里捏着一张崭新的二十英镑钞票。

"佩妮!"玛姬姑妈大声嚷嚷着,大步走过哈利身边,似乎只当他

CHAPTER TWO   Aunt Marge's Big Mistake

a hat-stand. Aunt Marge and Aunt Petunia kissed, or rather, Aunt Marge bumped her large jaw against Aunt Petunia's bony cheekbone.

Uncle Vernon now came in, smiling jovially as he shut the door.

'Tea, Marge?' he said. 'And what will Ripper take?'

'Ripper have some tea out of my saucer,' said Aunt Marge, as they all trooped into the kitchen, leaving Harry alone in the hall with the suitcase. But Harry wasn't complaining; any excuse not to be with Aunt Marge was fine by him, so he began to heave the case upstairs into the spare bedroom, taking as long as he could.

By the time he got back to the kitchen, Aunt Marge had been supplied with tea and fruitcake and Ripper was lapping noisily in the corner. Harry saw Aunt Petunia wince slightly as specks of tea and drool flecked her clean floor. Aunt Petunia hated animals.

'Who's looking after the other dogs, Marge?' Uncle Vernon asked.

'Oh, I've got Colonel Fubster managing them,' boomed Aunt Marge. 'He's retired now, good for him to have something to do. But I couldn't leave poor old Ripper. He pines if he's away from me.'

Ripper began to growl again as Harry sat down. This directed Aunt Marge's attention to Harry for the first time.

'So!' she barked. 'Still here, are you?'

'Yes,' said Harry.

'Don't you say "yes" in that ungrateful tone,' Aunt Marge growled. 'It's damn good of Vernon and Petunia to keep you. Wouldn't have done it myself. You'd have gone straight to an orphanage if you'd been dumped on *my* doorstep.'

Harry was bursting to say that he'd rather live in an orphanage than with the Dursleys, but the thought of the Hogsmeade form stopped him. He forced his face into a painful smile.

'Don't you smirk at me!' boomed Aunt Marge. 'I can see you haven't improved since I last saw you. I hoped school would knock some manners into you.' She took a large gulp of tea, wiped her moustache and said, 'Where is it that you send him, again, Vernon?'

'St Brutus's,' said Uncle Vernon promptly. 'It's a first-rate institution for hopeless cases.'

'I see,' said Aunt Marge. 'Do they use the cane at St Brutus's, boy?' she

第2章 玛姬姑妈的大错误

是个衣帽架。玛姬姑妈和佩妮姨妈互相亲吻,其实,是玛姬姑妈用她的大下巴重重地撞了一下佩妮姨妈干巴巴的瘦颧骨。

弗农姨父也进来了,脸上堆着愉快的笑容,把门关上了。

"喝点茶吧,玛姬?"他问,"利皮喝什么呢?"

"利皮就从我的茶碟里喝点茶好了。"玛姬姑妈说。他们鱼贯走进厨房,只留下哈利抱着箱子独自在门厅里。哈利正巴不得这样呢,只要有借口不跟玛姬姑妈待在一起就谢天谢地了。他开始慢慢地把箱子搬到楼上的客房,尽量拖延着时间。

等他回到厨房,玛姬姑妈面前已经摆上了茶和水果蛋糕,利皮正在墙角稀里呼噜地舔喝茶水。哈利看见佩妮姨妈微微皱起眉头,因为狗把茶水和口水溅到了她干净的地板上。佩妮姨妈不喜欢动物。

"别的那些狗由谁照料呢,玛姬?"弗农姨父问。

"噢,我请了法布斯特上校照看它们呢。"玛姬姑妈粗声大气地说,"他退休了,有点事情做做有好处。但我舍不得撇下可怜的老利皮。它离开我会憔悴的。"

哈利刚坐下,利皮又开始吼叫。这使玛姬姑妈的注意力第一次转向了哈利。

"怎么!"她吼了起来,"你还在这儿?"

"是啊。"哈利说。

"别用那种不知好歹的口气说'是啊',"玛姬姑妈咆哮起来,"弗农和佩妮能收留你就够好的了。换了我才不会这么做呢。当初如果他们把你扔在我家门口,你直接就去孤儿院了。"

哈利忍不住想说,他宁可住在孤儿院,也不愿跟德思礼家一起生活,但是想到去霍格莫德的许可表,他没有说话,脸上勉强挤出一丝苦笑。

"不许对我傻笑!"玛姬姑妈嚷道,"看得出来,从我上回看见你之后,你没有丝毫长进。我本来还指望上学能让你懂点规矩呢。"她喝了一大口茶,擦擦小胡子,接着说道:"弗农,你再说一遍,你把他送到哪儿去了?"

"圣布鲁斯,"弗农姨父马上接口,"是一流的少年犯学校。"

"知道了。"玛姬姑妈说,"圣布鲁斯那里用鞭子吗,小子?"她隔

CHAPTER TWO   Aunt Marge's Big Mistake

barked across the table.

'Er —'

Uncle Vernon nodded curtly behind Aunt Marge's back.

'Yes,' said Harry. Then, feeling he might as well do the thing properly, he added, 'All the time.'

'Excellent,' said Aunt Marge. 'I won't have this namby-pamby, wishy-washy nonsense about not hitting people who deserve it. A good thrashing is what's needed in ninety-nine cases out of a hundred. Have *you* been beaten often?'

'Oh, yeah,' said Harry, 'loads of times.'

Aunt Marge narrowed her eyes.

'I still don't like your tone, boy,' she said. 'If you can speak of your beatings in that casual way, they clearly aren't hitting you hard enough. Petunia, I'd write if I were you. Make it clear that you approve the use of extreme force in this boy's case.'

Perhaps Uncle Vernon was worried that Harry might forget their bargain; in any case, he changed the subject abruptly.

'Heard the news this morning, Marge? What about that escaped prisoner, eh?'

* * *

As Aunt Marge started to make herself at home, Harry caught himself thinking almost longingly of life at number four without her. Uncle Vernon and Aunt Petunia usually encouraged Harry to stay out of their way, which Harry was only too happy to do. Aunt Marge, on the other hand, wanted Harry under her eye at all times, so that she could boom out suggestions for his improvement. She delighted in comparing Harry with Dudley, and took huge pleasure in buying Dudley expensive presents while glaring at Harry, as though daring him to ask why he hadn't got a present too. She also kept throwing out dark hints about what made Harry such an unsatisfactory person.

'You mustn't blame yourself for the way the boy's turned out, Vernon,' she said over lunch on the third day. 'If there's something rotten on the *inside*, there's nothing anyone can do about it.'

Harry tried to concentrate on his food, but his hands shook and his face was starting to burn with anger. *Remember the form*, he told himself. *Think about Hogsmeade. Don't say anything. Don't rise —*

第 2 章 玛姬姑妈的大错误

着桌子吼道。

"嗯——"

弗农姨父在玛姬姑妈身后微微点了点头。

"用的。"哈利说。接着,他觉得应该把事情做得到位一些,又补充道,"一直用的。"

"太好了,"玛姬姑妈说,"我可不愿听那一套磨磨唧唧的无聊的废话,什么不能体罚之类,有些人就是该打。在百分之九十九的情况下,一顿臭揍就能解决问题。你经常挨打吗?"

"是啊,"哈利说,"挨过许多次呢。"

玛姬姑妈眯起了眼睛。

"我还是不喜欢你这副口气,小子。"她说,"你能这样轻描淡写地谈到你挨打的事,显然他们打你打得还不够狠。佩妮,如果我是你就会给他们写信,表明你赞成对这个男孩使用绝对的暴力。"

弗农姨父大概担心哈利会忘记他们之间的协定,他匆忙改变了话题。

"听了今天早晨的新闻吗,玛姬?那个在逃犯是怎么回事,嗯?"

玛姬姑妈舒舒服服地住了下来,就像在自己家里一样,哈利发现自己几乎怀念起了女贞路4号没有玛姬姑妈时的生活。弗农姨父和佩妮姨妈一般都想方设法不让哈利跟他们在一起,哈利也巴不得这样。可是,玛姬姑妈却希望哈利每时每刻都在她眼皮底下,这样她就能粗声恶气地给哈利提出改进的建议。她喜欢拿哈利跟达力作比较,最大的乐趣就是一边给达力买一些贵重的礼物,一边恶狠狠地瞪着哈利,似乎是在看哈利敢不敢问怎么没有他的份。她还经常含沙射影地暗示哈利为什么会成为这样一个没出息的人。

"弗农,这孩子变成这样,你千万别自责。"她在第三天吃午饭的时候这样说,"如果骨子里的东西坏了,谁也拿这没办法。"

哈利使劲把注意力集中在吃饭上,但还是忍不住双手发抖,怒火直往脸上烧。别忘了许可表,他对自己说,想想霍格莫德。什么也别说。别起身——

CHAPTER TWO   Aunt Marge's Big Mistake

Aunt Marge reached for her glass of wine.

'It's one of the basic rules of breeding,' she said. 'You see it all the time with dogs. If there's something wrong with the bitch, there'll be something wrong with the pup –'

At that moment, the wine glass Aunt Marge was holding exploded in her hand. Shards of glass flew in every direction and Aunt Marge spluttered and blinked, her great ruddy face dripping.

'Marge!' squealed Aunt Petunia. 'Marge, are you all right?'

'Not to worry,' grunted Aunt Marge, mopping her face with her napkin. 'Must have squeezed it too hard. Did the same thing at Colonel Fubster's the other day. No need to fuss, Petunia, I have a very firm grip ...'

But Aunt Petunia and Uncle Vernon were both looking at Harry suspiciously, so he decided he'd better skip pudding and escape from the table as soon as he could.

Outside in the hall, he leant against the wall, breathing deeply. It had been a long time since he'd lost control and made something explode. He couldn't afford to let it happen again. The Hogsmeade form wasn't the only thing at stake – if he carried on like that, he'd be in trouble with the Ministry of Magic.

Harry was still an underage wizard, and he was forbidden by wizard law to do magic outside school. His record wasn't exactly clean, either. Only last summer he'd got an official warning which had stated quite clearly that if the Ministry got wind of any more magic in Privet Drive, Harry would face expulsion from Hogwarts.

He heard the Dursleys leaving the table and hurried upstairs out of the way.

Harry got through the next three days by forcing himself to think about his *Handbook of Do-it-Yourself Broomcare* whenever Aunt Marge started on him. This worked quite well, though it seemed to give him a glazed look, because Aunt Marge started voicing the opinion that he was mentally subnormal.

At last, at long last, the final evening of Marge's stay arrived. Aunt Petunia cooked a fancy dinner and Uncle Vernon uncorked several bottles of wine. They got all the way through the soup and the salmon without a single mention of Harry's faults; during the lemon meringue pie, Uncle Vernon

第 2 章 玛姬姑妈的大错误

玛姬姑妈伸手去拿她的酒杯。

"这是遗传的一个基本法则,"她说,"在狗的身上经常能看到。如果母狗有毛病,狗崽子肯定也好不到哪儿去——"

就在这时,玛姬姑妈手里的酒杯突然爆炸了,玻璃碎片四下迸溅。玛姬姑妈结结巴巴说不出话来,呆呆地眨巴着眼睛,酒从她肥胖的红脸膛上滴下来。

"玛姬!"佩妮姨妈尖叫道,"玛姬,你没事吧?"

"别担心,"玛姬姑妈嘟哝道,用餐巾擦了擦脸,"准是捏得太使劲了。那天在法布斯特上校家也出过这种事。不用大惊小怪,佩妮,我的手劲儿很大……"

但佩妮姨妈和弗农姨父都怀疑地看着哈利,于是,哈利决定不吃布丁了,尽可能赶快离开餐桌。

他来到外面的门厅里,靠在墙上,大口做着深呼吸。他已经很长时间没有失去自控,让东西爆炸了。再也不能让这种事情发生了。如果继续这样行事,泡汤的可不只是去霍格莫德的许可表,到时候恐怕魔法部都会来找他的麻烦。

哈利还是个未成年的巫师,根据巫师法的规定,他不得在校外使用魔法。况且,他的记录不够清白。就在去年夏天,他得到一个正式警告,明确指出如果魔法部再得知女贞路有人使用魔法,哈利就将被霍格沃茨学校开除。

他听见德思礼一家离开饭桌的声音,便赶紧上楼躲开了。

接下来的三天,每当玛姬姑妈开始向哈利发难,哈利就强迫自己去想那本《飞天扫帚护理手册》。这一招还挺管用,但似乎会使他眼神发呆,因为玛姬姑妈开始大声谈论他智力低下了。

谢天谢地,终于熬到了玛姬姑妈在这里的最后一个夜晚。佩妮姨妈精心准备了一顿丰盛的晚餐,弗农姨父开了几瓶红酒。大家吃吃喝喝,汤上来了,鲑鱼肉也上来了,还一直没有谁来挑哈利的毛病。在吃柠檬蛋白甜饼时,弗农姨父长篇大论地谈起了他那家制造钻头的公司——

CHAPTER TWO   Aunt Marge's Big Mistake

bored them all with a long talk about Grunnings, his drill-making company; then Aunt Petunia made coffee and Uncle Vernon brought out a bottle of brandy.

'Can I tempt you, Marge?'

Aunt Marge had already had rather a lot of wine. Her huge face was very red.

'Just a small one, then,' she chuckled. 'A bit more than that ... and a bit more ... that's the boy.'

Dudley was eating his fourth slice of pie. Aunt Petunia was sipping coffee with her little finger sticking out. Harry really wanted to disappear into his bedroom, but he met Uncle Vernon's angry little eyes and knew he would have to sit it out.

'Aah,' said Aunt Marge, smacking her lips and putting the empty brandy glass back down. 'Excellent nosh, Petunia. It's normally just a fry-up for me of an evening, with twelve dogs to look after ...' She burped richly and patted her great tweed stomach. 'Pardon me. But I do like to see a healthy-sized boy,' she went on, winking at Dudley. 'You'll be a proper-sized man, Dudders, like your father. Yes, I'll have a spot more brandy, Vernon ...

'Now, this one here −'

She jerked her head at Harry, who felt his stomach clench. *The Handbook*, he thought quickly.

'This one's got a mean, runty look about him. You get that with dogs. I had Colonel Fubster drown one last year. Ratty little thing it was. Weak. Underbred.'

Harry was trying to remember page twelve of his book: *A Charm to Cure Reluctant Reversers*.

'It all comes down to blood, as I was saying the other day. Bad blood will out. Now, I'm saying nothing against your family, Petunia' − she patted Aunt Petunia's bony hand with her shovel-like one, 'but your sister was a bad egg. They turn up in the best families. Then she ran off with a wastrel and here's the result right in front of us.'

Harry was staring at his plate, a funny ringing in his ears. *Grasp your broom firmly by the tail*, he thought. But he couldn't remember what came next. Aunt Marge's voice seemed to be boring into him like one of Uncle Vernon's drills.

'This Potter,' said Aunt Marge loudly, seizing the brandy bottle and

格朗宁公司,听得大家不胜其烦。之后,佩妮姨妈去煮咖啡,弗农姨父拿出了一瓶白兰地。

"喝一点吧,玛姬?"

玛姬姑妈已经喝了很多红酒,一张大脸膛涨得通红。

"那就只来一小杯吧,"她轻笑着说,"再加一点……再加一点……好。"

达力在吃他的第四块甜饼。佩妮姨妈翘着兰花指,一小口一小口地啜着咖啡。哈利真想赶紧离开这里,钻进自己的卧室,可是他撞上了弗农姨父小眼睛里射出的愤怒眼神,知道必须捺着性子熬到最后。

"啊哈,"玛姬姑妈说着,咂咂嘴唇,把喝空的白兰地酒杯放了下来,"真是一顿美餐,佩妮。平常我晚饭只吃一盘简单的油煎快菜,没办法,有十二条狗要照料呢……"她响亮地打了个饱嗝,拍拍穿着花呢衣服的大肚子,"请原谅。不过我真高兴看见一个健健康康的男孩子,"她朝达力眨眨眼睛,继续说道,"你会成为一个体格健壮的男子汉,达达,就像你爸爸一样。好吧,再来一点儿白兰地,弗农……"

"再看看这位——"

她把脑袋朝哈利一偏,哈利顿时觉得心里一紧。手册,他赶紧提醒自己。

"这位就是一副獐头鼠目的窝囊样儿。有些狗就是这样。我去年就让法布斯特上校淹死过一条。那条狗活像一只小老鼠,病病歪歪,发育不良。"

哈利拼命回忆书上的第十二页:治疗不愿倒转的扫帚的咒语。

"就像我那天说的,这都是遗传。坏的遗传迟早都会冒头。哎哟,佩妮,我可不是在说你们家人的坏话——"她用铁铲般的手拍了拍佩妮姨妈瘦骨嶙峋的手,"不过你那个妹妹真是个败类。有时候好人家也会出现这样的人。后来她又跟一个无赖私奔,其结果现在就坐在我们面前。"

哈利眼睛盯着盘子,耳朵里嗡嗡作响。紧紧抓住扫帚尾巴,他想。可下面是什么呢?他想不起来了。玛姬姑妈的声音就像弗农姨父的电钻一样,直往他的脑袋里钻。

"那个叫波特的家伙,"玛姬姑妈大声说,一边抓起白兰地酒瓶,

CHAPTER TWO Aunt Marge's Big Mistake

splashing more into her glass and over the tablecloth, 'you never told me what he did?'

Uncle Vernon and Aunt Petunia were looking extremely tense. Dudley had even looked up from his pie to gape at his parents.

'He – didn't work,' said Uncle Vernon, with half a glance at Harry. 'Unemployed.'

'As I expected!' said Aunt Marge, taking a huge swig of brandy and wiping her chin on her sleeve. 'A no-account, good-for-nothing, lazy scrounger who –'

'He was not,' said Harry suddenly. The table went very quiet. Harry was shaking all over. He had never felt so angry in his life.

'MORE BRANDY!' yelled Uncle Vernon, who had gone very white. He emptied the bottle into Aunt Marge's glass. 'You, boy,' he snarled at Harry. 'Go to bed, go on –'

'No, Vernon,' hiccoughed Aunt Marge, holding up a hand, her tiny bloodshot eyes fixed on Harry's. 'Go on, boy, go on. Proud of your parents, are you? They go and get themselves killed in a car crash (drunk, I expect) –'

'They didn't die in a car crash!' said Harry, who found himself on his feet.

'They died in a car crash, you nasty little liar, and left you to be a burden on their decent, hardworking relatives!' screamed Aunt Marge, swelling with fury. 'You are an insolent, ungrateful little –'

But Aunt Marge suddenly stopped speaking. For a moment, it looked as though words had failed her. She seemed to be swelling with inexpressible anger – but the swelling didn't stop. Her great red face started to expand, her tiny eyes bulged and her mouth stretched too tightly for speech. Next second, several buttons burst from her tweed jacket and pinged off the walls – she was inflating like a monstrous balloon, her stomach bursting free of her tweed waistband, each of her fingers blowing up like a salami ...

'MARGE!' yelled Uncle Vernon and Aunt Petunia together, as Aunt Marge's whole body began to rise off her chair towards the ceiling. She was entirely round, now, like a vast life buoy with piggy eyes, and her hands and feet stuck out weirdly as she drifted up into the air, making apoplectic popping noises. Ripper came skidding into the room, barking madly.

哗哗地往她的酒杯里倒,许多酒都泼洒在桌布上,"你们从来没有跟我说过他是做什么的。"

弗农姨父和佩妮姨妈显得紧张极了,就连在一旁忙着吃甜饼的达力也抬起眼来,呆呆地望着他的父母。

"他——他没有工作,"弗农姨父说着,偷偷扫了哈利一眼,"失业。"

"我早就料到了!"玛姬姑妈说完,喝了一大口白兰地,用袖子擦了擦下巴,"一个废物、懒汉、骗子,一无是处的家伙,他——"

"他不是!"哈利突然说话了。饭桌上顿时一片寂静。哈利气得浑身发抖。他从来没这么生气过。

"**再来点儿白兰地!**"弗农姨父嚷道,脸色变得煞白。他把瓶里的酒都倒进了玛姬姑妈的杯子里。"你,小子,"他朝哈利咆哮道,"快睡觉去,快去——"

"不,弗农。"玛姬姑妈打着饱嗝,举起一只手,一双充血的小眼睛死死地盯住哈利的眼睛,"说下去,小子,说下去。你很为你的父母感到骄傲,是吗?他们在一起车祸中送了命(我猜准是喝醉了)——"

"他们不是死于车祸!"哈利说,发现自己站了起来。

"就是死于车祸,你这个谎话连篇的小坏蛋,他们撇下你,成为这些体面的、辛勤工作的亲戚们的累赘!"玛姬姑妈尖叫道,胸脯气得一鼓一鼓的,"你是个粗野无礼、忘恩负义的小——"

玛姬姑妈突然停住了。一时间,她似乎不会说话了。难以形容的怒气使她全身膨胀起来——而且这膨胀并没有停止。她红通通的大脸膛铺展开来,一双小眼睛往外凸起,嘴唇向两边伸长,绷得紧紧的说不出话来。接着,花呢衣服上的几粒纽扣绷开了,砰砰砸在墙上——她像一只巨大的气球在不断膨胀,肚子撑断了花呢衣服的腰带,每根手指都像吹了气似的,肿得像意大利蒜肠……

"玛姬!"弗农姨父和佩妮姨妈异口同声地喊。玛姬姑妈的身体从椅子上升了起来,朝天花板飘去。她在空中越升越高,身体已经变得滚圆,活像一个长着猪眼睛的救生圈,一双手脚怪里怪气地支棱出来,嘴里发出中风一般的噗噗声。利皮一溜小跑进了房间,疯狂地叫个不停。

CHAPTER TWO — Aunt Marge's Big Mistake

'NOOOOOOO!'

Uncle Vernon seized one of Marge's feet and tried to pull her down again, but was almost lifted from the floor himself. Next second, Ripper had leapt forward and sunk his teeth into Uncle Vernon's leg.

Harry tore from the dining room before anyone could stop him, heading for the cupboard under the stairs. The cupboard door burst magically open as he reached it. In seconds, he had heaved his trunk to the front door. He sprinted upstairs and threw himself under the bed, wrenched up the loose floorboard and grabbed the pillowcase full of his books and birthday presents. He wriggled out, seized Hedwig's empty cage and dashed back downstairs to his trunk, just as Uncle Vernon burst out of the dining room, his trouser leg in bloody tatters.

'COME BACK IN HERE!' he bellowed. 'COME BACK AND PUT HER RIGHT!'

But a reckless rage had come over Harry. He kicked his trunk open, pulled out his wand and pointed it at Uncle Vernon.

'She deserved it,' Harry said, breathing very fast. 'She deserved what she got. You keep away from me.'

He fumbled behind him for the catch on the door.

'I'm going,' Harry said. 'I've had enough.'

And next moment, he was out in the dark, quiet street, heaving his heavy trunk behind him, Hedwig's cage under his arm.

第 2 章　玛姬姑妈的大错误

"不——！"

弗农姨父抓住玛姬的一只脚,想把她拉下来,不料他自己也差点儿双脚离地被拖了起来。接着,利皮扑上前去,一口咬住了弗农姨父的腿。

没人来得及阻拦,哈利就飞快地离开餐厅,奔向楼梯下的储物间。刚到那里,储物间的门就神奇地自动打开了。他在几秒钟内把箱子搬到大门口,然后迅速奔到楼上,一头钻进床底下,撬开那块松动的地板,拽出装满课本和生日礼物的枕头套。他从床底下钻出来,抓起海德薇的空笼子,噔噔噔地冲下楼梯,朝箱子跑去。就在这时,弗农姨父从餐厅里冲了出来,一条裤腿被扯得稀烂,上面血迹斑斑。

"快回来！"他吼道,"回来把她弄好！"

然而哈利气得什么也顾不上了,他一脚把箱子盖踢开,抽出魔杖,指着弗农姨父。

"她活该,"哈利急促地喘着粗气说,"她这是自作自受。你给我闪开！"

他用手在背后摸索着门闩。

"我走了,"哈利说,"我受够了。"

转眼间,他就来到外面漆黑、静谧的街道上,身后拖着沉重的箱子,胳膊底下夹着海德薇的鸟笼。

CHAPTER THREE

The Knight Bus

Harry was several streets away before he collapsed onto a low wall in Magnolia Crescent, panting from the effort of dragging his trunk. He sat quite still, anger still surging through him, listening to the frantic thumping of his heart.

But after ten minutes alone in the dark street, a new emotion overtook him: panic. Whichever way he looked at it, he had never been in a worse fix. He was stranded, quite alone, in the dark Muggle world, with absolutely nowhere to go. And the worst of it was, he had just done serious magic, which meant that he was almost certainly expelled from Hogwarts. He had broken the Decree for the Restriction of Underage Wizardry so badly, he was surprised Ministry of Magic representatives weren't swooping down on him where he sat.

Harry shivered and looked up and down Magnolia Crescent. What was going to happen to him? Would he be arrested, or would he simply be outlawed from the wizarding world? He thought of Ron and Hermione, and his heart sank even lower. Harry was sure that, criminal or not, Ron and Hermione would want to help him now, but they were both abroad, and with Hedwig gone, he had no means of contacting them.

He didn't have any Muggle money, either. There was a little wizard gold in the money bag at the bottom of his trunk, but the rest of the fortune his parents had left him was stored in a vault at Gringotts Wizarding Bank in London. He'd never be able to drag his trunk all the way to London. Unless ...

He looked down at his wand, which he was still clutching in his hand. If he was already expelled (his heart was now thumping painfully fast), a bit more magic couldn't hurt. He had the Invisibility Cloak he had inherited from his father – what if he bewitched the trunk to make it feather-light, tied

第3章

骑士公共汽车

哈利拖着箱子走过几条街，瘫倒在木兰花新月街的一堵矮墙上，累得上气不接下气。他一动不动地坐在那里，听着自己的心嗵嗵狂跳，心里仍然腾腾地冒着怒火。

在漆黑的街道上独自待了十分钟后，一种新的情绪抓住了他：恐慌。不管从哪一方面来看，现在的情况都是前所未有的糟糕。他孤身一人流落在黑暗的麻瓜世界里，没有任何地方可去。最糟糕的是，他刚才使用了厉害的魔法，这意味着他几乎肯定要被霍格沃茨开除了。哈利甚至感到很吃惊：他如此严重地违反了《对未成年巫师加以合理约束法》，魔法部代表竟然没有扑过来抓他。

哈利浑身颤抖，朝木兰花新月街的两边看了看。会碰上什么情况呢？是会被抓起来，还是会被巫师世界驱逐？他想起了罗恩和赫敏，心情更加沉重了。哈利可以肯定，不管他有没有犯法，罗恩和赫敏都会愿意帮助他，可是他们俩此刻都在国外，而且海德薇也走了，他没有办法跟他们取得联系。

他身上也没有带着麻瓜钱。箱子底部的钱袋里倒有一些巫师金币，但父母留给他的其余财产都存在伦敦古灵阁巫师银行的地下金库里。他不可能拖着箱子一路走到伦敦。除非……

他低头看看仍然攥在手里的魔杖。既然已经要被开除（此刻他的心嗵嗵狂跳，令他难受），再多使用一点魔法也没什么关系了。他还有从父亲那里继承来的隐形衣——是不是可以给箱子施个魔法，把它变得像羽毛那么轻，拴在飞天扫帚上，然后他穿上隐形衣，一路飞到伦敦呢？

CHAPTER THREE The Knight Bus

it to his broomstick, covered himself in the Cloak and flew to London? Then he could get the rest of his money out of his vault and ... begin his life as an outcast. It was a horrible prospect, but he couldn't sit on this wall for ever or he'd find himself trying to explain to Muggle police why he was out in the dead of night with a trunkful of spellbooks and a broomstick.

Harry opened his trunk again and pushed the contents aside, looking for the Invisibility Cloak – but before he had found it, he straightened up suddenly, looking around him once more.

A funny prickling on the back of his neck had made Harry feel he was being watched, but the street appeared to be deserted, and no lights shone from any of the large square houses.

He bent over his trunk again, but almost immediately stood up once more, his hand clenched on his wand. He had sensed rather than heard it: someone or something was standing in the narrow gap between the garage and the fence behind him. Harry squinted at the black alleyway. If only it would move, then he'd know whether it was just a stray cat or – something else.

'*Lumos*,' Harry muttered, and a light appeared at the end of his wand, almost dazzling him. He held it high over his head, and the pebble-dashed walls of number two suddenly sparkled; the garage door gleamed, and between them, Harry saw, quite distinctly, the hulking outline of something very big, with wide, gleaming eyes.

Harry stepped backwards. His legs hit his trunk and he tripped. His wand flew out of his hand as he flung out an arm to break his fall, and he landed, hard, in the gutter.

There was a deafening BANG and Harry threw up his hands to shield his eyes against a sudden blinding light ...

With a yell, he rolled back onto the pavement, just in time. A second later, a gigantic pair of wheels and headlights had screeched to a halt exactly where Harry had just been lying. They belonged, as Harry saw when he raised his head, to a triple-decker, violently purple bus, which had appeared out of thin air. Gold lettering over the windscreen spelled *The Knight Bus*.

For a split second, Harry wondered if he had been knocked silly by his fall. Then a conductor in a purple uniform leapt out of the bus and began to speak loudly to the night.

'Welcome to the Knight Bus, emergency transport for the stranded witch

第3章 骑士公共汽车

这样,他就能把其余的钱都从地下金库里取出来……从此开始浪迹天涯。未来的日子令他恐惧,但是他不能永远呆坐在这堵墙上,弄得不好,他还得向麻瓜警察解释为什么半夜三更流落街头,还带着一箱子魔法书和一把飞天扫帚。

哈利又打开箱子,把里面的东西扒拉到一边,寻找那件隐形衣——衣服还没找到,他突然直起身子,又一次打量四周。

哈利感到脖颈上有一种异样的刺痛,似乎有人在盯他的梢,可是放眼望去,街道上空荡荡的,那些四四方方的大房子里也没有透出一丝灯光。

他又埋头在箱子里翻找,但紧接着再一次纵身跃起,把手里的魔杖攥得紧紧的。与其说他是听见,不如说他是感觉到有个什么人或什么东西,就在他身后车库和栅栏之间的窄巷里。哈利眯起眼睛盯着黑黢黢的小巷。只要那玩意儿动一动,他就能知道它是一只流浪猫还是——别的什么。

"荧光闪烁。"哈利低声说,他的魔杖头上立刻冒出一道亮光,刺得他几乎睁不开眼睛。他把魔杖高举过头顶,木兰花新月街2号的鹅卵石外墙一下子被照得亮闪闪的。车库的门反射着亮光。而在墙和车库之间,哈利清清楚楚地看见一个黑乎乎的大家伙,闪着一双贼亮的大眼睛。

哈利朝后退去,两条腿撞在箱子上,被绊了一下。他伸出一只胳膊稳住身体,魔杖从手里飞了出去。他重重地摔在了排水沟里。

随着**砰**的一声巨响,一道强光突然射了过来,哈利赶忙用双手挡住眼睛……

他尖叫一声,一骨碌滚到人行道上。幸亏躲得及时,一秒钟后,嘎吱一声,一对巨大的车轮和车灯就停在了哈利刚才躺着的地方。哈利抬头一看,这些车轮和车灯属于一辆艳紫色的三层公共汽车。它像是凭空冒出来的,挡风玻璃上用金色的字母写着骑士公共汽车。

一时间,哈利以为刚才那一跤把自己摔糊涂了。接着,一位穿紫色制服的售票员从公共汽车上跳出来,对着黑夜大声说起话来。

"欢迎乘坐骑士公共汽车——用于运送陷入困境的巫师的紧急交通

CHAPTER THREE   The Knight Bus

or wizard. Just stick out your wand hand, step on board and we can take you anywhere you want to go. My name is Stan Shunpike, and I will be your conductor this eve–'

The conductor stopped abruptly. He had just caught sight of Harry, who was still sitting on the ground. Harry snatched up his wand again and scrambled to his feet. Close to, he saw that Stan Shunpike was only a few years older than he was; eighteen or nineteen at most, with large, protruding ears and a fair few pimples.

'What were you doin' down there?' said Stan, dropping his professional manner.

'Fell over,' said Harry.

''Choo fall over for?' sniggered Stan.

'I didn't do it on purpose,' said Harry, annoyed. One of the knees in his jeans was torn, and the hand he had thrown out to break his fall was bleeding. He suddenly remembered why he had fallen over, and turned around quickly to stare at the alleyway between the garage and fence. The Knight Bus's headlamps were flooding it with light, and it was empty.

''Choo lookin' at?' said Stan.

'There was a big black thing,' said Harry, pointing uncertainly into the gap. 'Like a dog ... but massive ...'

He looked around at Stan, whose mouth was slightly open. With a feeling of unease, Harry saw Stan's eyes move to the scar on Harry's forehead.

'Woss that on your 'ead?' said Stan abruptly.

'Nothing,' said Harry quickly, flattening his hair over his scar. If the Ministry of Magic was looking for him, he didn't want to make it too easy for them.

'Woss your name?' Stan persisted.

'Neville Longbottom,' said Harry, saying the first name that came into his head. 'So – so this bus,' he went on quickly, hoping to distract Stan, 'did you say it goes *anywhere*?'

'Yep,' said Stan proudly, 'anywhere you like, long's it's on land. Can't do nuffink underwater. 'Ere,' he said, looking suspicious again, 'you *did* flag us down, dincha? Stuck out your wand 'and, dincha?'

'Yes,' said Harry quickly. 'Listen, how much would it be to get to London?'

工具。你只要伸出拿魔杖的手,登上车来,我们就能把你送到你想去的任何地方。我叫斯坦·桑帕克,今晚我是你的售票员——"

售票员突然停住话头。他这才看见仍然坐在地上的哈利。哈利重新抓起魔杖,挣扎着从地上站了起来。离近了看,他发现斯坦·桑帕克比他大不了多少,最多也就十八九岁,长着一对大大的招风耳,脸上还点缀着几颗粉刺。

"你坐在那地上干啥?"斯坦放下那副公事公办的派头,问道。

"摔了一跤。"哈利说。

"为啥摔跤?"斯坦轻轻笑着问。

"我又不是故意摔的。"哈利恼火地说。他的牛仔裤一条裤腿的膝盖处撕破了,刚才挥出去保持身体平衡的那只手在流血。他突然想起刚才为什么会摔倒了,赶紧转身朝车库和栅栏之间的小巷望去。骑士公共汽车的车灯把那里照得通明,小巷里空无一人。

"你在看啥?"斯坦问。

"刚才那儿有个黑乎乎的大家伙,"哈利不能确定地朝小巷里指着,"像是一条狗……但是大得吓人……"

他转过身来看着斯坦,斯坦的嘴巴微微张着。哈利看见斯坦的目光挪向了他的额头,顿时感到心里一阵不安。

"你脑门上是啥?"斯坦突然问道。

"没什么。"哈利赶紧说,一边把头发抹下来盖住伤疤。如果魔法部在找他,他可不想让他们轻易发现他的踪迹。

"你叫啥名字?"斯坦不依不饶地问。

"纳威·隆巴顿。"哈利脑子里想到什么名字就不假思索地说了出来,"那么——那么这辆公共汽车,"他急急忙忙地往下说,希望转移斯坦的注意力,"你刚才说它哪儿都能去?"

"没错,"斯坦得意地说,"你想去哪儿都行,只要是在陆地上。到水底下就不成了。对了,"他脸上又显出怀疑的神色,说,"刚才是你招呼我们停车的,是不?你伸出了你的魔杖,是不?"

"是啊,"哈利立刻回答,"那么,去伦敦要多少钱?"

CHAPTER THREE

The Knight Bus

'Eleven Sickles,' said Stan, 'but for firteen you get 'ot chocolate, and for fifteen you get an 'ot-water bottle an' a toofbrush in the colour of your choice.'

Harry rummaged once more in his trunk, extracted his money bag and shoved some silver into Stan's hand. He and Stan then lifted his trunk, with Hedwig's cage balanced on top, up the steps of the bus.

There were no seats; instead, half a dozen brass bedsteads stood beside the curtained windows. Candles were burning in brackets beside each bed, illuminating the wood-panelled walls. A tiny wizard in a nightcap at the rear of the bus muttered, 'Not now, thanks, I'm pickling some slugs,' and rolled over in his sleep.

'You 'ave this one,' Stan whispered, shoving Harry's trunk under the bed right behind the driver, who was sitting in an armchair in front of the steering wheel. 'This is our driver, Ernie Prang. This is Neville Longbottom, Ern.'

Ernie Prang, an elderly wizard wearing very thick glasses, nodded to Harry, who nervously flattened his fringe again and sat down on his bed.

'Take 'er away, Ern,' said Stan, sitting down in the armchair next to Ernie's.

There was another tremendous BANG, and next moment Harry found himself flat on his bed, thrown backwards by the speed of the Knight Bus. Pulling himself up, Harry stared out of the dark window and saw that they were now bowling along a completely different street. Stan was watching Harry's stunned face with great enjoyment.

'This is where we was before you flagged us down,' he said. 'Where are we, Ern? Somewhere in Wales?'

'Ar,' said Ernie.

'How come the Muggles don't hear the bus?' said Harry.

'Them!' said Stan contemptuously. 'Don' listen properly, do they? Don' look properly either. Never notice nuffink, they don'.'

'Best go wake up Madam Marsh, Stan,' said Ern. 'We'll be in Abergavenny in a minute.'

Stan passed Harry's bed and disappeared up a narrow wooden staircase. Harry was still looking out of the window, feeling increasingly nervous. Ernie didn't seem to have mastered the use of a steering wheel. The Knight Bus kept mounting the pavement, but it didn't hit anything; lines of lamp posts, letter-boxes and bins jumped out of its way as it approached and back into

第3章　骑士公共汽车

"十一个西可,"斯坦说,"付十三个就能喝到热巧克力,付十五个能拿到一个热水袋和一把牙刷,颜色随便挑。"

哈利又在箱子里翻找一通,拽出钱袋,把几个银币塞进斯坦手里。他和斯坦抬起箱子,登上了公共汽车,海德薇的鸟笼就放在箱子顶上。

车里没有座位,在拉着窗帘的窗边,摆着六七张黄铜架子床。每张床旁边的托架上都点着蜡烛,照亮了木板车壁。车尾附近一位戴睡帽的小个子巫师咕哝着:"谢谢你,现在不行,我在腌一些鼻涕虫。"在睡梦里翻了个身。

"你睡这张床。"斯坦小声说,把哈利的箱子推进司机身后那张床铺底下,司机坐在方向盘前的一把扶手椅上,"这是我们的司机,厄恩·普兰。厄恩,这位是纳威·隆巴顿。"

厄恩·普兰是一位上了年纪的巫师,戴着一副厚厚的眼镜。他朝哈利点点头,哈利又紧张地抹了抹刘海,在自己的床上坐了下来。

"开车吧,厄恩。"斯坦说着,坐在了厄恩身边的扶手椅上。

又是**砰**的一声巨响,紧接着哈利就发现自己仰面躺在了床上。骑士公共汽车速度太快了,把他向后抛去。哈利挣扎着坐起来,朝漆黑的窗外望去,看见他们正飞速行驶在另外一条完全不同的街道上。斯坦饶有兴趣地望着哈利惊愕的脸。

"刚才你招呼我们停车前,我们就在这里。"他说,"是在哪儿来着,厄恩?威尔士的某个地方?"

"嗯。"厄恩说。

"麻瓜们怎么听不见汽车的声音?"哈利问。

"他们!"斯坦轻蔑地说,"根本就不会好好地听,是不?也不会好好地看。他们啥都注意不到。"

"最好去把马什女士叫醒,斯坦,"厄恩说,"马上就到阿伯加文尼了。"

斯坦从哈利的床旁走过,顺着一道狭窄的木头楼梯去了上层。哈利仍然望着窗外,心里越来越紧张不安。厄恩似乎并没有掌握如何使用方向盘。骑士公共汽车不断地冲上人行道,好在并没有撞上什么东西;那些路灯、邮箱和垃圾桶,都在汽车开过去时自动跳开了,等汽车开

CHAPTER THREE   The Knight Bus

position once it had passed.

Stan came back downstairs, followed by a faintly green witch wrapped in a travelling cloak.

''Ere you go, Madam Marsh,' said Stan happily, as Ern stamped the brake and the beds slid a foot or so towards the front of the bus. Madam Marsh clamped a handkerchief to her mouth and tottered down the steps. Stan threw her bag out after her and rammed the doors shut; there was another loud BANG, and they were thundering down a narrow country lane, trees leaping out of the way.

Harry wouldn't have been able to sleep even if he had been travelling on a bus that didn't keep banging loudly and jumping a hundred miles at a time. His stomach churned as he fell back to wondering what was going to happen to him, and whether the Dursleys had managed to get Aunt Marge off the ceiling yet.

Stan had unfurled a copy of the *Daily Prophet* and was now reading with his tongue between his teeth. A large photograph of a sunken-faced man with long, matted hair blinked slowly at Harry from the front page. He looked strangely familiar.

'That man!' Harry said, forgetting his troubles for a moment. 'He was on the Muggle news!'

Stanley turned to the front page and chuckled.

'Sirius Black,' he said, nodding. ''Course 'e was on the Muggle news, Neville. Where you been?'

He gave a superior sort of chuckle at the blank look on Harry's face, removed the front page and handed it to Harry.

'You oughta read the papers more, Neville.'

Harry held the paper up to the candlelight and read:

BLACK STILL AT LARGE

Sirius Black, possibly the most infamous prisoner ever to be held in Azkaban fortress, is still eluding capture, the Ministry of Magic confirmed today.

'We are doing all we can to recapture Black,' said the Minister for Magic, Cornelius Fudge, this morning, 'and we beg the magical community to remain calm.'

第3章 骑士公共汽车

过又回到原来的位置。

斯坦又下楼来了,后面跟着一个身穿旅行斗篷、脸色有点发青的女巫。

"您这边走,马什女士。"斯坦愉快地说,厄恩一踩刹车,那些床都朝汽车前面滑出一尺左右。马什女士用手帕捂住嘴,跌跌撞撞地走下台阶。斯坦跟着把她的包扔了出去,重重地关上车门。又是**砰**的一声巨响,他们风驰电掣地驶过一条狭窄的乡村小路,树木纷纷闪开给他们让道。

即使坐的是一辆普通公共汽车,不像这样动不动就发出砰砰巨响,一步跳出一百英里,哈利也不可能入睡。他仰面躺倒,胃里一阵阵翻腾,心想不知道接下来会发生什么事,也不知道德思礼一家有没有把玛姬姑妈从天花板上弄下来。

斯坦展开一份《预言家日报》,牙齿咬着舌头,读得津津有味。第一版的一张大照片上,一个满脸憔悴、头发又长又乱的男人朝哈利慢慢地眨了眨眼睛。真是奇怪,他看着竟有点眼熟呢。

"就是那个人!"哈利说,暂时忘记了自己的烦恼,"麻瓜的新闻里也有他!"

斯坦重新翻到第一版,轻声笑了笑。

"小天狼星布莱克,"他点点头说,"麻瓜新闻里当然会有他,纳威,你待在哪儿来着啊?"

看到哈利脸上一片茫然,斯坦发出居高临下的笑声,扯下报纸的第一版,递给了哈利。

"你应该多读读报纸,纳威。"

哈利把报纸举到烛光下,读了起来:

布莱克仍然在逃

魔法部今天证实,小天狼星布莱克仍然逍遥法外,他大概是阿兹卡班监狱关押过的最臭名昭著的囚徒。

"我们正竭尽全力将布莱克重新捉拿归案,"魔法部部长康奈利·福吉今天早晨说,"恳请魔法界保持镇静。"

CHAPTER THREE   The Knight Bus

> Fudge has been criticised by some members of the International Federation of Warlocks for informing the Muggle Prime Minister of the crisis.
>
> 'Well, really, I had to, don't you know,' said an irritable Fudge. 'Black is mad. He's a danger to anyone who crosses him, magic or Muggle. I have the Prime Minister's assurance that he will not breathe a word of Black's true identity to anyone. And let's face it – who'd believe him if he did?'
>
> While Muggles have been told that Black is carrying a gun (a kind of metal wand which Muggles use to kill each other), the magical community lives in fear of a massacre like that of twelve years ago, when Black murdered thirteen people with a single curse.

Harry looked into the shadowed eyes of Sirius Black, the only part of the sunken face that seemed alive. Harry had never met a vampire, but he had seen pictures of them in his Defence Against the Dark Arts classes, and Black, with his waxy white skin, looked just like one.

'Scary-lookin' fing, inee?' said Stan, who had been watching Harry read.

'He murdered *thirteen people?*' said Harry, handing the page back to Stan, 'with *one curse?*'

'Yep,' said Stan. 'In front of witnesses an' all. Broad daylight. Big trouble it caused, dinnit, Ern?'

'Ar,' said Ern darkly.

Stan swivelled in his armchair, his hands on the back, the better to look at Harry.

'Black woz a big supporter of You-Know-'Oo,' he said.

'What, Voldemort?' said Harry, without thinking.

Even Stan's pimples went white; Ern jerked the steering wheel so hard that a whole farmhouse had to jump aside to avoid the bus.

'You outta your tree?' yelped Stan. ''Choo say 'is name for?'

'Sorry,' said Harry hastily. 'Sorry, I – I forgot –'

'Forgot!' said Stan weakly. 'Blimey, my 'eart's goin' that fast …'

'So – so Black was a supporter of You-Know-Who?' Harry prompted apologetically.

'Yeah,' said Stan, still rubbing his chest. 'Yeah, that's right. Very close to

第3章 骑士公共汽车

国际巫师联合会的一些成员指责福吉将这场危机通报给了麻瓜首相。

"说实在的,你们也知道,我这是没有办法,"福吉恼怒地说,"布莱克是个亡命徒。不管是魔法师还是麻瓜,谁碰到他都会有危险。我要求首相保证,决不把布莱克的真实身份透露给任何人。说句实话——即使他透露出去,又有谁会相信呢?"

麻瓜们被告知,布莱克携带一把枪(麻瓜们用来互相残杀的一种金属魔杖),而魔法界知道布莱克十二年前曾用一个咒语杀死了十三人,因此担心那样的大屠杀会再度出现。

哈利望着小天狼星布莱克阴郁的眼睛,那似乎是他憔悴不堪的脸上唯一有活力的地方。哈利从来没碰见过吸血鬼,但在黑魔法防御术课上看过吸血鬼的照片。布莱克的皮肤白森森的,看上去活像一个吸血鬼。

"看着怪吓人的,是不?"斯坦一直在注视着哈利读报,这时候问道。

"他杀死了十三个人?"哈利说着,把报纸递还给斯坦,"只用一个咒语?"

"没错,"斯坦说,"在光天化日、众目睽睽之下。惹出了大麻烦,是不,厄恩?"

"嗯。"厄恩沉着脸说。

斯坦在扶手椅里转了个圈,双手背在后面,仔细看着哈利。

"布莱克是神秘人的有力支持者。"他说。

"什么?伏地魔?"哈利不假思索地说。

斯坦脸上的粉刺都变白了,厄恩猛地一打方向盘,整个一座农宅跳到一边,躲开了疾驰而来的汽车。

"你脑子出毛病啦?"斯坦嚷道,"你干吗说他的名字?"

"对不起,"哈利赶紧说,"对不起,我……我忘记了——"

"忘记了!"斯坦有气无力地说,"天哪,我的心跳得那么快……"

"那么……那么,布莱克是支持神秘人的?"哈利带着歉意问道。

"没错,"斯坦仍然揉着胸脯,说,"没错,没错。他们说,他跟神

CHAPTER THREE   The Knight Bus

You-Know-'Oo, they say ... anyway, when little 'Arry Potter put paid to You-Know-'Oo' – Harry nervously flattened his fringe down again – 'all You-Know-'Oo's supporters was tracked down, wasn't they, Ern? Most of 'em knew it was all over, wiv You-Know-'Oo gone, and they came quiet. But not Sirius Black. I 'eard he thought 'e'd be second-in-command once You-Know-'Oo 'ad taken over.

'Anyway, they cornered Black in the middle of a street full of Muggles an' Black took out 'is wand and 'e blasted 'alf the street apart, an' a wizard got it, an' so did a dozen Muggles what got in the way. 'Orrible, eh? An' you know what Black did then?' Stan continued in a dramatic whisper.

'What?' said Harry.

'*Laughed*,' said Stan. 'Jus' stood there an' laughed. An' when reinforcements from the Ministry of Magic got there, 'e went wiv 'em quiet as anyfink, still laughing 'is 'ead off. 'Cos 'e's mad, inee, Ern? Inee mad?'

'If he weren't when he went to Azkaban, he will be now,' said Ern in his slow voice. 'I'd blow meself up before I set foot in that place. Serves him right, mind ... after what he did ...'

'They 'ad a job coverin' it up, din' they, Ern?' Stan said. "Ole street blown up an' all them Muggles dead. What was it they said 'ad 'appened, Ern?'

'Gas explosion,' grunted Ernie.

'An' now 'e's out,' said Stan, examining the newspaper picture of Black's gaunt face again. 'Never been a breakout from Azkaban before, 'as there, Ern? Beats me 'ow 'e did it. Frightenin', eh? Mind, I don't fancy 'is chances against them Azkaban guards, eh, Ern?'

Ernie suddenly shivered.

'Talk about summat else, Stan, there's a good lad. Them Azkaban guards give me the collywobbles.'

Stan put the paper away reluctantly and Harry leant against the window of the knight Bus, feeling worse than ever. He couldn't help imagining what Stan might be telling his passengers in a few nights' time.

"Ear about that 'Arry Potter? Blew up 'is Aunt! We 'ad 'im 'ere on the Knight Bus, di'n't we, Ern? 'E was tryin' to run for it ...'

第3章 骑士公共汽车

秘人走得很近……反正,当年小哈利·波特干掉了神秘人,"——哈利紧张地又把刘海往下抹了抹——"神秘人的所有支持者都被逮捕了,是不,厄恩?神秘人逃走后,他们大多数人都知道大势已去,不再兴风作浪。只有小天狼星布莱克例外。我听说,他认为一旦神秘人卷土重来,他就能坐上第二把交椅。

"反正,他们在一条满是麻瓜的街上把布莱克堵住了,布莱克掏出魔杖把半条街都炸烂了,击中了一个巫师,还有十几个碰巧在那儿的麻瓜。真可怕,是不?你知道布莱克接着做了啥?"斯坦继续用一种夸张的语气低声说。

"什么?"哈利问。

"放声大笑,"斯坦说,"站在那里放声大笑。后来魔法部的增援赶到,他乖乖地跟着他们走了,一边仍然不停地狂笑。他准是疯了。是不,厄恩?是不是疯了?"

"即使他去阿兹卡班的时候没疯,到这会儿肯定也疯了。"厄恩用低沉的声音说,"我宁可把自己炸死,也不愿踏进那个鬼地方。这是他应得的惩罚……竟然做出了那样的事……"

"他们好不容易才把事情抹平,是不,厄恩?"斯坦说,"街道炸飞了,那么多麻瓜送了命。他们是怎么解释的,厄恩?"

"煤气爆炸。"厄恩咕哝道。

"现在他又跑出来了。"斯坦说着,又仔细端详着报纸照片上布莱克那张瘦削的脸,"阿兹卡班还从来没发生过越狱的事呢,是不,厄恩?真不明白他是怎么得手的。怪吓人的,是不?说实在的,想象不出他居然对付得了阿兹卡班的那些看守。是不,厄恩?"

厄恩突然打了个寒战。

"说点别的吧,斯坦,有个本分的小伙子在车上呢。我一听到那些阿兹卡班的看守就会闹肚子。"

斯坦满不情愿地把报纸放到一边。哈利靠在骑士公共汽车的窗户上,心情从来没有这么糟过。他忍不住想象,几天后的某个夜晚,斯坦说不定会这样告诉他的乘客:

"听说过那个哈利·波特吗?他把他的姑妈吹胀了。后来还上了我们的骑士公共汽车呢。是不,厄恩?他当时拼命想逃跑……"

CHAPTER THREE   The Knight Bus

He, Harry, had broken wizard law just like Sirius Black. Was inflating Aunt Marge bad enough to land him in Azkaban? Harry didn't know anything about the wizard prison, though everyone he'd ever heard speak of it did so in the same fearful tone. Hagrid the Hogwarts gamekeeper had spent two months there only last year. Harry wouldn't soon forget the look of terror on Hagrid's face when he had been told where he was going, and Hagrid was one of the bravest people Harry knew.

The Knight Bus rolled through the darkness, scattering bushes and bollards, telephone boxes and trees, and Harry lay, restless and miserable, on his feather bed. After a while, Stan remembered that Harry had paid for hot chocolate, but poured it all over Harry's pillow when the bus moved abruptly from Anglesey to Aberdeen. One by one, wizards and witches in dressing-gowns and slippers descended from the upper floors to leave the bus. They all looked very pleased to go.

Finally, Harry was the only passenger left.

'Right then, Neville,' said Stan, clapping his hands, 'whereabouts in London?'

'Diagon Alley,' said Harry.

'Righto,' said Stan, ''old tight, then ...'

BANG!

They were thundering along Charing Cross Road. Harry sat up and watched buildings and benches squeezing themselves out of the Knight Bus's way. The sky was getting a little lighter. He would lie low for a couple of hours, go to Gringotts the moment it opened, then set off – where, he didn't know.

Ern slammed on the brakes and the Knight Bus skidded to a halt in front of a small and shabby-looking pub, the Leaky Cauldron, behind which lay the magical entrance to Diagon Alley.

'Thanks,' Harry said to Ern.

He jumped down the steps and helped Stan lower his trunk and Hedwig's cage onto the pavement.

'Well,' said Harry, 'bye then!'

But Stan wasn't paying attention. Still standing in the doorway to the bus, he was goggling at the shadowy entrance to the Leaky Cauldron.

'*There* you are, Harry,' said a voice.

Before Harry could turn, he felt a hand on his shoulder. At the same time,

第3章　骑士公共汽车

　　他，哈利，也像小天狼星布莱克一样违反了巫师法。吹胀了玛姬姑妈，是不是够到阿兹卡班坐牢呢？哈利对巫师监狱一无所知，不过他听每个人说起那个地方，用的都是同样畏惧的口吻。霍格沃茨猎场看守海格去年还在那里蹲了两个月。当海格得知要被关在那里时，脸上恐惧的神情令哈利很难忘记，而海格还是哈利知道的最勇敢的人之一呢。

　　骑士公共汽车在黑暗中摇摇晃晃地行驶着，冲散了灌木和垃圾桶、电话亭和树木。哈利躺在羽毛床垫上，心烦意乱，忧虑重重。过了一会儿，斯坦想起哈利付了热巧克力的钱，可是汽车突然从安格尔西岛跳到了阿伯丁，斯坦把巧克力都洒在了哈利的枕头上。那些穿着晨衣和便鞋的巫师一个个从上层走了下来，离开了汽车。他们似乎都巴不得赶紧下车。

　　最后，车上只剩下了哈利一名乘客。

　　"好了，纳威，"斯坦拍了拍手，说，"去伦敦什么地方？"

　　"对角巷。"哈利说。

　　"好嘞，"斯坦说，"抓紧了，走……"

　　砰！

　　他们闪电般地驶过查令十字街。哈利坐起身子，注视着窗外那些楼房和长椅全部挤到一边，给骑士公共汽车让路。天空有点放亮了。他可以找个地方躲两个小时，等古灵阁一开门就进去，然后就出发——去哪儿呢，他不知道。

　　厄恩重重地一踩刹车，骑士公共汽车停在了一家破破烂烂的小酒吧门前——破釜酒吧，它的后面就是通往对角巷的神秘入口。

　　"谢谢。"哈利对厄恩说。

　　他跳下台阶，帮着斯坦把他的箱子和海德薇的鸟笼搬到人行道上。

　　"好了，"哈利说，"再见了！"

　　但是斯坦没有理会哈利。他仍然站在车门处，瞪大眼睛看着破釜酒吧的阴暗入口。

　　"原来你在这里呢，哈利。"一个声音说。

　　哈利还没来得及转身，就感到一只手搭在了他的肩膀上。与此同时，

CHAPTER THREE   The Knight Bus

Stan shouted, 'Blimey! Ern, come 'ere! Come *'ere*!'

Harry looked up at the owner of the hand on his shoulder and felt a bucketful of ice cascade into his stomach – he had walked right into Cornelius Fudge, the Minister for Magic himself.

Stan leapt onto the pavement beside them.

'What didja call Neville, Minister?' he said excitedly.

Fudge, a portly little man in a long, pinstriped cloak, looked cold and exhausted.

'Neville?' he repeated, frowning. 'This is Harry Potter.'

'I knew it!' Stan shouted gleefully. 'Ern! Ern! Guess 'oo Neville is, Ern! 'E's 'Arry Potter! I can see 'is scar!'

'Yes,' said Fudge testily. 'Well, I'm very glad the Knight Bus picked Harry up, but he and I need to step inside the Leaky Cauldron now ...'

Fudge increased the pressure on Harry's shoulder, and Harry found himself being steered inside the pub. A stooping figure bearing a lantern appeared through the door behind the bar. It was Tom, the wizened, toothless landlord.

'You've got him, Minister!' said Tom. 'Will you be wanting anything? Beer? Brandy?'

'Perhaps a pot of tea,' said Fudge, who still hadn't let go of Harry.

There was a loud scraping and puffing from behind them, and Stan and Ern appeared, carrying Harry's trunk and Hedwig's cage and looking around excitedly.

''Ow come you di'n't tell us 'oo you are, eh, Neville?' said Stan, beaming at Harry, while Ernie's owlish face peered interestedly over Stan's shoulder.

'And a *private* parlour, please, Tom,' said Fudge pointedly.

'Bye,' Harry said miserably to Stan and Ern, as Tom beckoned Fudge towards the passage that led from the bar.

'Bye, Neville!' called Stan.

Fudge marched Harry along the narrow passage after Tom's lantern, and then into a small parlour. Tom clicked his fingers, a fire burst into life in the grate, and he bowed himself out of the room.

'Sit down, Harry,' said Fudge, indicating a chair by the fire.

Harry sat down, feeling goosebumps rising up his arms despite the glow of the fire. Fudge took off his pinstriped cloak and tossed it aside, then hitched

第3章 骑士公共汽车

斯坦喊道:"天哪!厄恩,快来!快来!"

哈利抬头朝他肩膀上那只手的主人望去,顿时感到一桶冰水倒进了他肚子里——他正好撞上了魔法部部长康奈利·福吉本人。

斯坦一步跳到人行道上,站在他们身边。

"你管纳威叫什么,部长?"他兴奋地问。

福吉是个小矮胖子,穿着一件长长的条纹斗篷,看上去又冷又累。

"纳威?"他皱起眉头说,"这是哈利·波特。"

"我就知道!"斯坦欢喜地叫了起来,"厄恩!厄恩!你猜纳威是谁,厄恩?是哈利·波特!我看见了他的伤疤!"

"是的,"福吉不耐烦地说,"我很高兴骑士公共汽车把哈利捎来了,但是现在我和他需要进破釜酒吧……"

福吉搭在哈利肩膀上的那只手加大了力度,哈利发现自己被推着进了酒吧。酒吧后面的门里闪出一个驼背的身影,手里提着一盏灯。正是那位消瘦干瘪、牙齿掉光的酒吧老板汤姆。

"您找到他了,部长!"汤姆说,"您需要点什么?啤酒?白兰地?"

"就来一壶茶吧。"福吉说,仍然抓住哈利不放。

身后传来响亮的摩擦声和粗重的喘息声,斯坦和厄恩抬着哈利的箱子和海德薇的鸟笼出现了,一边兴奋地东张西望着。

"你怎么不告诉我们你是谁呢,嗯,纳威?"斯坦笑嘻嘻地对哈利说,厄恩那张猫头鹰般的脸饶有兴趣地从斯坦肩膀上探了出来。

"请来一个单间,汤姆。"福吉毫不客气地说。

"再见。"哈利无奈地对斯坦和厄恩说,这时汤姆领着福吉朝吧台旁的通道走去。

"再见,纳威!"斯坦喊道。

福吉推着哈利,跟随汤姆的提灯走过狭窄的通道,进了一个小单间。汤姆打了个响指,炉栅里腾地冒起了火焰,他鞠着躬退出了房间。

"坐下吧,哈利。"福吉指着火炉旁的一把椅子说。

哈利坐了下来,尽管有火烘烤着,他还是感到胳膊上起了一层鸡皮疙瘩。福吉脱掉条纹斗篷扔到一边,把深绿色的西服裤子往上提了提,

CHAPTER THREE   The Knight Bus

up the trousers of his bottle-green suit and sat down opposite Harry.

'I am Cornelius Fudge, Harry. The Minister for Magic.'

Harry already knew this, of course; he had seen Fudge once before, but as he had been wearing his father's Invisibility Cloak at the time, Fudge wasn't to know that.

Tom the innkeeper reappeared, wearing an apron over his nightshirt and bearing a tray of tea and crumpets. He placed the tray on a table between Fudge and Harry, and left the parlour, closing the door behind him.

'Well, Harry,' said Fudge, pouring out tea, 'you've had us all in a right flap, I don't mind telling you. Running away from your aunt and uncle's house like that! I'd started to think ... but you're safe, and that's what matters.'

Fudge buttered himself a crumpet and pushed the plate towards Harry.

'Eat, Harry, you look dead on your feet. Now then ... You will be pleased to hear that we have dealt with the unfortunate blowing-up of Miss Marjorie Dursley. Two members of the Accidental Magic Reversal Squad were dispatched to Privet Drive a few hours ago. Miss Dursley has been punctured and her memory has been modified. She has no recollection of the incident at all. So that's that, and no harm done.'

Fudge smiled at Harry over the rim of his teacup, rather like an uncle surveying a favourite nephew. Harry, who couldn't believe his ears, opened his mouth to speak, couldn't think of anything to say, and closed it again.

'Ah, you're worrying about the reaction of your aunt and uncle?' said Fudge. 'Well, I won't deny that they are extremely angry, Harry, but they are prepared to take you back next summer as long as you stay at Hogwarts for the Christmas and Easter holidays.'

Harry unstuck his throat.

'I *always* stay at Hogwarts for the Christmas and Easter holidays,' he said, 'and I don't ever want to go back to Privet Drive.'

'Now, now, I'm sure you'll feel differently once you've calmed down,' said Fudge in a worried tone. 'They are your family, after all, and I'm sure you are fond of each other – er – *very* deep down.'

It didn't occur to Harry to put Fudge right. He was still waiting to hear what was going to happen to him now.

第3章　骑士公共汽车

坐在了哈利对面。

"哈利，我是魔法部部长康奈利·福吉。"

哈利当然知道他是谁。他见过福吉一次，但当时他穿着父亲的那件隐形衣，福吉并不知道。

酒吧老板汤姆又出现了，他在衬衫式长睡衣外面系了一条围裙，手里端着一个托盘，上面放着茶和烤面饼。他把托盘放在福吉和哈利中间，便离开单间，关上了房门。

"唉，哈利，"福吉一边倒茶一边说道，"实话跟你说吧，你真是把我们弄得手忙脚乱啊。竟然那样从你姨妈姨父家里逃了出来！我本来以为……不过你现在安全了，这是最重要的。"

福吉拿了一块烤面饼，往上面抹了点黄油，然后把盘子推给了哈利。

"吃吧，哈利，你看上去都快垮了。不过……我们已经把吹胀玛姬·德思礼小姐的不幸事件给摆平了，我想你听了肯定会高兴的。几个小时前，逆转偶发魔法事件小组的两位成员被派到女贞路。德思礼小姐已被放了气，她的记忆也被修改了。她对这件事一点儿印象也没有了。就是这样，没捅出什么大娄子。"

福吉从茶杯边上朝哈利微笑着，像是一位叔叔在端详他最喜欢的侄子。哈利简直不敢相信自己的耳朵，张嘴想说话，却不知道说什么才好，便又把嘴巴闭上了。

"啊，你是在担心你姨妈姨父的反应吧？"福吉说，"唉，不能否认，他们确实气到了极点，哈利，但他们还是准备明年让你回去过暑假，只要你能在霍格沃茨过圣诞节和复活节。"

哈利这才说得出话来。

"我一向是在霍格沃茨过圣诞节和复活节的，"他说，"而且我再也不想回女贞路了。"

"好了，好了，我相信等你平静下来，就不会这么想了，"福吉用担忧的口吻说，"他们毕竟是你的亲人嘛，我敢肯定你们实际上还是喜欢对方的——呃——在内心最深处。"

哈利根本就没想去纠正福吉的话。他仍然等着听他们打算怎么发落他。

CHAPTER THREE The Knight Bus

'So all that remains,' said Fudge, now buttering himself a second crumpet, 'is to decide where you're going to spend the last three weeks of your holidays. I suggest you take a room here at the Leaky Cauldron and –'

'Hang on,' blurted Harry, 'what about my punishment?'

Fudge blinked.

'Punishment?'

'I broke the law!' Harry said. 'The Decree for the Restriction of Underage Wizardry!'

'Oh, my dear boy, we're not going to punish you for a little thing like that!' cried Fudge, waving his crumpet impatiently. 'It was an accident! We don't send people to Azkaban just for blowing up their aunts!'

But this didn't tally at all with Harry's past dealings with the Ministry of Magic.

'Last year, I got an official warning just because a house-elf smashed a pudding in my uncle's house!' said Harry, frowning. 'The Ministry of Magic said I'd be expelled from Hogwarts if there was any more magic there!'

Unless Harry's eyes were deceiving him, Fudge was suddenly looking awkward.

'Circumstances change, Harry ... we have to take into account ... in the present climate ... surely you don't *want* to be expelled?'

'Of course I don't,' said Harry.

'Well then, what's all the fuss about?' laughed Fudge airily. 'Now, have a crumpet, Harry, while I go and see if Tom's got a room for you.'

Fudge strode out of the parlour and Harry stared after him. There was something extremely odd going on. Why had Fudge been waiting for him at the Leaky Cauldron, if not to punish him for what he'd done? And now Harry came to think of it, surely it wasn't usual for the Minister for Magic *himself* to get involved in matters of underage magic?

Fudge came back, accompanied by Tom the innkeeper.

'Room eleven's free, Harry,' said Fudge. 'I think you'll be very comfortable. Just one thing, and I'm sure you'll understand: I don't want you wandering off into Muggle London, all right? Keep to Diagon Alley. And you're to be back here before dark each night. Sure you'll understand. Tom will be keeping an eye on you for me.'

第3章 骑士公共汽车

"现在剩下来的,"福吉说着,又拿了第二块烤面饼给自己,抹上黄油,"就是要决定你在哪里度过暑假最后的这三个星期了。我建议你在破釜酒吧这里租一间房子——"

"等等,"哈利突然问道,"怎么惩罚我呢?"

福吉眨了眨眼睛。

"惩罚?"

"我犯了法!"哈利说,"《对未成年巫师加以合理约束法》!"

"噢,亲爱的孩子,我们不会为这样一件小事惩罚你的!"福吉不耐烦地挥着他的烤面饼,大声说道,"这是一起意外事故!我们不会因为谁吹胀了姑妈就把他送进阿兹卡班的!"

这可跟哈利过去跟魔法部打交道的情形大不一样。

"去年,就因为一个家养小精灵在我姨父家打烂了一块布丁,我就收到了正式警告!"哈利皱起眉头说,"魔法部说,如果那里再有人使用魔法,就把我从霍格沃茨开除!"

不知是不是哈利的眼睛看错了,福吉突然显得很尴尬。

"情况是在变化的嘛,哈利……我们必须考虑到……在目前的情况下……不用说,你肯定不愿意被开除吧?"

"当然不愿意。"哈利说。

"就是嘛,那你还纠缠这件事干什么?"福吉轻快地笑着说,"好了,吃一块烤甜饼吧。哈利,我去看看汤姆有没有房间可以给你住。"

福吉大步走出了单间,哈利盯着他的背影。这事儿真是蹊跷。福吉既然不想惩罚他的所作所为,为什么还要在破釜酒吧等他呢?哈利再仔细一想,魔法部部长本人亲自处理未成年巫师滥用魔法的事,这本身就很反常,不是吗?

福吉和酒吧老板汤姆一起回来了。

"11号房间空着,哈利,"福吉说,"我想你会住得很舒服的。只有一点,我相信你一定能理解:我不希望你擅自跑到伦敦的麻瓜世界去,明白吗?别离开对角巷。每天晚上天黑之前必须回到这里。你肯定能理解。汤姆会替我看住你的。"

CHAPTER THREE The Knight Bus

'OK,' said Harry slowly, 'but why –?'

'Don't want to lose you again, do we?' said Fudge with a hearty laugh. 'No, no ... best we know where you are ... I mean ...'

Fudge cleared his throat loudly and picked up his pinstriped cloak.

'Well, I'll be off, plenty to do, you know.'

'Have you had any luck with Black yet?' Harry asked.

Fudge's fingers slipped on the silver fastenings of his cloak.

'What's that? Oh, you've heard – well, no, not yet, but it's only a matter of time. The Azkaban guards have never yet failed ... and they are angrier than I've ever seen them.'

Fudge shuddered slightly.

'So, I'll say goodbye.'

He held out his hand and Harry, shaking it, had a sudden idea.

'Er – Minister? Can I ask you something?'

'Certainly,' smiled Fudge.

'Well, third-years at Hogwarts are allowed to visit Hogsmeade, but my aunt and uncle didn't sign the permission form. D'you think you could?'

Fudge was looking uncomfortable.

'Ah,' he said. 'No. No, I'm very sorry, Harry, but as I'm not your parent or guardian –'

'But you're the Minister for Magic,' said Harry eagerly. 'If you gave me permission –'

'No, I'm sorry, Harry, but rules are rules,' said Fudge flatly. 'Perhaps you'll be able to visit Hogsmeade next year. In fact, I think it best if you don't ... yes ... well, I'll be off. Enjoy your stay, Harry.'

And with a last smile and shake of Harry's hand, Fudge left the room. Tom now moved forward, beaming at Harry.

'If you'll follow me, Mr Potter,' he said. 'I've already taken your things up ...'

Harry followed Tom up a handsome wooden staircase to a door with a brass number eleven on it, which Tom unlocked and opened for him.

Inside was a very comfortable-looking bed, some highly polished oak furniture, a cheerfully crackling fire and, perched on top of the wardrobe –

第3章 骑士公共汽车

"好的,"哈利慢吞吞地说,"可是为什么——"

"我们不想再把你给丢了,不是吗?"福吉开怀大笑着说,"不,不……我是说……我们最好知道你在哪儿……"

福吉大声清了清喉咙,拿起他的条纹斗篷。

"好了,我得走了,还有一大堆事要做呢。"

"布莱克有下落吗?"哈利问。

福吉的手指在斗篷的银扣子上滑了一下。

"你说什么?噢,你也听说了——唉,没有,还没有消息,但这只是早晚的问题。阿兹卡班的看守从来都不是吃干饭的……而且我从来没见过他们这么恼火。"

福吉微微打了个寒战。

"好了,再见吧。"

他伸出一只手,哈利握了握,脑子里突然冒出一个念头。

"嗯——部长?我可以求你一件事吗?"

"当然。"福吉笑着说。

"嗯,霍格沃茨三年级的学生可以去霍格莫德村,可是我姨妈和姨父没有在许可表上签字。你是不是能帮我签一下呢?"

福吉显得很不自然。

"啊,"他说,"不行,不行,很抱歉,哈利,我不是你的家长或监护人——"

"但你是魔法部部长啊,"哈利急切地说,"如果你批准了——"

"不,很抱歉,哈利,规矩就是规矩。"福吉一口拒绝了,"也许你明年就能去霍格莫德村了。实际上,我认为你最好别去……是啊……好了,我要走了。祝你在这里住得愉快,哈利。"

福吉最后又笑了笑,跟哈利握握手,离开了房间。这时汤姆走上前,笑眯眯地看着哈利。

"请跟我来,波特先生,"他说,"我已经把你的东西搬上去了……"

哈利跟着汤姆走上一道漂亮的木头楼梯,来到一扇门前,门上贴着黄铜数字11号。汤姆开了锁,替哈利把门打开了。

里面是一张看上去非常舒适的床,几件锃光瓦亮的橡木家具,壁炉里燃着一蓬噼啪作响、令人喜悦的旺火,而在那衣柜顶上——

CHAPTER THREE The Knight Bus

'Hedwig!' Harry gasped.

The snowy owl clicked her beak and fluttered down onto Harry's arm.

'Very smart owl you've got there,' chuckled Tom. 'Arrived about five minutes after you did. If there's anything you need, Mr Potter, don't hesitate to ask.'

He gave another bow and left.

Harry sat on his bed for a long time, absent-mindedly stroking Hedwig. The sky outside the window was changing rapidly from deep, velvety blue to cold, steely grey and then, slowly, to pink shot with gold. Harry could hardly believe that he'd only left Privet Drive a few hours ago, that he wasn't expelled, and that he was now facing three completely Dursley-free weeks.

'It's been a very weird night, Hedwig,' he yawned.

And without even removing his glasses, he slumped back onto his pillows and fell asleep.

"海德薇!"哈利激动地喊。

雪白的猫头鹰敲了敲它的喙,呼扇着翅膀飞到哈利手臂上。

"你这只猫头鹰可真聪明,"汤姆轻声笑着说,"你刚来五分钟它就到了。波特先生,如果你有什么需要请尽管提。"

他又鞠了一躬,离开了。

哈利在床上坐了很长时间,心不在焉地抚摸着海德薇的羽毛。窗外天色迅速变化,从天鹅绒般的深蓝色变成阴冷的灰色,再慢慢变成夹着道道金光的粉红色。哈利简直不敢相信就在几个小时前他离开了女贞路,而且没有被开除,面前是三个星期彻底摆脱德思礼一家的日子。

"这个晚上真是太古怪了,海德薇。"他打了个哈欠。

他连眼镜都没有摘,一头倒在枕头上,进入了梦乡。

CHAPTER FOUR

The Leaky Cauldron

It took Harry several days to get used to his strange new freedom. Never before had he been able to get up whenever he wanted or eat whatever he fancied. He could even go wherever he liked, as long as it was in Diagon Alley, and as this long cobbled street was packed with the most fascinating wizarding shops in the world, Harry felt no desire to break his word to Fudge and stray back into the Muggle world.

Harry ate breakfast each morning in the Leaky Cauldron, where he liked watching the other guests: funny little witches from the country, up for a day's shopping; venerable-looking wizards arguing over the latest article in *Transfiguration Today*; wild-looking warlocks, raucous dwarfs and, once, what looked suspiciously like a hag, who ordered a plate of raw liver from behind a thick woollen balaclava.

After breakfast Harry would go out into the back yard, take out his wand, tap the third brick from the left above the dustbin, and stand back as the archway into Diagon Alley opened in the wall.

Harry spent the long sunny days exploring the shops and eating under the brightly coloured umbrellas outside cafés, where his fellow diners were showing each other their purchases ('it's a lunascope, old boy – no more messing around with moon charts, see?') or else discussing the case of Sirius Black ('personally, I won't let any of the children out alone until he's back in Azkaban'). Harry didn't have to do his homework under the blankets by torchlight any more; now he could sit in the bright sunshine outside Florean Fortescue's Ice-Cream Parlour, finishing all his essays with occasional help from Florean Fortescue himself, who, apart from knowing a great deal about medieval witch-burnings, gave Harry free sundaes every half hour.

第4章

破釜酒吧

过了几天,哈利才习惯了这种从未体验过的奇特的自由。以前,他从来不能想什么时候起床就什么时候起床,喜欢吃什么就吃什么。现在,他甚至可以想去哪儿就去哪儿,只要是在对角巷内,而这条长长的卵石街道上全是世界上最诱人的巫师商店。哈利一点儿也不想违反他对福吉的承诺,重新回到麻瓜世界里去。

哈利每天早晨在破釜酒吧吃早饭,他喜欢打量其他的顾客:从乡下来的怪模怪样的小个子女巫,大清早出来买东西;看上去弱不禁风的男巫,为《今日变形术》上的最新文章展开辩论;不修边幅的巫师;吵吵闹闹的小矮人……一次,还有一个活像老巫婆的人,戴着一顶厚厚的巴拉克拉瓦盔式羊毛帽,要了一盘生肝。

吃过早饭,哈利便走进后院,他掏出魔杖,敲敲垃圾箱上边从左边数的第三块砖,然后退后一步,看着对角巷的大门在墙上缓缓洞开。

那些漫长的阳光灿烂的白天,哈利就在商店里逛进逛出,在咖啡屋外色彩鲜艳的太阳伞下吃饭。和他一起用餐的顾客互相拿出购买的东西给对方看("老伙计,这是一台望月镜——再也用不着摆弄月亮图表了,是不是?"),或者谈论小天狼星布莱克的案子("从我个人来说,他没有回到阿兹卡班以前,我是不会让我的孩子单独出门的")。哈利再也不用躲在毯子底下,打着手电筒做家庭作业了。现在他可以坐在福洛林·福斯科冰淇淋店外面明亮的阳光里,完成他的那些论文。福洛林·福斯科有时还会帮他的忙,他不仅知道许多中世纪焚烧女巫的事,还每过半小时就给哈利一份免费的冰淇淋。

CHAPTER FOUR   The Leaky Cauldron

Once Harry had refilled his money bag with gold Galleons, silver Sickles and bronze Knuts from his vault at Gringotts, he needed to exercise a lot of self-control not to spend the whole lot at once. He had to keep reminding himself that he had five years to go at Hogwarts, and how it would feel to ask the Dursleys for money for spellbooks, to stop himself buying a handsome set of solid gold Gobstones (a wizarding game rather like marbles, in which the stones squirted a nasty-smelling liquid into the other player's face when they lost a point). He was sorely tempted, too, by the perfect, moving model of the galaxy in a large glass ball, which would have meant he never had to take another Astronomy lesson. But the thing that tested Harry's resolution most appeared in his favourite shop, Quality Quidditch Supplies, a week after he'd arrived at the Leaky Cauldron.

Curious to know what the crowd in the shop was staring at, Harry edged his way inside and squeezed in amongst the excited witches and wizards until he glimpsed a newly erected podium on which was mounted the most magnificent broom he had ever seen in his life.

'Just come out ... prototype ...' a square-jawed wizard was telling his companion.

'It's the fastest broom in the world, isn't it, Dad?' squeaked a boy younger than Harry, who was swinging off his father's arm.

'Irish International Side's just put in an order for seven of these beauties!' the proprietor of the shop told the crowd. 'And they're favourites for the World Cup!'

A large witch in front of Harry moved, and he was able to read the sign next to the broom:

THE FIREBOLT

This state-of-the-art racing broom sports a *STREAMLINED* super-fine handle of ash, treated with a *DIAMOND-HARD POLISH* and hand-numbered with its own registration number. Each individually selected birch twig in the broomtail has been honed to *AERODYNAMIC PERFECTION*, giving the Firebolt *UNSURPASSABLE BALANCE* and *PINPOINT PRECISION*. The Firebolt has an acceleration of 0-150 *MILES AN HOUR IN TEN SECONDS* and incorporates an *UNBREAKABLE BRAKING CHARM*.

PRICE ON REQUEST

第4章 破釜酒吧

哈利从古灵阁的地下金库里取出金加隆、银西可和铜纳特，把钱袋重新装满之后，就需要用很大的毅力克制自己，不要把钱一下子花光。他必须不断提醒自己还要在霍格沃茨上五年学，提醒自己向德思礼夫妇要钱买魔法书会是什么滋味。他忍住了没买那套漂亮的纯金高布石（一种很像弹子游戏的巫师玩具，那些石子会朝输了分数的人脸上喷射一种难闻的液体）。一个大玻璃球里的精美星系活动模型也让他非常动心，如果买下来，就用不着再去上天文课了。但是对哈利意志的最严峻考验，出现在他来到破釜酒吧一星期后，在他最喜欢的商店——魁地奇精品店里。

哈利想知道店里围了那么多人在看什么，便侧身钻了进去，挤过那些兴奋的男女巫师，好不容易看见一个刚搭起来的台子，上面放着一把他有生以来见过的最气派的扫帚。

"刚出来的……样品……"一位方下巴的男巫告诉他的同伴。

"这是世界上飞得最快的扫帚。是吗，爸爸？"一个比哈利年幼的男孩摇晃着父亲的胳膊，尖声问道。

"爱尔兰国际俱乐部刚下了订单，要买七把这样的精品！"店主告诉大家，"它们可是本届世界杯的抢手货啊！"

哈利前面一个大块头女巫挪开了，哈利终于看见了扫帚旁边的标牌：

火弩箭

　　本款最新高速飞天扫帚采用流线型设计，优质白蜡木柄，施以钻石硬度的增光剂，注册号码手工镌写。扫帚尾部每根精心挑选的白桦树枝都磨成流线型，使扫帚具有无与伦比的平衡性和精妙的准确性。火弩箭能在十秒钟内从静止加速到每小时一百五十英里，并内置牢不可破的制动咒。

　　价格面议。

CHAPTER FOUR The Leaky Cauldron

Price on request ... Harry didn't like to think how much gold the Firebolt would cost. He had never wanted anything so much in his whole life – but he had never lost a Quidditch match on his Nimbus Two Thousand, and what was the point in emptying his Gringotts vault for the Firebolt, when he had a very good broom already? Harry didn't ask for the price, but he returned, almost every day after that, just to look at the Firebolt.

There were, however, things that Harry needed to buy. He went to the apothecary to replenish his store of Potions' ingredients, and as his school robes were now several inches too short in the arm and leg, he visited Madam Malkin's Robes for All Occasions and bought new ones. Most important of all, he had to buy his new school books, which would include those for his two new subjects, Care of Magical Creatures and Divination.

Harry got a surprise as he looked in at the bookshop window. Instead of the usual display of gold-embossed spellbooks the size of paving slabs, there was a large iron cage behind the glass which held about a hundred copies of *The Monster Book of Monsters*. Torn pages were flying everywhere as the books grappled with each other, locked together in furious wrestling matches and snapping aggressively.

Harry pulled his booklist out of his pocket and consulted it for the first time. *The Monster Book of Monsters* was listed as the set book for Care of Magical Creatures. Now Harry understood why Hagrid had said it would come in useful. He felt relieved; he had been wondering whether Hagrid wanted help with some terrifying new pet.

As Harry entered Flourish and Blotts, the manager came hurrying towards him.

'Hogwarts?' he said abruptly. 'Come to get your new books?'

'Yes,' said Harry. 'I need –'

'Get out of the way,' said the manager impatiently, brushing Harry aside. He drew on a pair of very thick gloves, picked up a large, knobbly walking stick and proceeded towards the door of the *Monster Books'* cage.

'Hang on,' said Harry quickly, 'I've already got one of those.'

'Have you?' A look of enormous relief spread over the manager's face. 'Thank heavens for that, I've been bitten five times already this morning –'

A loud ripping noise rent the air; two of the *Monster Books* had seized a third and were pulling it apart.

第4章 破釜酒吧

价格面议……哈利不愿意去想火弩箭要卖多少钱。他一生中从没有这样渴望得到某件东西——但是，他用他的那把光轮2000没有输过一场比赛。既然已经有了一把很好的扫帚，有什么必要把他的古灵阁地下金库搬空，来买这把火弩箭呢？哈利没有去问价钱，可从那以后，他几乎每天都到店里去，只为了看看火弩箭。

不过，有些东西是哈利必须买的。他到药店去添置了魔药课所需的配料，而且校服的裤腿和袖子都短了几寸，他便到摩金夫人长袍专卖店买了新的。最重要的是，他要购买新课本，其中包括两门新课：保护神奇动物课和占卜课。

哈利朝书店的窗户里一看，不禁大吃一惊。店里平常都陈列着铺路石板那么厚的烫金魔法书，可现在玻璃后面放着的是一个很大的铁笼子，里面关着大约一百本《妖怪们的妖怪书》。这些书全都纠缠在一起，气势汹汹地互相厮打，像在进行激烈的摔跤比赛，破碎的纸片到处飞舞。

哈利从口袋里掏出书单，第一次好好看了看。《妖怪们的妖怪书》被列为保护神奇动物课的课本。哈利这才明白海格为什么说它会派上用场。他觉得松了口气；他一直担心海格要他帮着对付某种吓人的新宠物呢。

哈利走进了丽痕书店，经理三步两步走上前来。

"霍格沃茨的？"他唐突地问，"来买新课本？"

"是啊，"哈利说，"我需要——"

"闪开。"经理不耐烦地说，把哈利揉到一边。他戴上一副很厚的手套，操起一根布满节疤的大拐棍，朝着《妖怪们的妖怪书》的笼门走去。

"等等，"哈利赶紧说道，"那种书我已经有了。"

"是吗？"经理顿时显出如释重负的表情，"谢天谢地，今天上午我已经被咬了五次——"

一声响亮的哧啦划破了空气，两本《妖怪们的妖怪书》揪住第三本，把它扯成了两半。

CHAPTER FOUR The Leaky Cauldron

'Stop it! Stop it!' cried the manager, poking the walking stick through the bars and knocking the books apart. 'I'm never stocking them again, never! It's been bedlam! I thought we'd seen the worst when we bought two hundred copies of *The Invisible Book of Invisibility* – cost a fortune, and we never found them ... Well, is there anything else I can help you with?'

'Yes,' said Harry, looking down his booklist. 'I need *Unfogging the Future*, by Cassandra Vablatsky.'

'Ah, starting Divination, are you?' said the manager, stripping off his gloves and leading Harry into the back of the shop, where there was a corner devoted to fortune-telling. A small table was stacked with volumes such as *Predicting the Unpredictable: Insulate Yourself against Shocks* and *Broken Balls: When Fortunes Turn Foul.*

'Here you are,' said the manager, who had climbed a set of steps to take down a thick, black-bound book. '*Unfogging the Future*. Very good guide to all your basic fortune-telling methods – palmistry, crystal balls, bird entrails ...'

But Harry wasn't listening. His eyes had fallen on another book, which was among a display on a small table: *Death Omens: What to Do When You Know the Worst Is Coming.*

'Oh, I wouldn't read that if I were you,' said the assistant lightly, looking to see what Harry was staring at. 'You'll start seeing death omens everywhere, it's enough to frighten anyone to death.'

But Harry continued to stare at the front cover of the book; it showed a black dog large as a bear, with gleaming eyes. It looked oddly familiar ...

The assistant pressed *Unfogging the Future* into Harry's hands.

'Anything else?' he said.

'Yes,' said Harry, tearing his eyes away from the dog's and dazedly consulting his booklist. 'Er – I need *Intermediate Transfiguration* and *The Standard Book of Spells, Grade Three.*'

Harry emerged from Flourish and Blotts ten minutes later with his new books under his arms, and made his way back to the Leaky Cauldron, hardly noticing where he was going and bumping into several people.

He tramped up the stairs to his room, went inside and tipped his books onto his bed. Somebody had been in to tidy; the windows were open and sun was pouring inside. Harry could hear the buses rolling by in the unseen Muggle street behind him, and the sound of the invisible crowd below in

第4章 破釜酒吧

"住手！住手！"经理喊道，把拐棍捅进铁笼，敲打着那些书，使它们分开，"我再也不进这些货了，再也不了！真是闹得一团糟！那次我们买了两百本《隐形术的隐形书》——花了一大笔钱，后来连个影子都没找到……我还以为不会有比那更糟糕的呢……那么，你想要些别的什么吗？"

"是的，"哈利低头看着书单说，"我需要卡珊德拉·瓦布拉斯基写的《拨开迷雾看未来》。"

"啊，开始上占卜课了，是不是？"经理说着，脱掉手套，领着哈利走进商店后面，那里有个角落专门放着占卜方面的书。一个小桌子上堆满了《预言无法预言：使自己免受惊吓》《破碎的球：当厄运来临时》之类的大部头书。

"给，"经理爬上楼梯，取下一本黑封面的大厚书，"《拨开迷雾看未来》。很好的指南，教你学会所有最基本的占卜方法——看手相、水晶球、鸟类内脏……"

但是哈利没有听经理说话。他的目光落在小桌上陈列的另一本书上：《死亡预兆：当你知道厄运即将到来时该怎么办》。

"噢，换了我可不会读那本书。"经理看看哈利盯着的书，轻描淡写地说，"读完以后，你不管在哪儿都能看到死亡预兆，足以把你吓死。"

可是哈利还是盯着那本书的封面；上面是一条像熊那么大的黑狗，瞪着一双发亮的眼睛。奇怪，它看上去那么眼熟……

经理把《拨开迷雾看未来》塞进了哈利手里。

"还要些什么吗？"他问。

"哦，"哈利这才把目光从黑狗身上挪开，茫然地看了看手里的书单，"呃——我还需要《中级变形术》和《标准咒语，三级》。"

十分钟后，哈利胳膊底下夹着新课本从丽痕书店出来了。他心不在焉地往破釜酒吧走去，眼睛也不注意看路，一连撞了好几个人。

他脚步沉重地爬上楼走进房间，把课本一股脑儿都扔在床上。房间里有人进来打扫过了，窗户开着，阳光洒了进来。哈利可以听见身后那条看不见的麻瓜街道上的车水马龙声，还有楼下对角巷里那些看

CHAPTER FOUR   The Leaky Cauldron

Diagon Alley. He caught sight of himself in the mirror over the basin.

'It can't have been a death omen,' he told his reflection defiantly. 'I was panicking when I saw that thing in Magnolia Crescent. It was probably just a stray dog ...'

He raised his hand automatically and tried to make his hair lie flat.

'You're fighting a losing battle there, dear,' said his mirror in a wheezy voice.

As the days slipped by, Harry started looking wherever he went for a sign of Ron or Hermione. Plenty of Hogwarts students were arriving in Diagon Alley now, with the start of term so near. Harry met Seamus Finnigan and Dean Thomas, his fellow Gryffindors, in Quality Quidditch Supplies, where they, too, were ogling the Firebolt; he also ran into the real Neville Longbottom, a round-faced, forgetful boy, outside Flourish and Blotts. Harry didn't stop to chat; Neville appeared to have mislaid his booklist, and was being told off by his very formidable-looking grandmother. Harry hoped she never found out that he'd pretended to be Neville while on the run from the Ministry of Magic.

Harry woke on the last day of the holidays, thinking that he would at least meet Ron and Hermione tomorrow, on the Hogwarts Express. He got up, dressed, went for a last look at the Firebolt, and was just wondering where he'd have lunch, when someone yelled his name and he turned.

'Harry! HARRY!'

They were there, both of them, sitting outside Florean Fortescue's Ice-Cream Parlour, Ron looking incredibly freckly, Hermione very brown, both waving frantically at him.

'Finally!' said Ron, grinning at Harry as he sat down. 'We went to the Leaky Cauldron, but they said you'd left, and we went to Flourish and Blotts, and Madam Malkin's, and –'

'I got all my school stuff last week,' Harry explained. 'And how come you know I'm staying at the Leaky Cauldron?'

'Dad,' said Ron simply.

Mr Weasley, who worked at the Ministry of Magic, would of course have heard the whole story of what had happened to Aunt Marge.

'Did you *really* blow up your aunt, Harry?' said Hermione in a very serious voice.

第4章 破釜酒吧

不见的人群的嘈杂声。他突然瞥见了洗手池上方镜子里的自己。

"那不可能是死亡预兆，"他不服气地对镜子里的自己说，"我在木兰花新月街看见那东西时，心里太紧张了。那大概就是一条流浪狗……"

他下意识地举起手，想把头发抹平。

"你这是白费工夫，亲爱的。"镜子用呼哧带喘的声音说。

日子一天天过去，现在哈利不管走到哪儿，都留意着寻找罗恩和赫敏的身影。很快就要开学了，大批霍格沃茨的学生都拥进了对角巷。在魁地奇精品店里，哈利遇见了他在格兰芬多的同学西莫·斐尼甘和迪安·托马斯，他们也在那里眼馋地盯着火弩箭。在丽痕书店外面，他还碰到了真正的纳威·隆巴顿，一位特别爱忘事的团团脸男孩。哈利没有停下来跟他闲聊。纳威似乎忘记把他的书单放在什么地方了，他那位模样怪吓人的奶奶正在训他。哈利但愿她老人家永远不要发现他为了逃避魔法部的追捕，曾经冒充过纳威。

暑假的最后一天，哈利从梦中醒来，心想，明天在霍格沃茨特快列车上终于可以见到罗恩和赫敏了。他起床穿好衣服，又最后去看了一眼火弩箭。他正在考虑去哪儿吃午饭，突然听见有人喊他的名字，他转过身。

"哈利！**哈利！**"

嘿，他们俩都在那儿，坐在福洛林·福斯科冰淇淋店外面，罗恩脸上的雀斑那么显眼，赫敏晒得很黑，两人都在拼命朝他挥手。

"终于见到你了！"罗恩朝哈利笑着说，哈利坐了下来，"我们去了破釜酒吧，但他们说你走了，后来我们又去了丽痕书店、摩金夫人长袍店和……"

"我上个星期就把上学用的东西都买齐了。"哈利解释道，"你们怎么知道我住在破釜酒吧？"

"我爸说的。"罗恩淡淡地说了一句。

韦斯莱先生在魔法部工作，自然已经听说了玛姬姑妈那件事的前因后果。

"哈利，你真的把你姑妈吹胀了？"赫敏语气非常严肃地问。

CHAPTER FOUR The Leaky Cauldron

'I didn't mean to,' said Harry, while Ron roared with laughter. 'I just – lost control.'

'It's not funny, Ron,' said Hermione sharply. 'Honestly, I'm amazed Harry wasn't expelled.'

'So am I,' admitted Harry. 'Forget expelled, I thought I was going to be arrested.' He looked at Ron. 'Your dad doesn't know why Fudge let me off, does he?'

'Probably 'cause it's you, isn't it?' shrugged Ron, still chuckling. 'Famous Harry Potter and all that. I'd hate to see what the Ministry'd do to *me* if I blew up an aunt. Mind you, they'd have to dig me up first, because Mum would've killed me. Anyway, you can ask Dad yourself this evening. We're staying at the Leaky Cauldron tonight, too! So you can come to King's Cross with us tomorrow! Hermione's there as well!'

Hermione nodded, beaming. 'Mum and Dad dropped me off this morning with all my Hogwarts things.'

'Excellent!' said Harry happily. 'So, have you got all your new books and stuff?'

'Look at this,' said Ron, pulling a long thin box out of a bag and opening it. 'Brand-new wand. Fourteen inches, willow, containing one unicorn tail-hair. And we've got all our books' – he pointed at a large bag under his chair. 'What about those *Monster Books*, eh? The assistant nearly cried when we said we wanted two.'

'What's all that, Hermione?' Harry asked, pointing at not one, but three, bulging bags in the chair next to her.

'Well, I'm taking more new subjects than you, aren't I?' said Hermione. 'Those are my books for Arithmancy, Care of Magical Creatures, Divination, Study of Ancient Runes, Muggle Studies –'

'What are you doing Muggle Studies for?' said Ron, rolling his eyes at Harry. 'You're Muggle-born! Your mum and dad are Muggles! You already know all about Muggles!'

'But it'll be fascinating to study them from the wizarding point of view,' said Hermione earnestly.

'Are you planning to eat or sleep at all this year, Hermione?' asked Harry, while Ron sniggered. Hermione ignored them.

第4章 破釜酒吧

"我不是故意的。"哈利说,罗恩在一旁哈哈大笑起来,"我只是——一时控制不住。"

"这可不是闹着玩的事儿,罗恩!"赫敏严厉地说,"说实在的,哈利居然没被开除,真让我感到吃惊。"

"我也纳闷儿呢,"哈利承认道,"别说开除了,我还以为会被抓起来呢。"他看着罗恩,"你爸爸也不知道福吉为什么放我一马,是吗?"

"也许就因为是你吧?"罗恩耸了耸肩,仍然轻声笑着说,"大名鼎鼎的哈利·波特什么的。我可不敢想象,如果我把一个姑妈给吹胀了,魔法部会怎么收拾我。告诉你吧,他们首先要把我从地里刨出来,因为妈妈肯定已经把我弄死了。得,反正你今天晚上可以自己去问问我爸爸。我们今晚也住在破釜酒吧!这样你明天可以跟我们一起去国王十字车站!赫敏也住在那儿!"

赫敏开心地点点头。"爸爸妈妈今天早晨把我送到这里的,还有我在霍格沃茨要用的所有东西。"

"太棒了!"哈利高兴地说,"那,你们的新课本和用具买齐了吗?"

"看看这个,"罗恩说着,从袋子里抽出一个细细长长的盒子,打了开来,"新崭崭的魔杖。柳木,十四英寸长,里面是一根独角兽的尾毛。课本我们也都买了,"他指了指他椅子底下的一个大袋子,"那些《妖怪们的妖怪书》是怎么回事,啊?我们说要买两本,店员差点哭出来。"

"那些东西是什么,赫敏?"哈利指着赫敏旁边那张椅子上的三个鼓鼓囊囊的袋子问道。

"噢,我选的新课比你们多,不是吗?"赫敏说,"那些都是我的课本,天文占卜、保护神奇动物、占卜学、古代如尼文、麻瓜研究……"

"你学麻瓜研究干什么?"罗恩说,朝哈利翻了翻眼睛,"你本来就是麻瓜出身!你爸爸妈妈都是麻瓜!你对麻瓜的事已经全知道啦!"

"可是,从巫师的角度去研究他们肯定会很有趣的。"赫敏兴致勃勃地说。

"你这一年还打算吃饭和睡觉吗,赫敏?"哈利问,罗恩在一旁坏笑。赫敏没理他们。

CHAPTER FOUR   The Leaky Cauldron

'I've still got ten Galleons,' she said, checking her purse. 'It's my birthday in September, and Mum and Dad gave me some money to get myself an early birthday present.'

'How about a nice *book*?' said Ron innocently.

'No, I don't think so,' said Hermione composedly. 'I really want an owl. I mean, Harry's got Hedwig and you've got Errol –'

'I haven't,' said Ron. 'Errol's a family owl. All I've got is Scabbers.' He pulled his pet rat out of his pocket. 'And I want to get him checked over,' he added, placing Scabbers on the table in front of them. 'I don't think Egypt agreed with him.'

Scabbers was looking thinner than usual, and there was a definite droop to his whiskers.

'There's a magical-creature shop just over there,' said Harry, who knew Diagon Alley very well by now. 'You can see if they've got anything for Scabbers, and Hermione can get her owl.'

So they paid for their ice-creams and crossed the street to the Magical Menagerie.

There wasn't much room inside. Every inch of wall was hidden by cages. It was smelly and very noisy because the occupants of these cages were all squeaking, squawking, jabbering or hissing. The witch behind the counter was already advising a wizard on the care of double-ended newts, so Harry, Ron and Hermione waited, examining the cages.

A pair of enormous purple toads sat gulping wetly and feasting on dead blowflies. A gigantic tortoise with a jewel-encrusted shell was glittering near the window. Poisonous orange snails were oozing slowly up the side of their glass tank, and a fat white rabbit kept changing into a silk top hat and back again with a loud popping noise. Then there were cats of every colour, a noisy cage of ravens, a basket of funny custard-coloured furballs that were humming loudly, and, on the counter, a vast cage of sleek black rats which were playing some sort of skipping game using their long bald tails.

The double-ended-newt wizard left and Ron approached the counter.

'It's my rat,' he told the witch. 'He's been a bit off-colour ever since I brought him back from Egypt.'

'Bang him on the counter,' said the witch, pulling a pair of heavy black spectacles out of her pocket.

第4章 破釜酒吧

"我还有十个金加隆,"她看了看她的钱包,说,"九月份是我的生日,爸爸妈妈给了我一些钱,让我提前给自己买一份生日礼物。"

"买一本好书怎么样?"罗恩假装好心地说。

"不,我不想买书,"赫敏不动声色地说,"我特别想要一只猫头鹰。你看,哈利有海德薇,你有埃罗尔——"

"我没有,"罗恩说,"埃罗尔是全家的猫头鹰。我只有斑斑。"罗恩从口袋里掏出他的宠物老鼠。"我想带它去检查一下,"说着,他把斑斑放在他们面前的桌子上,"它在埃及好像有点水土不服。"

斑斑看上去比以前更瘦了,胡须也明显耷拉着。

"那边就有一家神奇动物商店。"哈利说,他已经把对角巷摸得很熟了,"你可以看看他们对斑斑有什么办法,赫敏也可以买到她的猫头鹰。"

于是,他们付了冰淇淋的钱,穿过马路朝神奇动物商店走去。

商店里面地方很小,墙上密密麻麻地挂满了笼子,空气里有一股臭味,而且声音嘈杂,因为关在笼子里的家伙都在吱吱哇哇、叽叽喳喳地尖叫,或者发出嘶嘶的声音。柜台后面的女巫正在告诉一位巫师怎么照料双尾水螈,哈利、罗恩和赫敏便在一旁等着,一边仔细端详着那些笼子。

两只巨大的紫色蟾蜍坐在那里狼吞虎咽地大吃死丽蝇,吃得口水滴答滴答直流。一只大得吓人的乌龟待在窗户旁边,背上的壳像宝石一样闪闪发亮。有毒的橘色蜗牛在玻璃缸的壁上慢慢蠕动。一只胖乎乎的白兔子啪的一声变成一顶绸缎高帽,又啪的一声变回来,就这样不停地变来变去。此外还有各种颜色的猫,一笼子吵吵闹闹的渡鸦,一筐蛋奶糕颜色的滑稽的绒毛球正发出嗡嗡的响声。柜台上有一只大笼子,里面那些油光水滑的黑老鼠正用光秃秃的长尾巴支着身体,玩一种跳跃的游戏。

买双尾水螈的巫师走了,罗恩走近柜台。

"我的老鼠,"他对女巫说,"自从我把它从埃及带回来以后,它的颜色就有点不对劲儿。"

"把它放在柜台上。"女巫说着,从口袋里抽出一副厚厚的黑眼镜。

CHAPTER FOUR The Leaky Cauldron

Ron lifted Scabbers out of his inside pocket and placed him next to the cage of his fellow rats, who stopped their skipping tricks and scuffled to the wire for a better look.

Like nearly everything Ron owned, Scabbers the rat was second-hand (he had once belonged to Ron's brother Percy) and a bit battered. Next to the glossy rats in the cage, he looked especially woebegone.

'Hm,' said the witch, picking Scabbers up. 'How old is this rat?'

'Dunno,' said Ron. 'Quite old. He used to belong to my brother.'

'What powers does he have?' said the witch, examining Scabbers closely.

'Er –' said Ron. The truth was that Scabbers had never shown the faintest trace of interesting powers. The witch's eyes moved from Scabbers's tattered left ear to his front paw, which had a toe missing, and tutted loudly.

'He's been through the mill, this one,' she said.

'He was like that when Percy gave him to me,' said Ron defensively.

'An ordinary, common or garden rat like this can't be expected to live longer than three years or so,' said the witch. 'Now, if you were looking for something a bit more hardwearing, you might like one of these ...'

She indicated the black rats, who promptly started skipping again. Ron muttered, 'Show-offs.'

'Well, if you don't want a replacement, you can try this Rat Tonic,' said the witch, reaching under the counter and bringing out a small red bottle.

'OK,' said Ron. 'How much – OUCH!'

Ron buckled as something huge and orange came soaring from the top of the highest cage, landed on his head and then propelled itself, spitting madly, at Scabbers.

'NO, CROOKSHANKS, NO!' cried the witch, but Scabbers shot from between her hands like a bar of soap, landed splay-legged on the floor and then scarpered for the door.

'Scabbers!' Ron shouted, haring out of the shop after him; Harry followed.

It took them nearly ten minutes to find Scabbers, who had taken refuge under a wastepaper bin outside Quality Quidditch Supplies. Ron stuffed the trembling rat back into his pocket and straightened up, massaging his head.

'What *was* that?'

第4章 破釜酒吧

罗恩从衣服内侧的口袋里把斑斑掏了出来,放在那一大笼老鼠旁边。那些老鼠不再玩跳跃的把戏,全都挤过来凑到铁丝笼边,仔细打量着斑斑。

老鼠斑斑和罗恩拥有的每件东西一样,也是二手货(本来属于罗恩的哥哥珀西)。它一副饱受虐待的样子,跟笼子里那些毛色光鲜的老鼠比起来,显得特别寒酸。

"哦,"女巫抓起斑斑说,"这只老鼠多大了?"

"不知道,"罗恩说,"很老了,以前是我哥哥的。"

"它有什么本事?"女巫仔细端详着斑斑问。

"呃——"罗恩支吾着。实际上,斑斑从没有表现出一丝一毫有趣的本事。女巫的目光从斑斑破损的左耳朵移向它的前爪,那里缺了一个脚趾,她大声咂了咂嘴。

"这只老鼠可吃了不少苦。"她说。

"珀西把它给我的时候就是这样的。"罗恩委屈地说。

"像这样一只普通老鼠或花园老鼠最多只能活三年左右。"女巫说,"我说,如果你想要个活得时间长一点的,也许愿意从这里面挑一只……"

她指指那些黑老鼠,它们立刻又开始玩起了跳跃游戏。罗恩咕哝道:"喜欢卖弄的家伙。"

"好吧,如果你不想换一只,不妨试试这种老鼠强身剂。"女巫说着,俯身从柜台底下拿出一只红色的小瓶子。

"好吧,"罗恩说,"多少钱——哎哟!"

一只姜黄色的大家伙突然从最高的笼子顶上蹿了出来,落在罗恩脑袋上,差点把他给砸趴下。那大家伙竖起身子,气势汹汹地朝斑斑龇牙咧嘴。

"别,克鲁克山,别!"女巫喊道,可是斑斑已经像一块肥皂似的从她手里蹿了出去,四脚朝天地落在地板上,然后跳起来夺门而逃。

"斑斑!"罗恩大喊,跟着追出了商店,哈利也跟了出去。

花了将近十分钟,他们才找到斑斑,原来它躲到了魁地奇精品店外面的一个废纸箱底下。罗恩把瑟瑟发抖的老鼠重新塞进口袋,直起身子,揉着自己的脑袋。

"刚才那是什么玩意儿?"

CHAPTER FOUR The Leaky Cauldron

'It was either a very big cat or quite a small tiger,' said Harry.

'Where's Hermione?'

'Probably getting her owl.'

They made their way back up the crowded street to the Magical Menagerie. As they reached it, Hermione came out, but she wasn't carrying an owl. Her arms were clamped tightly around the enormous ginger cat.

'You *bought* that monster?' said Ron, his mouth hanging open.

'He's *gorgeous*, isn't he?' said Hermione, glowing.

That was a matter of opinion, thought Harry. The cat's ginger fur was thick and fluffy, but it was definitely a bit bow-legged and its face looked grumpy and oddly squashed, as though it had run headlong into a brick wall. Now that Scabbers was out of sight, however, the cat was purring contentedly in Hermione's arms.

'Hermione, that thing nearly scalped me!' said Ron.

'He didn't mean to, did you, Crookshanks?' said Hermione.

'And what about Scabbers?' said Ron, pointing at the lump in his chest pocket. 'He needs rest and relaxation! How's he going to get it with that thing around?'

'That reminds me, you forgot your Rat Tonic,' said Hermione, slapping the small red bottle into Ron's hand. 'And stop *worrying*, Crookshanks will be sleeping in my dormitory and Scabbers in yours. What's the problem? Poor Crookshanks, that witch said he'd been in there for ages: no one wanted him.'

'I wonder why,' said Ron sarcastically, as they set off towards the Leaky Cauldron.

They found Mr Weasley sitting in the bar, reading the *Daily Prophet*.

'Harry!' he said, smiling as he looked up. 'How are you?'

'Fine, thanks,' said Harry, as he, Ron and Hermione joined Mr Weasley with all their shopping.

Mr Weasley put down his paper, and Harry saw the now familiar picture of Sirius Black staring up at him.

'They still haven't caught him, then?' he asked.

'No,' said Mr Weasley, looking extremely grave. 'They've pulled us all off our regular jobs at the Ministry to try and find him, but no luck so far.'

第4章 破釜酒吧

"要么是只大猫,要么是只小老虎。"哈利说。

"赫敏呢?"

"大概在买她的猫头鹰吧。"

他们顺着拥挤的街道返回神奇动物商店。刚走到门口,赫敏出来了,但是并没有抱着什么猫头鹰。她怀里紧紧搂着那只姜黄色的大猫。

"你把这怪物买下来了?"罗恩嘴巴张得老大,问道。

"它多漂亮啊,是不是?"赫敏说,高兴得满脸放光。

哈利想,这就见仁见智了。这只猫姜黄色的毛蓬松柔软,但它的脚明显有点儿内八字,而且表情阴沉,长着一张古怪的柿饼脸,好像曾经一头撞在砖墙上。这会儿看不见斑斑了,猫心满意足地在赫敏的怀里打起了呼噜。

"赫敏,这玩意儿差点把我的头皮剥掉!"罗恩说。

"它不是故意的,是不是,克鲁克山?"赫敏说。

"斑斑怎么办?"罗恩指着胸前口袋里鼓出来的那个小包,"它需要静养,需要放松!有这东西在旁边,它怎么可能放松呢?"

"这倒提醒了我,你把你的老鼠强身剂给忘了。"赫敏说着,把那个小红瓶塞进罗恩手里,"别担心了,克鲁克山睡在我的宿舍,斑斑睡在你们宿舍。有什么问题呢?可怜的克鲁克山,那个女巫说它在那里待了好久好久,没有一个人要它。"

"这可真是怪了。"罗恩讽刺地说。他们出发朝破釜酒吧走去。

进了酒吧,他们发现韦斯莱先生正坐在吧台边看《预言家日报》。

"哈利!"他抬头一看,笑着说道,"你好吗?"

"很好,谢谢。"哈利说,他和罗恩、赫敏带着他们买的东西,坐到了韦斯莱先生身边。

韦斯莱先生放下报纸,哈利看见那张他已熟悉的小天狼星布莱克的照片正朝他瞪着眼睛。

"他们还没有抓到他吗?"他问。

"没有,"韦斯莱先生神色十分严峻,"部里把我们都调离了正常岗位,全力以赴地去抓捕他,可是到目前为止毫无进展。"

CHAPTER FOUR The Leaky Cauldron

'Would we get a reward if we caught him?' asked Ron. 'It'd be good to get some more money —'

'Don't be ridiculous, Ron,' said Mr Weasley, who on closer inspection looked very strained. 'Black's not going to be caught by a thirteen-year-old wizard. It's the Azkaban guards who'll get him back, you mark my words.'

At that moment Mrs Weasley entered the bar, laden with shopping and followed by the twins, Fred and George, who were about to start their fifth year at Hogwarts, the newly elected Head Boy, Percy, and the Weasleys' youngest child and only girl, Ginny.

Ginny, who had always been very taken with Harry, seemed even more heartily embarrassed than usual when she saw him, perhaps because he had saved her life during their last term at Hogwarts. She went very red and muttered 'Hello' without looking at him. Percy, however, held out his hand solemnly as though he and Harry had never met and said, 'Harry. How nice to see you.'

'Hello, Percy,' said Harry, trying not to laugh.

'I hope you're well?' said Percy pompously, shaking hands. It was rather like being introduced to the mayor.

'Very well, thanks —'

'Harry!' said Fred, elbowing Percy out of the way and bowing deeply. 'Simply *splendid* to see you, old boy —'

'Marvellous,' said George, pushing Fred aside and seizing Harry's hand in turn. 'Absolutely spiffing.'

Percy scowled.

'That's enough, now,' said Mrs Weasley.

'Mum!' said Fred, as though he'd only just spotted her, and seized her hand, too. 'How really corking to see you —'

'I *said*, that's enough,' said Mrs Weasley, depositing her shopping in an empty chair. 'Hello, Harry, dear. I suppose you've heard our exciting news?' She pointed at the brand-new silver badge on Percy's chest. 'Second Head Boy in the family!' she said, swelling with pride.

'And last,' Fred muttered under his breath.

'I don't doubt that,' said Mrs Weasley, frowning suddenly. 'I notice they

"如果我们抓住了他，有奖金吗？"罗恩问，"再有些钱该多好——"

"别胡说八道，罗恩。"韦斯莱先生说，离近了看，他的神情显得非常紧张，"布莱克不可能被一个十三岁的小巫师抓住的。记住我的话吧，最后把他抓回去的肯定还是那些阿兹卡班的看守。"

就在这时，韦斯莱夫人走进了酒吧，手里大包小包地提着买的东西，后面跟着双胞胎兄弟弗雷德和乔治——他们将在霍格沃茨开始上五年级，还有刚被选为男生学生会主席的珀西，以及韦斯莱家最小的孩子，也是唯一的女孩——金妮。

金妮一向很喜欢哈利，现在看到哈利，似乎比平常更害羞了，这大概是因为上学期在霍格沃茨哈利曾经救过她的命。她脸涨得通红，低声说了句"你好"，眼睛都不敢看哈利。珀西则煞有介事地伸出手，就好像他和哈利不认识似的："哈利，见到你很高兴。"

"你好，珀西。"哈利忍着笑说。

"你一切都好吧？"珀西一边跟哈利握手，一边装模作样地说。这感觉像是被介绍给了市长。

"很好，谢谢——"

"哈利！"弗雷德说着，用胳膊肘把珀西推到一边，深深地鞠了一躬，"老伙计，见到你真是太美妙了——"

"绝妙无比，"乔治说，一把推开弗雷德，抢着抓住哈利的手，"绝对妙不可言。"

珀西皱起了眉头。

"行啦，够了。"韦斯莱夫人说。

"妈妈！"弗雷德好像刚看见她似的，也一把抓住她的手，说道，"看见你真是心花怒放——"

"听见没有，够了。"韦斯莱夫人说着，把买的东西放在一把空椅子上，"你好，哈利，亲爱的。我想你一定听说了我们的特大新闻吧？"她指着珀西胸前崭新的银徽章，"家里的第二个男生学生会主席！"她说，骄傲之情溢于言表。

"也是最后一位。"弗雷德压低声音咕哝道。

"这一点我毫不怀疑。"韦斯莱夫人突然皱起了眉头，"我注意到他

CHAPTER FOUR   The Leaky Cauldron

haven't made you two Prefects.'

'What do we want to be Prefects for?' said George, looking revolted at the very idea. 'It'd take all the fun out of life.'

Ginny giggled.

'You want to set a better example to your sister!' snapped Mrs Weasley.

'Ginny's got other brothers to set her an example, Mother,' said Percy loftily. 'I'm going up to change for dinner ...'

He disappeared and George heaved a sigh.

'We tried to shut him in a pyramid,' he told Harry. 'But Mum spotted us.'

Dinner that night was a very enjoyable affair. Tom the inn-keeper put three tables together in the parlour and the seven Weasleys, Harry and Hermione ate their way through five delicious courses.

'How're we getting to King's Cross tomorrow, Dad?' asked Fred, as they tucked into a sumptuous chocolate pudding.

'The Ministry's providing a couple of cars,' said Mr Weasley.

Everyone looked up at him.

'Why?' said Percy curiously.

'It's because of you, Perce,' said George seriously. 'And there'll be little flags on the bonnets, with HB on them –'

'– for Humungous Bighead,' said Fred.

Everyone except Percy and Mrs Weasley snorted into their pudding.

'Why are the Ministry providing cars, Father?' Percy asked again, in a dignified voice.

'Well, as we haven't got one any more,' said Mr Weasley, 'and as I work there, they're doing me a favour ...'

His voice was casual, but Harry couldn't help noticing that Mr Weasley's ears had gone red, just like Ron's did when he was under pressure.

'Good job, too,' said Mrs Weasley briskly. 'Do you realise how much luggage you've all got between you? A nice sight you'd be on the Muggle Underground ... You are all packed, aren't you?'

'Ron hasn't put all his new things in his trunk yet,' said Percy, in a long-suffering voice. 'He's dumped them on my bed.'

第4章 破釜酒吧

们没有选你们俩当级长。"

"我们要当级长干什么?"乔治说,似乎一想到这个念头就令他作呕,"它会使生活变得好没乐趣的。"

金妮咯咯地笑出声来。

"你们必须给妹妹树立一个好榜样!"韦斯莱夫人厉声说。

"金妮有别的哥哥给她树立榜样呢,妈妈。"珀西高傲地说,"我上楼换衣服,准备吃饭……"

他走了,乔治舒了口气。

"我们本来想把他关在一座金字塔里的,"他对哈利说,"可是被妈妈发现了。"

那天晚上的聚餐令人非常愉快。酒吧老板汤姆在大厅里把三张桌子拼在一起,韦斯莱一家七口、哈利和赫敏津津有味地品尝着五道鲜美的菜肴。

"爸爸,明天我们怎么去国王十字车站呢?"弗雷德问,这时他们正在大口地吃一块无比美味的巧克力布丁。

"部里派了两辆车。"韦斯莱先生说。

大家都抬起头来看着他。

"为什么?"珀西好奇地问。

"是因为你啊,珀西,"乔治一本正经地说,"引擎罩上还插着小旗子,上面写着 HB——"

"——奇大无比的脑袋。"弗雷德说。

除了珀西和韦斯莱夫人,桌上每个人都对着布丁笑出声来。

"爸爸,部里为什么要给我们派车?"珀西端着架子又问了一遍。

"噢,因为我们自己没有汽车了,"韦斯莱先生说,"而且我又在部里工作,他们就给我行了一个方便……"

韦斯莱先生的语气轻描淡写,但哈利注意到他的耳朵红了,就像罗恩内心承受压力时那样。

"这样太好了。"韦斯莱夫人轻快地说,"知道你们一共带了多少行李吗?在麻瓜地铁里肯定会引人注目……你们的东西都收拾好了吗?"

"罗恩还没有把他新买的东西都收进箱子,"珀西用一种忍耐了很久的口吻说,"他把它们都扔在了我的床上。"

CHAPTER FOUR   The Leaky Cauldron

'You'd better go and pack properly, Ron, because we won't have much time in the morning,' Mrs Weasley called down the table. Ron scowled at Percy.

After dinner everyone felt very full and sleepy. One by one they made their way upstairs to their rooms to check their things for the next day. Ron and Percy were next door to Harry. He had just closed and locked his own trunk when he heard angry voices through the wall, and went to see what was going on.

The door of number twelve was ajar and Percy was shouting.

'It was *here*, on the bedside table, I took it off for polishing –'

'I haven't touched it, all right?' Ron roared back.

'What's up?' said Harry.

'My Head Boy badge has gone,' said Percy, rounding on Harry.

'So's Scabbers's Rat Tonic,' said Ron, throwing things out of his trunk to look. 'I think I might've left it in the bar –'

'You're not going anywhere till you've found my badge!' yelled Percy.

'I'll get Scabbers's stuff, I'm packed,' Harry said to Ron, and he went downstairs.

Harry was halfway along the passage to the bar, which was now very dark, when he heard another pair of angry voices coming from the parlour. A second later, he recognised them as Mr and Mrs Weasley's. He hesitated, not wanting them to know he'd heard them rowing, when the sound of his own name made him stop, then move closer to the parlour door.

'... makes no sense not to tell him,' Mr Weasley was saying heatedly. 'Harry's got a right to know. I've tried to tell Fudge, but he insists on treating Harry like a child. He's thirteen years old and –'

'Arthur, the truth would terrify him!' said Mrs Weasley shrilly. 'Do you really want to send Harry back to school with that hanging over him? For heaven's sake, he's *happy* not knowing!'

'I don't want to make him miserable, I want to put him on his guard!' retorted Mr Weasley. 'You know what Harry and Ron are like, wandering off by themselves – they've even ended up in the Forbidden Forest! But Harry mustn't do that this year! When I think what could have happened

第4章 破釜酒吧

"你最好赶紧去收拾利索,罗恩,明天早上我们不会有多少时间的。"韦斯莱夫人朝桌子这头大声说。罗恩不满地瞪着珀西。

晚饭后,每个人都觉得饱饱的,昏昏欲睡。他们一个接一个地上楼回到自己的房间,检查第二天的东西是否收拾好了。罗恩和珀西住在哈利的隔壁。哈利刚关上门,锁好自己的箱子,就听见隔墙传来愤怒的说话声,于是出门去看个究竟。

12号房间的门开着一道缝,珀西正在大声叫嚷。

"它本来就在这儿,放在床头柜上的,我摘下来擦一擦——"

"我连碰都没碰一下,知道吗?"罗恩吼着回答。

"怎么啦?"哈利问。

"我的学生会主席徽章不见了。"珀西转向哈利说道。

"斑斑的老鼠强身剂也不见了。"罗恩把他箱子里的东西都扔出来寻找,"我想大概是忘在吧台上了——"

"不把徽章给我找到,你哪儿也别想去!"珀西嚷道。

"我去拿斑斑的药吧,我的东西已经收拾好了。"哈利对罗恩说,然后便下楼去了。

哈利朝现已漆黑一片的吧台走去,刚走到一半,突然听见一个单间里传来另外两个人愤怒的说话声,随即听出那是韦斯莱先生和韦斯莱夫人。他迟疑了,不想让他们知道他听见他们在吵架,可是,他突然听到了自己的名字,便停了下来,凑近单间的门。

"……不告诉他是不对的。"韦斯莱先生情绪激烈地说,"哈利有权知道。我本来想说服福吉,可他坚持要把哈利当小孩子看待。哈利已经十三岁了,他——"

"亚瑟,真相会把他吓坏的!"韦斯莱夫人尖叫着说,"那个危险随时存在,你真的想让哈利心里带着那样的阴影回学校吗?看在老天的分儿上,他蒙在鼓里倒会开心一些。"

"我不想让他难过,只想让他提高警惕!"韦斯莱先生厉声反驳,"你知道哈利和罗恩是个什么德行,他们经常自己到处乱逛——甚至跑到禁林里去!哈利这学期千万不能这么做了!我真不敢想象那天晚上他

CHAPTER FOUR The Leaky Cauldron

to him that night he ran away from home! If the Knight Bus hadn't picked him up, I'm prepared to bet he would have been dead before the Ministry found him.'

'But he's *not* dead, he's fine, so what's the point –'

'Molly, they say Sirius Black's mad, and maybe he is, but he was clever enough to escape from Azkaban, and that's supposed to be impossible. It's been a month now, and no one's seen hide nor hair of him, and I don't care what Fudge keeps telling the *Daily Prophet*, we're no nearer catching Black than inventing self-spelling wands. The only thing we know for sure is what Black's after –'

'But Harry will be perfectly safe at Hogwarts.'

'We thought Azkaban was perfectly safe. If Black can break out of Azkaban, he can break into Hogwarts.'

'But no one's really sure that Black's after Harry –'

There was a thud on wood, and Harry was sure Mr Weasley had banged his fist on the table.

'Molly, how many times do I have to tell you? They didn't report it in the press because Fudge wanted it kept quiet, but Fudge went out to Azkaban the night Black escaped. The guards told Fudge that Black's been talking in his sleep for a while now. Always the same words: "He's at Hogwarts ... he's at Hogwarts." Black is deranged, Molly, and he wants Harry dead. If you ask me, he thinks murdering Harry will bring You-Know-Who back to power. Black lost everything the night Harry stopped You-Know-Who, and he's had twelve years alone in Azkaban to brood on that ...'

There was a silence. Harry leant still closer to the door, desperate to hear more.

'Well, Arthur, you must do what you think is right. But you're forgetting Albus Dumbledore. I don't think anything could hurt Harry at Hogwarts while Dumbledore's Headmaster. I suppose he knows about all this?'

'Of course he knows. We had to ask him if he minds the Azkaban guards stationing themselves around the entrances to the school grounds. He wasn't happy about it, but he agreed.'

'Not happy? Why shouldn't he be happy, if they're there to catch Black?'

'Dumbledore isn't fond of the Azkaban guards,' said Mr Weasley heavily.

第4章　破釜酒吧

从家里逃出来会遭遇什么危险！如果骑士公共汽车没有把他接走，我敢肯定没等部里找到他，他就已经死了。"

"可是他没有死，他很好，有什么必要——"

"莫丽，他们说小天狼星布莱克疯了，没准他真是疯了，但他居然有本事从阿兹卡班逃出来，大家都认为那是不可能的事。现在已经一个月了，还没有任何人看见过他的影子。我不管福吉每天都在跟《预言家日报》说些什么，反正我们在逮捕布莱克的事情上，就像发明自动施咒魔杖一样毫无进展。只有一点可以肯定：布莱克在找——"

"可是哈利待在霍格沃茨是绝对安全的。"

"我们还以为阿兹卡班是绝对安全的呢。既然布莱克能从阿兹卡班越狱逃跑，肯定也有本事闯进霍格沃茨。"

"可是谁也不能真的肯定布莱克是在找哈利——"

咚，什么东西砸在木头上的声音，哈利猜想肯定是韦斯莱先生用拳头敲了一下桌子。

"莫丽，我还要告诉你多少遍呢？报纸上没有报道，因为福吉想捂盖子，可是布莱克逃跑的那天夜里福吉就去了阿兹卡班。看守们告诉福吉，很长时间以来，布莱克一直在说梦话，翻来覆去总是那一句话：'他在霍格沃茨……他在霍格沃茨。'布莱克精神错乱了，莫丽，他想要哈利的命。要我说，他以为杀死哈利就能使神秘人卷土重来。哈利阻止神秘人的那天夜里，布莱克失去了一切，他独自在阿兹卡班待了十二年，整天都在琢磨这件事……"

沉默。哈利往门上贴得更紧了，努力想多听到一些。

"好吧，亚瑟，你肯定是认为合适才这样做的。但是你忘记了阿不思·邓布利多。我认为，只要是邓布利多当校长，霍格沃茨就没有什么能够伤害到哈利。我想，这些情况邓布利多都知道吧？"

"他当然知道。我们得去问他是否同意阿兹卡班的看守在学校门口驻防。他对此不太高兴，但还是同意了。"

"不高兴？他们不是被派去抓布莱克的吗，他为什么不高兴？"

"邓布利多不喜欢阿兹卡班的看守。"韦斯莱先生语气沉重地说，"要

CHAPTER FOUR   The Leaky Cauldron

'Nor am I, if it comes to that ... but when you're dealing with a wizard like Black, you sometimes have to join forces with those you'd rather avoid.'

'If they save Harry –'

'– then I will never say another word against them,' said Mr Weasley wearily. 'It's late, Molly, we'd better go up ...'

Harry heard chairs move. As quietly as he could, he hurried down the passage to the bar and out of sight. The parlour door opened, and a few seconds later footsteps told him that Mr and Mrs Weasley were climbing the stairs.

The bottle of Rat Tonic was lying under the table they had sat at earlier. Harry waited until he heard Mr and Mrs Weasley's bedroom door close, then headed back upstairs with the bottle.

Fred and George were crouching in the shadows on the landing, heaving with laughter as they listened to Percy dismantling his and Ron's room in the search for his badge.

'We've got it,' Fred whispered to Harry. 'We've been improving it.'

The badge now read *Bighead Boy*.

Harry forced a laugh, went to give Ron the rat tonic, then shut himself in his room and lay down on his bed.

So Sirius Black was after him. That explained everything. Fudge had been lenient with him because he was so relieved to find him alive. He'd made Harry promise to stay in Diagon Alley, where there were plenty of wizards to keep an eye on him. And he was sending two Ministry cars to take them all to the station tomorrow, so that the Weasleys could look after Harry until he was on the train.

Harry lay listening to the muffled shouting next door and wondered why he didn't feel more scared. Sirius Black had murdered thirteen people with one curse; Mr and Mrs Weasley obviously thought Harry would be panic-stricken if he knew the truth. But Harry happened to agree wholeheartedly with Mrs Weasley that the safest place on earth was wherever Albus Dumbledore happened to be. Didn't people always say that Dumbledore was the only person Lord Voldemort had ever been afraid of? Surely Black, as Voldemort's right-hand man, would be just as frightened of him?

And then there were these Azkaban guards everyone kept talking about. They seemed to scare most people senseless, and if they were stationed all

第4章 破釜酒吧

说起来，其实我也不喜欢……但是要对付一个像布莱克那样的巫师，有时候不得不跟你本来避之唯恐不及的人联起手来。"

"如果他们救了哈利——"

"——那我再也不会说他们一个字的坏话。"韦斯莱先生疲倦地说，"太晚了，莫丽，我们最好上楼……"

哈利听见椅子挪动的声音，赶紧蹑手蹑脚地顺着过道跑到吧台后面躲了起来。单间的门开了，几秒钟后传来了脚步声，他知道韦斯莱夫妇上楼去了。

那瓶老鼠强身剂就在他们刚才坐过的桌子底下。哈利一直等到韦斯莱夫妇房间的门关上了，才拿着瓶子回到楼上。

弗雷德和乔治蹲在楼梯平台的暗处，笑得喘不过气来。他们听着珀西为了找他那枚徽章，正把他和罗恩的房间翻个底朝天。

"是我们拿的，"弗雷德小声对哈利说，"我们对它进行了改造。"

徽章上的字变成了大头鬼。

哈利忍住笑，过去把老鼠强身剂给了罗恩，然后便回屋关上门，躺在了床上。

这么说小天狼星布莱克是在找他。这下子就全明白了。福吉对他这么宽宏大量，是因为他看到哈利还活着大松了一口气。福吉叫哈利保证不离开对角巷，是因为这儿有这么多巫师可以照看他。福吉还从部里派了两辆车，明天送他们大家去车站，这样韦斯莱一家就可以照应哈利，一直到他安全坐上火车。

哈利躺在那里，听着隔壁传来的沉闷的叫嚷声，奇怪自己怎么并不觉得很害怕。小天狼星布莱克曾经用一个咒语杀害了十三个人，韦斯莱夫妇显然以为，哈利一旦知道真相肯定会十分恐慌。但哈利碰巧从心底里赞成韦斯莱夫人的观点，认为阿不思·邓布利多在哪里，哪里便是世界上最安全的地方。人们不是总说，伏地魔这辈子只害怕过邓布利多一个人吗？布莱克是伏地魔最得力的助手，肯定也同样害怕邓布利多。

还有人人都在谈论的那些阿兹卡班看守。他们似乎令大多数人闻风丧胆，有他们驻守在学校周围，布莱克闯进来的可能性似乎微乎其微。

CHAPTER FOUR The Leaky Cauldron

around the school, Black's chances of getting inside seemed very remote.

No, all in all, the thing that bothered Harry most was the fact that his chances of visiting Hogsmeade now looked like zero. Nobody would want Harry to leave the safety of the castle until Black was caught; in fact, Harry suspected his every move would be carefully watched until the danger had passed.

He scowled at the dark ceiling. Did they think he couldn't look after himself? He'd escaped Lord Voldemort three times, he wasn't completely useless ...

Unbidden, the image of the beast in the shadows of Magnolia Crescent crossed his mind. *What to do when you know the worst is coming ...*

'I'm not going to be murdered,' Harry said out loud.

'That's the spirit, dear,' said his mirror sleepily.

第4章 破釜酒吧

不过,最让哈利烦恼的,是他去霍格莫德村的希望现在看来完全破灭了。布莱克没有抓住,谁也不会让哈利离开安全的城堡的。事实上,哈利怀疑他的一举一动都会受到严密监视,直到危险过去。

他瞪眼望着漆黑的天花板。难道他们认为他不能照顾自己?他曾经三次逃脱了伏地魔的魔爪,他并不是一个毫无本事的废物……

突然,他脑海里浮现出木兰花新月街暗处那个兽类的身影。当你知道厄运即将到来时该怎么办……

"我不会被杀死的。"哈利大声说。

"这才是好样的,亲爱的。"他的镜子睡意蒙眬地说。

CHAPTER FIVE

The Dementor

Tom woke Harry next morning with his usual toothless grin and a cup of tea. Harry got dressed and was just persuading a disgruntled Hedwig to get back into her cage when Ron banged his way into the room, pulling a sweatshirt over his head and looking irritable.

'The sooner we get on the train, the better,' he said. 'At least I can get away from Percy at Hogwarts. Now he's accusing me of dripping tea on his photo of Penelope Clearwater. You know,' Ron grimaced, 'his *girlfriend*. She's hidden her face under the frame because her nose has gone all blotchy …'

'I've got something to tell you,' Harry began, but they were interrupted by Fred and George, who had looked in to congratulate Ron on infuriating Percy again.

They headed down to breakfast, where Mr Weasley was reading the front page of the *Daily Prophet* with a furrowed brow and Mrs Weasley was telling Hermione and Ginny about a Love Potion she'd made as a young girl. All three of them were rather giggly.

'What were you saying?' Ron asked Harry, as they sat down.

'Later,' Harry muttered, as Percy stormed in.

Harry had no chance to speak to Ron or Hermione in the chaos of leaving; they were too busy heaving all their trunks down the Leaky Cauldron's narrow staircase and piling them up near the door, with Hedwig and Hermes, Percy's screech owl, perched on top in their cages. A small wickerwork basket stood beside the heap of trunks, spitting loudly.

'It's all right, Crookshanks,' Hermione cooed through the wickerwork. 'I'll let you out on the train.'

第 5 章

摄 魂 怪

第二天早晨，汤姆像往常一样端来一杯茶，咧开没牙的嘴笑着，唤醒了哈利。哈利穿好衣服，把正在闹脾气的海德薇劝回了它的笼子，这时罗恩一头冲进了房间。他正在把一件无领长袖运动衫往脑袋上套，脸上是一副恼怒的样子。

"我巴不得赶紧上火车，"他说，"至少在霍格沃茨可以摆脱珀西。他这会儿又骂我把茶水滴在他那张佩内洛·克里瓦特的照片上了。你知道，"罗恩做了个鬼脸，"那是珀西的女朋友。她把脸藏到了镜框后面，因为鼻子上全是斑……"

"我有件事要告诉你……"哈利话没说完，就被弗雷德和乔治打断了，他们进来祝贺罗恩又一次惹恼了珀西。

下楼吃早饭时，韦斯莱先生皱着眉头在看《预言家日报》第一版，韦斯莱夫人在跟赫敏和金妮讲她年轻时制作的一种迷情剂，三个人不停地咯咯笑着。

"你刚才想说什么？"他们坐下来时，罗恩问哈利。

"待会儿再说吧。"哈利低声说，这时珀西气势汹汹地进来了。

出发前一片混乱，哈利没有机会跟罗恩或赫敏说话。他们都忙着把所有的箱子从破釜酒吧狭窄的楼梯上搬下来，堆在大门口，海德薇和赫梅斯——珀西的那只长耳猫头鹰——的笼子放在箱子顶上。箱子旁边有一只小小的柳条篮，里面传出很响的呼噜声。

"没关系的，克鲁克山，"赫敏隔着柳条篮轻声安慰道，"一上火车我就放你出来。"

CHAPTER FIVE   The Dementor

'You won't,' snapped Ron. 'What about poor Scabbers, eh?'

He pointed at his chest, where a large lump indicated that Scabbers was curled up in his pocket.

Mr Weasley, who had been outside waiting for the Ministry cars, stuck his head inside.

'They're here,' he said. 'Harry, come on.'

Mr Weasley marched Harry across the short stretch of pavement towards the first of two old-fashioned dark green cars, each of which was driven by a furtive-looking wizard, wearing a suit of emerald velvet.

'In you get, Harry,' said Mr Weasley, glancing up and down the crowded street.

Harry got into the back of the car, and was shortly joined by Hermione, Ron and, to Ron's disgust, Percy.

The journey to King's Cross was very uneventful compared to Harry's trip on the Knight Bus. The Ministry of Magic cars seemed almost ordinary, though Harry noticed that they could slide through gaps that Uncle Vernon's new company car certainly couldn't have managed. They reached King's Cross with twenty minutes to spare; the Ministry drivers found them trolleys, unloaded their trunks, touched their hats to Mr Weasley and drove away, somehow managing to jump to the head of an unmoving queue for the traffic lights.

Mr Weasley kept close to Harry's elbow all the way into the station.

'Right then,' he said, glancing around them. 'Let's do this in pairs, as there are so many of us. I'll go through first with Harry.'

Mr Weasley strolled towards the barrier between platforms nine and ten, pushing Harry's trolley and apparently very interested in the InterCity 125 that had just arrived at platform nine. With a meaningful look at Harry, he leant casually against the barrier. Harry imitated him.

Next moment, they had fallen sideways through the solid metal onto platform nine and three-quarters and looked up to see the Hogwarts Express, a scarlet steam engine, puffing smoke over a platform packed with witches and wizards seeing their children onto the train.

Percy and Ginny suddenly appeared behind Harry. They were panting, and had apparently taken the barrier at a run.

'Ah, there's Penelope!' said Percy, smoothing his hair and going pink again.

第5章 摄魂怪

"不行,"罗恩厉声地说,"可怜的斑斑怎么办,嗯?"

他指着自己的胸口,一个大鼓包显示斑斑正蜷着身子待在他口袋里。

韦斯莱先生一直在门外等候魔法部的车子,这时探进头来。

"他们来了,"他说,"哈利,快走吧。"

韦斯莱先生领着哈利大步走过那段短短的人行道,走向第一辆车。共有两辆老式的墨绿色汽车,司机都是神情诡秘的巫师,穿着鲜绿色的天鹅绒西服套装。

"你进去吧,哈利。"韦斯莱先生说着,望了望人来人往的街道两边。

哈利钻进了汽车后面,很快,赫敏、罗恩和珀西——令罗恩大倒胃口——也进来了。

跟哈利乘骑士公共汽车的经历相比,他们去国王十字车站的一路上真是风平浪静。魔法部的汽车看上去没什么特别,但是哈利注意到,它们可以毫不费力地穿过狭窄的缝隙,弗农姨父公司的新车肯定是做不到的。到了国王十字车站,离开车还有二十分钟的时间。魔法部的司机给他们找来小推车,搬出那些箱子,朝韦斯莱先生行了个触帽礼,便把车开走了,不知怎的,他们居然还蹿到了因红灯等在那里的一排汽车的前头。

韦斯莱先生贴着哈利的身子走进车站。

"好了。"他望望四周说,"我们人太多,两个两个地来。我和哈利先过去。"

韦斯莱先生推着哈利的小推车,慢悠悠地朝第9和第10站台之间的隔墙走去,装出对刚刚停靠在第9站台的那辆城际125号列车非常感兴趣的样子。随即,他意味深长地看了哈利一眼,貌似随意地往隔墙上一靠。哈利也学着他的样子。

一眨眼,他们就穿过了坚固的金属墙壁,来到了 $9\frac{3}{4}$ 站台。他们抬头看见了霍格沃茨特快列车——一辆深红色的蒸汽机车,正在那里喷吐着烟雾,站台上挤满了来送孩子上车的男女巫师。

珀西和金妮突然出现在哈利身后。他们气喘吁吁,显然是跑着穿过隔墙的。

"啊,佩内洛!"珀西说着,捋了捋头发,脸又涨成了粉红色。金

CHAPTER FIVE The Dementor

Ginny caught Harry's eye and they both turned away to hide their laughter as Percy strode over to a girl with long, curly hair, walking with his chest thrown out so that she couldn't miss his shiny badge.

Once the remaining Weasleys and Hermione had joined them, Harry and Mr Weasley led the way to the end of the train, past packed compartments, to a carriage that looked quite empty. They loaded the trunks onto it, stowed Hedwig and Crookshanks in the luggage rack, then went back outside to say goodbye to Mr and Mrs Weasley.

Mrs Weasley kissed all her children, then Hermione, and finally, Harry. He was embarrassed, but really quite pleased, when she gave him an extra hug.

'Do take care, won't you, Harry?' she said as she straightened up, her eyes oddly bright. Then she opened her enormous handbag and said, 'I've made you all sandwiches. Here you are, Ron ... no, they're not corned beef ... Fred? Where's Fred? Here you are, dear ...'

'Harry,' said Mr Weasley quietly, 'come over here a moment.'

He jerked his head towards a pillar, and Harry followed him behind it, leaving the others crowded around Mrs Weasley.

'There's something I've got to tell you before you leave –' said Mr Weasley, in a tense voice.

'It's all right, Mr Weasley,' said Harry, 'I already know.'

'You know? How could you know?'

'I – er – I heard you and Mrs Weasley talking last night. I couldn't help hearing,' Harry added quickly. 'Sorry –'

'That's not the way I'd have chosen for you to find out,' said Mr Weasley, looking anxious.

'No – honestly, it's OK. This way, you haven't broken your word to Fudge and I know what's going on.'

'Harry, you must be very scared –'

'I'm not,' said Harry sincerely. '*Really*,' he added, because Mr Weasley was looking disbelieving. 'I'm not trying to be a hero, but seriously, Sirius Black can't be worse than Voldemort, can he?'

Mr Weasley flinched at the sound of the name, but overlooked it.

'Harry, I knew you were, well, made of stronger stuff than Fudge seems to think, and I'm obviously pleased that you're not scared, but –'

第 5 章 摄魂怪

妮和哈利对了一下目光，两人都转过身去偷笑。珀西大踏步地朝一个留着长长鬈发的姑娘走去，故意把胸脯挺得老高，好让姑娘看清那枚闪闪发亮的徽章。

韦斯莱家的其他人和赫敏也过来了，哈利和韦斯莱先生领头走过一个个拥挤的车厢，来到火车尾部一节看着还比较空的包厢。他们把箱子搬上车，把海德薇和克鲁克山放在行李架上，然后出来跟韦斯莱夫妇告别。

韦斯莱夫人挨个儿亲吻她的孩子，接着是赫敏，最后是哈利。她格外多搂抱了哈利一会儿，哈利觉得有点不好意思，但心里还是很高兴的。

"一定要保重，知道吗，哈利？"她直起身子说，眼睛里闪烁着奇异的光。她打开那只巨大的手提包，说："我给你们大家都做了三明治。给，罗恩……不，不是咸牛肉的……弗雷德？弗雷德上哪儿去了？给，亲爱的……"

"哈利，"韦斯莱先生小声说，"你到这边来一下。"

他把头朝一个柱子偏了偏，哈利跟他走到柱子后面，其他人都还围在韦斯莱夫人身边。

"在你离开前，有件事我必须告诉你——"韦斯莱先生紧张地说。

"不用了，韦斯莱先生，"哈利说，"我已经知道了。"

"你知道了？怎么知道的？"

"我——呃——我昨晚听见了您和韦斯莱夫人的谈话。我忍不住听了，"哈利赶紧又说了句，"对不起——"

"我可不愿意你以那种方式知道这件事。"韦斯莱先生显得很担忧。

"没事——真的没事。这样，您没有违反对福吉的承诺，我也知道了是怎么回事。"

"哈利，你肯定吓坏了——"

"没有。"哈利认真地说。"真的，"他看到韦斯莱先生露出不相信的神情，便又补充道，"我不是想充好汉，但是说实在的，小天狼星布莱克不可能比伏地魔更可怕，对吗？"

韦斯莱先生听见这个名字，吓得缩了一下，但他未予理会。

"哈利，我知道你，嗯，比福吉所想的更勇敢坚强。看到你没有被吓着，我当然很高兴，可是——"

III

CHAPTER FIVE   The Dementor

'Arthur!' called Mrs Weasley, who was now shepherding the rest onto the train. 'Arthur, what are you doing? It's about to go!'

'He's coming, Molly!' said Mr Weasley, but he turned back to Harry and kept talking in a lower and more hurried voice. 'Listen, I want you to give me your word –'

'– that I'll be a good boy and stay in the castle?' said Harry gloomily.

'Not entirely,' said Mr Weasley, who looked more serious than Harry had ever seen him. 'Harry, swear to me you won't go *looking* for Black.'

Harry stared. 'What?'

There was a loud whistle. Guards were walking along the train, slamming all the doors shut.

'Promise me, Harry,' said Mr Weasley, talking more quickly still, 'that whatever happens –'

'Why would I go looking for someone I know wants to kill me?' said Harry blankly.

'Swear to me that whatever you might hear –'

'Arthur, quickly!' cried Mrs Weasley.

Steam was billowing from the train; it had started to move. Harry ran to the compartment door and Ron threw it open and stood back to let him on. They leant out of the window and waved at Mr and Mrs Weasley until the train turned a corner and blocked them from view.

'I need to talk to you in private,' Harry muttered to Ron and Hermione as the train picked up speed.

'Go away, Ginny,' said Ron.

'Oh, that's nice,' said Ginny huffily, and she stalked off.

Harry, Ron and Hermione set off down the corridor, looking for an empty compartment, but all were full except for the one at the very end of the train.

This only had one occupant, a man sitting fast asleep next to the window. Harry, Ron and Hermione checked on the threshold. The Hogwarts Express was usually reserved for students and they had never seen an adult there before, except for the witch who pushed the food trolley.

The stranger was wearing an extremely shabby set of wizard's robes which had been darned in several places. He looked ill and exhausted. Though he seemed quite young, his light-brown hair was flecked with grey.

'Who d'you reckon he is?' Ron hissed, as they sat down and slid the door shut, taking the seats furthest away from the window.

第5章 摄魂怪

"亚瑟！"韦斯莱夫人喊道，她已经在照顾其他人上火车了，"亚瑟，你在干什么？车要开了！"

"这就来，莫丽！"韦斯莱先生说，接着又转向哈利，用更低、更急促的声音说，"听着，我要你向我保证——"

"——保证做一个好孩子，不离开城堡？"哈利闷闷不乐地说。

"不完全是。"韦斯莱先生说，哈利从来没有见他这么严肃过，"哈利，你向我保证，你绝对不去找布莱克。"

哈利惊呆了。"什么？"

一声响亮的汽笛。警卫沿着列车走过来，把车门一扇扇关上。

"答应我，哈利，"韦斯莱先生的语速更快了，"不管发生什么——"

"我为什么要去找一个我明知会杀死我的人呢？"哈利不解地问。

"你向我发誓，不管你听到什么——"

"亚瑟，快点儿！"韦斯莱夫人喊道。

机车喷出蒸气，慢慢开动了。哈利跑向那节车厢的门，罗恩把门打开，闪开身让他上去。他们扑到窗口朝韦斯莱夫妇挥手，最后，火车拐了个弯，就再也看不见他们了。

"我需要跟你们单独谈谈。"哈利小声对罗恩和赫敏说，火车正在逐渐加速。

"金妮，你走开。"罗恩说。

"行，没问题。"金妮气鼓鼓地说，昂着脑袋走了。

哈利、罗恩和赫敏顺着过道往前走，想找一个没人的包厢，但是所有的包厢里都坐满了人，除了车尾的那个。

那个包厢里只有一个人，一个坐在窗边熟睡的男人。哈利、罗恩和赫敏站在门口看了看。霍格沃茨特快列车一般是学生专车，除了那个推着小车卖食品的女巫，他们以前从没在车上看见过别的成年人。

这个陌生人穿着一件破烂不堪的巫师长袍，长袍上好几个地方都是补过的。他看上去病恹恹的，一点儿力气也没有。虽说他的样子还很年轻，但浅棕色的头发已经有点花白了。

"你们说他是谁呀？"罗恩压低声音问，这时他们关上滑门，挑选离窗户最远的座位坐了下来。

CHAPTER FIVE   The Dementor

'Professor R. J. Lupin,' whispered Hermione at once.

'How d'you know that?'

'It's on his case,' replied Hermione, pointing at the luggage rack over the man's head, where there was a small, battered case held together with a large quantity of neatly knotted string. The name *Professor R. J. Lupin* was stamped across one corner in peeling letters.

'Wonder what he teaches?' said Ron, frowning at Professor Lupin's pallid profile.

'That's obvious,' whispered Hermione. 'There's only one vacancy, isn't there? Defence Against the Dark Arts.'

Harry, Ron and Hermione had already had two Defence Against the Dark Arts teachers, both of whom had only lasted one year. There were rumours that the job was jinxed.

'Well, I hope he's up to it,' said Ron doubtfully. 'He looks like one good hex would finish him off, doesn't he? Anyway ...' he turned to Harry, 'what were you going to tell us?'

Harry explained all about Mr and Mrs Weasley's argument and the warning Mr Weasley had just given him. When he'd finished, Ron looked thunderstruck, and Hermione had her hands over her mouth. She finally lowered them to say, 'Sirius Black escaped to come after *you*? Oh, Harry ... you'll have to be really, really careful. Don't go looking for trouble, Harry ...'

'I don't go looking for trouble,' said Harry, nettled. 'Trouble usually finds *me*.'

'How thick would Harry have to be, to go looking for a nutter who wants to kill him?' said Ron shakily.

They were taking the news worse than Harry had expected. Both Ron and Hermione seemed to be much more frightened of Black than he was.

'No one knows how he got out of Azkaban,' said Ron uncomfortably. 'No one's ever done it before. And he was a top-security prisoner, too.'

'But they'll catch him, won't they?' said Hermione earnestly. 'I mean, they've got all the Muggles looking out for him, too ...'

'What's that noise?' said Ron suddenly.

A faint, tinny sort of whistle was coming from somewhere. They looked all around the compartment.

第5章 摄魂怪

"R.J.卢平教授。"赫敏立刻小声说。

"你怎么知道的?"

"他的箱子上写着呢。"赫敏指着男人头顶上的行李架回答。那儿有一个破破烂烂的小箱子,用许多绳子绑着,绳子整整齐齐地打着结,R.J.卢平教授的名字就印在箱子的一角,字母已经有点剥落了。

"不知道他教哪门课?"罗恩皱起眉头望着卢平教授毫无生气的身影,问道。

"那还用问,"赫敏小声说,"只有一个位置空缺,不是吗?黑魔法防御术。"

哈利、罗恩和赫敏已经有过两位黑魔法防御术的老师了,都只教了一年。有传言说,这份工作被施了恶咒。

"好吧,我希望他能胜任。"罗恩怀疑地说,"瞧他这副样子,一个厉害的巫婆就能把他干掉,不是吗?不管他了……"他转向哈利,"你想跟我们说什么?"

哈利把韦斯莱夫妇争吵的内容,以及刚才韦斯莱先生警告他的话原原本本地说了一遍。他说完,罗恩惊得目瞪口呆,赫敏用双手捂住了嘴。最后她放下手,说:"小天狼星布莱克逃出来是为了找你?哦,哈利……你一定要特别特别小心。不要去找麻烦,哈利……"

"我没有找麻烦,"哈利恼火地说,"总是麻烦来找我。"

"去找一个想要杀死他的疯子,哈利不是傻到家了吗?"罗恩发着抖说。

哈利没有想到他们会把这个消息看得这么严重。罗恩和赫敏似乎都比他更害怕布莱克。

"谁也不知道他是怎么从阿兹卡班逃出来的,"罗恩不安地说,"以前从来没有人这么干过。而且他还是个被重点看守的犯人呢。"

"不过他们会抓住他的,不是吗?"赫敏认真地说,"我是说,他们让所有的麻瓜也都留意他……"

"什么声音?"罗恩突然问。

从什么地方传来了一种微弱的、若有若无的口哨声。他们在包厢里四下张望。

CHAPTER FIVE The Dementor

'It's coming from your trunk, Harry,' said Ron, standing up and reaching into the luggage rack. A moment later he had pulled the Pocket Sneakoscope out from between Harry's robes. It was spinning very fast in the palm of Ron's hand, and glowing brilliantly.

'Is that a *Sneakoscope?*' said Hermione interestedly, standing up for a better look.

'Yeah ... mind you, it's a very cheap one,' Ron said. 'It went haywire just as I was tying it to Errol's leg to send it to Harry.'

'Were you doing anything untrustworthy at the time?' said Hermione shrewdly.

'No! Well ... I wasn't supposed to be using Errol. You know he's not really up to long journeys ... but how else was I supposed to get Harry's present to him?'

'Stick it back in the trunk,' Harry advised, as the Sneakoscope whistled piercingly, 'or it'll wake him up.'

He nodded towards Professor Lupin. Ron stuffed the Sneakoscope into a particularly horrible pair of Uncle Vernon's old socks, which deadened the sound, then closed the lid of the trunk on it.

'We could get it checked in Hogsmeade,' said Ron, sitting back down. 'They sell that sort of thing in Dervish and Banges, magical instruments and stuff. Fred and George told me.'

'Do you know much about Hogsmeade?' asked Hermione keenly. 'I've read it's the only entirely non-Muggle settlement in Britain –'

'Yeah, I think it is,' said Ron in an offhand sort of way, 'but that's not why I want to go. I just want to get inside Honeydukes!'

'What's that?' said Hermione.

'It's this sweetshop,' said Ron, a dreamy look coming over his face, 'where they've got *everything* ... Pepper Imps – they make you smoke at the mouth – and great fat Chocoballs full of strawberry mousse and clotted cream, and really excellent sugar quills which you can suck in class and just look like you're thinking what to write next –'

'But Hogsmeade's a very interesting place, isn't it?' Hermione pressed on eagerly. 'In *Sites of Historical Sorcery* it says the inn was the headquarters for the 1612 goblin rebellion, and the Shrieking Shack's supposed to be the most severely haunted building in Britain –'

'– and massive sherbet balls that make you levitate a few inches off the ground while you're sucking them,' said Ron, who was plainly not listening to a word Hermione was saying.

第5章 摄魂怪

"是从你箱子里发出来的,哈利。"罗恩说着就站起来去够行李架。片刻之后,他从哈利的袍子里把那个袖珍窥镜拽了出来。窥镜在罗恩手心里转得飞快,发出耀眼的光芒。

"那是窥镜吗?"赫敏一边饶有兴趣地问,一边站起来想看个仔细。

"是啊……不瞒你说,是个便宜货。"罗恩说,"我把它拴在埃罗尔的脚上准备寄给哈利时,它突然出了毛病。"

"你当时不是在做什么离谱的事吧?"赫敏尖锐地问。

"没有!唉……我不应该用埃罗尔的。你们知道,它其实没有能力长途飞行……可是我还有什么办法把礼物送给哈利呢?"

"快把它塞回箱子里,"哈利听见窥镜发出刺耳的口哨声便建议道,"不然会把他吵醒的。"

他朝卢平教授点点头。罗恩把窥镜塞进了弗农姨父的一双特别难看的旧袜子里,声音立刻平息了,然后他把箱子盖上了。

"我们可以把它拿到霍格莫德去修修。"罗恩重新坐了下来,说道,"专卖魔法用品的德维斯-班斯店也有这玩意儿,弗雷德和乔治告诉我的。"

"你们对霍格莫德了解多吗?"赫敏兴致勃勃地问,"我在书里读到,它是英国唯一一个完全没有麻瓜的地方——"

"是啊,我想是吧,"罗恩用一种满不在乎的口气说,"但我想去那儿可不是为了这个。我只想到蜂蜜公爵去看看!"

"那是什么?"赫敏问。

"就是那家糖果店,"罗恩说,脸上浮现出一种梦幻般的表情,"那里什么都有……胡椒小顽童——会让你嘴里冒出烟来——还有胖嘟嘟的大巧克力球,里面全是草莓冻和奶油块,还有特别美妙的糖棒羽毛笔,可以在课堂上吮着吃,别人还以为你在琢磨下一句该写什么呢——"

"霍格莫德是一个非常有趣的地方,是不是?"赫敏热切地追问,"《魔法名胜古迹》里说,那家小酒馆是一六一二年妖精叛乱的指挥部;还有尖叫棚屋,据说是英国闹鬼闹得最厉害的一座房子——"

"——还有那么大的果汁奶冻球,你吸的时候,双脚会从地面升起几英寸呢。"罗恩说,显然一个字也没听赫敏在说什么。

CHAPTER FIVE   The Dementor

Hermione looked around at Harry.

'Won't it be nice to get out of school for a bit and explore Hogsmeade?'

''Spect it will,' said Harry heavily. 'You'll have to tell me when you've found out.'

'What d'you mean?' said Ron.

'I can't go. The Dursleys didn't sign my permission form, and Fudge wouldn't, either.'

Ron looked horrified.

'*You're not allowed to come?* But – no way – McGonagall or someone will give you permission –'

Harry gave a hollow laugh. Professor McGonagall, Head of Gryffindor house, was very strict.

'– or we can ask Fred and George, they know every secret passage out of the castle –'

'Ron!' said Hermione sharply. 'I don't think Harry should be sneaking out of school with Black on the loose –'

'Yeah, I expect that's what McGonagall will say when I ask for permission,' said Harry bitterly.

'But if *we're* with him,' said Ron spiritedly to Hermione, 'Black wouldn't dare –'

'Oh, Ron, don't talk rubbish,' snapped Hermione. 'Black's already murdered a whole bunch of people in the middle of a crowded street. Do you really think he's going to worry about attacking Harry just because *we're* there?'

She was fumbling with the straps of Crookshanks's basket as she spoke.

'Don't let that thing out!' Ron said, but too late; Crookshanks leapt lightly from the basket, stretched, yawned, and sprang onto Ron's knees; the lump in Ron's pocket trembled and he shoved Crookshanks angrily away.

'Get out of it!'

'Ron, don't!' said Hermione angrily.

Ron was about to answer back when Professor Lupin stirred. They watched him apprehensively, but he simply turned his head the other way, mouth slightly open, and slept on.

The Hogwarts Express moved steadily north and the scenery outside the window became wilder and darker while the clouds overhead thickened.

赫敏转过脸来看着哈利。

"偶尔离开学校，到霍格莫德去逛逛肯定很开心，是不是？"

"应该是吧，"哈利闷闷不乐地说，"只好等你们弄清楚再告诉我了。"

"你这话是什么意思？"罗恩说。

"我去不了。德思礼家没有在我的许可表上签字，福吉也不肯签。"

罗恩像是吓坏了。

"不让你去？可是——不可能——麦格或其他什么人会批准你——"

哈利干笑了一声。麦格教授是格兰芬多学院的院长，是个非常严厉的老师。

"——或者我们去问问弗雷德和乔治，他们知道通到城堡外面的每一条秘密通道——"

"罗恩！"赫敏厉声地说，"眼下布莱克还没有抓住，我认为哈利不应该偷偷溜出学校——"

"是啊，我想，如果我去请求麦格教授批准，她肯定也会这么说。"哈利郁闷地说。

"如果我们跟他在一起，"罗恩兴致勃勃地对赫敏说，"布莱克就不敢——"

"拜托，罗恩，别说蠢话了。"赫敏没好气地说，"布莱克曾经在拥挤的大街上杀死了一大群人，你真的以为就因为有我们在，他就不敢对哈利下手吗？"

她一边说话，一边摆弄着克鲁克山柳条篮的带子。

"别把那东西放出来！"罗恩说，可是已经晚了。克鲁克山敏捷地从篮子里跳出来，伸了个懒腰，打了个哈欠，纵身跳到罗恩膝头。罗恩口袋里的那个鼓包瑟瑟发抖，罗恩气愤地把克鲁克山推了下去。

"滚开！"

"罗恩，别这样！"赫敏生气地说。

罗恩刚要回话，卢平教授突然动了动。他们担心地看着他，却见他只是把脑袋转向了另一边，微微张着嘴巴，继续沉睡。

霍格沃茨特快列车一路向北行驶，窗外的景致变得越来越荒凉。随着高空云层的变厚，天色也暗了下来。人们追追跑跑地从他们包厢

CHAPTER FIVE   The Dementor

People were chasing backwards and forwards past the door of their compartment. Crookshanks had now settled in an empty seat, his squashed face turned towards Ron, his yellow eyes on Ron's top pocket.

At one o'clock the plump witch with the food trolley arrived at the compartment door.

'D'you think we should wake him up?' Ron asked awkwardly, nodding towards Professor Lupin. 'He looks like he could do with some food.'

Hermione approached Professor Lupin cautiously.

'Er – Professor?' she said. 'Excuse me – Professor?'

He didn't move.

'Don't worry, dear,' said the witch, as she handed Harry a large stack of Cauldron Cakes. 'If he's hungry when he wakes, I'll be up front with the driver.'

'I suppose he is asleep?' said Ron quietly, as the witch slid the compartment door closed. 'I mean – he hasn't died, has he?'

'No, no, he's breathing,' whispered Hermione, taking the Cauldron Cake Harry passed her.

He might not be very good company, but Professor Lupin's presence in their compartment had its uses. Mid-afternoon, just as it had started to rain, blurring the rolling hills outside the window, they heard footsteps in the corridor again, and their three least favourite people appeared at the door: Draco Malfoy, flanked by his cronies, Vincent Crabbe and Gregory Goyle.

Draco Malfoy and Harry had been enemies ever since they had met on their very first train journey to Hogwarts. Malfoy, who had a pale, pointed, sneering face, was in Slytherin house; he played Seeker on the Slytherin Quidditch team, the same position that Harry played on the Gryffindor team. Crabbe and Goyle seemed to exist to do Malfoy's bidding. They were both wide and muscly; Crabbe was the taller, with a pudding-basin haircut and a very thick neck; Goyle had short, bristly hair and long, gorilla arms.

'Well, look who it is,' said Malfoy in his usual lazy drawl, pulling open the compartment door. 'Potty and the Weasel.'

Crabbe and Goyle chuckled trollishly.

'I heard your father finally got his hands on some gold this summer, Weasley,' said Malfoy. 'Did your mother die of shock?'

第5章 摄魂怪

的门口经过。克鲁克山这会儿在一个空位子上安顿下来,那张柿饼脸朝着罗恩,一双黄眼睛盯着罗恩胸前的口袋。

一点钟的时候,推着食品车的胖女巫来到他们包厢的门口。

"你说我们是不是应该叫醒他?"罗恩冲卢平教授点点头,有点不知所措地问,"他看样子需要吃点东西。"

赫敏小心翼翼地走近卢平教授。

"呃——教授?"她说,"对不起——教授?"

他没有动。

"别担心,亲爱的,"女巫一边说,一边把一大摞坩埚形蛋糕递给哈利,"如果他醒来后感到肚子饿,我就在前面,跟司机在一起。"

"我想他是睡着了吧?"女巫把包厢的滑门关上后,罗恩轻声说,"我的意思是——他没死吧?"

"没有,没有,他还在呼吸呢。"赫敏小声说,接过哈利递给她的坩埚形蛋糕。

卢平教授虽说不是一个很好的旅伴,但有他在他们的包厢里,还是很有用的。下午三四点钟时,天开始下起雨来,窗外起伏的山峦变得模糊不清。就在这时,他们听见过道里又传来了脚步声,随即门口出现了三个他们最不喜欢的人。德拉科·马尔福,一左一右跟着他的两个死党:文森特·克拉布和格雷戈里·高尔。

在第一次去霍格沃茨的列车上,德拉科·马尔福和哈利一见面就成了死对头。马尔福长着一张苍白的、老带着讥笑的尖脸,在斯莱特林学院。他在斯莱特林魁地奇球队担任找球手,而哈利在格兰芬多球队里也是同样的位置。克拉布和高尔似乎只知道对马尔福言听计从。他们俩都体格粗壮,一身的腱子肉。克拉布略高一些,头发剪成布丁盆的形状,脖子很粗。高尔的头发又短又硬,两条胳膊跟大猩猩的一样长。

"嘿,看看这是谁。"马尔福拉开包厢的门,用他那懒洋洋的、拖着长腔的口吻说,"鼻涕和喂死鸡。"

克拉布和高尔像巨怪一样粗声大笑。

"我听说你爸爸今年夏天终于弄到了点儿金子,"马尔福说,"你妈妈是不是吃惊死了?"

CHAPTER FIVE   The Dementor

Ron stood up so quickly he knocked Crookshanks's basket to the floor. Professor Lupin gave a snort.

'Who's that?' said Malfoy, taking an automatic step backwards as he spotted Lupin.

'New teacher,' said Harry, who had got to his feet, too, in case he needed to hold Ron back. 'What were you saying, Malfoy?'

Malfoy's pale eyes narrowed; he wasn't fool enough to pick a fight right under a teacher's nose.

'C'mon,' he muttered resentfully to Crabbe and Goyle, and they disappeared.

Harry and Ron sat down again, Ron massaging his knuckles.

'I'm not going to take any rubbish from Malfoy this year,' he said angrily. 'I mean it. If he makes one more crack about my family, I'm going to get hold of his head and –'

Ron made a violent gesture in mid-air.

'Ron,' hissed Hermione, pointing at Professor Lupin, 'be *careful* ...'

But Professor Lupin was still fast asleep.

The rain thickened as the train sped yet further north; the windows were now a solid, shimmering grey, which gradually darkened until lanterns flickered into life all along the corridors and over the luggage racks. The train rattled, the rain hammered, the wind roared, but still, Professor Lupin slept.

'We must be nearly there,' said Ron, leaning forward to look past Professor Lupin at the now completely black window.

The words had hardly left him when the train started to slow down.

'Brilliant,' said Ron, getting up and walking carefully past Professor Lupin to try and see outside. 'I'm starving, I want to get to the feast ...'

'We can't be there yet,' said Hermione, checking her watch.

'So why're we stopping?'

The train was getting slower and slower. As the noise of the pistons fell away, the wind and rain sounded louder than ever against the windows.

Harry, who was nearest the door, got up to look into the corridor. All along the carriage, heads were sticking curiously out of their compartments.

The train came to a stop with a jolt and distant thuds and bangs told them that luggage had fallen out of the racks. Then, without warning, all the lamps went out and they were plunged into total darkness.

第5章 摄魂怪

罗恩腾地站起来,把克鲁克山的篮子碰翻在地。卢平哼了一声。

"那是谁?"马尔福说,他看见卢平,本能地向后退了一步。

"新来的老师。"哈利说着也站了起来,以便在需要的时候把罗恩拉回来,"你刚才说什么,马尔福?"

马尔福灰色的眼睛眯了起来。他不是傻瓜,不会在一位老师的眼皮底下惹是生非。

"走吧。"他懊丧地对克拉布和高尔说。三个人消失了。

哈利和罗恩重新坐了下来,罗恩揉着他的指关节。

"这学期我再也不会忍受马尔福的胡说八道。"他怒冲冲地说,"我说到做到,他要是再敢挖苦我们家人,我就揪住他的脑袋——"

罗恩在空中做了个猛烈的手势。

"罗恩,"赫敏指着卢平教授,压低声音说,"当心……"

可是卢平教授仍然睡得很沉。

火车继续朝北疾驰,雨越下越大,车窗外成了一片水汪汪的灰色,并且逐渐黑了下来。最后,过道里和行李架上的灯一下子都亮了。火车哐当哐当地响,雨点啪啪地敲,窗外狂风呼啸,但卢平教授仍然在睡觉。

"我们肯定快到了。"罗恩说着,探过身子,隔着卢平教授看看此刻已漆黑一片的车窗。

话音刚落,火车开始减速。

"太棒了!"罗恩说。他站起身,小心地走过卢平教授身边,想看清窗外的情况。"我饿坏了,真想参加宴会……"

"还不可能到呢。"赫敏看着手表说。

"那为什么停下了?"

火车越来越慢。车轮的声音逐渐听不见了,风声和雨声比以前更响地撞击着车窗。

哈利离门最近,他起身朝过道望去。整个车厢里,无数颗好奇的脑袋从包厢里探了出来。

火车咯噔一下停住了,远处传来乒乒乓乓的声音,准是行李从架子上掉了下来。接着,没来由地,所有的灯都灭了,他们陷入彻底的黑暗之中。

CHAPTER FIVE The Dementor

'What's going on?' said Ron's voice from behind Harry.

'Ouch!' gasped Hermione. 'Ron, that was my foot!'

Harry felt his way back to his seat.

'D'you think we've broken down?'

'Dunno ...'

There was a squeaking sound, and Harry saw the dim black outline of Ron, wiping a patch clean on the window and peering out.

'There's something moving out there,' Ron said. 'I think people are coming aboard ...'

The compartment door suddenly opened and someone fell painfully over Harry's legs.

'Sorry! D'you know what's going on? Ouch! Sorry –'

'Hello, Neville,' said Harry, feeling around in the dark and pulling Neville up by his cloak.

'Harry? Is that you? What's happening?'

'No idea! Sit down –'

There was a loud hissing and a yelp of pain; Neville had tried to sit on Crookshanks.

'I'm going to go and ask the driver what's going on,' came Hermione's voice. Harry felt her pass him, heard the door slide open again and then a thud and two loud squeals of pain.

'Who's that?'

'Who's *that*?'

'Ginny?'

'Hermione?'

'What are you doing?'

'I was looking for Ron –'

'Come in and sit down –'

'Not here!' said Harry hurriedly. 'I'm here!'

'Ouch!' said Neville.

'Quiet!' said a hoarse voice suddenly.

Professor Lupin appeared to have woken up at last. Harry could hear movements in his corner. None of them spoke.

There was a soft, crackling noise and a shivering light filled the compartment.

第5章 摄魂怪

"怎么回事?"罗恩的声音在哈利身后响起。

"哎哟!"赫敏倒抽了一口冷气,"罗恩,这是我的脚!"

哈利摸索着回到位子上。

"你们说是不是车坏了?"

"不知道……"

黑暗中传来刺耳的吱吱声,哈利看见了罗恩黑乎乎的模糊身影。他正在车窗上擦出一块干净的地方,往外面张望。

"外面有什么东西在动,"罗恩说,"好像有人在上车……"

包厢的门突然开了,有人被哈利的双腿绊住,痛苦地摔倒了。

"对不起!你知道是怎么回事吗?哎哟!对不起——"

"你好,纳威。"哈利在黑暗中摸索,提着纳威的袍子把他拉了起来。

"哈利?是你吗?出什么事了?"

"不知道!坐下吧——"

响亮的嘶嘶声,伴随着一声痛苦的尖叫,纳威差点儿坐到克鲁克山身上。

"我去问问司机是怎么回事。"赫敏的声音说。哈利感觉到赫敏从他面前经过,听见滑门又一次打开,接着砰的一声,又是两声痛苦的尖叫。

"是谁?"

"是谁?"

"金妮?"

"赫敏?"

"你在做什么?"

"我在找罗恩——"

"进来坐下——"

"别坐这儿!"哈利赶紧说,"这儿有我呢!"

"哎哟!"纳威说。

"安静!"一个沙哑的声音突然响起。

卢平教授似乎终于醒了。哈利听见他那个角落里有了动静。他们谁也没有说话。

随着一记轻微的爆裂声,一道颤巍巍的亮光照亮了包厢。卢平教

CHAPTER FIVE The Dementor

Professor Lupin appeared to be holding a handful of flames. They illuminated his tired grey face, but his eyes looked alert and wary.

'Stay where you are,' he said, in the same hoarse voice, and he got slowly to his feet with his handful of fire held out in front of him.

But the door slid slowly open before Lupin could reach it.

Standing in the doorway, illuminated by the shivering flames in Lupin's hand, was a cloaked figure that towered to the ceiling. Its face was completely hidden beneath its hood. Harry's eyes darted downwards, and what he saw made his stomach contract. There was a hand protruding from the cloak and it was glistening, greyish, slimy-looking and scabbed, like something dead that had decayed in water ...

It was visible only for a split second. As though the creature beneath the cloak sensed Harry's gaze, the hand was suddenly withdrawn into the folds of the black material.

And then the thing beneath the hood, whatever it was, drew a long, slow, rattling breath, as though it was trying to suck something more than air from its surroundings.

An intense cold swept over them all. Harry felt his own breath catch in his chest. The cold went deeper than his skin. It was inside his chest, it was inside his very heart ...

Harry's eyes rolled up into his head. He couldn't see. He was drowning in cold. There was a rushing in his ears as though of water. He was being dragged downwards, the roaring growing louder ...

And then, from far away, he heard screaming, terrible, terrified, pleading screams. He wanted to help whoever it was, he tried to move his arms, but couldn't ... a thick white fog was swirling around him, inside him –

'Harry! Harry! Are you all right?'

Someone was slapping his face.

'W-what?'

Harry opened his eyes. There were lanterns above him, and the floor was shaking – the Hogwarts Express was moving again and the lights had come back on. He seemed to have slid out of his seat onto the floor. Ron and Hermione were kneeling next to him, and above them he could see Neville and Professor Lupin watching. Harry felt very sick; when he put up his hand to push his glasses back on, he felt cold sweat on his face.

第5章 摄魂怪

授手里似乎攥着一把火焰,它们照亮了他疲倦的灰色脸庞,而他的眼睛显得十分警觉。

"待着别动。"他还是用那种沙哑的声音说,然后举着那把火焰,慢慢站起身来。

可是没等卢平走到门口,滑门慢慢打开了。

在卢平手里的颤巍巍的火苗映照下,可以看见门口站着一个穿斗篷的身影。这身影又高又大,差点儿碰着天花板,脸完全藏在兜帽下。哈利的目光往下一扫,看见的东西使他的胃揪成了一团。斗篷下伸出一只手,灰白色的,阴森森的闪着光,似乎布满了黏液和斑点,就像某种死了以后在水里腐烂的东西……

那只手随即就不见了。穿斗篷的家伙似乎意识到了哈利的目光,突然把手缩进了黑色斗篷的褶缝里。

接着,穿斗篷的家伙——不管是什么东西——慢慢地吸了一口长气,喉咙里发出咯咯的声音,似乎它吸进去的不只是周围的空气。

一股刺骨的寒意席卷了他们。哈利觉得喘不过气来。那寒意渗进他的皮肤,侵入他的胸膛,进入他的心脏……

哈利的眼睛往上一翻,什么也看不见了。他被寒意淹没,耳朵里呼呼作响,像在水里一样。什么东西在把他往下拽,呼呼声越来越响……

这时,他听见从很远的地方传来尖叫声,可怕的、惊惶的、哀求的尖叫声。他想去帮帮那个人,他想挪动一下胳膊,可是怎么也动不了……一团浓浓的白雾在他周围旋转,在他内心旋转——

"哈利!哈利!你没事吧?"

有人在拍打他的脸。

"什——什么?"

哈利睁开眼睛。头顶上灯光闪亮,地板在颤动——霍格沃茨特快列车又开动了,灯也重新亮了起来。他似乎从座位滑到了地板上。罗恩和赫敏跪在他身边,他看见纳威和卢平教授站在他们身后,都注视着他。哈利觉得非常难受,他抬起手把眼镜推上鼻梁时,摸到脸上满是冷汗。

CHAPTER FIVE The Dementor

Ron and Hermione heaved him back onto his seat.

'Are you OK?' Ron asked nervously.

'Yeah,' said Harry, looking quickly towards the door. The hooded creature had vanished. 'What happened? Where's that – that thing? Who screamed?'

'No one screamed,' said Ron, more nervously still.

Harry looked around the bright compartment. Ginny and Neville looked back at him, both very pale.

'But I heard screaming –'

A loud snap made them all jump. Professor Lupin was breaking an enormous slab of chocolate into pieces.

'Here,' he said to Harry, handing him a particularly large piece. 'Eat it. It'll help.'

Harry took the chocolate but didn't eat it.

'What was that thing?' he asked Lupin.

'A Dementor,' said Lupin, who was now giving chocolate to everyone else. 'One of the Dementors of Azkaban.'

Everyone stared at him. Professor Lupin crumpled up the empty chocolate wrapper and put it in his pocket.

'Eat,' he repeated. 'It'll help. I need to speak to the driver, excuse me ...'

He strolled past Harry and disappeared into the corridor.

'Are you sure you're OK, Harry?' said Hermione, watching Harry anxiously.

'I don't get it ... what happened?' said Harry, wiping more sweat off his face.

'Well – that thing – the Dementor – stood there and looked around (I mean, I think it did, I couldn't see its face) – and you – you –'

'I thought you were having a fit or something,' said Ron, who still looked scared. 'You went sort of rigid and fell out of your seat and started twitching –'

'And Professor Lupin stepped over you, and walked towards the Dementor, and pulled out his wand,' said Hermione. 'And he said, "None of us is hiding Sirius Black under our cloaks. Go." But the Dementor didn't move, so Lupin muttered something, and a silvery thing shot out of his wand at it, and it turned round and sort of glided away ...'

'It was horrible,' said Neville, in a higher voice than usual. 'Did you feel

第5章 摄魂怪

罗恩和赫敏把他扶回座位上。

"你没事吧?"罗恩紧张地问。

"没事。"哈利说着,迅速朝门口望去。穿斗篷的家伙已经不见了。"出什么事了?那个……那个东西到哪儿去了?谁在尖叫?"

"没有人尖叫啊。"罗恩说,显得更紧张了。

哈利在明亮的包厢里四下望了望。金妮和纳威朝他看着,两人脸色都很苍白。

"可是我听见了尖叫声——"

咔吧一声,把他们都吓了一跳。卢平教授把一大块巧克力掰成了好几片。

"给,"他把特别大的一片递给哈利,对他说道,"吃吧,会有帮助的。"

哈利接过巧克力,但没有吃。

"那东西是什么?"他问卢平。

"摄魂怪,"卢平一边把巧克力分给每个人,一边回答,"阿兹卡班的摄魂怪。"

大家都吃惊地瞪着他。卢平教授把空了的巧克力包装纸揉成一团,塞进了口袋。

"吃吧,"他又说道,"会有帮助的。请原谅,我需要跟司机谈谈……"

他从哈利身边走过,消失在过道里。

"你真的没事吗,哈利?"赫敏担忧地望着哈利说。

"我不明白……刚才是怎么回事?"哈利擦去脸上更多的冷汗,说道。

"嗯……那个家伙……那个摄魂怪……就站在那儿左右张望,我是说它似乎在左右张望,我看不见它的脸……然后你……你——"

"我还以为你发病了呢。"罗恩说,他看上去惊魂未定,"你好像变得僵硬了,从座位上摔了下去,开始抽搐——"

"然后卢平教授从你身上跨了过去,走到摄魂怪面前,掏出他的魔杖。"赫敏说,"他说:'我们谁也没有把小天狼星布莱克藏在袍子底下。快走。'可是摄魂怪没有动弹,卢平低声说了句什么,魔杖里就冒出一道银色的东西朝摄魂怪射去,摄魂怪转过身,飘飘悠悠地走了……"

"太可怕了。"纳威说,声音比平日要高,"你们有没有感觉到它进

CHAPTER FIVE The Dementor

how cold it went when it came in?'

'I felt weird,' said Ron, shifting his shoulders uncomfortably. 'Like I'd never be cheerful again ...'

Ginny, who was huddled in her corner looking nearly as bad as Harry felt, gave a small sob; Hermione went over and put a comforting arm around her.

'But didn't any of you – fall off your seats?' said Harry awkwardly.

'No,' said Ron, looking anxiously at Harry again. 'Ginny was shaking like mad, though ...'

Harry didn't understand. He felt weak and shivery, as though he was recovering from a bad bout of flu; he also felt the beginnings of shame. Why had he gone to pieces like that, when no one else had?

Professor Lupin had come back. He paused as he entered, looked around and said, with a small smile, 'I haven't poisoned that chocolate, you know ...'

Harry took a bite and to his great surprise felt warmth spread suddenly to the tips of his fingers and toes.

'We'll be at Hogwarts in ten minutes,' said Professor Lupin. 'Are you all right, Harry?'

Harry didn't ask how Professor Lupin knew his name.

'Fine,' he muttered, embarrassed.

They didn't talk much during the remainder of the journey. At long last, the train stopped at Hogsmeade station, and there was a great scramble to get out; owls hooted, cats miaowed, and Neville's pet toad croaked loudly from under his hat. It was freezing on the tiny platform; rain was driving down in icy sheets.

'Firs'-years this way!' called a familiar voice. Harry, Ron and Hermione turned and saw the gigantic outline of Hagrid at the other end of the platform, beckoning the terrified-looking new students forward for their traditional journey across the lake.

'All righ', you three?' Hagrid yelled over the heads of the crowd. They waved at him, but had no chance to speak to him because the mass of people around them was shunting them away along the platform. Harry, Ron and Hermione followed the rest of the school out onto a rough mud track, where at least a hundred stagecoaches awaited the remaining students, each pulled, Harry could only assume, by an invisible horse, because when they climbed inside one and shut the door, the coach set off all by itself, bumping and

第 5 章 摄魂怪

来时有多冷？"

"我感觉怪怪的，"罗恩说，不安地动了动肩膀，"就好像我再也快活不起来了……"

金妮蜷缩在角落里，看上去差不多跟哈利感觉一样糟糕。她发出一声轻轻的抽泣，赫敏过去用胳膊搂住了她。

"但是你们谁也没有——从座位上摔下来？"哈利尴尬地说。

"没有。"罗恩说，又忧心忡忡地看着哈利，"不过金妮抖得跟疯了似的……"

哈利真不明白。他觉得没有力气，全身都在发抖，好像患了一场重感冒刚刚恢复似的。他还隐约感到有点不好意思，为什么只有他那样失态，而别人都没事呢？

卢平教授回来了。他进门时停了一下，望望大家，微微笑着说："我可没有在那块巧克力里下毒呀……"

哈利咬了一口，非常吃惊地感到突然有一股热流涌向了他的脚趾尖和手指尖。

"再有十分钟就到霍格沃茨了。"卢平教授说，"你没事吧，哈利？"

哈利没有问卢平教授怎么知道他的名字。

"没事。"他不好意思地低声说。

在剩下来的旅程中，他们没有怎么说话。终于，火车在霍格莫德站停下了，大家纷纷下车，场面一片混乱。猫头鹰在叫，猫在叫，纳威的宠物蟾蜍也在他的帽子下边呱呱大叫。小小的站台上寒气逼人，冷入骨髓的大雨倾盆而下。

"一年级新生，这边走！"一个熟悉的声音喊道。哈利、罗恩和赫敏转身看见海格巨大的身影在站台那头，招呼那些惊慌失措的一年级新生过去，按传统的方式渡过湖水。

"你们三个还好吧？"海格从众人的脑袋上方嚷道。他们朝他挥挥手，可是没有机会跟他说话，因为周围的人群推挤着他们朝站台另一边走去。哈利、罗恩和赫敏跟着其他同学来到外面一条粗糙的泥泞小路上，那里至少有一百辆马车等着剩下来的同学，但是看不见马。哈利只能猜测每辆马车是由一匹隐形的马拉着，因为当他们钻进一辆马

131

CHAPTER FIVE The Dementor

swaying in procession.

The coach smelled faintly of mould and straw. Harry felt better since the chocolate, but still weak. Ron and Hermione kept looking at him sideways, as though frightened he might collapse again.

As the carriage trundled towards a pair of magnificent wrought-iron gates, flanked with stone columns topped with winged boars, Harry saw two more towering, hooded Dementors, standing guard on either side. A wave of cold sickness threatened to engulf him again; he leant back into the lumpy seat and closed his eyes until they had passed through the gates. The carriage picked up speed on the long, sloping drive up to the castle; Hermione was leaning out of the tiny window, watching the many turrets and towers draw nearer. At last, the carriage swayed to a halt, and Hermione and Ron got out.

As Harry stepped down, a drawling, delighted voice sounded in his ear.

'You *fainted*, Potter? Is Longbottom telling the truth? You actually *fainted*?'

Malfoy elbowed past Hermione to block Harry's way up the stone steps to the castle, his face gleeful and his pale eyes glinting maliciously.

'Shove off, Malfoy,' said Ron, whose jaw was clenched.

'Did you faint as well, Weasley?' said Malfoy loudly. 'Did the scary old Dementor frighten you, too, Weasley?'

'Is there a problem?' said a mild voice. Professor Lupin had just got out of the next carriage.

Malfoy gave Professor Lupin an insolent stare, which took in the patches on his robes and the dilapidated suitcase. With a tiny hint of sarcasm in his voice, he said, 'Oh, no – er – *Professor*,' then he smirked at Crabbe and Goyle, and led them up the steps into the castle.

Hermione prodded Ron in the back to make him hurry, and the three of them joined the crowd swarming up the steps, through the giant oak front doors, and into the cavernous Entrance Hall, which was lit with flaming torches and housed a magnificent marble staircase which led to the upper floors.

The door into the Great Hall stood open at the right; Harry followed the crowd towards it, but had barely glimpsed the enchanted ceiling, which was black and cloudy tonight, when a voice called, 'Potter! Granger! I want to see you both!'

Harry and Hermione turned around, surprised. Professor McGonagall,

第5章 摄魂怪

车、关上车门时，马车就自己移动起来，在队伍里颠簸摇晃着向前行进。

马车里有一股淡淡的霉味和稻草味。哈利吃过巧克力后感觉好一些了，但仍然浑身乏力。罗恩和赫敏不时地侧眼看着他，似乎担心他再次瘫倒。

马车驶向两扇气派非凡的锻铁大门，门两侧有石柱，柱子顶上是带翅膀的野猪。这时哈利又看见两个戴兜帽的阴森可怖的摄魂怪，一边一个在门口站岗。顿时，又有一种寒丝丝的难受感觉向他袭来，他赶紧缩进高低不平的座位里，闭上眼睛，直到从大门中间穿过。马车加速行驶在通向城堡的长长的上坡车道上。赫敏从小小的车窗探出头去，注视着那许多角楼和塔楼离他们越来越近。终于，马车摇摇晃晃地停下了，赫敏和罗恩下了车。

哈利从车上下来时，耳边传来一个拖着长腔的幸灾乐祸的声音。

"你晕倒了，波特？隆巴顿说的是真的吗？你果真晕倒了？"

马尔福用胳膊肘搡开赫敏，在通向城堡的石阶上挡住哈利，脸上乐开了花，一双灰色的眼睛里闪着恶毒的光。

"闪开，马尔福。"罗恩说，他牙关咬得紧紧的。

"你也晕倒了吗，韦斯莱？"马尔福大声说，"那个可怕的老摄魂怪也把你吓坏了吧，韦斯莱？"

"有麻烦吗？"一个温和的声音说。卢平教授刚从下一辆马车里出来。

马尔福傲慢无礼地瞪着卢平教授，把他长袍上的补丁和破烂不堪的箱子都看在了眼里。马尔福说："噢，没有……呃……教授。"他声音里隐约透着一丝讽刺。说罢，他朝克拉布和高尔假笑了一声，领着他们踏上石阶，进入了城堡。

赫敏捅了捅罗恩的后背，催他赶紧往前走，于是他们三人跟着人群走上石阶，穿过雄伟的橡木大门，进入宽敞幽深的门厅。那里点着燃烧的火把，有一道富丽堂皇的大理石楼梯通向楼上。

右边，礼堂的门开着，哈利跟着人群朝那里走去，刚看了一眼被施了魔法的天花板——今晚是黑沉沉的乌云密布的天空，就听见一个声音喊道："波特！格兰杰！我要见你们俩！"

哈利和赫敏吃惊地转过身。变形课老师、格兰芬多学院的院长麦

CHAPTER FIVE   The Dementor

Transfiguration teacher and Head of Gryffindor house, was calling over the heads of the crowd. She was a stern-looking witch who wore her hair in a tight bun; her sharp eyes were framed with square spectacles. Harry fought his way over to her with a feeling of foreboding; Professor McGonagall had a way of making him feel he must have done something wrong.

'There's no need to look so worried – I just want a word in my office,' she told them. 'Move along there, Weasley.'

Ron stared as Professor McGonagall ushered Harry and Hermione away from the chattering crowd; they accompanied her across the Entrance Hall, up the marble staircase and along a corridor.

Once they were in her office, a small room with a large, welcoming fire, Professor McGonagall motioned Harry and Hermione to sit down. She settled herself behind her desk and said abruptly, 'Professor Lupin sent an owl ahead to say that you were taken ill on the train, Potter.'

Before Harry could reply, there was a soft knock on the door and Madam Pomfrey, the matron, came bustling in.

Harry felt himself going red in the face. It was bad enough that he'd passed out, or whatever he had done, without everyone making all this fuss.

'I'm fine,' he said. 'I don't need anything –'

'Oh, it's you, is it?' said Madam Pomfrey, ignoring this and bending down to stare closely at him. 'I suppose you've been doing something dangerous again?'

'It was a Dementor, Poppy,' said Professor McGonagall.

They exchanged a dark look and Madam Pomfrey clucked disapprovingly.

'Setting Dementors around a school,' she muttered, pushing Harry's hair back and feeling his forehead. 'He won't be the first one who collapses. Yes, he's all clammy. Terrible things, they are, and the effect they have on people who are already delicate –'

'I'm not delicate!' said Harry crossly.

'Of course you're not,' said Madam Pomfrey absent-mindedly, now taking his pulse.

'What does he need?' said Professor McGonagall crisply. 'Bed rest? Should he perhaps spend tonight in the hospital wing?'

'I'm *fine*!' said Harry, jumping up. The idea of what Draco Malfoy would say if he had to go to the hospital wing was torture.

第 5 章　摄魂怪

格教授，正隔着众人的脑袋朝他们大喊。她是一位表情严肃的女巫，头发盘成一个紧紧的发髻，锐利的眼睛上戴着一副方形眼镜。哈利挤过人群朝她走去，内心有一种不祥的预感。麦格教授总是让他觉得自己做错了什么事情。

"没必要这么紧张——我只想在办公室里跟你们谈谈。"她对他们说，"到那边去吧，韦斯莱。"

罗恩瞪大眼睛，望着麦格教授领着哈利和赫敏离开了说说笑笑的人群。他们和麦格教授一起穿过门厅，上了大理石楼梯，然后顺着一条走廊往前走去。

麦格教授的办公室很小，却生着暖意融融的炉火。哈利和赫敏刚走进去，麦格教授就示意他们坐下，她自己也在办公桌后面落座，然后很突然地说："卢平教授提前派了一只猫头鹰来，说你在火车上不舒服了，波特。"

哈利还没来得及回答，便听见轻轻的敲门声，接着校医庞弗雷女士匆匆走了进来。

哈利觉得自己脸红了。他在火车上晕过去也好，还是别的什么也好，已经够糟糕的了，现在看到大家这样大惊小怪，他更觉得不好意思了。

"我挺好的。"他说，"我什么也不需要——"

"噢，是你啊！"庞弗雷女士像是没听见他的话，俯身仔细地打量着他，"我想你准是又在做什么危险的事情吧？"

"是摄魂怪，波比。"麦格教授说。

她们交换了一个凝重的目光，庞弗雷女士像母鸡一样不满地咯咯叫了起来。

"把摄魂怪派到学校周围。"她一边嘟囔，一边把哈利的头发往后一捋，摸了摸他的额头，"他不会是第一个晕倒的人。是啊，他身上又冷又湿。真是些可怕的家伙，它们对那些本身就很脆弱的人造成的影响——"

"我不脆弱！"哈利恼火地说。

"你当然不脆弱。"庞弗雷女士心不在焉地说，又开始摸他的脉搏。

"他需要什么？"麦格教授干脆利落地问，"卧床休息？也许他应该在校医院住一晚？"

"我挺好的！"哈利说着站了起来。一想到如果他不得不住院，德拉科·马尔福会说什么，他就觉得无法忍受。

CHAPTER FIVE   The Dementor

'Well, he should have some chocolate, at the very least,' said Madam Pomfrey, who was now trying to peer into Harry's eyes.

'I've already had some,' said Harry. 'Professor Lupin gave me some. He gave it to all of us.'

'Did he, now?' said Madam Pomfrey approvingly. 'So we've finally got a Defence Against the Dark Arts teacher who knows his remedies.'

'Are you sure you feel all right, Potter?' said Professor McGonagall sharply.

'*Yes*,' said Harry.

'Very well. Kindly wait outside while I have a quick word with Miss Granger about her timetable, then we can go down to the feast together.'

Harry went back into the corridor with Madam Pomfrey, who left for the hospital wing, muttering to herself. He only had to wait a few minutes; then Hermione emerged looking very happy about something, followed by Professor McGonagall, and the three of them made their way back down the marble staircase to the Great Hall.

It was a sea of pointed black hats; each of the long house tables was lined with students, their faces glimmering by the light of thousands of candles, which were floating over the tables in mid-air. Professor Flitwick, who was a tiny little wizard with a shock of white hair, was carrying an ancient hat and a three-legged stool out of the Hall.

'Oh,' said Hermione softly, 'we've missed the Sorting!'

New students at Hogwarts were sorted into houses by trying on the Sorting Hat, which shouted out the house they were best suited to (Gryffindor, Ravenclaw, Hufflepuff or Slytherin). Professor McGonagall strode off towards her empty seat at the staff table, and Harry and Hermione set off in the other direction, as quietly as possible, towards the Gryffindor table. People looked around at them as they passed along the back of the Hall, and a few of them pointed at Harry. Had the story of him collapsing in front of the Dementor travelled that fast?

He and Hermione sat down on either side of Ron, who had saved them seats.

'What was all that about?' he muttered to Harry.

Harry started to explain in a whisper, but at that moment the Headmaster stood up to speak, and he broke off.

Professor Dumbledore, though very old, always gave an impression of great energy. He had several feet of long silver hair and beard, half-

第 5 章 摄魂怪

"嗯,至少,他应该吃些巧克力。"庞弗雷女士说,这会儿她又在观察哈利的眼睛了。

"我已经吃了点儿,"哈利说,"卢平教授给了我一些。他把巧克力分给了我们大家。"

"是吗?"庞弗雷女士赞许地说,"我们终于有了一位知道对症下药的黑魔法防御术课老师了。"

"你真的感觉没事了吗,波特?"麦格教授严厉地问。

"是啊。"哈利说。

"很好。请到外面等一会儿,我跟格兰杰小姐说说她课程表的事,然后我们一起下楼参加宴会。"

哈利跟庞弗雷女士一起回到走廊上。庞弗雷女士一路嘟囔着回校医院去了。哈利只等了几分钟,赫敏就喜形于色地出来了,后面跟着麦格教授。他们三个从大理石楼梯下来,回到了礼堂。

礼堂里是一片尖顶黑帽的海洋,每一张长长的学院桌旁都坐满了学生,浮在桌子上空的几千支蜡烛把他们的脸庞映得闪闪发亮。弗立维教授,一个满头白发的小个子巫师,拿着一顶古色古香的帽子和一个三条腿的凳子走出了礼堂。

"哦,"赫敏轻声说,"我们没赶上分院仪式。"

霍格沃茨的新生都要戴一戴分院帽才被分到不同的学院,分院帽大声喊出学生最适合去哪个学院(格兰芬多、拉文克劳、赫奇帕奇和斯莱特林)。麦格教授大步流星地走向教工餐桌上她的空座位,哈利和赫敏则转向另一边,尽量蹑手蹑脚地朝格兰芬多餐桌走去。他们走过礼堂后面时,人们都转过脸来看他们,有几个人还对哈利指指点点。难道他在摄魂怪面前晕倒的事这么快就传开了?

罗恩给他们留了座位,他们分别坐在了罗恩两边。

"怎么回事?"罗恩轻声问哈利。

哈利刚想小声说给他听,这时校长站起来说话了,哈利便打住了话头。

邓布利多教授虽然年事已高,但总是给人一种精力充沛的感觉。他银白色的头发和胡子足有好几英尺长,戴着半月形眼镜,长着一个

CHAPTER FIVE   The Dementor

moon spectacles and an extremely crooked nose. He was often described as the greatest wizard of the age, but that wasn't why Harry respected him. You couldn't help trusting Albus Dumbledore, and as Harry watched him beaming around at the students, he felt really calm for the first time since the Dementor had entered the train compartment.

'Welcome!' said Dumbledore, the candlelight shimmering on his beard. 'Welcome to another year at Hogwarts! I have a few things to say to you all, and as one of them is very serious, I think it best to get it out of the way before you become befuddled by our excellent feast ...'

Dumbledore cleared his throat and continued. 'As you will all be aware after their search of the Hogwarts Express, our school is presently playing host to some of the Dementors of Azkaban, who are here on Ministry of Magic business.'

He paused, and Harry remembered what Mr Weasley had said about Dumbledore not being happy with the Dementors guarding the school.

'They are stationed at every entrance to the grounds,' Dumbledore continued, 'and while they are with us, I must make it plain that nobody is to leave school without permission. Dementors are not to be fooled by tricks or disguises – or even Invisibility Cloaks,' he added blandly, and Harry and Ron glanced at each other. 'It is not in the nature of a Dementor to understand pleading or excuses. I therefore warn each and every one of you to give them no reason to harm you. I look to the Prefects, and our new Head Boy and Girl, to make sure that no student runs foul of the Dementors.'

Percy, who was sitting a few seats along from Harry, puffed out his chest again and stared around impressively. Dumbledore paused again; he looked very seriously around the Hall, and nobody moved or made a sound.

'On a happier note,' he continued, 'I am pleased to welcome two new teachers to our ranks this year.

'Firstly, Professor Lupin, who has kindly consented to fill the post of Defence Against the Dark Arts teacher.'

There was some scattered, rather unenthusiastic, applause. Only those who had been in the compartment on the train with Professor Lupin clapped hard, Harry among them. Professor Lupin looked particularly shabby next to all the other teachers in their best robes.

'Look at Snape!' Ron hissed in Harry's ear.

Professor Snape, the Potions master, was staring along the staff table at

第5章 摄魂怪

特别歪扭的鼻子。人们常说他是当今最伟大的巫师，但哈利并不是因为这个才尊敬他的。阿不思·邓布利多总是使人不由自主地产生信任，此刻，哈利看着校长笑眯眯地面对全体同学，感到自从摄魂怪进入火车包厢后，他第一次真正镇静下来。

"欢迎！"邓布利多说，烛光照在他的胡子上闪闪发亮，"欢迎又回到霍格沃茨上学！我有几件事情要跟你们大家说说，其中一件非常重要，所以我想，最好在你们享受美味大餐、脑子变得糊涂之前就把它说清楚……"

邓布利多清了清嗓子，继续说道："我们学校目前迎来了几位阿兹卡班的摄魂怪，它们是魔法部派来执行公务的，这想必你们都已经知道了，因为它们对霍格沃茨特快列车进行了搜查。"

他停了停，哈利想起韦斯莱先生曾经说过，邓布利多对于派摄魂怪来看守学校不太高兴。

"它们驻守在学校的每个入口处，"邓布利多继续说，"我必须说清楚，它们在的时候，谁也不许擅自离开学校。任何诡计、花招和伪装都是骗不了摄魂怪的——甚至包括隐形衣。"他面无表情地补充道，哈利和罗恩对视了一下，"摄魂怪的本性不会理解辩解和求饶。因此我提醒在座的各位，不要让它们有理由伤害你们。我希望级长和我们新当选的男女学生会主席能确保不让一个学生与摄魂怪发生冲突。"

珀西与哈利隔着几个座位，他又挺起胸脯，神气活现地东张西望。邓布利多又停了停，表情非常严肃地环顾着礼堂，没有一个人动弹或发出声音。

"换个愉快一点的话题吧。"他继续说，"我很高兴欢迎两位新老师这学期加入我们的阵容。

"首先，是卢平教授，他欣然同意填补黑魔法防御术课的空缺。"

礼堂里响起几声冷淡的、稀稀拉拉的掌声。只有在火车上跟卢平教授同在一个车厢的同学拍手拍得比较起劲，哈利也是其中的一个。别的老师都穿着自己最好的长袍，卢平教授坐在他们身边更显得衣衫褴褛。

"快看斯内普！"罗恩贴着哈利的耳朵小声说。

斯内普教授是魔药课老师，此刻他正盯着教工餐桌那头的卢平教

CHAPTER FIVE   The Dementor

Professor Lupin. It was common knowledge that Snape wanted the Defence Against the Dark Arts job, but even Harry, who hated Snape, was startled at the expression twisting his thin, sallow face. It was beyond anger: it was loathing. Harry knew that expression only too well; it was the look Snape wore every time he set eyes on Harry.

'As to our second new appointment,' Dumbledore continued, as the lukewarm applause for Professor Lupin died away, 'well, I am sorry to tell you that Professor Kettleburn, our Care of Magical Creatures teacher, retired at the end of last year in order to enjoy more time with his remaining limbs. However, I am delighted to say that his place will be filled by none other than Rubeus Hagrid, who has agreed to take on this teaching job in addition to his gamekeeping duties.'

Harry, Ron and Hermione stared at each other, stunned. Then they joined in with the applause, which was tumultuous at the Gryffindor table in particular. Harry leant forward to see Hagrid, who was ruby red in the face and staring down at his enormous hands, his wide grin hidden in the tangle of his black beard.

'We should've known!' Ron roared, pounding the table. 'Who else would have set us a biting book?'

Harry, Ron and Hermione were the last to stop clapping, and as Professor Dumbledore started speaking again, they saw that Hagrid was wiping his eyes on the tablecloth.

'Well, I think that's everything of importance,' said Dumbledore. 'Let the feast begin!'

The golden plates and goblets before them filled suddenly with food and drink. Harry, suddenly ravenous, helped himself to everything he could reach and began to eat.

It was a delicious feast; the Hall echoed with talk, laughter and the clatter of knives and forks. Harry, Ron and Hermione, however, were eager for it to finish so that they could talk to Hagrid. They knew how much being made a teacher would mean to him. Hagrid wasn't a fully qualified wizard; he had been expelled from Hogwarts in his third year, for a crime he had not committed. It had been Harry, Ron and Hermione who had cleared Hagrid's name last year.

At long last, when the last morsels of pumpkin tart had melted from the golden platters, Dumbledore gave the word that it was time for them all to go to bed, and they got their chance.

授。大家都知道斯内普一直想得到黑魔法防御术课的教职，可是就连一向讨厌斯内普的哈利，看到斯内普枯黄的瘦脸上那副抽搐的表情，也感到很吃惊。那表情不只是愤怒，简直是憎恨。哈利太熟悉那副表情了，斯内普每次把目光落在哈利身上时，脸上都是这样的表情。

"至于我们的第二位新老师，"邓布利多等欢迎卢平教授的稀稀拉拉的掌声平静下来后，继续说道，"我很遗憾地告诉你们，我们的保护神奇动物课老师凯特尔伯恩教授，为了能有更多的时间享受他剩余的老胳膊老腿，上个学期末退休了。不过，我高兴地宣布，即将填补他的职位的不是别人，正是鲁伯·海格，他同意在承担猎场看守的职责之外，再接受这份教职。"

哈利、罗恩和赫敏惊讶得面面相觑。接着他们也和大家一起鼓起掌来，格兰芬多餐桌上的掌声格外热烈。哈利凑身向前，看见海格的脸涨得通红，低垂眼睛望着自己的一双大手，大大的笑容隐藏在那把蓬乱纠结的黑胡子后面。

"我们早该知道的！"罗恩捶着桌子大声嚷道，"还有谁会让我们准备一本会咬人的书呢？"

哈利、罗恩和赫敏是最后停止鼓掌的，这时邓布利多教授又开始说话了，他们看见海格正用桌布擦着眼睛。

"好了，重要的事情就这么多。"邓布利多说，"我们开宴吧！"

他们面前的金盘子和高脚酒杯里突然出现了满满的食物和饮料。哈利顿时胃口大开，把够得到的每样东西都取了一份，开始大吃起来。

这真是一场美味的盛宴。礼堂里回荡着欢声笑语，回荡着刀叉的碰撞声。不过，哈利、罗恩和赫敏急着赶紧吃完，好去跟海格说话。他们知道对海格来说，成为一名教师有多么重要。海格不是一个完全够资格的巫师，他在三年级时为了一桩莫须有的罪名，被霍格沃茨开除了。是哈利、罗恩和赫敏在上个学期为海格洗清了罪名。

终于，金色大浅盘子里的最后几块南瓜馅饼也消失了，邓布利多宣布大家可以上床睡觉了，他们这才有了机会。

CHAPTER FIVE The Dementor

'Congratulations, Hagrid!' Hermione squealed, as they reached the teachers' table.

'All down ter you three,' said Hagrid, wiping his shining face on his napkin as he looked up at them. 'Can' believe it ... great man, Dumbledore ... came straight down to me hut after Professor Kettleburn said he'd had enough ... it's what I always wanted ...'

Overcome with emotion, he buried his face in his napkin, and Professor McGonagall shooed them away.

Harry, Ron and Hermione joined the Gryffindors streaming up the marble staircase and, very tired now, along more corridors, up more and more stairs, to the hidden entrance to Gryffindor Tower. A large portrait of a fat lady in a pink dress asked them, 'Password?'

'Coming through, coming through!' Percy called from behind the crowd. 'The new password's *Fortuna Major*!'

'Oh no,' said Neville Longbottom sadly. He always had trouble remembering the passwords.

Through the portrait hole and across the common room, the girls and boys divided towards their separate staircases. Harry climbed the spiral stairs with no thought in his head except how glad he was to be back. They reached their familiar, circular dormitory with its five four-poster beds and Harry, looking around, felt he was home at last.

第5章 摄魂怪

"祝贺你,海格!"他们走到教工餐桌前,赫敏大声尖叫道。

"多亏了你们三个。"海格说着,用餐巾擦了擦油亮的面颊,抬起头看着他们,"真不敢相信……真是了不起的人,邓布利多……凯特尔伯恩教授说他受够了,邓布利多就直接来找我了……这正是我一直想得到的啊……"

他激动得难以自已,把脸埋在了餐巾里,麦格教授把他们赶走了。

哈利、罗恩和赫敏与格兰芬多的同学们一起走上大理石楼梯。他们已经很累了,走过一条又一条走廊,爬上一道又一道楼梯,终于来到格兰芬多塔楼隐蔽的入口处。一个穿着粉红色裙子的胖夫人的大肖像问他们:"口令?"

"快过去,快过去!"珀西在人群后面喊道,"新的口令是吉星高照!"

"哦,倒霉。"纳威·隆巴顿垂头丧气地说。他总是记不住口令。

穿过肖像洞口,走过公共休息室,男生女生分别朝不同的楼梯走去。哈利走上旋转楼梯,脑子里没有别的念头,只想着回到学校有多么高兴。他们来到熟悉的、摆着五张四柱床的圆形宿舍,哈利环顾四周,觉得自己终于到家了。

CHAPTER SIX

Talons and Tea Leaves

When Harry, Ron and Hermione entered the Great Hall for breakfast next day, the first thing they saw was Draco Malfoy, who seemed to be entertaining a large group of Slytherins with a very funny story. As they passed, Malfoy did a ridiculous impression of a swooning fit and there was a roar of laughter.

'Ignore him,' said Hermione, who was right behind Harry. 'Just ignore him, it's not worth it ...'

'Hey, Potter!' shrieked Pansy Parkinson, a Slytherin girl with a face like a pug. 'Potter! The Dementors are coming, Potter! *Wooooooooo!*'

Harry dropped into a seat at the Gryffindor table, next to George Weasley. 'New third-year timetables,' said George, passing them over. 'What's up with you, Harry?'

'Malfoy,' said Ron, sitting down on George's other side and glaring over at the Slytherin table.

George looked up in time to see Malfoy pretending to faint with terror again.

'That little git,' he said calmly. 'He wasn't so cocky last night when the Dementors were down our end of the train. Came running into our compartment, didn't he, Fred?'

'Nearly wet himself,' said Fred, with a contemptuous glance at Malfoy.

'I wasn't too happy myself,' said George. 'They're horrible things, those Dementors ...'

'Sort of freeze your insides, don't they?' said Fred.

'You didn't pass out, though, did you?' said Harry in a low voice.

'Forget it, Harry,' said George bracingly. 'Dad had to go out to Azkaban one time, remember, Fred? And he said it was the worst place he'd ever been. He came back all weak and shaking ... They suck the happiness out of a

第6章

鹰爪和茶叶

第二天早晨，哈利、罗恩和赫敏走进礼堂吃早饭时，一眼就看见了德拉科·马尔福，他似乎在给一大群斯莱特林同学讲一个特别滑稽的故事。他们经过时，马尔福故意拿腔作势地假装突然晕倒，引得大家一阵哄笑。

"别理他，"走在哈利身后的赫敏说，"别理他就是了，犯不着……"

"喂，波特！"斯莱特林的女生潘西·帕金森尖叫起来，她的脸长得像狮子狗一样，"波特！摄魂怪来了，波特！呜呜呜！"

哈利一屁股坐在格兰芬多餐桌旁的一个座位上，紧挨着乔治·韦斯莱。

"三年级的新课表。"乔治把课表递过来，说道，"你怎么啦，哈利？"

"马尔福。"罗恩说着，坐在了乔治的另一边，气冲冲地瞪着斯莱特林餐桌。

乔治抬起头，正好看见马尔福又在假装吓得晕死过去。

"那个小饭桶，"他心平气和地说，"昨晚摄魂怪来到车上时，他可没有这么趾高气扬。他一头钻进了我们的包厢，是不是，弗雷德？"

"差点儿尿湿了裤子。"弗雷德说着，轻蔑地扫了马尔福一眼。

"我自己也不太开心，"乔治说，"那些摄魂怪真是些可怕的家伙……"

"简直把你的五脏六腑都冻住了，是不是？"

"可是你们并没有晕过去，不是吗？"哈利低声说。

"别想它了，哈利。"乔治给他鼓劲儿，"爸爸有一次不得不去阿兹卡班，你还记得吗，弗雷德？他说他从来没见过那么可怕的地方。他回来时浑身瘫软，抖个不停……摄魂怪把欢乐都吸走了。那里的大多

CHAPTER SIX   Talons and Tea Leaves

place, Dementors. Most of the prisoners go mad in there.'

'Anyway, we'll see how happy Malfoy looks after our first Quidditch match,' said Fred. 'Gryffindor versus Slytherin, first game of the season, remember?'

The only time Harry and Malfoy had faced each other in a Quidditch match, Malfoy had definitely come off worse. Feeling slightly more cheerful, Harry helped himself to sausages and fried tomatoes.

Hermione was examining her new timetable.

'Ooh, good, we're starting some new subjects today,' she said happily.

'Hermione,' said Ron, frowning as he looked over her shoulder, 'they've messed up your timetable. Look – they've got you down for about ten subjects a day. There isn't enough *time*.'

'I'll manage. I've fixed it all with Professor McGonagall.'

'But look,' said Ron, laughing, 'see this morning? Nine o'clock, Divination. And underneath, nine o'clock, Muggle Studies. And –' Ron leant closer to the timetable, disbelieving, '*look* – underneath that, Arithmancy, *nine o'clock*. I mean, I know you're good, Hermione, but no one's *that* good. How're you supposed to be in three classes at once?'

'Don't be silly,' said Hermione shortly. 'Of course I won't be in three classes at once.'

'Well, then –'

'Pass the marmalade,' said Hermione.

'But –'

'Oh, Ron, what's it to you if my timetable's a bit full?' Hermione snapped. 'I told you, I've fixed it all with Professor McGonagall.'

Just then, Hagrid entered the Great Hall. He was wearing his long moleskin overcoat and was absent-mindedly swinging a dead polecat from one enormous hand.

'All righ'?' he said eagerly, pausing on the way to the staff table. 'Yer in my firs' ever lesson! Right after lunch! Bin up since five gettin' everythin' ready ... hope it's OK ... me, a teacher ... hones'ly ...'

He grinned broadly at them and headed off to the staff table, still swinging the polecat.

'Wonder what he's been getting ready?' said Ron, a note of anxiety in his voice.

第6章 鹰爪和茶叶

数犯人最后都疯了。"

"好吧，等我们打完第一场魁地奇比赛，看马尔福还会有多开心。"弗雷德说，"格兰芬多对斯莱特林，是本赛季的第一场比赛，记得吗？"

哈利和马尔福在魁地奇比赛中只交过一次手，那次马尔福无疑打得很糟糕。想到这点，哈利才觉得心情好了些，给自己拿了一些香肠和煎番茄。

赫敏正端详着她的新课程表。

"噢，太好了，我们今天要开始上几门新课了。"她高兴地说。

"赫敏，"罗恩从她肩膀后面看过来，皱着眉头说，"他们把你的课程表排得乱七八糟。看——你一天差不多要上十门课呢。哪有那么多时间啊。"

"我会有办法的。我已经跟麦格教授商量好了。"

"可是你看，"罗恩大笑着说，"看见今天上午的课了吗？九点，占卜课。下面，九点，麻瓜研究。还有……"罗恩凑近了那张课程表，似乎不相信自己的眼睛，"看——下面，算术占卜，九点。我知道你很优秀，赫敏，可是没人能优秀到那个份儿上。你怎么可能同时在三个教室里呢？"

"别说傻话了，"赫敏简短地说，"我当然不会同时在三个教室里。"

"那你……"

"把橘子酱递过来。"赫敏说。

"可是——"

"拜托，罗恩，即使我的课程表有点满，又关你什么事呢？"赫敏凶巴巴地说，"我告诉过你，我已经跟麦格教授商量好了。"

就在这时，海格走进了礼堂。他穿着那件长长的鼹鼠皮大衣，心不在焉地用一只大手甩着一只死鸡貂。

"怎么样？"他停住正往教工餐桌走去的脚步，兴致勃勃地说，"你们来上我的第一节课！一吃过午饭就上！我早晨五点就起来了，把所有的东西都准备好了……希望课上得顺利……我，终于当上老师了……真是……"

他朝他们开心地笑着，继续朝教工餐桌走去，手里仍然甩着那只死鸡貂。

"不知道他都在准备些什么？"罗恩说，声音里透着一丝担忧。

CHAPTER SIX   Talons and Tea Leaves

The Hall was starting to empty as people headed off towards their first lesson. Ron checked his timetable. 'We'd better go, look, Divination's at the top of North Tower. It'll take us ten minutes to get there ...'

They finished their breakfast hastily, said goodbye to Fred and George and walked back through the Hall. As they passed the Slytherin table, Malfoy did yet another impression of a fainting fit. The shouts of laughter followed Harry into the Entrance Hall.

The journey through the castle to North Tower was a long one. Two years at Hogwarts hadn't taught them everything about the castle, and they had never been inside North Tower before.

'There's – got – to – be – a – short – cut,' Ron panted, as they climbed their seventh long staircase and emerged on an unfamiliar landing, where there was nothing but a large painting of a bare stretch of grass hanging on the stone wall.

'I think it's this way,' said Hermione, peering down the empty passage to the right.

'Can't be,' said Ron. 'That's south. Look, you can see a bit of the lake out of the window ...'

Harry was watching the painting. A fat, dapple-grey pony had just ambled onto the grass and was grazing nonchalantly. Harry was used to the subjects of Hogwarts paintings moving around and leaving their frames to visit each other, but he always enjoyed watching them. A moment later, a short, squat knight in a suit of armour had clanked into the picture after his pony. By the look of the grass stains on his metal knees, he had just fallen off.

'Aha!' he yelled, seeing Harry, Ron and Hermione. 'What villains are these that trespass upon my private lands? Come to scorn at my fall, perchance? Draw, you knaves, you dogs!'

They watched in astonishment as the little knight tugged his sword out of its scabbard and began brandishing it violently, hopping up and down in rage. But the sword was too long for him; a particularly wild swing made him overbalance, and he landed face down in the grass.

'Are you all right?' said Harry, moving closer to the picture.

'Get back, you scurvy braggart! Back, you rogue!'

The knight seized his sword again and used it to push himself back up, but the blade sank deeply into the grass and, though he pulled with all his might, he couldn't get it out again. Finally he had to flop back down onto the grass and push up his visor to mop his sweating face.

第6章 鹰爪和茶叶

同学们都赶着去上他们的第一节课了,礼堂里的人渐渐少了。罗恩看了看他的课程表。"我们最好走吧,看,占卜课在北塔楼顶上呢。要十分钟才能赶到那儿……"

他们三口两口吃完早饭,跟弗雷德和乔治告了别,往礼堂外面走去。经过斯莱特林餐桌时,马尔福又在那里夸张地假装晕倒,哄笑声一直追着哈利传到了门厅。

穿过城堡到北塔楼去的路很长。他们虽说在霍格沃茨待了两年,却并没有对城堡了如指掌,北塔楼更是从来没有去过。

"肯定—有——条—近路。"罗恩气喘吁吁地说,这时他们爬上第七段长长的楼梯,来到一个陌生的平台上。平台上什么也没有,只是石墙上挂着一幅很大的图画,画面上是一片空荡荡的草地。

"我想就是这条路。"赫敏望着右边空空的走廊说。

"不可能,"罗恩说,"那是南面。看,窗外能看见一点湖面……"

哈利注视着那幅画。一匹胖胖的小灰斑马慢慢地走到草地上,正在漫不经心地吃草。哈利已经习惯了霍格沃茨画像里的人物会活动,还会离开各自的相框,互相串门,但他总是很喜欢观察它们。片刻之后,一位穿盔甲的矮胖骑士追着他的小马,哐啷哐啷地走进了画面。从他金属盔甲膝盖处的青草污渍看,他刚才准是从马上摔了下来。

"啊哈!"骑士看见哈利、罗恩和赫敏便喊道,"什么坏蛋,竟敢擅自闯入我的私人领地?或许是来笑话我摔倒的吧?拔剑吧,你们这些无赖,你们这些狗!"

他们惊愕地注视着小个子骑士把剑拔出了剑鞘,一边疯狂地挥舞着,一边怒气冲冲地上蹿下跳。可是,这把剑对他来说太长了,他一下用力过猛,身体失去平衡,脸朝下摔倒在草地上。

"你没事吧?"哈利凑近图画问道。

"滚开,你这讨厌的爱吹牛的家伙!滚开,你这恶棍!"

骑士又抓住他的剑,支撑着站了起来。可是剑刃在草地里陷得太深,他使出吃奶的力气拔呀拔呀,还是没能把它拔出来。最后他只好扑通倒在草地上,推开面罩,擦擦汗湿的脸。

CHAPTER SIX   Talons and Tea Leaves

'Listen,' said Harry, taking advantage of the knight's exhaustion, 'we're looking for the North Tower. You don't know the way, do you?'

'A quest!' The knight's rage seemed to vanish instantly. He clanked to his feet and shouted, 'Come follow me, dear friends, and we shall find our goal, or else shall perish bravely in the charge!'

He gave the sword another fruitless tug, tried and failed to mount the fat pony, and cried, 'On foot then, good sirs and gentle lady! On! On!'

And he ran, clanking loudly, into the left-hand side of the frame and out of sight.

They hurried after him along the corridor, following the sound of his armour. Every now and then they spotted him running through a picture ahead.

'Be of stout heart, the worst is yet to come!' yelled the knight, and they saw him reappear in front of an alarmed group of women in crinolines, whose picture hung on the wall of a narrow spiral staircase.

Puffing loudly, Harry, Ron and Hermione climbed the tightly spiralling steps, getting dizzier and dizzier, until at last they heard the murmur of voices above them, and knew they had reached the classroom.

'Farewell!' cried the knight, popping his head into a painting of some sinister-looking monks. 'Farewell, my comrades-in-arms! If ever you have need of noble heart and steely sinew, call upon Sir Cadogan!'

'Yeah, we'll call you,' muttered Ron, as the knight disappeared, 'if we ever need someone mental.'

They climbed the last few steps and emerged onto a tiny landing, where most of the class was already assembled. There were no doors off this landing; Ron nudged Harry and pointed at the ceiling, where there was a circular trap door with a brass plaque on it.

'Sybill Trelawney, Divination teacher,' Harry read. 'How're we supposed to get up there?'

As though in answer to his question, the trap door suddenly opened, and a silvery ladder descended right at Harry's feet. Everyone went quiet.

'After you,' said Ron, grinning, so Harry climbed the ladder first.

He emerged into the strangest-looking classroom he had ever seen. In fact, it didn't look like a classroom at all; more like a cross between someone's

第6章 鹰爪和茶叶

"听我说,"哈利趁骑士累得没劲儿了,赶紧说道,"我们在找北塔楼。你不知道路吧?"

"一次远征!"骑士的怒气似乎顿时烟消云散。他哐啷哐啷地站起来,喊道:"跟我来,亲爱的朋友们,我们一定要找到目标,不然就在冲锋中英勇地死去!"

他又用力拔了一下那把剑,还是没拔出来,再试着骑上那匹胖胖的小马,也没能成功,于是他叫道:"那就步行吧,尊贵的先生和文雅的女士!前进!前进!"

他哐啷哐啷地跑进相框的左边,不见了。

他们循着他盔甲的声音,在走廊上追着他跑。时不时地,看见他在前面一幅画里一跑而过。

"要有一颗顽强的心,最艰难的还在后头呢!"骑士嚷道,他们看见他出现在一群穿着圈环裙的惊慌失措的妇女们前面,她们的那幅画挂在一道狭窄的旋转楼梯的墙上。

哈利、罗恩和赫敏呼哧呼哧地喘着粗气,爬上一道道急速旋转的楼梯,感到越来越头晕眼花。最后,终于听见头顶上传来模模糊糊的说话声,这才知道教室到了。

"别了!"骑士喊道,一头扎进一幅画着几位阴险僧侣的图画里,"别了,我的战友!如果你们需要高贵的心灵和强健的体魄,就召唤卡多根爵士吧!"

"是啊,我们会召唤你的,"罗恩在骑士消失后低声说道,"如果我们需要一个疯子。"

他们爬上最后几级楼梯,来到一个小小的平台上,班上大部分同学已经聚集在这里了。平台上一扇门也没有。罗恩用胳膊肘捅捅哈利,指了指天花板,那儿有个圆形的活板门,上面嵌着一个黄铜牌子。

"西比尔·特里劳尼,占卜课教师。"哈利读道,"可是怎么上去呢?"

似乎为了回答他的问题,活板门突然开了,一把银色的梯子放下来,正好落在哈利脚边。大家都安静下来。

"你先上。"罗恩笑嘻嘻地说,于是哈利率先登上了梯子。

他来到一间他所见过的最最奇怪的教室。实际上,它看上去根本

CHAPTER SIX   Talons and Tea Leaves

attic and an old-fashioned teashop. At least twenty small, circular tables were crammed inside it, all surrounded by chintz armchairs and fat little pouffes. Everything was lit with a dim, crimson light; the curtains at the windows were all closed, and the many lamps were draped with dark red scarves. It was stiflingly warm, and the fire which was burning under the crowded mantelpiece was giving off a heavy, sickly sort of perfume as it heated a large copper kettle. The shelves running around the circular walls were crammed with dusty-looking feathers, stubs of candles, many packs of tattered playing cards, countless silvery crystal balls and a huge array of teacups.

Ron appeared at Harry's shoulder as the class assembled around them, all talking in whispers.

'Where is she?' Ron said.

A voice came suddenly out of the shadows, a soft, misty sort of voice.

'Welcome,' it said. 'How nice to see you in the physical world at last.'

Harry's immediate impression was of a large, glittering insect. Professor Trelawney moved into the firelight, and they saw that she was very thin; her large glasses magnified her eyes to several times their natural size, and she was draped in a gauzy spangled shawl. Innumerable chains and beads hung around her spindly neck, and her arms and hands were encrusted with bangles and rings.

'Sit, my children, sit,' she said, and they all climbed awkwardly into armchairs or sank onto pouffes. Harry, Ron and Hermione sat themselves around the same round table.

'Welcome to Divination,' said Professor Trelawney, who had seated herself in a winged armchair in front of the fire. 'My name is Professor Trelawney. You may not have seen me before. I find that descending too often into the hustle and bustle of the main school clouds my Inner eye.'

Nobody said anything in answer to this extraordinary pronouncement. Professor Trelawney delicately rearranged her shawl and continued, 'So you have chosen to study Divination, the most difficult of all magical arts. I must warn you at the outset that if you do not have the Sight, there is very little I will be able to teach you. Books can take you only so far in this field ...'

At these words, both Harry and Ron glanced, grinning, at Hermione, who looked startled at the news that books wouldn't be much help in this subject.

'Many witches and wizards, talented though they are in the area of loud

第6章 鹰爪和茶叶

不像教室，倒更像是阁楼和老式茶馆的混合物，里面至少挤放着二十张小圆桌，桌子周围放着印花布扶手椅和鼓鼓囊囊的小蒲团。房间里的一切都被一种朦朦胧胧的红光照着，窗帘拉得紧紧的，许多盏灯上都蒙着深红色的大围巾。这里热得让人透不过气来，在摆放得满满当当的壁炉台下面，火熊熊地烧着，上面放着一把很大的铜茶壶，散发出一股浓烈的、让人恶心的香味。圆形墙壁上一溜儿摆着许多架子，上面挤满了脏兮兮的羽毛笔、蜡烛头、许多破破烂烂的扑克牌、数不清的银光闪闪的水晶球和一大堆茶杯。

罗恩来到哈利身边，班上其他同学也都聚在他们周围窃窃私语。

"她在哪儿？"罗恩说。

阴影里突然响起一个声音，一个软绵绵的、含混不清的声音。

"欢迎，"那声音说，"终于在物质世界见到你们，真是太好了。"

哈利的第一感觉是见到了一只巨大的、闪闪发亮的昆虫。特里劳尼教授走到火光里，他们发现她体形很瘦，一副大眼镜把她的眼睛放大成原来的好几倍，她披着一条轻薄透明、缀着许多闪光金属片的披肩。又细又长的脖子上挂着数不清的珠子、链子，胳膊和手上也戴着许多镯子和戒指。

"坐下吧，我的孩子们，坐下吧。"她说，于是同学们局促不安地爬上了扶手椅，或跌坐在蒲团上。哈利、罗恩和赫敏围坐在同一张桌子旁。

"欢迎来上占卜课，"特里劳尼教授坐在炉火前的一把安乐椅上，对大家说，"我是特里劳尼教授。你们以前大概没有见过我。我发现，经常下到纷乱和嘈杂的校区生活中，会使我的天目变得模糊。"

听了这番奇谈怪论，谁也没有说什么。特里劳尼教授优雅地整了整她的披肩，继续说道："这么说，你们选修了占卜课，这是所有魔法艺术中最高深的一门学问。我必须把话说在前头，如果你们没有洞察力，我是无能为力的。在这个领域，书本能教给你们的也就这么一点点……"

听了这话，哈利和罗恩都笑着看了一眼赫敏。赫敏听到书本对这门学科没有多少帮助，显得非常惊愕。

"许多男女巫师尽管很有才能，弄出砰砰巨响、变出气味、让自己

CHAPTER SIX   Talons and Tea Leaves

bangs and smells and sudden disappearings, are yet unable to penetrate the veiled mysteries of the future,' Professor Trelawney went on, her enormous, gleaming eyes moving from face to nervous face. 'It is a Gift granted to few. You, boy,' she said suddenly to Neville, who almost toppled off his pouffe, 'is your grandmother well?'

'I think so,' said Neville tremulously.

'I wouldn't be so sure if I were you, dear,' said Professor Trelawney, the firelight glinting on her long emerald earrings. Neville gulped. Professor Trelawney continued placidly, 'We will be covering the basic methods of Divination this year. The first term will be devoted to reading the tea leaves. Next term we shall progress to palmistry. By the way, my dear,' she shot suddenly at Parvati Patil, 'beware a red-haired man.'

Parvati gave a startled look at Ron, who was right behind her, and edged her chair away from him.

'In the summer term,' Professor Trelawney went on, 'we shall progress to the crystal ball – if we have finished with fire-omens, that is. Unfortunately, classes will be disrupted in February by a nasty bout of flu. I myself will lose my voice. And around Easter, one of our number will leave us for ever.'

A very tense silence followed this pronouncement, but Professor Trelawney seemed unaware of it.

'I wonder, dear,' she said to Lavender Brown, who was nearest and shrank back in her chair, 'if you could pass me the largest silver teapot?'

Lavender, looking relieved, stood up, took an enormous teapot from the shelf and put it down on the table in front of Professor Trelawney.

'Thank you, my dear. Incidentally, that thing you are dreading – it will happen on Friday the sixteenth of October.'

Lavender trembled.

'Now, I want you all to divide into pairs. Collect a teacup from the shelf, come to me and I will fill it. Then sit down and drink; drink until only the dregs remain. Swill these around the cup three times with the left hand, then turn the cup upside-down on its saucer; wait for the last of the tea to drain away, then give your cup to your partner to read. You will interpret the patterns using pages five and six of *Unfogging the Future*. I shall move among you, helping and instructing. Oh, and dear –' she caught Neville by the arm

突然消失等，但却不能看透未来的神秘面纱。"特里劳尼教授继续说，一双大得吓人、闪闪发亮的眼睛，从一个紧张的面孔望向另一个紧张的面孔，"这是少数人具有的天赋。你，孩子，"她突然对纳威发话了，纳威吓得差点从蒲团上栽下去，"你奶奶好吗？"

"我想还好吧。"纳威战战兢兢地说。

"如果我是你，就不会这么肯定，亲爱的。"特里劳尼教授说，火光照得她长长的绿宝石耳坠熠熠发光。纳威倒抽了一口冷气。特里劳尼教授继续平静地说："今年我们将学习占卜的基本方法。第一学期集中学习解读茶叶。第二学期开始学习看手相。顺便说一句，我亲爱的，"她突然朝帕瓦蒂·佩蒂尔扔过去一句，"要警惕一个红头发男人。"

帕瓦蒂惊惶地看了看坐在她身后的罗恩，赶紧把椅子挪得离他远一点儿。

"在夏季学期，"特里劳尼教授接着往下说，"我们开始学习水晶球——我的意思是，如果学完了火焰预兆的话。不幸的是，二月份会因一场严重流感而停课。我自己会失音。复活节前后，我们中间的一位将会永远离开我们。"

这句话过后，是一片提心吊胆的沉默，但特里劳尼教授似乎没有意识到。

"亲爱的，"她对离她最近、吓得蜷缩在椅子上的拉文德·布朗说，"你能不能把那只最大的银色茶杯递给我？"

拉文德似乎松了口气，她站起身，从架子上取下一只巨大的茶杯，放在特里劳尼教授面前的桌子上。

"谢谢你，亲爱的。顺便说一句，你最害怕的那件事——会在十月十六日星期五发生。"

拉文德顿时发起抖来。

"现在，我要求你们分成两个人一组。每人从架子上拿一个茶杯，到我这里来，我给杯子里倒满茶。然后你们坐下去喝茶，喝到只剩下茶叶渣。用左手把茶叶渣在杯子里晃荡三下，再把杯子倒扣在托盘上，等最后一滴茶水都渗出来后，就把杯子递给你的搭档去解读。你们可以对照《拨开迷雾看未来》的第五、第六页来解读茶叶形状。我在你们中间巡视，帮助你们，指导你们。哦，亲爱的……"她一把拉住正

CHAPTER SIX   Talons and Tea Leaves

as he made to stand up, 'after you've broken your first cup, would you be so kind as to select one of the blue patterned ones? I'm rather attached to the pink.'

Sure enough, Neville had no sooner reached the shelf of teacups than there was a tinkle of breaking china. Professor Trelawney swept over to him holding a dustpan and brush and said, 'One of the blue ones, then, dear, if you wouldn't mind ... thank you ...'

When Harry and Ron had had their teacups filled, they went back to their table and tried to drink the scalding tea quickly. They swilled the dregs around as Professor Trelawney had instructed, then drained the cups and swapped them.

'Right,' said Ron, as they both opened their books at pages five and six. 'What can you see in mine?'

'A load of soggy brown stuff,' said Harry. The heavily perfumed smoke in the room was making him feel sleepy and stupid.

'Broaden your minds, my dears, and allow your eyes to see past the mundane!' Professor Trelawney cried through the gloom.

Harry tried to pull himself together.

'Right, you've got a wonky sort of cross ...' he said, consulting *Unfogging the Future*. 'That means you're going to have "trials and suffering" – sorry about that – but there's a thing that could be the sun. Hang on ... that means "great happiness" ... so you're going to suffer but be very happy ...'

'You need your Inner Eye testing, if you ask me,' said Ron, and they both had to stifle their laughs as Professor Trelawney gazed in their direction.

'My turn ...' Ron peered into Harry's teacup, his forehead wrinkled with effort. 'There's a blob a bit like a bowler hat,' he said. 'Maybe you're going to work for the Ministry of Magic ...'

He turned the teacup the other way up.

'But this way it looks more like an acorn ... what's that?' He scanned his copy of *Unfogging the Future*. '"A windfall, unexpected gold." Excellent, you can lend me some. And there's a thing here,' he turned the cup again, 'that looks like an animal. Yeah, if that was its head ... it looks like a hippo ... no, a sheep ...'

Professor Trelawney whirled around as Harry let out a snort of laughter.

第6章 鹰爪和茶叶

要站起来的纳威的胳膊,"在你打坏第一个茶杯之后,能不能麻烦你挑选一个蓝色图案的?我太喜欢那个粉红色的了。"

果然,纳威刚走到茶杯架子前,就传来了瓷器被打碎的脆响。特里劳尼教授拿着簸箕和扫帚快步走了过去,说道:"亲爱的,如果你不介意的话,拿一个蓝色的吧……谢谢……"

哈利和罗恩的茶杯灌满了,他们回到桌旁,三口两口喝掉滚烫的茶水。然后按照特里劳尼教授的指示,把茶叶渣晃荡了几下,沥干茶水,互相交换了杯子。

"好了,"罗恩说,这时他们都把课本翻到了第五和第六页,"你在我的杯子里能看到什么?"

"一堆湿乎乎的咖啡色的东西。"哈利说。房间里散发着的浓郁香味使他感到头脑发木,昏昏欲睡。

"开拓你们的思路,亲爱的,让你们的目光超越世俗的界限!"特里劳尼教授的声音在昏暗的教室里响起。

哈利强打起精神。

"对了,你杯子里有一个歪歪斜斜的十字架……"他对照着《拨开迷雾看未来》说,"那就是说,你将会有'磨难和痛苦'——真是抱歉——不过还有一个像是太阳的东西。等等……那意思是'巨大的欢乐'……所以,你将要受苦,但感到非常快乐……"

"要我说,你需要测试一下你的天目。"罗恩说,特里劳尼教授的目光朝这边瞪了过来,他们只好拼命忍住笑。

"该我了……"罗恩端详着哈利的茶杯,因为太用心,额头上都起了皱纹,"这一块有点像个圆顶高帽,"他说,"说不定你要去魔法部工作了……"

他把茶杯掉了个方向。

"可是这样一看,又更像是一颗橡实……那是什么呢?"他看了看他那本《拨开迷雾看未来》,"'一笔意外收入,一笔横财。'太棒了,你可以借给我一些。这里还有个东西,"他又把杯子转了转,"看上去像一只动物。没错,如果那是它的脑袋……就像一头河马……不,一只绵羊……"

哈利讥讽地笑了一声,特里劳尼教授忽地转过身来。

CHAPTER SIX   Talons and Tea Leaves

'Let me see that, my dear,' she said reprovingly to Ron, sweeping over and snatching Harry's cup from him. Everyone went quiet to watch.

Professor Trelawney was staring into the teacup, rotating it anti-clockwise.

'The falcon ... my dear, you have a deadly enemy.'

'But everyone knows *that*,' said Hermione in a loud whisper. Professor Trelawney stared at her.

'Well, they do,' said Hermione. 'Everybody knows about Harry and You-Know-Who.'

Harry and Ron stared at her with a mixture of amazement and admiration. They had never heard Hermione speak to a teacher like that before. Professor Trelawney chose not to reply. She lowered her huge eyes to Harry's cup again and continued to turn it.

'The club ... an attack. Dear, dear, this is not a happy cup ...'

'I thought that was a bowler hat,' said Ron sheepishly.

'The skull ... danger in your path, my dear ...'

Everyone was staring, transfixed, at Professor Trelawney, who gave the cup a final turn, gasped, and then screamed.

There was another tinkle of breaking china; Neville had smashed his second cup. Professor Trelawney sank into a vacant armchair, her glittering hand at her heart and her eyes closed.

'My dear boy – my poor dear boy – no – it is kinder not to say – no – don't ask me ...'

'What is it, Professor?' said Dean Thomas at once. Everyone had got to their feet, and slowly, they crowded around Harry and Ron's table, pressing close to Professor Trelawney's chair to get a good look at Harry's cup.

'My dear,' Professor Trelawney's huge eyes opened dramatically, 'you have the Grim.'

'The what?' said Harry.

He could tell that he wasn't the only one who didn't understand; Dean Thomas shrugged at him and Lavender Brown looked puzzled, but nearly everybody else clapped their hands to their mouths in horror.

'The Grim, my dear, the Grim!' cried Professor Trelawney, who looked shocked that Harry hadn't understood. 'The giant, spectral dog that haunts churchyards! My dear boy, it is an omen – the worst omen – of *death*!'

第6章 鹰爪和茶叶

"亲爱的,让我看看。"她不满地对罗恩说,一边快步走了过来,从他手里夺走了哈利的茶杯。同学们都安静下来注视着。

特里劳尼教授盯着茶杯,并按逆时针的方向转动着它。

"老鹰……亲爱的,你有一个死对头。"

"这是大家都知道的事。"赫敏故意说得让大家都听见。特里劳尼教授瞪着她。

"没错呀,"赫敏说,"每个人都知道哈利和神秘人的事。"

哈利和罗恩又吃惊又敬佩地望着赫敏。他们以前从没有听过赫敏对一位老师这么说话。特里劳尼教授没有回答。她垂下那双大得吓人的眼睛,再次打量哈利的茶杯,继续把茶杯转来转去。

"大头棒……一次袭击。天哪,天哪,这可不是一个令人愉快的杯子……"

"我还以为是一个圆顶高帽呢。"罗恩局促不安地说。

"骷髅……你的路上有危险,我亲爱的……"

每个人都呆呆地瞪着特里劳尼教授,她最后又把杯子转动了一下,大吸一口冷气,尖叫起来。

又传来一声瓷器打碎的脆响。纳威把他的第二个杯子也摔碎了。特里劳尼教授一屁股坐在一把空扶手椅上,用一只亮闪闪的手捂住胸口,闭上了眼睛。

"我亲爱的孩子——我可怜的亲爱的孩子——不——最好不要说出来——别来问我……"

"是什么呀,教授?"迪安·托马斯立刻问道。大家都站了起来,慢慢围拢在哈利和罗恩的桌旁,凑近特里劳尼教授的椅子,仔细看着哈利的茶杯。

"我亲爱的,"特里劳尼教授猛地睁开一双巨大的眼睛,"你有'不祥'。"

"什么?"哈利问。

他看得出来,听不懂的不止他一个人。迪安·托马斯冲他耸了耸肩膀,拉文德·布朗一脸迷惑,但其他人几乎都惊恐地用手捂住了嘴。

"不祥,亲爱的,不祥!"特里劳尼教授喊道,看到哈利竟然没有听懂,她似乎感到非常震惊,"那条在墓地出没的阴森森的大狗!亲爱的孩子,它是一个凶兆——最险恶的凶兆——死亡的凶兆!"

CHAPTER SIX   Talons and Tea Leaves

Harry's stomach lurched. That dog on the cover of *Death Omens* in Flourish and Blotts – the dog in the shadows of Magnolia Crescent ... Lavender Brown clapped her hands to her mouth, too. Everyone was looking at Harry; everyone except Hermione, who had got up and moved around to the back of Professor Trelawney's chair.

'*I* don't think it looks like a Grim,' she said flatly.

Professor Trelawney surveyed Hermione with mounting dislike.

'You'll forgive me for saying so, my dear, but I perceive very little aura around you. Very little receptivity to the resonances of the future.'

Seamus Finnigan was tilting his head from side to side.

'It looks like a Grim if you do this,' he said, with his eyes almost shut, 'but it looks more like a donkey from here,' he said, leaning to the left.

'When you've all finished deciding whether I'm going to die or not!' said Harry, taking even himself by surprise. Now nobody seemed to want to look at him.

'I think we will leave the lesson here for today,' said Professor Trelawney, in her mistiest voice. 'Yes ... please pack away your things ...'

Silently the class took their teacups back to Professor Trelawney, packed away their books and closed their bags. Even Ron was avoiding Harry's eyes.

'Until we meet again,' said Professor Trelawney faintly, 'fair fortune be yours. Oh, and dear –' she pointed at Neville, 'you'll be late next time, so mind you work extra hard to catch up.'

Harry, Ron and Hermione descended Professor Trelawney's ladder and the winding staircase in silence, then set off for Professor McGonagall's Transfiguration lesson. It took them so long to find her classroom that, early as they had left Divination, they were only just in time.

Harry chose a seat right at the back of the room, feeling as though he was sitting in a very bright spotlight; the rest of the class kept shooting furtive glances at him, as though he was about to drop dead at any moment. He hardly heard what Professor McGonagall was telling them about Animagi (wizards who could transform at will into animals), and wasn't even watching when she transformed herself in front of their eyes into a tabby cat with spectacle markings around her eyes.

'Really, what has got into you all today?' said Professor McGonagall,

第6章 鹰爪和茶叶

哈利的心揪紧了。丽痕书店里那本《死亡预兆》封面上的那条狗——木兰花新月街阴影里的那条狗——拉文德·布朗也用手捂住了嘴。每个人都看着哈利,只有赫敏除外,她已经站起身,绕到了特里劳尼教授的椅子后面。

"我认为这不像是不祥。"她冷静地说。

特里劳尼教授打量着赫敏,对她的厌恶逐渐增加。

"请原谅我这么说,亲爱的,但是我看见你周围的光环很小,对于未来并没有多少感知力。"

西莫·斐尼甘把脑袋从一边偏向另一边。

"这么一看,像是不祥,"他眼睛眯得几乎闭上了,说道,"可是从这里一看,更像是一头驴子。"他说着把头偏向了左边。

"你们什么时候才能定下来我是不是会死!"哈利突然开口说话,把自己也吓了一跳。现在似乎谁也不愿意看他一眼了。

"我想今天的课就上到这里吧。"特里劳尼教授用特别含混的声音说,"是的……请收拾好自己的东西……"

同学们默不作声地把茶杯还给特里劳尼教授,收拾起自己的书本,合上书包。就连罗恩也躲着哈利的眼睛。

"在我们下次见面之前,"特里劳尼教授有气无力地说,"祝你们好运。哦,亲爱的——"她指着纳威,"你下节课会迟到,所以要格外用功,把功课赶上来。"

哈利、罗恩和赫敏一言不发地顺着特里劳尼教授的梯子下来,走下旋转楼梯,赶去上麦格教授的变形课。尽管占卜课提早下课了,但他们花了很长时间寻找麦格教授的教室,到那里时刚刚赶上点儿。

哈利在教室后面挑了一个座位,觉得自己像是坐在刺眼的聚光灯下,班上其他同学不停地偷偷朝他张望,就好像他随时都会倒下来死掉。麦格教授在跟他们讲阿尼马格斯(会变成动物的巫师)的知识,哈利几乎没有听。麦格教授在全班同学面前变成了一只花斑猫,眼睛周围还有眼镜状的纹路,哈利也没有心思去看。

"我说,你们今天这是怎么啦?"麦格教授噗的一声把自己变回原

CHAPTER SIX   Talons and Tea Leaves

turning back into herself with a faint *pop*, and staring around at them all. 'Not that it matters, but that's the first time my transformation's not got applause from a class.'

Everybody's heads turned towards Harry again, but nobody spoke. Then Hermione raised her hand.

'Please, Professor, we've just had our first Divination class, and we were reading the tea leaves, and –'

'Ah, of course,' said Professor McGonagall, suddenly frowning. 'There is no need to say any more, Miss Granger. Tell me, which of you will be dying this year?'

Everyone stared at her.

'Me,' said Harry, finally.

'I see,' said Professor McGonagall, fixing Harry with her beady eyes. 'Then you should know, Potter, that Sybill Trelawney has predicted the death of one student a year since she arrived at this school. None of them has died yet. Seeing death omens is her favourite way of greeting a new class. If it were not for the fact that I never speak ill of my colleagues –' Professor McGonagall broke off, and they saw that her nostrils had gone white. She went on, more calmly, 'Divination is one of the most imprecise branches of magic. I shall not conceal from you that I have very little patience with it. True Seers are very rare, and Professor Trelawney ...'

She stopped again, and then said, in a very matter-of-fact tone, 'You look in excellent health to me, Potter, so you will excuse me if I don't let you off homework today. I assure you that if you die, you need not hand it in.'

Hermione laughed. Harry felt a bit better. It was harder to feel scared of a lump of tea leaves away from the dim red light and befuddling perfume of Professor Trelawney's classroom. Not everyone was convinced, however. Ron still looked worried, and Lavender whispered, 'But what about Neville's cup?'

When the Transfiguration class had finished, they joined the crowd thundering towards the Great Hall for lunch.

'Ron, cheer up,' said Hermione, pushing a dish of stew towards him. 'You heard what Professor McGonagall said.'

Ron spooned stew onto his plate and picked up his fork but didn't start.

'Harry,' he said, in a low, serious voice, 'you *haven't* seen a great black dog anywhere, have you?'

'Yeah, I have,' said Harry. 'I saw one the night I left the Dursleys.'

样,望着大家说道,"说来也没什么,只是我的变形第一次没有赢得同学们的掌声。"

大家又扭头看着哈利,谁也没有说话。这时赫敏举起了手。

"教授,我们刚才上了第一节占卜课,解读了茶叶,结果……"

"啊,明白了,"麦格教授皱起眉头,说,"用不着再说了,格兰杰小姐。告诉我,今年你们中间有谁会死?"

大家都吃惊地望着她。

"我。"最后哈利说道。

"明白了,"麦格教授用她那双亮晶晶的眼睛盯着哈利,说,"那么你应该知道,波特,西比尔·特里劳尼自从到这个学校之后,每年都预言一位学生会死。到现在为止,他们谁都没有死。她最喜欢用看凶兆的方式来迎接一个新的班级。要不是我从来不说同事的坏话——"麦格教授突然停住,他们看见她的鼻孔变白了。她平静一点后继续说:"占卜学是魔法分支里最不严谨的一门学问。不瞒你们说,我对它没有多少耐心。真正的先知少而又少,而特里劳尼教授……"

她又停住了,接着用一种实事求是的语气说:"在我看来,你的身体非常健康,所以,如果我没有免去你今天的家庭作业,请你原谅。我向你保证,万一你真的死了,就用不着交作业了。"

赫敏笑了起来。哈利也觉得轻松了一些。离开了特里劳尼教授教室里朦朦胧胧的红光和熏得人昏昏沉沉的香气,就很难被一堆茶叶吓住了。不过,并不是每个人都放下心来。罗恩看上去仍然忧心忡忡,拉文德·布朗小声说:"可纳威的杯子又是怎么回事呢?"

变形课结束后,他们随着人群,闹哄哄地去礼堂吃午饭。

"罗恩,高兴一点儿吧,"赫敏把一盘炖菜推到他面前,"麦格教授的话你都听见了。"

罗恩用勺子把炖菜舀进自己的盘子,拿起叉子,却没有吃。

"哈利,"他语气严肃地低声说,"你没有在什么地方看见过一条大黑狗吧?"

"看见过,"哈利说,"我离开德思礼家的那天夜里见过一条。"

CHAPTER SIX   Talons and Tea Leaves

Ron let his fork fall with a clatter.

'Probably a stray,' said Hermione calmly.

Ron looked at Hermione as though she had gone mad.

'Hermione, if Harry's seen a Grim, that's – that's bad,' he said. 'My – my Uncle Bilius saw one and – and he died twenty-four hours later!'

'Coincidence,' said Hermione airily, pouring herself some pumpkin juice.

'You don't know what you're talking about!' said Ron, starting to get angry. 'Grims scare the living daylights out of most wizards!'

'There you are, then,' said Hermione in a superior tone. 'They see the Grim and die of fright. The Grim's not an omen, it's the cause of death! And Harry's still with us because he's not stupid enough to see one and think, right, well, I'd better pop my clogs then!'

Ron mouthed wordlessly at Hermione, who opened her bag, took out her new Arithmancy book and propped it open against the juice jug.

'I think Divination seems very woolly,' she said, searching for her page. 'A lot of guesswork, if you ask me.'

'There was nothing woolly about the Grim in that cup!' said Ron hotly.

'You didn't seem quite so confident when you were telling Harry it was a sheep,' said Hermione coolly.

'Professor Trelawney said you didn't have the right aura! You just don't like being rubbish at something for a change!'

He had touched a nerve. Hermione slammed her Arithmancy book down on the table so hard that bits of meat and carrot flew everywhere.

'If being good at Divination means I have to pretend to see death omens in a lump of tea leaves, I'm not sure I'll be studying it much longer! That lesson was absolute rubbish compared to my Arithmancy class!'

She snatched up her bag and stalked away.

Ron frowned after her.

'What's she talking about?' he said to Harry. 'She hasn't been to an Arithmancy class yet.'

第6章 鹰爪和茶叶

罗恩的叉子咔嗒一声掉了下来。

"说不定就是一条流浪狗。"赫敏平静地说。

罗恩望着赫敏,就好像赫敏疯了似的。

"赫敏,如果哈利看见过不祥,那就——那就糟糕了。"他说,"我的——我的叔叔比利尔斯看见过一条,结果——结果他二十四小时之后就死了!"

"巧合。"赫敏满不在乎地说,给自己倒了一些南瓜汁。

"你根本不知道自己在说什么!"罗恩开始冒火了,"大多数巫师见了不祥都会吓得魂不附体!"

"就是这么回事,"赫敏用一种居高临下的口吻说,"他们看见不祥,就被吓死了。不祥不是凶兆,而是死亡的原因!哈利现在还和我们在一起,就是因为他还没有傻到那个份儿上,看见一个不祥就想,得,完了,这下子我小命完蛋了!"

罗恩朝赫敏不出声地说了句什么,赫敏打开书包,取出崭新的算术占卜课本,打开来支在果汁壶上。

"我觉得占卜课简直是一团糨糊,"她翻着课本说,"要我说,是在凭空乱猜。"

"那只杯子里的不祥可不是一团糨糊!"罗恩激动地说。

"你告诉哈利那是一只绵羊时,口气好像没有这么肯定。"赫敏冷淡地说。

"特里劳尼教授说你的光环不够!你只是逞强惯了,不愿意在什么事情上不行!"

他触到赫敏的痛处了。赫敏啪的一下把算术占卜课本摔到桌上,用劲过猛,肉末和胡萝卜末溅得到处都是。

"如果学好占卜课意味着我要假装在一堆茶叶里看见死亡预兆,那我说不定就不再学它了!跟我的算术占卜课比起来,这门课简直就是一堆垃圾!"

她一把抓起书包,气冲冲地走了。

罗恩皱起眉头望着她的背影。

"她在说些什么呀?"他对哈利说,"她还没有上过算术占卜课呢。"

CHAPTER SIX Talons and Tea Leaves

Harry was pleased to get out of the castle after lunch. Yesterday's rain had cleared; the sky was a clear, pale grey and the grass was springy and damp underfoot as they set off for their first ever Care of Magical Creatures class.

Ron and Hermione weren't speaking to each other. Harry walked beside them in silence as they went down the sloping lawns to Hagrid's hut on the edge of the Forbidden Forest. It was only when he spotted three only-too-familiar backs ahead of them that he realised they must be having these lessons with the Slytherins. Malfoy was talking animatedly to Crabbe and Goyle, who were chortling. Harry was quite sure he knew what they were talking about.

Hagrid was waiting for his class at the door of his hut. He stood in his moleskin overcoat, with Fang the boarhound at his heels, looking impatient to start.

'C'mon, now, get a move on!' he called, as the class approached. 'Got a real treat for yeh today! Great lesson comin' up! Everyone here? Right, follow me!'

For one nasty moment, Harry thought that Hagrid was going to lead them into the Forest; Harry had had enough unpleasant experiences in there to last him a lifetime. However, Hagrid strolled off around the edge of the trees, and five minutes later, they found themselves outside a kind of paddock. There was nothing in there.

'Everyone gather round the fence here!' he called. 'That's it – make sure yeh can see. Now, firs' thing yeh'll want ter do is open yer books –'

'How?' said the cold, drawling voice of Draco Malfoy.

'Eh?' said Hagrid.

'How do we open our books?' Malfoy repeated. He took out his copy of *The Monster Book of Monsters*, which he had bound shut with a length of rope. Other people took theirs out, too; some, like Harry, had belted their book shut; others had crammed them inside tight bags or clamped them together with bullclips.

'Hasn' – hasn' anyone bin able ter open their books?' said Hagrid, looking crestfallen.

The class all shook their heads.

'Yeh've got ter *stroke* 'em,' said Hagrid, as though this was the most obvious thing in the world. 'Look ...'

He took Hermione's copy and ripped off the Spellotape that bound it. The book tried to bite, but Hagrid ran a giant forefinger down its spine, and

第6章 鹰爪和茶叶

吃过午饭，哈利很高兴来到城堡外面。他们去上生平第一节保护神奇动物课。雨已经停了，天空是一种清清爽爽的淡灰色，脚下的青草湿漉漉的，踩上去很有弹性。

罗恩和赫敏互相不说话了。哈利默默地跟在他们身边，顺着草坡而下，朝禁林边海格的小屋走去。当他看见前面那三个再熟悉不过的后脑勺时，才意识到他们必须跟斯莱特林的学生一起上这门课。马尔福正在兴致勃勃地对克拉布和高尔说话，逗得那两个人粗声傻笑。哈利基本上可以肯定他们在谈论什么。

海格站在小屋门口等同学们。他穿着那件鼹鼠皮大衣，大猎狗牙牙站在他的脚边，似乎迫不及待地想要出发。

"来吧，来吧，抓紧点儿！"同学们走近时海格喊道，"今天有一样好东西给你们看！这堂课精彩极了！人都到齐了吗？好，跟我来吧！"

哈利以为海格要把他们领进禁林，心里一阵恐慌。哈利在禁林里有过许多很不愉快的经历，令他终生难忘。还好，海格绕着树林边缘往前走，五分钟后，同学们发现来到了一个小围场的外面。围场里什么也没有。

"大家都聚到这道栅栏周围！"海格喊道，"对了——保证自己能看得见。好，首先你们需要打开课本——"

"怎么打开？"是德拉科·马尔福那冰冷的、懒洋洋的声音。

"呃？"海格说。

"我们怎么打开课本？"马尔福又问了一遍。他拿出他那本用绳子绑着的《妖怪们的妖怪书》。其他同学也把课本拿了出来。有的像哈利一样把书捆得结结实实，有的把书塞在又窄又紧的包里，或是用大夹子把它们夹住。

"你们——你们谁也没能打开课本？"海格问，看上去有点儿失望。

全班同学都摇了摇头。

"要抚摸它们一下。"海格说，就好像这是世界上最明白不过的事情，"看……"

他拿过赫敏的课本，扯去上面捆着的魔法胶带。课本张嘴要咬，海格用粗大的食指顺着书脊往下一捋，课本颤抖了一下，摊开来静静

CHAPTER SIX Talons and Tea Leaves

the book shivered, and then fell open and lay quiet in his hand.

'Oh, how silly we've all been!' Malfoy sneered. 'We should have *stroked* them! Why didn't we guess!'

'I ... I thought they were funny,' Hagrid said uncertainly to Hermione.

'Oh, tremendously funny!' said Malfoy. 'Really witty, giving us books that try and rip our hands off!'

'Shut up, Malfoy,' said Harry quietly. Hagrid was looking downcast and Harry wanted Hagrid's first lesson to be a success.

'Righ' then,' said Hagrid, who seemed to have lost his thread, 'so ... so yeh've got yer books an' ... an' ... now yeh need the Magical Creatures. Yeah. So I'll go an' get 'em. Hang on ...'

He strode away from them into the Forest and out of sight.

'God, this place is going to the dogs,' said Malfoy loudly. 'That oaf teaching classes, my father'll have a fit when I tell him –'

'Shut up, Malfoy,' Harry repeated.

'Careful, Potter, there's a Dementor behind you –'

'Oooooooh!' squealed Lavender Brown, pointing towards the opposite side of the paddock.

Trotting towards them were a dozen of the most bizarre creatures Harry had ever seen. They had the bodies, hind legs and tails of horses, but the front legs, wings and heads of what seemed to be giant eagles, with cruel, steel-coloured beaks and large, brilliantly orange eyes. The talons on their front legs were half a foot long and deadly-looking. Each of the beasts had a thick leather collar around its neck, which was attached to a long chain, and the ends of all of these were held in the vast hands of Hagrid, who came jogging into the paddock behind the creatures.

'Gee up, there!' he roared, shaking the chains and urging the creatures towards the fence where the class stood. Everyone drew back slightly as Hagrid reached them and tethered the creatures to the fence.

'Hippogriffs!' Hagrid roared happily, waving a hand at them. 'Beau'iful, aren' they?'

Harry could sort of see what Hagrid meant. Once you had got over the first shock of seeing something that was half horse, half bird, you started to appreciate the Hippogriffs' gleaming coats, changing smoothly from feather

第6章 鹰爪和茶叶

地躺在他的手掌上。

"哦,我们大家多傻啊!"马尔福讥笑道,"应该抚摸它们的呀!我们为什么就没有猜到呢!"

"我……我认为它们挺好玩的。"海格不安地对赫敏说。

"没错,好玩极了!"马尔福说,"真是有趣,给我们的课本竟然想要扯断我们的手!"

"闭嘴,马尔福。"哈利轻声说。海格看上去垂头丧气,哈利希望海格的第一堂课上得成功。

"那好吧,"海格似乎乱了头绪,说道,"那么……那么你们都有了课本,现在……现在……现在需要的是神奇动物。是啊,我这就去把它们带来。等一等……"

海格撇下他们,走进禁林不见了。

"天哪,这学校算是完蛋了,"马尔福大声说,"那个笨蛋也来教课,我爸爸听说了准会发心脏病——"

"闭嘴,马尔福!"哈利又说了一遍。

"小心点儿,波特,你后面有个摄魂怪——"

"哦哦哦哦哦哦!"拉文德·布朗指着围场对面尖叫起来。

十几只动物朝他们小跑过来,哈利从来没见过这么古怪的动物。它们有着马的身体、后腿和尾巴,但前腿、翅膀和脑袋却像是老鹰的。冷酷的利喙是钢铁般的颜色,一双明亮的大眼睛是橘黄色的。它们前腿上的鹰爪有半英尺长,看上去令人生畏。每只怪兽的脖子上都围着一个粗粗的皮项圈,由一根长链子拴着。所有的链子都抓在海格那双大手里,他跟着这些怪兽慢慢走进围场。

"快走,那边!"他吼道,一边晃着链子,催促那些怪兽朝全班同学站的栅栏走来。海格走近,把怪兽们拴在栅栏上,同学们都稍稍往后退了退。

"鹰头马身有翼兽!"海格朝他们挥手,开心地吼道,"多漂亮啊,是不是?"

哈利有点儿明白海格的意思了。一旦克服了第一次见到半马半鸟怪物时的恐惧,便会开始赞叹鹰头马身有翼兽那一身光亮闪烁的皮毛,

CHAPTER SIX Talons and Tea Leaves

to hair, each of them a different colour: stormy grey, bronze, a pinkish roan, gleaming chestnut and inky black.

'So,' said Hagrid, rubbing his hands together and beaming around, 'if yeh wan' ter come a bit nearer ...'

No one seemed to want to. Harry, Ron and Hermione, however, approached the fence cautiously.

'Now, firs' thing yeh gotta know abou' Hippogriffs is they're proud,' said Hagrid. 'Easily offended, Hippogriffs are. Don't never insult one, 'cause it might be the last thing yeh do.'

Malfoy, Crabbe and Goyle weren't listening; they were talking in an undertone and Harry had a nasty feeling they were plotting how best to disrupt the lesson.

'Yeh always wait fer the Hippogriff ter make the firs' move,' Hagrid continued. 'It's polite, see? Yeh walk towards him, and yeh bow, an' yeh wait. If he bows back, yeh're allowed ter touch him. If he doesn' bow, then get away from him sharpish, 'cause those talons hurt.'

'Right – who wants ter go first?'

Most of the class backed further away in answer. Even Harry, Ron and Hermione had misgivings. The Hippogriffs were tossing their fierce heads and flexing their powerful wings; they didn't seem to like being tethered like this.

'No one?' said Hagrid, with a pleading look.

'I'll do it,' said Harry.

There was an intake of breath from behind him and both Lavender and Parvati whispered, 'Oooh, no, Harry, remember your tea leaves!'

Harry ignored them. He climbed over the paddock fence.

'Good man, Harry!' roared Hagrid. 'Right then – let's see how yeh get on with Buckbeak.'

He untied one of the chains, pulled the grey Hippogriff away from his fellows and slipped off his leather collar. The class on the other side of the paddock seemed to be holding its breath. Malfoy's eyes were narrowed maliciously.

'Easy, now, Harry,' said Hagrid quietly. 'Yeh've got eye contact, now try not ter blink – Hippogriffs don' trust yeh if yeh blink too much ...'

第6章 鹰爪和茶叶

从羽毛逐渐过渡到毛发。每头怪兽的颜色都不一样：暴风雨一般的灰色、青铜色、粉红的花斑色、晶莹闪烁的红棕色和墨一般的黑色。

"好，"海格搓了搓两只手，笑眯眯地看着大家说道，"如果你们想再走近一些……"

似乎谁也不想，只有哈利、罗恩和赫敏小心翼翼地靠近了栅栏。

"记住，关于鹰头马身有翼兽，你们首先需要知道的是它们都很骄傲，"海格说，"鹰头马身有翼兽很容易被冒犯。千万不要去羞辱它们，不然可能会送命的。"

马尔福、克拉布和高尔根本没听，他们凑在一起窃窃私语，哈利有一种很不好的感觉，似乎他们在琢磨着怎样把这堂课搅得一团糟。

"一定要等鹰头马身有翼兽先行动，"海格继续说道，"这是礼貌，明白吗？你朝它走过去，鞠一个躬，如果它也朝你鞠躬，你就可以摸它。如果它没有鞠躬，你就赶紧离开它，那些爪子会伤人的。"

"好了——谁愿意先来？"

听了这话，大多数同学又往后退了退，就连哈利、罗恩和赫敏也心存疑虑。那些鹰头马身有翼兽甩着凶恶的脑袋，伸展着强有力的翅膀，似乎不愿意被这样拴起来。

"没有人？"海格说，脸上带着祈求的表情。

"我来吧。"哈利说。

他身后传来倒吸冷气的声音，拉文德和帕瓦蒂异口同声地说："哟，不要，哈利，别忘了你的茶叶！"

哈利没有理睬她们。他翻过围场的栅栏。

"好样的，哈利！"海格粗声大气地说，"好吧——让我们看看你和巴克比克相处得怎么样。"

他解下一根链子，拉着那头灰色的鹰头马身有翼兽离开它的同伴，解下了它的皮项圈。站在围场另一边的同学们似乎全都屏住了呼吸。马尔福不怀好意地眯起眼睛。

"放松点儿，哈利，"海格轻声说，"你已经跟它对上了目光，别眨眼睛——如果你眼睛眨得太频繁，鹰头马身有翼兽就会不相信你……"

171

CHAPTER SIX   Talons and Tea Leaves

Harry's eyes immediately began to water, but he didn't shut them. Buckbeak had turned his great, sharp head, and was staring at Harry with one fierce orange eye.

'Tha's it,' said Hagrid. 'Tha's it, Harry ... now, bow ...'

Harry didn't feel much like exposing the back of his neck to Buckbeak, but he did as he was told. He gave a short bow and then looked up.

The Hippogriff was still staring haughtily at him. It didn't move.

'Ah,' said Hagrid, sounding worried. 'Right – back away, now, Harry, easy does it –'

But then, to Harry's enormous surprise, the Hippogriff suddenly bent his scaly front knees, and sank into what was an unmistakeable bow.

'Well done, Harry!' said Hagrid, ecstatic. 'Right – yeh can touch him! Pat his beak, go on!'

Feeling that a better reward would have been to back away, Harry moved slowly towards the Hippogriff and reached out towards him. He patted the beak several times and the Hippogriff closed his eyes lazily, as though enjoying it.

The class broke into applause, all except for Malfoy, Crabbe and Goyle, who were looking deeply disappointed.

'Righ' then, Harry,' said Hagrid, 'I reckon he migh' let yeh ride him!'

This was more than Harry had bargained for. He was used to a broomstick; but he wasn't sure a Hippogriff would be quite the same.

'Yeh climb up there, jus' behind the wing joint,' said Hagrid, 'an' mind yeh don' pull any of his feathers out, he won' like that ...'

Harry put his foot on the top of Buckbeak's wing and hoisted himself onto his back. Buckbeak stood up. Harry wasn't sure where to hold on; everything in front of him was covered in feathers.

'Go on, then!' roared Hagrid, slapping the Hippogriff's hindquarters.

Without warning, twelve-foot wings flapped open on either side of Harry; he just had time to seize the Hippogriff around the neck before he was soaring upwards. It was nothing like a broomstick, and Harry knew which one he preferred; the Hippogriff's wings were beating uncomfortably on either side of him, catching him under his legs and making him feel he was

第6章 鹰爪和茶叶

哈利很快就开始流眼泪了,但他没有闭上眼睛。巴克比克转动着尖尖的大脑袋,用一只凶狠的橘黄色眼睛盯着哈利。

"对了,"海格说,"对了,哈利……现在,鞠躬……"

哈利不愿意把自己的脖子后面暴露给巴克比克,但还是按海格的吩咐做了。他很快地鞠了一躬,抬起头来。

鹰头马身有翼兽仍然傲慢地盯着哈利。它没有动。

"啊,"海格说,声音里透着担忧,"好吧——现在往后退,哈利,轻松地往后退——"

然而,令哈利大为吃惊的是,鹰头马身有翼兽突然弯下它布满鳞片的前膝,做了一个确切无疑的鞠躬姿势。

"干得好,哈利!"海格欣喜若狂地说,"好了——你可以摸摸它了!拍拍它的嘴,去吧!"

哈利觉得还不如奖励他往后退退呢,他慢慢地朝鹰头马身有翼兽走去,向它伸出了手。哈利拍了几下鹰头马身有翼兽的嘴,它懒洋洋地闭上眼睛,似乎很喜欢的样子。

全班同学鼓起掌来,只有马尔福、克拉布和高尔除外,他们似乎失望极了。

"很好,哈利,"海格说,"我想它会让你骑它了!"

这可是哈利没有料到的。他骑飞天扫帚已经习惯了,但不能肯定骑鹰头马身有翼兽的感觉也是一样。

"你爬到那上面,就在翅膀关节的后面,"海格说,"记住,千万不要扯它的羽毛,它不会喜欢的……"

哈利把脚踏在巴克比克的翅膀上,向上爬到了它的背上。巴克比克站了起来。哈利不知道抓住哪儿。他面前的每处地方都覆盖着羽毛。

"走吧!"海格一拍鹰头马身有翼兽的后腿,吼道。

突然,十二英尺长的翅膀在哈利两边展开,他刚来得及一把抱住鹰头马身有翼兽的脖子,它就向空中飞去了。这跟骑飞天扫帚的感觉一点也不一样,哈利知道他更喜欢哪种。鹰头马身有翼兽的翅膀在他两侧扇动,使他感到很不舒服,并且时时绊住他的小腿,他觉得自己

CHAPTER SIX Talons and Tea Leaves

about to be thrown off; the glossy feathers slipped under his fingers and he didn't dare get a stronger grip; instead of the smooth action of his Nimbus Two Thousand, he now felt himself rocking backwards and forwards as the hindquarters of the Hippogriff rose and fell with his wings.

Buckbeak flew him once around the paddock and then headed back to the ground; this was the bit Harry had been dreading; he leant back as the smooth neck lowered, feeling he was going to slip off over the beak; then he felt a heavy thud as the four ill-assorted feet hit the ground, and just managed to hold on and push himself straight again.

'Good work, Harry!' roared Hagrid, as everyone except Malfoy, Crabbe and Goyle cheered. 'OK, who else wants a go?'

Emboldened by Harry's success, the rest of the class climbed cautiously into the paddock. Hagrid untied the Hippogriffs one by one, and soon people were bowing nervously, all over the paddock. Neville ran repeatedly backwards from his, which didn't seem to want to bend its knees. Ron and Hermione practised on the chestnut, while Harry watched.

Malfoy, Crabbe and Goyle had taken over Buckbeak. He had bowed to Malfoy, who was now patting his beak, looking disdainful.

'This is very easy,' Malfoy drawled, loud enough for Harry to hear him. 'I knew it must have been, if Potter could do it ... I bet you're not dangerous at all, are you?' he said to the Hippogriff. 'Are you, you ugly great brute?'

It happened in a flash of steely talons; Malfoy let out a high-pitched scream and next moment, Hagrid was wrestling Buckbeak back into his collar as he strained to get at Malfoy, who lay curled in the grass, blood blossoming over his robes.

'I'm dying!' Malfoy yelled, as the class panicked. 'I'm dying, look at me! It's killed me!'

'Yer not dyin'!' said Hagrid, who had gone very white. 'Someone help me – gotta get him outta here –'

Hermione ran to open the gate while Hagrid lifted Malfoy easily. As they passed, Harry saw that there was a long, deep gash in Malfoy's arm; blood splattered the grass and Hagrid ran with him, up the slope towards the castle.

Very shaken, the Care of Magical Creatures class followed at a walk. The Slytherins were all shouting about Hagrid.

第6章 鹰爪和茶叶

要被甩下来了。光洁的羽毛在他手指下面滑动,他不敢使劲揪住。他的光轮2000动作非常柔和,而此刻鹰头马身有翼兽的后腿随着翅膀的扇动上下起伏,他觉得自己在剧烈地上下颠簸。

巴克比克驮着他绕围场飞了一圈,返回地面。这是哈利最害怕的。当那光滑的脖子低下去时,他拼命往后靠,觉得自己就要滑到巴克比克的嘴上去了。接着,他听到砰的一声重响,巴克比克四只动作不协调的脚落了地,哈利勉强稳住身子,让自己重新坐好。

"干得漂亮,哈利!"海格大声吼道,除了马尔福、克拉布和高尔,同学们都在欢呼喝彩,"好了,谁还想试试?"

在哈利成功的鼓励下,班上其他同学也都小心翼翼地翻进围场。海格把鹰头马身有翼兽一只只地解下来,很快,在整个围场里,同学们都在紧张地鞠躬。纳威一次又一次地从他那头鹰头马身有翼兽面前后退,因为它似乎不肯弯下膝盖。罗恩和赫敏选中了那头红棕色的,哈利在一旁观看。

马尔福、克拉布和高尔选中了巴克比克。它已经向马尔福鞠了躬,马尔福正在拍它的嘴,摆出一副傲慢的派头。

"这很容易嘛,"马尔福拖着长腔说,声音大得让哈利能够听见,"我早就知道肯定是这样,既然波特都能做到……我敢说你一点儿也不危险,是不是?"他对鹰头马身有翼兽说,"是不是,你这只丑陋的大野兽?"

钢一般的利爪忽地一闪,马尔福发出一声刺耳的尖叫,巴克比克伸着脖子还要去咬马尔福。海格挣扎着给它重新套上了项圈,马尔福蜷着身子躺在草地上,鲜血染红了他的袍子。

"我要死了!"马尔福嚷嚷着,全班同学都惊慌失措,"我要死了,看看我!它要了我的命!"

"你不会死的!"海格说,他的脸色变得非常苍白,"谁来帮帮我……把他从这里弄走——"

赫敏跑过去打开大门,海格不费吹灰之力就把马尔福抱了起来。他们走过时,哈利看见马尔福的胳膊上有一道很长很深的伤口,鲜血溅在草地上,海格抱着他冲上山坡,向城堡跑去。

保护神奇动物课的同学们都吓傻了,慢慢地跟了过去。斯莱特林的学生都在大声埋怨海格。

CHAPTER SIX   Talons and Tea Leaves

'They should sack him straight away!' said Pansy Parkinson, who was in tears.

'It was Malfoy's fault!' snapped Dean Thomas. Crabbe and Goyle flexed their muscles threateningly.

They all climbed the stone steps into the deserted Entrance Hall.

'I'm going to see if he's OK!' said Pansy, and they all watched her run up the marble staircase. The Slytherins, still muttering about Hagrid, headed away in the direction of their dungeon common room; Harry, Ron and Hermione proceeded upstairs to Gryffindor Tower.

'D'you think he'll be all right?' said Hermione nervously.

''Course he will, Madam Pomfrey can mend cuts in about a second,' said Harry, who had had far worse injuries mended magically by the matron.

'That was a really bad thing to happen in Hagrid's first class, though, wasn't it?' said Ron, looking worried. 'Trust Malfoy to mess things up for him ...'

They were among the first to reach the Great Hall at dinner-time, hoping to see Hagrid, but he wasn't there.

'They *wouldn't* sack him, would they?' said Hermione anxiously, not touching her steak-and-kidney pudding.

'They'd better not,' said Ron, who wasn't eating either.

Harry was watching the Slytherin table. A large group including Crabbe and Goyle were huddled together, deep in conversation. Harry was sure they were cooking up their own version of how Malfoy had got injured.

'Well, you can't say it wasn't an interesting first day back,' said Ron gloomily.

They went up to the crowded Gryffindor common room after dinner and tried to do the homework Professor McGonagall had set them, but all three of them kept breaking off and glancing out of the tower window.

'There's a light on in Hagrid's window,' Harry said suddenly.

Ron looked at his watch.

'If we hurried, we could go down and see him, it's still quite early ...'

'I don't know,' Hermione said slowly, and Harry saw her glance at him.

'I'm allowed to walk across the *grounds*,' he said pointedly. 'Sirius Black hasn't got past the Dementors here, has he?'

So they put their things away and headed out of the portrait hole, glad

第6章 鹰爪和茶叶

"应该马上把他开除！"潘西·帕金森含着眼泪说。

"这都怪马尔福自己！"迪安·托马斯不客气地说。克拉布和高尔听了，气势汹汹地展示着他们的肌肉。

大家踏上石阶，来到空无一人的门厅。

"我去看看他怎么样了！"潘西说，大家看着她跑上大理石楼梯。斯莱特林们一边仍然嘀嘀咕咕说着海格的坏话，一边朝他们在地下室的公共休息室走去。哈利、罗恩和赫敏上楼来到格兰芬多塔楼。

"你们说他会有事吗？"赫敏不安地问。

"当然没事儿，庞弗雷女士一眨眼工夫就能把伤治好。"哈利说，他以前受的伤比这严重得多，都被校医奇迹般地治愈了。

"海格的第一节课就发生这种事情，真是太糟糕了，不是吗？"罗恩显得很担忧，"马尔福肯定会趁机给他捣乱……"

吃晚饭的时候，他们是第一批赶到礼堂的，希望能够见到海格，但是海格不在。

"他们不会开除他吧？"赫敏担心地问，碰也不碰她面前的牛排腰子布丁。

"最好不要。"罗恩说，他也没有心思吃东西。

哈利注视着斯莱特林餐桌，包括克拉布和高尔在内的一大群人聚在那里窃窃私语。哈利知道他们肯定在编造马尔福受伤的经过。

"唉，这开学第一天倒是过得挺有意思。"罗恩闷闷不乐地说。

吃过饭后，他们上楼来到拥挤的格兰芬多休息室，想完成麦格教授布置的家庭作业，可是三个人不时地停下来，向塔楼的窗外张望。

"海格的窗口有灯光。"哈利突然说道。

罗恩看了看手表。

"如果我们加快速度，可以下去看看他，时间还挺早的……"

"这样行吗？"赫敏慢慢地说，哈利看见她扫了自己一眼。

"我是可以穿过场地的，"他直截了当地说，"小天狼星布莱克没法通过这里的摄魂怪，是不是？"

于是他们收拾好东西，出了肖像洞口，一直来到大门口，还好，

177

not to meet anybody on their way to the front doors, as they weren't entirely sure they were supposed to be out.

The grass was still wet and looked almost black in the twilight. When they reached Hagrid's hut, they knocked, and a voice growled, 'C'min.'

Hagrid was sitting in his shirt-sleeves at his scrubbed wooden table; his boarhound, Fang, had his head in Hagrid's lap. One look told them that Hagrid had been drinking a lot; there was a pewter tankard almost as big as a bucket in front of him, and he seemed to be having difficulty in getting them into focus.

"Spect it's a record,' he said thickly, when he recognised them. 'Don' reckon they've ever had a teacher who on'y lasted a day before.'

'You haven't been sacked, Hagrid!' gasped Hermione.

'Not yet,' said Hagrid miserably, taking a huge gulp of whatever was in the tankard. 'But 's only a matter o' time, i'n't it, after Malfoy ...'

'How is he?' said Ron, as they all sat down. 'It wasn't serious, was it?'

'Madam Pomfrey fixed him best she could,' said Hagrid dully, 'but he's sayin' it's still agony ... covered in bandages ... moanin' ...'

'He's faking it,' said Harry at once. 'Madam Pomfrey can mend anything. She regrew half my bones last year. Trust Malfoy to milk it for all it's worth.'

'School gov'nors have bin told, o' course,' said Hagrid miserably. 'They reckon I started too big. Shoulda left Hippogriffs fer later ... done Flobberworms or summat ... jus' thought it'd make a good firs' lesson ... 's all my fault ...'

'It's all *Malfoy's* fault, Hagrid!' said Hermione earnestly.

'We're witnesses,' said Harry. 'You said Hippogriffs attack if you insult them. It's Malfoy's problem he wasn't listening. We'll tell Dumbledore what really happened.'

'Yeah, don't worry, Hagrid, we'll back you up,' said Ron.

Tears leaked out of the crinkled corners of Hagrid's beetle-black eyes. He grabbed both Harry and Ron and pulled them into a bone-breaking hug.

'I think you've had enough to drink, Hagrid,' said Hermione firmly. She took the tankard from the table and went outside to empty it.

'Ar, maybe she's right,' said Hagrid, letting go of Harry and Ron, who both staggered away, rubbing their ribs. Hagrid heaved himself out of his

第6章 鹰爪和茶叶

一路上没有碰到什么人,他们拿不准自己是不是可以出去。

草地仍然湿漉漉的,在暮色中看上去几乎是黑色的。他们来到海格的小屋前,敲了敲门,一个声音粗吼道:"进来。"

海格穿着衬衫坐在擦洗得很干净的木头桌子旁,他的猎狗牙牙把脑袋搁在他腿上。他们一眼就看出海格喝了不少酒,他面前放着一只水桶那么大的白镴大酒杯,而且他似乎两眼模糊,好不容易才看清了他们。

"这大概是破纪录了,"他认出是他们后,瓮声瓮气地说,"以前大概从来没有哪个老师只教了一天的课。"

"你没有被开除吧,海格?"赫敏吃惊地喘着气说。

"暂时还没有,"海格可怜巴巴地说,又喝了一大口大酒杯里的东西,"但这只是时间问题,不是吗?马尔福……"

"他怎么样了?"他们都坐下来时,罗恩问道,"伤得不严重吧?"

"庞弗雷女士尽力给他治了,"海格闷闷地说,"但他仍然说痛得要命……裹着绷带……哼哼唧唧……"

"他是装的,"哈利立刻说道,"庞弗雷女士什么伤都能治好。去年,她让我身上一半的骨头重新长了出来。马尔福准是想拿这件事情大做文章。"

"不用说,校董们肯定也知道了,"海格难过地说,"他们认为我一开始架势摆得太大。应该把鹰头马身有翼兽留到以后再说……先弄点弗洛伯毛虫什么的……我只想把第一节课上得精彩……这事儿都怪我……"

"都是马尔福自己活该,海格!"赫敏诚恳地说。

"我们都是证人,"哈利说,"你说过如果冒犯了鹰头马身有翼兽,它就会进攻。谁叫马尔福自己不认真听讲。我们要把当时的情况告诉邓布利多。"

"是啊,别担心,海格,我们都会支持你的。"罗恩说。

泪水从海格那双乌黑小眼睛的鱼尾纹里流了出来。他一把抓住哈利和罗恩,紧紧地搂在怀里,差点把他们的骨头都挤断了。

"海格,我看你已经喝得够多了。"赫敏认真地说。她把大酒杯从桌上拿起来,端到外面倒空了。

"啊,也许她是对的。"海格说着,放开了哈利和罗恩,两人揉着肋骨,

CHAPTER SIX Talons and Tea Leaves

chair and followed Hermione unsteadily outside. They heard a loud splash.

'What's he done?' said Harry nervously, as Hermione came back in with the empty tankard.

'Stuck his head in the water barrel,' said Hermione, putting the tankard away.

Hagrid came back, his long hair and beard sopping wet, wiping the water out of his eyes.

'Tha's better,' he said, shaking his head like a dog and drenching them all. 'Listen, it was good of yeh ter come an' see me, I really –'

Hagrid stopped dead, staring at Harry as though he'd only just realised he was there.

'WHAT D'YEH THINK YOU'RE DOIN', EH?' he roared, so suddenly that they jumped a foot in the air. 'YEH'RE NOT TO GO WANDERIN' AROUND AFTER DARK, HARRY! AN' YOU TWO! LETTIN' HIM!'

Hagrid strode over to Harry, grabbed his arm and pulled him to the door.

'C'mon!' Hagrid said angrily. 'I'm takin' yer all back up ter school, an' don' let me catch yeh walkin' down ter see me after dark again. I'm not worth that!'

第6章 鹰爪和茶叶

跟跟跄跄地后退。海格费力地从椅子上站起来，步履蹒跚地跟着赫敏走到屋外。他们听见了很响的泼水声。

"他在干什么？"哈利不安地问，这时赫敏拿着空酒杯进来了。

"把脑袋扎进了水桶里。"赫敏说着，把酒杯收了起来。

海格回来了，长长的头发和胡子都湿透了，他擦干眼睛里的水。

"这下好多了。"他说，一边像狗一样抖动脑袋，把水溅到他们三个身上，"我说，你们来看我真是太好了，我实在是……"

海格突然停住了，呆呆地望着哈利，好像刚刚意识到他在这里。

"你这是在干什么，嗯？"他突然大吼一声，把他们吓得惊跳起来，"天黑后不能到处乱跑，哈利！还有你们两个！居然让他这样做！"

海格大步走到哈利面前，揪住他的胳膊把他拉到门口。

"快！"海格气冲冲地说，"我把你们送回学校去，别再让我看见你们天黑后来这里看我。我不值得你们这么做！"

CHAPTER SEVEN

The Boggart in the Wardrobe

Malfoy didn't reappear in classes until late on Thursday morning, when the Slytherins and Gryffindors were halfway through double Potions. He swaggered into the dungeon, his right arm covered in bandages and bound up in a sling, acting, in Harry's opinion, as though he was the heroic survivor of some dreadful battle.

'How is it, Draco?' simpered Pansy Parkinson. 'Does it hurt much?'

'Yeah,' said Malfoy, putting on a brave sort of grimace. But Harry saw him wink at Crabbe and Goyle when Pansy had looked away.

'Settle down, settle down,' said Professor Snape idly.

Harry and Ron scowled at each other; Snape wouldn't have said 'settle down' if *they'd* walked in late, he'd have given them detention. But Malfoy had always been able to get away with anything in Snape's classes; Snape was Head of Slytherin house, and generally favoured his own students before all others.

They were making a new potion today, a Shrinking Solution. Malfoy set up his Cauldron right next to Harry and Ron, so that they were preparing their ingredients on the same table.

'Sir,' Malfoy called, 'sir, I'll need help cutting up these daisy roots, because of my arm —'

'Weasley, cut up Malfoy's roots for him,' said Snape, without looking up.

Ron went brick red.

'There's nothing wrong with your arm,' he hissed at Malfoy.

Malfoy smirked across the table.

'Weasley, you heard Professor Snape, cut up these roots.'

Ron seized his knife, pulled Malfoy's roots towards him and began to chop

第 7 章

衣柜里的博格特

直到星期四上午,马尔福才在课堂上露面,当时斯莱特林和格兰芬多的两节魔药课正上到一半。马尔福大摇大摆地走进地下教室,右胳膊上缠着绷带,用带子吊着。哈利觉得,他那副派头就像个在战场上九死一生的英雄。

"怎么样,德拉科?"潘西·帕金森傻笑着问,"还疼得厉害吗?"

"是啊。"马尔福说着,假装勇敢地做了个鬼脸。可是哈利看见,就在潘西看着别处时,他朝克拉布和高尔眨了眨眼睛。

"坐下吧,坐下吧。"斯内普教授懒懒地说。

哈利和罗恩气恼地对了一下目光。如果迟到的是他们,斯内普可不会说"坐下吧",他准会关他们的禁闭。而马尔福在斯内普的课上不管犯了什么错,都不会受到惩罚。斯内普是斯莱特林学院的院长,通常都偏袒他们学院的学生。

他们今天要做一种新的魔药:缩身药水。马尔福把他的坩埚架在哈利和罗恩的坩埚旁边,于是他们三个在同一张桌子上准备配料。

"先生,"马尔福喊道,"先生,我需要有人帮我切切这些雏菊的根,因为我的胳膊——"

"韦斯莱,替马尔福切根。"斯内普头也不抬地说。

罗恩脸涨得通红。

"你的胳膊根本就没事儿。"他压低声音对马尔福说。

马尔福在桌子那头得意地笑着。

"韦斯莱,你没有听见斯内普教授的话吗,快把这些根给我切了。"

罗恩抓起小刀,把马尔福的雏菊根拖到自己面前,胡乱地切了起来,

CHAPTER SEVEN   The Boggart in the Wardrobe

them roughly, so that they were all different sizes.

'Professor,' drawled Malfoy, 'Weasley's mutilating my roots, sir.'

Snape approached their table, stared down his hooked nose at the roots, then gave Ron an unpleasant smile from beneath his long, greasy black hair.

'Change roots with Malfoy, Weasley.'

'But sir –!'

Ron had spent the last quarter of an hour carefully shredding his own roots into exactly equal pieces.

'*Now*,' said Snape in his most dangerous voice.

Ron shoved his own beautifully cut roots across the table at Malfoy, then took up the knife again.

'And, sir, I'll need this Shrivelfig skinned,' said Malfoy, his voice full of malicious laughter.

'Potter, you can skin Malfoy's Shrivelfig,' said Snape, giving Harry the look of loathing he always reserved just for him.

Harry took Malfoy's Shrivelfig as Ron set about trying to repair the damage to the roots he now had to use. Harry skinned the Shrivelfig as fast as he could and flung it back across the table at Malfoy without speaking. Malfoy was smirking more broadly than ever.

'Seen your pal Hagrid lately?' he asked them quietly.

'None of your business,' said Ron jerkily, without looking up.

'I'm afraid he won't be a teacher much longer,' said Malfoy, in a tone of mock sorrow. 'Father's not very happy about my injury –'

'Keep talking, Malfoy, and I'll give you a real injury,' snarled Ron.

'– he's complained to the school governors. *And* to the Ministry of Magic. Father's got a lot of influence, you know. And a lasting injury like this –' he gave a huge, fake sigh, 'who knows if my arm'll ever be the same again?'

'So that's why you're putting it on,' said Harry, accidentally beheading a dead caterpillar because his hand was shaking in anger. 'To try and get Hagrid sacked.'

'Well,' said Malfoy, lowering his voice to a whisper, '*partly*, Potter. But there are other benefits, too. Weasley, slice my caterpillars for me.'

A few cauldrons away, Neville was in trouble. Neville regularly went

切得大大小小，很不均匀。

"教授，"马尔福拖着长腔说，"韦斯莱把我的雏菊根都切坏了，先生。"

斯内普走到他们桌前，低垂眼睛从鹰钩鼻上看了看那些根，他的脸在乌黑油腻的长头发下朝罗恩不怀好意地笑了笑。

"跟马尔福换一下根，韦斯莱。"

"可是，先生——"

罗恩刚花了一刻钟把自己的根仔仔细细切成均匀相等的小块儿。

"快换。"斯内普用他最咄咄逼人的声音说。

罗恩把自己那堆切得漂漂亮亮的雏菊根推到马尔福面前，又重新拿起小刀。

"还有，先生，我的这颗无花果需要剥皮。"马尔福说，声音里充满恶毒的笑意。

"波特，你帮马尔福剥无花果的皮。"斯内普说，厌恶地看了哈利一眼，这种目光是他一向在哈利身上专用的。

哈利拿过马尔福的缩皱无花果，罗恩继续切那堆现在归他自己用的乱糟糟的雏菊根。哈利三下五除二地给无花果剥了皮，一言不发地扔给了桌子那头的马尔福。马尔福笑得比任何时候都得意。

"最近见过你们的朋友海格吗？"他小声问他们。

"不用你管。"罗恩头也不抬，气冲冲地说。

"他恐怕当不成教师了，"马尔福装出一副悲伤的口吻说，"我爸爸对我受伤的事很不高兴——"

"马尔福，你再说下去，我就让你真的受点伤！"罗恩怒吼道。

"——他向校董事会提出抗议，还向魔法部提出抗议。你们知道，我爸爸是很有影响力的。像这样一种很难愈合的伤——"他假惺惺地长叹一口气，"谁知道我的胳膊还能不能恢复原样呢？"

"怪不得你这样装模作样。"哈利说，他气得手直抖，一不小心把一只死毛虫的脑袋切了下来，"就是想害得海格被开除。"

"这个嘛，"马尔福把声音压得低低地说，"说对了一部分，波特。但是还有别的好处呢。韦斯莱，替我把毛虫切成片。"

在隔着几只坩埚的那边，纳威遇到了麻烦。纳威在魔药课上经常弄得

CHAPTER SEVEN   The Boggart in the Wardrobe

to pieces in Potions lessons; it was his worst subject, and his great fear of Professor Snape made things ten times worse. His potion, which was supposed to be a bright, acid green, had turned –

'Orange, Longbottom,' said Snape, ladling some up and allowing it to splash back into the cauldron, so that everyone could see. 'Orange. Tell me, boy, does anything penetrate that thick skull of yours? Didn't you hear me say, quite clearly, that only one rat spleen was needed? Didn't I state plainly that a dash of leech juice would suffice? What do I have to do to make you understand, Longbottom?'

Neville was pink and trembling. He looked as though he was on the verge of tears.

'Please, sir,' said Hermione, 'please, I could help Neville put it right –'

'I don't remember asking you to show off, Miss Granger,' said Snape coldly, and Hermione went as pink as Neville. 'Longbottom, at the end of this lesson we will feed a few drops of this potion to your toad and see what happens. Perhaps that will encourage you to do it properly.'

Snape moved away, leaving Neville breathless with fear.

'Help me!' he moaned to Hermione.

'Hey, Harry,' said Seamus Finnigan, leaning over to borrow Harry's brass scales, 'have you heard? *Daily Prophet* this morning – they reckon Sirius Black's been sighted.'

'Where?' said Harry and Ron quickly. On the other side of the table, Malfoy looked up, listening closely.

'Not too far from here,' said Seamus, who looked excited. 'It was a Muggle who saw him. 'Course, she didn't really understand. The Muggles think he's just an ordinary criminal, don't they? So she 'phoned the telephone hotline. By the time the Ministry of Magic got there, he was gone.'

'Not too far from here ...' Ron repeated, looking significantly at Harry. He turned around and saw Malfoy watching closely. 'What, Malfoy? Need something else skinning?'

But Malfoy's eyes were shining malevolently, and they were fixed on Harry. He leant across the table.

'Thinking of trying to catch Black single-handed, Potter?'

'Yeah, that's right,' said Harry offhandedly.

一团糟。这是他学得最差的一门课,而且他对斯内普教授怕得要命,这就使事情更糟糕了十倍。他的药剂应该是一种鲜亮耀眼的绿色,结果却变成了……

"橘黄色,隆巴顿,"斯内普说着,用勺子舀起一些,慢慢倒回坩埚里,让大家都能看见,"橘黄色。告诉我,你这小子,有什么东西能够穿透你那颗榆木脑袋呢?难道你没有听见我说得明明白白,只需要一只老鼠的脾吗?难道我没有讲得清清楚楚,一点点蚂蟥汁就足够了吗?我要怎么样讲才能让你明白呢,隆巴顿?"

纳威涨红了脸,浑身发抖,眼看就要哭出来了。

"拜托,先生,"赫敏说,"拜托,我可以帮助纳威改过来——"

"我好像并没有请你出来炫耀自己,格兰杰小姐。"斯内普冷冰冰地说,赫敏的脸也涨得和纳威一样红,"隆巴顿,这节课结束时,我们要给你的癞蛤蟆喂几滴这种药剂,看看会发生什么情况。这样也许会激励你把药熬好。"

斯内普走开了,纳威吓得喘不过气来。

"帮帮我!"他呜咽着说。

"喂,哈利,"西莫·斐尼甘探过身来借哈利的铜天平,一边说道,"你听说了吗?今天早晨的《预言家日报》上说——他们认为有人看见了小天狼星布莱克。"

"在哪儿?"哈利和罗恩立刻问道。在桌子的另一端,马尔福抬起眼睛,仔细听着。

"离这儿不太远,"西莫似乎很兴奋,说,"是一个麻瓜看见的。当然啦,那麻瓜并不清楚到底是怎么回事。麻瓜们都以为他只是一个普通罪犯,不是吗?所以那麻瓜就打了热线电话。等魔法部的人赶到那儿,他已经不见了。"

"离这儿不太远……"罗恩重复了一遍这句话,意味深长地看着哈利。他转过身,看见马尔福在一旁留意地注视着他们,便问道:"怎么啦,马尔福?还有什么东西要剥皮吗?"

马尔福眼里闪着恶毒的光,他目不转睛地盯着哈利,从桌子那头探过身来。

"你想一个人抓住布莱克吗,波特?"

"是啊,没错。"哈利不假思索地说。

CHAPTER SEVEN   The Boggart in the Wardrobe

Malfoy's thin mouth was curving in a mean smile.

'Of course, if it was me,' he said quietly, 'I'd have done something before now. I wouldn't be staying in school like a good boy, I'd be out there looking for him.'

'What are you talking about, Malfoy?' said Ron roughly.

'Don't you *know*, Potter?' breathed Malfoy, his pale eyes narrowed.

'Know what?'

Malfoy let out a low, sneering laugh.

'Maybe you'd rather not risk your neck,' he said. 'Want to leave it to the Dementors, do you? But if it was me, I'd want revenge. I'd hunt him down myself.'

'*What are you talking about?*' said Harry angrily, but at that moment Snape called, 'You should have finished adding your ingredients by now. This potion needs to stew before it can be drunk; clear away while it simmers and then we'll test Longbottom's ...'

Crabbe and Goyle laughed openly, watching Neville sweat as he stirred his potion feverishly. Hermione was muttering instructions to him out of the corner of her mouth, so that Snape wouldn't see. Harry and Ron packed away their unused ingredients and went to wash their hands and ladles in the stone basin in the corner.

'What did Malfoy mean?' Harry muttered to Ron, as he stuck his hands under the icy jet that poured from a gargoyle's mouth. 'Why would I want revenge on Black? He hasn't done anything to me – yet.'

'He's making it up,' said Ron, savagely, 'he's trying to make you do something stupid ...'

The end of the lesson in sight, Snape strode over to Neville, who was cowering by his cauldron.

'Everyone gather round,' said Snape, his black eyes glittering, 'and watch what happens to Longbottom's toad. If he has managed to produce a Shrinking Solution, it will shrink to a tadpole. If, as I don't doubt, he has done it wrong, his toad is likely to be poisoned.'

The Gryffindors watched fearfully. The Slytherins looked excited. Snape picked up Trevor the toad in his left hand, and dipped a small spoon into Neville's potion, which was now green. He trickled a few drops down Trevor's throat.

There was a moment of hushed silence, in which Trevor gulped; then there was a small *pop*, and Trevor the tadpole was wriggling in Snape's palm.

第7章 衣柜里的博格特

马尔福薄薄的嘴唇拧成一个奸笑。

"当然啦，如果换了我，"他小声说，"我早就干出点事情来了。我才不会待在学校里做乖孩子呢，我肯定会出去找他的。"

"你在胡扯什么呀，马尔福？"罗恩没好气地说。

"你不知道吗，波特？"马尔福压低声音说，一双灰色的眼睛眯了起来。

"知道什么？"

马尔福发出低低的一声嗤笑。

"也许你不愿意拿你的小命冒险，"他说，"只想让摄魂怪去对付他，是吗？如果换了我，我肯定要复仇，我会亲自去追捕他。"

"你在说些什么呀？"哈利恼火地说。就在这时，斯内普说话了："现在你们应该添加完各种配料了。这种药剂需要文火熬一熬才能喝，趁它熬的时候，把东西收拾好，然后我们来测试一下隆巴顿的药剂……"

克拉布和高尔毫不掩饰地大笑起来，看着纳威在那里疯狂地搅拌药剂，汗流满面。赫敏压着嗓子悄悄告诉他怎么做，不让斯内普看见。哈利和罗恩把没有用完的配料收拾起来，然后到墙角的石盆那儿去洗手、洗勺子。

"马尔福是什么意思？"哈利低声问罗恩，一边把双手放在滴水嘴石兽里喷出的冰冷水柱下冲洗，"我为什么要去找布莱克报仇？他并没有对我做过什么啊——目前为止。"

"别听他胡编乱造，"罗恩恼怒地说，"他是想撺掇你去做傻事……"

眼看快要下课了，斯内普大步朝纳威走来，纳威战战兢兢地缩在他的坩埚旁。

"大家都围过来，"斯内普说，一双黑眼睛闪闪发亮，"看看隆巴顿的癞蛤蟆会变成什么样。如果他的缩身药水熬成了，癞蛤蟆就会缩成一只蝌蚪。如果熬得不对——对此我毫不怀疑，他的癞蛤蟆就很可能被毒死。"

格兰芬多的同学们担心地注视着。斯莱特林的同学却个个都很兴奋。斯内普用左手抓着纳威的蟾蜍莱福，然后把一只小勺伸进纳威的药水里。此刻药水已经变成了绿色，他往莱福的喉咙里灌了几滴。

教室里一时间鸦雀无声，只见莱福张嘴喘着粗气，然后就听噗的一声，变成了蝌蚪的莱福在斯内普的手心里扭来扭去。

CHAPTER SEVEN   The Boggart in the Wardrobe

The Gryffindors burst into applause. Snape, looking sour, pulled a small bottle from the pocket of his robe, poured a few drops on top of Trevor and he reappeared suddenly, fully grown.

'Five points from Gryffindor,' said Snape, which wiped the smiles from every face. 'I told you not to help him, Miss Granger. Class dismissed.'

Harry, Ron and Hermione climbed the steps to the Entrance Hall. Harry was still thinking about what Malfoy had said, while Ron was seething about Snape.

'Five points from Gryffindor because the potion was all right! Why didn't you lie, Hermione? You should've said Neville did it all by himself!'

Hermione didn't answer. Ron looked around.

'Where is she?'

Harry turned, too. They were at the top of the steps now, watching the rest of the class pass them, heading for the Great Hall and lunch.

'She was right behind us,' said Ron, frowning.

Malfoy passed them, walking between Crabbe and Goyle. He smirked at Harry and disappeared.

'There she is,' said Harry.

Hermione was panting slightly, hurrying up the stairs; one hand was clutching her bag, the other seemed to be tucking something down the front of her robes.

'How did you do that?' said Ron.

'What?' said Hermione, joining them.

'One minute you were right behind us, and next moment, you were back at the bottom of the stairs again.'

'What?' Hermione looked slightly confused. 'Oh – I had to go back for something. Oh, no ...'

A seam had split on Hermione's bag. Harry wasn't surprised; he could see that it was crammed with at least a dozen large and heavy books.

'Why are you carrying all these around with you?' Ron asked her.

'You know how many subjects I'm taking,' said Hermione breathlessly. 'Couldn't hold these for me, could you?'

'But –' Ron was turning over the books she had handed him, looking at the covers – 'you haven't got any of these subjects today. It's only Defence Against the Dark Arts this afternoon.'

第 7 章　衣柜里的博格特

格兰芬多的同学们顿时欢呼起来。斯内普显得很不高兴，从长袍口袋里掏出一个小瓶，倒了几滴液体在莱福身上，莱福一下子又变成了蟾蜍。

"格兰芬多扣五分。"斯内普说，大家脸上的笑容顿时不见了，"我告诉过你不许帮他的，格兰杰小姐。下课。"

哈利、罗恩和赫敏上楼往门厅走去。哈利还在想着马尔福说的话，罗恩一直在生斯内普的气。

"给格兰芬多扣五分，就因为药水熬对了！你为什么不说句假话，赫敏？你应该说是纳威自己完成的！"

赫敏没有回答，罗恩回过身。

"她跑哪儿去了？"

哈利也转过身。他们已经到了楼梯顶上，其他同学纷纷从他们身边走过，去礼堂吃午饭。

"她刚才就在我们后面的。"罗恩说着，皱起了眉头。

马尔福在克拉布和高尔的左右陪伴下，走过他们身边。他得意地朝哈利笑了一下，走了。

"她在那儿。"哈利说。

赫敏气喘吁吁地匆匆走上楼来，一只手抓着书包，另一只手似乎正把什么东西往袍子下面塞。

"你这是怎么弄的？"罗恩说。

"怎么啦？"赫敏追上他们问。

"你刚才还在我们后面，一眨眼的工夫，又跑到楼梯底下去了。"

"什么？"赫敏似乎有点儿摸不着头脑，"噢——我回去取点儿东西。哦，糟糕……"

赫敏的书包裂了一道缝。哈利一点儿也不吃惊，他看见书包里塞着至少十几本大部头的书。

"你把这些书带来带去的做什么？"罗恩问她。

"你知道我要上多少门课，"赫敏上气不接下气地说，"劳驾，帮我拿几本，好吗？"

"可是……"罗恩翻看着赫敏递给他的那些书的封面，"——你今天并没有这些课呀。今天下午只有黑魔法防御术课。"

CHAPTER SEVEN   The Boggart in the Wardrobe

'Oh, yes,' said Hermione vaguely, but she packed all the books back into her bag just the same. 'I hope there's something good for lunch, I'm starving,' she added, and she marched off towards the Great Hall.

'D'you get the feeling Hermione's not telling us something?' Ron asked Harry.

Professor Lupin wasn't there when they arrived at his first Defence Against the Dark Arts lesson. They all sat down, took out their books, quills and parchment, and were talking when he finally entered the room. Lupin smiled vaguely and placed his tatty old briefcase on the teacher's desk. He was as shabby as ever but looked healthier than he had on the train, as though he had had a few square meals.

'Good afternoon,' he said. 'Would you please put all your books back in your bags. Today's will be a practical lesson. You will only need your wands.'

A few curious looks were exchanged as the class put away their books. They had never had a practical Defence Against the Dark Arts before, unless you counted the memorable class last year when their old teacher had brought a cageful of pixies to class and set them loose.

'Right then,' said Professor Lupin, when everyone was ready, 'if you'd follow me.'

Puzzled but interested, the class got to its feet and followed Professor Lupin out of the classroom. He led them along the deserted corridor and around a corner, where the first thing they saw was Peeves the poltergeist, who was floating upside-down in mid-air and stuffing the nearest keyhole with chewing gum.

Peeves didn't look up until Professor Lupin was two feet away, then he wiggled his curly-toed feet and broke into song.

'Loony, loopy Lupin,' Peeves sang. 'Loony, loopy Lupin, loony, loopy Lupin –'

Rude and unmanageable as he almost always was, Peeves usually showed some respect towards the teachers. Everyone looked quickly at Professor Lupin to see how he would take this; to their surprise, he was still smiling.

'I'd take that gum out of the keyhole, if I were you, Peeves,' he said pleasantly. 'Mr Filch won't be able to get in to his brooms.'

Filch was the Hogwarts caretaker, a bad-tempered, failed wizard who waged a constant war against the students and, indeed, Peeves. However,

第7章 衣柜里的博格特

"是啊,是啊。"赫敏含含糊糊地应了一句,还是把那些书都塞进了书包,"真希望中午有好吃的,我饿坏了。"说完她就甩开大步朝礼堂走去。

"你是不是觉得赫敏有什么事儿瞒着我们?"罗恩问哈利。

他们赶去上卢平教授的第一节黑魔法防御术课时,卢平教授还没有到。他们坐下来,拿出课本、羽毛笔和羊皮纸,正在互相说话,卢平教授终于走进了教室。他脸上淡淡地笑着,把那只破破烂烂的旧公文包放在讲台上。他还是那样衣衫褴褛,但气色比在火车上的时候健康多了,似乎是因为好好地吃了几顿饱饭。

"下午好,"他说,"请大家把课本放回书包。今天上的是实践课。你们只需要魔杖。"

同学们把课本收了起来,相互交换了几个好奇的眼神。他们以前没有上过黑魔法防御术的实践课,除非把去年那一节令人难忘的课算上。在那节课上,前任教师把一笼子小精灵带到课堂上,并把它们都放了出来。

"好了,"卢平教授看到大家都准备好了,便说,"你们跟我来。"

同学们又疑惑又兴趣盎然,纷纷站起来跟着卢平教授走出教室。卢平教授领着他们穿过空荡荡的走廊,绕过一个拐角,他们一眼看见恶作剧精灵皮皮鬼头朝下悬在半空,正把口香糖往离他最近的那个钥匙孔里塞呢。

皮皮鬼直到卢平教授离他只有两英尺远时才抬起头来,扭动着脚趾弯曲的双脚,突然唱起歌来。

"卢平疯子大傻蛋,"皮皮鬼唱道,"卢平疯子大傻蛋,卢平疯子大傻蛋——"

皮皮鬼虽然一向粗鲁无礼,不服管教,但平常对教师还是比较尊敬的。大家赶紧望着卢平教授,看他对此作何反应。没想到,他竟然还是笑眯眯的。

"如果我是你,皮皮鬼,就会把口香糖从钥匙孔里拿出来,"他和颜悦色地说,"费尔奇先生没法进去拿扫帚了。"

费尔奇是霍格沃茨的管理员,一个坏脾气的、不成器的巫师,总是在找学生的碴儿,也跟皮皮鬼过不去。然而,皮皮鬼对卢平教授的

CHAPTER SEVEN   The Boggart in the Wardrobe

Peeves paid no attention to Professor Lupin's words, except to blow a loud wet raspberry.

Professor Lupin gave a small sigh and took out his wand.

'This is a useful little spell,' he told the class over his shoulder. 'Please watch closely.'

He raised the wand to shoulder height, said '*Waddiwasi!*' and pointed it at Peeves.

With the force of a bullet, the wad of chewing gum shot out of the keyhole and straight down Peeves's left nostril; he whirled right way up and zoomed away, cursing.

'Cool, sir!' said Dean Thomas in amazement.

'Thank you, Dean,' said Professor Lupin, putting his wand away again. 'Shall we proceed?'

They set off again, the class looking at shabby Professor Lupin with increased respect. He led them down a second corridor and stopped, right outside the staff-room door.

'Inside, please,' said Professor Lupin, opening it and standing back.

The staff room, a long, panelled room full of old, mismatched chairs, was empty except for one teacher. Professor Snape was sitting in a low armchair, and he looked around as the class filed in. His eyes were glittering and there was a nasty sneer playing around his mouth. As Professor Lupin came in and made to close the door behind him, Snape said, 'Leave it open, Lupin. I'd rather not witness this.' He got to his feet and strode past the class, his black robes billowing behind him. At the doorway he turned on his heel and said, 'Possibly no one's warned you, Lupin, but this class contains Neville Longbottom. I would advise you not to entrust him with anything difficult. Not unless Miss Granger is hissing instructions in his ear.'

Neville went scarlet. Harry glared at Snape; it was bad enough that he bullied Neville in his own classes, let alone doing it in front of other teachers.

Professor Lupin had raised his eyebrows.

'I was hoping that Neville would assist me with the first stage of the operation,' he said, 'and I am sure he will perform it admirably.'

Neville's face went, if possible, even redder. Snape's lip curled, but he left, shutting the door with a snap.

'Now, then,' said Professor Lupin, beckoning the class towards the end

第 7 章　衣柜里的博格特

话根本不在意，只是喷着唾沫狠狠地呸了一声。

卢平教授轻轻叹了口气，抽出魔杖。

"这是一个很有用的小咒语，"他扭头对全班同学说，"请注意看好。"

他把魔杖举到肩膀那么高，直指皮皮鬼，说了句"瓦迪瓦西"。

嗖的一下，那块口香糖像子弹一样从钥匙孔里飞出来，钻进了皮皮鬼的左鼻孔。皮皮鬼一个跟头腾空而起，嘴里骂骂咧咧，很快地飞走了。

"真棒，先生！"迪安·托马斯赞叹道。

"谢谢你，迪安。"卢平教授说着，把魔杖收了起来，"我们继续往前走吧？"

再次出发时，同学们用陡生敬意的目光看着衣衫褴褛的卢平教授。他领着他们走过第二道走廊，在教工休息室的门外停了下来。

"进去吧。"卢平教授说，他打开门，退后一步。

教工休息室是一间长长的屋子，堆满了不配套的旧椅子，四面墙上镶着木板。屋里只有一位教师。斯内普教授坐在一把低矮的扶手椅上。同学们鱼贯进屋时，他转过脸来，一双眼睛闪闪发光，嘴角泛起讥讽的冷笑。卢平教授进来后，正要回身关上房门，斯内普说："别关门，卢平。我还是不要目睹这一幕吧。"他站起来，大步从同学们身边走过，黑色的长袍在身后飘动。走到门外，他又转过身来说道："也许还没有人提醒过你，卢平，这个班里有一个纳威·隆巴顿。我建议你别把任何复杂的事情交给他去做。除非有格兰杰小姐对他咬耳朵，告诉他怎么做。"

纳威脸涨得通红。哈利气冲冲地瞪着斯内普。他在自己的课上欺负纳威就已经够恶劣了，没想到居然还当着别的教师的面这么做。

卢平教授扬起眉毛。

"我本来还希望纳威帮我完成第一步教学呢，"他说，"我相信他会表现得非常出色的。"

纳威的脸竟然涨得更红了。斯内普嘴角抽动着，但还是走了，砰的一声关上了房门。

"好了。"卢平教授说，示意同学们朝房间那头走去。那里只有一

CHAPTER SEVEN The Boggart in the Wardrobe

of the room, where there was nothing except an old wardrobe in which the teachers kept their spare robes. As Professor Lupin went to stand next to it, the wardrobe gave a sudden wobble, banging off the wall.

'Nothing to worry about,' said Professor Lupin calmly, as a few people jumped backwards in alarm. 'There's a Boggart in there.'

Most people seemed to feel that this *was* something to worry about. Neville gave Professor Lupin a look of pure terror, and Seamus Finnigan eyed the now rattling doorknob apprehensively.

'Boggarts like dark, enclosed spaces,' said Professor Lupin. 'Wardrobes, the gap beneath beds, the cupboards under sinks – I once met one that had lodged itself in a grandfather clock. *This* one moved in yesterday afternoon, and I asked the Headmaster if the staff would leave it to give my third-years some practice.

'So, the first question we must ask ourselves is, what is a Boggart?'

Hermione put up her hand.

'It's a shape-shifter,' she said. 'It can take the shape of whatever it thinks will frighten us most.'

'Couldn't have put it better myself,' said Professor Lupin, and Hermione glowed. 'So the Boggart sitting in the darkness within has not yet assumed a form. He does not yet know what will frighten the person on the other side of the door. Nobody knows what a Boggart looks like when he is alone, but when I let him out, he will immediately become whatever each of us most fears.

'This means,' said Professor Lupin, choosing to ignore Neville's small splutter of terror, 'that we have a huge advantage over the Boggart before we begin. Have you spotted it, Harry?'

Trying to answer a question with Hermione next to him, bobbing up and down on the balls of her feet with her hand in the air, was very off-putting, but Harry had a go.

'Er – because there are so many of us, it won't know what shape it should be?'

'Precisely,' said Professor Lupin, and Hermione put her hand down looking a little disappointed. 'It's always best to have company when you're dealing with a Boggart. He becomes confused. Which should he become, a headless corpse or a flesh-eating slug? I once saw a Boggart make that very mistake – tried to frighten two people at once and turned himself into half a slug. Not remotely frightening.

第 7 章 衣柜里的博格特

个旧衣柜,教师们把替换的长袍放在里面。卢平教授走过去站在衣柜旁边,衣柜突然抖动起来,嘭嘭地往墙上撞。

"用不着担心,"卢平教授看到几个同学惊得直往后跳,便心平气和地说,"里面有一只博格特。"

大多数同学似乎觉得这正是需要担心的。纳威惊恐万状地看了卢平教授一眼,西莫·斐尼甘心惊胆战地盯着正在咔嗒作响的柜门把手。

"博格特喜欢黑暗而封闭的空间,"卢平教授说,"衣柜、床底下的空隙、水池下的碗柜——有一次我还碰到一个住在老爷钟里的。这一个是昨天下午刚搬进来的,我请求校长让教师们把它留着,给我三年级的学生上实践课用。

"现在,我们要问自己的第一个问题是:什么是博格特?"

赫敏举起手来。

"是一种会变形的东西,"她说,"它认为什么最能吓住我们,就会变成什么。"

"我自己也没法解释得更清楚了。"卢平教授说,赫敏高兴得满脸放光,"所以,待在这漆黑的柜子里的博格特还没有具体的形状,因为它还不知道柜门外边的人害怕什么。谁也不知道博格特独处时是什么样子,但只要我把它放出来,它立刻就会变成我们每个人最害怕的东西。

"这就是说,"卢平教授接着说,纳威吓得语无伦次地嘀咕着什么,他只当没有听见,"我们在博格特面前有一个很大的优势。哈利,你发现这个优势了吗?"

哈利身边的赫敏把手高高举起,踮着脚尖跳上跳下,在这样的情况下要想回答问题是很别扭的,但是哈利还是试了一下。

"呃——因为我们有这么多人,它不知道应该变成什么形状?"

"非常正确。"卢平教授说,赫敏显得有点儿失望地把手放下了,"跟博格特打交道时,最好结伴而行。这样就把它弄糊涂了:是变成一个没有脑袋的骷髅呢,还是变成一条吃肉的鼻涕虫?我有一次就看见一个博格特犯了这种错误——它想同时吓住两个人,结果把自己变成了半条鼻涕虫,一点儿也不吓人。

CHAPTER SEVEN   The Boggart in the Wardrobe

'The charm that repels a Boggart is simple, yet it requires force of mind. You see, the thing that really finishes a Boggart is *laughter*. What you need to do is force it to assume a shape that you find amusing.

'We will practise the charm without wands first. After me, please ... *riddikulus*!'

'*Riddikulus*!' said the class together.

'Good,' said Professor Lupin. 'Very good. But that was the easy part, I'm afraid. You see, the word alone is not enough. And this is where you come in, Neville.'

The wardrobe shook again, though not as much as Neville, who walked forward as though he was heading for the gallows.

'Right, Neville,' said Professor Lupin. 'First things first: what would you say is the thing that frightens you most in the world?'

Neville's lips moved, but no noise came out.

'Didn't catch that, Neville, sorry,' said Professor Lupin cheerfully.

Neville looked around rather wildly, as though begging someone to help him, then said, in barely more than a whisper, 'Professor Snape.'

Nearly everyone laughed. Even Neville grinned apologetically. Professor Lupin, however, looked thoughtful.

'Professor Snape ... hmmm ... Neville, I believe you live with your grandmother?'

'Er – yes,' said Neville nervously. 'But – I don't want the Boggart to turn into her, either.'

'No, no, you misunderstand me,' said Professor Lupin, now smiling. 'I wonder, could you tell us what sort of clothes your grandmother usually wears?'

Neville looked startled, but said, 'Well ... always the same hat. A tall one with a stuffed vulture on top. And a long dress ... green, normally ... and sometimes a fox-fur scarf.'

'And a handbag?' prompted Professor Lupin.

'A big red one,' said Neville.

'Right then,' said Professor Lupin. 'Can you picture those clothes very clearly, Neville? Can you see them in your mind's eye?'

'Yes,' said Neville uncertainly, plainly wondering what was coming next.

第7章 衣柜里的博格特

"击退博格特的咒语非常简单,但需要强大的意志力量。要知道,真正让博格特彻底完蛋的是笑声。你们需要的是强迫它变成一种你们觉得很好笑的形象。

"我们先不拿魔杖练习一下咒语。请跟我念……滑稽滑稽!"

"滑稽滑稽!"全班同学一起说。

"很好,"卢平教授说,"非常好。但这还是比较简单的部分。要知道,光靠这个咒语是不够的。纳威,现在就看你的了。"

衣柜又抖动起来,但纳威抖得比它还要厉害。纳威战战兢兢地走上前,就像走上绞刑架。

"很好,纳威,"卢平教授说,"先说最要紧的:你说,在这个世界上你最害怕什么?"

纳威的嘴唇动了动,但没有发出声音。

"对不起,纳威,我没听清。"卢平教授和颜悦色地说。

纳威惊慌失措地左右张望了一下,似乎在请求谁能帮他一把。然后,他用低得几乎听不清的声音说:"斯内普教授。"

几乎每个人都笑了起来,就连纳威也不好意思地咧了咧嘴。卢平教授却是一副若有所思的样子。

"斯内普教授……哦……纳威,我想你是跟你奶奶一起生活的吧?"

"呃——是啊,"纳威局促不安地说,"可是——我也不想让博格特变成奶奶的样子。"

"不,不,你误会了。"卢平教授说,这时他的脸上绽开了笑容,"我想,你能不能跟我们说说,你奶奶平时穿什么衣服呢?"

纳威似乎吃了一惊,但他说道:"好的……她总是戴着那顶帽子。一顶高帽子,上面有一只秃鹫的标本。身上是一件长裙……一般是绿色的……有时还戴一条狐狸毛的围巾。"

"还有一个手袋对吗?"卢平教授提醒他说。

"一个红色的大手袋。"纳威说。

"好了,"卢平教授说,"纳威,你能不能非常清楚地想象出这些衣服?能不能在脑海里看见它们?"

"能。"纳威不敢肯定地说,显然在担心接下来会发生什么。

CHAPTER SEVEN The Boggart in the Wardrobe

'When the Boggart bursts out of this wardrobe, Neville, and sees you, it will assume the form of Professor Snape,' said Lupin. 'And you will raise your wand – thus – and cry "*Riddikulus*" – and concentrate hard on your grandmother's clothes. If all goes well, Professor Boggart Snape will be forced into that vulture-topped hat, that green dress, that big red handbag.'

There was a great shout of laughter. The wardrobe wobbled more violently.

'If Neville is successful, the Boggart is likely to turn his attention to each of us in turn,' said Professor Lupin. 'I would like all of you to take a moment now to think of the thing that scares you most, and imagine how you might force it to look comical ...'

The room went quiet. Harry thought ... What scared him most in the world?

His first thought was Lord Voldemort – a Voldemort returned to full strength. But before he had even started to plan a possible counter-attack on a Boggart-Voldemort, a horrible image came floating to the surface of his mind ...

A rotting, glistening hand, slithering back beneath a black cloak ... a long, rattling breath from an unseen mouth ... then a cold so penetrating it felt like drowning ...

Harry shivered, then looked around, hoping no one had noticed. Many people had their eyes shut tight. Ron was muttering to himself, 'Take its legs off.' Harry was sure he knew what that was about. Ron's greatest fear was spiders.

'Everyone ready?' said Professor Lupin.

Harry felt a lurch of fear. He wasn't ready. How could you make a Dementor less frightening? But he didn't want to ask for more time; everyone else was nodding and rolling up their sleeves.

'Neville, we're going to back away,' said Professor Lupin. 'Let you have a clear field, all right? I'll call the next person forward ... everyone back, now, so Neville can get a clear shot –'

They all retreated, backing against the walls, leaving Neville alone beside the wardrobe. He looked pale and frightened, but he had pushed up the sleeves of his robes and was holding his wand ready.

'On the count of three, Neville,' said Professor Lupin, who was pointing his own wand at the handle of the wardrobe. 'One – two – three – *now!*'

A jet of sparks shot from the end of Professor Lupin's wand and hit the

第7章 衣柜里的博格特

"纳威,当博格特从衣柜里冲出来看见你后,它就会变成斯内普教授的样子,"卢平说,"这时你就举起魔杖——像这样——大喊一声'滑稽滑稽'——然后集中精力去想你奶奶的衣服。如果一切顺利,博格特-斯内普教授就会被迫戴上那顶秃鹫帽子、穿上绿色长裙、拿着那个红色的大手袋。"

同学们哄堂大笑。衣柜摇晃得更厉害了。

"如果纳威成功了,博格特就会把注意力轮流转移到我们每个人身上。"卢平教授说,"我希望大家现在都花点时间考虑考虑你们最害怕什么,然后想象一下怎样才能让它变得滑稽可笑……"

教室里一片寂静。哈利在想……在这个世界上,他最害怕什么呢?

他首先想到了伏地魔——重新强大起来的伏地魔。可是,没等他开始考虑用什么来对付博格特-伏地魔,他脑海里突然浮现出一个恐怖的形象……

一只腐烂的、阴森森闪着冷光的手,飞快地缩回黑袍子下……从看不见的嘴里发出长长的呼噜呼噜的呼吸声……然后是一种渗透骨髓的寒意,如同被水淹没的感觉……

哈利打了个冷战,然后左右看看,希望没有人注意到他。许多同学都紧闭着眼睛,罗恩在那里喃喃自语:"把它的腿去掉。"哈利很清楚那是怎么回事。罗恩最害怕蜘蛛了。

"大家都准备好了吗?"卢平教授问。

哈利感到一阵恐慌。他还没有做好准备。怎样才能让摄魂怪看上去不那么吓人呢?但他又不愿意请求老师再给他一些时间。别的同学都一边点头,一边挽起了袖子。

"纳威,我们都往后退,"卢平教授说,"给你留出一块空地来,好吗?我会把下一个同学叫上前……好了,大家都退后,给纳威腾出地方——"

同学们都退到了墙边,只留下纳威一个人站在衣柜旁。他脸色苍白,看上去非常害怕,但已经挽起了长袍的袖子,举起魔杖做好了准备。

"我数到三,纳威,"卢平教授用他自己的魔杖指着衣柜的门把手,说道,"一——二——三——开始!"

卢平教授的魔杖尖上射出一串火星,击中了球形的门把手。衣柜

CHAPTER SEVEN The Boggart in the Wardrobe

doorknob. The wardrobe burst open. Hook-nosed and menacing, Professor Snape stepped out, his eyes flashing at Neville.

Neville backed away, his wand up, mouthing wordlessly. Snape was bearing down upon him, reaching inside his robes.

'*R-r-riddikulus!*' squeaked Neville.

There was a noise like a whip-crack. Snape stumbled; he was wearing a long, lace-trimmed dress and a towering hat topped with a moth-eaten vulture, and swinging a huge crimson handbag from his hand.

There was a roar of laughter; the Boggart paused, confused, and Professor Lupin shouted, 'Parvati! Forward!'

Parvati walked forward, her face set. Snape rounded on her. There was another crack, and where he had stood was a blood-stained, bandaged mummy; its sightless face was turned to Parvati and it began to walk towards her, very slowly, dragging its feet, its stiff arms rising –

'*Riddikulus!*' cried Parvati.

A bandage unravelled at the mummy's feet; it became entangled, fell face forwards and its head rolled off.

'Seamus!' roared Professor Lupin.

Seamus darted past Parvati.

Crack! Where the mummy had been was a woman with floor-length black hair and a skeletal, green-tinged face – a banshee. She opened her mouth wide, and an unearthly sound filled the room, a long, wailing shriek which made the hair on Harry's head stand on end –

'*Riddikulus!*' shouted Seamus.

The banshee made a rasping noise and clutched her throat; her voice was gone.

Crack! The banshee turned into a rat, which chased its tail in a circle, then – *crack*! – became a rattlesnake, which slithered and writhed before – *crack*! – becoming a single, bloody eyeball.

'It's confused!' shouted Lupin. 'We're getting there! Dean!'

Dean hurried forward.

Crack! The eyeball became a severed hand, which flipped over, and began to creep along the floor like a crab.

第7章 衣柜里的博格特

的门突然洞开,长着鹰钩鼻的斯内普教授气势汹汹地走了出来,眼睛恶狠狠地盯着纳威。

纳威连连后退,手里举着魔杖,嘴里却发不出声音。斯内普一步步朝他逼来,一边伸手到袍子里掏魔杖。

"滑—滑—滑稽滑稽!"纳威尖声叫道。

猛的一声脆响,像是抽了一记响鞭,斯内普脚步开始趔趄,只见他身穿一件带花边的长裙,头戴一顶高帽子,帽子上有一只被虫蛀过的秃鹫,手里还提着一个红色的大手袋。

同学们爆发出一阵大笑,博格特停住脚步,似乎被弄糊涂了,卢平教授喊道:"帕瓦蒂,上!"

帕瓦蒂神情果断地走上前去。斯内普转身朝她扑去。又是啪的一记脆响,斯内普不见了,原地站着一个血迹斑斑、裹着绷带的木乃伊,它那没有目光的脸转向了帕瓦蒂,拖着双脚、一步步地慢慢朝她走去,僵硬的胳膊也举了起来——

"滑稽滑稽!"帕瓦蒂喊道。

木乃伊脚下的一条绷带散开了,木乃伊被绊住,扑通栽倒在地,脑袋滚到了一边。

"西莫!"卢平教授大喊。

西莫从帕瓦蒂身边冲上前去。

啪!木乃伊不见了,出现了一个女人,黑黑的头发拖到地上,脸像个骷髅,泛着绿光——是个女鬼。她把嘴张得大大的,顿时,怪异可怕的声音在教室里回荡,是一种尖厉的长叫,哈利听得头发都竖了起来——

"滑稽滑稽!"西莫喊道。

女鬼发出粗哑刺耳的声音,一把抓住自己的喉咙,她的声音消失了。

啪!女鬼变成了一只老鼠,追着自己的尾巴直转圈儿,然后——啪!——变成了一条响尾蛇,扭动着身体在地上爬,然后——啪!变成了一个血淋淋的眼球。

"它已经糊涂了!"卢平大声说,"我们成功了!迪安!"

迪安冲了过去。

啪!眼球变成了一只被割断的手,它突然翻转过来,像螃蟹一样在地板上嗖嗖地爬行。

CHAPTER SEVEN   The Boggart in the Wardrobe

'*Riddikulus!*' yelled Dean.

There was a snap, and the hand was trapped in a mousetrap.

'Excellent! Ron, you next!'

Ron leapt forward.

'*Crack*!'

Quite a few people screamed. A giant spider, six feet tall and covered in hair, was advancing on Ron, clicking its pincers menacingly. For a moment, Harry thought Ron had frozen. Then –

'*Riddikulus!*' bellowed Ron, and the spider's legs vanished. It rolled over and over; Lavender Brown squealed and ran out of its way and it came to a halt at Harry's feet. He raised his wand, ready, but –

'Here!' shouted Professor Lupin suddenly, hurrying forward.

Crack!

The legless spider had vanished. For a second, everyone looked wildly around to see where it was. Then they saw a silvery white orb hanging in the air in front of Lupin, who said '*Riddikulus!*' almost lazily.

Crack!

'Forward, Neville, and finish him off!' said Lupin, as the Boggart landed on the floor as a cockroach. *Crack*! Snape was back. This time Neville charged forward looking determined.

'*Riddikulus!*' he shouted, and they had a split second's view of Snape in his lacy dress before Neville let out a great 'Ha!' of laughter, and the Boggart exploded, burst into a thousand tiny wisps of smoke, and was gone.

'Excellent!' cried Professor Lupin, as the class broke into applause. 'Excellent, Neville. Well done, everyone. Let me see … five points to Gryffindor for every person to tackle the Boggart – ten for Neville because he did it twice – and five each to Hermione and Harry.'

'But I didn't do anything,' said Harry.

'You and Hermione answered my questions correctly at the start of the class, Harry,' Lupin said lightly. 'Very well, everyone, an excellent lesson. Homework, kindly read the chapter on Boggarts and summarise it for me … to be handed in on Monday. That will be all.'

第7章 衣柜里的博格特

"滑稽滑稽！"迪安嚷道。

一声脆响，那只手被夹在了老鼠夹里。

"太棒了！罗恩，轮到你了！"

罗恩跑上前去。

啪！

好几个同学尖叫起来。一只足有六英尺高、浑身长满毛的大蜘蛛朝罗恩逼了过来，气势汹汹地张开了它的钳子。哈利一时还以为罗恩被吓傻了，接着——

"滑稽滑稽！"罗恩吼道，蜘蛛的腿顿时消失了。它在地上滚来滚去，拉文德·布朗尖叫着躲开。最后蜘蛛停在了哈利脚下，哈利举起魔杖，做好准备，可是——

"看这儿！"卢平教授突然喊道，抢先一步上前。

啪！

无腿的蜘蛛消失了。同学们都慌乱地东张西望，看它跑到哪儿去了。他们看见一个银白色的球悬在卢平教授面前，卢平教授几乎是懒洋洋地说了句："滑稽滑稽！"

啪！

"纳威，上前来，把它干掉！"卢平教授说。这时博格特已经变成一只蟑螂落在地板上。啪！斯内普又回来了。这次纳威信心十足地冲上前去。

"滑稽滑稽！"他喊道，他们只瞥见一眼斯内普穿花边长裙的模样，纳威就发出一阵响亮的哈哈大笑。博格特顿时爆炸，变成无数股细小的烟雾，消失不见了。

"太棒了！"卢平教授大声说，全班同学热烈鼓掌，"太棒了，纳威！同学们都做得不错。让我看看……给每个制服了博格特的格兰芬多同学加五分——给纳威加十分，因为他制服了两次——再给赫敏和哈利各加五分。"

"可是我什么也没做啊。"哈利说。

"刚开始上课时，你和赫敏正确地回答了我的问题，哈利，"卢平教授轻松地说，"每个人都表现很好，这堂课上得很成功。家庭作业，请阅读关于博格特的那一章，再用简单的话概括一下……星期一交。就这些。"

CHAPTER SEVEN   The Boggart in the Wardrobe

Talking excitedly, the class left the staff room. Harry, however, wasn't feeling cheerful. Professor Lupin had deliberately stopped him tackling the Boggart. Why? Was it because he'd seen Harry collapse on the train, and thought he wasn't up to much? Had he thought Harry would pass out again?

But no one else seemed to have noticed anything.

'Did you see me take that banshee?' shouted Seamus.

'And the hand!' said Dean, waving his own around.

'And Snape in that hat!'

'And my mummy!'

'I wonder why Professor Lupin's frightened of crystal balls?' said Lavender thoughtfully.

'That was the best Defence Against the Dark Arts lesson we've ever had, wasn't it?' said Ron excitedly, as they made their way back to the classroom to get their bags.

'He seems a very good teacher,' said Hermione approvingly. 'But I wish I could have had a turn with the Boggart –'

'What would it have been for you?' said Ron, sniggering. 'A piece of homework that only got nine out of ten?'

第7章 衣柜里的博格特

同学们兴奋地交谈着,离开了教工休息室。但哈利却感到闷闷不乐,卢平教授故意不让他去对付博格特,这是为什么呢?难道是因为他看见哈利在火车上晕倒,就以为哈利没有什么本事?难道他以为哈利还会再晕过去吗?

不过,其他同学似乎没有注意到什么。

"你们看见我怎么拿下那个女鬼的吗?"西莫嚷嚷着说。

"还有那只手!"迪安挥舞着自己的手说。

"还有戴着那顶帽子的斯内普!"

"还有我的木乃伊!"

"真不明白,卢平教授为什么会害怕水晶球呢?"拉文德若有所思地说。

"这是我们上过的最好的一节黑魔法防御术课,不是吗?"罗恩兴奋地说,这时他们正走回教室去拿书包。

"他好像是个很不错的老师呢,"赫敏赞许地说,"但我希望我也有机会对付那个博格特——"

"它在你面前会变成什么呢?"罗恩笑嘻嘻地说,"是一份没得着满分、只得了九分的作业吧?"

CHAPTER EIGHT

Flight of the Fat Lady

In no time at all, Defence Against the Dark Arts had become most people's favourite class. Only Draco Malfoy and his gang of Slytherins had anything bad to say about Professor Lupin.

'Look at the state of his robes,' Malfoy would say in a loud whisper as Professor Lupin passed. 'He dresses like our old house-elf.'

But no one else cared that Professor Lupin's robes were patched and frayed. His next few lessons were just as interesting as the first. After Boggarts, they studied Red Caps, nasty little goblin-like creatures that lurked wherever there had been bloodshed, in the dungeons of castles and the potholes of deserted battlefields, waiting to bludgeon those who had got lost. From Red Caps they moved on to Kappas, creepy water-dwellers that looked like scaly monkeys, with webbed hands itching to strangle unwitting waders in their ponds.

Harry only wished he was as happy with some of his other classes. Worst of all was Potions. Snape was in a particularly vindictive mood these days, and no one was in any doubt why. The story of the Boggart assuming Snape's shape, and the way that Neville had dressed it in his grandmother's clothes, had travelled through the school like wildfire. Snape didn't seem to find it funny. His eyes flashed menacingly at the very mention of Professor Lupin's name, and he was bullying Neville worse than ever.

Harry was also growing to dread the hours he spent in Professor Trelawney's stifling tower room, deciphering lop-sided shapes and symbols, trying to ignore the way Professor Trelawney's enormous eyes filled with tears every time she looked at him. He couldn't like Professor Trelawney, even though she was treated with respect bordering on reverence by many of the class. Parvati Patil and Lavender Brown had taken to haunting Professor

第 8 章

胖夫人逃跑

很快,黑魔法防御术就成了大多数人最喜欢的一门课程,只有德拉科·马尔福和他那帮斯莱特林的同党还在说卢平教授的坏话。

"看看他的袍子成了什么样儿。"卢平教授经过时,马尔福故意说得让别人都听见,"他穿得就像我们家以前的小精灵。"

除了他们,谁也不在意卢平教授的长袍打着补丁,已经磨损得很厉害。他接下来的几节课也像第一节课一样生动有趣。学完博格特,他们又学习了红帽子,这是一种类似小妖精的丑陋的小东西,潜伏在曾经流过血的地方,如城堡的地牢里、废弃的战场的坑道里,等着用大棒袭击迷路的人。红帽子之后,他们又开始学习卡巴,一种生活在水里的爬行动物,模样活像长着鳞片的猴子,手上带蹼,随时准备掐死在它们的池塘里涉水而过的毫无防备的人。

哈利只希望在上另外几门课时也能这样高兴。最糟糕的是魔药课。斯内普这些日子情绪特别恶劣,其中的原因大家都心知肚明。博格特变成斯内普的模样,纳威又给它穿上一身他奶奶的衣服,这消息像野火一样很快在学校里传遍了。斯内普似乎觉得这件事一点也不好玩。从此只要一听见有人提到卢平教授的名字,他的眼睛就恶狠狠地瞪了过去,而且他现在变本加厉地找纳威的碴儿。

哈利还越来越害怕在特里劳尼教授那间令人窒息的塔楼教室里上课。他要硬着头皮破译各种奇怪的形状和符号,还要强迫自己不去理会特里劳尼教授那双一看见他就泪汪汪的大眼睛。他没法喜欢特里劳尼教授,尽管班上许多同学对这位教授尊敬得近乎崇拜。帕瓦蒂·佩

CHAPTER EIGHT   Flight of the Fat Lady

Trelawney's tower room at lunchtimes, and always returned with annoyingly superior looks on their faces, as though they knew things the others didn't. They had also started using hushed voices whenever they spoke to Harry, as though he was on his deathbed.

Nobody really liked Care of Magical Creatures, which, after the action-packed first class, had become extremely dull. Hagrid seemed to have lost his confidence. They were now spending lesson after lesson learning how to look after Flobberworms, which had to be some of the most boring creatures in existence.

'Why would anyone *bother* looking after them?' said Ron, after yet another hour of poking shredded lettuce down the Flobberworms' slimy throats.

At the start of October, however, Harry had something else to occupy him, something so enjoyable it made up for his unsatisfactory classes. The Quidditch season was approaching, and Oliver Wood, captain of the Gryffindor team, called a meeting one Thursday evening to discuss tactics for the new season.

There were seven people on a Quidditch team: three Chasers, whose job it was to score goals by putting the Quaffle (a red, football-sized ball) through one of the fifty-foot-high hoops at each end of the pitch; two Beaters, who were equipped with heavy bats to repel the Bludgers (two heavy black balls which zoomed around trying to attack the players); a keeper, who defended the goalposts, and the Seeker, who had the hardest job of all, that of catching the Golden Snitch, a tiny, winged, walnut-sized ball, whose capture ended the game and earned the Seeker's team an extra one hundred and fifty points.

Oliver Wood was a burly seventeen-year-old, now in his seventh and final year at Hogwarts. There was a quiet sort of desperation in his voice as he addressed his six fellow team members in the chilly changing rooms on the edge of the darkening Quidditch pitch.

'This is our last chance – *my* last chance – to win the Quidditch Cup,' he told them, striding up and down in front of them. 'I'll be leaving at the end of this year. I'll never get another shot at it.

'Gryffindor haven't won for seven years now. OK, so we've had the worst luck in the world – injuries – then the tournament getting called off last year ...' Wood swallowed, as though the memory still brought a lump

第8章 胖夫人逃跑

蒂尔和拉文德·布朗中午吃饭时喜欢到特里劳尼教授的塔楼教室去，回来时脸上总是挂着一副讨厌的高深莫测的表情，似乎她们知道了一些别人不知道的事情。而且，现在她们每次跟哈利说话都把声音压得低低的，就好像哈利快要死了似的。

没有一个人真正喜欢保护神奇动物课。在刺激的第一节课后，这门课就变得特别乏味了。海格似乎失去了信心。现在，他们一节课又一节课地学习怎样照料弗洛伯毛虫，这种虫子肯定是世界上最没趣的动物了。

"为什么要费事照料它们呢？"罗恩说，他们刚才又花了一小时把切碎的莴苣叶塞进弗洛伯毛虫细细的喉咙里。

十月初，哈利的心思被另一件事所占据。这件事太有意思了，弥补了那些令人不快的课程带给他的烦恼。魁地奇赛季正在临近，一个星期四的晚上，格兰芬多球队的队长奥利弗·伍德召集大家开会，讨论新赛季的战术。

一支魁地奇球队由七人组成：三名追球手，负责把鬼飞球（一种足球大小的红球）打进球场两端五十英尺高的圆环，进球得分；两名击球手，用沉重的球棒击打游走球（两只蹿来蹿去地攻击球员的沉甸甸的黑球）；一名守门员，负责防守球门；还有就是找球手，他的工作最艰巨，要寻找并抓住金色飞贼。这是一个带翅膀的、胡桃那么大的小球，一旦把它抓住，比赛即刻结束。抓住飞贼的那支球队可加一百五十分。

奥利弗·伍德是个身材高大的十七岁小伙子，在霍格沃茨上七年级，也就是最后一个年级。在光线渐渐变暗的魁地奇球场边那间冷飕飕的更衣室里，他对六名队员训话，压抑的口气中透着一种决绝。

"要赢得魁地奇杯，这是我们的最后一次机会——我的最后一次机会，"他在队员面前大步踱来踱去，对他们说道，"这个学年结束我就要离开了，再也不会有下一次机会。

"格兰芬多已经七年没有赢过了。是啊，我们是世界上最倒霉的——受伤——去年又取消了联赛……"伍德咽了口唾沫，似乎这些往事仍然使他哽咽，"但我们也知道，我们是全校最好的——最棒的——球队。"说着，

CHAPTER EIGHT   Flight of the Fat Lady

to his throat. 'But we also know we've got the *best – ruddy – team – in – the – school*,' he said, punching a fist into his other hand, the old manic glint back in his eye.

'We've got three *superb* Chasers.'

Wood pointed at Alicia Spinnet, Angelina Johnson and Katie Bell.

'We've got two *unbeatable* Beaters.'

'Stop it, Oliver, you're embarrassing us,' said Fred and George Weasley together, pretending to blush.

'And we've got a Seeker who has *never failed to win us a match*!' Wood rumbled, glaring at Harry with a kind of furious pride. 'And me,' he added, as an afterthought.

'We think you're very good, too, Oliver,' said George.

'Cracking keeper,' said Fred.

'The point is,' Wood went on, resuming his pacing, 'the Quidditch Cup should have had our name on it these last two years. Ever since Harry joined the team, I've thought the thing was in the bag. But we haven't got it, and this year's the last chance we'll get to finally see our name on the thing ...'

Wood spoke so dejectedly that even Fred and George looked sympathetic.

'Oliver, this year's our year,' said Fred.

'We'll do it, Oliver!' said Angelina.

'Definitely,' said Harry.

Full of determination, the team started training sessions, three evenings a week. The weather was getting colder and wetter, the nights darker, but no amount of mud, wind or rain could tarnish Harry's wonderful vision of finally winning the huge silver Quidditch Cup.

Harry returned to the Gryffindor common room one evening after training, cold and stiff but pleased with the way practice had gone, to find the room buzzing excitedly.

'What's happened?' he asked Ron and Hermione, who were sitting in two of the best chairs by the fireside and completing some star charts for Astronomy.

'First Hogsmeade weekend,' said Ron, pointing at a notice that had appeared on the battered old noticeboard. 'End of October. Hallowe'en.'

'Excellent,' said Fred, who had followed Harry through the portrait hole. 'I need to visit Zonko's, I'm nearly out of Stink Pellets.'

第8章 胖夫人逃跑

他把一只拳头砸进另一只手的手心,眼睛里又闪出过去那种狂野的光芒。

"我们有三名最棒的追球手。"

伍德指着艾丽娅·斯平内特、安吉利娜·约翰逊和凯蒂·贝尔。

"有两名不可战胜的击球手。"

"打住,奥利弗,你说得我们怪不好意思的。"弗雷德和乔治·韦斯莱异口同声地说,假装羞红了脸。

"还有一位从来没输过比赛的找球手!"伍德继续说道,用一种激烈而骄傲的目光瞪着哈利,"还有我。"他好像后来才想起似的补了一句。

"我们认为你也很棒,奥利弗。"乔治说。

"呱呱叫的守门员。"弗雷德说。

"关键在于,"伍德接着说,一边又踱起步来,"最近这两年,魁地奇杯上应该写着我们的名字。自从哈利入队以来,我就一直认为这是十拿九稳的事。但是一直没能如愿。我们想看到自己的名字写在杯上,今年是最后一次机会了……"

伍德说得这么悲壮,就连弗雷德和乔治也为之动容。

"奥利弗,今年我们绝对没问题。"弗雷德说。

"我们会成功的,奥利弗!"安吉利娜说。

"肯定成功。"哈利说。

球队带着坚定的决心开始了训练,每星期三个晚上。天气越来越冷,雨水增多,夜晚变得更加黑暗,但是泥泞、狂风和暴雨都不能破坏哈利对最终赢得银光闪闪的魁地奇大奖杯的美好憧憬。

一天晚上训练结束后,哈利回到格兰芬多公共休息室,浑身冻得发僵,但对训练的进展非常满意。他发现公共休息室里叽叽喳喳,热闹非凡。

"出什么事了?"他问罗恩和赫敏,他们俩坐在火炉旁两把最好的椅子里,正在完成天文课的两张星星图表。

"第一次去霍格莫德过周末。"罗恩指着破破烂烂的布告栏上新贴出的一张通告,说,"十月底。万圣节前夕。"

"太棒了!"跟着哈利钻过肖像洞口的弗雷德说,"我要去一趟佐科笑话店,我的臭蛋快用完了。"

CHAPTER EIGHT   Flight of the Fat Lady

Harry threw himself into a chair beside Ron, his high spirits ebbing away. Hermione seemed to read his mind.

'Harry, I'm sure you'll be able to go next time,' she said. 'They're bound to catch Black soon, he's been sighted once already.'

'Black's not fool enough to try anything in Hogsmeade,' said Ron. 'Ask McGonagall if you can go this time, Harry, the next one might not be for ages –'

'*Ron!*' said Hermione. 'Harry's supposed to stay *in school* –'

'He can't be the only third-year left behind,' said Ron. 'Ask McGonagall, go on, Harry –'

'Yeah, I think I will,' said Harry, making up his mind.

Hermione opened her mouth to argue, but at that moment Crookshanks leapt lightly onto her lap. A large, dead spider was dangling from his mouth.

'Does he have to eat that in front of us?' said Ron, scowling.

'Clever Crookshanks, did you catch that all by yourself?' said Hermione.

Crookshanks slowly chewed up the spider, his yellow eyes fixed insolently on Ron.

'Just keep him over there, that's all,' said Ron irritably, turning back to his star chart. 'I've got Scabbers asleep in my bag.'

Harry yawned. He really wanted to go to bed, but he still had his own star chart to complete. He pulled his bag towards him, took out parchment, ink and quill, and started work.

'You can copy mine, if you like,' said Ron, labelling his last star with a flourish and shoving the chart towards Harry.

Hermione, who disapproved of copying, pursed her lips, but didn't say anything. Crookshanks was still staring unblinkingly at Ron, flicking the end of his bushy tail. Then, without warning, he pounced.

'OY!' Ron roared, seizing his bag, as Crookshanks sank four sets of claws deeply into it, and began tearing ferociously. 'GET OFF, YOU STUPID ANIMAL!'

Ron tried to pull the bag away from Crookshanks, but Crookshanks clung on, spitting and slashing.

'Ron, don't hurt him!' squealed Hermione. The whole common room was watching; Ron whirled the bag around, Crookshanks still clinging to it, and

第8章 胖夫人逃跑

哈利扑通坐在罗恩旁边的一把椅子里，满心的高兴劲儿一扫而光。赫敏似乎看透了他的心思。

"哈利，你下次一定能去。"她说，"他们肯定很快就能抓住布莱克，已经有人看见过他一次了。"

"布莱克又不是傻瓜，不可能跑到霍格莫德去轻举妄动。"罗恩说，"哈利，你问问麦格你这次能不能去，下次要等到猴年马月——"

"罗恩！"赫敏说，"哈利应该待在学校里——"

"不能就把他一个三年级学生留在学校。"罗恩说，"去问问麦格吧，哈利，快去——"

"好吧，我去问问。"哈利拿定了主意说。

赫敏张嘴想反驳，就在这时，克鲁克山轻轻跳上她的膝头，嘴里叼着一只很大的死蜘蛛。

"它非得当着我们的面吃那玩意儿吗？"罗恩皱着眉头问。

"聪明的克鲁克山，这是你自己抓住的吗？"赫敏说。

克鲁克山慢慢地把蜘蛛嚼着吃了，一双黄眼睛傲慢地盯着罗恩。

"就让它待在那儿别动。"罗恩恼怒地说，又埋头画他的星星图表，"斑斑在我的书包里睡觉呢。"

哈利打了个哈欠。他真想上床睡觉，可是他的星星图表还没画完呢。他把书包拖过来，掏出羊皮纸、墨水和羽毛笔，开始做功课。

"如果你愿意，可以抄我的。"罗恩说着，用花体字标出最后一颗星星，把图表推给了哈利。

赫敏不赞成抄袭，她噘起了嘴，但什么也没说。克鲁克山仍然眼睛一眨不眨地盯着罗恩，毛茸茸的尾巴尖轻轻摆动。突然，它猛扑过去。

"哎哟！"罗恩大吼一声，一把抓住书包，克鲁克山把四只爪子深深扎进包里，恶狠狠地撕扯着，"**滚开，你这个傻畜生！**"

罗恩想把书包从克鲁克山身下拽开，可是克鲁克山抓住不放，一边龇牙咧嘴，狠命撕扯。

"罗恩，别伤害它！"赫敏尖叫道。整个公共休息室里的同学都在看着。罗恩抓着书包抡了一圈，克鲁克山仍然抓住不放，斑斑却从书

CHAPTER EIGHT Flight of the Fat Lady

Scabbers came flying out of the top —

'CATCH THAT CAT!' Ron yelled, as Crookshanks freed himself from the remnants of the bag, sprang over the table and chased after the terrified Scabbers.

George Weasley made a lunge for Crookshanks but missed; Scabbers streaked through twenty pairs of legs and shot beneath an old chest of drawers. Crookshanks skidded to a halt, crouched low on his bandy legs and started making furious swipes beneath the chest of drawers with his front paw.

Ron and Hermione hurried over; Hermione grabbed Crookshanks around the middle and heaved him away; Ron threw himself onto his stomach and, with great difficulty, pulled Scabbers out by the tail.

'Look at him!' he said furiously to Hermione, dangling Scabbers in front of her. 'He's skin and bone! You keep that cat away from him!'

'Crookshanks doesn't understand it's wrong!' said Hermione, her voice shaking. 'All cats chase rats, Ron!'

'There's something funny about that animal!' said Ron, who was trying to persuade a frantically wiggling Scabbers back into his pocket. 'It heard me say that Scabbers was in my bag!'

'Oh, what rubbish,' said Hermione impatiently. 'Crookshanks could *smell* him, Ron, how else d'you think —'

'That cat's got it in for Scabbers!' said Ron, ignoring the people around him, who were starting to giggle. 'And Scabbers was here first, *and* he's ill!'

Ron marched through the common room and out of sight up the stairs to the boys' dormitories.

Ron was still in a bad mood with Hermione next day. He barely talked to her all through Herbology, even though he, Harry and Hermione were working together on the same Puffapod.

'How's Scabbers?' Hermione asked timidly, as they stripped fat pink pods from the plants and emptied the shining beans into a wooden pail.

'He's hiding at the bottom of my bed, shaking,' said Ron angrily, missing the pail and scattering beans over the greenhouse floor.

'Careful, Weasley, careful!' cried Professor Sprout, as the beans burst into bloom before their very eyes.

They had Transfiguration next. Harry, who had resolved to ask Professor

第8章 胖夫人逃跑

包口里飞了出来——

"抓住那只猫！"罗恩喊道，这时克鲁克山丢下散乱的书包，蹿到桌子那头，开始追赶惊慌失措的斑斑。

乔治·韦斯莱扑过去抓克鲁克山，没有抓住。斑斑一溜烟穿过二十双腿，一头钻到了一只旧五斗橱底下。克鲁克山刹住脚步，矮下罗圈腿，俯身把前爪伸到五斗橱底下拼命扒拉。

罗恩和赫敏匆匆赶了过来。赫敏抓住克鲁克山的腰，把它抱走了。罗恩趴在地上，费了不少劲儿，才揪着斑斑的尾巴把它拉了出来。

"你看看它！"他把斑斑拎到赫敏面前，气呼呼地对她说，"瘦得皮包骨头！你让那只猫离它远点儿！"

"克鲁克山不知道这样做不对！"赫敏声音发抖地说，"猫都喜欢追老鼠，罗恩！"

"那畜生有点儿怪！"罗恩一边说，一边哄劝疯狂扭动身体的斑斑重新钻进他的口袋，"它听见了我说斑斑在我书包里！"

"哦，别胡扯啦，"赫敏不耐烦地说，"克鲁克山能闻到斑斑的气味，罗恩，你以为——"

"那只猫就是盯住斑斑不放！"罗恩没理睬周围哧哧发笑的人群，"是斑斑先来的，而且它病了！"

罗恩气冲冲地大步穿过公共休息室，上楼去男生宿舍了。

第二天，罗恩仍然在跟赫敏闹别扭。草药课上，他几乎没跟赫敏说一句话，虽然他和哈利、赫敏分在一组剥泡泡豆荚。

"斑斑怎么样了？"赫敏怯生生地问，这时他们正从泡泡枝上摘下胖鼓鼓的粉红色豆荚，剥出亮晶晶的豆子，放到一只木桶里。

"躲在我的床脚发抖呢。"罗恩气呼呼地说，豆子没有扔进桶里，撒在了暖房的地上。

"当心，韦斯莱，当心！"斯普劳特教授喊道，地上的豆子在他们眼前开花了。

接下来是变形课。哈利已打定主意下课后要问问麦格教授他能不

CHAPTER EIGHT Flight of the Fat Lady

McGonagall after the lesson whether he could go into Hogsmeade with the rest, joined the queue outside the classroom, trying to decide how he was going to argue his case. He was distracted, however, by a disturbance at the front of the line.

Lavender Brown seemed to be crying. Parvati had her arm around her, and was explaining something to Seamus Finnigan and Dean Thomas, who were looking very serious.

'What's the matter, Lavender?' said Hermione anxiously, as she, Harry and Ron went to join the group.

'She got a letter from home this morning,' Parvati whispered. 'It's her rabbit, Binky. He's been killed by a fox.'

'Oh,' said Hermione. 'I'm sorry, Lavender.'

'I should have known!' said Lavender tragically. 'You know what day it is?'

'Er –'

'The sixteenth of October! "That thing you're dreading, it will happen on the sixteenth of October!" Remember? She was right, she was right!'

The whole class was gathered around Lavender now. Seamus shook his head seriously. Hermione hesitated; then she said, 'You – you were dreading Binky being killed by a fox?'

'Well, not necessarily by a *fox*,' said Lavender, looking up at Hermione with streaming eyes, 'but I was *obviously* dreading him dying, wasn't I?'

'Oh,' said Hermione. She paused again. Then –

'Was Binky an *old* rabbit?'

'N-no!' sobbed Lavender. 'H-he was only a baby!'

Parvati tightened her arm around Lavender's shoulders.

'But then, why would you dread him dying?' said Hermione.

Parvati glared at her.

'Well, look at it logically,' said Hermione, turning to the rest of the group. 'I mean, Binky didn't even die today, did he, Lavender just got the news today –' Lavender wailed loudly '– and she *can't* have been dreading it, because it's come as a real shock –'

'Don't mind Hermione, Lavender,' said Ron loudly, 'she doesn't think other people's pets matter very much.'

Professor McGonagall opened the classroom door at that moment, which was perhaps lucky; Hermione and Ron were looking daggers at each other,

第8章 胖夫人逃跑

能跟其他同学一起去霍格莫德,他排在教室外面的队伍里,心里盘算着到时候怎么说。可是,队伍前面出了点乱子,使他分了心。

拉文德·布朗好像在哭。帕瓦蒂一边用胳膊搂住她,一边向神情严肃的西莫·斐尼甘和迪安·托马斯解释着什么。

"怎么回事,拉文德?"赫敏焦急地问,跟哈利和罗恩一起凑了上去。

"她今天早晨收到了家里的一封信,"帕瓦蒂小声说,"她的兔子宾奇被一只狐狸咬死了。"

"哦,"赫敏说,"我为你难过,拉文德。"

"我早该知道的!"拉文德痛不欲生地说,"你知道今天是什么日子吗?"

"呃——"

"十月十六日!'你最害怕的那件事,会在十月十六日发生!'记得吗?她说得对,她说得对!"

此时,全班同学都聚在拉文德周围。西莫严肃地摇着头。赫敏迟疑了一下,说道:"你……你是一直害怕宾奇被一只狐狸咬死吗?"

"其实,也不一定是狐狸,"拉文德说,抬起泪汪汪的眼睛看着赫敏,"但我显然害怕兔子会死,不是吗?"

"噢。"赫敏说。她又顿了顿。然后——

"宾奇是一只老兔子吗?"

"不—不是!"拉文德抽抽搭搭地说,"是……是一只兔宝宝!"

帕瓦蒂把拉文德的肩膀搂得更紧了。

"那你为什么会害怕它死呢?"赫敏说。

帕瓦蒂没好气地瞪着她。

"理智地分析一下吧,"赫敏转向人群说道,"我的意思是,宾奇并不是今天死的,对吗?拉文德只是今天才得着消息,"——拉文德大声哀号——"而且她不可能一直在害怕这件事,因为她听到消息觉得非常震惊——"

"别理睬赫敏,拉文德,"罗恩大声说,"她根本不把别人的宠物当回事。"

幸好,这个时候麦格教授打开了教室的门。赫敏和罗恩怒目而视,

and when they got into class, they seated themselves either side of Harry, and didn't talk to each other all lesson.

Harry still hadn't decided what he was going to say to Professor McGonagall when the bell rang at the end of the lesson, but it was she who brought up the subject of Hogsmeade first.

'One moment, please!' she called, as the class made to leave. 'As you're all in my house, you should hand Hogsmeade permission forms to me before Hallowe'en. No form, no visiting the village, so don't forget!'

Neville put up his hand.

'Please, Professor, I – I think I've lost –'

'Your grandmother sent yours to me directly, Longbottom,' said Professor McGonagall. 'She seemed to think it was safer. Well, that's all, you may leave.'

'Ask her now,' Ron hissed at Harry.

'Oh, but –' Hermione began.

'Go for it, Harry,' said Ron stubbornly.

Harry waited for the rest of the class to disappear, then headed nervously for Professor McGonagall's desk.

'Yes, Potter?'

Harry took a deep breath.

'Professor, my aunt and uncle – er – forgot to sign my form,' he said.

Professor McGonagall looked over her square spectacles at him, but didn't say anything.

'So – er – d'you think it would be all right – I mean, will it be OK if I – if I go to Hogsmeade?'

Professor McGonagall looked down and began shuffling papers on her desk.

'I'm afraid not, Potter,' she said. 'You heard what I said. No form, no visiting the village. That's the rule.'

'But – Professor, my aunt and uncle – you know, they're Muggles, they don't really understand about – about Hogwarts forms and stuff,' Harry said, while Ron egged him on with vigorous nods. 'If you said I could go –'

'But I don't say so,' said Professor McGonagall, standing up and piling her papers neatly into a drawer. 'The form clearly states that the parent or guardian must give permission.' She turned to look at him, with an odd

第8章　胖夫人逃跑

进了教室。他们分坐在哈利的两边，整节课都没有互相说话。

下课铃响了，哈利还没有想好怎么跟麦格教授说，倒是她先提起了霍格莫德的话题。

"请等一下！"同学们起身离开时，麦格教授喊道，"你们都在我的学院，请在万圣节前把去霍格莫德的许可表交给我。不交表就不能去，千万别忘了！"

纳威把手举了起来。

"对不起，教授，我……我好像丢了——"

"你奶奶把你的表直接寄给我了，隆巴顿，"麦格教授说，"她似乎认为那样更安全。好了，就这样吧，你们可以走了。"

"快去问她。"罗恩压低声音对哈利说。

"哦，可是——"赫敏想说话。

"快去，哈利。"罗恩固执地说。

哈利等全班同学都离开后，才忐忑不安地朝麦格教授的讲台走去。

"什么事，波特？"

哈利深深吸了口气。

"教授，我的姨妈和姨父……呃……他们忘记在我的表上签字了。"他说。

麦格教授从她的方形眼镜上面看着哈利，什么也没说。

"所以……呃……你认为可不可以……我是说，能不能够……让我去霍格莫德？"

麦格教授垂下眼睛，开始整理桌上的讲义。

"恐怕不行，波特，"她说，"你听见我刚才说的话了。没有表就不能去。这是规定。"

"可是……教授，我的姨妈和姨父……你知道的，他们是麻瓜，他们其实根本不明白……不明白霍格沃茨发的表格之类的东西。"哈利说，罗恩在一旁拼命点头鼓励他，"如果你说我能去——"

"但是我不会说的，"麦格教授说着，站起身来，把讲义整整齐齐地放进抽屉，"表上说得很明白，必须由父母或监护人签字许可。"她

CHAPTER EIGHT   Flight of the Fat Lady

expression on her face. Was it pity? 'I'm sorry, Potter, but that's my final word. You had better hurry, or you'll be late for your next lesson.'

There was nothing to be done. Ron called Professor McGonagall a lot of names that greatly annoyed Hermione; Hermione assumed an 'all for the best' expression that made Ron even angrier, and Harry had to endure everyone in the class talking loudly and happily about what they were going to do first, once they got into Hogsmeade.

'There's always the feast,' said Ron, in an effort to cheer Harry up. 'You know, the Hallowe'en feast, in the evening.'

'Yeah,' said Harry, gloomily, 'great.'

The Hallowe'en feast was always good, but it would taste a lot better if he was coming to it after a day in Hogsmeade with everyone else. Nothing anyone said made him feel any better about being left behind. Dean Thomas, who was good with a quill, had offered to forge Uncle Vernon's signature on the form, but as Harry had already told Professor McGonagall he hadn't had it signed, that was no good. Ron half-heartedly suggested the Invisibility Cloak, but Hermione stamped on that one, reminding Ron what Dumbledore had told them about the Dementors being able to see through them. Percy had what were possibly the least helpful words of comfort.

'They make a fuss about Hogsmeade, but I assure you, Harry, it's not all it's cracked up to be,' he said seriously. 'All right, the sweetshop's rather good, but Zonko's Joke Shop's frankly dangerous, and yes, the Shrieking Shack's always worth a visit, but really, Harry, apart from that, you're not missing anything.'

On Hallowe'en morning, Harry awoke with the rest and went down to breakfast feeling thoroughly depressed, though doing his best to act normally.

'We'll bring you lots of sweets back from Honeydukes,' said Hermione, looking desperately sorry for him.

'Yeah, loads,' said Ron. He and Hermione had finally forgotten their squabble about Crookshanks in the face of Harry's disappointment.

'Don't worry about me,' said Harry, in what he hoped was an offhand voice. 'I'll see you at the feast. Have a good time.'

第8章　胖夫人逃跑

转身望着哈利，脸上的表情怪怪的。是同情吗？"很抱歉，波特，但事情只能这样了。你最好抓紧时间，不然下节课要迟到了。"

没有办法了。罗恩骂了麦格教授许多难听的话，使赫敏大为恼火。赫敏脸上摆出那副"都是为了你好"的表情，罗恩看了更加生气。班上每个人都在喜滋滋地大声谈论到了霍格莫德村先做什么，哈利只能干听着。

"不是还有宴会嘛，"罗恩想让哈利高兴起来，说道，"你知道的，万圣节前夕的宴会，在晚上举行。"

"是啊，"哈利闷闷不乐地说，"太棒了。"

万圣节前夕的宴会倒是不错，但如果他能跟其他人一样在霍格莫德玩了一天之后赴宴，那滋味将会更美妙。别人的安慰也没能使他感觉好受一点。迪安·托马斯笔头子很灵，提出要模仿弗农姨父的笔迹在表上签字，可是哈利已经跟麦格教授说了他没有签字，所以这招行不通。罗恩半真半假地建议用隐形衣，被赫敏断然否决。她提醒罗恩说，邓布利多告诉过他们，摄魂怪是能看透隐形衣的。而珀西的安慰话大概是最不管用的了。

"他们把霍格莫德吹得天花乱坠，可是我告诉你，哈利，其实根本就没有那么好。"他一本正经地说，"是啊，糖果店还是蛮不错的，但佐科笑话店很危险。噢，对了，尖叫棚屋倒是值得一去。可是除此之外，哈利，说实在的，你并没有错过什么。"

万圣节前一天早晨，哈利和其他同学一起醒来，下楼吃早饭时心情非常沮丧，但他尽量表现得跟平常一样。

"我们会从蜂蜜公爵带许多糖果回来给你。"赫敏说，她似乎为哈利感到难过极了。

"没错，带一大堆回来。"罗恩说。面对哈利的失望，他和赫敏终于忘记了他们关于克鲁克山的争吵。

"别替我担心啦，"哈利故意用满不在乎的口气说道，"宴会上见。好好玩吧。"

CHAPTER EIGHT   Flight of the Fat Lady

He accompanied them to the Entrance Hall, where Filch, the caretaker, was standing inside the front doors, checking off names against a long list, peering suspiciously into every face, and making sure that no one was sneaking out who shouldn't be going.

'Staying here, Potter?' shouted Malfoy, who was standing in line with Crabbe and Goyle. 'Scared of passing the Dementors?'

Harry ignored him and made his solitary way up the marble staircase, through the deserted corridors, and back to Gryffindor Tower.

'Password?' said the Fat Lady, jerking out of a doze.

'Fortuna Major,' said Harry listlessly.

The portrait swung open and he climbed through the hole into the common room. It was full of chattering first- and second-years, and a few older students who had obviously visited Hogsmeade so often the novelty had worn off.

'Harry! Harry! Hi, Harry!'

It was Colin Creevey, a second-year who was deeply in awe of Harry and never missed an opportunity to speak to him.

'Aren't you going to Hogsmeade, Harry? Why not? Hey –' Colin looked eagerly around at his friends, 'you can come and sit with us, if you like, Harry!'

'Er – no, thanks, Colin,' said Harry, who wasn't in the mood to have a lot of people staring avidly at the scar on his forehead. 'I – I've got to go to the library, got to get some work done.'

After that, he had no choice but to turn right around and head back out of the portrait hole again.

'What was the point of waking me up?' the Fat Lady called grumpily after him as he walked away.

Harry wandered dispiritedly towards the library, but halfway there he changed his mind; he didn't feel like working. He turned around and came face to face with Filch, who had obviously just seen off the last of the Hogsmeade visitors.

'What are you doing?' Filch snarled suspiciously.

'Nothing,' said Harry truthfully.

'Nothing!' spat Filch, his jowls quivering unpleasantly. 'A likely story! Sneaking around on your own, why aren't you in Hogsmeade buying Stink Pellets and Belch Powder and Whizzing Worms like the rest of your nasty little friends?'

第8章 胖夫人逃跑

他陪他们走到门厅,管理员费尔奇站在大门里面,核对着一份长长的名单,警惕地盯着每一张面孔,不让任何一个不该出去的人溜出大门。

"留在这儿了,波特?"马尔福喊道,他和克拉布、高尔一起排在队伍里,"不敢经过那些摄魂怪?"

哈利没有理他,独自走上大理石楼梯,穿过空无一人的走廊,返回格兰芬多塔楼。

"口令?"胖夫人从瞌睡中惊醒,问道。

"吉星高照。"哈利没精打采地说。

肖像画弹开了,哈利从洞口爬进公共休息室。里面满是叽叽喳喳的一、二年级学生,还有几个高年级的,显然是去过霍格莫德很多次,已经不再觉得新鲜了。

"哈利!哈利!嘿,哈利!"

是科林·克里维,一个二年级的学生,对哈利崇拜得五体投地,从不放过跟他说话的机会。

"你没有去霍格莫德吗,哈利?为什么?嘿——"科林热切地回头看看他那些朋友,"如果你愿意,可以过来跟我们坐在一起,哈利!"

"呃——不了,谢谢你,科林。"哈利说,他没有心情让一大堆人瞪眼盯着他额头上的伤疤,"我……我要去图书馆,有一些功课要做。"

说完,他别无选择,只能掉转身,又从肖像洞口爬了出来。

"为什么又把我叫醒?"胖夫人气呼呼地冲着他的背影喊道。

哈利灰心丧气地朝图书馆走去,走到半路,改变了主意。他并不想做功课。他转过身,不料却与费尔奇碰了个正着。费尔奇显然刚刚送走最后一批去霍格莫德的同学。

"你在干什么?"费尔奇怀疑地粗声问道。

"没干什么。"哈利实话实说。

"没干什么!"费尔奇厉声吼道,双下巴难看地抖动着,"编得倒像!一个人鬼鬼祟祟地溜达,你为什么没像你那些讨厌的小朋友那样,到霍格莫德去买臭弹、打嗝粉和飞鸣虫呢?"

CHAPTER EIGHT   Flight of the Fat Lady

Harry shrugged.

'Well, get back to your common room where you belong!' snapped Filch, and he stood glaring until Harry had passed out of sight.

But Harry didn't go back to the common room; he climbed a staircase, thinking vaguely of visiting the Owlery to see Hedwig, and was walking along another corridor when a voice from inside one of the rooms said, 'Harry?'

Harry doubled back to see who had spoken and met Professor Lupin, looking around his office door.

'What are you doing?' said Lupin, in a very different voice from Filch. 'Where are Ron and Hermione?'

'Hogsmeade,' said Harry, in a would-be casual voice.

'Ah,' said Lupin. He considered Harry for a moment. 'Why don't you come in? I've just taken delivery of a Grindylow for our next lesson.'

'A what?' said Harry.

He followed Lupin into his office. In the corner stood a very large tank of water. A sickly-green creature with sharp little horns had its face pressed against the glass, pulling faces and flexing its long, spindly fingers.

'Water demon,' said Lupin, surveying the Grindylow thoughtfully. 'We shouldn't have much difficulty with him, not after the Kappas. The trick is to break his grip. You notice the abnormally long fingers? Strong, but very brittle.'

The Grindylow bared its green teeth and then buried itself in a tangle of weed in a corner.

'Cup of tea?' Lupin said, looking around for his kettle. 'I was just thinking of making one.'

'All right,' said Harry awkwardly.

Lupin tapped the kettle with his wand and a blast of steam issued suddenly from the spout.

'Sit down,' said Lupin, taking the lid off a dusty tin. 'I've only got teabags, I'm afraid – but I daresay you've had enough of tea leaves?'

Harry looked at him. Lupin's eyes were twinkling.

'How did you know about that?' Harry asked.

'Professor McGonagall told me,' said Lupin, passing Harry a chipped mug of tea. 'You're not worried, are you?'

第8章 胖夫人逃跑

哈利耸了耸肩。

"好了，回你的公共休息室吧，你只能待在那儿！"费尔奇恶狠狠地说，他站在那里瞪着哈利，直到他从视线里消失。

可是哈利没有返回公共休息室。他爬了一段楼梯，心里隐约想着要去猫头鹰棚屋看看海德薇。他正走在另一条走廊上时，从一个房间里传出一个声音："哈利？"

哈利折回身来看是谁在说话，遇到了在办公室门口张望的卢平教授。

"你在做什么呢？"卢平问，语气跟费尔奇完全不同，"罗恩和赫敏呢？"

"在霍格莫德。"哈利说，努力让自己的口气显得随意些。

"啊。"卢平说，打量了哈利一会儿，"你干吗不进来？我刚收到一个格林迪洛，准备下节课用。"

"一个什么？"哈利问。

他跟着卢平走进办公室，墙角立着一只很大的水箱。一个令人恶心的、长着尖尖犄角的绿色怪物，把脸贴在玻璃上，一边做着各种怪相，一边不停地伸屈着瘦瘦长长的手指。

"水怪。"卢平若有所思地打量着格林迪洛，说道，"对付它不应该有什么困难，尤其是在对付过卡巴之后。诀窍是要挣脱它的手。你注意到它的手指长得出奇吗？很有力气，但是松脆易碎。"

格林迪洛龇了龇它的绿牙齿，然后把自己埋在了水箱角落里一堆纠结的水草中。

"喝杯茶吧？"卢平说，左右张望着找他的茶壶，"我刚才正想泡一壶茶呢。"

"好吧。"哈利局促不安地说。

卢平用魔杖敲了敲茶壶，壶嘴里突然喷出一股蒸汽。

"坐下吧，"卢平说，一边打开一个灰扑扑的罐子，"我恐怕只有茶叶包——不过我相信你已经受够了茶叶吧？"

哈利看着卢平。卢平眼里闪着诙谐的光。

"你怎么知道这事的？"哈利问。

"麦格教授告诉我的。"卢平说着，递给哈利一杯茶，杯子上有个缺口，"你并不担心，是吗？"

CHAPTER EIGHT — Flight of the Fat Lady

'No,' said Harry.

He thought for a moment of telling Lupin about the dog he'd seen in Magnolia Crescent, but decided not to. He didn't want Lupin to think he was a coward, especially since Lupin already seemed to think he couldn't cope with a Boggart.

Something of Harry's thoughts seemed to have shown on his face, because Lupin said, 'Anything worrying you, Harry?'

'No,' Harry lied. He drank a bit of tea and watched the Grindylow brandishing a fist at him. 'Yes,' he said suddenly, putting his tea down on Lupin's desk. 'You know that day we fought the Boggart?'

'Yes,' said Lupin slowly.

'Why didn't you let me fight it?' said Harry abruptly.

Lupin raised his eyebrows.

'I would have thought that was obvious, Harry,' he said, sounding surprised.

Harry, who had expected Lupin to deny that he'd done any such thing, was taken aback.

'Why?' he said again.

'Well,' said Lupin, frowning slightly, 'I assumed that if the Boggart faced you, it would assume the shape of Lord Voldemort.'

Harry stared. Not only was this the last answer he'd expected, but Lupin had said Voldemort's name. The only person Harry had ever heard say the name aloud (apart from himself) was Professor Dumbledore.

'Clearly, I was wrong,' said Lupin, still frowning at Harry. 'But I didn't think it a good idea for Lord Voldemort to materialise in the staff room. I imagined that people would panic.'

'I did think of Voldemort first,' said Harry honestly. 'But then I – I remembered those Dementors.'

'I see,' said Lupin thoughtfully. 'Well, well ... I'm impressed.' He smiled slightly at the look of surprise on Harry's face. 'That suggests that what you fear most of all is – fear. Very wise, Harry.'

Harry didn't know what to say to that, so he drank some more tea.

'So you've been thinking that I didn't believe you capable of fighting the Boggart?' said Lupin shrewdly.

'Well ... yeah,' said Harry. He was suddenly feeling a lot happier. 'Professor

第8章 胖夫人逃跑

"是的。"哈利说。

他很想把在木兰花新月街看到那条狗的事告诉卢平，但转念一想还是算了。他不愿意卢平把他想成一个胆小鬼，特别是卢平似乎已经认为他没有能力对付博格特了。

大概是他的一些想法在脸上有所表现，只听卢平问道："你有什么烦心的事吗，哈利？"

"没有。"哈利没说实话。他喝了点儿茶，注视着格林迪洛冲他挥舞一只拳头。"有，"他突然说道，把茶杯放在卢平的书桌上，"你还记得我们对付博格特的那天吗？"

"记得。"卢平慢悠悠地说。

"你为什么不让我对付它？"哈利突兀地问。

卢平扬起眉毛。

"我认为那是明摆着的呀，哈利。"卢平的口气有些惊讶。

哈利本以为卢平会否认这件事，听了这话很是吃惊。

"为什么？"他又问了一遍。

"是这样，"卢平微微蹙起眉头说道，"我想当然地认为，如果让博格特面对你，它会变成伏地魔的形象。"

哈利怔住了。他没有料到卢平会这样回答，而且，卢平竟然说出了伏地魔的名字。除了他自己，哈利只听见邓布利多教授大声说过这个名字。

"显然，我错了。"卢平仍然皱着眉头对哈利道，"但当时我认为不应该让伏地魔在教工休息室里显形。我想这会把别人吓坏的。"

"我确实先想到了伏地魔，"哈利坦诚地说，"可是后来我……我想起了那些摄魂怪。"

"我明白了，"卢平若有所思地说，"是啊，嗯……挺不寻常的。"看到哈利脸上惊讶的神情，他微微笑了笑，"这就说明，你最恐惧的是——恐惧本身。很有智慧，哈利。"

哈利不知道如何作答，便又喝了几口茶。

"这么说，你一直以为我不相信你有能力对付博格特？"卢平敏锐地问。

"这个……是啊。"哈利说，突然觉得开心多了，"卢平教授，你知

CHAPTER EIGHT   Flight of the Fat Lady

Lupin, you know the Dementors –'

He was interrupted by a knock on the door.

'Come in,' called Lupin.

The door opened, and in came Snape. He was carrying a goblet, which was smoking faintly, and stopped at the sight of Harry, his black eyes narrowing.

'Ah, Severus,' said Lupin, smiling. 'Thanks very much. Could you leave it here on the desk for me?'

Snape set the smoking goblet down, his eyes wandering between Harry and Lupin.

'I was just showing Harry my Grindylow,' said Lupin pleasantly, pointing at the tank.

'Fascinating,' said Snape, without looking at it. 'You should drink that directly, Lupin.'

'Yes, yes, I will,' said Lupin.

'I made an entire cauldronful,' Snape continued. 'If you need more.'

'I should probably take some again tomorrow. Thanks very much, Severus.'

'Not at all,' said Snape, but there was a look in his eye Harry didn't like. He backed out of the room, unsmiling and watchful.

Harry looked curiously at the goblet. Lupin smiled.

'Professor Snape has very kindly concocted a potion for me,' he said. 'I have never been much of a potion-brewer and this one is particularly complex.' He picked up the goblet and sniffed it. 'Pity sugar makes it useless,' he added, taking a sip and shuddering.

'Why –?' Harry began. Lupin looked at him and answered the unfinished question.

'I've been feeling a bit off-colour,' he said. 'This potion is the only thing that helps. I am very lucky to be working alongside Professor Snape; there aren't many wizards who are up to making it.'

Professor Lupin took another sip and Harry had a mad urge to knock the goblet out of his hands.

'Professor Snape's very interested in the Dark Arts,' he blurted out.

'Really?' said Lupin, looking only mildly interested as he took another gulp of potion.

第8章 胖夫人逃跑

道那些摄魂怪——"

有人敲门，打断了他的话。

"进来。"卢平大声说。

门开了，斯内普走了进来，手里拿着一个微微冒烟的高脚酒杯。看见哈利，他停住脚步，一双黑眼睛眯了起来。

"啊，西弗勒斯，"卢平微笑着说，"非常感谢。你把它放在桌子上好吗？"

斯内普放下冒烟的酒杯，目光来回打量着哈利和卢平。

"我刚才在给哈利看我的格林迪洛。"卢平心情愉快地指着水箱说道。

"真有意思。"斯内普看也不看地说，"你应该马上把它喝掉，卢平。"

"好的，好的，我会喝的。"卢平说。

"我熬了满满一锅，"斯内普继续说，"怕你还需要。"

"我大概明天还应该再喝一些。非常感谢，西弗勒斯。"

"不必客气。"斯内普说，但眼里的神情是哈利不喜欢的。他面无笑容，十分警惕地退出了房间。

哈利好奇地看着高脚酒杯。卢平笑了。

"斯内普教授好意为我熬制了一种药剂。"他说，"我对制药不大在行，而这种药又特别复杂。"他端起酒杯，闻了闻，"真可惜，加了糖就不管用了。"说完，他啜了一口，打了个哆嗦。

"为什么——？"哈利想问个明白。卢平看着他，回答了他没有说完的问题。

"我一直感到有点儿不舒服，"卢平说，"只有这种药能管用。我运气真好，跟斯内普教授在一起工作。能够调制这种药的巫师可不多啊。"

卢平教授又啜了一口，哈利产生了一种强烈的冲动，想把他手里的酒杯打掉。

"斯内普教授对黑魔法很感兴趣。"他冒冒失失地说了一句。

"真的吗？"卢平说，似乎只是略感好奇，他又喝了一大口药。

CHAPTER EIGHT — Flight of the Fat Lady

'Some people reckon –' Harry hesitated, then plunged recklessly on, 'some people reckon he'd do anything to get the Defence Against the Dark Arts job.'

Lupin drained the goblet and pulled a face.

'Disgusting,' he said. 'Well, Harry, I'd better get back to work. I'll see you at the feast later.'

'Right,' said Harry, putting his empty teacup down.

The empty goblet was still smoking.

* * *

'There you go,' said Ron. 'We got as much as we could carry.'

A shower of brilliantly coloured sweets fell into Harry's lap. It was dusk, and Ron and Hermione had just turned up in the common room, pink-faced from the cold wind and looking as though they'd had the time of their lives.

'Thanks,' said Harry, picking up a packet of tiny black Pepper Imps. 'What's Hogsmeade like? Where did you go?'

By the sound of it – everywhere. Dervish and Banges, the wizarding equipment shop, Zonko's Joke Shop, into the Three Broomsticks for foaming mugs of hot Butterbeer and many places besides.

'The post office, Harry! About two hundred owls, all sitting on shelves, all colour-coded depending on how fast you want your letter to get there!'

'Honeydukes have got a new kind of fudge, they were giving out free samples, there's a bit, look –'

'We *think* we saw an ogre, honestly, they get all sorts at the Three Broomsticks –'

'Wish we could have brought you some Butterbeer, really warms you up –'

'What did you do?' said Hermione, looking anxious. 'Did you get any work done?'

'No,' said Harry. 'Lupin made me a cup of tea in his office. And then Snape came in ...'

He told them all about the goblet. Ron's mouth fell open.

'*Lupin drank it?*' he gasped. 'Is he mad?'

Hermione checked her watch.

'We'd better go down, you know, the feast'll be starting in five minutes ...' They hurried through the portrait hole and into the crowd, still discussing Snape.

第8章　胖夫人逃跑

"有人认为……"哈利迟疑了一下，然后不顾一切地说了下去，"有人认为，为了得到黑魔法防御术课的教职，他什么都做得出来。"

卢平喝光了酒杯里的药，做了个苦脸。

"真难喝，"他说，"好了，哈利，我要接着工作了。待会儿宴会上见。"

"好的。"哈利说着，放下了空茶杯。

那只喝空了的高脚酒杯仍在冒烟。

"给，"罗恩说，"我们能拿多少就拿了多少。"

一大堆五颜六色的糖果阵雨一样落在哈利的腿上。天已擦黑，罗恩和赫敏刚刚走进公共休息室，脸蛋被寒风吹得红扑扑的，看上去他们玩得别提多开心了。

"谢谢。"哈利说着，拿起一包胡椒小顽童，"霍格莫德怎么样？你们去了哪儿？"

听他们的口气——好像哪儿都去了。专卖魔法用品的德维斯-班斯店、佐科笑话店，还进三把扫帚喝了热腾腾的黄油啤酒，此外还去了许多别的地方。

"邮局，哈利！有差不多两百只猫头鹰，都蹲在架子上，都标着颜色代码，就看你想让你的信走多快了！"

"蜂蜜公爵推出了一种新的乳汁软糖，还让我们免费尝了几块，这里就有，看——"

"我们好像看见了一个吃人妖，真的，三把扫帚里什么货色都有——"

"真希望能给你带一些黄油啤酒啊，确实让你感到全身热乎乎的——"

"你做什么了？"赫敏显得很担忧地问，"你做了什么功课没有？"

"没有，"哈利说，"卢平在他的办公室里请我喝茶。后来斯内普进去了……"

他把高脚酒杯的事告诉了他们。罗恩的嘴一下子张大了。

"卢平喝了？"他吃惊地问，"他疯了吗？"

赫敏看了看表。

"我们得下去了，知道吗？再过五分钟宴会就要开始了……"他们匆匆爬出肖像洞口，汇入人群，一边仍在谈论着斯内普。

CHAPTER EIGHT — Flight of the Fat Lady

'But if he – you know –' Hermione dropped her voice, glancing nervously around, 'if he was trying to – to poison Lupin – he wouldn't have done it in front of Harry.'

'Yeah, maybe,' said Harry, as they reached the Entrance Hall and crossed into the Great Hall. It had been decorated with hundreds and hundreds of candle-filled pumpkins, a cloud of fluttering live bats and many flaming orange streamers, which were swimming lazily across the stormy ceiling like brilliant watersnakes.

The food was delicious; even Hermione and Ron, who were full to bursting with Honeydukes sweets, managed second helpings of everything. Harry kept glancing at the staff table. Professor Lupin looked cheerful and as well as he ever did; he was talking animatedly to tiny little Professor Flitwick, the Charms teacher. Harry moved his eyes along the table, to the place where Snape sat. Was he imagining it, or were Snape's eyes flickering towards Lupin more often than was natural?

The feast finished with an entertainment provided by the Hogwarts ghosts. They popped out of the walls and tables to do a spot of formation gliding; Nearly Headless Nick, the Gryffindor ghost, had a great success with a re-enactment of his own botched beheading.

It had been such a good evening that Harry's good mood couldn't even be spoiled by Malfoy, who shouted through the crowd as they all left the Hall, 'The Dementors send their love, Potter!'

Harry, Ron and Hermione followed the rest of the Gryffindors along the usual path to Gryffindor Tower, but when they reached the corridor which ended with the portrait of the Fat Lady, they found it jammed with students.

'Why isn't anyone going in?' said Ron curiously.

Harry peered over the heads in front of him. The portrait seemed to be closed.

'Let me through, please,' came Percy's voice, and he came bustling importantly through the crowd. 'What's the hold-up here? You can't all have forgotten the password – excuse me, I'm Head Boy –'

And then a silence fell over the crowd, from the front first, so that a chill seemed to spread down the corridor. They heard Percy say, in a suddenly sharp voice, 'Somebody get Professor Dumbledore. Quick.'

People's heads turned; those at the back were standing on tiptoe.

'What's going on?' said Ginny, who had just arrived.

第8章 胖夫人逃跑

"可是，如果他——你知道的——"赫敏压低声音，不安地扫了一眼周围，"如果他想要——想要毒死卢平——是不会当着哈利的面这么做的。"

"是啊，大概吧。"哈利说，他们到了门厅，往礼堂走去。礼堂里装饰着成百上千个点着蜡烛的南瓜，一大群飞来飞去的活蝙蝠，还有许多燃着火苗的橘黄色横幅，它们像色彩斑斓的水蛇一样，在酝酿着风暴的天花板上懒洋洋地飘荡。

食物美味极了，就连肚子里已经塞满蜂蜜公爵糖果的罗恩和赫敏，也每样都添了一份。哈利不住地去看教工餐桌。卢平教授看上去很快乐，跟平常没有什么两样，正跟小个子魔咒课老师弗立维教授聊得起劲儿。哈利的目光扫过教工餐桌，落在斯内普的座位上。难道是他的幻觉吗？他觉得斯内普的眼睛在频频瞥向卢平，次数多得不正常。

宴会的结尾是霍格沃茨幽灵们表演的节目。他们纷纷从墙壁和桌子里蹿出来，组成各种阵形表演滑行。格兰芬多的差点没头的尼克把他的砍头经历又重演了一遍，大获成功。

这个晚上过得太愉快了，就连离开礼堂时马尔福隔着人群冲哈利大喊"波特，摄魂怪向你问好！"也没有影响哈利的好心情。

哈利、罗恩和赫敏跟着格兰芬多的其他同学，顺着平常的路线往格兰芬多塔楼走去。可是，走到通向胖夫人肖像的那条走廊时，却发现那里挤满了学生。

"为什么都不进去？"罗恩好奇地说。

哈利越过前面同学的头顶望去。肖像洞口似乎是关着的。

"劳驾，让我过去。"传来了珀西的声音，他煞有介事地匆匆穿过人群，"为什么都堵在这儿？你们不可能都忘记口令了吧——对不起，我是学生会主席——"

突然，人群安静下来，从前排开始，似乎有一股寒意顺着走廊蔓延。他们听见珀西用一种变得尖厉的声音说道："谁去叫一下邓布利多教授。快！"

人们纷纷转过脑袋。站在后面的人踮起了脚尖。

"出什么事了？"刚走过来的金妮问道。

CHAPTER EIGHT   Flight of the Fat Lady

Next moment, Professor Dumbledore was there, sweeping towards the portrait; the Gryffindors squeezed together to let him through, and Harry, Ron and Hermione moved closer to see what the trouble was.

'Oh, my –' Hermione exclaimed and grabbed Harry's arm.

The Fat Lady had vanished from her portrait, which had been slashed so viciously that strips of canvas littered the floor; great chunks of it had been torn away completely.

Dumbledore took one quick look at the ruined painting and turned, his eyes sombre, to see Professors McGonagall, Lupin and Snape hurrying towards him.

'We need to find her,' said Dumbledore. 'Professor McGonagall, please go to Mr Filch at once and tell him to search every painting in the castle for the Fat Lady.'

'You'll be lucky!' said a cackling voice.

It was Peeves the poltergeist, bobbing over the crowd and looking delighted, as he always did, at the sight of wreckage or worry.

'What do you mean, Peeves?' said Dumbledore calmly, and Peeves's grin faded a little. He didn't dare taunt Dumbledore. Instead he adopted an oily voice that was no better than his cackle.

'Ashamed, Your Headship, sir. Doesn't want to be seen. She's a horrible mess. Saw her running through the landscape up on the fourth floor, sir, dodging between the trees. Crying something dreadful,' he said happily. 'Poor thing,' he added, unconvincingly.

'Did she say who did it?' said Dumbledore quietly.

'Oh, yes, Professorhead,' said Peeves, with the air of one cradling a large bombshell in his arms. 'He got very angry when she wouldn't let him in, you see.' Peeves flipped over, and grinned at Dumbledore from between his own legs. 'Nasty temper he's got, that Sirius Black.'

第8章 胖夫人逃跑

接着，邓布利多教授出现了，他快步朝肖像走去。格兰芬多的同学挤作一团让他通过，哈利、罗恩和赫敏凑过去看是怎么回事。

"哦，天哪——"赫敏惊叫一声，一把抓住了哈利的胳膊。

胖夫人从她的肖像上消失了，肖像被狠狠砍过，画布碎片散落在地板上，还有一大块画布干脆被撕走了。

邓布利多迅速扫了一眼被毁坏的肖像，转过身来，目光凝重，看着快步朝他走来的麦格教授、卢平和斯内普。

"我们需要找到她。"邓布利多说，"麦格教授，请立刻去找费尔奇先生，叫他搜查城堡里的每一幅画，寻找胖夫人。"

"祝你好运！"一个声音咯咯地笑着说。

是恶作剧精灵皮皮鬼，他在众人头顶上跳来跳去，看到这不幸和烦恼的场面，他像平常一样欢天喜地。

"你说什么，皮皮鬼？"邓布利多心平气和地问，皮皮鬼脸上的笑容收敛了一些。他可不敢嘲笑邓布利多。他换了一种谄媚讨好的口吻，却并不比刚才的咯咯怪笑好听多少。

"她太难为情了，校长大人。不愿被人看见。惨得一塌糊涂。看见她跑过五楼的那幅风景画，先生，躲在树丛里。哭得别提多伤心了。"他快活地说，"可怜的人。"他又假心假意地补了一句。

"她有没有说是谁干的？"邓布利多轻声问道。

"噢，说了，教授头儿。"皮皮鬼说，那神情就像怀里抱着一个大炸弹，"你瞧，胖夫人不肯放他进来，他很生气。"皮皮鬼忽地翻了个跟头，从两条腿中间朝邓布利多咧着嘴笑，"他的脾气可真吓人——那个小天狼星布莱克。"

CHAPTER NINE

Grim Defeat

Professor Dumbledore sent all the Gryffindors back to the Great Hall, where they were joined ten minutes later by the students from Hufflepuff, Ravenclaw and Slytherin, who all looked extremely confused.

'The teachers and I need to conduct a thorough search of the castle,' Professor Dumbledore told them as Professors McGonagall and Flitwick closed all doors into the Hall. 'I'm afraid that, for your own safety, you will have to spend the night here. I want the Prefects to stand guard over the entrances to the Hall and I am leaving the Head Boy and Girl in charge. Any disturbance should be reported to me immediately,' he added to Percy, who was looking immensely proud and important. 'Send word with one of the ghosts.'

Professor Dumbledore paused, about to the leave the Hall, and said, 'Oh, yes, you'll be needing …'

One casual wave of his wand and the long tables flew to the edges of the Hall and stood themselves against the walls; another wave, and the floor was covered with hundreds of squashy purple sleeping bags.

'Sleep well,' said Professor Dumbledore, closing the door behind him.

The Hall immediately began to buzz excitedly; the Gryffindors were telling the rest of the school what had just happened.

'Everyone into their sleeping bags!' shouted Percy. 'Come on now, no more talking! Lights out in ten minutes!'

'C'mon,' Ron said to Harry and Hermione; they seized three sleeping bags and dragged them into a corner.

'Do you think Black's still in the castle?' Hermione whispered anxiously.

'Dumbledore obviously thinks he might be,' said Ron.

'It's very lucky he picked tonight, you know,' said Hermione, as they

第 9 章

不祥的失败

邓布利多教授命令格兰芬多全体同学返回礼堂。十分钟后，赫奇帕奇、拉文克劳和斯莱特林的同学们也进来了，每个人脸上都很困惑。

"我和教师们需要对城堡展开全面搜查。"邓布利多教授告诉大家，这时麦格和弗立维教授关上了礼堂所有的门，"为了自身安全，你们恐怕只能在这里过夜了。希望级长守住礼堂入口，我委托男女生学生会主席负责管理。若有什么情况，立即向我汇报，"他又对一旁得意非凡、煞有介事的珀西说道，"派一个幽灵传递消息。"

邓布利多教授停住话头，正准备离开礼堂，却又说道："哦，对了，你们需要……"

他轻轻一挥魔杖，一张张长桌子便飞到礼堂边上，自动靠墙站着；又是轻轻一挥，地上出现了几百个软绵绵的紫色睡袋。

"好好睡吧。"邓布利多教授说完，便走出去关上了门。

礼堂里立刻响起了叽叽喳喳的议论声，格兰芬多的同学把刚才发生的事情告诉了其他学院的同学。

"大家都钻进睡袋！"珀西喊道，"快点儿，不许再说话了！十分钟后熄灯！"

"过来。"罗恩对哈利和赫敏说。他们抓过三个睡袋，拖到墙角。

"你们说，布莱克还在城堡里吗？"赫敏担忧地小声问。

"邓布利多好像认为他还在。"罗恩说。

"幸亏他挑了今天晚上。"赫敏说，他们和衣钻进了睡袋，用胳膊

CHAPTER NINE — Grim Defeat

climbed fully dressed into their sleeping bags and propped themselves on their elbows to talk. 'The one night we weren't in the Tower ...'

'I reckon he's lost track of time, being on the run,' said Ron. 'Didn't realise it was Hallowe'en. Otherwise he'd have come bursting in here.'

Hermione shuddered.

All around them, people were asking each other the same question: '*How did he get in?*'

'Maybe he knows how to Apparate,' said a Ravenclaw a few feet away. 'Just appear out of thin air, you know.'

'Disguised himself, probably,' said a Hufflepuff fifth-year.

'He could've flown in,' suggested Dean Thomas.

'Honestly, am I the *only* person who's ever bothered to read *Hogwarts, A History*?' said Hermione crossly to Harry and Ron.

'Probably,' said Ron. 'Why?'

'Because the castle's protected by more than *walls*, you know,' said Hermione. 'There are all sorts of enchantments on it, to stop people entering by stealth. You can't just Apparate in here. And I'd like to see the disguise that could fool those Dementors. They're guarding every single entrance to the grounds. They'd have seen him fly in, too. And Filch knows all the secret passages, they'll have them covered ...'

'The lights are going out now!' Percy shouted. 'I want everyone in their sleeping bags and no more talking!'

The candles all went out at once. The only light now came from the silvery ghosts, who were drifting about talking seriously to the Prefects, and the enchanted ceiling, which, like the sky outside, was scattered with stars. What with that, and the whispering that still filled the Hall, Harry felt as though he was sleeping out of doors in a light wind.

Once every hour, a teacher would reappear in the Hall to check that everything was quiet. Around three in the morning, when many students had finally fallen asleep, Professor Dumbledore came in. Harry watched him looking around for Percy, who had been prowling between the sleeping bags, telling people off for talking. Percy was only a short way away from Harry, Ron and Hermione, who quickly pretended to be asleep as Dumbledore's footsteps drew nearer.

'Any sign of him, Professor?' asked Percy in a whisper.

支着脑袋聊天,"今晚我们不在塔楼里……"

"我想,他出逃在外,已经没有时间概念了,"罗恩说,"不知道今天是万圣节前夕。不然他肯定冲到这里来了。"

赫敏打了个哆嗦。

在他们周围,同学们互相询问着同样的问题:"他是怎么进来的?"

"也许他知道怎样幻影显形,"几步之外的一位拉文克劳同学说,"就一下子凭空出现了。"

"没准他把自己伪装起来了。"赫奇帕奇的一位五年级学生说。

"他可能是飞进来的。"迪安·托马斯说。

"拜托,难道只有我一个人花时间读过《霍格沃茨:一段校史》吗?"赫敏恼火地对哈利和罗恩说。

"大概是吧,"罗恩说,"怎么啦?"

"因为城堡不光有城墙保护,"赫敏说,"还有各种各样的魔法,阻止外人偷偷闯入。你不可能在这里幻影显形。还有,我倒想看看什么样的伪装能骗过那些摄魂怪。它们把守着学校的每一个入口。如果他飞进来,它们肯定会看见的。另外,费尔奇知道所有的秘密通道,都已派人严加看守……"

"现在熄灯!"珀西大声说,"我要求每个人都钻进睡袋,别再说话!"

蜡烛立刻全部熄灭了。只有那些银色的幽灵发出些许光亮,飘来飘去地跟级长们严肃地交谈着什么。施了魔法的天花板看上去跟外面的天空一样,点缀着许多星星。在这样的天花板下,听着礼堂里仍然响着的窃窃私语声,哈利觉得自己好像睡在户外的微风里一样。

每过一个小时,就有一位教师出现在礼堂里,查看是否平安无事。大约凌晨三点的时候,许多同学终于睡着了,邓布利多教授走了进来。哈利注视着他在四处寻找珀西。珀西在一排排睡袋间巡行,训斥那些说话的同学。他离哈利、罗恩和赫敏不远,邓布利多的脚步声越来越近了,他们三个立刻假装睡着。

"教授,有他的线索吗?"珀西小声问。

CHAPTER NINE   Grim Defeat

'No. All well here?'

'Everything under control, sir.'

'Good. There's no point moving them all now. I've found a temporary guardian for the Gryffindor portrait hole. You'll be able to move them back in tomorrow.'

'And the Fat Lady, sir?'

'Hiding in a map of Argyllshire on the second floor. Apparently she refused to let Black in without the password, so he attacked. She's still very distressed, but once she's calmed down, I'll have Mr Filch restore her.'

Harry heard the door of the Hall creak open again, and more footsteps.

'Headmaster?' It was Snape. Harry kept quite still, listening hard. 'The whole of the third floor has been searched. He's not there. And Filch has done the dungeons; nothing there, either.'

'What about the Astronomy Tower? Professor Trelawney's room? The Owlery?'

'All searched ...'

'Very well, Severus. I didn't really expect Black to linger.'

'Have you any theory as to how he got in, Professor?' asked Snape.

Harry raised his head very slightly off his arms to free his other ear.

'Many, Severus, each of them as unlikely as the next.'

Harry opened his eyes a fraction and squinted up to where they stood; Dumbledore's back was to him, but he could see Percy's face, rapt with attention, and Snape's profile, which looked angry.

'You remember the conversation we had, Headmaster, just before – ah – the start of term?' said Snape, who was barely opening his lips, as though trying to block Percy out of the conversation.

'I do, Severus,' said Dumbledore, and there was something like warning in his voice.

'It seems – almost impossible – that Black could have entered the school without inside help. I did express my concerns when you appointed –'

'I do not believe a single person inside this castle would have helped Black enter it,' said Dumbledore, and his tone made it so clear that the subject was closed that Snape didn't reply. 'I must go down to the Dementors,' said Dumbledore. 'I said I would inform them when our search was complete.'

'Didn't they want to help, sir?' said Percy.

第9章 不祥的失败

"没有。这里没事吧？"

"一切正常，先生。"

"很好。现在没有必要惊动他们。我给格兰芬多肖像洞口找了个临时看守。明天早晨你就可以让他们搬回去了。"

"胖夫人呢，先生？"

"躲在三楼的阿盖尔郡地图里。看来，当时她没听到口令就不让布莱克进去，布莱克就动了手。她的情绪仍然很糟糕，等她平静下来后，我再让费尔奇先生把她修复。"

哈利听见礼堂的门又吱嘎一声打开了，传来更多的脚步声。

"校长？"是斯内普。哈利一动不动，仔细倾听。"整个四楼都搜过了。他不在那儿。费尔奇也到地下教室看过了，那儿也没有。"

"天文塔呢？特里劳尼教授的房间呢？猫头鹰棚屋呢？"

"都搜过了……"

"很好，西弗勒斯。我也料到布莱克不会在这里逗留。"

"你有没有想过他是怎么进来的，教授？"斯内普问。

哈利把脑袋从胳膊上微微抬起一些，好让另一只耳朵也能听见。

"想法很多，西弗勒斯，可每一种都同样站不住脚。"

哈利把眼睛睁开一条缝，朝他们站的地方望去。邓布利多背对着他，但他能看到珀西的脸，一副全神贯注的样子，还能看到斯内普怒气冲冲的侧影。

"你还记得我们的那次谈话吗，校长，就在——呃——就在开学前？"斯内普说话时嘴唇几乎不动，似乎不想让珀西参与他们的谈话。

"记得，西弗勒斯。"邓布利多说，声音里透出某种类似警告的意思。

"布莱克不依靠内援就闯进学校——这似乎是——不可能的。我表达过我的担忧，当你指定——"

"我不相信这座城堡里有哪一个人会帮助布莱克闯入。"邓布利多说，他的语气明确表示这个话题到此为止，斯内普便没再说话。"我必须下去找那些摄魂怪，"邓布利多说，"我说过，等我们搜查完了就通知它们。"

"它们不是想来帮忙的吗，先生？"珀西说。

CHAPTER NINE   Grim Defeat

'Oh yes,' said Dumbledore coldly. 'But I'm afraid no Dementor will cross the threshold of this castle while I am Headmaster.'

Percy looked slightly abashed. Dumbledore left the Hall, walking quickly and quietly. Snape stood for a moment, watching the Headmaster with an expression of deep resentment on his face, then he, too, left.

Harry glanced sideways at Ron and Hermione. Both of them had their eyes open, too, reflecting the starry ceiling.

'What was all that about?' Ron mouthed.

The school talked of nothing but Sirius Black for the next few days. The theories about how he had entered the castle became wilder and wilder; Hannah Abbott, from Hufflepuff, spent much of their next Herbology class telling anyone who'd listen that Black could turn into a flowering shrub.

The Fat Lady's ripped canvas had been taken off the wall and replaced with the portrait of Sir Cadogan and his fat grey pony. Nobody was very happy about this. Sir Cadogan spent half his time challenging people to duels, and the rest thinking up ridiculously complicated passwords, which he changed at least twice a day.

'He's barking mad,' said Seamus Finnigan angrily to Percy. 'Can't we get anyone else?'

'None of the other pictures wanted the job,' said Percy. 'Frightened of what happened to the Fat Lady. Sir Cadogan was the only one brave enough to volunteer.'

Sir Cadogan, however, was the least of Harry's worries. He was now being closely watched. Teachers found excuses to walk along corridors with him and Percy Weasley (acting, Harry suspected, on his mother's orders) was tailing him everywhere like an extremely pompous guard dog. To cap it all, Professor McGonagall summoned Harry into her office, with such a sombre expression on her face Harry thought someone must have died.

'There's no point hiding it from you any longer, Potter,' she said, in a very serious voice. 'I know this will come as a shock to you, but Sirius Black –'

'I know he's after me,' said Harry wearily. 'I heard Ron's dad telling his mum. Mr Weasley works for the Ministry of Magic.'

第9章 不祥的失败

"哦,是的,"邓布利多冷冷地说,"但只要我还是校长,恐怕没有一个摄魂怪能跨过这座城堡的门槛。"

珀西显得有点儿尴尬。邓布利多离开了礼堂,走得很快,悄无声息。斯内普站了一会儿,注视着校长的背影,脸上带着很深的怨恨。然后,他也离开了。

哈利望了望旁边的罗恩和赫敏。他们俩也都睁着眼睛,眼里映着星光闪烁的天花板。

"这都是怎么回事?"罗恩不出声地问。

接下来的几天里,全校只有一个话题,就是小天狼星布莱克。关于他怎么闯进城堡的说法越来越离奇。在接下来的一节草药课上,赫奇帕奇的汉娜·艾博花了好多时间告诉别人——只要有人肯听——布莱克会变成一丛开花的灌木。

被撕坏的胖夫人肖像从墙上拿了下来,换上了卡多根爵士和他那匹肥灰马的画像。这弄得大家都很不开心。卡多根爵士用一半时间挑逗别人跟他决斗,用另一半时间想出一些复杂得近乎荒唐的口令,而且一天至少要换两次。

"他彻底疯了,"西莫·斐尼甘气恼地对珀西说,"就不能换个别人吗?"

"别的画像都不肯接这份活儿,"珀西说,"被胖夫人的遭遇吓坏了。只有卡多根爵士很勇敢,居然自告奋勇。"

不过,跟哈利担心的其他事情比起来,卡多根爵士根本算不了什么。现在哈利被严密监视着。教师们寻找借口陪他穿过走廊,珀西·韦斯莱(哈利怀疑是听从他母亲的吩咐)到处跟着他,就像一条特别神气活现的警犬。更糟糕的是,麦格教授还把哈利叫到她的办公室,她脸上的表情那么凝重,哈利还以为一定是谁死了。

"再瞒着你也没有意义了,波特,"她用非常严肃的口吻说道,"我知道这对你来说是一个打击,小天狼星布莱克——"

"我知道他是来找我的,"哈利无奈地说,"罗恩的爸爸告诉他妈妈时我听见了。韦斯莱先生在魔法部工作。"

CHAPTER NINE Grim Defeat

Professor McGonagall seemed very taken aback. She stared at Harry for a moment or two, then said, 'I see! Well, in that case, Potter, you'll understand why I don't think it's a good idea for you to be practising Quidditch in the evenings. Out on the pitch with only your team members, it's very exposed, Potter –'

'We've got our first match on Saturday!' said Harry, outraged. 'I've got to train, Professor!'

Professor McGonagall considered him intently. Harry knew she was deeply interested in the Gryffindor team's prospects; it had been she, after all, who'd suggested him as Seeker in the first place. He waited, holding his breath.

'Hmm ...' Professor McGonagall stood up and stared out of the window at the Quidditch pitch, just visible through the rain. 'Well ... goodness knows, I'd like to see us win the Cup at last ... but all the same, Potter ... I'd be happier if a teacher were present. I'll ask Madam Hooch to oversee your training sessions.'

The weather worsened steadily as the first Quidditch match drew nearer. Undaunted, the Gryffindor team were training harder than ever under the eye of Madam Hooch. Then, at their final training session before Saturday's match, Oliver Wood gave his team some unwelcome news.

'We're not playing Slytherin!' he told them, looking very angry. 'Flint's just been to see me. We're playing Hufflepuff instead.'

'Why?' chorused the rest of the team.

'Flint's excuse is that their Seeker's arm's still injured,' said Wood, grinding his teeth furiously. 'But it's obvious why they're doing it. Don't want to play in this weather. Think it'll damage their chances ...'

There had been strong winds and heavy rain all day, and as Wood spoke, they heard a distant rumble of thunder.

'There's *nothing wrong* with Malfoy's arm!' said Harry furiously. 'He's faking it!'

'I know that, but we can't prove it,' said Wood bitterly. 'And we've been practising all those moves assuming we're playing Slytherin, and instead it's Hufflepuff, and their style's quite different. They've got a new captain and Seeker, Cedric Diggory –'

Angelina, Alicia and Katie suddenly giggled.

第9章 不祥的失败

麦格教授看上去非常吃惊。她瞪着哈利看了一会儿，然后说道："我明白了！好吧，那样的话，波特，我想你能理解我为什么认为你不宜再参加晚上的魁地奇训练。在外面的球场上，身边只有你们球队的人，这是很暴露的，波特——"

"星期六我们就要进行第一场比赛了！"哈利激动地说，"我必须参加训练，教授！"

麦格教授专注地打量着他。哈利知道她对格兰芬多球队的输赢也非常关注。毕竟，当初就是她建议哈利当找球手的。哈利屏住呼吸等待着。

"哦……"麦格教授站起身，望着窗外雨中隐约可见的魁地奇球场，"好吧……看在老天的分儿上，我也愿意看到我们最终赢得奖杯……不过，话说回来，波特……如果有一位教师在场就好多了。我去请霍琦女士监督你们训练。"

第一场魁地奇比赛日益临近，天气越来越恶劣。勇敢无畏的格兰芬多球队在霍琦女士的监督下，训练得更辛苦了。在星期六比赛前的最后一次训练中，奥利弗·伍德告诉了队员们一个不太好的消息。

"我们不和斯莱特林队比赛了！"他非常恼火地对他们说，"弗林特刚才找过我。我们要打赫奇帕奇。"

"为什么？"队员们异口同声地问。

"弗林特的理由是他们找球手的胳膊仍然有伤。"伍德怒气冲冲地咬着牙说，"他们这么做的原因是明摆着的。不想在这种天气比赛，认为这会减少他们赢的机会……"

狂风暴雨肆虐了一整天，伍德说话时，他们还能听见远处传来隆隆的雷声。

"马尔福的胳膊根本就没问题！"哈利愤怒地说，"他是假装的！"

"这我知道，但是没法证明啊。"伍德恨恨地说，"我们一直是按照对付斯莱特林的战术训练的，结果却要打赫奇帕奇，他们的风格完全不同。他们新换了队长和找球手，是塞德里克·迪戈里——"

安吉利娜、艾丽娅和凯蒂突然咯咯地笑了起来。

CHAPTER NINE   Grim Defeat

'What?' said Wood, frowning at this light-hearted behaviour.

'He's that tall, good-looking one, isn't he?' said Angelina.

'Strong and silent,' said Katie, and they started to giggle again.

'He's only silent because he's too thick to string two words together,' said Fred impatiently. 'I don't know why you're worried, Oliver, Hufflepuff are a pushover. Last time we played them, Harry caught the Snitch in about five minutes, remember?'

'We were playing in completely different conditions!' Wood shouted, his eyes bulging slightly. 'Diggory's put a very strong side together! He's an excellent Seeker! I was afraid you'd take it like this! We mustn't relax! We must keep our focus! Slytherin are trying to wrong-foot us! We *must* win!'

'Oliver, calm down!' said Fred, looking slightly alarmed. 'We're taking Hufflepuff very seriously. *Seriously*.'

The day before the match, the winds reached howling point and the rain fell harder than ever. It was so dark inside the corridors and classrooms that extra torches and lanterns were lit. The Slytherin team were looking very smug indeed, and none more so than Malfoy.

'Ah, if only my arm was feeling a bit better!' he sighed, as the gale outside pounded the windows.

Harry had no room in his head to worry about anything except the match next day. Oliver Wood kept hurrying up to him between classes and giving him tips. The third time this happened, Wood talked for so long that Harry suddenly realised he was ten minutes late for Defence Against the Dark Arts, and set off at a run with Wood shouting after him, 'Diggory's got a very fast swerve, Harry, so you might want to try looping him –'

Harry skidded to a halt outside the Defence Against the Dark Arts classroom, pulled the door open and dashed inside.

'Sorry I'm late, Professor Lupin, I –'

But it wasn't Professor Lupin who looked up at him from the teacher's desk; it was Snape.

'This lesson began ten minutes ago, Potter, so I think we'll make it ten points from Gryffindor. Sit down.'

But Harry didn't move.

第9章 不祥的失败

"笑什么?"伍德说,皱起眉头看着这种轻浮的行为。

"他就是那个高个儿帅哥,是不是?"安吉利娜说。

"身材结实,不爱说话。"凯蒂说,她们又咯咯地笑开了。

"他不爱说话,是因为他脑子太笨,连不成句子。"弗雷德不耐烦地说,"我不知道你担心什么,奥利弗,赫奇帕奇不过是小菜一碟。上次我们跟他们比,大约五分钟哈利就抓住了金色飞贼,记得吗?"

"那时我们是在完全不同的情况下比赛的!"伍德大声嚷道,眼珠子微微突了出来,"迪戈里组织了强大的阵容!他是个出色的找球手!恐怕你们都要认识到这一点!我们决不能放松!必须集中精力!斯莱特林想打乱我们的阵脚!我们必须获胜!"

"奥利弗,镇静!"弗雷德显得有点惊慌,说道,"我们会非常认真地对待赫奇帕奇的。非常认真。"

比赛前一天,狂风呼啸,雨下得比任何时候都猛。走廊和教室里太昏暗了,又多点了一些火把和灯笼。斯莱特林的队员都露出幸灾乐祸的表情,最得意的就数马尔福了。

"唉,但愿我的胳膊能感觉好一点儿!"他叹着气说,外面狂风撞击着窗户。

哈利满脑子都想着第二天的比赛,没有心思考虑其他的事。奥利弗·伍德总是在课间跑过来找他,给他支招儿。第三次发生这种情况时,伍德说话时间太长,哈利突然意识到黑魔法防御术课已经开始十分钟了,赶紧拔腿就跑,伍德还在后面大喊:"迪戈里转身特别快,哈利,所以你必须想办法缠住他——"

哈利在黑魔法防御术课教室外面刹住脚步,拉开门,冲了进去。

"对不起,我迟到了,卢平教授,我——"

然而,在讲台上抬眼望着他的不是卢平教授,而是斯内普。

"这堂课十分钟以前就开始了,波特,所以我认为应该给格兰芬多扣掉十分。坐下。"

哈利没有动弹。

CHAPTER NINE   Grim Defeat

'Where's Professor Lupin?' he said.

'He says he is feeling too ill to teach today,' said Snape with a twisted smile. 'I believe I told you to sit down?'

But Harry stayed where he was.

'What's wrong with him?'

Snape's black eyes glittered.

'Nothing life-threatening,' he said, looking as though he wished it was. 'Five more points from Gryffindor, and if I have to ask you to sit down again, it will be fifty.'

Harry walked slowly to his seat and sat down. Snape looked around at the class.

'As I was saying before Potter interrupted, Professor Lupin has not left any record of the topics you have covered so far –'

'Please, sir, we've done Boggarts, Red Caps, Kappas and Grindylows,' said Hermione quickly, 'and we're just about to start –'

'Be quiet,' said Snape coldly. 'I did not ask for information. I was merely commenting on Professor Lupin's lack of organisation.'

'He's the best Defence Against the Dark Arts teacher we've ever had,' said Dean Thomas boldly, and there was a murmur of agreement from the rest of the class. Snape looked more menacing than ever.

'You are easily satisfied. Lupin is hardly over-taxing you – I would expect first-years to be able to deal with Red Caps and Grindylows. Today we shall discuss –'

Harry watched him flick through the textbook, to the very back chapter, which he must know they hadn't covered.

'– werewolves,' said Snape.

'But, sir,' said Hermione, seemingly unable to restrain herself, 'we're not supposed to do werewolves yet, we're due to start Hinkypunks –'

'Miss Granger,' said Snape, in a voice of deadly calm, 'I was under the impression that I was taking this lesson, not you. And I am telling you all to turn to page three hundred and ninety-four.' He glanced around again. '*All* of you! *Now!*'

With many bitter sidelong looks and some sullen muttering, the class opened their books.

'Which of you can tell me how we distinguish between the werewolf and

第9章 不祥的失败

"卢平教授呢？"他问。

"他说他今天很不舒服，不能来上课了。"斯内普狞笑着说，"我好像叫你坐下的吧？"

可哈利还是待在原地没动。

"他怎么啦？"

斯内普的黑眼睛闪闪发亮。

"没有生命危险。"他说，看他的神情，似乎希望有生命危险似的，"格兰芬多再扣五分，如果我必须第三遍叫你坐下，就扣五十分。"

哈利慢慢走向自己的座位，坐了下来。斯内普环视着全班同学。

"在波特打断我之前，我说到关于你们所学过的内容，卢平教授没有留下任何记录——"

"对不起，先生，我们学了博格特、红帽子、卡巴和格林迪洛，"赫敏敏捷地说，"正准备开始学——"

"安静，"斯内普冷冷地说，"我没有提问。我只是批评卢平教授的教学缺少章法。"

"他是教过我们的最棒的黑魔法防御术课老师。"迪安·托马斯大胆地说，其他同学也纷纷小声表示赞同。斯内普看上去比任何时候都更加气势汹汹。

"你们太容易满足了。卢平教授并没有给你们增加什么负担——我认为一年级学生就应该有能力对付红帽子和格林迪洛了。今天我们要讨论——"

哈利注视着他哗哗地翻课本，一直翻到最后一章，他知道他们肯定还没有学到。

"——狼人。"斯内普说。

"可是，先生，"赫敏似乎没法控制自己了，说道，"我们还不该学习狼人呢，现在应该开始学欣克庞克——"

"格兰杰小姐，"斯内普用一种平静得令人恐惧的声音说道，"我好像记得教这堂课的是我，不是你。现在我叫你们所有的人都把书翻到第 394 页。"他又扫了一眼全班同学，"所有的人！快！"

同学们愤愤不平地翻着白眼，一边小声嘀咕，一边翻开课本。

the true wolf?' said Snape.

Everyone sat in motionless silence; everyone except Hermione, whose hand, as it so often did, had shot straight into the air.

'Anyone?' Snape said, ignoring Hermione. His twisted smile was back. 'Are you telling me that Professor Lupin hasn't even taught you the basic distinction between –'

'We told you,' said Parvati suddenly, 'we haven't got as far as werewolves yet, we're still on –'

'*Silence*!' snarled Snape. 'Well, well, well, I never thought I'd meet a third-year class who wouldn't even recognise a werewolf when they saw one. I shall make a point of informing Professor Dumbledore how very behind you all are …'

'Please, sir,' said Hermione, whose hand was still in the air, 'the werewolf differs from the true wolf in several small ways. The snout of the werewolf –'

'That is the second time you have spoken out of turn, Miss Granger,' said Snape coolly. 'Five more points from Gryffindor for being an insufferable know-it-all.'

Hermione went very red, put down her hand and stared at the floor with her eyes full of tears. It was a mark of how much the class loathed Snape that they were all glaring at him, because every one of them had called Hermione a know-it-all at least once, and Ron, who told Hermione she was a know-it-all at least twice a week, said loudly, 'You asked us a question and she knows the answer! Why ask if you don't want to be told?'

The class knew instantly he'd gone too far. Snape advanced on Ron slowly, and the room held its breath.

'Detention, Weasley,' Snape said silkily, his face very close to Ron's. 'And if I ever hear you criticise the way I teach a class again, you will be very sorry indeed.'

No one made a sound throughout the rest of the lesson. They sat and made notes on werewolves from the textbook, while Snape prowled up and down the rows of desks, examining the work they had been doing with Professor Lupin.

'Very poorly explained … that is incorrect, the Kappa is more commonly found in Mongolia … Professor Lupin gave this eight out of ten? I wouldn't have given it three …'

第9章 不祥的失败

"你们有谁能告诉我，如何区别狼人和真狼？"斯内普问。

大家都一动不动、一言不发地坐着，只有赫敏例外，她又像往常那样，忽地把手举得老高。

"谁能回答？"斯内普没有理睬赫敏，继续问道，脸上又露出了那种狞笑，"难道你们是说，卢平教授没有告诉你们这两者的根本差别——"

"我们跟你说了，"帕瓦蒂突然说道，"狼人那一章还没有学到呢，我们还在学——"

"安静！"斯内普恶声恶气地说，"是啊，是啊，是啊，真想不到，我居然会遇到一班见到狼人都认不出来的三年级学生。我必须跟邓布利多教授说说你们落后了多少……"

"拜托，先生，"赫敏仍然把手举得高高的，说，"狼人与真狼在几个小地方存在差别。狼人的口鼻部——"

"这是你第二次擅自发言，格兰杰小姐。"斯内普冷冷地说，"因为一个令人无法容忍的万事通，格兰芬多再扣五分。"

赫敏脸涨得通红，把手放了下来，眼泪汪汪地盯着地面。全班同学都气呼呼地瞪着斯内普，这足以说明大家有多恨他，因为其实同学们都叫过赫敏"万事通"，每人至少一次。罗恩呢，一星期至少会说赫敏两回"万事通"，此刻他却大声说道："你提了一个问题，她知道答案！如果你不要人回答，干吗要问呢？"

全班同学立刻知道罗恩越界了。斯内普慢慢地向罗恩走去，同学们都屏住了呼吸。

"关禁闭，韦斯莱！"斯内普把脸凑近罗恩的脸，柔声细语地说，"如果我再听见你对我的教学方式提出批评，你可就后悔也来不及了。"

接下来的课上，谁也不敢出声了。他们坐在那里，从书上抄写有关狼人的笔记，斯内普在课桌间来回巡视，检查卢平教授布置他们做的功课。

"解释得很不清楚……说得不准确，卡巴在蒙古更为常见……卢平教授还给了八分？我连三分都不会给……"

CHAPTER NINE Grim Defeat

When the bell rang at last, Snape held them back.

'You will each write an essay, to be handed in to me, on the ways you recognise and kill werewolves. I want two rolls of parchment on the subject, and I want them by Monday morning. It is time somebody took this class in hand. Weasley, stay behind, we need to arrange your detention.'

Harry and Hermione left the room with the rest of the class, who waited until they were well out of earshot, then burst into a furious tirade about Snape.

'Snape's never been like this with any of our other Defence Against the Dark Arts teachers, even if he did want the job,' Harry said to Hermione. 'Why's he got it in for Lupin? D'you think this is all because of the Boggart?'

'I don't know,' said Hermione pensively. 'But I really hope Professor Lupin gets better soon ...'

Ron caught up with them five minutes later, in a towering rage.

'D'you know what that –' (he called Snape something that made Hermione say '*Ron!*') '– is making me do? I've got to scrub out the bedpans in the hospital wing. *Without magic!*' He was breathing deeply, his fists clenched. 'Why couldn't Black have hidden in Snape's office, eh? He could have finished him off for us!'

Harry woke extremely early next morning; so early that it was still dark. For a moment he thought the roaring of the wind had woken him, then he felt a cold breeze on the back of his neck and sat bolt upright – Peeves the poltergeist had been floating next to him, blowing hard in his ear.

'What did you do that for?' said Harry furiously.

Peeves puffed out his cheeks, blew hard and zoomed backwards out of the room, cackling.

Harry fumbled for his alarm clock and looked at it. It was half past four. Cursing Peeves, he rolled over and tried to get back to sleep, but it was very difficult, now he was awake, to ignore the sounds of the thunder rumbling overhead, the pounding of the wind against the castle walls and the distant creaking of the trees in the Forbidden Forest. In a few hours he would be out on the Quidditch pitch, battling through that gale. Finally he gave up any thought of more sleep, got up, dressed, picked up his Nimbus Two Thousand and walked quietly out of the dormitory.

第9章 不祥的失败

下课铃终于响了，但斯内普没让他们离开。

"每人写一篇论文交给我，内容是如何识别和杀死狼人。我要求你们就这个题目写满两卷羊皮纸，星期一早晨交。这个班需要有人好好管管了。韦斯莱，你先别走，我们需要安排一下关你禁闭的事。"

哈利和赫敏跟其他同学一起离开了教室，同学们都忍着怒气，等走到斯内普听不见的地方，才开始七嘴八舌地激烈声讨斯内普。

"斯内普从来没有这样对待过我们的另外几个黑魔法防御术课老师，虽然他很想得到这份工作，"哈利对赫敏说，"他为什么要跟卢平过不去呢？你说，难道是因为那次博格特的事吗？"

"不知道，"赫敏忧心忡忡地说，"我真希望卢平教授能赶快好起来……"

五分钟后，罗恩追了上来，气得不得了。

"你们知道那个……"（他骂了斯内普一句难听的话，惊得赫敏喊了声"罗恩！"）"要我干什么吗？要我擦洗医院的便盆。还不许用魔法！"他呼呼直喘粗气，两个拳头捏得紧紧的，"为什么布莱克不能藏在斯内普的办公室里呢，嗯？他可以替我们干掉他！"

第二天，哈利醒得特别早，天还没有亮。起初，他以为是狂风呼啸把他给惊醒了，接着感到一股凉风吹到脖子后面，他腾地坐得笔直——恶作剧精灵皮皮鬼在他身旁飘来飘去，正使劲儿往他耳朵里吹气。

"你这是干什么？"哈利气愤地问。

皮皮鬼鼓起腮帮子用力一吹，然后嗖地蹿出房间，一边咯咯狂笑着。

哈利摸到闹钟看了看，才凌晨四点半。他心里骂着皮皮鬼，翻了个身想接着睡，可是现在醒了，就很难不去理会头顶上闷雷滚滚、狂风撞击城堡墙壁，以及远处禁林里树枝嘎嘎折断的声音。再过几个小时，他就要在外面的魁地奇球场跟这狂风暴雨搏斗了。最后，他不再指望自己能重新入睡，起身穿好衣服，拿起他的光轮2000，悄没声儿地离开了宿舍。

CHAPTER NINE — Grim Defeat

As Harry opened the door, something brushed against his leg. He bent down just in time to grab Crookshanks by the end of his bushy tail, and drag him outside.

'You know, I reckon Ron was right about you,' Harry told Crookshanks suspiciously. 'There are plenty of mice around this place, go and chase them. Go on,' he added, nudging Crookshanks down the spiral staircase with his foot, 'leave Scabbers alone.'

The noise of the storm was even louder in the common room. Harry knew better than to think the match would be cancelled; Quidditch matches weren't called off for trifles such as thunderstorms. Nevertheless, he was starting to feel very apprehensive. Wood had pointed out Cedric Diggory to him in the corridor; Diggory was a fifth-year and a lot bigger than Harry. Seekers were usually light and speedy, but Diggory's weight would be an advantage in this weather because he was less likely to be blown off course.

Harry whiled away the hours until dawn in front of the fire, getting up every now and then to stop Crookshanks sneaking up the boys' staircase again. At long last Harry thought it must be time for breakfast, so he headed through the portrait hole alone.

'Stand and fight, you mangy cur!' yelled Sir Cadogan.

'Oh, shut up,' Harry yawned.

He revived a bit over a large bowl of porridge, and by the time he'd started on toast, the rest of the team had turned up.

'It's going to be a tough one,' said Wood, who wasn't eating anything.

'Stop worrying, Oliver,' said Alicia soothingly, 'we don't mind a bit of rain.'

But it was considerably more than a bit of rain. Such was the popularity of Quidditch that the whole school turned out to watch the match as usual, but they ran down the lawns towards the Quidditch pitch, heads bowed against the ferocious wind, umbrellas being whipped out of their hands as they went. Just before he entered the changing room, Harry saw Malfoy, Crabbe and Goyle laughing and pointing at him from under an enormous umbrella on their way to the stadium.

The team changed into their scarlet robes and waited for Wood's usual pre-match pep talk, but it didn't come. He tried to speak several times, made an odd gulping noise, then shook his head hopelessly and beckoned them to follow him.

第9章 不祥的失败

哈利刚把门打开,就感到有什么东西蹭了他的腿。他赶紧一弯腰,正好抓住克鲁克山毛茸茸的尾巴尖儿,把它拖到了外面。

"告诉你,我觉得罗恩对你的看法是对的。"哈利怀疑地对克鲁克山说,"这地方有不少老鼠,快去捉它们。快去,"说着,他用脚把克鲁克山往旋转楼梯下面推,"别来找斑斑的麻烦。"

到了公共休息室,风暴的声音更响了。哈利心里很清楚比赛不会被取消。魁地奇比赛是不会因为雷电风暴这样的小事而取消的。尽管如此,他还是开始感到忧心忡忡。伍德曾经在走廊里把塞德里克·迪戈里指给他看过。迪戈里是五年级学生,个头比哈利大得多。找球手一般体格轻盈,身手敏捷,但是在这种天气里,迪戈里的体重倒成了一种优势,他不大容易被风刮得东倒西歪。

哈利在炉火前消磨时间,等待天亮,时不时地起身阻止克鲁克山再次溜上男生宿舍的楼梯。好不容易,他觉得吃早饭的时间肯定到了,就独自钻出了肖像洞口。

"站住,决斗吧,你这条癞皮狗!"卡多根爵士嚷道。

"哦,闭嘴吧。"哈利打着哈欠说。

他吃了一大碗粥,感到振作了一些。开始吃面包时,其他队员也来了。

"肯定是一场恶战。"伍德说,他什么也没吃。

"别担心,奥利弗,"艾丽娅安慰他说,"我们不在乎这点毛毛雨。"

然而这绝不是一点毛毛雨。魁地奇运动特别受欢迎,全校师生都像平常一样出来观看比赛。他们顺着草坪朝球场跑去,低着头抵挡剧烈的狂风,因为半路上手里的雨伞被风刮跑了。哈利刚要走进更衣室,就看见马尔福、克拉布和高尔撑着一把大伞朝露天体育场走去,一边对着他指指点点,哈哈大笑。

队员们换上深红色的队袍,等着伍德像往常一样给他们做赛前讲话,可是没有等到。伍德试了几次,却只发出一种古怪的哽咽声,便无奈地摇摇头,示意他们跟着他走。

CHAPTER NINE   Grim Defeat

The wind was so strong that they staggered sideways as they walked out onto the pitch. If the crowd was cheering they couldn't hear it over the fresh rolls of thunder. Rain was splattering over Harry's glasses. How on earth was he going to see the Snitch in this?

The Hufflepuffs were approaching from the opposite side of the pitch, wearing canary-yellow robes. The captains walked up to each other and shook hands; Diggory smiled at Wood but Wood now looked as though he had lockjaw and merely nodded. Harry saw Madam Hooch's mouth form the words, 'Mount your brooms.' He pulled his right foot out of the mud with a squelch and swung it over his Nimbus Two Thousand. Madam Hooch put her whistle to her lips and gave it a blast that sounded shrill and distant – they were off.

Harry rose fast, but his Nimbus was swerving slightly with the wind. He held it as steady as he could and turned, squinting into the rain.

Within five minutes Harry was soaked to his skin and frozen, hardly able to see his team-mates, let alone the tiny Snitch. He flew backwards and forwards across the pitch, past blurred red and yellow shapes, with no idea of what was happening in the rest of the game. He couldn't hear the commentary over the wind. The crowd was hidden beneath a sea of cloaks and battered umbrellas. Twice Harry came very close to being unseated by a Bludger; his vision was so clouded by the rain on his glasses he hadn't seen them coming.

He lost track of time. It was getting harder and harder to hold his broom straight. The sky was getting darker, as though night had decided to come early. Twice Harry nearly hit another player, without knowing whether it was a team-mate or opponent; everyone was now so wet, and the rain so thick, he could hardly tell them apart ...

With the first flash of lightning came the sound of Madam Hooch's whistle; Harry could just see the outline of Wood through the thick rain, gesturing him to the ground. The whole team splashed down into the mud.

'I called for time out!' Wood roared at his team. 'Come on, under here –'

They huddled at the edge of the pitch under a large umbrella; Harry took off his glasses and wiped them hurriedly on his robes.

'What's the score?'

'We're fifty points up,' said Wood, 'but unless we get the Snitch soon, we'll be playing into the night.'

'I've got no chance with these on,' Harry said exasperatedly, waving his glasses.

第9章 不祥的失败

风刮得太猛了,他们向球场走去时被刮得左右摇晃。又是一阵滚滚雷声,即使观众在欢呼喝彩,他们也不可能听见。雨水打在哈利的眼镜上。这种状况下,他怎么可能看见金色飞贼呢?

赫奇帕奇队员穿着淡黄色的队袍,从球场对面走来。两位队长走到一起,互相握手。迪戈里朝伍德微笑,可是伍德像患了破伤风一样牙关紧闭,只是点了点头。哈利看见霍琦女士的嘴在说"骑上扫帚"。他叽咕一声把右脚从烂泥浆里拔出来,跨上他的光轮2000。霍琦女士把哨子塞到唇间吹了一下,声音尖细,像是从远处传来——比赛开始了。

哈利迅速上升,可是他的光轮在风里拐来拐去。他尽量稳住扫帚,转了个身,眯起眼睛看着雨中。

短短五分钟,哈利就淋得透湿,全身都冻僵了。他几乎看不见他的队友,更不用说小小的飞贼了。他在球场上空来回穿梭,身边掠过一些红色或黄色的人影,根本不知道比赛打得怎么样了。风声呼啸,他听不清评论。人群隐藏在一片密密麻麻的斗篷和破雨伞底下。有两次,哈利差点儿被游走球撞得摔下扫帚。镜片上的雨水使他眼前一片模糊,所以他没看见向他飞来的游走球。

他也不知道比赛进行了多久。抓牢扫帚变得越来越难。天空昏暗,似乎夜晚决定提前到来。哈利有两次险些撞上另一位球员,也不知是队友还是对手。每个人都像落汤鸡,雨又这么大,他很难分得清……

随着第一道闪电划过,传来霍琦女士的哨声。隔着厚厚的雨帘,哈利只能看见伍德的轮廓,伍德示意他降到地面。噼里啪啦,队员们全都落在烂泥地上。

"我叫了暂停!"伍德冲他的队员吼道,"快,到这底下来——"

他们挤在球场边的一把大伞下。哈利摘下眼镜,用袍子匆匆擦着。

"比分怎么样了?"

"我们领先五十分,"伍德说,"但除非很快抓住飞贼,不然比到入夜也比不完。"

"戴着这副眼镜,我是没指望了。"哈利挥着眼镜,绝望地说。

CHAPTER NINE   Grim Defeat

At that very moment, Hermione appeared at his shoulder; she was holding her cloak over her head and was, inexplicably, beaming.

'I've had an idea, Harry! Give me your glasses, quick!'

He handed them to her and, as the team watched in amazement, Hermione tapped them with her wand and said, '*Impervius!*'

'There!' she said, handing them back to Harry. 'They'll repel water!'

Wood looked as though he could have kissed her.

'Brilliant!' he called hoarsely after her, as she disappeared into the crowd. 'OK, team, let's go for it!'

Hermione's spell had done the trick. Harry was still numb with cold, still wetter than he'd ever been in his life, but he could see. Full of fresh determination, he urged his broom through the turbulent air, staring in every direction for the Snitch, avoiding a Bludger, ducking beneath Diggory, who was streaking in the opposite direction ...

There was another clap of thunder, followed immediately by forked lightning. This was getting more and more dangerous. Harry needed to get the Snitch quickly –

He turned, intending to head back towards the middle of the pitch, but at that moment, another flash of lightning illuminated the stands, and Harry saw something that distracted him completely: the silhouette of an enormous shaggy black dog, clearly imprinted against the sky, motionless in the topmost, empty row of seats.

Harry's numb hands slipped on the broom handle and his Nimbus dropped a few feet. Shaking his sodden fringe out of his eyes, he squinted back into the stands. The dog had vanished.

'Harry!' came Wood's anguished yell from the Gryffindor goalposts. 'Harry, behind you!'

Harry looked wildly around. Cedric Diggory was pelting up the pitch, and a tiny speck of gold was shimmering in the rain-filled air between them ...

With a jolt of panic, Harry threw himself flat to the broom handle and zoomed towards the Snitch.

'Come on!' he growled at his Nimbus, as the rain whipped his face. '*Faster!*'

But something odd was happening. An eerie silence was falling across the stadium. The wind, though as strong as ever, was forgetting to roar. It was as though someone had turned off the sound, as though Harry had gone suddenly deaf – what was going on?

第9章 不祥的失败

就在这时，赫敏出现在他身边，她用斗篷遮住脑袋，不知为什么满脸笑眯眯的。

"我有一个主意，哈利！把眼镜给我，快！"

哈利把眼镜递给了赫敏。在队员们惊异的注视下，赫敏用魔杖轻轻敲了敲眼镜，说了声："防水防湿！"

"给！"说着，她把眼镜还给了哈利，"现在不怕水了！"

伍德看样子简直要上去吻她了。

"太精彩了！"赫敏跑回人群时，伍德冲着她的背影用沙哑的声音喊道，"好了，全体队员，上吧！"

赫敏的咒语真灵验。哈利虽然还是冻得全身发僵，比以前任何时候都湿得更透，但是他能看见了。他重新下定决心，驾着扫帚在狂风骤雨中穿梭，四处张望着寻找飞贼。他躲过一只游走球，又一猫腰从迎面飞来的迪戈里身下穿过……

又是一声霹雳，紧接着是之字形的闪电。情况越来越危险了。哈利必须赶快抓到飞贼——

他转过身，打算返回球场中央。这时又是一道闪电照亮了看台，哈利看见了什么，注意力被分散了：一条毛发蓬乱的大黑狗的轮廓，被天空衬托得十分清晰，就在最上面那排空座位上。

哈利冻僵的手在扫帚把上滑了一下，光轮2000下坠了几英尺。他甩掉挡住眼睛的湿漉漉的刘海，再次眯眼朝看台上望去。那条狗消失了。

"哈利！"格兰芬多球门那儿传来伍德痛苦的喊叫，"哈利，在你后面！"

哈利赶紧回头张望。塞德里克·迪戈里迅速飞过球场，在他们俩之间的大雨中，闪着一个金灿灿的小点……

哈利紧张得一个激灵，扑倒在扫帚把上，朝飞贼嗖地直冲过去。

"快！"他对他的光轮吼道，大雨啪啪地打在他脸上，"再快点儿！"

然而一件奇怪的事出现了。整个体育场里掠过一片诡异的寂静。风虽然还是那样猛烈，却忘了发出怒吼，就好像有人关掉了音量，就好像哈利突然变成了聋子——怎么回事？

CHAPTER NINE Grim Defeat

And then a horribly familiar wave of cold swept over him, inside him, just as he became aware of something moving on the pitch below ...

Before he'd had time to think, Harry had taken his eyes off the Snitch and looked down.

At least a hundred Dementors, their hidden faces pointing up at him, were standing below. It was as though freezing water was rising in his chest, cutting at his insides. And then he heard it again ... someone was screaming, screaming inside his head ... a woman ...

'*Not Harry, not Harry, please not Harry!*'

'*Stand aside, you silly girl ... stand aside, now ...*'

'*Not Harry, please no, take me, kill me instead —*'

Numbing, swirling white mist was filling Harry's brain ... What was he doing? Why was he flying? He needed to help her ... she was going to die ... she was going to be murdered ...

He was falling, falling through the icy mist.

'*Not Harry! Please ... have mercy ... have mercy ...*'

A shrill voice was laughing, the woman was screaming, and Harry knew no more.

'Lucky the ground was so soft.'

'I thought he was dead for sure.'

'But he didn't even break his glasses.'

Harry could hear the voices whispering, but they made no sense whatsoever. He didn't have a clue where he was, or how he'd got there, or what he'd been doing before he got there. All he knew was that every inch of him was aching as though it had been beaten.

'That was the scariest thing I've ever seen in my life.'

Scariest ... the scariest thing ... hooded black figures ... cold ... screaming ...

Harry's eyes snapped open. He was lying in the hospital wing. The Gryffindor Quidditch team, spattered with mud from head to foot, was gathered around his bed. Ron and Hermione were also there, looking as though they'd just climbed out of a swimming pool.

'Harry!' said Fred, who looked extremely white underneath the mud. 'How're you feeling?'

It was as though Harry's memory was on fast forward. The lightning ...

第9章 不祥的失败

随后，一股熟悉得可怕的寒意朝他袭来，侵入他的体内，同时他意识到下面球场上有东西在动——

他没有来得及思考，就把目光从飞贼上挪开，朝下面望去……

至少有一百个摄魂怪站在下面，那些隐藏的脸全都抬起来望着他。似乎有冰冷的水涌上了他的胸膛，切割着他的内脏。接着，他又听见了……有人在尖叫，在他脑海里尖叫……是一个女人……

"别碰哈利，别碰哈利，求求你别碰哈利！"

"闪开，你这个蠢女人……快给我闪开……"

"别碰哈利，求求你，杀我吧，把我杀了吧——"

缭绕的白雾在哈利脑海里弥漫，使他变得麻木……他在做什么？他为什么要飞？他必须去帮助她……她就要死了……她就要被杀死了……

他坠落下去，落进了寒冷刺骨的迷雾。

"别碰哈利！求求你……发发慈悲……发发慈悲吧……"

一个刺耳的声音在狂笑，一个女人在尖叫，哈利什么也不知道了。

"幸亏地面那么软。"

"我还以为他肯定死了呢。"

"没想到他连眼镜都没摔碎。"

哈利听见人们在窃窃私语，但不明白他们在说些什么。他不知道自己在哪儿，也不知道是怎么到这儿来的，来之前在做什么。他只知道身上没有一处不疼，好像遭了毒打似的。

"这是我这一辈子见过的最可怕的事情。"

最可怕的……最可怕的事情……戴着兜帽的黑影……寒冷……尖叫……

哈利猛地睁开眼睛。他躺在医院里。格兰芬多魁地奇球队的队员们围在他的床边，从头到脚都沾着泥浆。罗恩和赫敏也在，那模样就像刚从游泳池里爬出来的。

"哈利！"弗雷德说，泥浆下面的脸显得格外苍白，"你感觉怎么样？"

哈利的记忆似乎在迅速跳跃。闪电……不祥……金色飞贼……摄

CHAPTER NINE   Grim Defeat

the Grim ... the Snitch ... and the Dementors ...

'What happened?' he said, sitting up so suddenly they all gasped.

'You fell off,' said Fred. 'Must've been – what – fifty feet?'

'We thought you'd died,' said Alicia, who was shaking.

Hermione made a small, squeaky noise. Her eyes were extremely bloodshot.

'But the match,' said Harry. 'What happened? Are we having a replay?'

No one said anything. The horrible truth sank into Harry like a stone.

'We didn't – *lose?*'

'Diggory got the Snitch,' said George. 'Just after you fell. He didn't realise what had happened. When he looked back and saw you on the ground, he tried to call it off. Wanted a re-match. But they won fair and square ... even Wood admits it.'

'Where is Wood?' said Harry, suddenly realising he wasn't there.

'Still in the showers,' said Fred. 'We think he's trying to drown himself.'

Harry put his face to his knees, his hands gripping his hair. Fred grabbed his shoulder and shook it roughly.

'C'mon, Harry, you've never missed the Snitch before.'

'There had to be one time you didn't get it,' said George.

'It's not over yet,' said Fred. 'We lost by a hundred points, right? So if Hufflepuff lose to Ravenclaw and we beat Ravenclaw and Slytherin ...'

'Hufflepuff'll have to lose by at least two hundred points,' said George.

'But if they beat Ravenclaw ...'

'No way, Ravenclaw are too good. But if Slytherin lose against Hufflepuff ...'

'It all depends on the points – a margin of a hundred either way –'

Harry lay there, not saying a word. They had lost ... for the first time ever, he had lost a Quidditch match.

After ten minutes or so, Madam Pomfrey came over to tell the team to leave him in peace.

'We'll come and see you later,' Fred told him. 'Don't beat yourself up, Harry, you're still the best Seeker we've ever had.'

The team trooped out, trailing mud behind them. Madam Pomfrey shut the door behind them, looking disapproving. Ron and Hermione moved nearer to Harry's bed.

第 9 章 不祥的失败

魂怪……

"出什么事了？"他腾地坐了起来，把大家都吓了一跳。

"你摔下来了，"弗雷德说，"准有——多少来着——五十英尺吧？"

"我们还以为你死了呢。"艾丽娅发着抖说。

赫敏发出一个短促的小声音，眼睛又红又肿。

"可是比赛，"哈利说，"怎么样了？我们还能重赛吗？"

谁也没有说话。可怕的事实像石头一样，沉入哈利心中。

"我们没有——输吧？"

"迪戈里抓到了飞贼，"乔治说，"就在你摔下来之后。他不知道发生了什么事。他一回头，看见你摔在地上，便想叫暂停，希望来一次复赛。可是他们赢得公平，赢得光明正大……就连伍德也承认。"

"伍德呢？"哈利突然发现伍德不在，问道。

"还在浴室呢，"弗雷德说，"我们认为他想把自己淹死。"

哈利把脸埋在两个膝盖之间，用手揪着头发。弗雷德抓住他的肩膀，粗暴地摇了摇。

"行啦，哈利，你以前从没漏掉过飞贼。"

"你总得有一次抓不住吧。"乔治说。

"还不算完呢，"弗雷德说，"我们输了一百分，对吗？所以只有赫奇帕奇输给拉文克劳，我们再打败了拉文克劳和斯莱特林……"

"赫奇帕奇必须至少输二百分。"乔治说。

"但如果他们打败了拉文克劳……"

"不可能，拉文克劳太厉害了。但如果斯莱特林输给了赫奇帕奇……"

"要看比分——输赢都差一百分——"

哈利躺在那里，一句话也没说。他们输了……第一次，他输了魁地奇比赛。

大约十分钟之后，庞弗雷女士过来叫队员们离开，让哈利休息。

"我们以后再来看你，"弗雷德对他说，"别自责啦，你仍然是我们遇到过的最棒的找球手。"

队员们排着队出去了，留下一串泥迹。他们走后，庞弗雷女士关上房门，显出很不满的样子。罗恩和赫敏走近哈利的床边。

CHAPTER NINE Grim Defeat

'Dumbledore was really angry,' Hermione said in a quaking voice. 'I've never seen him like that before. He ran onto the pitch as you fell, waved his wand, and you sort of slowed down before you hit the ground. Then he whirled his wand at the Dementors. Shot silver stuff at them. They left the stadium straight away ... he was furious they'd come into the grounds, we heard him –'

'Then he magicked you onto a stretcher,' said Ron. 'And walked up to school with you floating on it. Everyone thought you were ...'

His voice faded away, but Harry hardly noticed. He was thinking about what the Dementors had done to him ... about the screaming voice. He looked up and saw Ron and Hermione looking at him so anxiously that he quickly cast around for something matter-of-fact to say.

'Did someone get my Nimbus?'

Ron and Hermione looked quickly at each other.

'Er –'

'What?' said Harry, looking from one to the other.

'Well ... when you fell off, it got blown away,' said Hermione hesitantly.

'And?'

'And it hit – it hit – oh, Harry – it hit the Whomping Willow.'

Harry's insides lurched. The Whomping Willow was a very violent tree which stood alone in the middle of the grounds.

'And?' he said, dreading the answer.

'Well, you know the Whomping Willow,' said Ron. 'It – it doesn't like being hit.'

'Professor Flitwick brought it back just before you came round,' said Hermione in a very small voice.

Slowly, she reached down for a bag at her feet, turned it upside-down and tipped a dozen bits of splintered wood and twig onto the bed, the only remains of Harry's faithful, finally beaten broomstick.

第9章 不祥的失败

"邓布利多气坏了,"赫敏用颤抖的声音说,"我以前从没见过他那个样子。你摔下来时,他冲到球场上,挥舞着魔杖,你落地的速度似乎就减慢了。然后他把魔杖转向了那些摄魂怪,朝它们射出银色的东西。摄魂怪们立刻就离开了体育场……他气极了,它们居然跑进了校内,我们听见他——"

"后来他用魔法把你放到一个担架上,"罗恩说,"你在担架上飘浮着,他步行把你送到学校。大家都以为你……"

他的声音低得听不见了,可是哈利没怎么注意。他在想那些摄魂怪对他做的事情……在想那尖叫的声音。他抬起目光,看见罗恩和赫敏都那样忧心忡忡地望着他,于是赶紧绞尽脑汁想一个比较平淡的话题。

"有谁拿了我的光轮吗?"

罗恩和赫敏快速交换了一下目光。

"呃——"

"怎么啦?"哈利看看这个,又看看那个,问道。

"是这样……你摔下来的时候,它被风刮跑了。"赫敏犹犹豫豫地说。

"后来呢?"

"后来撞在——撞在——哦,哈利——撞在了那棵打人柳上。"

哈利的内脏都抽紧了。打人柳是一棵非常凶狠的树,孤零零地伫立在场地中央。

"后来呢?"他问,却又害怕听到回答。

"唉,你知道那棵打人柳,"罗恩说,"它——它可不喜欢被撞的滋味。"

"就在你苏醒前,弗立维教授刚把它送回来。"赫敏用很小的声音说。

她慢慢地俯身拿起脚边的一个口袋,把它倒过来,十几块碎木片和细枝落在床上,这就是哈利那把忠诚的、最终被打烂的飞天扫帚的残骸。

CHAPTER TEN

The Marauder's Map

Madam Pomfrey insisted on keeping Harry in the hospital wing for the rest of the weekend. He didn't argue or complain, but he wouldn't let her throw away the shattered remnants of his Nimbus Two Thousand. He knew he was being stupid, knew that the Nimbus was beyond repair, but Harry couldn't help it; he felt as though he'd lost one of his best friends.

He had a stream of visitors, all intent on cheering him up. Hagrid sent him a bunch of earwiggy flowers that looked like yellow cabbages and Ginny Weasley, blushing furiously, turned up with a 'get well' card she had made herself, which sang shrilly unless Harry kept it shut under his bowl of fruit. The Gryffindor team visited again on Sunday morning, this time accompanied by Wood, who told Harry, in a hollow, dead sort of voice, that he didn't blame him in the slightest. Ron and Hermione only left Harry's bedside at night. But nothing anyone said or did could make Harry feel any better, because they only knew half of what was troubling him.

He hadn't told anyone about the Grim, not even Ron and Hermione, because he knew Ron would panic and Hermione would scoff. The fact remained, however, that it had now appeared twice, and both appearances had been followed by near-fatal accidents; the first time, he had nearly been run over by the Knight Bus; the second, fallen fifty feet from his broomstick. Was the Grim going to haunt him until he actually died? Was he going to spend the rest of his life looking over his shoulder for the beast?

And then there were the Dementors. Harry felt sick and humiliated every time he thought of them. Everyone said the Dementors were horrible, but no one else collapsed every time they went near one ... no one else heard echoes in their head of their dying parents.

第 10 章

活点地图

庞弗雷女士坚持周末把哈利留在校医院，哈利没有争辩也没有抱怨，但就是不肯让她扔掉光轮 2000 的残骸。他知道这是犯傻，也知道光轮 2000 修不好了。但哈利控制不了自己，觉得像是失去了最好的朋友。

来看他的人络绎不绝，都一门心思要逗他开心。海格捎来了一束长满了地蜈蚣的花，看上去像黄色的卷心菜；金妮·韦斯莱满面绯红，带来了一张她自制的祝愿康复卡，那张卡一直尖声尖气地唱个不停，哈利只好用装水果的钵子把它压住。格兰芬多球队的队员星期天早上又来探望他，这次伍德也来了，用一种空洞、沉闷的声音说他一点也不怪哈利。罗恩和赫敏只有晚上才会离开哈利床边——然而，不管别人说什么或做什么，都无法让哈利感觉好一点，因为他们对于他的烦恼只了解一半。

他没有对任何人提起"不祥"，对罗恩和赫敏都没有，因为他知道罗恩会惊慌失措，赫敏会嗤之以鼻。但实际情况是，不祥已经出现了两次，而且随后都发生了近乎致命的事故。第一次他差点被骑士公共汽车撞死，第二次从飞天扫帚上坠落五十英尺。不祥会不会一直尾随着他，直到他真的一命呜呼呢？他是不是整个余生一直都要提防这头畜生呢？

还有摄魂怪。哈利每次想到它们就觉得恶心和耻辱。人人都说摄魂怪很恐怖，但别人靠近它们时都没有晕倒……别人也没有在脑子里听到死去的爸爸妈妈的声音。

CHAPTER TEN — The Marauder's Map

For Harry knew who that screaming voice belonged to now. He had heard her words, heard them over and over again during the night hours in the hospital wing while he lay awake, staring at the strips of moonlight on the ceiling. When the Dementors approached him, he heard the last moments of his mother's life, her attempts to protect him, Harry, from Lord Voldemort, and Voldemort's laughter before he murdered her ... Harry dozed fitfully, sinking into dreams full of clammy, rotted hands and petrified pleading, jerking awake only to dwell again on the sound of his mother's voice.

It was a relief to return on Monday to the noise and bustle of the main school, where he was forced to think about other things, even if he had to endure Draco Malfoy's taunting. Malfoy was almost beside himself with glee at Gryffindor's defeat. He had finally taken off his bandages, and celebrated having the full use of both arms again by doing spirited imitations of Harry falling off his broom. Malfoy spent much of their next Potions class doing Dementor imitations across the dungeon; Ron finally cracked, flinging a large, slippery crocodile heart at Malfoy, which hit him in the face and caused Snape to take fifty points from Gryffindor.

'If Snape's taking Defence Against the Dark Arts again, I'm going off sick,' said Ron, as they headed towards Lupin's classroom after lunch. 'Check who's in there, Hermione.'

Hermione peered around the classroom door.

'It's OK!'

Professor Lupin was back at work. It certainly looked as though he had been ill. His old robes were hanging more loosely on him and there were dark shadows beneath his eyes; nevertheless, he smiled at the class as they took their seats, and they burst at once into an explosion of complaints about Snape's behaviour while Lupin had been ill.

'It's not fair, he was only filling in, why should he set us homework?'

'We don't know anything about werewolves —'

'— two rolls of parchment! '

'Did you tell Professor Snape we haven't covered them yet?' Lupin asked, frowning slightly.

The babble broke out again.

'Yes, but he said we were really behind —'

第 10 章 活点地图

哈利现在知道那尖叫声是谁的了。他听到了她说话,夜里躺在校医院时,眼睁睁地盯着天花板上的一道道月光,那声音一次次在他耳边回响。当摄魂怪靠近时,他听到了妈妈生命中最后时刻的声音,听到她试图保护他——哈利,不受伏地魔的伤害,还听到伏地魔杀害她之前的大笑……哈利迷迷糊糊,时而陷入梦境,梦中充满了冰冷黏湿、已经腐烂的手和恐惧的哀求。猛然惊醒,又听到妈妈的声音。

星期一回到喧闹而忙碌的学校,能逼着自己去想别的事情,真是一种解脱,尽管他不得不忍受德拉科·马尔福的奚落。格兰芬多失败之后,马尔福乐得几乎得意忘形。他终于拆掉了绷带,为庆祝自己又能使用两条胳膊,他一个劲儿地模仿哈利摔下扫帚的狼狈样子。在接下来的魔药课上,马尔福大部分时间都在地下教室里模仿摄魂怪;罗恩终于控制不住,朝马尔福扔了一颗巨大的、滑溜溜的鳄鱼心脏,正中他的面部。结果斯内普扣了格兰芬多五十分。

"如果斯内普再来教黑魔法防御术,我就装病逃课。"午饭后,他们朝卢平的教室走去时,罗恩说道,"看看里面是谁,赫敏。"

赫敏在教室门口张望了一下。

"这下好了!"

卢平教授回来教课了。当然他看起来好像病了一场,旧袍子更加松松垮垮,眼睛下面有暗黑的阴影;同学们就座时,他微笑地望着大家,但他们立刻爆发出一片控诉之声,七嘴八舌地抱怨卢平生病期间斯内普的行为。

"这不公平。他不过是代课,凭什么给我们布置家庭作业?"

"我们根本不知道什么狼人——"

"——两卷羊皮纸啊!"

"你们有没有告诉斯内普教授,我们还没有教到那儿?"卢平问道,微微蹙起眉头。

又是一片七嘴八舌。

"告诉了,可是他说我们落后太多了——"

CHAPTER TEN   The Marauder's Map

'– he wouldn't listen –'

'– *two rolls of parchment!*'

Professor Lupin smiled at the look of indignation on every face.

'Don't worry. I'll speak to Professor Snape. You don't have to do the essay.'

'Oh *no*,' said Hermione, looking very disappointed. 'I've already finished it!'

They had a very enjoyable lesson. Professor Lupin had brought along a glass box containing a Hinkypunk, a little one-legged creature who seemed as though he was made of wisps of smoke, rather frail and harmless-looking.

'Lures travellers into bogs,' said Professor Lupin, as they took notes. 'You notice the lantern dangling from his hand? Hops ahead – people follow the light – then –'

The Hinkypunk made a horrible squelching noise against the glass.

When the bell rang, everyone gathered up their things and headed for the door, Harry amongst them, but –

'Wait a moment, Harry,' Lupin called, 'I'd like a word.'

Harry doubled back and watched Professor Lupin covering the Hinkypunk's box with a cloth.

'I heard about the match,' said Lupin, turning back to his desk and starting to pile books into his briefcase, 'and I'm sorry about your broomstick. Is there any chance of fixing it?'

'No,' said Harry. 'The tree smashed it to bits.'

Lupin sighed.

'They planted the Whomping Willow the same year that I arrived at Hogwarts. People used to play a game, trying to get near enough to touch the trunk. In the end, a boy called Davey Gudgeon nearly lost an eye, and we were forbidden to go near it. No broomstick would have a chance.'

'Did you hear about the Dementors, too?' said Harry with difficulty.

Lupin looked at him quickly.

'Yes, I did. I don't think any of us have seen Professor Dumbledore that angry. They have been growing restless for some time ... furious at his refusal to let them inside the grounds ... I suppose they were the reason you fell?'

'Yes,' said Harry. He hesitated, and then the question he had to ask burst from him before he could stop himself. '*Why*? Why do they affect me like that? Am I just –?'

第10章 活点地图

"他不听——"

"——两卷羊皮纸啊!"

卢平教授微笑地看着每一张义愤填膺的面孔。

"别担心。我会跟斯内普谈谈。你们不用写那篇论文。"

"哦,别呀,"赫敏一脸失望地说,"我已经写完了!"

他们上了非常愉快的一堂课,卢平教授带来了一个玻璃箱,里面装着一只欣克庞克,那是一种单腿小生物,看上去像是由一缕缕烟雾组成,相当脆弱,似乎也没有什么危险。

"它会把旅行的人引入泥沼,"卢平教授说道,同学们记着笔记,"注意到它手上提的灯笼了吗?跳动前行——人们跟随亮光——然后——"

欣克庞克贴在玻璃壁上,发出可怕的、嘎吱嘎吱的声音。

下课铃响起,大家都收拾东西朝门外走去,哈利也在其中,但——

"等一等,哈利,"卢平叫道,"我想说句话。"

哈利返回来,看着卢平教授用布把欣克庞克的箱子罩上。

"我听说了比赛的事,"卢平说,转身回到讲台前,开始把书收进公文包,"很为你的飞天扫帚惋惜,有没有可能修好呢?"

"没有可能了,"哈利说,"那棵树把它打成了碎片。"

卢平叹息了一声。

"那棵打人柳是我到霍格沃茨的那一年他们栽的。人们过去经常玩一个游戏,就是设法去摸那树干。后来有个叫戴维·格杰恩的男生差点瞎了一只眼睛,学校就不许我们再靠近它了。没有一把飞天扫帚能够顶得住的。"

"你也听说摄魂怪了吗?"哈利艰难地问。

卢平迅速看了他一眼。

"听说了。我想谁都没见过邓布利多教授发那么大的火。这些家伙蠢蠢欲动有一段时间了——邓布利多拒绝允许它们进入校内,它们非常恼火……我猜它们是你摔下来的原因吧?"

"是的。"哈利说。他犹豫了一下,然后他想问的问题便忍不住脱口而出:"为什么?为什么它们会对我有那样的影响?难道我——?"

CHAPTER TEN   The Marauder's Map

'It has nothing to do with weakness,' said Professor Lupin sharply, as though he had read Harry's mind. 'The Dementors affect you worse than the others because there are horrors in your past that the others don't have.'

A ray of wintry sunlight fell across the classroom, illuminating Lupin's grey hairs and the lines on his young face.

'Dementors are among the foulest creatures that walk this earth. They infest the darkest, filthiest places, they glory in decay and despair, they drain peace, hope and happiness out of the air around them. Even Muggles feel their presence, though they can't see them. Get too near a Dementor and every good feeling, every happy memory, will be sucked out of you. If it can, the Dementor will feed on you long enough to reduce you to something like itself – soulless and evil. You'll be left with nothing but the worst experiences of your life. And the worst that has happened to *you*, Harry, is enough to make anyone fall off their broom. You have nothing to feel ashamed of.'

'When they get near me –' Harry stared at Lupin's desk, his throat tight, 'I can hear Voldemort murdering my mum.'

Lupin made a sudden motion with his arm as though he had made to grip Harry's shoulder, but thought better of it. There was a moment's silence; then –

'Why did they have to come to the match?' said Harry bitterly.

'They're getting hungry,' said Lupin coolly, shutting his briefcase with a snap. 'Dumbledore won't let them into the school, so their supply of human prey has dried up ... I don't think they could resist the large crowd around the Quidditch pitch. All that excitement ... emotions running high ... it was their idea of a feast.'

'Azkaban must be terrible,' Harry muttered. Lupin nodded grimly.

'The fortress is set on a tiny island, way out to sea, but they don't need walls and water to keep the prisoners in, not when they're all trapped inside their own heads, incapable of a single cheerful thought. Most of them go mad within weeks.'

'But Sirius Black escaped from them,' Harry said slowly. 'He got away ...'

Lupin's briefcase slipped from the desk; he had to stoop quickly to catch it.

'Yes,' he said, straightening up. 'Black must have found a way to fight them. I wouldn't have believed it possible ... Dementors are supposed to

第10章 活点地图

"这与软弱没有关系。"卢平教授断然说道,仿佛看穿了哈利的思想,"摄魂怪对你的影响比对别人大,是因为你过去的经历中有过别人未曾有过的恐惧。"

一道冬日的阳光射进教室,照亮了卢平花白的头发和他年轻面庞上的皱纹。

"摄魂怪是世上最丑恶的东西之一。它们在最黑暗、最污秽的地方出没,在腐烂和绝望中生活,它们把和平、希望和欢乐从周围的空气中吸走。就连麻瓜也能感觉到摄魂怪的存在,尽管麻瓜们看不见它们。摄魂怪靠近时,所有美好的感觉,所有快乐的回忆都会从你身上被吸走。如果可能的话,摄魂怪会一直把你吸到跟它一样……没有灵魂,充满邪恶。你只剩下一生中最坏的经历。而你最坏的经历,哈利,足以让任何人从飞天扫帚上摔下来。你不用感到羞愧。"

"当它们靠近我时——"哈利盯着卢平的书桌,嗓子发紧,"我听到伏地魔在杀害我的妈妈。"

卢平的胳膊突然一动,仿佛要抓住哈利的肩膀,但他克制住了。片刻的沉默,然后——

"它们为什么要去赛场呢?"哈利怨恨地问。

"它们饿了。"卢平冷静地说,啪嗒一声关上了公文包,"邓布利多不让它们进学校,所以它们的猎物来源枯竭了……我想它们是无法抗拒魁地奇球场周围那一大群人的诱惑。那种兴奋激动……情绪高涨……它们觉得这是一场盛宴。"

"阿兹卡班一定很恐怖。"哈利喃喃地说。卢平阴沉地点了点头。

"那座堡垒建在茫茫大海中一个孤零零的小岛上,其实并不需要高墙和海水把人关住,因为犯人都被囚禁在自己的脑子里,无法唤起一丝快乐的念头。大部分人几星期之后就疯了。"

"但小天狼星布莱克躲过了它们,"哈利缓缓地说,"他逃走了……"

卢平的公文包从桌上滑了下去,他忙俯身把它接住。

"是的,"他直起身子说,"布莱克一定找到了什么抵抗它们的办法。我本来以为这是不可能的……据说,如果巫师跟摄魂怪在一起时间太

CHAPTER TEN The Marauder's Map

drain a wizard of his powers if he is left with them too long ...'

'*You* made that Dementor on the train back off,' said Harry suddenly.

'There are – certain defences one can use,' said Lupin. 'But there was only one Dementor on the train. The more there are, the more difficult it becomes to resist.'

'What defences?' said Harry at once. 'Can you teach me?'

'I don't pretend to be an expert at fighting Dementors, Harry – quite the contrary ...'

'But if the Dementors come to another Quidditch match, I need to be able to fight them –'

Lupin looked into Harry's determined face, hesitated, then said, 'Well ... all right. I'll try and help. But it'll have to wait until next term, I'm afraid. I have a lot to do before the holidays. I chose a very inconvenient time to fall ill.'

What with the promise of Anti-Dementor lessons from Lupin, the thought that he might never have to hear his mother's death again, and the fact that Ravenclaw flattened Hufflepuff in their Quidditch match at the end of November, Harry's mood took a definite upturn. Gryffindor were not out of the running after all, although they could not afford to lose another match. Wood became repossessed of his manic energy, and worked his team as hard as ever in the chilly haze of rain that persisted into December. Harry saw no hint of a Dementor within the grounds. Dumbledore's anger seemed to be keeping them at their stations at the entrances.

Two weeks before the end of term, the sky lightened suddenly to a dazzling, opaline white and the muddy grounds were revealed one morning covered in glittering frost. Inside the castle, there was a buzz of Christmas in the air. Professor Flitwick, the Charms teacher, had already decorated his classroom with shimmering lights that turned out to be real, fluttering fairies. The students were all happily discussing their plans for the holidays. Both Ron and Hermione had decided to remain at Hogwarts, and though Ron said it was because he couldn't stand two weeks with Percy, and Hermione insisted she needed to use the library, Harry wasn't fooled; they were doing it to keep him company, and he was very grateful.

To everyone's delight except Harry's, there was to be another Hogsmeade trip on the very last weekend of term.

第 10 章 活点地图

久,摄魂怪能把巫师的法力吸干……"

"你让火车上那个摄魂怪后退了。"哈利突然说。

"还是有——某些防御办法的,"卢平说,"但火车上只有一个摄魂怪。它们数量越多,就越难抵御。"

"什么防御办法?"哈利马上问,"你能教我吗?"

"我可不敢自称是抵御摄魂怪的专家,哈利,相反……"

"可是如果下次摄魂怪又来魁地奇赛场,我得有办法抵御它们啊——"

卢平望着哈利坚决的表情,犹豫着,然后说道:"嗯……好吧。我试试看。但恐怕只能等到下学期了。放假前我有很多事要做。我病得真不是时候。"

想到可以跟卢平学习抵御摄魂怪的功课,想到他也许再也不用听到妈妈临死时的声音,又得知拉文克劳十一月底打败了赫奇帕奇,哈利的心情才真正好转起来。毕竟,格兰芬多还没有被淘汰出局,不过他们一场球也不能再输了。伍德恢复了他那疯狂的精力,率领队员们在霏霏冷雨中一如既往地刻苦训练,这雨一直持续到十二月。哈利在校园里看不到摄魂怪的踪迹。邓布利多的盛怒似乎使它们留在了校门外的岗位上。

离学期结束还有两个星期。天空突然放晴,变成了明亮耀眼的蛋白色。一天清晨,泥泞的场地上蒙了一层晶莹的白霜。城堡里洋溢着一种圣诞节的忙碌气氛。教魔咒课的弗立维教授已经在他的教室里装饰了五光十色的彩灯,大家后来发现那些是真的小仙子,呼扇着翅膀。同学们都在愉快地讨论假期计划。罗恩和赫敏决定留在霍格沃茨。虽然罗恩说是受不了跟珀西一起过两个星期,赫敏坚持说她需要上图书馆,但这瞒不过哈利,他知道他们留下来是为了陪他,内心十分感激。

最后一个周末又要去霍格莫德游玩,除了哈利大家都兴高采烈。

CHAPTER TEN   The Marauder's Map

'We can do all our Christmas shopping there!' said Hermione. 'Mum and Dad would really love those Toothflossing Stringmints from Honeydukes!'

Resigned to the fact that he would be the only third-year staying behind again, Harry borrowed a copy of *Which Broomstick* from Wood, and decided to spend the day reading up on the different makes. He had been riding one of the school brooms at team practice, an ancient Shooting Star, which was very slow and jerky; he definitely needed a new broom of his own.

On the Saturday morning of the Hogsmeade trip, Harry bid goodbye to Ron and Hermione, who were wrapped in cloaks and scarves, then turned up the marble staircase alone, and headed back towards Gryffindor Tower. Snow had started to fall outside the windows, and the castle was very still and quiet.

'Psst – Harry!'

He turned, halfway along the third-floor corridor, to see Fred and George peering out at him from behind a statue of a humpbacked, one-eyed witch.

'What are you doing?' said Harry curiously. 'How come you're not going to Hogsmeade?'

'We've come to give you a bit of festive cheer before we go,' said Fred, with a mysterious wink. 'Come in here …'

He nodded towards an empty classroom to the left of the one-eyed statue. Harry followed Fred and George inside. George closed the door quietly and then turned, beaming, to look at Harry.

'Early Christmas present for you, Harry,' he said.

Fred pulled something from inside his cloak with a flourish and laid it on one of the desks. It was a large, square, very worn piece of parchment with nothing written on it. Harry, suspecting one of Fred and George's jokes, stared at it.

'What's that supposed to be?'

'This, Harry, is the secret of our success,' said George, patting the parchment fondly.

'It's a wrench, giving it to you,' said Fred, 'but we decided last night, your need's greater than ours.'

'Anyway, we know it off by heart,' said George. 'We bequeath it to you. We don't really need it any more.'

'And what do I need with a bit of old parchment?' said Harry.

'A bit of old parchment!' said Fred, closing his eyes with a grimace as

"我们可以在那儿把圣诞节要买的东西全买了!"赫敏说,"爸爸妈妈可喜欢蜂蜜公爵的那些牙线薄荷糖了!"

哈利又是唯一一个留守的三年级学生,他无可奈何地向伍德借了一本《飞天扫帚大全》,决定那天仔细研读一下不同的扫帚品牌。他在球队训练时骑的是一把学校的飞天扫帚,老古董"流星",速度很慢而且有点跌跌撞撞。无疑他需要一把自己的新扫帚。

在大家去霍格莫德的那个星期六早上,哈利跟裹在斗篷和围巾里的罗恩和赫敏道别,然后独自登上大理石楼梯,走回格兰芬多塔楼。窗外飘起了雪花,城堡里静悄悄的。

"嘘——哈利!"

他转过身,在四楼走廊的一半处,看到弗雷德和乔治正在一个驼背独眼女巫的雕像后面向他窥视。

"你们在干什么?"哈利好奇地问,"怎么没去霍格莫德?"

"我们走之前来给你搞一点节日气氛。"弗雷德神秘地眨了眨眼睛说,"进去……"

他朝独眼雕像左边的一间空教室摆了摆头。哈利跟着弗雷德和乔治走了进去。乔治轻轻关上门,转身笑嘻嘻地看着哈利。

"提前给你的圣诞节礼物,哈利。"他说。

弗雷德夸张地从斗篷里抽出一样东西,放在课桌上。那是一张大大的正方形羊皮纸,磨损得很厉害,上面什么也没有。哈利盯着它,怀疑又是弗雷德和乔治的恶作剧。

"这是什么?"

"这个呀,哈利,是我们成功的秘密。"乔治珍爱地拍着羊皮纸说。

"还真舍不得送给你,"弗雷德说,"但我们昨晚决定了,你比我们更需要它。"

"反正我们也已经记熟了。"乔治说,"现在郑重地传给你,我们用不着了。"

"我要一块旧羊皮纸有什么用呢?"哈利问。

"一块旧羊皮纸!"弗雷德闭起眼睛做了个鬼脸,仿佛哈利深深地

CHAPTER TEN   The Marauder's Map

though Harry had mortally offended him. 'Explain, George.'

'Well ... when we were in our first year, Harry – young, carefree and innocent –'

Harry snorted. He doubted whether Fred and George had ever been innocent.

'– well, more innocent than we are now – we got into a spot of bother with Filch.'

'We let off a Dungbomb in the corridor and it upset him for some reason –'

'So he hauled us off to his office and started threatening us with the usual –'

'– detention –'

'– disembowelment –'

'– and we couldn't help noticing a drawer in one of his filing cabinets marked *Confiscated and Highly Dangerous*.'

'Don't tell me –' said Harry, starting to grin.

'Well, what would you've done?' said Fred. 'George caused a diversion by dropping another Dungbomb, I whipped the drawer open and grabbed – *this*.'

'It's not as bad as it sounds, you know,' said George. 'We don't reckon Filch ever found out how to work it. He probably suspected what it was, though, or he wouldn't have confiscated it.'

'And you know how to work it?'

'Oh yes,' said Fred, smirking. 'This little beauty's taught us more than all the teachers in this school.'

'You're winding me up,' said Harry, looking at the ragged old bit of parchment.

'Oh, are we?' said George.

He took out his wand, touched the parchment lightly and said, '*I solemnly swear that I am up to no good.*'

And at once, thin ink lines began to spread like a spider's web from the point that George's wand had touched. They joined each other, they crisscrossed, they fanned into every corner of the parchment; then words began to blossom across the top, great, curly green words, that proclaimed:

Messrs Moony, Wormtail, Padfoot and Prongs
Purveyors of Aids to Magical Mischief-Makers
are proud to present

THE MARAUDER'S MAP

伤害了他,"解释一下,乔治。"

"是这样,哈利……我们一年级时——年轻,无忧无虑,天真无邪——"

哈利扑哧笑了,怀疑弗雷德和乔治是否有过天真无邪的时候。

"——啊哈,比现在天真无邪——那会儿我们跟费尔奇闹了点儿别扭。"

"我们在走廊里放了一个大粪弹,由于某种原因,这让他很恼火——"

"于是他把我们拉进了他的办公室,开始用惯常的那一套威胁我们——"

"——关禁闭——"

"——开膛破肚——"

"——而我们忍不住瞄上了他的一只档案柜抽屉,那上面标着:没收物品,高度危险。"

"该不会是——"哈利咧嘴笑了。

"嘿,换了你会怎么做?"弗雷德说,"乔治又扔了一个大粪弹转移他的注意力,我马上打开抽屉,抓到了——这个。"

"其实没那么糟糕,你知道,"乔治说,"我们估计费尔奇从来没弄明白怎么使用。但他可能猜到了它是什么,不然也不会把它没收。"

"你们知道怎么用吗?"

"哦,知道。"弗雷德得意地笑道,"这小宝贝教给我们的东西比全校老师教的都多。"

"你们在吊我胃口呢。"哈利盯着那块破旧的羊皮纸说。

"哦,是吗?"乔治说。

他拔出魔杖,轻轻敲了敲羊皮纸,说道:"我庄严宣誓我不干好事。"

刹那间,细细的墨水线条像蜘蛛网那样,从乔治魔杖尖碰过的地方蔓延开来,相互连接,纵横交错,扩展到羊皮纸的每个角落;然后顶上现出了字样,是绿色的花体大字:

月亮脸、虫尾巴、大脚板和尖头叉子

专为魔法恶作剧制造者提供帮助的诸位先生

隆重推出

活点地图

CHAPTER TEN   The Marauder's Map

It was a map showing every detail of the Hogwarts castle and grounds. But the truly remarkable thing was the tiny ink dots moving around it, each labelled with a name in minuscule writing. Astounded, Harry bent over it. A labelled dot in the top left corner showed that Professor Dumbledore was pacing his study; the caretaker's cat, Mrs Norris, was prowling the second floor, and Peeves the poltergeist was currently bouncing around the trophy room. And as Harry's eyes travelled up and down the familiar corridors, he noticed something else.

This map showed a set of passages he had never entered. And many of them seemed to lead –

'Right into Hogsmeade,' said Fred, tracing one of them with his finger. 'There are seven in all. Now, Filch knows about these four –' he pointed them out, '– but we're sure we're the only ones who know about *these*. Don't bother with the one behind the mirror on the fourth floor. We used it until last winter, but it's caved in – completely blocked. And we don't reckon anyone's ever used this one, because the Whomping Willow's planted right over the entrance. But this one here, this one leads right into the cellar of Honeydukes. We've used it loads of times. And as you might've noticed, the entrance is right outside this room, through that one-eyed old crone's hump.'

'Moony, Wormtail, Padfoot and Prongs,' sighed George, patting the heading of the map. 'We owe them so much.'

'Noble men, working tirelessly to help a new generation of law-breakers,' said Fred solemnly.

'Right,' said George briskly, 'don't forget to wipe it after you've used it –'

'– or anyone can read it,' Fred said warningly.

'Just tap it again and say, "Mischief managed!" And it'll go blank.'

'So, young Harry,' said Fred, in an uncanny impersonation of Percy, 'mind you behave yourself.'

'See you in Honeydukes,' said George, winking.

They left the room, both smirking in a satisfied sort of way.

Harry stood there, gazing at the miraculous map. He watched the tiny ink Mrs Norris turn left and pause to sniff at something on the floor. If Filch really didn't know … he wouldn't have to pass the Dementors at all …

But even as he stood there, flooded with excitement, something Harry had once heard Mr Weasley say came floating out of his memory.

第10章 活点地图

这张地图绘出了霍格沃茨城堡和场地的所有细节，但最不同寻常的是，有许多小黑点在图上移动，每个都用极小的字体标出了名字。哈利惊奇地俯身细看，左上角一个带标记的黑点显示邓布利多教授正在书房踱步；管理员费尔奇的猫洛丽丝夫人正在三楼逡巡；恶作剧精灵皮皮鬼此刻正在奖品陈列室里蹦蹦跳跳。哈利的目光沿着那些熟悉的走廊上下扫视，忽然发现了一些新的东西。

地图上还有一些他从没走过的通道，许多似乎都通往——

"霍格莫德，"弗雷德一边说，一边用手指描着一条通道的路线，"一共有七条。费尔奇知道这四条——"他一条条指出来，"——我们相信这三条只有我们俩知道。别考虑五楼镜子后面的那条。去年冬天以前我们还用过，但现在已经塌陷——完全堵死了。这一条估计也没人用过，因为打人柳正好栽在它的入口处。剩下的这条，直接通到蜂蜜公爵的地窖，我们用过好多次。你大概也注意到了，入口就在这间教室的外面，穿过独眼老太婆的驼背。"

"月亮脸、虫尾巴、大脚板和尖头叉子。"乔治拍着地图的标题感叹，"多亏了他们啊。"

"高尚的人哪，为帮助新一代违纪学生而不知疲倦地工作。"弗雷德庄严地说。

"对啊，"乔治轻快地附和，"别忘了用完之后要消掉——"

"——不然别人都能看见。"弗雷德警告道。

"只要再敲敲它，念道：'恶作剧完毕！'它就又变成一张白纸了。"

"好了，小哈利，"弗雷德怪腔怪调地模仿着珀西说，"你好自为之吧！"

"蜂蜜公爵见。"乔治眨了眨眼。

他们俩走出教室，都心满意足地笑着。

哈利站在那儿，凝视着那张奇妙的地图。他看到洛丽丝夫人的小黑点向左一转，停下来嗅着地上的什么东西。如果费尔奇真的不知道……他就不用经过那些摄魂怪了……

但正当他站在那儿满怀兴奋的时候，记忆中突然浮现出以前听韦斯莱先生说过的话。

CHAPTER TEN — The Marauder's Map

Never trust anything that can think for itself, if you can't see where it keeps its brain.

This map was one of those dangerous magical objects Mr Weasley had been warning against ... *Aids to Magical Mischief-Makers* ... but then, Harry reasoned, he only wanted to use it to get into Hogsmeade, it wasn't as though he wanted to steal anything or attack anyone ... and Fred and George had been using it for years without anything horrible happening ...

Harry traced the secret passage to Honeydukes with his finger.

Then, quite suddenly, as though following orders, he rolled up the map, stuffed it inside his robes, and hurried to the door of the classroom. He opened it a couple of inches. There was no one outside. Very carefully, he edged out of the room and slipped behind the statue of the one-eyed witch.

What did he have to do? He pulled out the map again and saw, to his astonishment, that a new ink figure had appeared upon it, labelled *Harry Potter*. This figure was standing exactly where the real Harry was standing, about halfway down the third-floor corridor. Harry watched carefully. His little ink self appeared to be tapping the witch with his minute wand. Harry quickly took out his real wand and tapped the statue. Nothing happened. He looked back at the map. The tiniest speech bubble had appeared next to his figure. The word inside said *'Dissendium'*.

'Dissendium!' Harry whispered, tapping the stone witch again.

At once, the statue's hump opened wide enough to admit a fairly thin person. Harry glanced quickly up and down the corridor, then tucked the map away again, hoisted himself into the hole head first, and pushed himself forwards.

He slid a considerable way down what felt like a stone slide, then landed on cold, damp earth. He stood up, looking around. It was pitch dark. He held up his wand, muttered, *'Lumos!'* and saw that he was in a very narrow, low, earthy passageway. He raised the map, tapped it with the tip of his wand and muttered, 'Mischief managed!' The map went blank at once. He folded it carefully, tucked it inside his robes, then, heart beating fast, both excited and apprehensive, he set off.

The passage twisted and turned, more like the burrow of a giant rabbit than anything else. Harry hurried along it, stumbling now and then on the uneven floor, holding his wand out in front of him.

It took ages, but Harry had the thought of Honeydukes to sustain him. After what felt like an hour, the passage began to rise. Panting, Harry sped

第10章 活点地图

永远不要相信任何能够独立思考的东西,除非你看清了它把头脑藏在什么地方。

这张地图就是韦斯莱先生警告过的那种危险的魔法物品之一……为恶作剧制造者提供帮助……可是,哈利思忖,他只想用它进入霍格莫德,并不想偷东西或袭击什么人……而弗雷德和乔治用了它好多年,也没有发生什么可怕的事情……

哈利用手描着通往蜂蜜公爵的秘道。

突然,仿佛听到了什么指令似的,他卷起地图,塞进袍子,匆匆走到教室门口。他把门打开一道缝,外面没人。哈利小心翼翼地溜出教室,躲到独眼女巫的雕像后面。

该怎么做呢?他又摸出地图,吃惊地看到图上出现了一个新的黑点,标着哈利·波特。这黑点正站在哈利实际站的地方,四楼走廊的一半处。哈利定睛细看,小黑点哈利好像在用小小的魔杖敲那女巫。哈利迅速抽出他的魔杖,敲了敲雕像,毫无效果。他又看了看地图,他的黑点旁边冒出了一个极小极小的泡泡,里面写着左右分离。

"左右分离!"哈利小声念道,又敲了敲石头雕像。

顿时,雕像的驼背打开了,能容一个体形较瘦的人钻入。哈利迅速扫视一下走廊两边,随即把地图重新揣好,头朝前钻进洞里,往前走去。

他好像在石滑梯上滑了长长的一段,然后掉到了又冷又湿的泥土地上。哈利站起来环顾四周,一片漆黑。他举起魔杖念道:"荧光闪烁!"这才看清自己是在一条逼仄低矮的泥土通道里。他举起地图,用杖尖敲了敲,小声说:"恶作剧完毕!"图上立刻变得一片空白。他小心地把它折好,塞进袍子里,心脏剧烈地跳着,又是兴奋又是害怕。他往前走去。

通道迂回曲折,更像一个巨型的兔子洞。哈利急急地走着,把魔杖举在前面,时而在高低不平的地上绊一下。

好漫长啊,但哈利有蜂蜜公爵的念头在支撑着自己。过了仿佛一个小时,通道开始上升,哈利喘着气加快了脚步,他面孔发烫,双脚

CHAPTER TEN — The Marauder's Map

却很凉。

十分钟后,哈利来到一道破旧石梯的底部,石梯一直延伸到上面看不见的地方。他开始往上爬,小心地不发出响声。一百级,两百级,数着数着就数不清了,他盯着自己的脚……冷不防,脑袋撞到了什么硬东西上。

好像是个活板门。哈利站在那儿揉着脑袋,一边仔细聆听。听不到顶上有什么声音,他慢慢地推开活板门,从门边往里面窥视。

是一个地窖,堆满了板条箱和其他木箱子。哈利爬了上去,又把活板门关好——它和灰蒙蒙的地板浑然一体,根本看不出来。哈利慢慢朝通往上层的木楼梯爬去。现在他分明听见了说话声,更不用说叮咚的铃声和开门关门的响声了。

他正在寻思怎么办时,突然听到更近处的一扇门开了,有人要下楼来。

"再拿一箱果冻鼻涕虫,亲爱的,他们简直把咱们这儿都买空了——"一个女人的声音说。

有一双脚正走下楼梯,哈利忙跳到一个大板条箱子后面,等着脚步声过去。他听见那人正在搬动对面墙边的箱子。也许再也没有别的机会了——

哈利悄悄地从隐蔽处迅速闪出来,爬上楼梯;他回头望了一眼,只见一个庞大的后背和一个光亮的秃顶埋在一个箱子里。哈利爬到楼梯顶上的门口,悄悄溜了进去,发现自己正站在蜂蜜公爵的柜台后面——他猫下腰,蹑手蹑脚地走到一边,然后直起身来。

蜂蜜公爵里挤满了霍格沃茨的学生,没人朝哈利多看一眼。他在人群中侧身而行,扫视四周。达力要是看到哈利在什么地方,他那张胖猪脸上会露出怎样的表情呢?这想象让哈利差点笑出声来。

一排排架子上摆满了最最美味诱人的糖果,大块乳黄的奶油杏仁糖、亮晶晶的粉色椰子冰糕、蜜汁色的太妃糖,几百种摆放得整整齐齐的巧克力,一大桶比比多味豆,还有一大桶滋滋蜜蜂糖,就是罗恩提到过的那种能让人飘到空中的果汁奶冻球;靠着另一面墙的都是"特

CHAPTER TEN The Marauder's Map

along yet another wall were 'Special Effects' sweets: Drooble's Best Blowing Gum (which filled a room with bluebell-coloured bubbles that refused to pop for days), the strange, splintery Toothflossing Stringmints, tiny black Pepper Imps ('breathe fire for your friends!'), Ice Mice ('hear your teeth chatter and squeak!'), peppermint creams shaped like toads ('hop realistically in the stomach!'), fragile sugar-spun quills and exploding bonbons.

Harry squeezed himself through a crowd of sixth-years and saw a sign hanging in the furthest corner of the shop (*Unusual Tastes*). Ron and Hermione were standing underneath it, examining a tray of blood-flavoured lollipops. Harry sneaked up behind them.

'Urgh, no, Harry won't want one of those, they're for vampires, I expect,' Hermione was saying.

'How about these?' said Ron, shoving a jar of Cockroach Cluster under Hermione's nose.

'Definitely not,' said Harry.

Ron nearly dropped the jar.

'*Harry!*' squealed Hermione. 'What are you doing here? How – how did you –?'

'Wow!' said Ron, looking very impressed. 'You've learnt to Apparate!'

''Course I haven't,' said Harry. He dropped his voice so that none of the sixth-years could hear him and told them all about the Marauder's Map.

'How come Fred and George never gave it to *me*!' said Ron, outraged. 'I'm their brother!'

'But Harry isn't going to keep it!' said Hermione, as though the idea was ludicrous. 'He's going to hand it in to Professor McGonagall, aren't you, Harry?'

'No, I'm not!' said Harry.

'Are you mad?' said Ron, goggling at Hermione. 'Hand in something that good?'

'If I hand it in, I'll have to say where I got it! Filch would know Fred and George nicked it!'

'But what about Sirius Black?' Hermione hissed. 'He could be using one of the passages on that map to get into the castle! The teachers have got to know!'

'He can't be getting in through a passage,' said Harry quickly. 'There are seven secret tunnels on the map, right? Fred and George reckon Filch already knows about four of them. And the other three – one of them's caved in, so no one can get through it. One of them's got the Whomping Willow planted

第10章　活点地图

效"糖果：吹宝超级泡泡糖（能让房间里飘满蓝铃花颜色的泡泡，好几天都不破），还有那奇异而松脆易碎的牙线薄荷糖，又小又黑的胡椒小顽童（"为你的朋友喷火！"），冰老鼠（"听到你的牙齿吱吱叫！"），蟾蜍形状的薄荷冰淇淋（"真的会在胃里跳动！"），糖丝织成的薄脆羽毛糖，还有爆炸夹心软糖。

哈利从一群六年级学生中间挤过去，看到店里最远的角落那儿挂着一个牌子（特殊口味）。罗恩和赫敏站在那下面，正在研究一盘血腥味的棒棒糖。哈利悄悄走到他们俩身后。

"呃，不行，我猜哈利不会要这种东西，它们是给吸血鬼的。"赫敏说。

"这些怎么样？"罗恩说，把一罐蟑螂串塞到赫敏鼻子底下。

"绝对不行。"哈利说。

罗恩差点儿把罐子扔掉。

"哈利！"赫敏尖叫一声，"你在这儿干什么？你怎么……怎么——？"

"哇！"罗恩佩服得五体投地，"你学会幻影显形了！"

"当然没有。"哈利说。为了不让那帮六年级学生听见，他压低了嗓门，跟他们俩讲了活点地图的事。

"弗雷德和乔治怎么从来没有给我呢！"罗恩来气了，"我是他们的亲弟弟啊！"

"但哈利不会留着它的！"赫敏说，好像这想法很是荒唐可笑，"他要交给麦格教授，是不是，哈利？"

"我不交！"哈利说。

"你疯了吗？"罗恩瞪着赫敏，"把这么好的东西交出去？"

"如果交出去，我就必须说出从哪儿得来的！费尔奇就会知道这是弗雷德和乔治偷的！"

"可是小天狼星布莱克呢？"赫敏从牙缝里挤出声音说，"他会利用图上的某条秘密通道潜入城堡！老师们必须知道！"

"他不可能从秘密通道进来。"哈利马上说，"图上有七条秘密通道，对吧？弗雷德和乔治估计费尔奇已经知道其中四条了。另外三条——一条已经塌陷，没人能穿过。另一条的洞口栽了打人柳，没办法躲得开。

CHAPTER TEN   The Marauder's Map

over the entrance, so you can't get out of it. And the one I just came through – well – it's really hard to see the entrance to it down in the cellar – so unless he knew it was there –'

Harry hesitated. What if Black did know the passage was there? Ron, however, cleared his throat significantly, and pointed to a notice pasted on the inside of the sweetshop door.

BY ORDER OF THE MINISTRY OF MAGIC
Customers are reminded that until further notice, Dementors will be patrolling the streets of Hogsmeade every night after sundown. This measure has been put in place for the safety of Hogsmeade residents and will be lifted upon the recapture of Sirius Black. It is therefore advisable that you complete your shopping well before nightfall.
Merry Christmas!

'See?' said Ron quietly. 'I'd like to see Black try and break into Honeydukes with Dementors swarming all over the village. Anyway, Hermione, the Honeydukes owners would hear a break-in, wouldn't they? They live over the shop!'

'Yes, but – but –' Hermione seemed to be struggling to find another problem. 'Look, Harry still shouldn't be coming into Hogsmeade, he hasn't got a signed form! If anyone finds out, he'll be in so much trouble! And it's not nightfall yet – what if Sirius Black turns up today? Now?'

'He'd have a job spotting Harry in this,' said Ron, nodding through the mullioned windows at the thick, swirling snow. 'Come on, Hermione, it's Christmas, Harry deserves a break.'

Hermione bit her lip, looking extremely worried.

'Are you going to report me?' Harry asked her, grinning.

'Oh – of course not – but honestly, Harry –'

'Seen the Fizzing Whizzbees, Harry?' said Ron, grabbing him and leading him over to their barrel. 'And the Jelly Slugs? And the Acid Pops? Fred gave me one of those when I was seven – it burnt a hole right through my tongue. I remember Mum walloping him with her broomstick.' Ron stared broodingly into the Acid Pop box. 'Reckon Fred'd take a bit of Cockroach

我刚才用的这一条——嗯——地窖里的洞口很难看出来,所以除非他知道那儿有通道……"

哈利迟疑了。如果布莱克确实知道那儿有通道呢?但罗恩煞有介事地清了清嗓子,指着糖果店门后的一张告示。

魔法部令

顾客请注意,若无另外通知,每天日落时分起都有摄魂怪在霍格莫德街头巡逻。此项措施乃为保护霍格莫德居民之安全,待小天狼星布莱克落网后方可解除。因此请所有顾客在日落前结束购物。

圣诞快乐!

"看到了吧?"罗恩悄声说,"满街都是摄魂怪,我倒想看看布莱克怎么闯进蜂蜜公爵。再说,赫敏,蜂蜜公爵的店主也会听见的,是不是?他们就住在店铺楼上!"

"这倒不假,可是,可是——"赫敏似乎竭力想再挑出什么问题,"听我说,哈利还是不应该来霍格莫德。他没有签过字的许可表!如果被人发现,他的麻烦就大了!现在还没到日落——如果小天狼星布莱克今天就来了呢?就在现在?"

"他在这种天气里想要发现哈利可不容易。"罗恩说,朝直棂窗户外纷纷扬扬的大雪点了点头,"好了,赫敏,圣诞节嘛,哈利该轻松一下了。"

赫敏咬着嘴唇,看上去担忧极了。

"你会告发我吗?"哈利笑嘻嘻地问她。

"哦——当然不会——但说实话,哈利——"

"看到滋滋蜜蜂糖了吗,哈利?"罗恩把他拽到那个大桶前,"还有果冻鼻涕虫?还有酸味爆爆糖?我七岁时弗雷德给过我一颗——把我舌头烧了一个洞。我记得妈妈用飞天扫帚狠狠揍了他一顿。"罗恩若有所思地看着酸味爆爆糖盒子里面,"如果我跟他说是花生,弗雷德会

CHAPTER TEN   The Marauder's Map

Cluster if I told him they were peanuts?'

When Ron and Hermione had paid for all their sweets, the three of them left Honeydukes for the blizzard outside.

Hogsmeade looked like a Christmas card; the little thatched cottages and shops were all covered in a layer of crisp snow; there were holly wreaths on the doors and strings of enchanted candles hanging in the trees.

Harry shivered; unlike the other two, he didn't have his cloak. They headed up the street, heads bowed against the wind, Ron and Hermione shouting through their scarves.

'That's the Post Office –'

'Zonko's is up there –'

'We could go up to the Shrieking Shack –'

'Tell you what,' said Ron, his teeth chattering, 'shall we go for a Butterbeer in the Three Broomsticks?'

Harry was more than willing; the wind was fierce and his hands were freezing, so they crossed the road, and in a few minutes were entering the tiny inn.

It was extremely crowded, noisy, warm and smoky. A curvy sort of woman with a pretty face was serving a bunch of rowdy warlocks up at the bar.

'That's Madam Rosmerta,' said Ron. 'I'll get the drinks, shall I?' he added, going slightly red.

Harry and Hermione made their way to the back of the room, where there was a small, vacant table between the window and a handsome Christmas tree which stood next to the fireplace. Ron came back five minutes later, carrying three foaming tankards of hot Butterbeer.

'Happy Christmas!' he said happily, raising his tankard.

Harry drank deeply. It was the most delicious thing he'd ever tasted and seemed to heat every bit of him from the inside.

A sudden breeze ruffled his hair. The door of the Three Broomsticks had opened again. Harry looked over the rim of his tankard and choked.

Professors McGonagall and Flitwick had just entered the pub in a flurry of snowflakes, shortly followed by Hagrid, who was deep in conversation with a portly man in a lime-green bowler hat and a pinstriped cloak: Cornelius Fudge, Minister for Magic.

第10章 活点地图

尝一点蟑螂串吗？"

罗恩和赫敏付钱买了一大堆糖果之后，三人离开了蜂蜜公爵，走到暴风雪中。

霍格莫德看上去像一张圣诞卡，茅草顶的小屋和店铺上覆了一层新落的白雪，房门上都挂着冬青花环，树上点缀着一串串施了魔法的蜡烛。

哈利打了个哆嗦；他跟他们俩不一样，没有穿斗篷。三人在街上低头顶着风往前走，罗恩和赫敏隔着围巾喊话。

"那是邮局——"

"佐科笑话店就在前面——"

"我们可以去尖叫棚屋——"

"我说，"罗恩牙齿格格打战地说，"我们去三把扫帚喝杯黄油啤酒怎么样？"

哈利正求之不得。寒风凛冽，他的手都冻僵了。于是三人穿过马路，几分钟后就钻进了那家小酒吧。

里面极其拥挤嘈杂，热烘烘的，烟雾缭绕。一位相貌标致、曲线优美的妇人正在吧台前招呼着一群吵吵嚷嚷的男巫。

"那是罗斯默塔女士。"罗恩说，"我去拿饮料，好吗？"他加了一句，脸有点红。

哈利和赫敏挤到酒吧后边，在窗户和一棵漂亮的圣诞树之间有一张小小的空桌子，靠着壁炉。五分钟后罗恩也来了，端着三大杯冒着泡沫的热黄油啤酒。

"圣诞快乐！"他举起酒杯快活地说。

哈利痛饮了一口，他从没尝过这么美妙的东西，好像体内的每一寸地方都暖和起来了。

突然一阵凉风拂乱了他的头发。三把扫帚的门开了，哈利从杯沿上望过去，呛了一口。

麦格教授和弗立维教授卷着一阵风雪走进了酒吧，随后是海格，他正在跟一个胖子亲密交谈。那胖子戴着一顶黄绿色的圆顶硬礼帽，身披细条纹斗篷——是康奈利·福吉，魔法部部长。

CHAPTER TEN   The Marauder's Map

In an instant, Ron and Hermione had both placed hands on the top of Harry's head and forced him off his stool and under the table. Dripping with Butterbeer and crouching out of sight, Harry clutched his empty tankard and watched the teachers' and Fudge's feet move towards the bar, pause, then turn and walk right towards him.

Somewhere above him, Hermione whispered, '*Mobiliarbus!*'

The Christmas tree beside their table rose a few inches off the ground, drifted sideways and landed with a soft thump right in front of their table, hiding them from view. Staring through the dense lower branches, Harry saw four sets of chair legs move back from the table right beside theirs, then heard the grunts and sighs of the teachers and Minister as they sat down.

Next he saw another pair of feet, wearing sparkly turquoise high heels, and heard a woman's voice.

'A small Gillywater –'

'Mine,' said Professor McGonagall's voice.

'Four pints of mulled mead –'

'Ta, Rosmerta,' said Hagrid.

'A cherry syrup and soda with ice and umbrella –'

'Mmm!' said Professor Flitwick, smacking his lips.

'So you'll be the redcurrant rum, Minister.'

'Thank you, Rosmerta, m'dear,' said Fudge's voice. 'Lovely to see you again, I must say. Have one yourself, won't you? Come and join us ...'

'Well, thank you very much, Minister.'

Harry watched the glittering heels march away and back again. His heart was pounding uncomfortably in his throat. Why hadn't it occurred to him that this was the last weekend of term for the teachers, too? And how long were they going to sit there? He needed time to sneak back into Honeydukes if he wanted to return to school tonight ... Hermione's leg gave a nervous twitch next to him.

'So, what brings you to this neck of the woods, Minister?' came Madam Rosmerta's voice.

Harry saw the lower part of Fudge's thick body twist in his chair as though he was checking for eavesdroppers. Then he said in a quiet voice, 'What else, m'dear, but Sirius Black? I daresay you heard what happened up at the school at Hallowe'en?'

'I did hear a rumour,' admitted Madam Rosmerta.

第10章　活点地图

霎时间，罗恩和赫敏同时一把按住哈利的头顶，把他从凳子上按下去，藏到了桌子底下。哈利躲在暗处，嘴边流着黄油啤酒，手里抓着他的空酒杯。只见几位老师和福吉的脚走向吧台，停住，然后脚跟一转，向他这边走来。

在他上面的某个地方，赫敏悄声念道："移形幻影！"

桌子旁边的圣诞树从地面升起几英寸，向旁边飘移，轻轻落在他们的桌子前，把他们遮住了。透过树下方茂密的枝叶，哈利看到四把椅子的腿从旁边那张桌子跟前退去，然后听到老师们和部长入座时的嘟哝和叹息声。

随后他又看到一双脚，穿着亮闪闪的青绿色高跟鞋，又听到一个女人的声音："一小杯鳃囊草水——"

"我的。"麦格教授说。

"四品脱热蜂蜜酒——"

"谢了，罗斯默塔。"海格说。

"一杯加冰和伞的樱桃糖浆苏打水——"

"嗯！"弗立维教授咂着嘴唇说。

"那您的就是红醋栗朗姆酒了，部长。"

"谢谢你，罗斯默塔，亲爱的。"福吉的声音说，"我必须说，又见到你真高兴。你也来一份吧，好吗？来跟我们一起……"

"哦，非常感谢您，部长。"

哈利看到亮闪闪的高跟鞋又走了回来。他的心脏在喉咙口不舒服地跳着。他怎么没想到这也是教师们这学期的最后一个周末呢？他们会在这儿坐多久？如果他今晚想回学校，就得及时溜回蜂蜜公爵……赫敏的腿在他旁边紧张地抽搐了一下。

"什么风把您吹到这旮旯来了，部长？"罗斯默塔女士的声音传来。

哈利看到福吉肥胖的下半身在椅子里扭动了一下，似乎在检查周围有没有人窃听。然后他小声说道："还能有什么，亲爱的，还不是小天狼星布莱克？我猜你也听到学校万圣节前夕发生的事情了吧？"

"我确实听到一些谣传。"罗斯默塔女士承认。

CHAPTER TEN   The Marauder's Map

'Did you tell the whole pub, Hagrid?' said Professor McGonagall exasperatedly.

'Do you think Black's still in the area, Minister?' whispered Madam Rosmerta.

'I'm sure of it,' said Fudge shortly.

'You know that the Dementors have searched my pub twice?' said Madam Rosmerta, a slight edge to her voice. 'Scared all my customers away ... it's very bad for business, Minister.'

'Rosmerta, m'dear, I don't like them any more than you do,' said Fudge uncomfortably. 'Necessary precaution ... unfortunate, but there you are ... I've just met some of them. They're in a fury against Dumbledore – he won't let them inside the castle grounds.'

'I should think not,' said Professor McGonagall sharply. 'How are we supposed to teach with those horrors floating around?'

'Hear, hear!' squeaked tiny Professor Flitwick, whose feet were dangling a foot from the ground.

'All the same,' demurred Fudge, 'they are here to protect you all from something much worse ... we all know what Black's capable of ...'

'Do you know, I still have trouble believing it,' said Madam Rosmerta thoughtfully. 'Of all the people to go over to the Dark side, Sirius Black was the last I'd have thought ... I mean, I remember him when he was a boy at Hogwarts. If you'd told me then what he was going to become, I'd have said you'd had too much mead.'

'You don't know the half of it, Rosmerta,' said Fudge gruffly. 'The worst he did isn't widely known.'

'The worst?' said Madam Rosmerta, her voice alive with curiosity. 'Worse than murdering all those poor people, you mean?'

'I certainly do,' said Fudge.

'I can't believe that. What could possibly be worse?'

'You say you remember him at Hogwarts, Rosmerta,' murmured Professor McGonagall. 'Do you remember who his best friend was?'

'Naturally,' said Madam Rosmerta, with a small laugh. 'Never saw one without the other, did you? The number of times I had them in here – ooh, they used to make me laugh. Quite the double act, Sirius Black and James Potter!'

第 10 章 活点地图

"你是不是告诉了整个酒吧的人,海格?"麦格教授恼火地问。

"你认为布莱克还在这一带吗,部长?"罗斯默塔女士小声问。

"我相信还在。"福吉简短地说。

"您知道摄魂怪已经把我的酒吧搜查了两遍吗?"罗斯默塔女士的语气有一点尖锐,"把我的客人全吓跑了……对生意影响很大,部长。"

"罗斯默塔,亲爱的,我也不喜欢它们啊。"福吉尴尬地说,"必要的预防措施……很遗憾,可是你瞧……我刚刚还碰到了几个。它们对邓布利多非常恼火——他不肯让它们进入城堡的场地。"

"我看也不能让它们进来,"麦格教授尖刻地说,"那些恐怖的东西到处游荡,我们还怎么教课啊?"

"对啊,对啊!"瘦小的弗立维教授尖声说,他的双脚悬在离地面一英尺处。

"可是,"福吉争辩道,"它们是来保护大家免遭更可怕的威胁的……我们都知道布莱克能干出什么……"

"您知道吗,我至今都难以相信。"罗斯默塔女士沉吟地说,"在所有投靠黑魔势力的人中,小天狼星布莱克是我最想不到的……我是说,我还记得他在霍格沃茨上学时的样子。如果当时您告诉我他会变成什么人,我准会说你蜂蜜酒喝多了。"

"你知道的还不到一半,罗斯默塔。"福吉粗声说,"很少有人知道他干过的最恶劣的事情。"

"最恶劣的?"罗斯默塔女士的声音中充满好奇,"您是说,比杀死那么多无辜的人还要恶劣?"

"当然。"福吉答道。

"我无法相信。还能有什么更恶劣的呢?"

"你说你记得他在霍格沃茨时的样子,罗斯默塔,"麦格教授轻声说,"你记不记得他最好的朋友是谁?"

"当然记得,"罗斯默塔女士轻笑道,"从没看到他们俩分开过,是不是?他们在我这儿的那几次——哦,逗得我直笑,像演双簧一样,小天狼星布莱克和詹姆·波特!"

CHAPTER TEN   The Marauder's Map

Harry dropped his tankard with a loud clunk. Ron kicked him.

'Precisely,' said Professor McGonagall. 'Black and Potter. Ringleaders of their little gang. Both very bright, of course – exceptionally bright, in fact – but I don't think we've ever had such a pair of troublemakers –'

'I dunno,' chuckled Hagrid. 'Fred and George Weasley could give 'em a run fer their money.'

'You'd have thought Black and Potter were brothers!' chimed in Professor Flitwick. 'Inseparable!'

'Of course they were,' said Fudge. 'Potter trusted Black beyond all his other friends. Nothing changed when they left school. Black was best man when James married Lily. Then they named him godfather to Harry. Harry has no idea, of course. You can imagine how the idea would torment him.'

'Because Black turned out to be in league with You-Know-Who?' whispered Madam Rosmerta.

'Worse even than that, m'dear ...' Fudge dropped his voice and proceeded in a sort of low rumble. 'Not many people are aware that the Potters knew You-Know-Who was after them. Dumbledore, who was of course working tirelessly against You-Know-Who, had a number of useful spies. One of them tipped him off, and he alerted James and Lily at once. He advised them to go into hiding. Well, of course, You-Know-Who wasn't an easy person to hide from. Dumbledore told them that their best chance was the Fidelius Charm.'

'How does that work?' said Madam Rosmerta, breathless with interest. Professor Flitwick cleared his throat.

'An immensely complex spell,' he said squeakily, 'involving the magical concealment of a secret inside a single, living soul. The information is hidden inside the chosen person, or Secret Keeper, and is henceforth impossible to find – unless, of course, the Secret Keeper chooses to divulge it. As long as the Secret Keeper refused to speak, You-Know-Who could search the village where Lily and James were staying for years and never find them, not even if he had his nose pressed against their sitting-room window!'

'So Black was the Potters' Secret Keeper?' whispered Madam Rosmerta.

'Naturally,' said Professor McGonagall. 'James Potter told Dumbledore that Black would die rather than tell where they were, that Black was planning to go into hiding himself ... and yet, Dumbledore remained worried. I remember him offering to be the Potters' Secret Keeper himself.'

哈利的大酒杯掉到地上，发出响亮的当啷一声，罗恩踢了他一脚。

"正是，"麦格教授说，"布莱克和波特，是他们那个小团体的头头。当然，两人都非常聪明——绝顶聪明，但好像我们也从没见过这样一对捣蛋鬼——"

"也不一定。"海格咔咔地笑道，"弗雷德和乔治·韦斯莱倒是跟他们有一拼。"

"你会以为布莱克和波特是亲兄弟呢！"弗立维教授插话道，"形影不离！"

"可不是嘛，"福吉说，"波特信任布莱克胜过信任他的任何一个朋友。毕业后也没有变。詹姆和莉莉结婚时布莱克是伴郎。后来他们又让他当了哈利的教父。当然，哈利毫不知情。你们可以相信知道这些事会带给他怎样的折磨。"

"因为布莱克跟神秘人是一伙的？"罗斯默塔女士轻声问。

"比这还要糟糕，亲爱的……"福吉压低嗓门，低沉地嘟哝道，"没有多少人了解波特夫妇知道神秘人在找他们。邓布利多那时当然在不懈地跟神秘人做斗争，他有一些能干的密探，其中一个向他吐露了消息。他立刻提醒了詹姆和莉莉，建议他们躲一躲。当然啦，要躲过神秘人可不是件容易的事。邓布利多告诉他们，最好的办法是使用赤胆忠心咒。"

"那咒语怎么用？"罗斯默塔女士好奇地屏息问道。弗立维教授清了清嗓子。

"一个极其复杂的咒语。"他尖声解释道，"用魔法将某个秘密藏在一个活人的灵魂中。那秘密藏在被选定的人——即保密人的心里，因此永远不会被发现——当然，除非保密人主动泄露。只要保密人不说，神秘人即使在莉莉和詹姆住的村子里搜寻千年万载都不会发现他们，哪怕他把鼻子贴在他们起居室的窗户外面！"

"这么说，布莱克是波特的保密人？"罗斯默塔女士悄声问。

"自然。"麦格教授说，"詹姆·波特告诉邓布利多，布莱克宁死也不会说出他们在哪儿的，而且布莱克本人也准备躲起来……然而邓布利多还是不放心。我记得他提出要亲自担任波特夫妇的保密人。"

CHAPTER TEN   The Marauder's Map

'He suspected Black?' gasped Madam Rosmerta.

'He was sure that somebody close to the Potters had been keeping You-Know-Who informed of their movements,' said Professor McGonagall darkly. 'Indeed, he had suspected for some time that someone on our side had turned traitor and was passing a lot of information to You-Know-Who.'

'But James Potter insisted on using Black?'

'He did,' said Fudge heavily. 'And then, barely a week after the Fidelius Charm had been performed —'

'Black betrayed them?' breathed Madam Rosmerta.

'He did indeed. Black was tired of his double-agent role, he was ready to declare his support openly for You-Know-Who, and he seems to have planned this for the moment of the Potters' death. But, as we all know, You-Know-Who met his downfall in little Harry Potter. Powers gone, horribly weakened, he fled. And this left Black in a very nasty position indeed. His Master had fallen at the very moment when he, Black, had shown his true colours as a traitor. He had no choice but to run for it —'

'Filthy, stinkin' turncoat!' Hagrid said, so loudly that half the bar went quiet.

'Shh!' said Professor McGonagall.

'I met him!' growled Hagrid. 'I musta bin the last ter see him before he killed all them people! It was me what rescued Harry from Lily an' James's house after they was killed! Jus' got him outta the ruins, poor little thing, with a great slash across his forehead, an' his parents dead ... an' Sirius Black turns up, on that flyin' motorbike he used ter ride. Never occurred ter me what he was doin' there. I didn' know he'd bin Lily an' James's Secret Keeper. Thought he'd jus' heard the news o' You-Know-Who's attack an' come ter see what he could do. White an' shakin', he was. An' yeh know what I did? I COMFORTED THE MURDERIN' TRAITOR!' Hagrid roared.

'Hagrid, please!' said Professor McGonagall. 'Keep your voice down!'

'How was I ter know he wasn' upset abou' Lily an' James? It was You-Know-Who he cared abou'! An' then he says, "Give Harry ter me, Hagrid, I'm his godfather, I'll look after him —" Ha! But I'd had me orders from Dumbledore, an' I told Black no, Dumbledore said Harry was ter go ter his aunt an' uncle's. Black argued, but in the end he gave in. Told me ter take his motorbike ter get Harry there. "I won' need it any more," he says.

"他怀疑布莱克?"罗斯默塔女士吃惊地问。

"他断定波特夫妇身边的某个人一直在向神秘人报告他们的动向。"麦格教授神情阴郁地说,"实际上,在之前的一段时间里,他就已经在怀疑我们中间有人叛变了,为神秘人提供了许多情报。"

"但詹姆坚持用布莱克?"

"是的,"福吉沉重地说,"然后,赤胆忠心咒才施了不到一个星期——"

"布莱克就出卖了他们?"罗斯默塔低声问。

"是的。布莱克厌倦了他的双料间谍角色,准备公开宣布支持神秘人,而且似乎计划在波特夫妇死去的那一刻宣布。但是,我们知道,神秘人在小哈利·波特面前一败涂地。他失去了法力,变得极其虚弱,只能落荒而逃。这使得布莱克的处境非常尴尬。偏偏在他暴露了叛徒的本质时,他的主子垮台了。他别无选择,只能狼狈出逃——"

"卑鄙、龌龊的叛徒!"海格大叫一声,半个酒吧都静了下来。

"嘘——"麦格教授提醒海格。

"我碰到他了!"海格咆哮道,"我一定是在他害死那些人之前最后一个看见他的人!在莉莉和詹姆死后,是我把哈利从他家的房子里抢救出来的!我刚把哈利从废墟中抱出来,可怜的小东西,前额上有一道长长的伤口,爸爸妈妈都死了……这时小天狼星布莱克就出现了,骑着他以前的那辆会飞的摩托。我压根也没想到他在那儿干了什么勾当。我不知道他是莉莉和詹姆的保密人,还以为他刚听到神秘人袭击的消息,赶来相救呢。那小子脸色苍白,浑身发抖。你知道我干了什么吗?**我还安慰了那个杀人的叛徒!**"海格怒吼道。

"海格,拜托!"麦格教授说,"声音放低点儿!"

"我怎么知道他并不是为莉莉和詹姆难过呢?他关心的是神秘人!然后他说:'把哈利给我,海格,我是他的教父。我会照顾他——'哈!但我有邓布利多的命令,我就对布莱克说,不行,邓布利多说了哈利要去他的姨妈和姨父家。布莱克跟我争辩,但后来让步了,叫我用他的摩托车送哈利去。'我用不着它了。'他说。

CHAPTER TEN   The Marauder's Map

'I shoulda known there was somethin' fishy goin' on then. He loved that motorbike, what was he givin' it ter me for? Why wouldn' he need it any more? Fact was, it was too easy ter trace. Dumbledore knew he'd bin the Potters' Secret Keeper. Black knew he was goin' ter have ter run fer it that night, knew it was a matter o' hours before the Ministry was after him.

'*But what if I'd given Harry to him, eh?* I bet he'd've pitched him off the bike halfway out ter sea. His bes' friend's son! But when a wizard goes over ter the dark side, there's nothin' and no one that matters to 'em any more ...'

A long silence followed Hagrid's story. Then Madam Rosmerta said with some satisfaction, 'But he didn't manage to disappear, did he? The Ministry of Magic caught up with him next day!'

'Alas, if only we had,' said Fudge bitterly. 'It was not we who found him. It was little Peter Pettigrew – another of the Potters' friends. Maddened by grief, no doubt, and knowing that Black had been the Potters' Secret Keeper, he went after Black himself.'

'Pettigrew ... that fat little boy who was always tagging around after them at Hogwarts?' said Madam Rosmerta.

'Hero-worshipped Black and Potter,' said Professor McGonagall. 'Never quite in their league, talent-wise. I was often rather sharp with him. You can imagine how I – how I regret that now ...' She sounded as though she had a sudden head cold.

'There, now, Minerva,' said Fudge kindly, 'Pettigrew died a hero's death. Eye-witnesses – Muggles, of course, we wiped their memories later – told us how Pettigrew cornered Black. They say he was sobbing. "Lily and James, Sirius! How could you!" And then he went for his wand. Well, of course, Black was quicker. Blew Pettigrew to smithereens ...'

Professor McGonagall blew her nose and said thickly, 'Stupid boy ... foolish boy ... he was always hopeless at duelling ... should have left it to the Ministry ...'

'I tell yeh, if I'd got ter Black before little Pettigrew did, I wouldn't've messed around with wands – I'd've ripped him limb – from – limb,' Hagrid growled.

'You don't know what you're talking about, Hagrid,' said Fudge sharply. 'Nobody but trained Hit Wizards from the Magical Law Enforcement Squad would have stood a chance against Black once he was cornered. I was Junior

第10章 活点地图

"我当时就应该想到这里面有些可疑。那辆摩托车是他心爱的东西,为什么会送给我呢?他为什么用不着了呢?实际上是摩托车太容易被追踪了。邓布利多了解他是波特夫妇的保密人。布莱克知道自己必须连夜逃走,知道还有几小时魔法部就会通缉他。

"要是我把哈利交给了他会怎么样呢?我打赌他会在大海中央把那孩子从车上扔下去。他好朋友的儿子!当一个巫师投靠了黑势力,就会什么也不顾,什么人也不认……"

海格的故事讲完之后,一阵良久的沉默。后来罗斯默塔女士带着一丝快意说:"可是他没有逃得掉,是不是?魔法部第二天就把他逮住了!"

"唉,如果是我们就好了。"福吉苦涩地说,"并不是我们找到他的。是小矮星彼得——波特夫妇的另一个朋友。他一定是悲伤得发了狂,知道布莱克是波特夫妇的保密人,就自己去追布莱克。"

"小矮星……那个小胖墩男孩,在霍格沃茨总是像跟屁虫一样跟着他们的?"罗斯默塔女士问道。

"把布莱克和波特当英雄一样崇拜。"麦格教授说,"从天赋上讲,他跟他们从来不是一个级别的。我对他经常很严厉。你们可以想象我——我现在有多么后悔……"听声音她好像突然得了感冒。

"好了,米勒娃。"福吉温和地说,"小矮星死得很英勇。目击证人——当然都是麻瓜,我们后来消掉了他们的记忆——说小矮星截住了布莱克,哭着叫道:'莉莉和詹姆!小天狼星,你怎么下得了手?'然后他就拔魔杖。当然,布莱克比他敏捷,把小矮星炸成了碎片……"

麦格教授擤了一下鼻涕,瓮声瓮气地说:"傻孩子……傻孩子……他决斗总是没有什么希望的……应该交给魔法部的……"

"跟你说,要是我在小矮星之前堵住布莱克,我才不会浪费时间去拔魔杖——我会把他撕成一块一块的!"海格粗声说。

"你不知道自己在说什么,海格。"福吉尖刻地说,"要堵住布莱克,只有训练有素的魔法法律执行队的打击手才可能有些胜算。当时我是魔法灾难司的副司长,布莱克把那些人统统杀死之后,我是最先赶到

CHAPTER TEN   The Marauder's Map

Minister in the Department of Magical Catastrophes at the time, and I was one of the first on the scene after Black murdered all those people. I – I will never forget it. I still dream about it sometimes. A crater in the middle of the street, so deep it had cracked the sewer below. Bodies everywhere. Muggles screaming. And Black standing there laughing, with what was left of Pettigrew in front of him ... a heap of blood-stained robes and a few – a few fragments –'

Fudge's voice stopped abruptly. There was the sound of five noses being blown.

'Well, there you have it, Rosmerta,' said Fudge thickly. 'Black was taken away by twenty members of the Magical Law Enforcement Patrol and Pettigrew received the Order of Merlin, First Class, which I think was some comfort to his poor mother. Black's been in Azkaban ever since.'

Madam Rosmerta let out a long sigh.

'Is it true he's mad, Minister?'

'I wish I could say that he was,' said Fudge slowly. 'I certainly believe his master's defeat unhinged him for a while. The murder of Pettigrew and all those Muggles was the action of a cornered and desperate man – cruel ... pointless. Yet I met Black on my last inspection of Azkaban. You know, most of the prisoners in there sit muttering to themselves in the dark, there's no sense in them ... but I was shocked at how *normal* Black seemed. He spoke quite rationally to me. It was unnerving. You'd have thought he was merely bored – asked if I'd finished with my newspaper, cool as you please, said he missed doing the crossword. Yes, I was astounded at how little effect the Dementors seemed to be having on him – and he was one of the most heavily guarded in the place, you know. Dementors outside his door, day and night.'

'But what do you think he's broken out to do?' said Madam Rosmerta. 'Good gracious, Minister, he isn't trying to rejoin You-Know-Who, is he?'

'I daresay that is his – er – eventual plan,' said Fudge evasively. 'But we hope to catch Black long before that. I must say, You-Know-Who alone and friendless is one thing ... but give him back his most devoted servant, and I shudder to think how quickly he'll rise again ...'

There was a small chink of glass on wood. Someone had set down their glass.

'You know, Cornelius, if you're dining with the Headmaster, we'd better head back up to the castle,' said Professor McGonagall.

第 10 章 活点地图

现场的人之一。我——永远忘不了那一幕，至今有时还会梦到。街心炸了一个大坑，深得连下水道都裂开了。尸横遍野，麻瓜们哭天喊地。布莱克站在那儿哈哈大笑，他面前的小矮星只剩下……一堆血染的袍子和些许——些许碎片——"

福吉的话音突然中断了，只听见五人擤鼻子的声音。

"就是这样，罗斯默塔。"福吉声音发闷地说，"布莱克被二十名魔法法律执行队的队员带走了，小矮星被颁以梅林爵士团一级勋章。我想这对他可怜的妈妈也算是一丝安慰吧。布莱克此后就一直关在阿兹卡班。"

罗斯默塔女士发出一声长叹。

"他现在真的疯了吗，部长？"

"我希望能说是的，"福吉缓缓说道，"我确实相信他主子的垮台让他精神失常了一段时间。杀害小矮星和那么多麻瓜就是一种狗急跳墙的行为——残忍……毫无意义。可是我上次去视察阿兹卡班时碰到了布莱克。你们知道，那儿的大部分囚徒都坐在黑暗中自言自语，没有正常的意识……但我惊讶地发现布莱克看上去很正常。他相当理智地跟我说话。这令我感到不安。你会觉得他只是闷得慌——问我报纸看完了没有，要多冷静有多冷静，还说他很想做报纸上的填字游戏。这真让我大吃一惊，摄魂怪对他的影响似乎非常小——要知道，他还是那里被看守得最严密的要犯之一呢。摄魂怪日夜守在他的门外。"

"可是您认为他越狱出来想干什么呢？"罗斯默塔女士问，"天哪，不会是想去投奔神秘人吧？"

"我猜这是布莱克的——呃——最终计划。"福吉含糊其词地说，"但我们希望在那之前就抓住他。我必须说，神秘人在孤立无援的情况下是一种局面……但如果让他找回最忠心的仆人，他会迅速卷土重来。一想到这里我就不寒而栗……"

玻璃碰到木头的轻微叮当声，有人放下了杯子。

"你知道，康奈利，如果你要跟校长一起吃晚饭，最好现在就返回城堡。"麦格教授说。

CHAPTER TEN — The Marauder's Map

One by one, the pairs of feet in front of Harry took the weight of their owners once more; hems of cloaks swung into sight and Madam Rosmerta's glittering heels disappeared behind the bar. The door of the Three Broomsticks opened again, there was another flurry of snow, and the teachers disappeared.

'Harry?'

Ron and Hermione's faces appeared under the table. They were both staring at him, lost for words.

第10章 活点地图

　　哈利面前的几双脚依次重新支撑起主人的重量；袍子的下摆飘入他的眼帘，罗斯默塔女士亮闪闪的高跟鞋消失在吧台后面。三把扫帚的大门再次打开，一阵风雪再次卷入，教师们不见了。

　　"哈利？"

　　罗恩和赫敏的面孔出现在桌子底下，他们都呆呆地望着他，不知说什么好。

CHAPTER ELEVEN

The Firebolt

Harry didn't have a very clear idea of how he had managed to get back into the Honeydukes cellar, through the tunnel and into the castle once more. All he knew was that the return trip seemed to take no time at all, and that he hardly noticed what he was doing, because his head was still pounding with the conversation he had just heard.

Why had nobody ever told him? Dumbledore, Hagrid, Mr Weasley, Cornelius Fudge ... why hadn't anyone ever mentioned the fact that Harry's parents had died because their best friend had betrayed them?

Ron and Hermione watched Harry nervously all through dinner, not daring to talk about what they'd overheard, because Percy was sitting close by them. When they went upstairs to the crowded common room, it was to find Fred and George had set off half a dozen Dungbombs in a fit of end-of-term high spirits. Harry, who didn't want Fred and George asking him whether he'd reached Hogsmeade or not, sneaked quietly up to the empty dormitory, and headed straight for his bedside cabinet. He pushed his books aside and quickly found what he was looking for – the leather-bound photo album Hagrid had given him two years ago, which was full of wizard pictures of his mother and father. He sat down on his bed, drew the hangings around him, and started turning the pages, searching, until ...

He stopped on a picture of his parents' wedding day. There was his father waving up at him, beaming, the untidy black hair Harry had inherited standing up in all directions. There was his mother, alight with happiness, arm in arm with his dad. And there ... that must be him. Their best man ... Harry had never given him a thought before.

If he hadn't known it was the same person, he would never have guessed it was Black in this old photograph. His face wasn't sunken and waxy, but

第 11 章

火 弩 箭

哈利不大清楚他是怎么回到蜂蜜公爵地窖,又是怎么穿地道返回城堡的。他只知道回去的路上似乎没花多少时间。他也没有注意自己在做什么,因为脑袋里还在嗡嗡回响着刚才听到的那些话。

为什么没有人告诉过他呢?邓布利多、海格、韦斯莱先生、康奈利·福吉……为什么没人提到过,哈利的父母是因为最好的朋友背叛了他们才惨遭杀害的?

吃晚饭时,罗恩和赫敏一直紧张不安地看着哈利,不敢议论他们听到的消息,因为珀西就坐在旁边。当他们上楼来到挤满了人的公共休息室时,却看到弗雷德和乔治因为期末即将到来而兴奋不已,引爆了半打粪弹。哈利不希望弗雷德和乔治问他有没有去霍格莫德,便悄悄溜进了无人的宿舍,径直走到自己的床头柜前。他推开书本,很快就找到了他要找的东西——海格两年前给他的那本皮面相册,里面都是他父母的魔法照片。他坐到床上,拉好帷帐,开始一页页翻看相册,寻找着……

他翻到了一张爸爸妈妈婚礼上的照片,停住了。爸爸满面春风地向他挥手,那一头遗传给哈利的蓬乱的黑发向四面八方支棱着。妈妈容光焕发,幸福地与爸爸手挽着手。还有……一定就是他了。他们的伴郎……哈利以前压根儿没想到过他。

如果不知道是同一个人,他怎么也猜不到这张老照片上的人就是布莱克。他的面孔并不是蜡黄凹陷,而是十分英俊,笑容可掬。拍摄

CHAPTER ELEVEN The Firebolt

handsome, full of laughter. Had he already been working for Voldemort when this picture had been taken? Was he already planning the deaths of the two people next to him? Did he realise he was facing twelve years in Azkaban, twelve years which would make him unrecognisable?

But the Dementors don't affect him, Harry thought, staring into the handsome, laughing face. *He doesn't have to hear my mum screaming if they get too close –*

Harry slammed the album shut, reached over and stuffed it back into his cabinet, took off his robes and glasses and got into bed, making sure the hangings were hiding him from view.

The dormitory door opened.

'Harry?' said Ron's voice uncertainly.

But Harry lay still, pretending to be asleep. He heard Ron leave again, and rolled over on his back, his eyes wide open.

A hatred such as he had never known before was coursing through Harry like poison. He could see Black laughing at him through the darkness, as though somebody had pasted the picture from the album over his eyes. He watched, as though somebody was playing him a piece of film, Sirius Black blasting Peter Pettigrew (who resembled Neville Longbottom) into a thousand pieces. He could hear (though he had no idea what Black's voice might sound like) a low, excited mutter. 'It has happened, my Lord ... the Potters have made me their Secret Keeper ...' And then came another voice, laughing shrilly, the same laugh that Harry heard inside his head whenever the Dementors drew near ...

'Harry, you – you look terrible.'

Harry hadn't got to sleep until daybreak. He had awoken to find the dormitory deserted, dressed and gone down the spiral staircase to a common room that was completely empty except for Ron, who was eating a Peppermint Toad and massaging his stomach, and Hermione, who had spread her homework over three tables.

'Where is everyone?' said Harry.

'Gone! It's the first day of the holidays, remember?' said Ron, watching Harry closely. 'It's nearly lunchtime, I was going to come and wake you up in a minute.'

Harry slumped into a chair next to the fire. Snow was still falling outside the windows. Crookshanks was spread out in front of the fire like a large, ginger rug.

这张照片时，他是否已经在为伏地魔效劳了呢？他是否已经在谋划身边这两个人的死期？他是否意识到自己将面临十二年阿兹卡班的牢狱生涯，这十二年将使他变得面目全非？

但是摄魂怪对他没有影响，哈利盯着那张英俊的、笑容可掬的面孔想道，他不用在摄魂怪逼近时听到我妈妈的惨叫。

哈利用力合上相册，欠身把它塞回柜子里，然后脱了袍子，摘下眼镜，躺到床上，并确保帷帐将自己完全遮住。

宿舍的门开了。

"哈利？"罗恩的声音迟疑地问。

哈利躺着没动，假装睡着了。听到罗恩走了，他翻身仰面躺着，眼睛睁得大大的。

一股前所未有的仇恨，像毒药一般流遍哈利的全身。他看到布莱克在黑暗中向他大笑，就像有人把相册里的照片贴在了他的眼前。他又像放电影一样，看到小天狼星布莱克把小矮星彼得（他看上去像纳威·隆巴顿）炸成了碎片。他还听到了一个声音（虽然不知道布莱克的声音是什么样的）在兴奋地低语："成功了，主人……波特夫妇让我做他们的保密人。"接着是另一个声音，尖厉地狂笑，正是每当摄魂怪逼近时哈利脑海中回响的那种笑声……

"哈利，你——你脸色很难看。"

哈利天亮时才睡着，醒来时发现宿舍里已经没人了。他穿上衣服，走下旋转楼梯，公共休息室里空荡荡的，只有罗恩在揉着肚子吃薄荷蟾蜍糖，赫敏把作业摊满了三张桌子。

"人都哪儿去了？"哈利问。

"走啦！今天是放假第一天，记得吗？"罗恩仔细打量着哈利说，"快到午饭时间了，我正打算去把你叫醒呢。"

哈利颓然坐到壁炉旁的一把椅子上。雪花仍在窗外飞舞。克鲁克山趴在壁炉前面，像一块姜黄色的大皮毯子。

CHAPTER ELEVEN   The Firebolt

'You really don't look well, you know,' Hermione said, peering anxiously into his face.

'I'm fine,' said Harry.

'Harry, listen,' said Hermione, exchanging a look with Ron, 'you must be really upset about what we heard yesterday. But the thing is, you mustn't go doing anything stupid.'

'Like what?' said Harry.

'Like trying to go after Black,' said Ron sharply.

Harry could tell they had rehearsed this conversation while he had been asleep. He didn't say anything.

'You won't, will you, Harry?' said Hermione.

'Because Black's not worth dying for,' said Ron.

Harry looked at them. They didn't seem to understand at all.

'D'you know what I see and hear every time a Dementor gets too near me?' Ron and Hermione shook their heads, looking apprehensive. 'I can hear my mum screaming and pleading with Voldemort. And if you'd heard your mum screaming like that, just about to be killed, you wouldn't forget it in a hurry. And if you found out someone who was supposed to be a friend of hers betrayed her and sent Voldemort after her –'

'There's nothing you can do!' said Hermione, looking stricken. 'The Dementors will catch Black and he'll go back to Azkaban and – and serve him right!'

'You heard what Fudge said. Black isn't affected by Azkaban like normal people are. It's not a punishment for him like it is for the others.'

'So what are you saying?' said Ron, looking very tense. 'You want to – to kill Black or something?'

'Don't be silly,' said Hermione in a panicky voice. 'Harry doesn't want to kill anyone, do you, Harry?'

Again, Harry didn't answer. He didn't know what he wanted to do. All he knew was that the idea of doing nothing, while Black was at liberty, was almost more than he could stand.

'Malfoy knows,' he said abruptly. 'Remember what he said to me in Potions? "If it was me, I'd hunt him down myself ... I'd want revenge."'

'You're going to take Malfoy's advice instead of ours?' said Ron furiously. 'Listen ... you know what Pettigrew's mother got back after Black had

第11章 火弩箭

"你脸色真的不好。"赫敏担忧地望着哈利的面孔说。

"我没事儿。"哈利说。

"哈利,听我说,"赫敏跟罗恩交换了一下眼色,说道,"昨天我们听到的事一定让你非常难过,但要紧的是,你不能做任何傻事。"

"比如什么?"哈利问。

"比如去找布莱克。"罗恩一针见血地说。

哈利看得出,他们在他睡觉时已经把这段对话排练过了。他什么也没说。

"你不会的,是吗,哈利?"赫敏问。

"为布莱克送命不值得。"罗恩说。

哈利看着两个朋友,他们似乎一点儿也不理解他。

"你们知道每次摄魂怪离我太近时,我就会看到什么、听到什么吗?"罗恩和赫敏摇了摇头,面露惧色。"我听到我妈妈在尖叫,在向伏地魔哀求。如果你们听到自己的妈妈被杀死之前那样惨叫,你们也不会很快忘掉的。一旦得知有个据说是她朋友的人背叛了她,让伏地魔来追杀她——"

"你做不了什么!"赫敏惊慌地说,"摄魂怪会抓住布莱克,把他送回阿兹卡班的——那是他活该!"

"你听到了福吉说的,布莱克不像一般人那样受阿兹卡班的影响。对他来说那儿并不像对别人那样,是一种可怕的惩罚。"

"那你想说什么?"罗恩问,显得非常紧张,"你想——杀了布莱克还是怎么着?"

"别说傻话,"赫敏说,语气十分恐慌,"哈利不想杀谁,是不是,哈利?"

哈利又没有回答。他也不知道自己想做些什么。他只知道一点:布莱克逍遥法外,他却无所作为,这几乎是他无法忍受的。

"马尔福知道,"他突然说,"还记得他在魔药课上是怎么对我说的吗?'如果换了我,我肯定要复仇,我会亲自去追捕他。'"

"你要听马尔福的,却不听我们的劝告?"罗恩气急败坏地说,"听着……你知道布莱克下手之后,小矮星的妈妈得到的是什么吗?爸爸

CHAPTER ELEVEN   The Firebolt

finished with him? Dad told me – the Order of Merlin, First Class, and Pettigrew's finger in a box. That was the biggest bit of him they could find. Black's a madman, Harry, and he's dangerous –'

'Malfoy's dad must have told him,' said Harry, ignoring Ron. 'He was right in Voldemort's inner circle –'

'*Say You-Know-Who, will you?*' interjected Ron angrily.

'– so obviously, the Malfoys knew Black was working for Voldemort –'

'– and Malfoy'd love to see you blown into about a million pieces, like Pettigrew! Get a grip, Malfoy's just hoping you'll get yourself killed before he has to play you at Quidditch.'

'Harry, *please*,' said Hermione, her eyes now shining with tears, '*please* be sensible. Black did a terrible, terrible thing, but d-don't put yourself in danger, it's what Black wants ... oh, Harry, you'd be playing right into Black's hands if you went looking for him. Your mum and dad wouldn't want you to get hurt, would they? They'd never want you to go looking for Black!'

'I'll never know what they'd have wanted because, thanks to Black, I've never spoken to them,' said Harry shortly.

There was a silence, in which Crookshanks stretched luxuriously, flexing his claws. Ron's pocket quivered.

'Look,' said Ron, obviously casting around for a change of subject, 'it's the holidays! It's nearly Christmas! Let's – let's go down and see Hagrid. We haven't visited him for ages!'

'No!' said Hermione quickly. 'Harry isn't supposed to leave the castle, Ron –'

'Yeah, let's go,' said Harry, sitting up, 'and I can ask him how come he never mentioned Black when he told me all about my parents!'

Further discussion of Sirius Black plainly wasn't what Ron had had in mind.

'Or we could have a game of chess,' he said hastily, 'or Gobstones. Percy left a set –'

'No, let's visit Hagrid,' said Harry firmly.

So they got their cloaks from their dormitories and set off through the portrait hole ('Stand and fight, you yellow-bellied mongrels!'), down through the empty castle and out through the oak front doors.

They made their way slowly down the lawn, making a shallow trench in the glittering, powdery snow, their socks and the hems of their cloaks soaked

第11章 火弩箭

告诉我——梅林爵士团一级勋章,还有小矮星的一根手指头,装在盒子里。那是他们能找到的最大的一片残骸。布莱克是个丧心病狂的疯子,哈利,他非常危险——"

"马尔福的爸爸一定跟他讲过,"哈利说,没有理睬罗恩,"他就在伏地魔的核心圈子里——"

"说神秘人,行不行?"罗恩气呼呼地插话。

"——所以显然,马尔福一家知道布莱克在为伏地魔效劳——"

"——而且马尔福很乐意看到你像小矮星那样被炸成无数碎片!清醒清醒吧。马尔福只希望你在魁地奇比赛之前就把小命送掉。"

"哈利,求求你,"赫敏说,眼睛里泪光闪闪,"求求你理智一点儿。布莱克做了一件非常非常可怕的事情,但是不要——不要冒险,那会正中布莱克的下怀……哦,哈利,如果你去找他,就正好让布莱克占了便宜。你爸爸妈妈不希望你受伤,是不是?他们绝不会希望你去找布莱克!"

"我永远也不知道他们希望什么了,就因为布莱克,我从来就没跟他们说过话。"哈利断然说道。

一阵静默,克鲁克山大大地伸了个懒腰,屈伸着爪子。罗恩的口袋在颤动。

"我说,"罗恩显然是努力想转换话题,"这是假期!就快过圣诞节了!我们——我们到下面去看看海格吧,都好久没去看过他了!"

"不行!"赫敏马上说,"哈利不能离开城堡,罗恩——"

"好,我们去吧。"哈利坐直了身体,说,"我还可以问问他,在跟我讲我爸爸妈妈的事时,为什么从没提过布莱克!"

罗恩显然不想再继续谈论布莱克。

"或者我们可以玩一盘象棋,"他急忙说道,"或是高布石。珀西留了一副——"

"不,去海格那儿。"哈利坚决地说。

于是三人从宿舍拿了斗篷,爬出了肖像洞口("站住,决斗吧,你们这些黄肚皮的杂种!"),走下空荡荡的城堡,出了橡木大门。

他们在草坪上慢慢走着,细粉一般晶莹的雪地上留下一道浅浅的

CHAPTER ELEVEN The Firebolt

and freezing. The Forbidden Forest looked as though it had been enchanted, each tree smattered with silver, and Hagrid's cabin looked like an iced cake.

Ron knocked, but there was no answer.

'He's not out, is he?' said Hermione, who was shivering under her cloak.

Ron had his ear to the door.

'There's a weird noise,' he said. 'Listen – is that Fang?'

Harry and Hermione put their ears to the door, too. From inside the cabin came a series of low, throbbing moans.

'Think we'd better go and get someone?' said Ron nervously.

'Hagrid!' called Harry, thumping the door. 'Hagrid, are you in there?'

There was a sound of heavy footsteps, then the door creaked open. Hagrid stood there with his eyes red and swollen; tears splashing down the front of his leather waistcoat.

'Yeh've heard!' he bellowed, and he flung himself onto Harry's neck.

Hagrid being at least twice the size of a normal man, this was no laughing matter. Harry, about to collapse under Hagrid's weight, was rescued by Ron and Hermione, who each seized Hagrid under an arm and heaved him, Harry helping, back into the cabin. Hagrid allowed himself to be steered into a chair and slumped over the table, sobbing uncontrollably, his face glazed with tears which dripped down into his tangled beard.

'Hagrid, what *is* it?' said Hermione, aghast.

Harry spotted an official-looking letter lying open on the table.

'What's this, Hagrid?'

Hagrid's sobs redoubled, but he shoved the letter towards Harry, who picked it up and read aloud:

> Dear Mr Hagrid,
>
> Further to our inquiry into the attack by a Hippogriff on a student in your class, we have accepted the assurances of Professor Dumbledore that you bear no responsibility for the regrettable incident.

'Well, that's OK, then, Hagrid!' said Ron, clapping Hagrid on the shoulder. But Hagrid continued to sob, and waved one of his gigantic hands, inviting Harry to read on.

第11章 火弩箭

沟痕。袜子和斗篷的下摆都湿了,还结了冰。禁林看上去仿佛被施了魔法,每一棵树都银光闪闪,海格的小屋像一块撒了糖霜的蛋糕。

罗恩敲了敲门,没人应声。

"他不会出去了吧?"赫敏说,她裹着斗篷直打哆嗦。

罗恩把耳朵贴到门上。

"有一种奇怪的声音,"他说,"听——是牙牙吗?"

哈利和赫敏也把耳朵贴到门上。小屋里传出一声声低低的、抽搐的呻吟。

"要不要去叫人来?"罗恩紧张地问。

"海格!"哈利捶着门喊道,"海格,你在里面吗?"

一阵沉重的脚步声,门吱呀一声打开了。海格站在那儿,眼睛红肿,泪水啪嗒啪嗒地滴在皮背心的前襟上。

"你们都听说了?"他低吼道,一把搂住了哈利的脖子。

海格的身躯至少是常人的两倍,这可不是闹着玩的。哈利差点被他的重量压垮,幸亏罗恩和赫敏及时抢救,一边一个扶住海格的胳膊,把他搀回了屋里。海格顺从地被领到一把椅子里,一下扑到桌上,不可收拾地哭了起来。泪水亮晶晶地流了满脸,滴到乱蓬蓬的胡子里。

"海格,到底怎么啦?"赫敏震惊地问。

哈利发现桌上摊着一封公文样的信。

"这是什么,海格?"

海格的哭声更响了,他把信推向了哈利。哈利拿起来念道:

亲爱的海格先生:
  关于发生在您课堂上的鹰头马身有翼兽袭击学生一事,经进一步调查,我们接受了邓布利多教授的担保,相信在这一令人遗憾的事件中您没有责任。

"那不是没事了吗,海格?"罗恩拍着海格的肩膀说。但海格仍在哭泣,他挥了挥一只巨手,要哈利再往下念。

CHAPTER ELEVEN   The Firebolt

However, we must register our concern about the Hippogriff in question. We have decided to uphold the official complaint of Mr Lucius Malfoy, and this matter will therefore be taken to the Committee for the Disposal of Dangerous Creatures. The hearing will take place on April 20th, and we ask you to present yourself and your Hippogriff at the Committee's offices in London on that date. In the meantime, the Hippogriff should be kept tethered and isolated.

Yours in fellowship ...

There followed a list of the school governors.

'Oh,' said Ron. 'But you said Buckbeak isn't a bad Hippogriff, Hagrid. I bet he'll get off –'

'Yeh don' know them gargoyles at the Committee fer the Disposal o' Dangerous Creatures!' choked Hagrid, wiping his eyes on his sleeve. 'They've got it in fer interestin' creatures!'

A sudden sound from the corner of Hagrid's cabin made Harry, Ron and Hermione whip around. Buckbeak the Hippogriff was lying in the corner, chomping on something that was oozing blood all over the floor.

'I couldn' leave him tied up out there in the snow!' choked Hagrid. 'All on his own! At Christmas!'

Harry, Ron and Hermione looked at each other. They had never seen eye to eye with Hagrid about what he called 'interesting creatures' and other people called 'terrifying monsters'. On the other hand, there didn't seem to be any particular harm in Buckbeak. In fact, by Hagrid's usual standards, he was positively cute.

'You'll have to put up a good strong defence, Hagrid,' said Hermione, sitting down and laying a hand on Hagrid's massive forearm. 'I'm sure you can prove Buckbeak is safe.'

'Won' make no diff'rence!' sobbed Hagrid. 'Them Disposal devils, they're all in Lucius Malfoy's pocket! Scared o' him! An' if I lose the case, Buckbeak –'

Hagrid drew his finger swiftly across his throat, then gave a great wail and lurched forwards, his face in his arms.

'What about Dumbledore, Hagrid?' said Harry.

第11章 火弩箭

但我们不得不对该鹰头马身有翼兽表示担忧。现已决定支持卢修斯·马尔福先生的正式投诉,将此案提交处置危险动物委员会。开庭日期定于4月20日,届时请您携带鹰头马身有翼兽前往该委员会的伦敦办事处报到。在此期间,鹰头马身有翼兽应妥善拴系隔离。

谨致衷心的问候……

下面是校董事会成员名单。

"哦,"罗恩说,"可你说过巴克比克不是一头作恶的鹰头马身有翼兽呀,海格。我相信它不会有事的。"

"你不了解处置危险动物委员会那些滴水嘴石兽一样的家伙,"海格哽咽道,用袖子擦着眼睛,"他们专跟有趣的动物作对!"

海格木屋的角落里突然传来一阵响动,哈利、罗恩和赫敏迅速转过身。鹰头马身有翼兽巴克比克躺在屋角,大声咀嚼着什么血淋淋的东西,血流了一地。

"我不能把它拴在外面的雪地里!"海格哽咽着说,"孤零零的。在圣诞节里!"

哈利、罗恩和赫敏面面相觑。他们从未完全赞同海格对他所谓"有趣的动物"的看法,这些动物别人会称之为"可怕的怪物"。然而,巴克比克似乎并没有什么特别的危险。实际上,按照海格通常的标准,它真算得上是很可爱的。

"你必须准备充足有力的辩护,海格。"赫敏坐下来,把手放在海格粗大的胳膊上,"我相信你能证明巴克比克是安全的。"

"没有用!"海格抽泣道,"处置委员会的那帮魔鬼,他们都是受卢修斯·马尔福指使的,都怕他!如果我败诉了,巴克比克——"

海格迅速用手指在喉咙处划了一下,发出一声长号,又一下扑倒在桌上,脸埋在胳膊里。

"邓布利多怎么说呢,海格?"哈利说。

CHAPTER ELEVEN   The Firebolt

'He's done more'n enough fer me already,' groaned Hagrid. 'Got enough on his plate what with keepin' them Dementors outta the castle, an' Sirius Black lurkin' around –'

Ron and Hermione looked quickly at Harry, as though expecting him to start berating Hagrid for not telling him the truth about Black. But Harry couldn't bring himself to do it, not now he saw Hagrid so miserable and scared.

'Listen, Hagrid,' he said, 'you can't give up. Hermione's right, you just need a good defence. You can call us as witnesses –'

'I'm sure I've read about a case of Hippogriff-baiting,' said Hermione thoughtfully, 'where the Hippogriff got off. I'll look it up for you, Hagrid, and see exactly what happened.'

Hagrid howled still more loudly. Harry and Hermione looked at Ron to help them.

'Er – shall I make a cup of tea?' said Ron.

Harry stared at him.

'It's what my mum does whenever someone's upset,' Ron muttered, shrugging.

At last, after many more assurances of help, with a steaming mug of tea in front of him, Hagrid blew his nose on a handkerchief the size of a tablecloth and said, 'Yer right. I can' afford to go ter pieces. Gotta pull meself together ...'

Fang the boarhound came timidly out from under the table and laid his head on Hagrid's knee.

'I've not bin meself lately,' said Hagrid, stroking Fang with one hand and mopping his face with the other. 'Worried abou' Buckbeak, an' no one likin' me classes –'

'We do like them!' lied Hermione at once.

'Yeah, they're great!' said Ron, crossing his fingers under the table. 'Er – how are the Flobberworms?'

'Dead,' said Hagrid gloomily. 'Too much lettuce.'

'Oh, no!' said Ron, his lip twitching.

'An' them Dementors make me feel ruddy terrible an' all,' said Hagrid, with a sudden shudder. 'Gotta walk past 'em ev'ry time I want a drink in the Three Broomsticks. 'S like bein' back in Azkaban –'

He fell silent, gulping his tea. Harry, Ron and Hermione watched him

"他已经为我做得太多了,"海格呜咽道,"而且手头的事也够他忙的,要把摄魂怪挡在城堡外面,还有小天狼星就藏在附近——"

罗恩和赫敏立刻看了哈利一眼,仿佛以为哈利会责备海格没有告诉他布莱克的真相。但哈利不忍那么做,他看到海格那么难过,那么恐惧。

"听我说,海格。"他说,"你不能放弃。赫敏说得对,你只需要一场有力的辩护。你可以让我们当证人——"

"我看到过一个鹰头马身有翼兽发狂的案子。"赫敏动着脑筋,"那头鹰头马身有翼兽被开释了。我去帮你查一下,海格,看看经过是怎么样的。"

海格哭得更响了。哈利和赫敏求助地望着罗恩。

"嗯——我去冲杯茶好吗?"罗恩说。

哈利瞪了他一眼。

"每次有人难过时,我妈妈总是这么做的。"罗恩耸耸肩,咕哝道。

终于,在得到许多帮忙的保证,还有一杯热腾腾的茶摆在面前之后,海格用桌布那么大的手帕擤了擤鼻子,说道:"你们说得对。我不能崩溃,必须振作起来……"

猎狗牙牙怯生生地从桌子底下钻出来,把脑袋搁在海格的膝头。

"我最近不大正常,"海格用一只手抚摸牙牙,另一只手抹了把脸,"担心巴克比克,而且没人喜欢我的课——"

"我们喜欢!"赫敏当即撒了个谎。

"是啊,你的课棒极了!"罗恩说,在桌子底下把中指和食指交叉在一起,"呃——弗洛伯毛虫怎么样啦?"

"死了。"海格哭丧着脸说,"莴苣吃多了。"

"哦,真糟糕!"罗恩说,嘴唇在颤抖。

"还有那些摄魂怪让我感觉特别糟糕,"海格说着,猛然打了个激灵,"每次我想去三把扫帚喝酒都要从它们跟前经过。好像又回到了阿兹卡班——"

他沉默了,大口喝着茶。哈利、罗恩和赫敏都屏住呼吸看着他。

CHAPTER ELEVEN   The Firebolt

breathlessly. They had never heard Hagrid talk about his brief spell in Azkaban before. After a brief pause, Hermione said timidly, 'Is it awful in there, Hagrid?'

'Yeh've no idea,' said Hagrid quietly. 'Never bin anywhere like it. Thought I was goin' mad. Kep' goin' over horrible stuff in me mind ... the day I got expelled from Hogwarts ... day me dad died ... day I had ter let Norbert go ...'

His eyes filled with tears. Norbert was the baby dragon Hagrid had once won in a game of cards.

'Yeh can' really remember who yeh are after a while. An' yeh can' see the point o' livin' at all. I used ter hope I'd jus' die in me sleep ... when they let me out, it was like bein' born again, ev'rythin' came floodin' back, it was the bes' feelin' in the world. Mind, the Dementors weren't keen on lettin' me go.'

'But you were innocent!' said Hermione.

Hagrid snorted.

'Think that matters to them? They don' care. Long as they've got a couple o' hundred humans stuck there with 'em, so they can leech all the happiness out of 'em, they don' give a damn who's guilty an' who's not.'

Hagrid went quiet for a moment, staring into his tea. Then he said quietly, 'Thought o' jus' letting Buckbeak go ... tryin' ter make him fly away ... but how d'yeh explain ter a Hippogriff it's gotta go inter hidin'? An' – an' I'm scared o' breakin' the law ...' He looked up at them, tears leaking down his face again. 'I don' ever want ter go back ter Azkaban.'

The trip to Hagrid's, though far from fun, had nevertheless had the effect Ron and Hermione had hoped. Though Harry had by no means forgotten about Black, he couldn't brood constantly on revenge if he wanted to help Hagrid win his case against the Committee for the Disposal of Dangerous Creatures. He, Ron and Hermione went to the library next day, and returned to the empty common room laden with books which might help prepare a defence for Buckbeak. The three of them sat in front of the roaring fire, slowly turning the pages of dusty volumes about famous cases of marauding beasts, speaking occasionally when they ran across something relevant.

'Here's something ... there was a case in 1722 ... but the Hippogriff was convicted – urgh, look what they did to it, that's disgusting –'

'This might help, look – a Manticore savaged someone in 1296, and they

第11章 火弩箭

他们从没有听海格讲过他在阿兹卡班短暂的关押经历。停了一会儿，赫敏小心翼翼地问："那里是不是很可怕，海格？"

"你们不知道，"海格轻声说，"从没到过那样的地方。我以为自己要疯了，脑子里总想着可怕的事情……我被赶出霍格沃茨的那天……我爸爸去世的那天……我被迫让诺伯离开的那天……"

他眼里噙满了泪水。诺伯是海格在一次玩牌时赢到的小火龙。

"你过一阵子就想不起自己是谁了，根本看不到活下去的意义。我曾经希望就在睡梦中死掉……他们把我放出来的时候，真好像获得重生一样，一切全都想起来了。那真是世界上最美妙的感觉。要知道，摄魂怪可不乐意放我出来。"

"可你是无辜的呀！"赫敏说。

海格哼了一声。

"那关它们什么事？它们才不管呢。只要有几百个人关在那里，让它们把所有的快乐都吸走，它们才不在乎谁有罪谁没罪呢。"

海格又沉默了片刻，盯着他的茶。然后轻声说道："我想把巴克比克放走……想让它飞走……可是你怎么向一头鹰头马身有翼兽解释说它必须躲起来呢？而且——我很怕犯法……"他抬头望着他们，泪水又流下了面颊，"我不想再回阿兹卡班。"

这次拜访海格远远谈不上开心，倒是达到了罗恩和赫敏希望的效果。哈利心里绝对没有忘记布莱克，但也不能老是想着报仇了，因为他们要帮助海格打赢与处置危险动物委员会的官司。他和罗恩、赫敏第二天就去了图书馆，抱着一大堆书回到空无一人的公共休息室，这些书都是为巴克比克辩护可能用得着的。三个人坐在熊熊的炉火前，慢慢翻动着灰扑扑的卷宗，查阅关于劫掠性怪兽的著名案例，碰到相关的资料时偶尔会交谈几句。

"这儿有一条……一七七二年有个案子……但那头鹰头马身有翼兽被宣判有罪——啊，看他们对它干了什么，好恶心——"

"这个也许有用，看——一二九六年有一头人头狮身蝎尾兽袭击

CHAPTER ELEVEN The Firebolt

let the Manticore off – oh – no, that was only because everyone was too scared to go near it ...'

Meanwhile, in the rest of the castle, the usual magnificent Christmas decorations had been put up, despite the fact that hardly any of the students remained to enjoy them. Thick streamers of holly and mistletoe were strung along the corridors, mysterious lights shone from inside every suit of armour and the Great Hall was filled with its usual twelve Christmas trees, glittering with golden stars. A powerful and delicious smell of cooking pervaded the corridors, and by Christmas Eve, it had grown so strong that even Scabbers poked his nose out of the shelter of Ron's pocket to sniff hopefully at the air.

On Christmas morning, Harry was woken by Ron throwing his pillow at him.

'Oy! Presents!'

Harry reached for his glasses and put them on, squinting through the semi-darkness to the foot of his bed, where a small heap of parcels had appeared. Ron was already ripping the paper off his own presents.

'Another jumper from Mum ... maroon *again* ... see if you've got one.'

Harry had. Mrs Weasley had sent him a scarlet jumper with the Gryffindor lion knitted on the front, also a dozen home-baked mince pies, some Christmas cake and a box of nut brittle. As he moved all these things aside, he saw a long, thin package lying underneath.

'What's that?' said Ron, looking over, a freshly unwrapped pair of maroon socks in his hand.

'Dunno ...'

Harry ripped the parcel open and gasped as a magnificent, gleaming broomstick rolled out onto his bedspread. Ron dropped his socks and jumped off his bed for a closer look.

'I don't believe it,' he said hoarsely.

It was a Firebolt, identical to the dream broom Harry had gone to see every day in Diagon Alley. Its handle glittered as he picked it up. He could feel it vibrating, and let go; it hung in mid-air, unsupported, at exactly the right height for him to mount it. His eyes moved from the golden registration number at the top of the handle right down to the perfectly smooth, streamlined birch twigs that made up the tail.

'Who sent it to you?' said Ron in a hushed voice.

第11章 火弩箭

了一个人,被释放了——哦——不,那只是因为所有的人都不敢靠近它……"

这时候,在城堡的其他地方,五光十色的圣诞节装饰像往年一样布置起来了,尽管并没有几个学生留下来欣赏。走廊上拉起了冬青和槲寄生组成的粗彩带,每套盔甲里都闪烁着神秘的灯光。礼堂里照例摆着那十二棵圣诞树,树上有金色的星星闪闪发光。一股浓郁诱人的烹饪香味在走廊里弥漫,到了平安夜时,香味浓得连斑斑都把鼻子从罗恩的口袋里伸了出来,满怀希望地向空中嗅着。

圣诞节的早上,哈利被罗恩扔来的枕头砸醒了。

"嘿!礼物!"

哈利伸手摸到眼镜戴上,在半明半暗中眯眼向床脚望去。那里出现了一小堆包裹。罗恩已经在撕扯他自己礼物上的包装纸。

"妈妈送的又是一件毛衣……又是暗红色的……看看你是不是也有。"

哈利也有。韦斯莱夫人给他寄的是一件猩红色的毛衣,胸前还织出了格兰芬多的狮子图案。另外还有一打家里烤的小圆百果馅饼、一些圣诞糕点和一盒果仁脆糖。哈利把这些东西拿开时,发现底下还躺着一个狭长的包裹。

"那是什么?"罗恩望着这边问道,手里是一双刚拆包的暗红色袜子。

"不知道……"

哈利撕开包裹,倒吸了一口气,一把闪闪发光、精美绝伦的飞天扫帚滚到他的床单上。罗恩丢掉他的袜子,从床上跳下来细看。

"我真不敢相信。"他声音沙哑地说。

是一把火弩箭,跟哈利在对角巷时每天去看的那把梦寐以求的飞天扫帚一模一样。他把它拿在手中,扫帚把熠熠生辉。他能感觉到它在颤动,于是松开了手。扫帚便悬在半空中,恰好是他可以骑上去的高度。他用目光抚摸着它,从扫帚把顶端的金色登记号,细细地看到那白桦细枝做成的、柔韧光滑的流线型扫帚尾。

"谁送给你的呀?"罗恩压低声音问。

CHAPTER ELEVEN The Firebolt

'Look and see if there's a card,' said Harry.

Ron ripped apart the Firebolt's wrappings.

'Nothing! Blimey, who'd spend that much on you?'

'Well,' said Harry, feeling stunned, 'I'm betting it wasn't the Dursleys.'

'I bet it was Dumbledore,' said Ron, now walking round and round the Firebolt, taking in every glorious inch. 'He sent you the Invisibility Cloak anonymously ...'

'That was my dad's, though,' said Harry. 'Dumbledore was just passing it on to me. He wouldn't spend hundreds of Galleons on me. He can't go giving students stuff like this –'

'That's why he wouldn't say it was from him!' said Ron. 'In case some git like Malfoy said it was favouritism. Hey, Harry –' Ron gave a great whoop of laughter, '*Malfoy*! Wait 'til he sees you on this! He'll be sick as a pig! This is an *international*-standard broom, this is!'

'I can't believe this,' Harry muttered, running a hand along the Firebolt, while Ron sank onto Harry's bed, laughing his head off at the thought of Malfoy. '*Who* –?'

'I know,' said Ron, controlling himself. 'I know who it could've been – Lupin!'

'*What*?' said Harry, now starting to laugh himself. '*Lupin*? Listen, if he had this much gold, he'd be able to buy himself some new robes.'

'Yeah, but he likes you,' said Ron. 'And he was away when your Nimbus got smashed, and he might've heard about it and decided to visit Diagon Alley and get this for you –'

'What d'you mean, he was away?' said Harry. 'He was ill when I was playing in that match.'

'Well, he wasn't in the hospital wing,' said Ron. 'I was there, cleaning out the bedpans on that detention from Snape, remember?'

Harry frowned at Ron.

'I can't see Lupin affording something like this.'

'What're you two laughing about?'

Hermione had just come in, wearing her dressing-gown and carrying Crookshanks, who was looking very grumpy, with a string of tinsel tied around his neck.

'Don't bring him in here!' said Ron, hurriedly snatching Scabbers from

第11章 火弩箭

"看看有没有卡片。"哈利说。

罗恩撕开火弩箭的包装。

"没有！我的天哪，谁会为你花这么多钱呢？"

"嗯，"哈利说，他完全蒙了，"我打赌不是德思礼家。"

"我打赌是邓布利多。"罗恩一边说，一边围着火弩箭转来转去，欣赏那光彩夺目的每一寸，"他匿名给你送了隐形衣……"

"但那是我爸爸的，"哈利说，"邓布利多只是把它转交给我。他不会为我花几百个金加隆的。他不可能给学生送这样的礼物——"

"所以他才不说是他送的！"罗恩说，"怕马尔福那样的饭桶说这是偏心。嘿，哈利——"罗恩高声大笑起来，"马尔福！等他看到你骑着这个吧！他会像瘟猪一样萎掉的！这可是一把国际水准的飞天扫帚，没错！"

"真不敢相信。"哈利喃喃道，一只手抚摸着火弩箭，而罗恩倒在哈利的床上，为想象中的马尔福的窘样狂笑不已，"是谁——？"

"我知道了，"罗恩控制住自己，说道，"我知道可能是谁了——卢平！"

"什么？"哈利说，现在轮到他大笑起来，"卢平？我说，他要有那么多金子，就能给自己买几件新袍子了。"

"是啊，可是他喜欢你。"罗恩说，"你的光轮摔坏时他正好不在，也许他听说后就决定去对角巷给你买把这个——"

"你说什么，他不在？"哈利说，"我那次比赛时他正病着呢。"

"哦，他不在校医院。"罗恩说，"当时我在校医院关禁闭，斯内普罚我清洗便盆，记得吗？"

哈利皱眉看着罗恩。

"我看不出卢平能买得起这样的东西。"

"你们两个在笑什么？"

赫敏刚刚进来，穿着晨衣，抱着克鲁克山。克鲁克山看上去脾气很恶劣，脖子上挂了一圈金箔装饰。

"别把它带到这儿来！"罗恩急忙把斑斑从床里面抓起来，塞进自

CHAPTER ELEVEN The Firebolt

the depths of his bed and stowing him in his pyjama pocket. But Hermione wasn't listening. She dropped Crookshanks onto Seamus's empty bed and stared, open-mouthed, at the Firebolt.

'Oh, *Harry*! Who sent you *that*?'

'No idea,' said Harry. 'There wasn't a card or anything with it.'

To his great surprise, Hermione did not appear either excited or intrigued by this news. On the contrary, her face fell, and she bit her lip.

'What's the matter with you?' said Ron.

'I don't know,' said Hermione slowly, 'but it's a bit odd, isn't it? I mean, this is supposed to be quite a good broom, isn't it?'

Ron sighed exasperatedly.

'It's the best broom there is, Hermione,' he said.

'So it must've been really expensive ...'

'Probably cost more than all the Slytherins' brooms put together,' said Ron happily.

'Well ... who'd send Harry something as expensive as that, and not even tell him they'd sent it?' said Hermione.

'Who cares?' said Ron, impatiently. 'Listen, Harry, can I have a go on it? Can I?'

'I don't think anyone should ride that broom just yet!' said Hermione shrilly.

Harry and Ron looked at her.

'What d'you think Harry's going to do with it – sweep the floor?' said Ron.

But before Hermione could answer, Crookshanks sprang from Seamus's bed, right at Ron's chest.

'GET – HIM – OUT – OF – HERE!' Ron bellowed, as Crookshanks's claws ripped his pyjamas and Scabbers attempted a wild escape over his shoulder. Ron seized Scabbers by the tail and aimed a misjudged kick at Crookshanks which hit the trunk at the end of Harry's bed, knocking it over and causing Ron to hop on the spot, howling with pain.

Crookshanks's fur suddenly stood on end. A shrill, tinny whistling was filling the room. The Pocket Sneakoscope had become dislodged from Uncle Vernon's old socks and was whirling and gleaming on the floor.

'I forgot about that!' Harry said, bending down and picking up the Sneakoscope. 'I never wear those socks if I can help it ...'

第11章 火弩箭

己的睡衣口袋里。但赫敏根本没听,她把克鲁克山丢到西莫的空床上,张大了嘴巴瞪着火弩箭。

"哦,哈利!这是谁送给你的?"

"不知道。"哈利说,"没附卡片什么的。"

令他大为意外的是,赫敏对于这个新闻似乎既不兴奋也不感兴趣。相反,她脸色一沉,咬起了嘴唇。

"你怎么啦?"罗恩问。

"我不知道。"赫敏慢吞吞地说,"可是有点奇怪,不是吗?我是说,这应该是一把蛮好的扫帚,是不是?"

罗恩又急又恼地叹了口气。

"它是最好的飞天扫帚,赫敏。"

"所以肯定很贵……"

"可能比斯莱特林队所有的扫帚加起来都贵。"罗恩开心地说。

"那么……谁会送给哈利一件这么贵重的东西,而且还不告诉他是谁送的呢?"赫敏问。

"管他呢。"罗恩不耐烦地说,"喂,哈利,我可以骑一下吗?可以吗?"

"我想目前谁都不能骑这把扫帚!"赫敏尖声叫道。

哈利和罗恩望着她。

"那你说哈利用它做什么——扫地?"罗恩说。

赫敏还没回答,克鲁克山从西莫的床上一跃而起,正好扑到罗恩胸口。

"把——它——带——走!"罗恩吼道。克鲁克山的爪子在撕扯他的睡衣,而斑斑拼命想从他肩上逃走。罗恩抓住斑斑的尾巴,朝克鲁克山一脚踢去,却踢到了哈利床脚的箱子。箱子翻了。罗恩跳着脚,痛得哇哇大叫。

克鲁克山突然把毛竖起来,一种尖锐的呼啸声响彻了整个房间。袖珍窥镜从弗农姨父的旧袜子里掉了出来,在地上旋转着,闪闪发光。

"我把它给忘了!"哈利俯身捡起窥镜,"我尽量不穿这双袜子的……"

CHAPTER ELEVEN The Firebolt

The Sneakoscope whirled and whistled in his palm. Crookshanks was hissing and spitting at it.

'You'd better take that cat out of here, Hermione,' said Ron furiously; he was sitting on Harry's bed nursing his toe. 'Can't you shut that thing up?' he added to Harry, as Hermione strode out of the room, Crookshanks's yellow eyes still fixed maliciously on Ron.

Harry stuffed the Sneakoscope back inside the socks and threw it back into his trunk. All that could be heard now was Ron's stifled moans of pain and rage. Scabbers was huddled in Ron's hands. It had been a while since Harry had seen him out of Ron's pocket, and he was unpleasantly surprised to see that Scabbers, once so fat, was now very skinny; patches of fur seemed to have fallen out, too.

'He's not looking too good, is he?' Harry said.

'It's stress!' said Ron. 'He'd be fine if that stupid great furball left him alone!'

But Harry, remembering what the woman at the Magical Menagerie had said about rats only living three years, couldn't help feeling that unless Scabbers had powers he had never revealed, he was reaching the end of his life. And despite Ron's frequent complaints that Scabbers was both boring and useless, he was sure Ron would be very miserable if Scabbers died.

Christmas spirit was definitely thin on the ground in the Gryffindor common room that morning. Hermione had shut Crookshanks in her dormitory, but was furious with Ron for trying to kick him; Ron was still fuming about Crookshanks's fresh attempt to eat Scabbers. Harry gave up trying to make them talk to each other, and devoted himself to examining the Firebolt, which he had brought down to the common room with him. For some reason this seemed to annoy Hermione as well; she didn't say anything, but she kept looking darkly at the broom as though it, too, had been criticising her cat.

At lunchtime they went down to the Great Hall, to find that the house tables had been moved against the walls again, and that a single table, set for twelve, stood in the middle of the room. Professors Dumbledore, McGonagall, Snape, Sprout and Flitwick were there, along with Filch, the caretaker, who had taken off his usual brown coat and was wearing a very old and rather mouldy-looking tail coat. There were only three other students: two extremely nervous-looking first-years and a sullen-faced Slytherin fifth-year.

第 11 章 火弩箭

窥镜在他手中旋转尖啸，克鲁克山朝它嘶嘶喷着唾沫。

"你最好把那只猫带走，赫敏。"罗恩暴躁地说，坐到哈利的床上揉着他的脚趾，"你就不能把那玩意儿关掉吗？"赫敏大步走出房间后，他对哈利说。克鲁克山被带出门时，一双黄眼睛仍恶狠狠地盯着罗恩。

哈利重新把窥镜塞到袜子里，丢进了箱子。现在只能听到罗恩在痛苦而气恼地低声呻吟了。斑斑蜷缩在罗恩的手里。哈利已经很长一段时间没见到它离开罗恩的口袋了，此刻惊讶地发现以前胖乎乎的斑斑现在变成了皮包骨，还掉了一块块的毛，看上去让人很不舒服。

"它看上去不大健康，是不是？"哈利说。

"心理压力太大了吧！"罗恩说，"如果那个蠢笨的大毛球离它远点儿，它就没事了。"

但哈利想起神奇动物商店里那位女士说过老鼠只能活三年，不禁想道，斑斑除非有未曾显露的法力，否则就要走到生命的尽头了。虽说罗恩经常抱怨斑斑既乏味又无用，但哈利相信如果斑斑死了，他还是会很难过的。

那天早上，格兰芬多公共休息室里的圣诞气氛显然很淡。赫敏把克鲁克山关在她的宿舍了，但对于罗恩想踢它非常生气。罗恩仍在为克鲁克山又想吃斑斑而恼火。哈利放弃了让他们跟对方说话的努力，专心研究他的火弩箭——他把它带到了公共休息室。不知为什么，这似乎也让赫敏很生气；她倒没说什么，但总是脸色阴沉地瞪着那把飞天扫帚，好像它也得罪过她的猫似的。

午饭时他们下楼来到礼堂，发现学院餐桌又都被移到了墙边，一张十二人的餐桌摆在礼堂中央，邓布利多、麦格、斯内普、斯普劳特和弗立维教授坐在那儿，还有管理员费尔奇。费尔奇脱掉平素穿的那件棕色外套，换上了一件年头很久、看上去发了霉的燕尾服。另外只有三个学生，两个非常紧张的一年级学生，还有一个耷拉着脸的斯莱特林五年级学生。

CHAPTER ELEVEN   The Firebolt

'Merry Christmas!' said Dumbledore, as Harry, Ron and Hermione approached the table. 'As there are so few of us, it seemed foolish to use the house tables ... sit down, sit down!'

Harry, Ron and Hermione sat down side by side at the end of the table.

'Crackers!' said Dumbledore enthusiastically, offering the end of a large silver one to Snape, who took it reluctantly and tugged. With a bang like a gunshot, the cracker flew apart to reveal a large, pointed witch's hat topped with a stuffed vulture.

Harry, remembering the Boggart, caught Ron's eye and they both grinned; Snape's mouth thinned and he pushed the hat towards Dumbledore, who swapped it for his wizard's hat at once.

'Tuck in!' he advised the table, beaming around.

As Harry was helping himself to roast potatoes, the doors of the Great Hall opened again. It was Professor Trelawney, gliding towards them as though on wheels. She had put on a green sequined dress in honour of the occasion, making her look more than ever like a glittering, oversize dragonfly.

'Sybill, this is a pleasant surprise!' said Dumbledore, standing up.

'I have been crystal-gazing, Headmaster,' said Professor Trelawney, in her mistiest, most faraway voice, 'and to my astonishment, I saw myself abandoning my solitary luncheon and coming to join you. Who am I to refuse the promptings of fate? I at once hastened from my tower, and I do beg you to forgive my lateness ...'

'Certainly, certainly,' said Dumbledore, his eyes twinkling. 'Let me draw you up a chair –'

And he did indeed draw a chair in mid-air with his wand, which revolved for a few seconds before falling with a thud between Professors Snape and McGonagall. Professor Trelawney, however, did not sit down; her enormous eyes had been roving around the table, and she suddenly uttered a kind of soft scream.

'I dare not, Headmaster! If I join the table, we shall be thirteen! Nothing could be more unlucky! Never forget that when thirteen dine together, the first to rise will be the first to die!'

'We'll risk it, Sybill,' said Professor McGonagall impatiently. 'Do sit down, the turkey's getting stone cold.'

Professor Trelawney hesitated, then lowered herself into the empty chair,

第11章 火弩箭

"圣诞快乐!"哈利、罗恩和赫敏走到桌前时,邓布利多说道,"我们这么少的人,用学院餐桌显得有点傻……坐,坐吧!"

哈利、罗恩和赫敏并排坐到桌子末端。

"爆竹!"邓布利多兴高采烈地说,把一个银色大爆竹的尾端递给斯内普,斯内普不情愿地拉了一下。一声放炮般的巨响,爆竹炸开,露出了一顶大大的尖顶女巫帽,上面顶着一只秃鹫标本。

哈利想起了那个博格特,与罗恩相视一笑。斯内普的嘴唇抿得更薄了,他把帽子朝邓布利多一推。邓布利多马上用它换下了自己头上的那顶男巫帽。

"痛快地吃吧!"他招呼道,笑眯眯地环视着全桌。

在哈利拿烤土豆时,礼堂大门又打开了,是特里劳尼教授,她像踩着轮子一样朝他们滑了过来。为了庆祝节日,她穿了一件缀满金属亮片的绿衣服,看上去更像一只闪闪发光的超大号蜻蜓了。

"西比尔,真是让人喜出望外!"邓布利多站起来说道。

"我刚才在看水晶球,校长。"特里劳尼教授用她最虚无缥缈的声音说道,"令我吃惊的是,我看到自己抛下了孤独的午宴,来加入你们的欢宴。我怎能拒绝命运的昭示呢?我急忙从我的塔楼下来,恳请你们原谅我来迟了……"

"没问题,没问题,"邓布利多眼里闪烁着光芒,"我来给你弄一把椅子——"

他果然用魔杖从空中变出了一把椅子。椅子旋转了几秒钟,噗地落在斯内普和麦格中间。然而特里劳尼教授没有坐下,她的大眼睛滴溜溜地向桌边看了一圈,突然发出一声低低的尖叫。

"我不敢,校长!如果我坐到桌边,就是正好十三位!这是最不吉利的!别忘了,当十三个人一起用餐时,第一个站起来的肯定会第一个死去!"

"我们愿意冒险,西比尔。"麦格教授不耐烦地说,"坐下吧,火鸡都凉得跟石头一样了。"

特里劳尼教授犹豫了一会儿,然后慢慢坐到空椅子上。她闭上眼睛,

CHAPTER ELEVEN   The Firebolt

eyes shut and mouth clenched tight, as though expecting a thunderbolt to hit the table. Professor McGonagall poked a large spoon into the nearest tureen.

'Tripe, Sybill?'

Professor Trelawney ignored her. Eyes open again, she looked around once more and said, 'But where is dear Professor Lupin?'

'I'm afraid the poor fellow is ill again,' said Dumbledore, indicating that everybody should start serving themselves. 'Most unfortunate that it should happen on Christmas Day.'

'But surely you already knew that, Sybill?' said Professor McGonagall, her eyebrows raised.

Professor Trelawney gave Professor McGonagall a very cold look.

'Certainly I knew, Minerva,' she said quietly. 'But one does not parade the fact that one is All-Knowing. I frequently act as though I am not possessed of the Inner Eye, so as not to make others nervous.'

'That explains a great deal,' said Professor McGonagall tartly.

Professor Trelawney's voice suddenly became a good deal less misty.

'If you must know, Minerva, I have seen that poor Professor Lupin will not be with us for very long. He seems aware, himself, that his time is short. He positively fled when I offered to crystal-gaze for him –'

'Imagine that,' said Professor McGonagall drily.

'I doubt,' said Dumbledore, in a cheerful but slightly raised voice, which put an end to Professor McGonagall and Professor Trelawney's conversation, 'that Professor Lupin is in any immediate danger. Severus, you've made the Potion for him again?'

'Yes, Headmaster,' said Snape.

'Good,' said Dumbledore. 'Then he should be up and about in no time ... Derek, have you had any of these chipolatas? They're excellent.'

The first-year boy went furiously red on being addressed directly by Dumbledore, and took the platter of sausages with trembling hands.

Professor Trelawney behaved almost normally until the very end of Christmas dinner, two hours later. Full to bursting with Christmas dinner and still wearing their cracker hats, Harry and Ron got up first from the table and she shrieked loudly.

'My dears! Which of you left his seat first? Which?'

'Dunno,' said Ron, looking uneasily at Harry.

第11章 火弩箭

紧抿双唇,仿佛在等着雷电击中餐桌。麦格教授将一把大勺子插进了最近的汤碗里。

"牛肚要吗,西比尔?"

特里劳尼教授没有理睬。她睁开眼睛,环视了一遍周围,说道:"可是,亲爱的卢平教授在哪儿?"

"我担心那个可怜的人又病了。"邓布利多说,示意大家自己动手,"正赶上圣诞节,真是太不幸了。"

"可是你想必已经知道了吧,西比尔?"麦格教授扬起眉毛问。

特里劳尼教授冷冷地看了麦格教授一眼。

"我当然知道,米勒娃。"她淡淡地说,"但我们不会炫耀自己无所不知。我经常假装像是没有天目一样,免得让别人感到紧张。"

"原来如此。"麦格教授辛辣地说。

特里劳尼教授的声音突然变得不那么虚幻了。

"如果你非要知道的话,米勒娃,我看到可怜的卢平教授在我们这里待不长了。他似乎也知道自己时日无多。我说要给他看水晶球时,他几乎是匆匆逃走的——"

"可以想象。"麦格教授冷淡地说。

"我表示怀疑。"邓布利多说,语气轻松愉快,但稍稍提高了一点声音,这就结束了麦格教授和特里劳尼教授的对话,"我不相信卢平教授有什么迫在眉睫的危险。西弗勒斯,你又给他配制魔药了吗?"

"配了,校长。"斯内普答道。

"很好,"邓布利多说,"那他应该很快就能起来活动了……德雷克,你有没有尝过这些小香肠?味道好极了。"

被邓布利多招呼的那个一年级学生满面通红,用颤抖的双手接过了那盘香肠。

在两个小时的圣诞大餐中,特里劳尼教授的表现还算正常。哈利和罗恩被美味佳肴撑得肚子都快爆炸了,头上还戴着各自的爆竹帽子。午餐结束时,哈利和罗恩首先从桌旁站了起来,特里劳尼教授大声尖叫:

"亲爱的!你们哪个先站起来的?哪个?"

"不知道。"罗恩不安地看着哈利。

335

CHAPTER ELEVEN   The Firebolt

'I doubt it will make much difference,' said Professor McGonagall coldly, 'unless a mad axe-man is waiting outside the doors to slaughter the first into the Entrance Hall.'

Even Ron laughed. Professor Trelawney looked highly affronted.

'Coming?' Harry said to Hermione.

'No,' Hermione muttered. 'I want a quick word with Professor McGonagall.'

'Probably trying to see if she can take any more classes,' yawned Ron as they made their way into the Entrance Hall, which was completely devoid of mad axe-men.

When they reached the portrait hole they found Sir Cadogan enjoying a Christmas party with a couple of monks, several previous Headmasters of Hogwarts and his fat pony. He pushed up his visor and toasted them with a flagon of mead.

'Merry – hic – Christmas! Password?'

'Scurvy cur,' said Ron.

'And the same to you, sir!' roared Sir Cadogan, as the painting swung forward to admit them.

Harry went straight up to the dormitory, collected his Firebolt and the Broomstick Servicing Kit Hermione had given him for his birthday, brought them downstairs and tried to find something to do to the Firebolt; however, there were no bent twigs to clip, and the handle was so shiny already it seemed pointless to polish it. He and Ron simply sat admiring it from every angle, until the portrait hole opened, and Hermione came in, accompanied by Professor McGonagall.

Though Professor McGonagall was Head of Gryffindor house, Harry had only seen her in the common room once before, and that had been to make a very grave announcement. He and Ron stared at her, both holding the Firebolt. Hermione walked around them, sat down, picked up the nearest book and hid her face behind it.

'So that's it, is it?' said Professor McGonagall beadily, walking over to the fireside and staring at the Firebolt. 'Miss Granger has just informed me that you have been sent a broomstick, Potter.'

Harry and Ron looked around at Hermione. They could see her forehead reddening over the top of her book, which was upside-down.

'May I?' said Professor McGonagall, but she didn't wait for an answer

第11章 火弩箭

"我不相信这有多大区别,"麦格教授冷冷地说,"除非有个丧心病狂的刀斧手在门外等着,要砍死第一个走进门厅的人。"

连罗恩都笑了起来。特里劳尼教授似乎受了莫大的侮辱。

"走吗?"哈利问赫敏。

"不,"赫敏小声说,"我想跟麦格教授说句话。"

"大概是想问问她能不能再多上几门课吧。"罗恩打着哈欠说。两人走进门厅,根本没有看到什么丧心病狂的刀斧手。

来到肖像洞口,他们看到卡多根爵士正在跟两三个僧侣、几位霍格沃茨的前校长,以及他那匹肥肥的小灰斑马一起享用圣诞晚餐。他把头盔推上去,举起一壶蜂蜜酒向他们致意。

"圣诞——呃——快乐!口令?"

"下流的杂种狗。"罗恩说。

"你也一样,先生!"卡多根爵士高叫,肖像向前弹开,让他们进去了。

哈利径直回到宿舍,拿了他的火弩箭和赫敏送给他的生日礼物——飞天扫帚护理工具箱,下楼来想看看能对火弩箭做点什么。可是并没有折掉的短枝要修剪,扫帚把也光滑锃亮,似乎没有必要擦拭。他和罗恩只是坐在那里从各个角度欣赏它。忽然,肖像洞口再次打开,赫敏进来了,还有麦格教授。

麦格教授是格兰芬多学院的院长,但哈利以前只有一次在公共休息室里看到过她,那次她来是宣布一条非常重要的消息。此刻,哈利和罗恩都抓紧了火弩箭,呆呆地望着她。赫敏从他们旁边绕过去坐下,顺手抄起一本书挡住了自己的脸。

"就是这把,对不对?"麦格教授目光敏锐地说,走到壁炉前端详着火弩箭,"格兰杰小姐刚刚告诉我,有人送给你一把飞天扫帚,波特。"

哈利和罗恩都回头看赫敏,她露在书上方的额头正在变红,而且书都拿颠倒了。

"给我看看行吗?"麦格教授问,她没等回答,就把火弩箭从他们

CHAPTER ELEVEN The Firebolt

before pulling the Firebolt out of their hands. She examined it carefully from handle to twig-ends. 'Hmm. And there was no note at all, Potter? No card? No message of any kind?'

'No,' said Harry blankly.

'I see ...' said Professor McGonagall. 'Well, I'm afraid I will have to take this, Potter.'

'W-what?' said Harry, scrambling to his feet. 'Why?'

'It will need to be checked for jinxes,' said Professor McGonagall. 'Of course, I'm no expert, but I daresay Madam Hooch and Professor Flitwick will strip it down –'

'Strip it down?' repeated Ron, as though Professor McGonagall was mad.

'It shouldn't take more than a few weeks,' said Professor McGonagall. 'You will have it back if we are sure it is jinx-free.'

'There's nothing wrong with it!' said Harry, his voice shaking slightly. 'Honestly, Professor –'

'You can't know that, Potter,' said Professor McGonagall, quite kindly, 'not until you've flown it, at any rate, and I'm afraid that is out of the question until we are certain that it has not been tampered with. I shall keep you informed.'

Professor McGonagall turned on her heel and carried the Firebolt out of the portrait hole, which closed behind her. Harry stood staring after her, the tin of High-Finish Polish still clutched in his hands. Ron, however, rounded on Hermione.

'*What did you go running to McGonagall for?*'

Hermione threw her book aside. She was still pink in the face, but stood up and faced Ron defiantly.

'Because I thought – and Professor McGonagall agrees with me – that that broom was probably sent to Harry by Sirius Black!'

第11章 火弩箭

手中抽了过去,从头到尾仔细察看起来。"嗯,一张字条也没有吗,波特?没有卡片?没有任何信息?"

"没有。"哈利茫然答道。

"我知道了……"麦格教授说,"嗯,恐怕我要把这个拿走,波特。"

"什——什么?"哈利说着,慌忙站了起来,"为什么?"

"需要检查一下它上面有没有恶咒。"麦格教授说,"当然,我不是专家,但我想霍琦女士和弗立维教授会把它拆开——"

"拆开?"罗恩不相信地问,好像觉得麦格教授疯了。

"这要不了几个星期。"麦格教授说,"如果我们确认它不带恶咒,你就可以把它拿回来。"

"它没有问题!"哈利说,声音有点儿颤抖,"真的,教授——"

"你无法知道,波特。"麦格教授说,语气十分和蔼,"至少要等你骑它飞过之后才能知道。但在我们确定它没有被做过手脚之前,你恐怕不能骑它。有什么情况我会及时通知你的。"

麦格教授一转身,带着火弩箭出了肖像洞口。洞门在她身后关闭了。哈利站在那儿望着她消失的地方,那一罐速洁把手增光剂还抓在手里。罗恩则把气撒到了赫敏头上。

"你跑去找麦格教授干什么?"

赫敏把书丢到一边,脸上依然泛着红晕,但她站直身体,不服气地面对罗恩。

"因为我想——麦格教授也这么想——那把飞天扫帚可能是小天狼星布莱克送给哈利的!"

CHAPTER TWELVE

The Patronus

Harry knew that Hermione had meant well, but that didn't stop him being angry with her. He had been the owner of the best broom in the world for a few short hours, and now, because of her interference, he didn't know whether he would ever see it again. He was positive that there was nothing wrong with the Firebolt now, but what sort of state would it be in once it had been subjected to all sorts of anti-jinx tests?

Ron was furious with Hermione, too. As far as he was concerned, the stripping-down of a brand-new Firebolt was nothing less than criminal damage. Hermione, who remained convinced that she had acted for the best, started avoiding the common room. Harry and Ron supposed she had taken refuge in the library, and didn't try and persuade her to come back. All in all, they were glad when the rest of the school returned shortly after New Year, and Gryffindor Tower became crowded and noisy again.

Wood sought Harry out on the night before term started.

'Had a good Christmas?' he said, and then, without waiting for an answer, he sat down, lowered his voice and said, 'I've been doing some thinking over Christmas, Harry. After the last match, you know. If the Dementors come to the next one ... I mean ... we can't afford you to – well –'

Wood broke off, looking awkward.

'I'm working on it,' said Harry quickly. 'Professor Lupin said he'd train me to ward the Dementors off. We should be starting this week; he said he'd have time after Christmas.'

'Ah,' said Wood, his expression clearing. 'Well, in that case – I really didn't want to lose you as Seeker, Harry. And have you ordered a new broom yet?'

'No,' said Harry.

第12章

守 护 神

哈利知道赫敏的用意是好的,但还是忍不住生她的气。世界上最好的飞天扫帚,他拿到手里才短短几个小时,就因为赫敏横插一杠子,现在还不知道这辈子能不能再见到它。哈利可以肯定火弩箭目前没有一点毛病,但是在做了各种反恶咒的检测之后,会是什么模样,那就只有天知道了。

罗恩也很生赫敏的气。在他看来,将一把崭新的火弩箭拆开等于是犯罪行为。赫敏仍然认为自己这么做是为了哈利好,但她现在不到公共休息室来了。哈利和罗恩以为她躲到图书馆去了,也就没想着把她劝回来。总的来说,他们很高兴新年过后不久同学们就回来了,格兰芬多塔楼又变得拥挤和嘈杂起来。

开学前一天晚上,伍德找到哈利。

"圣诞节过得好吧?"他说,然后不等哈利回答,他就坐下来,压低嗓门说道,"过节的时候我好好想了想,哈利。上次比赛之后我一直在想。如果下次比赛摄魂怪再来……我的意思是……我们可禁不起你——怎么说呢——"

伍德顿住了,显得有些尴尬。

"我在努力呢,"哈利赶紧说道,"卢平教授说他要训练我抵御摄魂怪。应该从这个星期就开始。他说过完圣诞节他就有时间了。"

"啊,"伍德说着,脸上的表情变得开朗了,"如果是这样——我其实也不愿失去你这位找球手,哈利。还有,你订购新扫帚没有?"

"没有。"哈利说。

CHAPTER TWELVE   The Patronus

'What! You'd better get a move on, you know – you can't ride that Shooting Star against Ravenclaw!'

'He got a Firebolt for Christmas,' said Ron.

'A *Firebolt*? No! Seriously? A – a real *Firebolt*?'

'Don't get excited, Oliver,' said Harry gloomily. 'I haven't got it any more. It was confiscated.' And he explained all about how the Firebolt was now being checked for jinxes.

'Jinxed? How could it be jinxed?'

'Sirius Black,' Harry said wearily. 'He's supposed to be after me. So McGonagall reckons he might have sent it.'

Waving aside the information that a famous murderer was after his Seeker, Wood said, 'But Black couldn't have bought a Firebolt! He's on the run! The whole country's on the lookout for him! How could he just walk into Quality Quidditch Supplies and buy a broomstick?'

'I know,' said Harry, 'but McGonagall still wants to strip it down –'

Wood went pale.

'I'll go and talk to her, Harry,' he promised. 'I'll make her see reason ... a Firebolt ... a real Firebolt, on our team ... she wants Gryffindor to win as much as we do ... I'll make her see sense ... a *Firebolt* ...'

Lessons started again next day. The last thing anyone felt like doing was spending two hours in the grounds on a raw January morning, but Hagrid had provided a bonfire full of salamanders for their enjoyment, and they spent an unusually good lesson collecting dry wood and leaves to keep the fire blazing, while the flame-loving lizards scampered up and down the crumbling, white-hot logs. The first Divination lesson of the new term was much less fun; Professor Trelawney was now teaching them palmistry, and she lost no time in informing Harry that he had the shortest life-lines she had ever seen.

It was Defence Against the Dark Arts that Harry was keen to get to; after his conversation with Wood, he wanted to get started on his Anti-Dementor lessons as soon as possible.

'Ah yes,' said Lupin, when Harry reminded him of his promise at the end of class. 'Let me see ... how about eight o'clock on Thursday evening? The History of Magic classroom should be large enough ... I'll have to think

第12章 守护神

"什么！最好抓紧吧，要知道——你可不能骑着那把流星去打拉文克劳！"

"他圣诞节收到了一把火弩箭。"罗恩说。

"火弩箭？不可能！当真？一把——一把真的火弩箭？"

"别激动，奥利弗，"哈利闷闷不乐地说，"现在已经没有了，被没收了。"然后他一五一十地解释火弩箭怎样被拿去检测是否有恶咒了。

"恶咒？怎么可能有恶咒呢？"

"小天狼星布莱克，"哈利厌倦地说，"据说他要追杀的人是我。所以麦格教授认为扫帚可能是他送来的。"

听到大名鼎鼎的杀人犯要追杀他的找球手，伍德只是漫不经心地挥挥手，说："可是布莱克不可能买到一把火弩箭！他是在逃犯！全国都在通缉他！他怎么可能大摇大摆地走进魁地奇精品店去买扫帚呢？"

"我知道，"哈利说，"但麦格教授还是想把它拆开——"

伍德的脸发白了。

"我去找她谈谈，哈利。"他保证道，"我要让她想清楚……一把火弩箭……一把如假包换的火弩箭，在我们球队……麦格教授跟我们一样盼着格兰芬多赢……我要让她明白过来……一把火弩箭……"

第二天，学校恢复了上课。在这个阴冷潮湿的一月的上午，大家最不愿意的就是在场地上待两个小时，没想到海格为了让他们高兴，弄出了一堆篝火，里面都是火蜥蜴。这节课上得特别有意思，同学们收集柴火树叶，让火不断燃烧，那些喜欢火焰的蜥蜴，在烧得噼啪作响的木柴里蹿来蹿去。新学期的第一节占卜课就没劲多了，特里劳尼教授现在教他们看手相了。她一逮着机会就告诉哈利，他的生命线是她见过的最短的。

哈利盼望的课是黑魔法防御术。跟伍德交谈过之后，他希望抵御摄魂怪的训练课程能尽早开始。

下课后，哈利提醒卢平别忘记他答应的事。"是的，"卢平回答，"让我想想……星期四晚上八点怎么样？魔法史教室应该够大了……我必须仔细想想该怎么做……我们不可能把一个真的摄魂怪带进城堡里来

CHAPTER TWELVE The Patronus

carefully about how we're going to do this ... we can't bring a real Dementor into the castle to practise on ...'

'Still looks ill, doesn't he?' said Ron, as they walked down the corridor, heading to dinner. 'What d'you reckon's the matter with him?'

There was a loud and impatient 'tuh' from behind them. It was Hermione, who had been sitting at the feet of a suit of armour, repacking her bag, which was so full of books it wouldn't close.

'And what are you tutting at us for?' said Ron irritably.

'Nothing,' said Hermione in a lofty voice, heaving her bag back over her shoulder.

'Yes, you were,' said Ron. 'I said I wonder what's wrong with Lupin, and you –'

'Well, isn't it *obvious*?' said Hermione, with a look of maddening superiority.

'If you don't want to tell us, don't,' snapped Ron.

'Fine,' said Hermione haughtily, and she marched off.

'She doesn't know,' said Ron, staring resentfully after Hermione. 'She's just trying to get us to talk to her again.'

At eight o'clock on Thursday evening, Harry left Gryffindor Tower for the History of Magic classroom. It was dark and empty when he arrived, but he lit the lamps with his wand and had waited only five minutes when Professor Lupin turned up, carrying a large packing case, which he heaved onto Professor Binns' desk.

'What's that?' said Harry.

'Another Boggart,' said Lupin, stripping off his cloak. 'I've been combing the castle ever since Tuesday, and very luckily, I found this one lurking inside Mr Filch's filing cabinet. It's the nearest we'll get to a real Dementor. The Boggart will turn into a Dementor when he sees you, so we'll be able to practise on him. I can store him in my office when we're not using him; there's a cupboard under my desk he'll like.'

'OK,' said Harry, trying to sound as though he wasn't apprehensive at all and merely glad that Lupin had found such a good substitute for a real Dementor.

'So ...' Professor Lupin had taken out his own wand, and indicated that Harry should do the same. 'The spell I am going to try and teach you is highly advanced magic, Harry – well beyond Ordinary Wizarding Level. It is called the Patronus Charm.'

第12章 守护神

练习……"

"他的脸色还是不好,是吗?"罗恩说,这时他们顺着走廊去礼堂吃晚饭,"你说他究竟是怎么回事呢?"

身后传来一声很响、很不耐烦的咂嘴声。是赫敏,她坐在一套铠甲的脚上整理书包,书太多了,撑得书包都合不上了。

"你朝我们咂什么嘴啊?"罗恩恼火地说。

"没什么。"赫敏用清高自傲的语气说,把书包背到了肩上。

"你就是咂嘴了。"罗恩说,"我说不知道卢平是怎么回事,然后你就——"

"这不是明摆着的事吗?"赫敏带着令人气恼的优越感说。

"如果你不想告诉我们,就别说。"罗恩没好气地说。

"很好。"赫敏傲慢地说,然后大步流星地走开了。

"她其实不知道,"罗恩气呼呼地瞪着赫敏的背影,说,"她只是想让我们重新跟她说话。"

星期四晚上八点,哈利离开格兰芬多塔楼去魔法史教室。到了那儿,教室里空荡荡的,一片漆黑。他用魔杖把灯点亮,只等了五分钟,卢平教授就出现了,手里提着一个大货箱。他把货箱放在宾斯教授的讲台上。

"那是什么?"哈利问。

"另外一个博格特。"卢平说着,脱掉斗篷,"我从星期二就开始在城堡里四处搜寻,还算走运,我发现这家伙躲在费尔奇先生的档案柜里。这是我们能找到的最接近摄魂怪的东西了。博格特一看见你就会变成摄魂怪,我们就可以拿它来练习。用不着的时候,我把它存在我的办公室里。我桌子底下有个柜子,它会喜欢的。"

"好吧。"哈利说,尽量使语气听起来好像他一点也不担心,正为卢平找到这么一个理想的摄魂怪替代品而感到高兴。

"那么……"卢平教授抽出自己的魔杖,示意哈利也照着做,"我马上要演示并教给你的咒语,哈利,是一种非常高深的魔法——远远超出了普通巫师等级考试的水平。这个咒语名叫守护神咒。"

345

CHAPTER TWELVE   The Patronus

'How does it work?' said Harry nervously.

'Well, when it works correctly, it conjures up a Patronus,' said Lupin, 'which is a kind of Anti-Dementor – a guardian which acts as a shield between you and the Dementor.'

Harry had a sudden vision of himself crouching behind a Hagrid-sized figure holding a large club. Professor Lupin continued, 'The Patronus is a kind of positive force, a projection of the very things that the Dementor feeds upon – hope, happiness, the desire to survive – but it cannot feel despair, as real humans can, so the Dementors can't hurt it. But I must warn you, Harry, that the Charm might be too advanced for you. Many qualified wizards have difficulty with it.'

'What does a Patronus look like?' said Harry curiously.

'Each one is unique to the wizard who conjures it.'

'And how do you conjure it?'

'With an incantation, which will work only if you are concentrating, with all your might, on a single, very happy memory.'

Harry cast about for a happy memory. Certainly, nothing that had happened to him at the Dursleys' was going to do. Finally, he settled on the moment when he had first ridden a broomstick.

'Right,' he said, trying to recall as exactly as possible the wonderful, soaring sensation in his stomach.

'The incantation is this –' Lupin cleared his throat, '*expecto patronum!*'

'*Expecto patronum,*' Harry repeated under his breath, '*expecto patronum.*'

'Concentrating hard on your happy memory?'

'Oh – yeah –' said Harry, quickly forcing his thoughts back to that first broom-ride. '*Expecto patrono* – no, *patronum* – sorry – *expecto patronum, expecto patronum* –'

Something whooshed suddenly out of the end of his wand; it looked like a wisp of silvery gas.

'Did you see that?' said Harry excitedly. 'Something happened!'

'Very good,' said Lupin, smiling. 'Right then – ready to try it on a Dementor?'

'Yes,' Harry said, gripping his wand very tightly, and moving into the middle of the deserted classroom. He tried to keep his mind on flying, but something else kept intruding ... any second now, he might hear his mother

第12章 守护神

"有什么作用呢?"哈利紧张地问。

"是这样的,如果做得正确,就会变出一个守护神,"卢平说,"它是摄魂怪克星——是一个守护者,像盾牌一样挡在你和摄魂怪之间。"

哈利脑子里突然闪过一个画面:自己躲在一个海格那么庞大、拿着大棒的身影后面。卢平教授继续说道:"守护神是一种积极的力量,是摄魂怪赖以为生的那些东西的外化表现——希望、快乐、求生的欲望——但它不像真人一样能感受到绝望,所以摄魂怪奈何不了它。不过我必须提醒你,哈利,这个咒语对你来说可能太艰深了,许多合格的巫师都没能够掌握。"

"守护神是什么样子?"哈利好奇地问。

"每个守护神都是变它出来的巫师所独有的。"

"是怎么变出来的呢?"

"念一个咒语,必须把所有的意念都集中在某个特别愉快的时刻,这咒语才会生效。"

哈利绞尽脑汁想一个愉快的时刻。毫无疑问,他在德思礼家的所有遭遇都不能考虑。最后,他选定了第一次骑飞天扫帚的时刻。

"好了。"他说,尽量准确地回忆心里那种奇妙的、飞翔的感觉。

"咒语是——"卢平清了清嗓子,"呼神护卫!"

"呼神护卫,"哈利不出声地重复着,"呼神护卫。"

"你把意念都集中在那愉快的回忆上了吗?"

"噢——是啊——"哈利说,赶紧强迫自己的思绪回到第一次骑飞天扫帚的时候,"呼神护佑——不对,护卫——对不起——呼神护卫,呼神护卫——"

突然,什么东西从他的魔杖尖上蹿了出来,看上去像一团银白色的气体。

"看见了吗?"哈利兴奋地说,"有反应了!"

"很好,"卢平微笑着说,"那么——准备好在摄魂怪身上练习了吗?"

"准备好了。"哈利说着,把魔杖攥得紧紧的,走到空荡荡的教室中央。他努力让自己只想着那次飞行,可是别的东西总是闯进来……

CHAPTER TWELVE The Patronus

again ... but he shouldn't think that, or he *would* hear her again, and he didn't want to ... or did he?

Lupin grasped the lid of the packing case and pulled.

A Dementor rose slowly from the box, its hooded face turned towards Harry, one glistening, scabbed hand gripping its cloak. The lamps around the classroom flickered and went out. The Dementor stepped from the box and started to sweep silently towards Harry, drawing a deep, rattling breath. A wave of piercing cold broke over him –

'*Expecto patronum!*' Harry yelled. '*Expecto patronum! Expecto –*'

But the classroom and the Dementor were dissolving ... Harry was falling again through thick white fog, and his mother's voice was louder than ever, echoing inside his head – '*Not Harry! Not Harry! Please – I'll do anything –*'

'*Stand aside – stand aside, girl –*'

'Harry!'

Harry jerked back to life. He was lying flat on his back on the floor. The classroom lamps were alight again. He didn't have to ask what had happened.

'Sorry,' he muttered, sitting up and feeling cold sweat trickling down behind his glasses.

'Are you all right?' said Lupin.

'Yes ...' Harry pulled himself up on one of the desks and leant against it.

'Here –' Lupin handed him a Chocolate Frog. 'Eat this before we try again. I didn't expect you to do it first time. In fact, I would have been astounded if you had.'

'It's getting worse,' Harry muttered, biting the Frog's head off. 'I could hear her louder that time – and him – Voldemort –'

Lupin looked paler than usual.

'Harry, if you don't want to continue, I will more than understand –'

'I do!' said Harry fiercely, stuffing the rest of the Chocolate Frog into his mouth. 'I've got to! What if the Dementors turn up at our match against Ravenclaw? I can't afford to fall off again. If we lose this game we've lost the Quidditch Cup!'

'All right then ...' said Lupin. 'You might want to select another memory, a happy memory, I mean, to concentrate on ... that one doesn't seem to have been strong enough ...'

第12章 守护神

现在，他随时都可能再次听见妈妈的声音……但是他不应该这么想，不然肯定会再次听见她的声音，他不愿听见……难道他愿意听见吗？

卢平抓住货箱的盖子，猛地一掀。

一个摄魂怪慢慢地从箱子里冒了出来，戴兜帽的脸朝哈利这边转来，一只闪着寒光、生着疥癣的手抓着斗篷。教室里的灯闪了几闪，熄灭了。摄魂怪从箱子里走出来，开始悄没声儿地朝哈利快速逼近，同时发出低沉的、呼噜呼噜的喘息声。一股渗透骨髓的寒意笼罩了哈利——

"呼神护卫！"哈利大喊，"呼神护卫！呼神……"

然而，教室和摄魂怪在消失……哈利再度坠入厚厚的白色浓雾，妈妈的声音比以往任何时候都更加响亮，在他脑海里回荡——"别碰哈利！别碰哈利！求求你——要我怎样都行——"

"闪开——闪开，女人——"

"哈利！"

哈利猛地醒转过来。他仰面躺在地板上。教室的灯又亮了。他不需要问刚才发生了什么。

"对不起。"他低声说，坐了起来，感觉冷汗在眼镜后面往下流。

"你没事吧？"卢平说。

"没事……"哈利扶着一张桌子站了起来，然后靠在桌上。

"给——"卢平递给他一只巧克力蛙，"把它吃了，我们再试一次。我本来就没指望你能一次成功。说实在的，如果你真的成功了，我倒会感到震惊呢。"

"更糟糕了，"哈利嘟哝着说，一口咬掉了巧克力蛙的脑袋，"这次我听见她的声音更响了——还有他——伏地魔——"

卢平的脸色比平素更加苍白。

"哈利，如果你不想继续，我完全能够理解——"

"我想继续！"哈利情绪激动地说，把剩下来的巧克力蛙全部塞进了嘴里，"我必须继续！如果我们跟拉文克劳比赛的时候，摄魂怪突然出现了怎么办？我可不能再摔下来了。要是这场比赛再输了，我们的魁地奇杯就丢了！"

"那好吧……"卢平说，"你可能需要另外挑选一段回忆，我是说一段愉快的回忆，把意念集中在上面……刚才那个好像还不够强烈……"

CHAPTER TWELVE The Patronus

Harry thought hard, and decided his feelings when Gryffindor had won the House Championship last year had definitely qualified as very happy. He gripped his wand tightly again, and took up his position in the middle of the classroom.

'Ready?' said Lupin, gripping the box lid.

'Ready,' said Harry, trying hard to fill his head with happy thoughts about Gryffindor winning, and not dark thoughts about what was going to happen when the box opened.

'Go!' said Lupin, pulling off the lid. The room went icily cold and dark once more. The Dementor glided forwards, drawing its rattly breath; one rotting hand was extending towards Harry –

'*Expecto patronum!*' Harry yelled. '*Expecto patronum! Expecto pat–*'

White fog obscured his senses ... big, blurred shapes were moving around him ... then came a new voice, a man's voice, shouting, panicking –

'*Lily, take Harry and go! It's him! Go! Run! I'll hold him off –*'

The sounds of someone stumbling from a room – a door bursting open – a cackle of high-pitched laughter –

'Harry! Harry ... wake up ...'

Lupin was tapping Harry hard on the face. This time it was a minute before Harry understood why he was lying on a dusty classroom floor.

'I heard my dad,' Harry mumbled. 'That's the first time I've ever heard him – he tried to take on Voldemort himself, to give my mum time to run for it ...'

Harry suddenly realised that there were tears on his face mingling with the sweat. He bent his face low as possible, wiping them off on his robes, pretending to do up his shoelace, so that Lupin wouldn't see.

'You heard James?' said Lupin, in a strange voice.

'Yeah ...' Face dry, Harry looked up. 'Why – you didn't know my dad, did you?'

'I – I did, as a matter of fact,' said Lupin. 'We were friends at Hogwarts. Listen, Harry – perhaps we should leave it here for tonight. This charm is ridiculously advanced ... I shouldn't have suggested putting you through this ...'

'No!' said Harry. He got up again. 'I'll have one more go! I'm not thinking of happy enough things, that's what it is ... hang on ...'

第12章 守护神

哈利使劲地想着,认为去年格兰芬多赢得学院杯冠军赛时,他的心情无疑是非常愉快的。他再次紧紧抓住魔杖,在教室中央摆好了姿势。

"准备好了吗?"卢平抓着箱子盖问道。

"好了。"哈利说,拼命让格兰芬多获胜的愉快想法占据自己的大脑,而不去想箱子打开后会发生的可怕事情。

"开始!"卢平说,一把掀开盖子。教室里再一次变得寒冷刺骨,一片黑暗。摄魂怪向前滑行,发出呼哧呼哧的喘息声,一只腐烂的手直朝哈利伸来——

"呼神护卫!"哈利大喊,"呼神护卫!呼神护——"

白色的雾气笼罩了他的意识……周围移动着一些大而模糊的身影……接着传来一个新的声音,一个男人的声音,正在紧张地高叫——

"莉莉,带着哈利快走!是他!快走!快跑!我来拖住他——"

有人从房间里跌跌撞撞跑出来——一扇门猛地打开——一阵刺耳的嘎嘎狂笑——

"哈利!哈利……醒醒……"

卢平用力拍打着哈利的面颊。这次,哈利过了一分钟才弄清自己为什么躺在一间灰扑扑的教室的地板上。

"我听见我爸爸的声音了,"哈利喃喃地说,"这是我第一次听见他的声音——他想自己牵制住伏地魔,让我妈妈有时间逃生……"

哈利突然意识到脸上有泪水跟汗水混在一起。为了不让卢平看见,他假装系鞋带,尽量把脸埋得很低,在袍子上擦去泪水。

"你听见詹姆的声音了?"卢平问,声音有些异样。

"是啊……"哈利擦干了脸,抬起头来,"怎么——你不认识我爸爸,是吗?"

"我——我,实际上我认识,"卢平说,"我们在霍格沃茨是朋友。听着,哈利——也许今晚应该到此为止了。这个咒语特别高深……我不应该提出让你经历这个……"

"不!"哈利说,重新站起身来,"我还要再试一次!我想的事情不够愉快,所以才会这样……等一等……"

CHAPTER TWELVE — The Patronus

He racked his brains. A really, really happy memory ... one that he could turn into a good, strong Patronus ...

The moment when he'd first found out he was a wizard, and would be leaving the Dursleys for Hogwarts! If that wasn't a happy memory, he didn't know what was ... concentrating very hard on how he had felt when he'd realised he'd be leaving Privet Drive, Harry got to his feet and faced the packing case once more.

'Ready?' said Lupin, who looked as though he was doing this against his better judgement. 'Concentrating hard? All right – go!'

He pulled off the lid of the case for the third time, and the Dementor rose out of it; the room fell cold and dark –

'*EXPECTO PATRONUM!*' Harry bellowed. '*EXPECTO PATRONUM! EXPECTO PATRONUM!*'

The screaming inside Harry's head had started again – except this time, it sounded as though it was coming from a badly tuned radio. Softer and louder and softer again ... and he could still see the Dementor ... it had halted ... and then a huge, silver shadow came bursting out of the end of Harry's wand, to hover between him and the Dementor, and though Harry's legs felt like water, he was still on his feet ... though for how much longer, he wasn't sure ...

'*Riddikulus!*' roared Lupin, springing forwards.

There was a loud crack, and Harry's cloudy Patronus vanished along with the Dementor; he sank into a chair, feeling as exhausted as if he'd just run a mile, his legs shaking. Out of the corner of his eye, he saw Professor Lupin forcing the Boggart back into the packing case with his wand; it had turned into a silvery orb again.

'Excellent!' Lupin said, striding over to where Harry sat. 'Excellent, Harry! That was definitely a start!'

'Can we have another go? Just one more go?'

'Not now,' said Lupin firmly. 'You've had enough for one night. Here –'

He handed Harry a large bar of Honeydukes' best chocolate.

'Eat the lot, or Madam Pomfrey will be after my blood. Same time next week?'

'OK,' said Harry. He took a bite of the chocolate and watched Lupin extinguishing the lamps that had rekindled with the disappearance of the Dementor. A thought had just occurred to him.

'Professor Lupin?' he said. 'If you knew my dad, you must've known Sirius

第12章　守护神

他搜肠刮肚。一段特别特别愉快的记忆……他可以用它变出一个强壮有力的守护神……

当他第一次发现自己是个巫师，要离开德思礼家去霍格沃茨上学的那一刻！如果那还不能算愉快的记忆，他就不知道还有什么才能算了……哈利集中意念体会当时得知自己将要离开女贞路的感觉。他站稳脚跟，再一次面对那个货箱。

"准备好了？"卢平说，看上去他似乎在做一件违心的事情，"集中意念了？好——开始！"

他第三次掀开箱盖，摄魂怪从里面冒了出来，教室里一片寒冷、黑暗——

"**呼神护卫！**"哈利吼道，"**呼神护卫！呼神护卫！**"

哈利脑海里的尖叫声又出现了——不过这次像是从一台没有调准的收音机里发出来的。忽高，忽低，忽高，忽低……他仍然能看见摄魂怪……摄魂怪已经停住了……接着一个巨大的银色影子从哈利的魔杖尖上喷了出来，悬在他和摄魂怪之间。哈利虽然两腿软弱无力，但仍然站着……他没有把握自己还能站多久……

"滑稽滑稽！"卢平大吼着，冲上前来。

啪的一声，哈利那只模糊不清的守护神随着摄魂怪一起消失了。他跌坐在椅子上，感到精疲力竭，就好像刚跑了一英里似的，双腿不住地发抖。他眼角瞥见卢平教授用魔杖把博格特驱赶进了货箱里。博格特已经又变成了银色的圆球。

"很出色！"卢平说着，大步走到哈利面前，"很出色，哈利！终于有起色了！"

"我们再试一次行吗？就一次？"

"现在不行，"卢平坚决地说，"一个晚上练这么多就够了。给——"他递给哈利一大块蜂蜜公爵最好的巧克力。

"把它吃了，不然庞弗雷女士会来找我算账的。下星期还是这个时间？"

"好的。"哈利说。他咬了一口巧克力，望着卢平把刚才摄魂怪消失后重新亮起的灯再次熄灭。他脑海里突然闪过一个念头。

"卢平教授？"他说，"既然你认识我爸爸，那么也一定认识小天

CHAPTER TWELVE The Patronus

Black as well.'

Lupin turned very quickly.

'What gives you that idea?' he said sharply.

'Nothing – I mean, I just knew they were friends at Hogwarts, too ...'

Lupin's face relaxed.

'Yes, I knew him,' he said shortly. 'Or I thought I did. You'd better get off, Harry, it's getting late.'

Harry left the classroom, walked along the corridor and around a corner, then took a detour behind a suit of armour and sank down on its plinth to finish his chocolate, wishing he hadn't mentioned Black, as Lupin was obviously not keen on the subject. Then Harry's thoughts wandered back to his mother and father ...

He felt drained and strangely empty, even though he was so full of chocolate. Terrible though it was to hear his parents' last moments replayed inside his head, these were the only times Harry had heard their voices since he was a very small child. But he'd never be able to produce a proper Patronus if he half wanted to hear his parents again ...

'They're dead,' he told himself sternly. 'They're dead, and listening to echoes of them won't bring them back. You'd better get a grip on yourself if you want that Quidditch Cup.'

He stood up, crammed the last bit of chocolate into his mouth and headed back to Gryffindor Tower.

Ravenclaw played Slytherin a week after the start of term. Slytherin won, though narrowly. According to Wood, this was good news for Gryffindor, who would take second place if they beat Ravenclaw too. He therefore increased the number of team practices to five a week. This meant that with Lupin's Anti-Dementor classes, which in themselves were more draining than six Quidditch practices, Harry had just one night a week to do all his homework. Even so, he wasn't showing the strain nearly as much as Hermione, whose immense workload finally seemed to be getting to her. Every night, without fail, Hermione was to be seen in a corner of the common room, several tables spread with books, Arithmancy charts, Rune dictionaries, diagrams of Muggles lifting heavy objects, and file upon file of extensive notes; she barely spoke to anybody, and snapped when she was interrupted.

第12章 守护神

狼星布莱克了。"

卢平迅速转过身来。

"你怎么会这么想?"他严厉地问。

"没什么——我的意思是,我知道他们在霍格沃茨也是朋友……"卢平的表情放松了。

"对,我认识他,"他简短地说,"或者,我以为我认识他。你最好离开吧,哈利,时间不早了。"

哈利离开了教室,顺着走廊往前走,转过一个弯,绕到一套铠甲后面,一屁股坐在铠甲底座上,吃起了那块巧克力。他后悔自己刚才提到了布莱克,卢平显然对这个话题没有兴趣。接着,哈利的思绪又飘回他的爸爸妈妈身上……

他觉得全身无力,并且有一种奇怪的空落落的感觉,虽然吃了这么多巧克力。听见父母的最后时刻在自己脑海里回放,这固然很可怕,但是从很小的时候起,哈利只有这几次听见了他们的声音。不过,如果他隐约期待再次听见父母的声音,就永远不可能变出一个像样的守护神……

"他们死了,"他严厉地告诫自己,"他们死了,反复听他们的声音并不能使他们复活。如果想得到魁地奇杯,你最好控制住自己。"

他站了起来,把最后一点巧克力塞进嘴里,朝格兰芬多塔楼走去。

开学一星期后,拉文克劳跟斯莱特林比赛了一场。斯莱特林赢了,赢得很险。照伍德的说法,这对格兰芬多是个好消息,如果他们也打败了拉文克劳,就能排到第二名。于是,伍德把球队训练的次数增加到了每星期五次。这就意味着,算上卢平的抵御摄魂怪训练课——它比六次魁地奇训练还要累人——哈利每星期只有一个晚上可以用来做所有的家庭作业。尽管如此,他也不像赫敏那样表现得紧张兮兮。赫敏繁重的功课似乎终于令她招架不住了。每天晚上都能看见赫敏坐在公共休息室的一个角落,面前的几张桌子上全摊着课本、算术占卜图表、如尼文词典、麻瓜搬动重物的图解,还有一份又一份密密麻麻的笔记。她几乎不跟任何人说话,被人打扰时总是恶语相向。

CHAPTER TWELVE   The Patronus

'How's she doing it?' Ron muttered to Harry one evening, as Harry sat finishing a nasty essay on Undetectable Poisons for Snape. Harry looked up. Hermione was barely visible behind a tottering pile of books.

'Doing what?'

'Getting to all her classes!' Ron said. 'I heard her talking to Professor Vector, that Arithmancy witch, this morning. They were going on about yesterday's lesson, but Hermione can't've been there, because she was with us in Care of Magical Creatures! And Ernie McMillan told me she's never missed a Muggle Studies class, but half of them are at the same time as Divination, and she's never missed one of them, either!'

Harry didn't have time to fathom the mystery of Hermione's impossible timetable at the moment; he really needed to get on with Snape's essay. Two seconds later, however, he was interrupted again, this time by Wood.

'Bad news, Harry. I've just been to see Professor McGonagall about the Firebolt. She – er – got a bit shirty with me. Told me I'd got my priorities wrong. Seemed to think I cared more about winning the Cup than I do about you staying alive. Just because I told her I didn't care if it threw you off, as long as you caught the Snitch on it first.' Wood shook his head in disbelief. 'Honestly, the way she was yelling at me ... you'd think I'd said something terrible. Then I asked her how much longer she was going to keep it ...' He screwed up his face and imitated Professor McGonagall's severe voice, '"As long as necessary, Wood" ... I reckon it's time you ordered a new broom, Harry. There's an order form at the back of *Which Broomstick* ... you could get a Nimbus Two Thousand and One, like Malfoy's got.'

'I'm not buying anything Malfoy thinks is good,' said Harry flatly.

January faded imperceptibly into February, with no change in the bitterly cold weather. The match against Ravenclaw was drawing nearer and nearer, but Harry still hadn't ordered a new broom. He was now asking Professor McGonagall for news of the Firebolt after every Transfiguration lesson, Ron standing hopefully at his shoulder, Hermione rushing past with her face averted.

'No, Potter, you can't have it back yet,' Professor McGonagall told him the twelfth time this happened, before he'd even opened his mouth. 'We've checked for most of the usual curses, but Professor Flitwick believes the

第12章 守护神

"她是怎么弄的?"一天晚上罗恩小声问哈利,哈利正坐在那里写斯内普布置的一篇关于不可检测药剂的讨厌论文。哈利抬头一看,赫敏几乎被一大堆摇摇欲坠的书完全挡住了。

"弄什么?"

"上她所有的课呀!"罗恩说,"今天上午我听见她跟维克多教授,就是那个教算术占卜课的女巫说话。她们在谈论昨天的课,可是赫敏不可能去上课呀,那会儿她正跟我们一起上保护神奇动物课呢!还有,厄尼·麦克米兰告诉我,赫敏从来没有落下一堂麻瓜研究课,但那门课半数都跟占卜课的时间冲突,而她占卜课居然也一堂没落!"

哈利眼下没有时间去探究赫敏那张令人难以置信的时间表的奥秘。他真的需要赶紧把斯内普的论文写完。可是,两秒钟后,他又一次被打断了,这次是伍德。

"情况不妙,哈利。我为了火弩箭的事去找了麦格教授。她——呃——有点儿跟我发火了。说我弄错了事情的轻重缓急。她好像认为我关心赢奖杯胜过关心你能不能活着。就因为我对她说,只要你能先抓住金色飞贼,我不在乎你是不是被甩下扫帚。"伍德难以置信地摇摇头,"天哪,她朝我嚷嚷的那副样子……你会以为我说了什么混账话呢。后来我问她还要把扫帚留在手里多久……"他扭歪了脸,学着麦格教授严肃的声音说,"'需要多久就多久,伍德。'……我认为你应该再订一把新扫帚了,哈利。《飞天扫帚大全》背面有一张订单……你可以订一把光轮2001,就像马尔福的那把。"

"凡是马尔福认为好的东西,我都不会买。"哈利淡淡地说。

一月不知不觉变成了二月,寒冷刺骨的天气没有丝毫变化。跟拉文克劳队的比赛一天天临近了,哈利仍然没有订购新的扫帚。现在,每次上完变形课,他都要向麦格教授询问火弩箭的消息,罗恩满怀希望地站在他身后,赫敏则把脸扭向一边,匆匆走过。

"不行,波特,你还不能把它拿回去。"第十二次的时候,哈利还没有张口,麦格教授就对他说道,"我们检测了大部分惯常的魔咒,但

CHAPTER TWELVE The Patronus

broom might be carrying a Hurling Hex. I shall *tell* you once we've finished checking it. Now, please stop badgering me.'

To make matters even worse, Harry's Anti-Dementor lessons were not going nearly as well as he had hoped. Several sessions on, he was able to produce an indistinct, silvery shadow every time the Boggart-Dementor approached him, but his Patronus was too feeble to drive the Dementor away. All it did was hover, like a semi-transparent cloud, draining Harry of energy as he fought to keep it there. Harry felt angry with himself, guilty about his secret desire to hear his parents' voices again.

'You're expecting too much of yourself,' said Professor Lupin sternly, in their fourth week of practice. 'For a thirteen-year-old wizard, even an indistinct Patronus is a huge achievement. You aren't passing out any more, are you?'

'I thought a Patronus would – charge the Dementors down or something,' said Harry dispiritedly. 'Make them disappear –'

'The true Patronus does do that,' said Lupin. 'But you've achieved a great deal in a very short space of time. If the Dementors put in an appearance at your next Quidditch match, you will be able to keep them at bay long enough to get back to the ground.'

'You said it's harder if there are loads of them,' said Harry.

'I have complete confidence in you,' said Lupin, smiling. 'Here – you've earned a drink. Something from the Three Broomsticks, you won't have tried it before –'

He pulled two bottles out of his briefcase.

'Butterbeer!' said Harry, without thinking. 'Yeah, I like that stuff!'

Lupin raised an eyebrow.

'Oh – Ron and Hermione brought me some back from Hogsmeade,' Harry lied quickly.

'I see,' said Lupin, though he still looked slightly suspicious. 'Well – let's drink to a Gryffindor victory against Ravenclaw! Not that I'm supposed to take sides, as a teacher …' he added hastily.

They drank the Butterbeer in silence, until Harry voiced something he'd been wondering for a while.

'What's under a Dementor's hood?'

第12章 守护神

弗立维教授相信扫帚上可能带有一种投掷咒。等检测完了我会立刻告诉你。现在请你别再缠着我了。"

更糟糕的是，哈利的抵御摄魂怪训练课完全不像他希望的那样顺利。几次课后，每当博格特变的摄魂怪朝他逼来时，他虽能变出一个模模糊糊的银白色影子，但是他的守护神太弱了，不足以把摄魂怪赶跑。守护神只是像一团半透明的云一样悬在那里。哈利为了不让它消失，耗尽了全部的精力。哈利很生自己的气，为内心暗暗渴望再次听见父母的声音而感到愧疚。

"你对自己期望太高了，"在第四个星期的训练课上，卢平教授严肃地说，"对于一个十三岁的巫师来说，模糊不清的守护神也是一个了不起的成绩。你现在不再晕倒了，不是吗？"

"我以为守护神会——把摄魂怪赶跑什么的呢，"哈利沮丧地说，"让它们消失——"

"真正的守护神确实能做到这点，"卢平说，"但是你在很短时间内取得了很大的进展。如果下次魁地奇比赛时摄魂怪再出现，你就能暂时把它们控制住，让自己安全降到地面。"

"你说过，如果它们数量很多，就比较难以对付。"哈利说。

"我对你完全有信心。"卢平微笑着说，"好了——你给自己赢得了一点饮料。是三把扫帚里的东西，你恐怕还没有尝过——"

他从公文包里掏出两个瓶子。

"黄油啤酒！"哈利不假思索地说，"是啊，我喜欢这东西！"

卢平扬起一条眉毛。

"噢——罗恩和赫敏从霍格莫德带了一些给我。"哈利赶紧撒谎道。

"明白了。"卢平说，但脸上仍然带着一丝怀疑，"好了——让我们祝愿格兰芬多战胜拉文克劳！其实我作为一个老师不应该有偏心……"他赶紧加了一句。

他们默默地喝着黄油啤酒，最后哈利说出了已经困扰他一段时间的疑问。

"摄魂怪的兜帽下面是什么？"

CHAPTER TWELVE The Patronus

Professor Lupin lowered his bottle thoughtfully.

'Hmmm ... well, the only people who really know are in no condition to tell us. You see, the Dementor only lowers its hood to use its last and worst weapon.'

'What's that?'

'They call it the Dementor's Kiss,' said Lupin, with a slightly twisted smile. 'It's what Dementors do to those they wish to destroy utterly. I suppose there must be some kind of mouth under there, because they clamp their jaws upon the mouth of the victim and – and suck out his soul.'

Harry accidentally spat out a bit of Butterbeer.

'What – they kill –?'

'Oh, no,' said Lupin. 'Much worse than that. You can exist without your soul, you know, as long as your brain and heart are still working. But you'll have no sense of self any more, no memory, no ... anything. There's no chance at all of recovery. You'll just – exist. As an empty shell. And your soul is gone for ever ... lost.'

Lupin drank a little more Butterbeer, then said, 'It's the fate that awaits Sirius Black. It was in the *Daily Prophet* this morning. The Ministry have given the Dementors permission to perform it if they find him.'

Harry sat stunned for a moment at the idea of someone having their soul sucked out through their mouth. But then he thought of Black.

'He deserves it,' he said suddenly.

'You think so?' said Lupin lightly. 'Do you really think anyone deserves that?'

'Yes,' said Harry defiantly. 'For ... for some things ...'

He would have liked to have told Lupin about the conversation he'd overheard about Black in the Three Broomsticks, about Black betraying his mother and father, but it would have involved revealing that he'd gone to Hogsmeade without permission, and he knew Lupin wouldn't be very impressed by that. So he finished his Butterbeer, thanked Lupin, and left the History of Magic classroom.

Harry half wished that he hadn't asked what was under a Dementor's hood, the answer had been so horrible, and he was so lost in unpleasant thoughts of what it would feel like to have your soul sucked out of you that he walked headlong into Professor McGonagall halfway up the stairs.

第12章 守护神

卢平教授若有所思地放下酒瓶。

"哦……是这样,那些真正了解实情的人,他们的状况很差,不可能告诉我们。要知道,摄魂怪只在使用它最后的也是最毒辣的武器时才会放下兜帽。"

"那是什么呢?"

"人们称之为'摄魂怪的吻'。"卢平带着一丝嘲讽的微笑说,"摄魂怪用这一招来对付那些它们想要彻底摧毁的人。我猜想那下面肯定有类似嘴的东西,因为它们把下巴压在受害者的嘴上——吸走他的灵魂。"

哈利一不留神喷出了一些黄油啤酒。

"什么?它们杀人——?"

"噢,不,"卢平说,"比这厉害得多。你知道,只要大脑和心脏还在工作,即使没有灵魂你也能活着。但是不再有自我意识,不再有记忆,不再有……任何东西,而且没有丝毫康复的希望。只是——活着。一具空空的躯壳。你的灵魂丢失了……一去不复返。"

卢平又喝了点黄油啤酒,然后说道:"等待小天狼星布莱克的就是这种命运。今天早晨的《预言家日报》上写着呢。魔法部已经指示摄魂怪,一旦找到布莱克就用这种方式处置。"

哈利呆呆地坐在那里。把人的灵魂从嘴里吸走,这想法令他震惊。接着,他又想起了布莱克。

"他这是活该。"他突然说。

"你这么认为?"卢平轻轻地问道,"你真的认为有人活该得到这种惩罚?"

"对,"哈利倔强地说,"因为……因为他做的事情……"

他真想告诉卢平他在三把扫帚听到的关于布莱克、关于布莱克背叛他父母的那段对话,但是如果那么做,就会暴露他未经许可擅自去了霍格莫德,他知道卢平对此肯定会不高兴的。于是他喝完黄油啤酒,谢过卢平,就离开了魔法史教室。

哈利有点后悔自己问了摄魂怪的兜帽下面是什么,那答案太恐怖了。上楼的时候,他满脑子都想着一个人的灵魂被吸走时是什么感觉,结果一头撞在了麦格教授身上。

CHAPTER TWELVE   The Patronus

'Do watch where you're going, Potter!'

'Sorry, Professor —'

'I've just been looking for you in the Gryffindor common room. Well, here it is, we've done everything we could think of, and there doesn't seem to be anything wrong with it at all — you've got a very good friend somewhere, Potter ...'

Harry's jaw dropped. She was holding out his Firebolt, and it looked as magnificent as ever.

'I can have it back?' Harry said weakly. 'Seriously?'

'Seriously,' said Professor McGonagall, and she was actually smiling. 'I daresay you'll need to get the feel of it before Saturday's match, won't you? And Potter — *do* try and win, won't you? Or we'll be out of the running for the eighth year in a row, as Professor Snape was kind enough to remind me only last night ...'

Speechless, Harry carried the Firebolt back upstairs towards Gryffindor Tower. As he turned a corner, he saw Ron dashing towards him, grinning from ear to ear.

'She gave it to you? Excellent! Listen, can I still have a go on it? Tomorrow?'

'Yeah ... anything ...' said Harry, his heart lighter than it had been in a month. 'You know what — we should make it up with Hermione. She was only trying to help ...'

'Yeah, all right,' said Ron. 'She's in the common room now — working, for a change.'

They turned into the corridor to Gryffindor Tower and saw Neville Longbottom, pleading with Sir Cadogan, who seemed to be refusing him entrance.

'I wrote them down,' Neville was saying tearfully, 'but I must've dropped them somewhere!'

'A likely tale!' roared Sir Cadogan. Then, spotting Harry and Ron, 'Good even, my fine young yeomen! Come clap this loon in irons, he is trying to force entry to the chambers within!'

'Oh, shut up,' said Ron, as he and Harry drew level with Neville.

'I've lost the passwords!' Neville told them miserably. 'I made him tell me what passwords he was going to use this week, because he keeps changing them, and now I don't know what I've done with them!'

第12章 守护神

"走路好好看着,波特!"

"对不起,教授——"

"我刚才到格兰芬多公共休息室去找你。好了,给你吧,我们采取了所能想到的各种措施,看来它没有什么问题——波特,你在某个地方有一位很好的朋友呢……"

哈利吃惊地张大了嘴巴。麦格教授手里举着他的火弩箭,看上去跟以前一样精美。

"我可以拿回来了?"哈利轻声问,"真的?"

"真的。"麦格教授说,脸上居然露出了微笑,"我相信你需要在星期六的比赛前找感觉,是不是?波特——一定要争取获胜,行吗?不然我们就连续八年与奖杯无缘了,这是昨天晚上斯内普教授好意提醒我的……"

哈利说不出话来,拿着火弩箭上楼返回格兰芬多塔楼。他拐过一个弯,看见罗恩朝他冲来,嘴巴咧得好大,笑得正欢。

"她给你了?太棒了!听我说,能不能让我骑上试试?明天?"

"行……怎么都行……"哈利说,一个月来,他的心情从没有这么轻松过,"对了——我们应该跟赫敏和解了。她当时只是想帮……"

"好吧,好吧。"罗恩说,"她眼下就在公共休息室呢——在做功课,为了换换脑子——"

他们拐进通向格兰芬多塔楼的走廊,看见纳威·隆巴顿正在苦苦哀求卡多根爵士,看样子是卡多根爵士不让他进去。

"我把它们都写下来了,"纳威眼泪汪汪地说,"可是肯定掉在什么地方了!"

"编得倒像!"卡多根爵士吼道。他转眼看见哈利和罗恩:"晚上好,我年轻的优秀骑兵!快给这无赖戴上镣铐,他正试图闯入里面的房间!"

"哦,闭嘴。"罗恩说着,和哈利一起站在纳威身边。

"我把口令丢了!"纳威可怜巴巴地告诉他们,"我让他把这星期要用的口令都告诉我,因为他老是变来变去的,可是我那些口令不知道哪儿去了!"

CHAPTER TWELVE The Patronus

'Oddsbodikins,' said Harry to Sir Cadogan, who looked extremely disappointed and reluctantly swung forwards to let them into the common room. There was a sudden, excited murmur as every head turned and the next moment, Harry was surrounded by people exclaiming over his Firebolt.

'Where'd you get it, Harry?'

'Will you let me have a go?'

'Have you ridden it yet, Harry?'

'Ravenclaw'll have no chance, they're all on Cleansweep Sevens!'

'Can I just *hold* it, Harry?'

After ten minutes or so, during which the Firebolt was passed around and admired from every angle, the crowd dispersed and Harry and Ron had a clear view of Hermione, the only person who hadn't rushed over to them, bent over her work, and carefully avoiding their eyes. Harry and Ron approached her table and at last, she looked up.

'I got it back,' said Harry, grinning at her and holding up the Firebolt.

'See, Hermione? There wasn't anything wrong with it!' said Ron.

'Well – there *might* have been!' said Hermione. 'I mean, at least you know now that it's safe!'

'Yeah, I suppose so,' said Harry. 'I'd better put it upstairs –'

'I'll take it!' said Ron eagerly. 'I've got to give Scabbers his Rat Tonic.'

He took the Firebolt, and, holding it as if it were made of glass, carried it away up the boys' staircase.

'Can I sit down, then?' Harry asked Hermione.

'I suppose so,' said Hermione, moving a great stack of parchment off a chair.

Harry looked around at the cluttered table, at the long Arithmancy essay on which the ink was still glistening, at the even longer Muggle Studies essay ('Explain why Muggles Need Electricity') and at the Rune translation Hermione was now poring over.

'How are you getting through all this stuff?' Harry asked her.

'Oh, well – you know – working hard,' said Hermione. Close to, Harry saw that she looked almost as tired as Lupin.

'Why don't you just drop a couple of subjects?' Harry asked, watching her

第12章 守护神

"奇身怪皮。"哈利对卡多根爵士说,爵士显得失望极了,极不情愿地向前转开,放他们进了公共休息室。一阵兴奋的低语声突然响起,每个人都把脑袋转了过来,紧接着,那些为火弩箭大呼小叫的人就把哈利围在了中间。

"你从哪儿弄来的,哈利?"

"能让我试试吗?"

"你骑过没有,哈利?"

"拉文克劳肯定没戏了,他们骑的都是横扫七星!"

"能让我拿一下吗,哈利?"

人们把火弩箭传来传去,从每一个角度细细欣赏。过了十分钟左右,人群渐渐散去,哈利和罗恩总算看见了赫敏。赫敏是唯一没有冲到他们身边的人,她埋头做着功课,小心地避开他们的目光。哈利和罗恩向她的桌子走去,最后,她终于抬起头来。

"我拿回来了。"哈利笑眯眯地看着她,把火弩箭举得高高的。

"看见了吗,赫敏?根本就没有任何问题!"罗恩说。

"可是——当时说不定呀!"赫敏说,"我是说,至少你现在知道它是安全的了。"

"是啊,我也是这样想的。"哈利说,"我最好把它放到楼上去——"

"我来拿!"罗恩积极地说,"我正好要给斑斑喂强身剂呢。"

他接过火弩箭,小心翼翼地捧着走上了男生宿舍的楼梯,就好像那扫帚是玻璃做的。

"好了,我可以坐下来吗?"哈利问赫敏。

"我想可以。"赫敏说着,把一张椅子上的一大堆羊皮纸挪开。

哈利看看堆得乱七八糟的桌子,看看墨迹未干的算术占卜的长篇论文,看看篇幅更长的麻瓜研究论文(《试论麻瓜为何需要用电》),再看看赫敏正在埋头钻研的如尼文翻译。

"这么多功课,你是怎么对付下来的?"哈利问她。

"哦,没什么——就是——刻苦用功呗。"赫敏说。哈利凑近了看,发现她几乎跟卢平一样憔悴。

"你为什么不少学两门课呢?"哈利问,一边注视着赫敏搬开书本

CHAPTER TWELVE The Patronus

lifting books as she searched for her Rune dictionary.

'I couldn't do that!' said Hermione, looking scandalised.

'Arithmancy looks terrible,' said Harry, picking up a very complicated-looking number chart.

'Oh, no, it's wonderful!' said Hermione earnestly. 'It's my favourite subject! It's –'

But exactly what was wonderful about Arithmancy, Harry never found out. At that precise moment, a strangled yell echoed down the boys' staircase. The whole common room fell silent, staring, petrified, at the entrance. There came hurried footsteps, growing louder and louder – and then, Ron came leaping into view, dragging with him a bedsheet.

'LOOK!' he bellowed, striding over to Hermione's table. 'LOOK!' he yelled, shaking the sheets in her face.

'Ron, what –?'

'SCABBERS! LOOK! SCABBERS!'

Hermione was leaning away from Ron, looking utterly bewildered. Harry looked down at the sheet Ron was holding. There was something red on it. Something that looked horribly like –

'BLOOD!' Ron yelled into the stunned silence. 'HE'S GONE! AND YOU KNOW WHAT WAS ON THE FLOOR?'

'N-no,' said Hermione, in a trembling voice.

Ron threw something down onto Hermione's Rune translation. Hermione and Harry leant forward. Lying on top of the weird, spiky shapes were several long, ginger cat hairs.

第12章 守护神

寻找如尼文词典。

"我办不到！"赫敏显得十分愤慨地说。

"算术占卜看着怪吓人的。"哈利说，拿起一张看上去十分复杂的数字图表。

"噢，不，它很奇妙！"赫敏一本正经地说，"是我最喜欢的一门课！它——"

可是，算术占卜究竟奇妙在哪儿，哈利恐怕永远也不会知道了。就在那一刻，男生宿舍的楼梯上传来一声哽咽的尖叫。整个公共休息室顿时安静下来，大家呆呆地盯着楼梯口。急匆匆的脚步声传来，越来越响——接着，罗恩蹦了出来，手里拖着一条床单。

"看！"他咆哮道，大步走向赫敏的桌子，"看！"他吼着，在赫敏面前抖着床单。

"罗恩，怎么——？"

"斑斑！看！斑斑！"

赫敏躲闪着罗恩，脸上的表情十分困惑。哈利低头看看罗恩手里的床单，上面有一块红色的东西。真可怕，看上去就像——

"血！"罗恩在人们的惊愕和静默中喊道，"**它死了！你知道地板上有什么吗**？"

"不—不知道。"赫敏用颤抖的声音说。

罗恩把什么东西扔在赫敏的如尼文翻译作业上。赫敏和哈利赶紧凑上去看。在那些古怪的、尖头尖脑的文字上，躺着几根长长的姜黄色猫毛。

CHAPTER THIRTEEN

Gryffindor versus Ravenclaw

It looked like the end of Ron and Hermione's friendship. Each was so angry with the other that Harry couldn't see how they'd ever make it up.

Ron was enraged that Hermione had never taken Crookshanks's attempts to eat Scabbers seriously, hadn't bothered to keep a close enough watch on him and was still trying to pretend that Crookshanks was innocent by suggesting Ron look for Scabbers under all the boys' beds. Hermione, meanwhile, maintained fiercely that Ron had no proof that Crookshanks had eaten Scabbers, that the ginger hairs might have been there since Christmas, and that Ron had been prejudiced against her cat ever since Crookshanks had landed on Ron's head in the Magical Menagerie.

Personally, Harry was sure that Crookshanks had eaten Scabbers, and when he tried to point out to Hermione that the evidence all pointed that way, she lost her temper with Harry, too.

'OK, side with Ron, I knew you would!' she said shrilly. 'First the Firebolt, now Scabbers, everything's my fault, isn't it! Just leave me alone, Harry, I've got a lot of work to do!'

Ron had taken the loss of his rat very hard indeed.

'Come on, Ron, you were always saying how boring Scabbers was,' said Fred bracingly. 'And he's been off-colour for ages, he was wasting away. It was probably better for him to snuff it quickly. One swallow – he probably didn't feel a thing.'

'*Fred!*' said Ginny indignantly.

'All he did was eat and sleep, Ron, you said it yourself,' said George.

'He bit Goyle for us once!' Ron said miserably. 'Remember, Harry?'

'Yeah, that's true,' said Harry.

第 13 章

格兰芬多对拉文克劳

看起来，罗恩和赫敏的友谊到此结束了。彼此都恨得牙痒痒，哈利不知道他俩怎么才能言归于好。

罗恩生气，因为赫敏从来没有认真对待过克鲁克山想吃斑斑这件事，没有费心好好看住克鲁克山，而且直到现在还想诡称它是无辜的，并建议罗恩到所有男生的床底下去寻找斑斑。而赫敏则情绪激动地咬定罗恩没有证据证明克鲁克山吃了斑斑，说那几根姜黄色猫毛大概从圣诞节就在那里了，还说自从克鲁克山在神奇动物店里砸在罗恩脑袋上以后，罗恩就一直对它抱有成见。

哈利私下里相信是克鲁克山吃了斑斑，当他向赫敏提出所有的证据都指向这一点时，赫敏也朝哈利发起了脾气。

"好，跟罗恩站在一边吧，我就知道你会这样！"她尖着嗓子说，"先是火弩箭，现在是斑斑，每件事都是我的错，对吗？别来烦我了，哈利，我还有很多功课要做呢！"

罗恩实在难以接受他的老鼠的离去。

"好了，罗恩，你以前总是说斑斑多么没劲，"弗雷德安慰他说，"它很长时间都病恹恹的，年老不中用啦。突然一命呜呼对它来说或许更好呢。啊呜一口——它大概什么感觉都没有。"

"弗雷德！"金妮气愤地说。

"它整天除了吃就是睡，罗恩，这可是你自己说的。"乔治说。

"有一次它还帮我们咬了高尔呢！"罗恩难过地说，"记得吗，哈利？"

"是啊，没错。"哈利说。

CHAPTER THIRTEEN   Gryffindor versus Ravenclaw

'His finest hour,' said Fred, unable to keep a straight face. 'Let the scar on Goyle's finger stand as a lasting tribute to his memory. Oh, come on, Ron, get yourself down to Hogsmeade and buy a new rat. What's the point of moaning?'

In a last-ditch attempt to cheer Ron up, Harry persuaded him to come along to the Gryffindor team's final practice before the Ravenclaw match, so that he could have a go on the Firebolt after they'd finished. This did seem to take Ron's mind off Scabbers for a moment ('Brilliant! Can I try and shoot a few goals on it?') so they set off for the Quidditch pitch together.

Madam Hooch, who was still overseeing Gryffindor practices to keep an eye on Harry, was just as impressed with the Firebolt as everyone else had been. She took it in her hands before take-off and gave them the benefit of her professional opinion.

'Look at the balance on it! If the Nimbus series has a fault, it's a slight list to the tail-end – you often find they develop a drag after a few years. They've updated the handle, too, a bit slimmer than the Cleansweeps, reminds me of the old Silver Arrows – a pity they've stopped making them, I learnt to fly on one, and a very fine old broom it was too ... '

She continued in this vein for some time, until Wood said, 'Er – Madam Hooch? Is it OK if Harry has the Firebolt back? Only we need to practise ...'

'Oh – right – here you are, then, Potter,' said Madam Hooch. 'I'll sit over here with Weasley ...'

She and Ron left the pitch to sit in the stadium, and the Gryffindor team gathered around Wood for his final instructions for tomorrow's match.

'Harry, I've just found out who Ravenclaw are playing as Seeker. It's Cho Chang. She's a fourth-year, and she's pretty good ... I really hoped she wouldn't be fit, she's had some problems with injuries ...' Wood scowled his displeasure that Cho Chang had made a full recovery, then said, 'On the other hand, she rides a Comet Two Sixty, which is going to look like a joke next to the Firebolt.' He gave Harry's broom a look of fervent admiration, then said, 'OK, everyone, let's go –'

And at long last, Harry mounted his Firebolt, and kicked off from the ground.

It was better than he'd ever dreamed. The Firebolt turned with the lightest touch; it seemed to obey his thoughts rather than his grip. It sped across

第13章 格兰芬多对拉文克劳

"那是它最辉煌的时刻,"弗雷德说,忍不住要发笑,"就让高尔手指上的伤疤成为对它永久的纪念吧。哦,好了,罗恩,到霍格莫德去给自己买一只新老鼠吧。这么唉声叹气有什么用呢?"

为了让罗恩高兴,哈利做了最后的努力,劝罗恩陪他一起去观看格兰芬多跟拉文克劳比赛前的最后一次训练,等训练结束后罗恩可以骑上火弩箭试试。这似乎确实让罗恩暂时忘记了斑斑("太棒了!我可以骑着它来几次射门吗?"),于是他们一起出发去了魁地奇球场。

为了照看哈利,霍琦女士仍在监督格兰芬多的训练。她像别人一样,对火弩箭爱不释手。训练开始前,她把扫帚拿在手里,向队员们发表了一番专业性的意见。

"看看它的平衡能力!要说光轮有什么缺陷,那就是尾部稍微有些倾斜——用了几年之后,就会发现它们有点儿拖泥带水。他们对扫帚把也做了改进,比横扫系列更纤细一些,让我想起过去的'银箭'——真可惜现在不再生产了,我就是骑着银箭学飞的,那是一种非常精美的老扫帚……"

她就这个话题又说了一会儿,最后伍德说道:"呃——霍琦女士,是不是让哈利把火弩箭拿回去?不为别的,我们需要训练了……"

"哦——行——给你吧,波特,"霍琦女士说,"我和韦斯莱一起坐在那儿……"

她和罗恩离开球场,坐在看台上。格兰芬多队员们聚集在伍德周围,听他做明天比赛前的最后指示。

"哈利,我刚打听清楚拉文克劳的找球手是谁。是秋·张。她上四年级,打得很好……我本来真希望她不能参加比赛,她有一些伤病……"伍德皱起眉头,对秋·张的彻底痊愈表示不满,然后又说:"不过,她骑的是一把彗星260,跟火弩箭一比,那简直像个笑料。"他带着狂热的崇拜看了一眼哈利的扫帚,接着说道,"好了,每位队员,开始吧——"

哈利终于骑上了他的火弩箭,用脚一蹬离开了地面。

那感觉比他梦想的还要美妙。他轻轻一触,火弩箭就有了反应。它顺从的似乎是哈利的思想,而不是他的掌控。扫帚飞一般地掠过球场,速

CHAPTER THIRTEEN   Gryffindor versus Ravenclaw

the pitch at such speed that the stadium turned into a green and grey blur; Harry turned it so sharply that Alicia Spinnet screamed, then he went into a perfectly controlled dive, brushing the grassy pitch with his toes before rising thirty, forty, fifty feet into the air again –

'Harry, I'm letting the Snitch out!' Wood called.

Harry turned and raced a Bludger towards the goalposts; he outstripped it easily, saw the Snitch dart out from behind Wood and within ten seconds had caught it tightly in his hand.

The team cheered madly. Harry let the Snitch go again, gave it a minute's head start, then tore after it, weaving in and out of the others; he spotted it lurking near Katie Bell's knee, looped her easily, and caught it again.

It was the best practice ever; the team, inspired by the presence of the Firebolt in their midst, performed their best moves faultlessly, and by the time they hit the ground again, Wood didn't have a single criticism to make, which, as George Weasley pointed out, was a first.

'I can't see what's going to stop us tomorrow!' said Wood. 'Not unless – Harry, you've sorted your Dementor problem, haven't you?'

'Yeah,' said Harry, thinking of his feeble Patronus and wishing it was stronger.

'The Dementors won't turn up again, Oliver, Dumbledore'd do his nut,' said Fred confidently.

'Well, let's hope not,' said Wood. 'Anyway – good work, everyone. Let's get back to the Tower – turn in early ...'

'I'm staying out for a bit, Ron wants a go on the Firebolt,' Harry told Wood, and while the rest of the team headed off to the changing rooms, Harry strode over to Ron, who vaulted the barrier to the stands and came to meet him. Madam Hooch had fallen asleep in her seat.

'Here you go,' said Harry, handing Ron the Firebolt.

Ron, an expression of ecstasy on his face, mounted the broom and zoomed off into the gathering darkness while Harry walked around the edge of the pitch, watching him. Night had fallen before Madam Hooch awoke with a start, told Harry and Ron off for not waking her, and insisted that they go back to the castle.

Harry shouldered the Firebolt and he and Ron walked out of the shadowy stadium, discussing the Firebolt's superbly smooth action, its phenomenal

度之快，使看台变成了绿莹莹和灰蒙蒙的一片。哈利猛地拐了个弯，惊得艾丽娅·斯平内特失声尖叫，然后他做了一个控制完美的俯冲，脚尖擦过青草覆盖的场地，随即又迅疾升向空中，三十英尺，四十英尺，五十英尺——

"哈利，我把飞贼放出来了！"伍德喊道。

哈利转了个身，追着一只游走球朝球门柱飞去。他很轻松地超过了游走球，看见飞贼从伍德身后蹿了出来。不出十秒钟，他就把它紧紧抓在手里了。

队员们疯狂地欢呼。哈利又把飞贼放出去，让它先飞一分钟，随即迅速追了上去，左躲右闪地在队员之间穿梭。他看见飞贼躲在凯蒂·贝尔膝盖周围，便轻松绕过凯蒂，再次把飞贼抓住了。

这是最好的一次训练。火弩箭出现在队员们中间，使他们大受鼓舞，都发挥出了自己的最高水平，表现近乎完美。当大家再次落回地面时，伍德没有一句批评的话可说，用乔治·韦斯莱的话讲，这可是破天荒的一次。

"我看明天没有什么能够阻挡我们！"伍德说，"除非——哈利，摄魂怪的问题你已经解决了，是不是？"

"是啊。"哈利说着，想起了他那柔弱的守护神，暗自希望它能变得强壮一些。

"摄魂怪不会再出现了，奥利弗，不然邓布利多非气疯了不可。"弗雷德信心十足地说。

"好吧，但愿如此。"伍德说，"不管怎样——大家练得不错。我们回塔楼去吧——早点睡觉……"

"我再稍微待一会儿，罗恩想骑骑火弩箭。"哈利对伍德说。其他队员都朝更衣室走去，哈利大步走向罗恩。罗恩翻过看台的栅栏，迎面跑了过来。霍琦女士已经在座位上睡着了。

"给你。"哈利说，把火弩箭递给了罗恩。

罗恩脸上带着狂喜的表情，骑上扫帚，嗖地蹿入逐渐昏暗的天空。哈利绕着球场边缘行走，注视着他。夜幕降临，霍琦女士突然惊醒了。她责备哈利和罗恩没有叫醒她，并坚持要他们赶紧返回城堡。

哈利把火弩箭扛在肩上，和罗恩一起走出幽暗的球场，一边议论

CHAPTER THIRTEEN   Gryffindor versus Ravenclaw

acceleration and its pinpoint turning. They were halfway towards the castle when Harry, glancing to his left, saw something that made his heart turn over – a pair of eyes, gleaming out of the darkness.

Harry stopped dead, his heart banging against his ribs.

'What's the matter?' said Ron.

Harry pointed. Ron pulled out his wand and muttered, '*Lumos!*'

A beam of light fell across the grass, hit the bottom of a tree and illuminated its branches; there, crouching amongst the budding leaves, was Crookshanks.

'Get out of it!' Ron roared, and he stooped down and seized a stone lying on the grass, but before he could do anything else, Crookshanks had vanished with one swish of his long ginger tail.

'See?' Ron said furiously, chucking the stone down again. 'She's still letting him wander about wherever he wants – probably washing down Scabbers with a couple of birds now ...'

Harry didn't say anything. He took a deep breath as relief seeped through him; he had been sure for a moment that those eyes had belonged to the Grim. They set off for the castle once more. Slightly ashamed of his moment of panic, Harry didn't say anything to Ron – nor did he look left or right until they had reached the well lit Entrance Hall.

Harry went down to breakfast next morning with the rest of the boys in his dormitory, all of whom seemed to think the Firebolt deserved a sort of guard of honour. As Harry entered the Great Hall, heads turned in the direction of the Firebolt, and there was a good deal of excited muttering. Harry saw, with enormous satisfaction, that the Slytherin team were all looking thunderstruck.

'Did you see his face?' said Ron gleefully, looking back at Malfoy. 'He can't believe it! This is brilliant!'

Wood, too, was basking in the reflected glory of the Firebolt.

'Put it here, Harry,' he said, laying the broom in the middle of the table and carefully turning it so that its name faced upwards. People from the Ravenclaw and Hufflepuff tables were soon coming over to look. Cedric Diggory came over to congratulate Harry on having acquired such a superb replacement for his Nimbus, and Percy's Ravenclaw girlfriend, Penelope Clearwater, asked if she could actually hold the Firebolt.

第13章 格兰芬多对拉文克劳

着火弩箭不同凡响的精彩表现，它出色的加速能力以及转弯时的精确性。走到半路，哈利向左边扫了一眼，看到了使他心慌意乱的东西——一双眼睛在暗中闪闪发光。

哈利猛地停住脚步，心怦怦地撞击着他的胸膛。

"怎么啦？"罗恩问。

哈利指了指。罗恩抽出魔杖，低声说了句："荧光闪烁！"

一道亮光掠过草地，照到一棵树的根部，照亮了树枝。在刚刚萌芽的树叶中间，蹲着的是克鲁克山。

"滚开！"罗恩吼道，弯腰抓起草地上的一块石头。可是没等他再做什么，克鲁克山忽地一甩姜黄色的长尾巴，消失了。

"看见了吗？"罗恩气呼呼地说，又把石头扔了回去，"她还让它由着性子乱逛——大概想再吃两只小鸟帮着消化斑斑……"

哈利什么也没说。他深深吸了口气，觉得心里一阵轻松。他刚才还以为那肯定是"不祥"的眼睛呢。他们又拔腿朝城堡走去。哈利为自己刚才的紧张感到有些羞愧，什么也没有对罗恩说——也没有再往两边看，就这样一直走到灯火通明的门厅。

第二天早晨，哈利跟宿舍里的同学一起下楼吃早饭，他们似乎都认为火弩箭需要一支仪仗队。哈利走进礼堂，同学们都把脑袋转向了火弩箭，礼堂里一片兴奋的叽叽喳喳。哈利看到斯莱特林队员们一个个目瞪口呆，不由得感到极大的满足。

"你看见他的脸了吗？"罗恩回头看看马尔福，开心地说，"他不敢相信！真是太棒了！"

伍德也为火弩箭的辉煌感到得意。

"把它放在这里，哈利。"说着，他把扫帚放在桌子中央，小心地转动着，让它的牌子朝上。很快，拉文克劳和赫奇帕奇的同学纷纷过来观看。塞德里克·迪戈里上前祝贺哈利得到这样一把出色的扫帚来代替那把光轮，珀西的女朋友佩内洛·克里瓦特问能不能让她拿一下火弩箭。

CHAPTER THIRTEEN   Gryffindor versus Ravenclaw

'Now, now, Penny, no sabotage!' said Percy heartily, as she examined the Firebolt closely. 'Penelope and I have got a bet on,' he told the team. 'Ten Galleons on the outcome of the match!'

Penelope put the Firebolt down again, thanked Harry and went back to her table.

'Harry – make sure you win,' said Percy, in an urgent whisper. '*I haven't got ten Galleons*. Yes, I'm coming, Penny!' And he bustled off to join her in a piece of toast.

'Sure you can manage that broom, Potter?' said a cold, drawling voice.

Draco Malfoy had arrived for a closer look, Crabbe and Goyle right behind him.

'Yeah, reckon so,' said Harry casually.

'Got plenty of special features, hasn't it?' said Malfoy, eyes glittering maliciously. 'Shame it doesn't come with a parachute – in case you get too near a Dementor.'

Crabbe and Goyle sniggered.

'Pity you can't attach an extra arm to yours, Malfoy,' said Harry. 'Then it could catch the Snitch for you.'

The Gryffindor team laughed loudly. Malfoy's pale eyes narrowed, and he stalked away. They watched him rejoin the rest of the Slytherin team, who put their heads together, no doubt asking Malfoy whether Harry's broom really was a Firebolt.

At a quarter to eleven, the Gryffindor team set off for the changing rooms. The weather couldn't have been more different from their match against Hufflepuff. It was a clear, cool day, with a very light breeze; there would be no visibility problems this time, and Harry, though nervous, was starting to feel the excitement only a Quidditch match could bring. They could hear the rest of the school moving into the stadium beyond. Harry took off his black school robes, removed his wand from his pocket, and stuck it inside the T-shirt he was going to wear under his Quidditch robes. He only hoped he wouldn't need it. He wondered suddenly whether Professor Lupin was in the crowd, watching.

'You know what we've got to do,' said Wood, as they prepared to leave the changing rooms. 'If we lose this match, we're out of the running. Just – just fly like you did in practice yesterday, and we'll be OK!'

第13章 格兰芬多对拉文克劳

"好了，好了，佩内洛，不许破坏！"佩内洛仔细端详火弩箭时，珀西兴奋地说。"佩内洛和我打了个赌，"他告诉队员们，"十个加隆赌比赛结果！"

佩内洛放下火弩箭，谢过哈利，返回她的餐桌去了。

"哈利——你们可一定要赢啊，"珀西急切地低声说道，"我可没有十个加隆。来了，来了，佩内洛！"他赶紧跑过去跟她一起吃一块烤面包。

"你对付那把扫帚没问题吧，波特？"一个冷冷的、拖腔拖调的声音说。

德拉科·马尔福也过来看扫帚了，身后跟着克拉布和高尔。

"我想是吧。"哈利漫不经心地说。

"这扫帚有许多特殊性能，是不是？"马尔福说，眼睛里闪着不怀好意的光，"真可惜它没有带着降落伞——以防你跟一个摄魂怪靠得太近。"

克拉布和高尔哧哧地笑了起来。

"真可惜你不能给自己再接一条手臂，马尔福，"哈利说，"不然它就可以替你抓住飞贼了。"

格兰芬多队员们哈哈大笑。马尔福眯起灰色的眼睛，大步走开了。大家注视着他走到斯莱特林的其他队员中间，他们把脑袋凑在一起，无疑是在向马尔福打听哈利的扫帚是不是真的火弩箭。

十点三刻，格兰芬多队出发去更衣室。天气跟他们同赫奇帕奇队比赛的那天完全不一样，晴朗，凉爽，微风习习。这次不会存在能见度的问题。哈利虽然紧张，却也开始感到只有魁地奇比赛才能带来的那种兴奋了。他们听见了全校同学拥进外面体育场的声音。哈利脱掉黑色校袍，从口袋里抽出魔杖，塞进他准备穿在魁地奇球服下面的T恤衫里。但愿不要用到魔杖。他突然想知道卢平教授是不是也在人群里观看比赛。

"你们知道要怎么做。"大家准备离开更衣室时，伍德说道，"如果输了这场比赛，我们就彻底没希望了。就像——就像昨天训练的时候那样飞，我们肯定没问题！"

CHAPTER THIRTEEN Gryffindor versus Ravenclaw

They walked out onto the pitch to tumultuous applause. The Ravenclaw team, dressed in blue, were already standing in the middle of the pitch. Their Seeker, Cho Chang, was the only girl in their team. She was shorter than Harry by about a head, and Harry couldn't help noticing, nervous as he was, that she was extremely pretty. She smiled at Harry as the teams faced each other behind their captains, and he felt a slight jolt in the region of his stomach that he didn't think had anything to do with nerves.

'Wood, Davies, shake hands,' Madam Hooch said briskly, and Wood shook hands with the Ravenclaw captain.

'Mount your brooms ... on my whistle ... three – two – one –'

Harry kicked off into the air and the Firebolt zoomed higher and faster than any other broom; he soared around the stadium and began squinting around for the Snitch, listening all the while to the commentary, which was being provided by the Weasley twins' friend, Lee Jordan.

'They're off, and the big excitement this match is the Firebolt which Harry Potter is flying for Gryffindor. According to *Which Broomstick*, the Firebolt's going to be the broom of choice for the national teams at this year's World Championship –'

'Jordan, would you mind telling us what's going on in the match?' interrupted Professor McGonagall's voice.

'Right you are, Professor – just giving a bit of background information. The Firebolt, incidentally, has a built-in autobrake and –'

'Jordan!'

'OK, OK, Gryffindor in possession, Katie Bell of Gryffindor heading for goal ...'

Harry streaked past Katie in the opposite direction, gazing around for a glint of gold and noticing that Cho Chang was tailing him closely. She was undoubtedly a very good flier – she kept cutting across him, forcing him to change direction.

'Show her your acceleration, Harry!' Fred yelled, as he whooshed past in pursuit of a Bludger that was aiming for Alicia.

Harry urged the Firebolt forward as they rounded the Ravenclaw goalposts and Cho fell behind. Just as Katie succeeded in scoring the first goal of the match, and the Gryffindor end of the pitch went wild, he saw it – the Snitch was close to the ground, flitting near one of the barriers.

第13章 格兰芬多对拉文克劳

他们走到外面的球场上，欢呼声震耳欲聋。身穿蓝色队袍的拉文克劳队已经站在球场中央。他们的找球手秋·张是队里唯一的女生，她比哈利大约矮一个头。哈利虽然紧张得要命，也忍不住注意到她漂亮得惊人。双方队员面对面站在各自的队长身后，秋·张微笑地看着哈利。哈利觉得肚子那儿异样地抽动了一下，他想这抽动与紧张没有关系。

"伍德，戴维斯，握手。"霍琦女士干脆利落地说，伍德与拉文克劳队的队长握了握手。

"骑上扫帚……听我的哨声……三——二——一——"

哈利双脚一蹬，蹿到空中，火弩箭比别的扫帚都飞得快，蹿得高。哈利在球场上空盘旋，开始眯着眼睛寻找飞贼，同时留神倾听场上的评论。解说员是韦斯莱双胞胎兄弟的朋友李·乔丹。

"比赛开始了，本场比赛最大的兴奋点是火弩箭，哈利·波特骑着它代表格兰芬多参赛。《飞天扫帚大全》上说，火弩箭是国家队在今年世界杯上的首选扫帚——"

"乔丹，你能不能跟我们说说比赛的情况？"麦格教授的声音插了进来。

"没问题，教授——介绍一点背景消息嘛。顺便说一句，火弩箭有一个内置的自动制动装置，可以——"

"乔丹！"

"好的，好的，现在格兰芬多控球，格兰芬多的凯蒂·贝尔准备投球射门……"

哈利迎面掠过凯蒂身边，一边东张西望地寻找金色的亮光，却发现秋·张紧紧地跟在他身后。毫无疑问，秋·张是个很出色的飞行手——她频繁地超到哈利前面，逼迫他改变方向。

"让她见识一下你的加速，哈利！"弗雷德一边飞过去追赶一只瞄准艾丽娅的游走球，一边喊道。

绕过拉文克劳的门柱时，哈利催促火弩箭加快速度，秋落后了。就在凯蒂投中全场比赛的第一个球，格兰芬多那边的球场上一片沸腾时，哈利看见了——飞贼就在靠近地面的地方，在一处栅栏旁飞来飞去。

CHAPTER THIRTEEN Gryffindor versus Ravenclaw

Harry dived; Cho saw what he was doing and tore after him. Harry was speeding up, excitement flooding him; dives were his speciality. He was ten feet away –

Then a Bludger, hit by one of the Ravenclaw Beaters, came pelting out of nowhere; Harry veered off course, avoiding it by an inch, and in those few, crucial seconds, the Snitch had vanished.

There was a great 'Ooooooh' of disappointment from the Gryffindor supporters, but much applause for their Beater from the Ravenclaw end. George Weasley vented his feelings by hitting the second Bludger directly at the offending Beater, who was forced to roll right over in mid-air to avoid it.

'Gryffindor lead by eighty points to zero, and look at that Firebolt go! Potter's really putting it through its paces now. See it turn – Chang's Comet is just no match for it. The Firebolt's precision-balance is really noticeable in these long –'

'JORDAN! ARE YOU BEING PAID TO ADVERTISE FIREBOLTS? GET ON WITH THE COMMENTARY!'

Ravenclaw were pulling back; they had now scored three goals, which put Gryffindor only fifty points ahead – if Cho got the Snitch before him, Ravenclaw would win. Harry dropped lower, narrowly avoiding a Ravenclaw Chaser, scanning the pitch frantically. A glint of gold, a flutter of tiny wings – the Snitch was circling the Gryffindor goalpost ...

Harry accelerated, eyes fixed on the speck of gold ahead – but next second, Cho had appeared out of thin air, blocking him –

'HARRY, THIS IS NO TIME TO BE A GENTLEMAN!' Wood roared, as Harry swerved to avoid a collision. 'KNOCK HER OFF HER BROOM IF YOU HAVE TO!'

Harry turned and caught sight of Cho; she was grinning. The Snitch had vanished again. Harry turned his Firebolt upwards and was soon twenty feet above the game. Out of the corner of his eye, he saw Cho following him ... she'd decided to mark him rather than search for the Snitch herself. Right then ... if she wanted to tail him, she'd have to take the consequences ...

He dived again, and Cho, thinking he'd seen the Snitch, tried to follow. Harry pulled out of the dive very sharply, she hurtled downwards; he rose fast as a bullet once more, and then saw it, for the third time: the Snitch was glittering way above the pitch at the Ravenclaw end.

第 13 章 格兰芬多对拉文克劳

哈利俯冲下去，秋看见他这么做，立刻追了上来。哈利不断加速，心里兴奋极了。俯冲是他的强项。还有十英尺了——

这时，拉文克劳的一位击球手打出的一只游走球突然冒了出来。哈利赶紧往旁边一闪，差一英寸就撞上了，而在这关键的几秒钟里，飞贼消失了。

"哦！"格兰芬多的支持者们发出一片失望的叹息，拉文克劳那头却在为他们的击球手喝彩欢呼。乔治·韦斯莱为了发泄自己的情绪，把第二只游走球直接击向那位惹祸的击球手。他为了躲避，在空中翻了个跟头。

"格兰芬多八十比〇领先，快看火弩箭的身手！波特此刻正在测试它的性能呢。看见它转身了吗——秋·张的彗星根本没法儿跟它比。火弩箭的精确平衡能力尤其体现在长时间的——"

"**乔丹！火弩箭花了钱要你做广告吗？赶快解说比赛！**"

拉文克劳把比分追了上来，他们接连进了三个球，格兰芬多只领先五十分了——如果秋在哈利之前抓到飞贼，拉文克劳就赢了。哈利降低高度，目光焦急地扫视球场，差点儿撞上拉文克劳的一位追球手。一道金光，一对呼扇的小翅膀——飞贼正在格兰芬多球门柱周围盘旋呢……

哈利加快速度，眼睛盯着前面那个金色的小点——可是一眨眼间，秋·张凭空出现，挡住了他——

"哈利，现在可不能当绅士！"伍德吼道，因为哈利猛一转身避免相撞，"**如果需要，把她从扫帚上撞下去！**"

哈利转脸看见了秋。她脸上带着笑容。飞贼又消失了。哈利把火弩箭往上一转，很快就升到了球场二十英尺的上空。他从眼角看见秋在跟踪他……秋已经决定自己不找飞贼，只管留意哈利。好啊……如果她想跟踪他，就必须承担这样做的后果……

哈利又一个俯冲，秋以为他看见了飞贼，想赶紧跟上来。哈利突然停止俯冲，秋·张却刹不住，一个劲儿地往下降落。哈利再次像子弹一般飞速上升，于是他看见了，第三次看见了：飞贼在拉文克劳那边的球场上空闪闪发光。

CHAPTER THIRTEEN   Gryffindor versus Ravenclaw

He accelerated; so, many feet below, did Cho. He was winning, gaining on the Snitch with every second – then –

'Oh!' screamed Cho, pointing.

Distracted, Harry looked down.

Three Dementors, three tall, black, hooded Dementors, were looking up at him.

He didn't stop to think. Plunging a hand down the neck of his robes, he whipped out his wand and roared, *'Expecto patronum!'*

Something silver white, something enormous, erupted from the end of his wand. He knew it had shot directly at the Dementors but didn't pause to watch; his mind still miraculously clear, he looked ahead – he was nearly there. He stretched out the hand still grasping his wand and just managed to close his fingers over the small, struggling Snitch.

Madam Hooch's whistle sounded, Harry turned around in mid-air and saw six scarlet blurs bearing down on him. Next moment, the whole team were hugging him so hard he was nearly pulled off his broom. Down below he could hear the roars of the Gryffindors in the crowd.

'That's my boy!' Wood kept yelling. Alicia, Angelina and Katie had all kissed Harry, and Fred had him in a grip so tight Harry felt as though his head would come off. In complete disarray, the team managed to make its way back to the ground. Harry got off his broom and looked up to see a gaggle of Gryffindor supporters sprinting onto the pitch, Ron in the lead. Before he knew it, he had been engulfed by the cheering crowd.

'Yes!' Ron yelled, yanking Harry's arm into the air. 'Yes! Yes!'

'Well *done*, Harry!' said Percy, looking delighted. 'Ten Galleons to me! Must find Penelope, excuse me –'

'Good on you, Harry!' roared Seamus Finnigan.

'Ruddy brilliant!' boomed Hagrid over the heads of the milling Gryffindors.

'That was quite some Patronus,' said a voice in Harry's ear.

Harry turned around to see Professor Lupin, who looked both shaken and pleased.

'The Dementors didn't affect me at all!' Harry said excitedly. 'I didn't feel a thing!'

'That would be because they – er – weren't Dementors,' said Professor

第13章 格兰芬多对拉文克劳

哈利加速，在许多英尺之下，秋也跟着加速。他要赢了，飞贼眼看着就要到手了——这时——

"哦！"秋大喊一声，用手指着。

哈利分了神，低头看去。

三个摄魂怪，三个又高又黑、戴着兜帽的摄魂怪，正抬起头看着他呢。

哈利没有停下来思考。他把一只手塞进球袍颈口，抽出魔杖，大吼一声："呼神护卫！"

一个银白色的庞然大物从魔杖尖上冒了出来。哈利知道它径直射向了那些摄魂怪，但他没有停下来细看。他的头脑仍然奇迹般清醒，眼睛望着前面——快要到了。他伸出那只仍然抓着魔杖的手，正好把那挣扎着的小飞贼团在了手指间。

霍琦女士的哨声响了，哈利在空中转了个身，看见六个深红色的模糊身影朝他飞来。接着，队员们都在使劲地搂抱他，弄得他差点儿从扫帚上摔下去。他听见了下面人群中格兰芬多们的喧嚣。

"真是好样儿的！"伍德一遍又一遍地喊。艾丽娅、安吉利娜和凯蒂都亲吻了哈利，弗雷德一把抓住哈利，哈利感觉脑袋都快掉了。在一片混乱中，队员们总算降落到地面。哈利离开扫帚，抬眼看见一群格兰芬多支持者们正飞快地跑向球场，跑在最前面的是罗恩。没等反应过来，哈利就被欢呼的人群团团围住了。

"赢了！"罗恩喊道，使劲把哈利的胳膊举向空中，"赢了！赢了！"

"干得漂亮，哈利！"珀西显得很高兴，说道，"我赢了十个加隆！对不起，我得找到佩内洛——"

"你可真棒啊，哈利！"西莫·斐尼甘嚷道。

"实在太精彩了！"海格在格兰芬多人群的头顶上粗声大气地说。

"那个守护神很像回事儿。"一个声音在哈利耳边说。

哈利一转脸，看见了卢平教授，他显得既担忧又高兴。

"摄魂怪根本没有影响到我！"哈利兴奋地说，"我什么感觉也没有！"

"那是因为他们——呃——不是摄魂怪，"卢平教授说，"你过

CHAPTER THIRTEEN   Gryffindor versus Ravenclaw

Lupin. 'Come and see –'

He led Harry out of the crowd until they were able to see the edge of the pitch.

'You gave Mr Malfoy quite a fright,' said Lupin.

Harry stared. Lying in a crumpled heap on the ground were Malfoy, Crabbe, Goyle and Marcus Flint, the Slytherin team captain, all struggling to remove themselves from long, black, hooded robes. It looked as though Malfoy had been standing on Goyle's shoulders. Standing over them, with an expression of the utmost fury on her face, was Professor McGonagall.

'An unworthy trick!' she was shouting. 'A low and cowardly attempt to sabotage the Gryffindor Seeker! Detention for all of you, and fifty points from Slytherin! I shall be speaking to Professor Dumbledore about this, make no mistake! Ah, here he comes now!'

If anything could have set the seal on Gryffindor's victory, it was this. Ron, who had fought his way through to Harry's side, doubled up with laughter as they watched Malfoy fighting to extricate himself from the robe, Goyle's head still stuck inside it.

'Come on, Harry!' said George, fighting his way over. 'Party! Gryffindor common room, now!'

'Right,' said Harry, and feeling happier than he had done in ages, he and the rest of the team led the way, still in their scarlet robes, out of the stadium and back up to the castle.

* * *

It felt as though they had already won the Quidditch Cup; the party went on all day and well into the night. Fred and George Weasley disappeared for a couple of hours and returned with armfuls of bottles of Butterbeer, pumpkin fizz and several bags full of Honeydukes sweets.

'How did you do that?' squealed Angelina Johnson, as George started throwing Peppermint Toads into the crowd.

'With a little help from Moony, Wormtail, Padfoot and Prongs,' Fred muttered in Harry's ear.

Only one person wasn't joining in the festivities. Hermione, incredibly, was sitting in a corner, attempting to read an enormous book entitled *Home Life and Social Habits of British Muggles*. Harry broke away from the table where Fred and George had started juggling Butterbeer bottles, and went over to her.

来看——"

他领着哈利走出人群,来到能看到球场边缘的地方。

"你把马尔福同学吓得够呛。"卢平说。

哈利惊讶地瞪大了眼睛。在球场上跌作一团的是马尔福、克拉布、高尔和斯莱特林队的队长马库斯·弗林特,他们正手忙脚乱地从长长的、带兜帽的黑袍子里挣脱出来。看样子,刚才马尔福是站在高尔的肩膀上来着。麦格教授站在他们身边,脸上的神情十分愤怒。

"可耻的诡计!"她喊道,"卑鄙、懦弱,想给格兰芬多队的找球手使坏!罚你们每个人都关禁闭,斯莱特林扣除五十分!我要跟邓布利多教授谈谈这事,澄清是非!啊,他来了!"

要说有什么能给格兰芬多的胜利画上一个圆满的句号,那就是这一幕了。罗恩从人群中挤过来,跟哈利一起注视马尔福挣扎着从袍子里脱出身,而高尔的脑袋还缠在袍子里。他们笑得腰都直不起来了。

"快点儿,哈利!"乔治匆忙挤过来说,"联欢会!格兰芬多公共休息室,现在!"

"好嘞。"哈利说,觉得自己好久没有这么开心了。他和队员们仍然穿着深红色球袍,领头走出体育场,返回城堡。

感觉就好像他们已经赢得了魁地奇杯。联欢会开了一整天,又一直延续到深夜。弗雷德和乔治·韦斯莱消失了几个小时,他们俩回来的时候怀里抱着一大堆黄油啤酒、南瓜汽水和满满几大袋蜂蜜公爵的糖果。

"你们怎么弄到的?"乔治把薄荷蟾蜍糖抛向人群时,安吉利娜·约翰逊问道。

"靠了月亮脸、虫尾巴、大脚板和尖头叉子的一点帮助。"弗雷德对着哈利的耳朵低声说。

只有一个人没有参加庆祝活动。赫敏这时居然坐在墙角,埋头阅读一本名叫《英国麻瓜的家庭生活和社交习惯》的大部头书。弗雷德和乔治用黄油啤酒瓶玩起了杂耍,哈利离开桌子,朝赫敏走去。

CHAPTER THIRTEEN   Gryffindor versus Ravenclaw

'Did you even come to the match?' he asked her.

'Of course I did,' said Hermione, in a strangely high-pitched voice, not looking up. 'And I'm very glad we won, and I think you did really well, but I need to read this by Monday.'

'Come on, Hermione, come and have some food,' Harry said, looking over at Ron and wondering whether he was in a good enough mood to bury the hatchet.

'I can't, Harry, I've still got four hundred and twenty-two pages to read!' said Hermione, now sounding slightly hysterical. 'Anyway ...' she glanced over at Ron, too, '*he* doesn't want me to join in.'

There was no arguing with this, as Ron chose that moment to say loudly, 'If Scabbers hadn't just been *eaten*, he could have had some of these Fudge Flies, he used to really like them –'

Hermione burst into tears. Before Harry could say or do anything, she had tucked the enormous book under her arm, and, still sobbing, run towards the staircase to the girls' dormitories and out of sight.

'Can't you give her a break?' Harry asked Ron quietly.

'No,' said Ron flatly. 'If she just acted like she was sorry – but she'll never admit she's wrong, Hermione. She's still acting like Scabbers has gone on holiday or something.'

The Gryffindor party only ended when Professor McGonagall turned up in her tartan dressing-gown and hair-net at one in the morning, to insist that they all went to bed. Harry and Ron climbed the stairs to their dormitory, still discussing the match. At last, exhausted, Harry climbed into bed, twitched the hangings of his four-poster shut to block out a ray of moonlight, lay back and felt himself almost instantly drifting off to sleep ...

He had a very strange dream. He was walking through a forest, his Firebolt over his shoulder, following something silvery white. It was winding its way through the trees ahead, and he could only catch glimpses of it between the leaves. Anxious to catch up with it, he sped up, but as he moved faster, so did his quarry. Harry broke into a run and ahead, he heard hooves gathering speed. Now he was running flat out, and ahead he could hear galloping. Then he turned a corner into a clearing and –

'AAAAAAAAAAAAARRRRRRRRRRGGGHHHHH! NOOOOOOOOOOOOOOOOO!'

第13章 格兰芬多对拉文克劳

"你没去看比赛吗?"他问赫敏。

"当然去了。"赫敏说,她连头也没抬,声音尖得奇怪,"我很高兴我们赢了,我认为你的表现确实很棒,但我需要在星期一之前把这本书读完。"

"来吧,赫敏,过来吃点东西。"哈利一边说,一边看了看那边的罗恩,不知道他此刻情绪是不是特别好,能够跟赫敏握手言和。

"我不能,哈利,我还有四百二十二页要读呢!"赫敏说,她此刻的声音听起来有点歇斯底里了,"而且……"她瞥了一眼罗恩,"他也不希望我参加。"

哈利对此无话可说,因为罗恩偏偏在这个时候大声说道:"如果斑斑没被吃掉,就可以吃几块这种乳脂软糖苍蝇了,它以前特别喜欢的——"

赫敏哭了起来。没等哈利再说什么或做什么,她就把大部头书夹在胳膊底下,一路哭着跑向女生宿舍的楼梯,消失不见了。

"你就不能饶过她吗?"哈利小声问罗恩。

"不能。"罗恩一口回绝,"哪怕她表现出一点难过的样子也行啊——可是她死活不承认她错了,这就是赫敏。她仍然不当回事儿,就好像斑斑出去度假了什么的。"

到了深夜一点,麦格教授穿着格子晨衣、戴着发网出现了,她坚持叫大家都上床去睡觉,格兰芬多的联欢会这才散了。哈利和罗恩上楼回宿舍,一路仍在谈论着比赛。终于,精疲力竭的哈利爬到床上,把四柱床的帷帐合上掖紧,挡住月光,平躺下来,觉得自己好像立刻就进入了梦乡……

他做了一个很奇怪的梦。他肩上扛着火弩箭,跟着一个银白色的东西,走在森林里。那东西在前面的树丛里迂回穿梭,他只能看见它在树叶间忽隐忽现。他急于赶上它,便加快了速度,可是他走得越快,前面那东西走得更快。哈利跑了起来,听见前面的蹄声也在嘚嘚地加速。现在他是全速奔跑了,前面传来飞奔的蹄声。然后,他转了个弯,来到一片空地上——

"啊——!不——!"

CHAPTER THIRTEEN — Gryffindor versus Ravenclaw

Harry woke as suddenly as though he'd been hit in the face. Disorientated in the total darkness, he fumbled with his hangings – he could hear movements around him, and Seamus Finnigan's voice from the other side of the room.

'What's going on?'

Harry thought he heard the dormitory door slam. At last finding the divide in his curtains, he ripped them back, and at the same moment, Dean Thomas lit his lamp.

Ron was sitting up in bed, the hangings torn from one side, a look of the utmost terror on his face.

'Black! Sirius Black! With a knife!'

'*What?*'

'Here! Just now! Slashed the curtains! Woke me up!'

'You sure you weren't dreaming, Ron?' said Dean.

'Look at the curtains! I tell you, he was here!'

They all scrambled out of bed; Harry reached the dormitory door first, and they sprinted back down the staircase. Doors opened behind them, and sleepy voices called after them.

'Who shouted?'

'What're you doing?'

The common room was lit by the glow of the dying fire, still littered with debris from the party. It was deserted.

'Are you *sure* you weren't dreaming, Ron?'

'I'm telling you, I saw him!'

'What's all the noise?'

'Professor McGonagall told us to go to bed!'

A few of the girls had come down their staircase, pulling on dressing-gowns and yawning. Boys, too, were reappearing.

'Excellent, are we carrying on?' said Fred Weasley brightly.

'Everyone back upstairs!' said Percy, hurrying into the common room and pinning his Head Boy badge to his pyjamas as he spoke.

'Perce – Sirius Black!' said Ron faintly. 'In our dormitory! With a knife! Woke me up!'

The common room went very still.

第 13 章 格兰芬多对拉文克劳

哈利猛地惊醒,好像脸上被人打了一下似的。他在黑暗中辨不清方向,胡乱地摸索着帷帐——他听见周围有动静,西莫·斐尼甘的声音从房间的另一边传来。

"怎么回事?"

哈利好像听见宿舍的门砰地关上了。他终于找到了帷帐的开口处,把它们拉开,就在这时,迪安·托马斯把灯点亮了。

罗恩坐在床上,帷帐的一边被扯了下来,他脸上的神情极度恐惧。

"布莱克!小天狼星布莱克!拿着刀!"

"什么?"

"这儿!就在刚才!用刀刺帷帐!把我惊醒了!"

"你能肯定不是在做梦,罗恩?"迪安问。

"看看帷帐!我说得没错,他刚才就在这儿!"

大家手忙脚乱地下了床,哈利首先奔到宿舍门口,他们顺着楼梯跑下来。身后一扇扇门打开了,睡意蒙眬的声音追着他们问道:

"谁在喊?"

"你们在干吗?"

公共休息室里,未燃尽的余火放出些许亮光,到处都乱糟糟地扔着联欢会的东西。没有人。

"你真的不是在做梦吗,罗恩?"

"我告诉你,我看见他了!"

"这么多声音是怎么回事?"

"麦格教授叫我们都上床睡觉!"

几个女生从楼上下来了,裹着晨衣,打着哈欠。男生也在不断拥来。

"太棒了,我们继续联欢吗?"弗雷德·韦斯莱兴高采烈地说。

"所有的人都上楼去!"珀西匆匆走进公共休息室,一边说话,一边把男生学生会主席的徽章别在睡衣上。

"珀西——小天狼星布莱克!"罗恩胆战心惊地说,"在我们宿舍!拿着刀子!把我弄醒了!"

公共休息室里一片寂静。

CHAPTER THIRTEEN   Gryffindor versus Ravenclaw

'Nonsense!' said Percy, looking startled. 'You had too much to eat, Ron – had a nightmare –'

'I'm telling you –'

'Now, really, enough's enough!'

Professor McGonagall was back. She slammed the portrait behind her as she entered the common room and stared furiously around.

'I am delighted that Gryffindor won the match, but this is getting ridiculous! Percy, I expected better of you!'

'I certainly didn't authorise this, Professor!' said Percy, puffing himself up indignantly. 'I was just telling them all to get back to bed! My brother Ron here had a nightmare –'

'IT WASN'T A NIGHTMARE!' Ron yelled. 'PROFESSOR, I WOKE UP, AND SIRIUS BLACK WAS STANDING OVER ME, HOLDING A KNIFE!'

Professor McGonagall stared at him.

'Don't be ridiculous, Weasley, how could he possibly have got through the portrait hole?'

'Ask him!' said Ron, pointing a shaking finger at the back of Sir Cadogan's picture. 'Ask him if he saw –'

Glaring suspiciously at Ron, Professor McGonagall pushed the portrait back open and went outside. The whole common room listened with bated breath.

'Sir Cadogan, did you just let a man enter Gryffindor Tower?'

'Certainly, good lady!' cried Sir Cadogan.

There was a stunned silence, both inside and outside the common room.

'You – you *did*?' said Professor McGonagall. 'But – but the password!'

'He had 'em!' said Sir Cadogan proudly. 'Had the whole week's, my lady! Read 'em off a little piece of paper!'

Professor McGonagall pulled herself back through the portrait hole to face the stunned crowd. She was white as chalk.

'Which person,' she said, her voice shaking, 'which abysmally foolish person wrote down this week's passwords and left them lying around?'

There was utter silence, broken by the smallest of terrified squeaks. Neville Longbottom, trembling from head to fluffy-slippered toes, raised his hand slowly into the air.

第13章 格兰芬多对拉文克劳

"胡说！"珀西神色惊讶地说，"你吃得太多了，罗恩——做了噩梦——"

"我告诉你——"

"够了，够了，别再说了！"

麦格教授回来了。她重重地关上肖像洞门，走进公共休息室，怒气冲冲地四下张望。

"我很高兴格兰芬多赢了比赛，但是这也太过分了！珀西，我原指望你能管好大家呢！"

"这不是我批准的，教授！"珀西说，气得胸脯都鼓了起来，"我正要叫他们都上床睡觉呢！我弟弟罗恩做了一个噩梦——"

"**不是噩梦！**"罗恩嚷了起来，"**教授，我醒了，看见小天狼星布莱克站在我床边，手里拿着刀！**"

麦格教授吃惊地瞪着他。

"别丢人现眼啦，韦斯莱，他怎么可能通过肖像洞口呢？"

"问他！"罗恩举起颤抖的手指，指着卡多根爵士肖像的背面说道，"问他有没有看见——"

麦格教授怀疑地瞪了罗恩一眼，推开肖像，走到外面。公共休息室里的人们都屏住呼吸听着。

"卡多根爵士，你刚才有没有放一个男人进入格兰芬多塔楼？"

"当然有啊，尊贵的女士！"卡多根爵士大声说。

公共休息室内外一片惊愕的沉默。

"你——你真的这么做了？"麦格教授说，"可是——可是口令呢？"

"他有口令！"卡多根爵士骄傲地说，"有一星期的口令呢，我的女士！照着一张小纸条念的！"

麦格教授从肖像洞口钻了回来，面对呆若木鸡的学生，她的脸白得像粉笔一样。

"是谁，"她声音颤抖地问，"是哪个十足的笨蛋，写下这星期的口令到处乱扔？"

一片沉默中，响起一个战战兢兢的细小声音。纳威·隆巴顿，慢慢地举起了他的手，他从脑袋到穿着绒毛拖鞋的脚趾都在发抖。

CHAPTER FOURTEEN

Snape's Grudge

No one in Gryffindor Tower slept that night. They knew that the castle was being searched again, and the whole house stayed awake in the common room, waiting to hear whether Black had been caught. Professor McGonagall came back at dawn, to tell them that he had again escaped.

Everywhere they went next day they saw signs of tighter security; Professor Flitwick could be seen teaching the front doors to recognise a large picture of Sirius Black; Filch was suddenly bustling up and down the corridors, boarding up everything from tiny cracks in the walls to mouse holes. Sir Cadogan had been sacked. His portrait had been taken back to its lonely landing on the seventh floor, and the Fat Lady was back. She had been expertly restored, but was still extremely nervous, and had only agreed to return to her job on condition that she was given extra protection. A bunch of surly security trolls had been hired to guard her. They paced the corridor in a menacing group, talking in grunts and comparing the size of their clubs.

Harry couldn't help noticing that the statue of the one-eyed witch on the third floor remained unguarded and unblocked. It seemed that Fred and George had been right in thinking that they – and now Harry, Ron and Hermione – were the only ones who knew about the hidden passageway within it.

'D'you reckon we should tell someone?' Harry asked Ron.

'We know he's not coming in through Honeydukes,' said Ron dismissively. 'We'd've heard if the shop had been broken into.'

Harry was glad Ron took this view. If the one-eyed witch was boarded up too, he would never be able to go into Hogsmeade again.

Ron had become an instant celebrity. For the first time in his life, people

第 14 章

斯内普怀恨在心

那一夜,格兰芬多塔楼里没有一个人睡觉。大家知道又在搜查城堡了。全院学生都待在公共休息室里,保持着清醒状态,等着布莱克被抓获的消息。黎明时麦格教授回来,告诉大家布莱克又逃脱了。

第二天,他们看到到处都加强了保安措施。弗立维教授在教城堡大门的看守辨认小天狼星布莱克的大照片;费尔奇突然忙得不可开交,在走廊里跑来跑去堵缺口,从墙上最小的裂缝到老鼠洞都不放过。卡多根爵士被撤职了,他的肖像又被送回八楼那个冷冷清清的楼梯平台上。胖夫人又回来了,她经过了专家修复,但还是极其神经质,要求给予她特别保护才肯回到岗位上。一帮粗暴的巨怪保安被雇来保护她。他们三五成群凶神恶煞般地在走廊里巡逻,粗声大气,互相比较着手中棒子的大小。

哈利无意中注意到四楼的独眼女巫雕像依然无人看守,也没有被封死。看来弗雷德和乔治说得不错,只有他们(现在还有哈利、罗恩和赫敏)知道那里有一条秘密通道。

"你说要不要告诉别人?"哈利问罗恩。

"我们知道他不会从蜂蜜公爵那边进来,"罗恩不以为然地说,"如果他闯进了糖果店,我们会得到消息的。"

哈利很高兴罗恩这么看。要是独眼女巫也被封死了,他就没法再去霍格莫德了。

罗恩一下子出了名。平生第一次,他比哈利受到了人们更多的关

CHAPTER FOURTEEN   Snape's Grudge

were paying more attention to him than to Harry, and it was clear that Ron was rather enjoying the experience. Though still severely shaken by the night's events, he was happy to tell anyone who asked, what had happened, with a wealth of detail.

'... I was asleep, and I heard this ripping noise, and I thought it was in my dream, you know? But then there was this draught ... I woke up and one side of the hangings on my bed had been pulled down ... I rolled over ... and I saw him standing over me ... like a skeleton, with loads of filthy hair ... holding this great long knife, must've been twelve inches ... and he looked at me, and I looked at him, and then I yelled, and he scarpered.

'Why, though?' Ron added to Harry, as the group of second-year girls who had been listening to his chilling tale departed. 'Why did he scarper?'

Harry had been wondering the same thing. Why had Black, having got the wrong bed, not silenced Ron and proceeded to Harry? Black had proved twelve years ago that he didn't mind murdering innocent people, and this time he had been facing five unarmed boys, four of whom were asleep.

'He must've known he'd have a job getting back out of the castle once you'd yelled and woken people up,' said Harry thoughtfully. 'He'd've had to kill the whole house to get back through the portrait hole ... then he would've met the teachers ...'

Neville was in total disgrace. Professor McGonagall was so furious with him she had banned him from all future Hogsmeade visits, given him a detention and forbidden anyone to give him the password into the Tower. Poor Neville was forced to wait outside the common room every night for somebody to let him in, while the security trolls leered unpleasantly at him. None of these punishments, however, came close to matching the one his grandmother had in store for him. Two days after Black's break-in, she sent Neville the very worst thing a Hogwarts student could receive over breakfast – a Howler.

The school owls swooped into the Great Hall, carrying the post as usual, and Neville choked as a huge barn owl landed in front of him, a scarlet envelope clutched in its beak. Harry and Ron, who were sitting opposite him, recognised the letter as a Howler at once – Ron had got one from his mother the year before.

'Run for it, Neville,' Ron advised.

Neville didn't need telling twice. He seized the envelope and, holding it before him like a bomb, sprinted out of the Hall, while the Slytherin table

第 14 章 斯内普怀恨在心

注。罗恩显然很喜欢这种感觉。他虽然还因昨晚的事惊魂未定,但只要有人来问,他总是很乐意绘声绘色、详详细细地向他们讲述他的历险经过。

"……我正在睡觉,忽然听到撕东西的声音,我还以为是在做梦呢,你知道吧?可是一阵冷风……我醒了,帷帐的一边被扯下来了……我翻过身……看到他站在我跟前……像一具骷髅,一大蓬脏兮兮的头发……举着一把这么老长的刀子,准有十二英寸长……他看着我,我看着他,然后我大叫一声,他就噌地跑了。"

"可是为什么呢?"罗恩问哈利,这时一群二年级女生听完他那瘆人的故事刚刚走开,"他为什么要跑呢?"

哈利也在纳闷这个问题。布莱克走错了床铺之后,为什么没有杀了罗恩灭口,接着去找哈利呢?布莱克十二年前就已经证明,他不在乎屠杀无辜,这次他面对的是五个手无寸铁的男孩,其中四个还在熟睡。

"他大概知道,你嚷嚷起来把人吵醒后,他想要撤出城堡就难了。"哈利思索着说,"他必须杀光全院的学生才能从肖像洞口出去……然后还会碰到教师……"

纳威丢尽了脸。麦格教授对他大发雷霆,禁止他以后再去霍格莫德,关了他的禁闭,还不许任何人告诉他进塔楼的口令。可怜的纳威每天晚上只能待在公共休息室外面,眼巴巴地等着有谁能带他进去,而那些巨怪保安还在一旁不怀好意地斜瞟着他。但这些与他奶奶给他的惩罚相比,还算是小巫见大巫呢。布莱克闯入塔楼的两天之后,纳威的奶奶给他寄来了霍格沃茨学生早餐时可能接到的最可怕的东西———一封吼叫信。

学校的猫头鹰像往常一样呼啦啦飞进礼堂,带来了邮件。纳威看到一只巨大的谷仓猫头鹰落在他面前,嘴里叼着一个大红信封,他惊得噎住了。哈利和罗恩坐在他对面,一下子认出那是一封吼叫信——罗恩的妈妈去年给罗恩寄过一封。

"快跑,纳威。"罗恩提醒道。

纳威不需要提醒第二遍,他抓起信封,像捧炸弹一样把它举在身前,箭一般地冲出了礼堂。看到他那副狼狈样,斯莱特林那一桌爆发出一

CHAPTER FOURTEEN   Snape's Grudge

exploded with laughter at the sight of him. They heard the Howler go off in the Entrance Hall – Neville's grandmother's voice, magically magnified to a hundred times its usual volume, shrieking about how he had brought shame on the whole family.

Harry was too busy feeling sorry for Neville to notice immediately that he had a letter, too. Hedwig got his attention by nipping him sharply on the wrist.

'Ouch! Oh – thanks, Hedwig …'

Harry tore open the envelope while Hedwig helped herself to some of Neville's cornflakes. The note inside said:

> DEAR HARRY AND RON,
> HOW ABOUT HAVING TEA WITH ME THIS EVENING ROUND SIX? I'LL COME AND COLLECT YOU FROM THE CASTLE. <u>WAIT FOR ME IN THE ENTRANCE HALL, YOU'RE NOT ALLOWED OUT ON YOUR OWN.</u>
> CHEERS,
> HAGRID

'He probably wants to hear all about Black!' said Ron.

So at six o'clock that evening, Harry and Ron left Gryffindor Tower, passed the security trolls at a run, and headed down to the Entrance Hall.

Hagrid was already waiting for them.

'All right, Hagrid!' said Ron. 'S'pose you want to hear about Saturday night, do you?'

'I've already heard all abou' it,' said Hagrid, opening the front doors and leading them outside.

'Oh,' said Ron, looking slightly put out.

The first thing they saw on entering Hagrid's cabin was Buckbeak, who was stretched out on top of Hagrid's patchwork quilt, his enormous wings folded tight to his body, enjoying a large plate of dead ferrets. Averting his eyes from this unpleasant sight, Harry saw a gigantic, hairy brown suit and a very horrible yellow and orange tie hanging from the top of Hagrid's wardrobe door.

'What are they for, Hagrid?' said Harry.

'Buckbeak's case against the Committee fer the Disposal o' Dangerous Creatures,' said Hagrid. 'This Friday. Him an' me'll be goin' down ter

阵大笑。他们听到吼叫信在门厅炸响了——纳威奶奶的声音用了魔法，比平常说话的音量放大了一百倍，尖叫着谴责他给整个家族带来了耻辱。

哈利光顾着为纳威感到难过，一时没发现他也有一封信。海德薇狠狠啄了啄他的手腕，引起他的注意。

"哎哟！哦——谢谢，海德薇……"

哈利扯开信封，海德薇自行去啄食纳威的玉米片了。这张纸条上写着：

亲爱的哈利和罗恩：

今天下午六点左右陪我喝茶好吗？我到城堡来接你们。**在门厅里等我；你们不能出来。**

祝开心。

海　格

"他可能想听听布莱克的事！"罗恩说。

于是，下午六点钟，哈利和罗恩离开了格兰芬多塔楼，从巨怪保安旁边快步跑过，下楼来到门厅。

海格已经等在那里。

"嘿嘿，海格！"罗恩说，"你是想听听星期六夜里的事情吧？"

"我已经全听说了。"海格说着，打开大门带他们出去。

"哦。"罗恩显得有点讪讪的。

进了海格的小屋，一眼就看见巴克比克舒展着四肢倚在海格的拼花被子上，巨大的翅膀收拢在体侧，正在享用一大盘死白鼬。哈利把目光从这令人不舒服的一幕移开，看到一件特大号的、毛乎乎的棕色外套和一条黄橙相间、丑陋不堪的领带，挂在海格衣柜的门上。

"这些是干吗用的，海格？"哈利问。

"巴克比克跟处置危险动物委员会的案子，"海格说，"就在这星期

CHAPTER FOURTEEN   Snape's Grudge

London together. I've booked two beds on the Knight Bus ...'

Harry felt a nasty pang of guilt. He had completely forgotten that Buckbeak's trial was so near, and judging by the uneasy look on Ron's face, he had, too. They had also forgotten their promise about helping him prepare Buckbeak's defence; the arrival of the Firebolt had driven it clean out of their minds.

Hagrid poured them tea and offered them a plate of Bath buns, but they knew better than to accept; they had had too much experience of Hagrid's cooking.

'I got somethin' ter discuss with you two,' said Hagrid, sitting himself between them and looking uncharacteristically serious.

'What?' said Harry.

'Hermione,' said Hagrid.

'What about her?' said Ron.

'She's in a righ' state, that's what. She's bin comin' down ter visit me a lot since Chris'mas. Bin feelin' lonely. Firs' yeh weren' talking to her because o' the Firebolt, now yer not talkin' to her because her cat —'

'— ate Scabbers!' Ron interjected angrily.

'Because her cat acted like all cats do,' Hagrid continued doggedly. 'She's cried a fair few times, yeh know. Goin' through a rough time at the moment. Bitten off more'n she can chew, if yeh ask me, all the work she's tryin' ter do. Still found time ter help me with Buckbeak's case, mind ... she's found some really good stuff fer me ... reckon he'll stand a good chance now ...'

'Hagrid, we should've helped as well — sorry —' Harry began awkwardly.

'I'm not blamin' yeh!' said Hagrid, waving Harry's apology aside. 'Gawd knows yeh've had enough ter be gettin' on with, I've seen yeh practisin' Quidditch ev'ry hour o' the day an' night — but I gotta tell yeh, I thought you two'd value yer friend more'n broomsticks or rats. Tha's all.'

Harry and Ron exchanged uncomfortable looks.

'Really upset, she was, when Black nearly stabbed yeh, Ron. She's got her heart in the right place, Hermione has, an' you two not talkin' to her —'

'If she'd just get rid of that cat, I'd speak to her again!' Ron said angrily. 'But she's still sticking up for it! It's a maniac, and she won't hear a word against it!'

'Ah, well, people can be a bit stupid abou' their pets,' said Hagrid wisely.

第14章 斯内普怀恨在心

五,我要和它去伦敦,我在骑士公共汽车上订了两个铺位……"

哈利感到一阵深深的内疚,他竟然完全忘记了对巴克比克的审讯已迫在眉睫。从罗恩不安的表情看,他也很愧疚。他们俩还忘记了自己保证过要帮海格准备巴克比克的辩护词——火弩箭的到来使他们把这一切都忘到了脑后。

海格给他们倒了茶,又端出一盘巴斯圆面包,但他们不敢接受——他们已经多次领教过海格的厨艺了。

"我有点事要跟你们俩谈谈。"海格在他俩中间坐下,神情严肃,一反常态。

"什么事?"哈利问。

"赫敏。"海格说。

"她怎么啦?"罗恩问。

"她情况不大妙,就是这样。圣诞节之后她来看过我好多次,觉得孤单。你们起先不理她,因为火弩箭,现在又不跟她说话,因为她的猫——"

"——吃掉了斑斑!"罗恩愤怒地插嘴。

"因为她的猫做了所有的猫都可能做的事,"海格固执地说下去,"她哭了好几回,你们知道吧?她现在的日子不好过,揽的事儿太多啦,我觉得。要完成那么多的功课,还要抽出时间来帮我准备巴克比克的诉讼,想想吧……她给我找了一些很好的材料……估计现在有希望了……"

"海格,我们也应该帮忙的——对不起——"哈利窘迫地说。

"我不怪你们!"海格一摆手,没理会哈利的歉意,"上帝知道你们也够忙的。我看到你没日没夜地练魁地奇。但我必须说一句,我觉得你们两个应该把朋友看得比飞天扫帚和老鼠更重要。就是这样。"

哈利和罗恩难为情地对视了一下。

"她真的很难过,因为布莱克差点杀了你,罗恩。她有一颗善良的心啊,赫敏。可你们两个不跟她说话——"

"只要她把那只猫弄走,我就跟她说话!"罗恩没好气地说,"结果她还袒护它!那只猫疯了!可是赫敏听不得一句数落它的话!"

"啊,是啊,人们对于宠物会有点犯糊涂。"海格机智地说。在他身后,

CHAPTER FOURTEEN   Snape's Grudge

Behind him, Buckbeak spat a few ferret bones onto Hagrid's pillow.

They spent the rest of their visit discussing Gryffindor's improved chances for the Quidditch Cup. At nine o'clock, Hagrid walked them back up to the castle.

A large group of people was bunched around the noticeboard when they returned to the common room.

'Hogsmeade, next weekend!' said Ron, craning over the heads to read the new notice. 'What d'you reckon?' he added quietly to Harry, as they went to sit down.

'Well, Filch hasn't done anything about the passage into Honeydukes ...' Harry said, even more quietly.

'Harry!' said a voice in his right ear. Harry started and looked around at Hermione, who was sitting at the table right behind them and clearing a space in the wall of books that had been hiding her.

'Harry, if you go into Hogsmeade again ... I'll tell Professor McGonagall about that map!' said Hermione.

'Can you hear someone talking, Harry?' growled Ron, not looking at Hermione.

'Ron, how can you let him go with you? After what Sirius Black nearly did to *you*! I mean it, I'll tell –'

'So now you're trying to get Harry expelled!' said Ron furiously. 'Haven't you done enough damage this year?'

Hermione opened her mouth to respond, but with a soft hiss, Crookshanks leapt onto her lap. Hermione took one frightened look at the expression on Ron's face, gathered Crookshanks up and hurried away towards the girls' dormitories.

'So how about it?' Ron said to Harry, as though there had been no interruption. 'Come on, last time we went you didn't see anything. You haven't even been inside Zonko's yet!'

Harry looked around to check that Hermione was well out of earshot.

'OK,' he said. 'But I'm taking the Invisibility Cloak this time.'

On Saturday morning, Harry packed his Invisibility Cloak in his bag, slipped the Marauder's Map into his pocket and went down to breakfast with everyone else. Hermione kept shooting suspicious looks down the table at him, but he avoided her eye, and was careful to let her see him walking back

巴克比克把几块白鼬骨头吐到了海格的枕头上。

在剩下的时间里，他们一直在讨论格兰芬多夺取魁地奇杯的新希望。九点钟，海格把他们送回了城堡。

回到公共休息室，他们看到一大群人围在布告栏前。

"霍格莫德，下个周末！"罗恩伸着脖子看那张新贴的通知。"你是怎么想的？"坐下之后他轻声问哈利。

"嗯，费尔奇还没有对那条通往蜂蜜公爵的秘密通道动手……"哈利声音更轻地说。

"哈利！"他右耳边有人叫他。哈利吓了一跳，回头一看是赫敏，就坐在他们后边的座位上，正把桌上挡住她的一面书墙清理出一个缺口。

"哈利，如果你再去霍格莫德……我就把地图的事告诉麦格教授！"赫敏说。

"你听到有人在说话吗，哈利？"罗恩吼道，看也不看赫敏。

"罗恩，你怎么能让他跟你一起去呢？在小天狼星差点对你下手之后！我说到做到，我会告诉——"

"现在你又想害得哈利被开除！"罗恩火冒三丈，"你今年搞的破坏还不够吗？"

赫敏张开嘴正要分辩，忽然随着一声哈气声，克鲁克山跳到了她的膝头。赫敏害怕地看了一眼罗恩的脸色，抱起克鲁克山，匆匆走向女生宿舍。

"怎么样？"罗恩对哈利说，好像刚才没被打断一样，"去吧，上次我们去的时候你什么都没看着。你还没进佐科店里看过呢！"

哈利回头看看赫敏是否已经听不见他们说话了。

"好吧，"他说，"但这次我要带上隐形衣。"

星期六早上，哈利把隐形衣放进书包，把活点地图塞进口袋，下去和大家一起吃早饭。赫敏在桌旁不时朝他投来怀疑的目光，但他避免与她视线相交，并且在别人都朝门口走去时，故意让她看到他在门

CHAPTER FOURTEEN   Snape's Grudge

up the marble staircase in the Entrance Hall as everybody else proceeded to the front doors.

'Bye!' Harry called to Ron. 'See you when you get back!'

Ron grinned and winked.

Harry hurried up to the third floor, slipping the Marauder's Map out of his pocket as he went. Crouching behind the one-eyed witch, he smoothed it out. A tiny dot was moving in his direction. Harry squinted at it. The minuscule writing next to it read *Neville Longbottom*.

Harry quickly pulled out his wand, muttered '*Dissendium!* ' and shoved his bag into the statue, but before he could climb in himself, Neville came around the corner.

'Harry! I forgot you weren't going to Hogsmeade either!'

'Hi, Neville,' said Harry, moving swiftly away from the statue and pushing the map back into his pocket. 'What are you up to?'

'Nothing,' shrugged Neville. 'Want a game of Exploding Snap?'

'Er – not now – I was going to go to the library and do that vampire essay for Lupin –'

'I'll come with you!' said Neville brightly. 'I haven't done it either!'

'Er – hang on – yeah, I forgot, I finished it last night!'

'Brilliant, you can help me!' said Neville, his round face anxious. 'I don't understand that thing about the garlic at all – do they have to eat it, or –'

Neville broke off with a small gasp, looking over Harry's shoulder.

It was Snape. Neville took a quick step behind Harry.

'And what are you two doing here?' said Snape, coming to a halt and looking from one to the other. 'An odd place to meet –'

To Harry's immense disquiet, Snape's black eyes flicked to the doorways on either side of them, and then to the one-eyed witch.

'We're not – meeting here,' said Harry. 'We just – met here.'

'Indeed?' said Snape. 'You have a habit of turning up in unexpected places, Potter, and you are rarely there for no reason ... I suggest the pair of you return to Gryffindor Tower, where you belong.'

Harry and Neville set off without another word. As they turned the corner, Harry looked back. Snape was running one of his hands over the one-eyed witch's head, examining it closely.

第14章 斯内普怀恨在心

厅里顺着大理石楼梯上去了。

"再见!"哈利对罗恩喊道,"等你回来再见!"

罗恩咧嘴一笑,眨了眨眼睛。

哈利快步爬到四楼,一边走一边从口袋里抽出活点地图。他蹲在独眼女巫背后,展开地图,有个小黑点正在朝他这边移动。哈利眯眼细看。黑点旁边的小字写的是纳威·隆巴顿。

哈利迅速拔出魔杖,低声念道:"左右分离!"他把背包塞进雕像里,但自己还没来得及爬进去,纳威已在拐角出现了。

"哈利!我忘了你也不去霍格莫德!"

"嘿,纳威!"哈利迅速离开雕像,把地图塞回口袋里,"你打算做什么?"

"没事做,"纳威耸耸肩,"想玩噼啪爆炸牌吗?"

"呃——现在不行——我要去图书馆写卢平布置的那篇关于吸血鬼的论文——"

"我跟你一起去!"纳威高兴地说,"我也没写呢!"

"呃——等等——对了,瞧我这记性,我昨晚已经写完了!"

"太好了,你可以帮帮我!"纳威说着,圆脸上显出焦急的神情,"我根本没搞懂大蒜那一节——大蒜是必须吃的,还是……?"

他突然住口,轻轻倒吸了一口气,望着哈利的身后。

是斯内普。纳威急忙躲到哈利的后面。

"你们两个在这儿干什么?"斯内普停住脚步,扫视着两人,"在这里碰头真是奇怪——"

令哈利极度紧张的是,斯内普的黑眼睛朝两边的房门一扫,然后把目光射向了独眼女巫。

"我们不是——在这儿碰头,"哈利说,"我们只是——正好碰到了。"

"是吗?"斯内普说,"你惯于在别人意想不到的地方出现,波特,而且很少有正当理由……我建议你们两个回格兰芬多塔楼去,那才是你们该待的地方。"

哈利和纳威马上逃走了,一句话也没说。来到拐角处,哈利回头看了看,斯内普正用一只手抚摩着独眼女巫的头部,仔细检查。

CHAPTER FOURTEEN   Snape's Grudge

Harry managed to shake Neville off at the Fat Lady by telling him the password, then pretending he'd left his vampire essay in the library and doubling back. Once out of sight of the security trolls, he pulled out the map again and held it close to his nose.

The third-floor corridor seemed to be deserted. Harry scanned the map carefully and saw, with a leap of relief, that the tiny dot labelled *Severus Snape* was now back in its office.

He sprinted back to the one-eyed witch, opened her hump, heaved himself inside and slid down to meet his bag at the bottom of the stone chute. He wiped the Marauder's Map blank again, then set off at a run.

Harry, completely hidden beneath the Invisibility Cloak, emerged into the sunlight outside Honeydukes and prodded Ron in the back.

'It's me,' he muttered.

'What kept you?' Ron hissed.

'Snape was hanging around ...'

They set off up the High Street.

'Where are you?' Ron kept muttering out of the corner of his mouth. 'Are you still there? This feels weird ...'

They went to the Post Office; Ron pretended to be checking the price of an owl to Bill in Egypt so that Harry could have a good look around. The owls sat hooting softly down at him, at least three hundred of them; from Great Greys right down to tiny little Scops owls ('Local Deliveries Only') which were so small they could have sat in the palm of Harry's hand.

Then they visited Zonko's, which was so packed with students Harry had to exercise great care not to tread on anyone and cause a panic. There were jokes and tricks to fulfil even Fred and George's wildest dreams; Harry gave Ron whispered orders and passed him some gold from under the Cloak. They left Zonko's with their money bags considerably lighter than they had been on entering, but their pockets bulging with Dungbombs, Hiccough Sweets, Frog Spawn Soap and a Nose-Biting Teacup apiece.

The day was fine and breezy, and neither of them felt like staying indoors, so they walked past the Three Broomsticks and climbed a slope to visit the Shrieking Shack, the most haunted dwelling in Britain. It stood a little way above the rest of the village, and even in daylight was slightly creepy, with its

第14章 斯内普怀恨在心

哈利在胖夫人跟前终于把纳威甩掉了,他把口令告诉了纳威,然后假装自己把吸血鬼论文忘在图书馆了,又折了回来。到了巨怪保安的视线以外,他重新抽出地图,举到眼前查看。

四楼走廊上似乎没人了,哈利仔细搜索了一番,看到标着西弗勒斯·斯内普的小黑点已回到他的办公室,不觉大大松了一口气。

他飞奔到独眼女巫跟前,打开她的驼背钻了进去,出溜到石头滑道的底部,捡到了他的书包。然后他消掉活点地图上的字迹,撒腿跑了起来。

哈利纹丝不露地藏在隐形衣里,来到蜂蜜公爵门外的阳光下,捅了捅罗恩的后背。

"是我。"他小声说。

"怎么这么晚?"罗恩悄声问。

"斯内普在那儿转悠。"

他们沿着大街往前走。

"你在哪儿?"罗恩不停地从嘴角发出声音轻轻说,"你还在那儿吗?这种感觉好怪……"

走进邮局,罗恩假装询问给埃及的比尔发一只猫头鹰要多少钱,让哈利有时间好好参观。许多猫头鹰栖在那里向他轻声叫唤,起码有三百只。从大灰鸮到角鸮(仅送当地邮件),什么都有,角鸮小得都可以托在哈利的掌心里。

接着他们去了佐科,店里挤满了学生。哈利不得不十分小心,免得踩到别人引起恐慌。那里有许多恶作剧和变戏法用的材料,能满足弗雷德和乔治最异想天开的念头。哈利悄声告诉罗恩要买什么,并从隐形衣下面给了他一些金币。离开佐科时,他们的钱包比来时轻了许多,但口袋里都塞满了粪弹、打嗝糖、蛙卵肥皂,每人还有一只咬鼻子茶杯。

天气很好,凉风习习,两人都不想待在室内,就走过三把扫帚酒吧,爬上山坡去看尖叫棚屋,那是英国闹鬼闹得最厉害的一座房子。它比村子里的其他房屋稍高一些,白天看着也有点瘆人,窗户都封上了,

CHAPTER FOURTEEN   Snape's Grudge

boarded windows and dank overgrown garden.

'Even the Hogwarts ghosts avoid it,' said Ron, as they leaned on the fence, looking up at it. 'I asked Nearly Headless Nick ... he says he's heard a very rough crowd live here. No one can get in. Fred and George tried, obviously, but all the entrances are sealed shut ...'

Harry, feeling hot from their climb, was just considering taking off the Cloak for a few minutes, when they heard voices nearby. Someone was climbing towards the house from the other side of the hill; moments later, Malfoy had appeared, followed closely by Crabbe and Goyle. Malfoy was speaking.

'... should have an owl from Father any time now. He had to go to the hearing to tell them about my arm ... about how I couldn't use it for three months ...'

Crabbe and Goyle sniggered.

'I really wish I could hear that great hairy moron trying to defend himself ... "There's no 'arm in 'im, 'onest –" ... that Hippogriff's as good as dead –'

Malfoy suddenly caught sight of Ron. His pale face split in a malevolent grin.

'What are you doing, Weasley?'

Malfoy looked up at the crumbling house behind Ron.

'Suppose you'd love to live here, wouldn't you, Weasley? Dreaming about having your own bedroom? I heard your family all sleep in one room – is that true?'

Harry seized the back of Ron's robes to stop him leaping on Malfoy.

'Leave him to me,' he hissed in Ron's ear.

The opportunity was too perfect to miss. Harry crept silently around behind Malfoy, Crabbe and Goyle, bent down and scooped a large handful of mud out of the path.

'We were just discussing your friend Hagrid,' Malfoy said to Ron. 'Just trying to imagine what he's saying to the Committee for the Disposal of Dangerous Creatures. D'you think he'll cry when they cut off his Hippogriff's –'

SPLAT!

Malfoy's head jerked forwards as the mud hit him; his silver-blond hair was suddenly dripping in muck.

'What the –?'

第14章 斯内普怀恨在心

花园里野草丛生。

"连霍格沃茨的幽灵都躲着它。"罗恩说,他们俩靠在篱笆上,抬头望着棚屋,"我问了差点没头的尼克……他听说有一帮非常粗野的家伙住在这儿。谁也进不去。弗雷德和乔治显然试过,但现在所有的入口都被封了……"

哈利爬山爬得浑身发热,正在考虑把隐形衣脱掉几分钟,忽然听见附近有说话声。有人从山对面向着棚屋爬了上来。过了一会儿,马尔福出现了,后面紧跟着克拉布和高尔。马尔福在说话。

"……应该很快就收到我爸爸的猫头鹰了,他要出庭去跟他们说我的胳膊……说我三个月都不能用这条胳膊……"

克拉布和高尔嘿嘿傻笑着。

"真希望能听到那个毛乎乎的大蠢货使劲儿为自己辩护……'它没有危险,真的——'那头鹰头马身有翼兽死定了——"

马尔福突然看到了罗恩,苍白的脸上绽出一个恶毒的笑容。

"你在干什么,韦斯莱?"

马尔福抬头望着罗恩身后摇摇欲倒的棚屋。

"你大概很愿意住在这里吧,韦斯莱?梦想着有你自己的卧室?我听说你全家都睡在一个房间里——是真的吗?"

哈利抓住罗恩袍子的后背,不让他朝马尔福扑过去。

"交给我吧。"他对罗恩耳语道。

这个机会太好了,绝不能错过。哈利蹑手蹑脚地走到马尔福、克拉布和高尔身后,俯身从路上抓了一大捧泥巴。

"我们正在谈论你的朋友海格,"马尔福对罗恩说,"正在想象他会对处置危险生物委员会说些什么。你认为他会哭吗?当他们砍掉他那头鹰头马身有翼兽的——"

啪!

马尔福的脑袋往前一倾,淡金色的头发上突然全是泥浆,直往下滴答。

"什么——?"

CHAPTER FOURTEEN   Snape's Grudge

Ron had to hold onto the fence to keep himself standing, he was laughing so hard. Malfoy, Crabbe and Goyle spun stupidly on the spot, staring wildly around, Malfoy trying to wipe his hair clean.

'What was that? Who did that?'

'Very haunted up here, isn't it?' said Ron, with the air of one commenting on the weather.

Crabbe and Goyle were looking scared. Their bulging muscles were no use against ghosts. Malfoy was staring madly around at the deserted landscape.

Harry sneaked along the path, where a particularly sloppy puddle yielded some foul-smelling, green sludge.

SPLATTER!

Crabbe and Goyle caught some this time. Goyle hopped furiously on the spot, trying to rub it out of his small, dull eyes.

'It came from over there!' said Malfoy, wiping his face, and staring at a spot some six feet to the left of Harry.

Crabbe blundered forwards, his long arms outstretched like a zombie. Harry dodged around him, picked up a stick, and lobbed it at Crabbe's back. Harry doubled up with silent laughter as Crabbe did a kind of pirouette in mid-air, trying to see who had thrown it. As Ron was the only person Crabbe could see, it was Ron he started towards, but Harry stuck out his leg. Crabbe stumbled – and his huge, flat foot caught the hem of Harry's Cloak. Harry felt a great tug, then the Cloak slid off his face.

For a split second, Malfoy stared at him.

'AAARGH!' he yelled, pointing at Harry's head. Then he turned tail and ran, at breakneck speed, back down the hill, Crabbe and Goyle behind him.

Harry tugged the Cloak up again, but the damage was done.

'Harry!' Ron said, stumbling forward and staring hopelessly at the point where Harry had disappeared, 'you'd better run for it! If Malfoy tells anyone – you'd better get back to the castle, quick –'

'See you later,' said Harry, and without another word, he tore back down the path towards Hogsmeade.

Would Malfoy believe what he had seen? Would anyone believe Malfoy? Nobody knew about the Invisibility Cloak – nobody except Dumbledore. Harry's stomach turned over – Dumbledore would know exactly what had happened, if Malfoy said anything –

第14章 斯内普怀恨在心

罗恩笑得前仰后合，不得不抓住篱笆让自己站稳。马尔福、克拉布和高尔傻瓜似的原地转圈，狂乱地四处搜寻。马尔福拼命想把头发擦干净。

"刚才是怎么回事？谁干的？"

"这儿经常闹鬼，是不是？"罗恩用谈论天气的口吻说。

克拉布和高尔显得很害怕，他们隆起的肌肉对付鬼魂就没有用了。马尔福疯狂地扫视着周围荒无人烟的景致。

哈利从小路上悄悄向前走去，一个特别脏烂的水塘里有一些发臭的绿色淤泥。

啪！

这次克拉布和高尔分到了一些。高尔气急败坏地原地跳脚，想把烂泥从他那呆滞的小眼睛里揉掉。

"是从那儿过来的！"马尔福擦着脸说，盯着哈利左边约六英尺处。

克拉布跌跌撞撞地走过去，长胳膊像僵尸那样伸着。哈利闪身绕开，捡起一根木棍，抛到克拉布的背上。哈利不出声地笑弯了腰。克拉布脚尖点地来了个空中转体，想看清是谁扔的。由于只能看见罗恩，他就朝罗恩扑了过去，哈利把腿一伸，克拉布绊了一跤，他的大脚板钩到了哈利的隐形衣。哈利感到有人猛力一扯，隐形衣从他的脸上滑落下来。

一瞬间，马尔福直勾勾地瞪着他。

"啊——！"他指着哈利的脑袋大叫，然后掉头没命地朝山下跑去，克拉布和高尔紧随其后。

哈利把隐形衣拉好，但后果已经酿成。

"哈利！"罗恩踉踉跄跄走上前，绝望地看着哈利刚刚消失的地方，"你快跑吧！要是马尔福告诉了别人——你最好赶紧回城堡，快——"

"再见。"哈利没再说别的，顺着小路向霍格莫德飞奔而去。

马尔福会相信他看到的那一幕吗？会有人相信马尔福吗？没有人知道隐形衣的事——除了邓布利多。哈利胃里翻腾起来——邓布利多会知道是怎么回事，如果马尔福说了——

CHAPTER FOURTEEN Snape's Grudge

Back into Honeydukes, back down the cellar steps, across the stone floor, through the trapdoor – Harry pulled off the Cloak, tucked it under his arm, and ran, flat out, along the passage ... Malfoy would get back first ... how long would it take him to find a teacher? Panting, a sharp pain in his side, Harry didn't slow down until he reached the stone slide. He would have to leave the Cloak where it was, it was too much of a giveaway if Malfoy had tipped off a teacher. He hid it in a shadowy corner, then started to climb, fast as he could, his sweaty hands slipping on the sides of the chute. He reached the inside of the witch's hump, tapped it with his wand, stuck his head through and hoisted himself out; the hump closed, and just as Harry jumped out from behind the statue, he heard quick footsteps approaching.

It was Snape. He approached Harry at a swift walk, his black robes swishing, then stopped in front of him.

'So,' he said.

There was a look of suppressed triumph about him. Harry tried to look innocent, all too aware of his sweaty face and his muddy hands, which he quickly hid in his pockets.

'Come with me, Potter,' said Snape.

Harry followed him downstairs, trying to wipe his hands clean on the inside of his robes without Snape noticing. They walked down the stairs to the dungeons and then into Snape's office.

Harry had only been in here once before, and he had been in very serious trouble then, too. Snape had acquired a few more horrible slimy things in jars since last time, all standing on shelves behind his desk, glinting in the firelight and adding to the threatening atmosphere.

'Sit,' said Snape.

Harry sat. Snape, however, remained standing.

'Mr Malfoy has just been to see me with a strange story, Potter,' said Snape.

Harry didn't say anything.

'He tells me that he was up by the Shrieking Shack when he ran into Weasley – apparently alone.'

Still, Harry didn't speak.

'Mr Malfoy states that he was standing talking to Weasley, when a large amount of mud hit him on the back of the head. How do you think that could have happened?'

第14章 斯内普怀恨在心

回到蜂蜜公爵，下到地窖，走过石头地板，钻进活板门——哈利扯下隐形衣夹在胳肢窝里，沿着地道全速狂奔……马尔福会先到的……他找到老师要花多长时间？哈利气喘吁吁，肋下生疼，但不敢放慢脚步，一直跑到了石头滑道跟前。他必须把隐形衣丢在什么地方，如果马尔福告诉了老师，那可就怎么也藏不住了——他把隐形衣藏在一个黑暗的角落里，然后开始尽快往上爬，汗湿的双手在滑道边上直打滑。他到了女巫的驼背里，用魔杖敲了敲，把脑袋伸到外面，然后整个身体爬了出来。女巫的驼背关上了。哈利刚从雕像后面跳出来，就听到急促的脚步声正在临近。

是斯内普。他正快步朝哈利走来，黑袍子嗖嗖飘动，他停在了哈利面前。

"原来如此。"他说。

他带着一种压抑的得意神情。哈利努力装作无辜的样子，可是他很清楚自己脸上满是汗水，手上全是泥污，于是忙把双手插进了口袋里。

"跟我来，波特。"斯内普说。

哈利跟着斯内普下了楼，趁他不注意，偷偷在袍子里面把手擦干净。他们走下通往地下教室的台阶，然后进了斯内普的办公室。

哈利以前只来过这里一次，那次也是遇到了非常大的麻烦。斯内普在那以后又搞到了几样黏糊糊的可怕东西装在大口瓶子里，都搁在他办公桌后的架子上，在火光中冷冷地闪烁着，增添了恐怖的气氛。

"坐。"斯内普说。

哈利坐了下来，但斯内普仍然站着。

"马尔福同学刚才来找过我，讲了一个奇怪的故事，波特。"斯内普说。

哈利一言不发。

"他告诉我，他在尖叫棚屋碰到了韦斯莱——似乎是独自一人。"

哈利仍然一声不吭。

"马尔福同学说，他正在跟韦斯莱说话时，一大团烂泥砸到了他的后脑勺上。你认为那是怎么回事？"

CHAPTER FOURTEEN   Snape's Grudge

Harry tried to look mildly surprised.

'I don't know, Professor.'

Snape's eyes were boring into Harry's. It was exactly like trying to stare out a Hippogriff. Harry tried hard not to blink.

'Mr Malfoy then saw an extraordinary apparition. Can you imagine what it might have been, Potter?'

'No,' said Harry, now trying to sound innocently curious.

'It was your head, Potter. Floating in mid-air.'

There was a long silence.

'Maybe he'd better go to Madam Pomfrey,' said Harry. 'If he's seeing things like —'

'What would your head have been doing in Hogsmeade, Potter?' said Snape softly. 'Your head is not allowed in Hogsmeade. No part of your body has permission to be in Hogsmeade.'

'I know that,' said Harry, striving to keep his face free of guilt or fear. 'It sounds like Malfoy's having hallucin—'

'Malfoy is not having hallucinations,' snarled Snape, and he bent down, a hand on each arm of Harry's chair, so that their faces were a foot apart. 'If your head was in Hogsmeade, so was the rest of you.'

'I've been up in Gryffindor Tower,' said Harry. 'Like you told —'

'Can anyone confirm that?'

Harry didn't say anything. Snape's thin mouth curled into a horrible smile.

'So,' he said, straightening up again. 'Everyone from the Minister for Magic downwards has been trying to keep famous Harry Potter safe from Sirius Black. But famous Harry Potter is a law unto himself. Let the ordinary people worry about his safety! Famous Harry Potter goes where he wants to, with no thought for the consequences.'

Harry stayed silent. Snape was trying to provoke him into telling the truth. He wasn't going to do it. Snape had no proof – yet.

'How extraordinarily like your father you are, Potter,' Snape said suddenly, his eyes glinting. 'He, too, was exceedingly arrogant. A small amount of talent on the Quidditch pitch made him think he was a cut above the rest of us, too. Strutting around the place with his friends and admirers ... the resemblance between you is uncanny.'

第14章 斯内普怀恨在心

哈利努力做出略微有些惊奇的样子。

"我不知道，教授。"

斯内普的目光像锥子似的直盯着哈利的眼睛，就跟要用目光制伏鹰头马身有翼兽一样，哈利竭尽全力不眨眼睛。

"然后，马尔福同学看到一个奇异的景象。你能猜到是什么吗，波特？"

"猜不到。"哈利说，现在又使劲装出一副天真好奇的语气。

"是你的脑袋，波特，浮在半空中。"

一阵长长的沉默。

"也许他该去找庞弗雷女士，"哈利说，"如果他有那样的幻觉——"

"你的脑袋在霍格莫德做什么，波特？"斯内普轻声问，"你的脑袋不可以进入霍格莫德。你身体的任何部分都不可以进入霍格莫德。"

"我知道。"哈利说，努力让自己脸上不露出负疚或恐惧的表情，"听起来马尔福好像产生了幻——"

"马尔福没有产生幻觉，"斯内普吼道，他俯下身，双手按在哈利椅子两边的扶手上，两人的脸相距只有一英尺，"如果你的脑袋在霍格莫德，那你的身子也在那儿。"

"我一直待在格兰芬多塔楼里，"哈利说，"就像你吩咐的——"

"有人能证明吗？"

哈利没有说话。斯内普的薄嘴唇扭曲成一个可怕的微笑。

"好啊，"他直起身子说，"从魔法部部长开始，所有的人都在努力保护著名的哈利·波特不受小天狼星布莱克的威胁。可是著名的哈利·波特一意孤行，让普通人去为他的安全担心吧！著名的哈利·波特想去哪儿就去哪儿，丝毫不考虑后果。"

哈利保持沉默。斯内普想刺激他说出真相，他才不会上当的。斯内普没有证据——目前还没有。

"你跟你父亲真是像极了，波特，"斯内普突然说，眼睛里射出冷光，"他也是极其傲慢，魁地奇球场上一点雕虫小技就让他以为自己比我们大家都高出一等。带着一帮朋友和崇拜者趾高气扬地到处招摇……你们两个真是相像得不可思议。"

CHAPTER FOURTEEN Snape's Grudge

'My dad didn't *strut*,' said Harry, before he could stop himself. 'And nor do I.'

'Your father didn't set much store by rules, either,' Snape went on, pressing his advantage, his thin face full of malice. 'Rules were for lesser mortals, not Quidditch Cup-winners. His head was so swollen –'

'SHUT UP!'

Harry was suddenly on his feet. Rage such as he had not felt since his last night in Privet Drive was thundering through him. He didn't care that Snape's face had gone rigid, the black eyes flashing dangerously.

'*What did you say to me, Potter?*'

'I told you to shut up about my dad!' Harry yelled. 'I know the truth, all right? He saved your life! Dumbledore told me! You wouldn't even be here if it weren't for my dad!'

Snape's sallow skin had gone the colour of sour milk.

'And did the Headmaster tell you the circumstances in which your father saved my life?' he whispered. 'Or did he consider the details too unpleasant for precious Potter's delicate ears?'

Harry bit his lip. He didn't know what had happened and didn't want to admit it – but Snape seemed to have guessed the truth.

'I would hate you to run away with a false idea of your father, Potter,' he said, a terrible grin twisting his face. 'Have you been imagining some act of glorious heroism? Then let me correct you – your saintly father and his friends played a highly amusing joke on me that would have resulted in my death if your father hadn't got cold feet at the last moment. There was nothing brave about what he did. He was saving his own skin as much as mine. Had their joke succeeded, he would have been expelled from Hogwarts.'

Snape's uneven, yellowish teeth were bared.

'Turn out your pockets, Potter!' he spat suddenly.

Harry didn't move. There was a pounding in his ears.

'Turn out your pockets, or we go straight to the Headmaster! Pull them out, Potter!'

Cold with dread, Harry slowly pulled out the bag of Zonko's tricks and the Marauder's Map.

Snape picked up the Zonko's bag.

第14章 斯内普怀恨在心

"我爸爸没有趾高气扬,"哈利来不及控制自己,脱口说道,"我也没有。"

"你父亲也不大重视法规。"斯内普乘胜追击,瘦削的脸上充满恶意,"法规是给小人物遵守的,魁地奇冠军不用遵守。他脑袋膨胀得——"

"闭嘴!"

哈利一下子站了起来,一股怒火冲遍全身,自从女贞路最后一夜以来他从没有如此愤怒过。他已不在乎斯内普那变得僵硬的面孔,以及那双黑眼睛里闪出的危险的光芒。

"你刚才对我说什么,波特?"

"我叫你闭嘴,不许说我爸爸!"哈利喊道,"我知道真相,明白吗?他救过你的命!邓布利多告诉我的!要不是我爸爸,你现在根本不会站在这儿!"

斯内普的黄皮肤变成了变质牛奶的颜色。

"校长有没有告诉你,你父亲是在什么情况下救了我的命?"他低声问,"或者他认为那些细节对于宝贝波特那娇贵的耳朵来说太不中听?"

哈利咬住嘴唇。他不知道当时的情况,可又不想承认——但斯内普似乎猜到了。

"我可不愿意让你带着对你父亲的错误认识离开,波特。"他说,一个可怕的笑容扭曲了他的面孔,"你是不是想象出了某种英雄壮举?那么让我来纠正一下——你那神圣的父亲和他的朋友对我开了一个非常有趣的玩笑,要不是你父亲在最后一刻胆怯了一下,那会置我于死地。他保住我的性命也是为了保全他自己。他们的玩笑如果成功,他就会被霍格沃茨开除。"

斯内普那口参差不齐的黄牙暴露了出来。

"把口袋翻过来,波特!"他突然喝道。

哈利没有动,耳朵里嗡嗡作响。

"把你的口袋翻过来,不然我们直接去找校长!掏出来,波特!"

哈利吓得浑身冰凉,慢慢掏出了在佐科买的一袋魔术用品和那张活点地图。

斯内普捡起了佐科的袋子。

CHAPTER FOURTEEN   Snape's Grudge

'Ron gave them to me,' said Harry, praying he'd get a chance to tip Ron off before Snape saw him. 'He – brought them back from Hogsmeade last time –'

'Indeed? And you've been carrying them round ever since? How very touching ... and what is this?'

Snape had picked up the map. Harry tried with all his might to keep his face impassive.

'Spare bit of parchment,' he shrugged.

Snape turned it over, his eyes on Harry.

'Surely you don't need such a very *old* piece of parchment?' he said. 'Why don't I just – throw this away?'

His hand moved towards the fire.

'No!' Harry said quickly.

'So!' said Snape, his long nostrils quivering. 'Is this another treasured gift from Mr Weasley? Or is it – something else? A letter, perhaps, written in invisible ink? Or – instructions to get into Hogsmeade without passing the Dementors?'

Harry blinked. Snape's eyes gleamed.

'Let me see, let me see ...' he muttered, taking out his wand and smoothing the map out on his desk. 'Reveal your secret!' he said, touching the wand to the parchment.

Nothing happened. Harry clenched his hands to stop them shaking.

'Show yourself!' Snape said, tapping the map sharply.

It stayed blank. Harry was taking deep, calming breaths.

'Professor Severus Snape, master of this school, commands you to yield the information you conceal!' Snape said, hitting the map with his wand.

As though an invisible hand was writing upon it, words appeared on the smooth surface of the map.

'*Mr Moony presents his compliments to Professor Snape, and begs him to keep his abnormally large nose out of other people's business.*'

Snape froze. Harry stared, dumbstruck, at the message. But the map didn't stop there. More writing was appearing beneath the first.

'*Mr Prongs agrees with Mr Moony, and would like to add that Professor Snape is an ugly git.*'

It would have been very funny if the situation hadn't been so serious. And

"是罗恩给我的。"哈利一边说,一边祈祷能有机会在斯内普见到罗恩之前跟他通个气,"他——上次从霍格莫德带回来的——"

"是吗?然后你就一直随身带着?多么动人啊……这又是什么?"

斯内普捡起了地图,哈利努力让自己做到面无表情。

"空白羊皮纸。"他耸耸肩说。

斯内普把它翻过来,眼睛盯着哈利。

"你当然不需要这样一张破旧的羊皮纸吧?"他说,"我为什么不——把它扔掉呢?"

他的手朝火炉一扬。

"不要!"哈利马上叫道。

"哦!"斯内普的长鼻孔颤动着,"这又是韦斯莱同学送的一件珍贵礼物?或者是——别的什么?也许是一封信,用隐形墨水写的?或者是——写着如何能避开摄魂怪进入霍格莫德?"

哈利的目光躲闪了一下。斯内普的眼睛放出光来。

"我来看看,我来看看……"他嘀咕着,抽出魔杖,把地图平摊在桌上。"显示你的秘密!"他用魔杖点着羊皮纸说。

没有丝毫反应。哈利攥紧拳头让双手不要颤抖。

"现出原形!"斯内普用力敲了敲地图,叫道。

纸上还是一片空白。哈利做着深呼吸,让自己镇静。

"本院院长西弗勒斯·斯内普教授,命令你现出隐藏的信息!"斯内普用魔杖敲着地图说。

仿佛有一只无形的手在书写一般,地图光滑的表面显出了字迹。

月亮脸先生向斯内普教授致意,并恳请他不要把大得变态的鼻子伸到别人那里多管闲事。

斯内普僵住了。哈利目瞪口呆地看着那行字。但地图并没有到此为止。更多的字迹在下面显现出来。

尖头叉子先生同意月亮脸的观点,并要补充一句:斯内普教授是个饭桶、丑八怪。

如果眼下的局面不是这样严峻的话,这倒是蛮好玩的。后面

CHAPTER FOURTEEN   Snape's Grudge

there was more ...

'*Mr Padfoot would like to register his astonishment that an idiot like that ever became a Professor.*'

Harry closed his eyes in horror. When he'd opened them, the map had had its last word.

'*Mr Wormtail bids Professor Snape good day, and advises him to wash his hair, the slimeball.*'

Harry waited for the blow to fall.

'So ...' said Snape softly. 'We'll see about this ...'

He strode across to his fire, seized a fistful of glittering powder from a jar on the fireplace, and threw it into the flames.

'Lupin!' Snape called into the fire. 'I want a word!'

Utterly bewildered, Harry stared at the fire. A large shape had appeared in it, revolving very fast. Seconds later, Professor Lupin was clambering out of the fireplace, brushing ash off his shabby robes.

'You called, Severus?' said Lupin mildly.

'I certainly did,' said Snape, his face contorted with fury as he strode back to his desk. 'I have just asked Potter to empty his pockets. He was carrying this.'

Snape pointed at the parchment, on which the words of Messrs Moony, Wormtail, Padfoot and Prongs were still shining. An odd, closed expression appeared on Lupin's face.

'Well?' said Snape.

Lupin continued to stare at the map. Harry had the impression that Lupin was doing some very quick thinking.

'*Well?*' said Snape again. 'This parchment is plainly full of Dark Magic. This is supposed to be your area of expertise, Lupin. Where do you imagine Potter got such a thing?'

Lupin looked up and, by the merest half glance in Harry's direction, warned him not to interrupt.

'Full of Dark Magic?' he repeated mildly. 'Do you really think so, Severus? It looks to me as though it is merely a piece of parchment that insults anybody who tries to read it. Childish, but surely not dangerous? I imagine Harry got it from a joke-shop –'

'Indeed?' said Snape. His jaw had gone rigid with anger. 'You think a joke-shop could supply him with such a thing? You don't think it more likely that

第14章 斯内普怀恨在心

还有……

大脚板先生在此表示吃惊，那样一个白痴居然当上了教授。

哈利惊恐地闭上了眼睛。等他睁开眼时，地图上已经显出了最后一句话。

虫尾巴先生向斯内普教授问好，并建议他洗洗头发，大泥球。

哈利等着大难临头。

"好啊……"斯内普轻声说道，"我们来查一查……"

他大步走到壁炉边，从壁炉台上的瓶子里抓了一把闪闪发光的粉末，抛进火焰中。

"卢平！"斯内普向火中喊道，"我有话要说！"

哈利一头雾水，他盯着炉火，火中出现了一个大大的身形，在高速旋转。几秒钟后，卢平教授从壁炉里爬了出来，掸着那件旧袍子上的炉灰。

"你叫我，西弗勒斯？"卢平温和地问。

"当然。"斯内普的脸都气歪了，他大步走回桌边，"我刚才叫波特掏出口袋里的东西。他带着这个。"

斯内普指着羊皮纸，月亮脸、尖头叉子、大脚板和虫尾巴先生的话还在纸上闪闪发亮。卢平脸上现出了一丝古怪的、诡秘的表情。

"怎么说？"斯内普问。

卢平继续盯着地图。哈利觉得卢平在迅速地思考着什么。

"怎么说？"斯内普又说，"这张羊皮纸上显然充满了黑魔法。而这应该是你精通的领域啊，卢平。你估计波特是从哪儿搞到这东西的？"

卢平抬起头，目光十分微妙地朝哈利这边瞥了一下，警告他不要插嘴。

"充满了黑魔法？"他温和地重复道，"你真的这么想吗，西弗勒斯？在我看来这好像只是一张会侮辱任何读它的人的羊皮纸，幼稚无聊，但显然没有什么危险吧？我猜哈利是从一家玩笑商店里搞来的——"

"是吗？"斯内普气得脸都僵硬了，"你认为玩笑商店能给他提供这种东西？你难道不认为，他更有可能是直接从制造者那儿得到的？"

CHAPTER FOURTEEN   Snape's Grudge

he got it *directly from the manufacturers?*'

Harry didn't understand what Snape was talking about. Nor, apparently, did Lupin.

'You mean, from Mr Wormtail or one of these people?' he said. 'Harry, do you know any of these men?'

'No,' said Harry quickly.

'You see, Severus?' said Lupin, turning back to Snape. 'It looks like a Zonko product to me –'

Right on cue, Ron came bursting into the office. He was completely out of breath, and stopped just short of Snape's desk, clutching the stitch in his chest and trying to speak.

'I – gave – Harry – that – stuff,' he choked. 'Bought – it – in Zonko's – ages – ago ...'

'Well!' said Lupin, clapping his hands together and looking around cheerfully. 'That seems to clear that up! Severus, I'll take this back, shall I?' He folded the map and tucked it inside his robes. 'Harry, Ron, come with me, I need a word about my vampire essay. Excuse us, Severus.'

Harry didn't dare look at Snape as they left his office. He, Ron and Lupin walked all the way back into the Entrance Hall before speaking. Then Harry turned to Lupin.

'Professor, I –'

'I don't want to hear explanations,' said Lupin shortly. He glanced around the empty Entrance Hall and lowered his voice. 'I happen to know that this map was confiscated by Mr Filch many years ago. Yes, I know it's a map,' he said, as Harry and Ron looked amazed. 'I don't want to know how it fell into your possession. I am, however, *astounded* that you didn't hand it in. Particularly after what happened the last time a student left information about the castle lying around. And I can't let you have it back, Harry.'

Harry had expected that, and was too keen for explanations to protest.

'Why did Snape think I'd got it from the manufacturers?'

'Because ...' Lupin hesitated, 'because these mapmakers would have wanted to lure you out of school. They'd think it extremely entertaining.'

'Do you *know* them?' said Harry, impressed.

'We've met,' he said shortly. He was looking at Harry more seriously than ever before.

第14章 斯内普怀恨在心

哈利不明白斯内普在说什么。卢平似乎也不明白。

"你是说虫尾巴先生或这几个人当中的一个？"他问，"哈利，你认识这些人吗？"

"不认识。"哈利马上说。

"看到了吧，西弗勒斯？"卢平转身对斯内普说，"我看它像是佐科的产品——"

正在此时，罗恩冲进了办公室。他上气不接下气，直冲到斯内普的桌前，捂着生疼的胸口，努力想说话。

"我——给——哈利——的，"他呼吸艰难地说，"在佐科——买的……好久——以前……"

"好了！"卢平双手一拍，愉快地看看大家，"这似乎就清楚了！西弗勒斯，我把这个带回去，好吗？"他折起地图，塞进自己的袍子里，"哈利、罗恩，跟我来，我需要谈谈那篇吸血鬼论文。请原谅，西弗勒斯——"

离开办公室时，哈利不敢看斯内普。他和罗恩、卢平一直走到门厅才开口说话。哈利转向卢平。

"教授，我——"

"我不想听解释。"卢平简单地说。他扫视了一下空荡荡的门厅，又压低了声音说："不过我恰好知道这张地图是许多年前费尔奇先生没收的。是的，我知道它是地图。"看到哈利和罗恩惊奇的表情，他补充道："我不想弄清它怎么到了你们手里。但我非常震惊你竟然没有把它交出去，尤其是在上次有一名学生把城堡的信息随便乱扔之后。我不能把它还给你了，哈利。"

哈利已有心理准备，他顾不上提出抗议，一心只想问个明白。

"斯内普为什么认为我是从制造者那里得到的？"

"因为……"卢平犹豫着，"因为这些地图制造者可能想把你引出学校。他们会觉得这非常有趣。"

"你认识他们吗？"哈利问，一脸钦佩的神情。

"见过。"他简单地说，然后异常严肃地望着哈利。

CHAPTER FOURTEEN Snape's Grudge

'Don't expect me to cover up for you again, Harry. I cannot make you take Sirius Black seriously. But I would have thought that what you have heard when the Dementors draw near you would have had more of an effect on you. Your parents gave their lives to keep you alive, Harry. A poor way to repay them – gambling their sacrifice for a bag of magic tricks.'

He walked away, leaving Harry feeling worse by far than he had at any point in Snape's office. Slowly, he and Ron mounted the marble staircase. As Harry passed the one-eyed witch, he remembered the Invisibility Cloak – it was still down there, but he didn't dare go and get it.

'It's my fault,' said Ron abruptly. 'I persuaded you to go. Lupin's right, it was stupid, we shouldn't've done it –'

He broke off; they had reached the corridor where the security trolls were pacing, and Hermione was walking towards them. One look at her face convinced Harry that she had heard what had happened. His heart plummeted – had she told Professor McGonagall?

'Come to have a good gloat?' said Ron savagely, as she stopped in front of them. 'Or have you just been to tell on us?'

'No,' said Hermione. She was holding a letter in her hands and her lip was trembling. 'I just thought you ought to know ... Hagrid lost his case. Buckbeak is going to be executed.'

第14章 斯内普怀恨在心

"别指望我下次还会替你掩饰,哈利。我没法让你把小天狼星布莱克当回事。但我以为,你在摄魂怪靠近时听到的声音会对你有比较大的作用。你的父母牺牲了生命保护你,让你活下来,哈利。用这种方式报答他们真不应该——就为了一袋魔术把戏,拿他们的牺牲去冒险。"

卢平走了,哈利觉得比待在斯内普办公室里的时候还要难受。他和罗恩慢慢爬上大理石楼梯。走过独眼女巫雕像旁边时,哈利想起了隐形衣——它还在下面,但他不敢去拿。

"都怪我,"罗恩突然说,"是我劝你去的。卢平说得对,这很愚蠢,我们不该那么做——"

他打住话头,他们来到了有巨怪保安巡逻的走廊,赫敏迎面走来。一看她的脸色,哈利就相信她已经听说了发生的事。他的心猛地一沉——她告诉麦格教授了吗?

"是来幸灾乐祸的吧?"她停在他们面前时,罗恩恶狠狠地问,"或者你刚刚去打了小报告?"

"没有。"赫敏说,她手里拿着一封信,嘴唇颤抖着,"我只是觉得应该让你们知道……海格败诉了。巴克比克要被处死了。"

CHAPTER FIFTEEN

The Quidditch Final

'He – he sent me this,' Hermione said, holding out the letter. Harry took it. The parchment was damp, and enormous teardrops had smudged the ink so badly in places that it was very difficult to read.

> DEAR HERMIONE,
> WE LOST. I'M ALLOWED TO BRING HIM BACK TO HOGWARTS. EXECUTION DATE TO BE FIXED. BEAKY HAS ENJOYED LONDON.
> I WON'T FORGET ALL THE HELP YOU GAVE US.
> HAGRID

'They can't do this,' said Harry. 'They can't. Buckbeak isn't dangerous.'

'Malfoy's dad's frightened the Committee into it,' said Hermione, wiping her eyes. 'You know what he's like. They're a bunch of doddery old fools, and they were scared. There'll be an appeal, though, there always is. Only I can't see any hope ... nothing will have changed.'

'Yeah, it will,' said Ron fiercely. 'You won't have to do all the work alone this time, Hermione. I'll help.'

'Oh, Ron!'

Hermione flung her arms around Ron's neck and broke down completely. Ron, looking quite terrified, patted her very awkwardly on the top of the head. Finally, Hermione drew away.

'Ron, I'm really, really sorry about Scabbers ...' she sobbed.

'Oh – well – he was old,' said Ron, looking thoroughly relieved that she

第 15 章

魁地奇决赛

"**他**——他送来的。"赫敏举着信说。

哈利接过信,羊皮纸是潮的,有几处墨迹被大颗的泪水弄得模糊,很难辨读。

亲爱的赫敏:

  我们败诉了。我获准把它带回霍格沃茨。处决日期待定。
  比克很喜欢伦敦。
  我不会忘记你们给我们的所有帮助。

海 格

"他们不能那么干,"哈利说,"不能!巴克比克没有危险。"

"马尔福的爸爸胁迫委员会这么干的。"赫敏擦着眼睛说,"你们知道他的为人。委员会里都是一帮昏聩的老朽,心里害怕。不过还可以上诉,总是可以的。只是我看不到任何希望……什么也改变不了。"

"会改变的,"罗恩狂怒地说,"这次不再全由你一个人来做了,赫敏,我也要帮忙。"

"哦,罗恩!"

赫敏双臂搂住罗恩的脖子,失声痛哭。罗恩似乎被吓着了,笨手笨脚地轻轻拍拍她的头顶。最后,赫敏抽身离开了。

"罗恩,斑斑的事我真的、真的很抱歉……"她抽泣道。

"哦——没事——它老了,"见她终于放开了自己,罗恩如释重负,

CHAPTER FIFTEEN   The Quidditch Final

had let go of him. 'And he was a bit useless. You never know, Mum and Dad might get me an owl now.'

The safety measures imposed on the students since Black's second break-in made it impossible for Harry, Ron and Hermione to go and visit Hagrid in the evenings. Their only chance of talking to him was during Care of Magical Creatures lessons.

He seemed numb with shock at the verdict.

"S all my fault. Got all tongue-tied. They was all sittin' there in black robes an' I kep' droppin' me notes and forgettin' all them dates yeh looked up fer me, Hermione. An' then Lucius Malfoy stood up an' said his bit, and the Committee jus' did exac'ly what he told 'em ...'

'There's still the appeal!' said Ron fiercely. 'Don't give up yet, we're working on it!'

They were walking back up to the castle with the rest of the class. Ahead they could see Malfoy, who was walking with Crabbe and Goyle, and kept looking back, laughing derisively.

"S no good, Ron,' said Hagrid sadly as they reached the castle steps. 'That Committee's in Lucius Malfoy's pocket. I'm jus' gonna make sure the rest o' Beaky's time is the happiest he's ever had. I owe him that ...'

Hagrid turned round and hurried back towards his cabin, his face buried in his handkerchief.

'Look at him blubber!'

Malfoy, Crabbe and Goyle had been standing just inside the castle doors, listening.

'Have you ever seen anything quite as pathetic?' said Malfoy. 'And he's supposed to be our teacher!'

Harry and Ron both made furious moves towards Malfoy, but Hermione got there first – SMACK!

She had slapped Malfoy around the face with all the strength she could muster. Malfoy staggered. Harry, Ron, Crabbe and Goyle stood flabbergasted as Hermione raised her hand again.

'Don't you *dare* call Hagrid pathetic, you foul – you evil –'

'Hermione!' said Ron weakly, and he tried to grab her hand as she swung it back.

'Get *off*, Ron!'

"而且它本来就不大中用。谁知道呢,爸爸妈妈现在说不定会给我一只猫头鹰呢。"

布莱克第二次闯入城堡之后,学校加强了针对学生们的安全措施,哈利、罗恩和赫敏晚上无法去看望海格了。他们只有在上保护神奇动物课的时候才能跟他说上话。

海格似乎被判决吓蒙了。

"都怪我,笨嘴笨舌的。他们都穿着黑袍子坐在那儿,我手里的笔记老往下掉,还把你帮我查的日期全忘了,赫敏。后来卢修斯·马尔福站起来说了一些话,委员会就照他说的办了……"

"还可以上诉呢!"罗恩情绪激烈地说,"别放弃,我们会想办法的!"

他们跟全班同学一起走回城堡时,看见马尔福在前面跟克拉布和高尔走在一起,不时回头张望,嘲弄地大笑。

"没有用的,罗恩。"海格悲哀地说,他们走到了城堡外的台阶前,"委员会是受卢修斯·马尔福摆布的。我只是想保证比克在余下的时间里能过得非常快乐。这是我欠它的……"

海格转过身,快步朝他的小屋走去,脸捂在手帕里。

"看他那哭哭啼啼的样子!"

马尔福、克拉布和高尔刚才就站在城堡大门里听着。

"你们见过那样的可怜虫吗?"马尔福说,"他居然还算我们的老师呢!"

哈利和罗恩都愤怒地冲向了马尔福,但赫敏比他们两个都快——啪!

她使出浑身力气抽了马尔福一记耳光。马尔福被打了个趔趄。哈利、罗恩、克拉布和高尔都惊呆了。赫敏又扬起手。

"你敢说海格是可怜虫,你这龌龊的——邪恶的——"

"赫敏!"罗恩无力地说,试图抓住她的手,但她把手一甩。

"放开,罗恩!"

CHAPTER FIFTEEN   The Quidditch Final

Hermione pulled out her wand. Malfoy stepped backwards. Crabbe and Goyle looked at him for instructions, thoroughly bewildered.

'C'mon,' Malfoy muttered, and next moment, all three of them had disappeared into the passageway to the dungeons.

'*Hermione!*' Ron said again, sounding both stunned and impressed.

'Harry, you'd better beat him in the Quidditch final!' Hermione said shrilly. 'You just better had, because I can't stand it if Slytherin win!'

'We're due in Charms,' said Ron, still goggling at Hermione. 'We'd better go.'

They hurried up the marble staircase towards Professor Flitwick's classroom.

'You're late, boys!' said Professor Flitwick reprovingly, as Harry opened the classroom door. 'Come along, quickly, wands out, we're experimenting with Cheering Charms today. We've already divided into pairs –'

Harry and Ron hurried to a desk at the back and opened their bags. Ron looked behind him.

'Where's Hermione gone?'

Harry looked around, too. Hermione hadn't entered the classroom, yet Harry knew she had been right next to him when he had opened the door.

'That's weird,' said Harry, staring at Ron. 'Maybe – maybe she went to the bathroom or something?'

But Hermione didn't turn up all lesson.

'She could've done with a Cheering Charm on her, too,' said Ron, as the class left for lunch, all grinning broadly – the Cheering Charms had left them with a feeling of great contentment.

Hermione wasn't at lunch either. By the time they had finished their apple pie, the after-effects of the Cheering Charms were wearing off, and Harry and Ron had started to get slightly worried.

'You don't think Malfoy did something to her?' Ron said anxiously, as they hurried upstairs towards Gryffindor Tower.

They passed the security trolls, gave the Fat Lady the password ('Flibbertigibbet') and scrambled through the portrait hole into the common room.

Hermione was sitting at a table, fast asleep, her head resting on an open Arithmancy book. They went to sit down either side of her. Harry prodded her awake.

'Wh-what?' said Hermione, waking with a start, and staring wildly

第15章 魁地奇决赛

赫敏拔出了魔杖，马尔福向后倒退了一步，克拉布和高尔呆呆望着他等待指示，全然不知所措。

"走。"马尔福咕哝道，一眨眼，他们三个消失在了通往地下教室的通道里。

"赫敏！"罗恩又叫了一声，又是吃惊又是敬佩。

"哈利，你最好在魁地奇决赛中把他打得一败涂地！"赫敏厉声说，"你必须，如果斯莱特林赢了，我会受不了的！"

"魔咒课时间到了，"罗恩说，仍然呆呆地瞪着赫敏，"我们走吧。"

三人匆匆跑上大理石楼梯，向弗立维教授的教室奔去。

"你们迟到了，孩子们！"哈利推开教室的门时，弗立维教授责备地说，"快来吧，举起魔杖，我们今天要试验快乐咒，全班已经分成两人一组——"

哈利和罗恩快步走到后排一张课桌前，打开书包。罗恩回头看了看。

"赫敏呢？"

哈利也四下张望，赫敏没有进教室。可是哈利记得他推门时赫敏就在身后啊。

"怪了。"哈利茫然地望着罗恩说，"也许……也许她去盥洗室了？"

可是赫敏直到下课都没有出现。

"她倒是挺需要一个快乐咒的。"罗恩说道。全班同学都咧着大嘴笑嘻嘻去吃午饭——快乐咒让他们感到心满意足。

赫敏也没来吃午饭。等到吃完苹果馅饼时，快乐咒的影响逐渐减退，哈利和罗恩开始有些担心了。

"马尔福不会对她做什么吧？"两人匆匆爬上楼梯朝格兰芬多塔楼走去时，罗恩焦急地说。

他们经过巨怪保安旁边，对胖夫人说了口令（"花花公子哥儿"），从肖像洞口钻进了公共休息室。

赫敏坐在桌前睡得正香，脑袋搁在一本打开的算术占卜课本上。他们俩一边一个坐到她旁边。哈利把她捅醒了。

"怎——怎么？"赫敏吃了一惊，茫然四顾，"是不是该走了？现在

CHAPTER FIFTEEN   The Quidditch Final

around. 'Is it time to go? W-which lesson have we got now?'

'Divination, but it's not for another twenty minutes,' said Harry. 'Hermione, why didn't you come to Charms?'

'What? Oh no!' Hermione squeaked. 'I forgot to go to Charms!'

'But how could you forget?' said Harry. 'You were with us till we were right outside the classroom!'

'I don't believe it!' Hermione wailed. 'Was Professor Flitwick angry? Oh, it was Malfoy, I was thinking about him and I lost track of things!'

'You know what, Hermione?' said Ron, looking down at the enormous Arithmancy book Hermione had been using as a pillow. 'I reckon you're cracking up. You're trying to do too much.'

'No, I'm not!' said Hermione, brushing her hair out of her eyes and staring hopelessly around for her bag. 'I just made a mistake, that's all! I'd better go and see Professor Flitwick and say sorry ... I'll see you in Divination!'

Hermione joined them at the foot of the ladder to Professor Trelawney's classroom twenty minutes later, looking extremely harassed.

'I can't believe I missed Cheering Charms! And I bet they come up in our exams. Professor Flitwick hinted they might!'

Together they climbed the ladder into the dim, stifling tower room. Glowing on every little table was a crystal ball full of pearly white mist. Harry, Ron and Hermione sat down together at the same rickety table.

'I thought we weren't starting crystal balls until next term,' Ron muttered, casting a wary eye around for Professor Trelawney, in case she was lurking nearby.

'Don't complain, this means we've finished palmistry,' Harry muttered back. 'I was getting sick of her flinching every time she looked at my hands.'

'Good day to you!' said the familiar, misty voice, and Professor Trelawney made her usual dramatic entrance out of the shadows. Parvati and Lavender quivered with excitement, their faces lit by the milky glow of their crystal ball.

'I have decided to introduce the crystal ball a little earlier than I had planned,' said Professor Trelawney, seating herself with her back to the fire and gazing around. 'The fates have informed me that your examination in June will concern the Orb, and I am anxious to give you sufficient

第15章 魁地奇决赛

是什——什么课啦？"

"占卜。不过还有二十分钟呢。"哈利说，"赫敏，你怎么没去上魔咒课呢？"

"什么？哦，糟了！"赫敏尖叫起来，"我忘了上魔咒课！"

"可你怎么会忘记呢？"哈利问，"走到教室门口的时候，你还跟我们在一起啊！"

"我简直不能相信！"赫敏哀叫道，"弗立维教授生气了吗？哦，都怪马尔福，我一直想着他的事，后来就什么都忘了！"

"你知道吗，赫敏？"罗恩低头望着赫敏当枕头用的那本大部头算术占术书，"我觉得你快要崩溃了，你想做的事太多了。"

"不，我不会的！"赫敏拂开挡住眼睛的头发，焦急地四下寻找她的书包，"我只是犯了个错误而已！我最好去找弗立维教授道歉……占卜课上见！"

二十分钟后，赫敏在通向特里劳尼教授课堂的梯子脚下与他们会合了，看上去万分沮丧。

"我真不能相信我竟然错过了快乐咒！我打赌考试会考到的。弗立维教授暗示说会有！"

他们一起登着梯子进了那间昏暗闷热的顶楼房间。每张小桌上都有一个发着幽光的水晶球，里面满是珍珠白的雾。哈利、罗恩和赫敏一起坐在一张摇摇晃晃的桌子旁。

"我以为要下学期才学水晶球呢。"罗恩嘀咕着，警惕地瞄了一眼四周，生怕特里劳尼教授就藏在附近。

"不要抱怨，这意味着手相终于学完了，"哈利悄声回答，"她每次看到我的手掌都要哆嗦一下，我烦透了。"

"大家好！"那熟悉的、恍惚的声音说道，特里劳尼教授照例戏剧性地从黑暗处走了出来。帕瓦蒂和拉文德激动得浑身发抖，脸上映着水晶球乳白色的幽光。

"我决定比原计划稍稍提前一点介绍水晶球，"特里劳尼教授背对着壁炉坐下，环视全班同学，"命运女神告诉我，你们六月的考试将涉

CHAPTER FIFTEEN — The Quidditch Final

practice.'

Hermione snorted.

'Well, honestly ... "the fates have informed her" ... who sets the exam? She does! What an amazing prediction!' she said, not troubling to keep her voice low.

It was hard to tell whether Professor Trelawney had heard them, as her face was hidden in shadow. She continued, however, as though she had not.

'Crystal-gazing is a particularly refined art,' she said dreamily. 'I do not expect any of you to See when first you peer into the Orb's infinite depths. We shall start by practising relaxing the conscious mind and external eyes' – Ron began to snigger uncontrollably, and had to stuff his fist in his mouth to stifle the noise – 'so as to clear the Inner Eye and the superconscious. Perhaps, if we are lucky, some of you will See before the end of the class.'

And so they began. Harry, at least, felt extremely foolish, staring blankly at the crystal ball, trying to keep his mind empty when thoughts such as 'this is stupid' kept drifting across it. It didn't help that Ron kept breaking into silent giggles and Hermione kept tutting.

'Seen anything yet?' Harry asked them, after a quarter of an hour's quiet crystal-gazing.

'Yeah, there's a burn on this table,' said Ron, pointing. 'Someone's spilled their candle.'

'This is such a waste of time,' Hermione hissed. 'I could be practising something useful. I could be catching up on Cheering Charms –'

Professor Trelawney rustled past.

'Would anyone like me to help them interpret the shadowy portents within their Orb?' she murmured over the clinking of her bangles.

'I don't need help,' Ron whispered. 'It's obvious what this means. There's going to be loads of fog tonight.'

Both Harry and Hermione burst out laughing.

'Now, really!' said Professor Trelawney, as everyone's heads turned in their direction. Parvati and Lavender were looking scandalised. 'You are disturbing the clairvoyant vibrations!' She approached their table and peered into their crystal ball. Harry felt his heart sinking. He was sure he knew what was coming ...

'There is something here!' Professor Trelawney whispered, lowering her

及这只灵球,我希望给你们足够的机会练习。"

赫敏嗤之以鼻。

"哼,得了吧……'命运女神告诉她',考题由谁出?她出!多么神奇的预言!"赫敏说,连声音都没有压低。

特里劳尼教授的面孔隐在阴影中,很难看出她有没有听到这些话。但她仿佛没听见似的继续说了下去。

"水晶球占卜是一门极其高深的学问,"她梦呓般地说道,"我并不指望各位第一次凝视那无限深邃的灵球时就能看到什么。我们将首先练习放松意识和外眼,"——罗恩开始控制不住地咻咻窃笑,不得不把拳头塞进嘴里堵住笑声——"好让天目和超意识清晰起来。也许,幸运的话,有些同学能在下课之前看到什么。"

于是他们就开始看了。至少哈利感觉这么做很傻。他茫然地盯着水晶球,努力让自己的脑子一片空白,可是"这样真傻"的想法不停地冒出来。罗恩在一旁不时地悄声偷笑,赫敏不时地咂嘴,这更给哈利帮了倒忙。

"看到什么了吗?"对着水晶球默默凝视了一刻钟之后,哈利问。

"嗯,桌上有块焦斑,"罗恩指着说,"有人把蜡烛打翻了。"

"真是浪费时间,"赫敏从牙缝里挤出声音说,"我本来可以练习点有用的东西,可以补习快乐咒——"

特里劳尼教授衣裙沙沙作响地走了过来。

"有谁愿意让我帮他解释一下灵球里模糊的征兆吗?"她在手镯脚镯的叮当声中喃喃低语。

"我不需要帮助,"罗恩小声说,"这征兆很明显,今夜会有大雾。"

哈利和赫敏都笑出了声。

"注意!"特里劳尼教授说道,所有的人都扭头朝他们这边看了过来。帕瓦蒂和拉文德露出嫌恶的表情。"你们在扰乱超视感应!"特里劳尼走到他们桌前,查看每人的水晶球。哈利的心一沉,他已料到下面会发生什么——

"这儿有点东西!"特里劳尼教授轻声说,把脸凑到水晶球跟前,

CHAPTER FIFTEEN — The Quidditch Final

face to the ball, so that it was reflected twice in her huge glasses. 'Something moving ... but what is it?'

Harry was prepared to bet everything he owned, including his Firebolt, that it wasn't good news, whatever it was. And sure enough ...

'My dear ...' Professor Trelawney breathed, gazing up at Harry. 'It is here, plainer than ever before ... my dear, stalking towards you, growing ever closer ... the Gr—'

'Oh, for *goodness*' sake!' said Hermione, loudly. 'Not that ridiculous Grim *again*!'

Professor Trelawney raised her enormous eyes to Hermione's face. Parvati whispered something to Lavender, and they both glared at Hermione, too. Professor Trelawney stood up, surveying Hermione with unmistakeable anger.

'I am sorry to say that from the moment you have arrived in this class, my *dear*, it has been apparent that you do not have what the noble art of Divination requires. Indeed, I don't remember ever meeting a student whose mind was so hopelessly Mundane.'

There was a moment's silence. Then —

'Fine!' said Hermione suddenly, getting up and cramming *Unfogging the Future* back into her bag. 'Fine!' she repeated, swinging the bag over her shoulder and almost knocking Ron off his chair. 'I give up! I'm leaving!'

And to the whole class's amazement, Hermione strode over to the trapdoor, kicked it open, and climbed down the ladder out of sight.

It took a few minutes for the class to settle down again. Professor Trelawney seemed to have forgotten all about the Grim. She turned abruptly from Harry and Ron's table, breathing rather heavily as she tugged her gauzy shawl more closely to her.

'Ooooo!' said Lavender suddenly, making everyone start. 'Oooooo, Professor Trelawney, I've just remembered! You saw her leaving, didn't you? Didn't you, Professor? *"Around Easter, one of our number will leave us for ever!"* You said it *ages* ago, Professor!'

Professor Trelawney gave her a dewy smile.

'Yes, my dear, I did indeed know that Miss Granger would be leaving us. One hopes, however, that one might have mistaken the Signs ... the Inner Eye can be a burden, you know ...'

Lavender and Parvati looked deeply impressed, and moved over so that

球在她那巨大的眼镜里映成了两个,"有东西在动……但那是什么呢?"

哈利愿意用他的全部财产——包括火弩箭来打赌,不管那是什么,肯定不是什么好消息。果然——

"亲爱的,"特里劳尼教授轻呼道,抬头望着哈利,"它就在这里,比以前更加清晰……正在朝你走来,亲爱的,越来越近……不祥——"

"哦,看在上帝的分儿上!"赫敏大声说,"别再提起那个荒谬的不祥了!"

特里劳尼教授抬起大眼睛望着赫敏的脸,帕瓦蒂和拉文德窃窃私语,两人都对赫敏怒目而视。特里劳尼教授站起来,带着明显的怒气打量赫敏。

"我很遗憾地说,亲爱的,从你第一次踏进这个课堂,就显然不具备高贵的占卜学所需要的天赋。实际上,我不记得我见过哪个学生的脑子如此平庸、无可救药。"

全班鸦雀无声,然后——

"好!"赫敏突然说道,起身把《拨开迷雾看未来》塞进书包。"好!"她又说了一遍,把书包甩到肩上,差点把罗恩从椅子上撞倒,"我放弃!我走!"

全班同学目瞪口呆,赫敏大步走到活板门旁,一脚把它踢开,噔噔噔爬下梯子不见了。

过了几分钟教室里才安静下来。特里劳尼教授好像把不祥忘到了脑后。她猛一转身离开了哈利和罗恩的课桌,喘着粗气,拉紧了纱巾。

"哦——!"拉文德突然叫了起来,把大家吓了一跳。"哦——!特里劳尼教授,我想起来了!您预见到她要走的,是不是,教授?'复活节前后,我们中间的一位将会永远离开我们!'您早就说过的,教授!"

特里劳尼教授给了她一个泪光莹莹的微笑。

"对,亲爱的,我确实早就知道格兰杰小姐要离开我们。但人总希望是自己看错了征兆……天目有时是一种负担,你知道……"

拉文德和帕瓦蒂看上去佩服得五体投地,她们挪了挪位子,好让

CHAPTER FIFTEEN The Quidditch Final

Professor Trelawney could join their table instead.

'Some day Hermione's having, eh?' Ron muttered to Harry, looking awed.

'Yeah ...'

Harry glanced into the crystal ball, but saw nothing but swirling white mist. Had Professor Trelawney really seen the Grim again? Would he? The last thing he needed was another near-fatal accident, with the Quidditch final drawing ever nearer.

The Easter holidays were not exactly relaxing. The third-years had never had so much homework. Neville Longbottom seemed close to a nervous collapse, and he wasn't the only one.

'Call this a holiday!' Seamus Finnigan roared at the common room one afternoon. 'The exams are ages away, what're they playing at?'

But nobody had as much to do as Hermione. Even without Divination, she was taking more subjects than anybody else. She was usually last to leave the common room at night, first to arrive at the library next morning; she had shadows like Lupin's under her eyes, and seemed constantly close to tears.

Ron had taken over responsibility for Buckbeak's appeal. When he wasn't doing his own work, he was poring over enormously thick volumes with names like *The Handbook of Hippogriff Psychology* and *Fowl or Foul? A Study of Hippogriff Brutality*. He was so absorbed, he even forgot to be horrible to Crookshanks.

Harry, meanwhile, had to fit in his homework around Quidditch practice every day, not to mention endless discussions of tactics with Wood. The Gryffindor–Slytherin match would take place on the first Saturday after the Easter holidays. Slytherin were leading the tournament by exactly two hundred points. This meant (as Wood constantly reminded his team) that they needed to win the match by more than that amount to win the Cup. It also meant that the burden of winning fell largely on Harry, because capturing the Snitch was worth one hundred and fifty points.

'So you must *only* catch it if we're *more* than fifty points up,' Wood told Harry constantly. 'Only if we're more than fifty points up, Harry, or we win the match but lose the Cup. You've got that, haven't you? You must only catch the Snitch if we're –'

'I KNOW, OLIVER!' Harry yelled.

第 15 章　魁地奇决赛

特里劳尼教授坐到她们的桌子旁边。

"赫敏有一天会离开,呃?"罗恩低声对哈利说,面露畏惧之色。

"是啊……"

哈利注视着水晶球,但只看到旋转的白雾,特里劳尼教授真的又看到不祥了吗?他会看见吗?魁地奇决赛日益临近了,他可不想再来一场险些送命的事故。

复活节假期并不轻松。三年级学生从没做过这么多作业。纳威·隆巴顿似乎要神经崩溃了,而且不止他一个人这样。

"这也叫过节!"一天下午,西莫·斐尼甘在公共休息室里嚷嚷道,"离考试还远着呢,他们这是干吗呀?"

但是谁都没有赫敏那么忙。即使没有了占卜课,她上的课还是比别人多。她通常是夜里最晚离开公共休息室,第二天早上又第一个到图书馆。她像卢平那样眼睛下面有了黑圈,而且总是一副快要哭出来的样子。

罗恩把巴克比克上诉的事接了过去。不做作业时,他便埋头翻阅厚厚的书籍,诸如《鹰头马身有翼兽心理手册》《珍禽还是恶兽:鹰头马身有翼兽之残暴性研究》等。他太投入了,以至于忘记了要对克鲁克山凶狠一点。

哈利则不得不在每天的魁地奇训练之余见缝插针地做作业,更不用说还要跟伍德没完没了地讨论战术。格兰芬多对斯莱特林的比赛将于复活节后的第一个星期六举行。斯莱特林队在联赛中整整领先两百分,也就是说哈利他们需要赢两百分以上才能夺杯(伍德经常对队员们提起这一点)。这还意味着获胜的压力大部分都落在哈利的头上,因为抓住金色飞贼就能得到一百五十分。

"所以,你只能在我们领先五十分以上时抓住它,"伍德不断地对哈利说,"只能在领先五十分以上的时候,哈利,不然我们就会赢了比赛而输掉奖杯。你明白吗?你必须抓住飞贼,但只能在我们——"

"**我知道了,奥利弗!**"哈利喊道。

CHAPTER FIFTEEN — The Quidditch Final

The whole of Gryffindor house was obsessed with the coming match. Gryffindor hadn't won the Quidditch Cup since the legendary Charlie Weasley (Ron's second-oldest brother) had been Seeker. But Harry doubted whether any of them, even Wood, wanted to win as much as he did. The enmity between Harry and Malfoy was at its highest point ever. Malfoy was still smarting about the mud-throwing incident in Hogsmeade, and even more furious that Harry had somehow wormed his way out of punishment. Harry hadn't forgotten Malfoy's attempt to sabotage him in the match against Ravenclaw, but it was the matter of Buckbeak that made him most determined to beat Malfoy in front of the entire school.

Never, in anyone's memory, had a match approached in such a highly charged atmosphere. By the time the holidays were over, tension between the two teams and their houses was at breaking-point. A number of small scuffles broke out in the corridors, culminating in a nasty incident in which a Gryffindor fourth-year and a Slytherin sixth-year ended up in the hospital wing with leeks sprouting out of their ears.

Harry was having a particularly bad time of it. He couldn't walk to class without Slytherins sticking out their legs and trying to trip him up; Crabbe and Goyle kept popping up wherever he went, and slouching away looking disappointed when they saw him surrounded by people. Wood had given instructions that Harry should be accompanied everywhere, in case the Slytherins tried to put him out of action. The whole of Gryffindor house took up the challenge enthusiastically, so that it was impossible for Harry to get to classes on time because he was surrounded by a vast, chattering crowd. Harry was more concerned for his Firebolt's safety than his own. When he wasn't flying it, he locked it securely in his trunk, and frequently dashed back up to Gryffindor Tower at break-times to check that it was still there.

All usual pursuits were abandoned in the Gryffindor common room the night before the match. Even Hermione had put down her books.

'I can't work, I can't concentrate,' she said nervously.

There was a great deal of noise. Fred and George Weasley were dealing with the pressure by being louder and more exuberant than ever. Oliver Wood was crouched over a model of a Quidditch pitch in the corner, prodding little figures across it with his wand and muttering to himself. Angelina, Alicia and

第15章 魁地奇决赛

整个格兰芬多学院都心系这场即将来临的比赛。继传奇人物查理·韦斯莱（罗恩的二哥）担任找球手的时代之后，格兰芬多还一直没有夺得过魁地奇杯。不过，哈利怀疑没有任何一个人（包括伍德）像他这么想赢。他和马尔福之间的敌意达到了顶峰。马尔福还在为霍格莫德村被扔了泥巴的事耿耿于怀，而哈利居然逃脱了惩罚，更令他气破了肚皮。哈利没有忘记马尔福在格兰芬多对拉文克劳那场比赛中对他使的坏，而巴克比克的事更让他下定决心要在全校师生面前打败马尔福。

在所有人的记忆中，没有一场比赛是在这样充满火药味的气氛中来临的。复活节后，两支球队以及两个学院之间的紧张关系达到了一触即发的程度。走廊里发生了一些小混战，在最恶劣的一起中，一名格兰芬多四年级学生和一名斯莱特林六年级学生进了校医院，他们的耳朵里都冒出了韭菜。

哈利的日子特别难过。他去上课时，总有斯莱特林的学生伸出腿来绊他；无论他走到哪儿，克拉布和高尔总会冒出来，看见他被人围着，便失望地挪到一边。伍德吩咐哈利到哪里都必须有人陪伴，防止斯莱特林的人害得他不能上场。格兰芬多全院学生都踊跃承担这一任务，弄得哈利都无法按时走进课堂，因为身边总是围着一大群叽叽喳喳的人。哈利对火弩箭的安全比对他自己更关心。不飞的时候，他把火弩箭小心地锁在箱子里，课间经常冲回格兰芬多塔楼去看看它还在不在。

比赛的前一天晚上，格兰芬多学院公共休息室里的一切日常活动都停止了，连赫敏都放下了书本。

"我没法学习，精神集中不起来。"她紧张地说。

公共休息室里很吵。弗雷德和乔治·韦斯莱对付压力的办法是比往常更加闹腾。奥利弗·伍德蹲在角落里的一个魁地奇赛场模型前，一边用魔杖指挥小人移来移去，一边自言自语。安吉利娜、艾丽娅和凯蒂听了弗雷德和乔治的笑话哈哈大笑。哈利跟罗恩和赫敏坐在一起，

CHAPTER FIFTEEN   The Quidditch Final

Katie were laughing at Fred and George's jokes. Harry was sitting with Ron and Hermione, removed from the centre of things, trying not to think about the next day, because every time he did, he had the horrible sensation that something very large was fighting to get out of his stomach.

'You're going to be fine,' Hermione told him, though she looked positively terrified.

'You've got a *Firebolt*!' said Ron.

'Yeah ...' said Harry, his stomach writhing.

It came as a relief when Wood suddenly stood up and yelled, 'Team! Bed!'

Harry slept badly. First he dreamed that he had overslept, and that Wood was yelling, 'Where were you? We had to use Neville instead!' Then he dreamed that Malfoy and the rest of the Slytherin team arrived for the match riding dragons. He was flying at breakneck speed, trying to avoid a spurt of flames from Malfoy's steed's mouth, when he realised he had forgotten his Firebolt. He fell through the air and woke with a start.

It was a few seconds before Harry remembered that the match hadn't taken place yet, that he was safe in bed and that the Slytherin team definitely wouldn't be allowed to play on dragons. He was feeling very thirsty. As quietly as he could, he got out of his four-poster and went to pour himself some water from the silver jug beneath the window.

The grounds were still and quiet. No breath of wind disturbed the treetops in the Forbidden Forest; the Whomping Willow was motionless and innocent-looking. It looked as though conditions for the match would be perfect.

Harry set down his goblet and was about to turn back to his bed when something caught his eye. An animal of some kind was prowling across the silvery lawn.

Harry dashed to his bedside table, snatched up his glasses and put them on, then hurried back to the window. It couldn't be the Grim – not now – not right before the match –

He peered out at the grounds again and, after a minute's frantic searching, spotted it. It was skirting the edge of the Forest now ... it wasn't the Grim at all ... it was a cat ... Harry clutched the window-ledge in relief as he recognised the bottle-brush tail. It was only Crookshanks ...

Or *was* it only Crookshanks? Harry squinted, pressing his nose flat against the glass. Crookshanks seemed to have come to a halt. Harry was sure he could see something else moving in the shadow of the trees, too.

第15章 魁地奇决赛

远离热闹的中心，努力不去想明天，因为每次一想，就会有一种可怕的感觉，好像胃里有一个很大的东西要挣脱出来。

"你肯定没问题的。"赫敏宽慰哈利说，尽管她看上去也是提心吊胆的。

"你有火弩箭呢！"罗恩说。

"是啊……"哈利说，胃里在翻腾。

谢天谢地，伍德突然站起来喊道："全体队员，睡觉！"

哈利睡得不好，先是梦见自己睡过头了，伍德吼道："你上哪儿去了？我们只好让纳威替补！"然后又梦见马尔福和斯莱特林的其他队员骑着火龙来比赛。哈利以惊险的速度飞行，努力躲开马尔福的坐骑喷出的火焰，忽然想起他没带火弩箭，一下子从空中摔下去，猛地惊醒了。

过了几秒钟，哈利才想起比赛还没有开始，他还安安稳稳地躺在床上，而且斯莱特林队决不会获准骑着火龙来参赛。他感到口干舌燥，轻手轻脚地从他的四柱床上爬起来，端起窗下的银罐子给自己倒了点水喝。

外面静悄悄的，没有一丝微风拂过禁林的树梢，打人柳一动不动，一副很无辜的样子。看来比赛的天气会很理想。

哈利放下杯子，正要转身上床，忽然有个东西吸引了他的目光，像是什么动物在银色的草坪上徘徊。

哈利冲到床头柜旁，抓起眼镜戴上，又奔回窗前。不会是不祥吧——偏偏在这个时候——在比赛之前——

他再次朝操场上望去，急切地搜寻了一分钟后，终于找到了那只动物，此刻是在禁林的边缘……那不是什么不祥……那是一只猫……哈利认出了那毛茸茸的尾巴，他如释重负地抓住窗台，原来是克鲁克山……

只是克鲁克山吗？哈利眯起眼睛，鼻子紧贴在玻璃上。克鲁克山似乎停下来了。哈利确信他看到树影中还有一个东西在动。

CHAPTER FIFTEEN The Quidditch Final

And next moment, it had emerged: a gigantic, shaggy black dog, moving stealthily across the lawn, Crookshanks trotting at its side. Harry stared. What did this mean? If Crookshanks could see the dog as well, how could it be an omen of Harry's death?

'Ron!' Harry hissed. 'Ron! Wake up!'

'Huh?'

'I need you to tell me if you can see something!'

"S all dark, Harry,' Ron muttered thickly. 'What're you on about?'

'Down here –'

Harry looked quickly back out of the window.

Crookshanks and the dog had vanished. Harry climbed onto the window-sill to look right down into the shadows of the castle, but they weren't there. Where had they gone?

A loud snore told him Ron had fallen asleep again.

Harry and the rest of the Gryffindor team entered the Great Hall next day to enormous applause. Harry couldn't help grinning broadly as he saw that both the Ravenclaw and Hufflepuff tables were clapping them, too. The Slytherin table hissed loudly as they passed. Harry noticed that Malfoy looked even paler than usual.

Wood spent the whole of breakfast urging his team to eat, while touching nothing himself. Then he hurried them off to the pitch before anyone else had finished, so they could get an idea of the conditions. As they left the Great Hall, everyone applauded again.

'Good luck, Harry!' called Cho Chang. Harry felt himself blushing.

'OK ... no wind to speak of ... sun's a bit bright, that could impair your vision, watch out for it ... ground's fairly hard, good, that'll give us a fast kick-off ...'

Wood paced the pitch, staring around with the team behind him. Finally they saw the front doors of the castle open in the distance, and the rest of the school spill onto the lawn.

'Changing rooms,' said Wood tersely.

None of them spoke as they changed into their scarlet robes. Harry wondered if they were feeling like he was: as though he'd eaten something extremely wriggly for breakfast. In what seemed like no time at all, Wood was

第15章 魁地奇决赛

就在这时,它出来了——一条毛蓬蓬的大黑狗,悄悄地穿过草坪,克鲁克山小跑着跟在它旁边。哈利瞪大了眼睛。怎么回事?如果克鲁克山也看得见那条狗,它怎么会是哈利的死亡预兆呢?

"罗恩!"哈利轻声说,"罗恩!醒醒!"

"嗯?"

"我要你帮我看一个东西,看你能不能看清楚!"

"黑咕隆咚的,哈利,"罗恩含混不清地咕哝道,"你在搞什么名堂呢?"

"过来——"

哈利急忙回头看着窗外。

克鲁克山和那条狗不见了。哈利爬上窗台,低头朝城堡的阴影中望去,也没有。它们去哪儿了呢?

响亮的鼾声告诉他,罗恩又睡着了。

第二天,哈利与格兰芬多的队友们走进礼堂时,受到了热烈的掌声欢迎。看到拉文克劳和赫奇帕奇餐桌上的同学也在为他们鼓掌,哈利不禁露出了开心的笑容。斯莱特林在他们走过时大发嘘声,哈利看到马尔福的脸色比平常更加苍白。

伍德全部早餐时间都在动员队员们多吃,自己却什么都没碰。然后他在大家还没吃完时就催他们先去球场熟悉情况。他们离开礼堂时,大家又鼓起掌来。

"祝你好运,哈利!"秋·张喊道。哈利感到自己脸红了。

"好……没什么风……太阳有点亮,会晃眼睛,要当心……地面挺硬的,很好,这样起飞快……"

伍德在球场上走来走去,看看这个看看那个,队员们跟在后面。终于,他们望见远处的城堡大门打开了,全校同学拥上了草坪。

"去更衣室。"伍德一声令下。

球员们换上深红色袍子时谁都没有说话。哈利想知道别人是不是跟他感觉一样,好像早餐吃了什么超级蠕虫。似乎才一眨眼的工夫,

CHAPTER FIFTEEN — The Quidditch Final

saying, 'OK, it's time, let's go ...'

They walked out onto the pitch to a tidal wave of noise. Three-quarters of the crowd were wearing scarlet rosettes, waving scarlet flags with the Gryffindor lion upon them or brandishing banners with slogans such as 'GO GRYFFINDOR!' and 'LIONS FOR THE CUP!' Behind the Slytherin goalposts, however, two hundred people were wearing green; the silver serpent of Slytherin glittered on their flags, and Professor Snape sat in the very front row, wearing green like everyone else, and a very grim smile.

'And here are the Gryffindors!' yelled Lee Jordan, who was acting as commentator as usual. 'Potter, Bell, Johnson, Spinnet, Weasley, Weasley and Wood. Widely acknowledged as the best side Hogwarts has seen in a good few years –'

Lee's comments were drowned by a tide of 'boos' from the Slytherin end.

'And here come the Slytherin team, led by captain Flint. He's made some changes in the line-up and seems to be going for size rather than skill –'

More boos from the Slytherin crowd. Harry, however, thought Lee had a point. Malfoy was easily the smallest person on the Slytherin team; the rest of them were enormous.

'Captains, shake hands!' said Madam Hooch.

Flint and Wood approached each other and grasped each other's hands very tightly; it looked as though each was trying to break the other's fingers.

'Mount your brooms!' said Madam Hooch. 'Three ... two ... one ...'

The sound of her whistle was lost in the roar from the crowd as fourteen brooms rose into the air. Harry felt his hair fly back off his forehead; his nerves left him in the thrill of the flight; he glanced around, saw Malfoy on his tail, and sped off in search of the Snitch.

'And it's Gryffindor in possession, Alicia Spinnet of Gryffindor with the Quaffle, heading straight for the Slytherin goalposts, looking good, Alicia! Argh, no – Quaffle intercepted by Warrington, Warrington of Slytherin tearing up the pitch – WHAM! – nice Bludger work there by George Weasley, Warrington drops the Quaffle, it's caught by – Johnson, Gryffindor back in possession, come on, Angelina – nice swerve round Montague – *duck, Angelina, that's a Bludger!* – SHE SCORES! TEN–ZERO TO GRYFFINDOR!'

Angelina punched the air as she soared round the end of the pitch; the sea of scarlet below was screaming its delight –

第15章 魁地奇决赛

伍德就说:"好,时间到了,走吧——"

他们走出更衣室,走向球场,喧闹的声浪扑面而来。四分之三的观众戴着深红色的玫瑰形徽章,挥舞着绘有格兰芬多狮子的红旗子,或是打着"**格兰芬多加油!**""**狮子夺杯!**"等字样的横幅。斯莱特林的球门柱后面有两百号人佩戴着绿色饰物,银蛇的图样在他们旗子上闪闪发亮。斯内普教授坐在第一排,也戴着绿色饰物,脸上挂着阴沉的笑容。

"格兰芬多队上场了!"照常担任解说员的李·乔丹高叫道,"波特、贝尔、约翰逊、斯平内特、韦斯莱兄弟和伍德。人们普遍认为这是霍格沃茨几年来最好的球队——"

李的解说淹没在斯莱特林那边发出的一片嘘声中。

"斯莱特林队也上场了,率队的是弗林特队长。他对阵容做了一些调整,似乎更侧重于个头而非技术——"

斯莱特林的那帮人嘘声更大了,但哈利觉得李说得有些道理。马尔福在队里明显个子最小,其他队员都又高又壮。

"两位队长握手!"霍琦女士说。

弗林特和伍德走上前紧紧握了握手,好像都想把对方的手指捏断似的。

"骑上飞天扫帚!"霍琦女士说,"三……二……一……"

她的哨声被观众的喝彩声淹没了,十四把扫帚升上天空。哈利感到额上的头发向后飘起,紧张的感觉在飞翔的兴奋中消失了。他放眼四望,看到马尔福跟在后面,便赶忙加速疾驰去寻找飞贼。

"现在格兰芬多队在控球。格兰芬多的艾丽娅·斯平内特带着鬼飞球,直奔斯莱特林的球门而去,势头不错,艾丽娅!啊,不好——鬼飞球被沃林顿截走了。斯莱特林的沃林顿在场上猛冲——**哇!**——乔治·韦斯莱这一记游走球打得漂亮,沃林顿丢掉了鬼飞球,它被——约翰逊抢到,格兰芬多又控制球了。加油,安吉利娜——漂亮,晃过了蒙太——小心,安吉利娜,游走球!——**她得分了!十比〇,格兰芬多队领先!**"

安吉利娜绕着球场一端滑翔,得意地挥舞拳头,下面深红色的海洋一片欢呼——

CHAPTER FIFTEEN   The Quidditch Final

'OUCH!'

Angelina was nearly thrown from her broom as Marcus Flint went smashing into her.

'Sorry!' said Flint, as the crowd below booed. 'Sorry, didn't see her!'

Next moment, Fred Weasley had chucked his Beater's club at the back of Flint's head. Flint's nose smashed into the handle of his broom and began to bleed.

'That will do!' shrieked Madam Hooch, zooming between them. 'Penalty to Gryffindor for an unprovoked attack on their Chaser! Penalty to Slytherin for deliberate damage to *their* Chaser!'

'Come off it, Miss!' howled Fred, but Madam Hooch blew her whistle and Alicia flew forward to take the penalty.

'Come on, Alicia!' yelled Lee into the silence that had descended on the crowd. 'YES! SHE'S BEATEN THE KEEPER! TWENTY–ZERO TO GRYFFINDOR!'

Harry turned the Firebolt sharply to watch Flint, still bleeding freely, fly forwards to take the Slytherin penalty. Wood was hovering in front of the Gryffindor goalposts, his jaw clenched.

"Course, Wood's a superb keeper!' Lee Jordan told the crowd, as Flint waited for Madam Hooch's whistle. 'Superb! Very difficult to pass – very difficult indeed – YES! I DON'T BELIEVE IT! HE'S SAVED IT!'

Relieved, Harry zoomed away, gazing around for the Snitch, but still making sure he caught every word of Lee's commentary. It was essential that he hold Malfoy off the Snitch until Gryffindor was more than fifty points up …

'Gryffindor in possession, no, Slytherin in possession – no! – Gryffindor back in possession and it's Katie Bell, Katie Bell for Gryffindor with the Quaffle, she's streaking up the pitch – THAT WAS DELIBERATE!'

Montague, a Slytherin Chaser, had swerved in front of Katie, and instead of seizing the Quaffle, had grabbed her head. Katie cartwheeled in the air, managed to stay on her broom but dropped the Quaffle.

Madam Hooch's whistle rang out again as she soared over to Montague and began shouting at him. A minute later, Katie had put another penalty past the Slytherin keeper.

'THIRTY–ZERO! TAKE THAT, YOU DIRTY, CHEATING –'

'Jordan, if you can't commentate in an unbiased way –!'

第 15 章 魁地奇决赛

"哎哟!"

安吉利娜差点从扫帚上摔下去,是马库斯·弗林特狠狠地撞了她一下。

"对不起!"弗林特在观众的嘘声中说,"对不起,没看见!"

稍后,弗雷德·韦斯莱用球棒照着弗林特的后脑勺敲了一下。弗林特的鼻子撞到扫帚把上,流出血来。

"够了!"霍琦女士厉声喊道,嗖地蹿到两人之间,"追球手受到无端袭击,由格兰芬多罚球!追球手受到故意伤害,由斯莱特林罚球!"

"别呀,女士!"弗雷德叫了起来,但霍琦女士吹响了哨子,艾丽娅飞上前去罚球。

"加油,艾丽娅!"李在观众的寂静中大声说,"**好!她突破了守门员!格兰芬多队二十比〇领先!**"

哈利迅速拨转火弩箭,看鼻子仍在流血的弗林特飞上前为斯莱特林罚球。伍德守在格兰芬多队的球门前,紧咬牙关。

"当然,伍德是一流的守门员!"弗林特在等待霍琦女士的哨声时,李·乔丹对观众说,"一流的!很难攻破——难而又难——**好!真是难以置信!他把球扑出去了!**"

哈利松了口气,急速上升,四下寻找飞贼,但仍在一字不落地留心听着李·乔丹的解说。他不能让马尔福碰到飞贼,一定要等到格兰芬多领先五十分以上……

"格兰芬多控球,不,斯莱特林控制球了——不!——格兰芬多又把球夺了回来,是凯蒂·贝尔,格兰芬多的凯蒂·贝尔拿到了鬼飞球,在场上飞驰——**这是故意的!**"

斯莱特林的追球手蒙太转到了凯蒂前面,他没有抢鬼飞球,而是去抓凯蒂的脑袋。凯蒂在空中横翻了个跟头,总算还骑在扫帚上,但是鬼飞球丢了。

霍琦女士的哨子又响了。她飞向蒙太,开始大声训斥。一分钟后,凯蒂又罚进一球。

"三十比〇!接受教训吧,你们这些卑鄙、无耻的——"

"乔丹,如果你不能中立地解说——"

CHAPTER FIFTEEN   The Quidditch Final

'I'm telling it like it is, Professor!'

Harry felt a huge jolt of excitement. He had seen the Snitch – it was shimmering at the foot of one of the Gryffindor goalposts – but he mustn't catch it yet. And if Malfoy saw it ...

Faking a look of sudden concentration, Harry pulled his Firebolt round and sped off towards the Slytherin end. It worked. Malfoy went haring after him, clearly thinking Harry had seen the Snitch there ...

WHOOSH.

One of the Bludgers came streaking past Harry's right ear, hit by the gigantic Slytherin Beater, Derrick. Next moment –

WHOOSH.

The second Bludger had grazed Harry's elbow. The other Beater, Bole, was closing in.

Harry had a fleeting glimpse of Bole and Derrick zooming towards him, clubs raised –

He turned the Firebolt upwards at the last second, and Bole and Derrick collided with a sickening crunch.

'Ha haaa!' yelled Lee Jordan, as the Slytherin Beaters lurched away from each other, clutching their heads. 'Too bad, boys! You'll need to get up earlier than that to beat a Firebolt! And it's Gryffindor in possession again, as Johnson takes the Quaffle – Flint alongside her – poke him in the eye, Angelina! – it was a joke, Professor, it was a joke – oh, no – Flint in possession, Flint flying towards the Gryffindor goalposts, come on, now, Wood, save –!'

But Flint had scored; there was an eruption of cheers from the Slytherin end and Lee swore so badly that Professor McGonagall tried to tug the magical megaphone away from him.

'Sorry, Professor, sorry! Won't happen again! So, Gryffindor in the lead, thirty points to ten, and Gryffindor in possession –'

It was turning into the dirtiest match Harry had ever played in. Enraged that Gryffindor had taken such an early lead, the Slytherins were rapidly resorting to any means to take the Quaffle. Bole hit Alicia with his club and tried to say he'd thought she was a Bludger. George Weasley elbowed Bole in the face in retaliation. Madam Hooch awarded both teams penalties, and Wood pulled off another spectacular save, making the score forty–ten to Gryffindor.

第15章 魁地奇决赛

"我是实事求是的，教授！"

哈利感到一阵强烈的激动，他发现金色飞贼了——就在格兰芬多的一根门柱下方闪烁——但他还不能去抓它——要是马尔福也看到了——

哈利突然装出全神贯注的样子，掉转火弩箭朝斯莱特林那头迅速冲去——成功了，马尔福紧跟上来，他显然以为哈利看到飞贼在那边……

嗖！

一个游走球贴着哈利的左耳疾飞过去，是高大的斯莱特林击球手德里克打来的。紧接着又是——

嗖！

第二个游走球擦到了哈利的胳膊肘。另一名击球手博尔包抄过来。

哈利在匆匆一瞥中看到博尔和德里克朝他冲来，都举起了球棒——

他在最后一秒钟掉转火弩箭急速上升，博尔和德里克撞到一起，发出可怕的咣当声。

"哈哈哈！"李·乔丹叫道，那两名斯莱特林击球手抱着脑袋摇摇晃晃地分开了，"很遗憾，哥们儿！要想胜过火弩箭，你们应该起得更早一点儿！格兰芬多又控制球了，约翰逊拿着鬼飞球——弗林特跟在旁边——戳他的眼睛，安吉利娜！——说着玩儿的，教授，说着玩儿的——哦，不好——弗林特拿到球了，弗林特朝格兰芬多的球门飞去。注意，伍德，防住——！"

但弗林特得分了。斯莱特林那头爆发出一阵欢呼，李·乔丹骂得太难听了，麦格教授要把魔法麦克风从他手里夺走。

"对不起，教授，对不起！再也不了！现在，格兰芬多队领先，三十比十，格兰芬多控球——"

这场比赛逐渐变成了哈利参加过的最肮脏的一场比赛。看到格兰芬多这么早就领先，斯莱特林的队员气急败坏，很快就开始不择手段地争夺鬼飞球。博尔用球棒打了艾丽娅，还狡辩说以为她是游走球。乔治·韦斯莱用胳膊肘撞了博尔的脸以示报复。霍琦女士判双方各罚球一次。伍德又完成了一次精彩的救球，把比分拉大到四十比十。

CHAPTER FIFTEEN The Quidditch Final

The Snitch had disappeared again. Malfoy was still keeping close to Harry as he soared over the match, looking around for it – once Gryffindor were fifty points ahead ...

Katie scored. Fifty–ten. Fred and George Weasley were swooping around her, clubs raised, in case any of the Slytherins were thinking of revenge. Bole and Derrick took advantage of Fred and George's absence to aim both Bludgers at Wood; they caught him in the stomach, one after the other, and he rolled over in the air, clutching his broom, completely winded.

Madam Hooch was beside herself.

'*You do not attack the Keeper unless the Quaffle is within the scoring area*!' she shrieked at Bole and Derrick. 'Gryffindor penalty!'

And Angelina scored. Sixty–ten. Moments later, Fred Weasley pelted a Bludger at Warrington, knocking the Quaffle out of his hands; Alicia seized it and put it through the Slytherin goal: seventy–ten.

The Gryffindor crowd below were screaming themselves hoarse – Gryffindor were sixty points in the lead, and if Harry caught the Snitch now, the Cup was theirs. Harry could almost feel hundreds of eyes following him as he soared around the pitch, high above the rest of the game, with Malfoy speeding along behind him.

And then he saw it. The Snitch was sparkling twenty feet above him.

Harry put on a huge burst of speed, the wind roaring in his ears; he stretched out his hand, but suddenly, the Firebolt was slowing down –

Horrified, he looked around. Malfoy had thrown himself forward, grabbed hold of the Firebolt's tail and was pulling it back.

'You –'

Harry was angry enough to hit Malfoy, but he couldn't reach. Malfoy was panting with the effort of holding onto the Firebolt, but his eyes were sparkling maliciously. He had achieved what he'd wanted – the Snitch had disappeared again.

'Penalty! Penalty to Gryffindor! I've never seen such tactics!' Madam Hooch screeched, shooting up to where Malfoy was sliding back onto his Nimbus Two Thousand and One.

'YOU CHEATING SCUM!' Lee Jordan was howling into the megaphone, dancing out of Professor McGonagall's reach. 'YOU FILTHY, CHEATING B–'

第15章 魁地奇决赛

金色飞贼又消失了。马尔福依然紧跟在哈利身后,哈利升到高空,举目寻找———一旦格兰芬多领先五十分——

凯蒂得分了,五十比十。弗雷德和乔治·韦斯莱高举球棒飞旋在她旁边保驾,防止斯莱特林的队员报复。博尔和德里克趁弗雷德和乔治不注意把两只游走球打向伍德,一先一后击中了他的肚子。伍德在空中打了个滚,抓紧扫帚,呼吸困难。

霍琦女士勃然大怒。

"鬼飞球不在得分区,不可以袭击守门员!"她朝博尔和德里克尖叫道,"格兰芬多罚球!"

安吉利娜得分,六十比十。稍后,弗雷德·韦斯莱朝沃林顿打出一个游走球,把他手里的鬼飞球打掉了,艾丽娅抓住球,丢进了斯莱特林的球门,七十比十。

下面的格兰芬多球迷嗓子都快喊哑了——格兰芬多领先六十分。如果哈利现在抓到飞贼,奖杯就是他们的了。哈利几乎能感到几百双眼睛都盯在他身上。他在高空绕着球场飞,马尔福在后面加速追赶。

看到了。金色飞贼正在他上方二十英尺处闪耀。

哈利猛然加速,风在他耳边呼啸。他伸出手,可是火弩箭突然慢了下来——

哈利大惊,回头一看,是马尔福扑上来抓住了火弩箭的尾部,在把它往后拉。

"你——"

哈利气得想揍马尔福,可是够不着。马尔福因为拽着火弩箭而气喘吁吁,但眼里闪着恶毒的光。他达到了目的——金色飞贼又消失了。

"罚球!格兰芬多罚球!我从没见过这么干的!"霍琦女士尖声大叫,嗖地冲上去,马尔福正在滑回他的光轮2001。

"**无耻的流氓!**"李·乔丹一边冲着麦克风咆哮,一边跳到麦格教授够不到他的地方,"**卑鄙、无耻的杂——**"

451

CHAPTER FIFTEEN   The Quidditch Final

Professor McGonagall didn't even bother to tell him off. She was actually shaking her fist in Malfoy's direction; her hat had fallen off, and she, too, was shouting furiously.

Alicia took Gryffindor's penalty, but she was so angry she missed by several feet. The Gryffindor team was losing concentration and the Slytherins, delighted by Malfoy's foul on Harry, were being spurred on to greater heights.

'Slytherin in possession, Slytherin heading for goal – Montague scores –' Lee groaned. 'Seventy–twenty to Gryffindor ...'

Harry was now marking Malfoy so closely their knees kept hitting each other. Harry wasn't going to let Malfoy anywhere near the Snitch ...

'Get out of it, Potter!' Malfoy yelled in frustration, as he tried to turn and found Harry blocking him.

'Angelina Johnson gets the Quaffle for Gryffindor, come on, Angelina, COME ON!'

Harry looked round. Every single Slytherin player apart from Malfoy, even the Slytherin Keeper, was streaking up the pitch towards Angelina – they were all going to block her –

Harry wheeled the Firebolt about, bent so low he was lying flat along the handle and kicked it forwards. Like a bullet, he shot towards the Slytherins.

'AAAAAAARRRGH!'

They scattered as the Firebolt zoomed towards them; Angelina's way was clear.

'SHE SCORES! SHE SCORES! Gryffindor lead by eighty points to twenty!'

Harry, who had almost pelted headlong into the stands, skidded to a halt in mid-air, reversed and zoomed back into the middle of the pitch.

And then he saw something to make his heart stand still. Malfoy was diving, a look of triumph on his face – there, a few feet above the grass below, was a tiny, golden glimmer.

Harry urged the Firebolt downwards but Malfoy was miles ahead.

'Go! Go! Go!' Harry urged his broom. They were gaining on Malfoy ... Harry flattened himself to the broom handle as Bole sent a Bludger at him ... he was at Malfoy's ankles ... he was level –.

Harry threw himself forwards, taking both hands off his broom. He knocked Malfoy's arm out of the way and –

第 15 章 魁地奇决赛

麦格教授甚至没有训斥乔丹。她也冲着马尔福的方向晃动拳头，气愤地大喊，她的帽子都掉了。

艾丽娅为格兰芬多罚球，但是她太生气了，球偏离了球门几英尺。格兰芬多球队有点分神，斯莱特林队员受到马尔福对哈利犯规的鼓舞，更加嚣张起来。

"斯莱特林控球，斯莱特林投球射门——蒙太得分——"李·乔丹呻吟道，"七十比二十，格兰芬多领先……"

哈利现在把马尔福盯得很紧，两人的膝盖经常碰到一起。哈利不让马尔福有机会靠近飞贼……

"滚开，波特！"马尔福恼火地叫道，因为他想转弯，却发现被哈利挡着。

"安吉利娜·约翰逊为格兰芬多队抢到了鬼飞球，加油，安吉利娜，**加油！**"

哈利回头一看，除了马尔福之外，斯莱特林的每一位队员都在冲向安吉利娜，连斯莱特林的守门员都出来了——他们都想堵住安吉利娜——

哈利掉转火弩箭，身体完全伏在扫帚把上，驱帚向前，像一枚子弹般朝斯莱特林的队员们冲去。

"啊——！"

他们看到火弩箭射来，纷纷躲闪，被迫为安吉利娜让出了路。

"**她得分了！她得分了！**格兰芬多八十比二十领先！"

哈利差点冲到了看台上，但他在半空滑行着刹住扫帚，掉头冲回中场。

眼前的一幕让他的心脏停止了跳动。马尔福在俯冲，脸上带着胜利的表情——在他下方，在离草坪几英尺的高处，有一点小小的金光——

哈利催动火弩箭加速俯冲，但马尔福比他近得多——

"快！快！快！"哈利催动着他的火弩箭，逼近马尔福——博尔打来游走球，他伏到扫帚把上躲开了——他追到了马尔福的脚边——他跟马尔福并排了——

哈利向前扑去，双手都放开了飞天扫帚，他撞开了马尔福的胳膊——

CHAPTER FIFTEEN The Quidditch Final

'YES!'

He pulled out of his dive, his hand in the air, and the stadium exploded. Harry soared above the crowd, an odd ringing in his ears. The tiny golden ball was held tight in his fist, beating its wings hopelessly against his fingers.

Then Wood was speeding towards him, half-blinded by tears; he seized Harry around the neck and sobbed unrestrainedly into his shoulder. Harry felt two large thumps as Fred and George hit them; then Angelina, Alicia and Katie's voices, '*We've won the Cup! We've won the Cup!*' Tangled together in a many-armed hug, the Gryffindor team sank, yelling hoarsely, back to earth.

Wave upon wave of crimson supporters was pouring over the barriers onto the pitch. Hands were raining down on their backs. Harry had a confused impression of noise and bodies pressing in on him. Then he, and the rest of the team, were hoisted onto the shoulders of the crowd. Thrust into the light, he saw Hagrid, plastered with crimson rosettes – 'Yeh beat 'em, Harry, yeh beat 'em! Wait till I tell Buckbeak!' There was Percy, jumping up and down like a maniac, all dignity forgotten. Professor McGonagall was sobbing harder even than Wood, wiping her eyes with an enormous Gryffindor flag; and there, fighting their way towards Harry, were Ron and Hermione. Words failed them. They simply beamed, as Harry was borne towards the stands, where Dumbledore stood waiting with the enormous Quidditch Cup.

If only there had been a Dementor around ... As a sobbing Wood passed Harry the Cup, as he lifted it into the air, Harry felt he could have produced the world's best Patronus.

第15章 魁地奇决赛

"抓住了!"

他直起身来,手举在空中,全场沸腾了。哈利高高地飞在人群上空,耳朵里响着奇怪的嗡嗡声。小小的金球被他紧紧攥在手里,绝望地拍打着翅膀。

伍德泪眼模糊地冲过来,搂住哈利的脖子,趴在他肩上纵情地哭泣。哈利感到两下重重的撞击,弗雷德和乔治扑上来了,然后是安吉利娜、艾丽娅和凯蒂的声音:"我们夺杯了!我们夺杯了!"许多条胳膊搂在一起,格兰芬多的队员们抱成一团,嘶哑地叫喊着,落回到地面。

一股股红色的洪流冲过围栏涌进球场。无数只手雨点般地落到他们背上。混乱中哈利只觉得许多声音和身体向他压来,然后他和其他球员被人群扛了起来。他一下子被举到了亮处,看见了身上别满深红色玫瑰形徽章的海格——"你打败了他们,哈利,你打败了他们!我要告诉巴克比克!"还有珀西,疯子一样跳上跳下,完全忘记了体面。麦格教授比伍德哭得还厉害,正用一面格兰芬多的大旗子擦眼泪。那边,罗恩和赫敏正在努力朝哈利跟前挤,激动得说不出话来,只是望着他笑。哈利被抬向看台,邓布利多站在那里,手里捧着巨大的魁地奇奖杯。

要是附近有摄魂怪……当哈利从抽泣的伍德手中接过奖杯,高高举起时,他感到自己能够变出全世界最好的守护神。

CHAPTER SIXTEEN

Professor Trelawney's Prediction

Harry's euphoria at finally winning the Quidditch Cup lasted at least a week. Even the weather seemed to be celebrating; as June approached, the days became cloudless and sultry, and all anybody felt like doing was strolling into the grounds and flopping down on the grass with several pints of iced pumpkin juice, perhaps playing a casual game of Gobstones or watching the giant squid propel itself dreamily across the surface of the lake.

But they couldn't. The exams were nearly upon them, and instead of lazing around outside, the students were forced to remain inside the castle, trying to bully their brains into concentrating while enticing wafts of summer air drifted in through the windows. Even Fred and George Weasley had been spotted working; they were about to take their O.W.L.s (Ordinary Wizarding Levels). Percy was getting ready to sit his N.E.W.T.s (Nastily Exhausting Wizarding Tests), the highest qualification Hogwarts offered. As Percy hoped to enter the Ministry of Magic, he needed top grades. He was becoming increasingly edgy, and gave very severe punishments to anybody who disturbed the quiet of the common room in the evenings. In fact, the only person who seemed more anxious than Percy was Hermione.

Harry and Ron had given up asking her how she was managing to attend several classes at once, but they couldn't restrain themselves when they saw the exam timetable she had drawn up for herself. The first column read:

MONDAY
9 o'clock, Arithmancy
9 o'clock, Transfiguration
Lunch
1 o'clock, Charms
1 o'clock, Ancient Runes

第 16 章

特里劳尼教授的预言

终于夺得了魁地奇杯,哈利的兴奋劲儿至少维持了一个星期。连天气都像是在庆祝。临近六月,白天变得晴朗无云,热烘烘的,让人只想带上几品脱冰镇南瓜汁溜达到场地上,一屁股坐在草地上,也许可以随意玩上几局高布石,或者看着巨乌贼在湖面上梦幻般地游动。

可是不行。考试临头,学生们不能在外面逍遥,而不得不待在城堡里,逼着自己的大脑集中思想,任凭窗外飘来阵阵诱人的夏风。连弗雷德和乔治·韦斯莱都在用功了,他们要参加 O.W.L.(普通巫师等级考试)。珀西准备通过 N.E.W.T.(终极巫师考试),这是霍格沃茨提供的最高学历。珀西想进魔法部,所以需要成绩优异。他越来越神经质了,不管是谁在晚上打扰了公共休息室的安静,他都会给以很重的惩罚。实际上,只有一个人比珀西更紧张,那就是赫敏。

哈利和罗恩已经不再问她怎么能同时上好几堂课,可是看到她自己给自己制订的考试时间表,他们又忍不住了。这张表的第一栏上列着:

星期一

9 点,算术占卜

9 点,变形

午餐

1 点,魔咒

1 点,古代如尼文

CHAPTER SIXTEEN — Professor Trelawney's Prediction

'Hermione?' Ron said cautiously, because she was liable to explode when interrupted these days. 'Er – are you sure you've copied down these times right?'

'What?' snapped Hermione, picking up the exam timetable and examining it. 'Yes, of course I have.'

'Is there any point asking how you're going to sit two exams at once?' said Harry.

'No,' said Hermione shortly. 'Has either of you seen my copy of *Numerology and Grammatica*?'

'Oh, yeah, I borrowed it for a bit of bedtime reading,' said Ron, but very quietly. Hermione started shifting heaps of parchment around on her table, looking for the book. Just then, there was a rustle at the window and Hedwig fluttered through it, a note clutched tightly in her beak.

'It's from Hagrid,' said Harry, ripping the note open. 'Buckbeak's appeal – it's set for the sixth.'

'That's the day we finish our exams,' said Hermione, still looking everywhere for her Arithmancy book.

'And they're coming up here to do it,' said Harry, still reading from the letter. 'Someone from the Ministry of Magic and – and an executioner.'

Hermione looked up, startled.

'They're bringing the executioner to the appeal! But that sounds as though they've already decided!'

'Yeah, it does,' said Harry slowly.

'They can't!' Ron howled. 'I've spent *ages* reading up stuff for him, they can't just ignore it all!'

But Harry had a horrible feeling that the Committee for the Disposal of Dangerous Creatures had had its mind made up for it by Mr Malfoy. Draco, who had been noticeably subdued since Gryffindor's triumph in the Quidditch final, seemed to regain some of his old swagger over the next few days. From sneering comments Harry overheard, Malfoy was certain Buckbeak was going to be killed, and seemed thoroughly pleased with himself for bringing it about. It was all Harry could do to stop himself imitating Hermione and hitting Malfoy in the face on these occasions. And the worst thing of all was that they had no time or opportunity to go and see Hagrid, because the strict new security measures had not been lifted, and Harry didn't dare retrieve his Invisibility Cloak from below the one-eyed witch.

"赫敏,"罗恩小心地问,因为这些天赫敏被打搅时很容易发怒,"呃——你确定这些时间都抄对了吗?"

"什么?"赫敏尖声说,抓起那张时间表来仔细检查,"没错,当然对了。"

"我是否有必要问一句,你怎么能同时坐在两个考场里?"哈利说。

"没有。"赫敏干脆地说,"你们有谁看见我的《数字学和语法学》了?"

"哦,对了,我借去了,睡觉前翻翻。"罗恩说,但声音憋在嗓子眼里。赫敏开始把桌上那一堆堆羊皮纸挪来挪去,寻找那本书。这时窗口一阵响动,海德薇拍着翅膀飞进来,嘴里紧衔着一张便条。

"是海格的,"哈利说着,扯开了便条,"巴克比克的上诉——定在六号。"

"正是我们考完试那天。"赫敏说,她仍在到处寻找她的算术占卜课本。

"他们要到这儿来,"哈利继续看信,"魔法部的人和——和一名行刑官。"

赫敏惊愕地抬起头。

"他们要带行刑官来听取上诉!怎么听着像已经做出了判决呀!"

"是啊。"哈利沉吟着说。

"不行!"罗恩吼了起来,"我花了那么多时间为它查资料,他们不能置若罔闻!"

但是哈利有一种可怕的预感,觉得处置危险生物委员会已经接受了马尔福先生的决定。自从格兰芬多在魁地奇决赛中获胜之后,德拉科明显收敛了不少,但这几天他似乎又恢复了一些往日的嚣张。从刮到哈利耳朵里的冷嘲热讽看,马尔福确信巴克比克将被处决,而且他好像还为自己促成了此事而扬扬得意呢。这种时候,哈利竭力克制住情绪,才没有像赫敏那样打马尔福的耳光。最糟糕的是他们没有时间,也没有机会去见海格,因为严格的新保安措施还没有撤销,哈利不敢从独眼女巫雕像下面取回他的隐形衣。

CHAPTER SIXTEEN   Professor Trelawney's Prediction

Exam week began and an unnatural hush fell over the castle. The third-years emerged from Transfiguration at lunchtime on Monday limp and ashen-faced, comparing results and bemoaning the difficulty of the tasks they had been set, which had included turning a teapot into a tortoise. Hermione irritated the rest by fussing about how her tortoise had looked more like a turtle, which was the least of everyone else's worries.

'Mine still had a spout for a tail, what a nightmare ...'

'Were the tortoises *supposed* to breathe steam?'

'It still had a willow-patterned shell, d'you think that'll count against me?'

Then, after a hasty lunch, it was straight back upstairs for the Charms exam. Hermione had been right; Professor Flitwick did indeed test them on Cheering Charms. Harry slightly overdid his out of nerves and Ron, who was partnering him, ended up in fits of hysterical laughter and had to be led away to a quiet room for an hour before he was ready to perform the Charm himself. After dinner, the students hurried back to their common rooms, not to relax, but to start revising for Care of Magical Creatures, Potions and Astronomy.

Hagrid presided over the Care of Magical Creatures exam the following morning with a very preoccupied air indeed; his heart didn't seem to be in it at all. He had provided a large tub of fresh Flobberworms for the class, and told them that, to pass the test, their Flobberworm had to still be alive at the end of one hour. As Flobberworms flourished best if left to their own devices, it was the easiest exam any of them had ever sat, and also gave Harry, Ron and Hermione plenty of opportunity to speak to Hagrid.

'Beaky's gettin' a bit depressed,' Hagrid told them, bending low on the pretence of checking that Harry's Flobberworm was still alive. 'Bin cooped up too long. But still ... we'll know day after tomorrow – one way or the other.'

They had Potions that afternoon, which was an unqualified disaster. Try as Harry might, he couldn't get his Confusing Concoction to thicken, and Snape, standing watching with an air of vindictive pleasure, scribbled something that looked suspiciously like a zero onto his notes before moving away.

Then came Astronomy at midnight, up on the tallest tower; History of Magic on Wednesday morning, in which Harry scribbled everything Florean Fortescue had ever told him about medieval witch hunts, while wishing he could have had one of Fortescue's choco-nut sundaes with him in the stifling

第16章 特里劳尼教授的预言

考试周开始了，城堡里寂静异常。星期一吃午饭的时候，三年级学生从变形课考场出来，一个个精神委顿，面色苍白，一边比较着成绩，一边抱怨考题太难，有道题竟要他们把茶壶变成乌龟。赫敏大惊小怪地说她变出的乌龟看上去像海龟，把人气得够呛，因为在别人看来这是根本不用担心的。

"我变出的乌龟尾巴还是壶嘴的样子，多可怕……"

"乌龟该不该吐蒸气？"

"我变出的乌龟壳子上还有柳树花纹，你说会不会扣分呀？"

然后，大家匆匆吃完午饭，马上又回到楼上去考魔咒。赫敏说中了，弗立维教授果然考了快乐咒。哈利由于紧张，动作有点过，跟他搭档的罗恩爆发出一阵阵歇斯底里的大笑，最后只好被带到一间安静的屋子里，待了一小时才能去完成他自己的咒语。晚饭后，学生们又赶着回到公共休息室，不是去休息，而是开始复习保护神奇动物、魔药和天文学。

第二天上午，海格主持保护神奇动物的考试。他显得心事重重，心思好像根本不在考场上。他给学生准备了一大桶新鲜的弗洛伯毛虫，说他们要想通过考试，必须保证自己的弗洛伯毛虫一小时后还活着。因为弗洛伯毛虫在放任自由的情况下活得最好，所以这是他们所有人参加过的最容易的考试，也使哈利、罗恩和赫敏有很多机会和海格说话。

"比克有点儿抑郁，"海格对他们说，身子弯得低低的，假装在检查哈利的弗洛伯毛虫是否还活着，"关得太久了。不过……后天就知道了——是吉是凶——"

下午考魔药，那是一场彻头彻尾的灾难。哈利无论如何也没法使他的迷乱药变稠。斯内普带着一脸的快意在旁边看着，走开之前在笔记簿上记了点什么，看上去很像是个零蛋。

半夜里考了天文学，在最高的塔楼顶上。魔法史是星期三上午考，哈利把福洛林·福斯科对他讲过的中世纪搜捕女巫的那些事情统统写了上去，一边渴望在这闷热的考场上能有一份福斯科的巧克力坚果冰

CHAPTER SIXTEEN — Professor Trelawney's Prediction

classroom. Wednesday afternoon meant Herbology, in the greenhouses under a baking hot sun; then back to the common room once more, with the backs of their necks sunburnt, thinking longingly of this time next day, when it would all be over.

Their second from last exam, on Thursday morning, was Defence Against the Dark Arts. Professor Lupin had compiled the most unusual exam any of them had ever taken; a sort of obstacle course outside in the sun, where they had to wade across a deep paddling pool containing a Grindylow, cross a series of potholes full of Red Caps, squish their way across a patch of marsh, ignoring the misleading directions from a Hinkypunk, then climb into an old trunk and battle with a new Boggart.

'Excellent, Harry,' Lupin muttered, as Harry climbed out of the trunk, grinning. 'Full marks.'

Flushed with his success, Harry hung around to watch Ron and Hermione. Ron did very well until he reached the Hinkypunk, which successfully confused him into sinking waist-high into the quagmire. Hermione did everything perfectly until she reached the trunk with the Boggart in it. After about a minute inside it, she burst out again, screaming.

'Hermione!' said Lupin, startled. 'What's the matter?'

'P-P-Professor McGonagall!' Hermione gasped, pointing into the trunk. 'Sh-she said I'd failed everything!'

It took a little while to calm Hermione down. When at last she had regained a grip on herself, she, Harry and Ron went back to the castle. Ron was still slightly inclined to laugh at Hermione's Boggart, but an argument was averted by the sight that met them on the top of the steps.

Cornelius Fudge, sweating slightly in his pinstriped cloak, was standing there staring out at the grounds. He started at the sight of Harry.

'Hello there, Harry!' he said. 'Just had an exam, I expect? Nearly finished?'

'Yes,' said Harry. Hermione and Ron, not being on speaking terms with the Minister for Magic, hovered awkwardly in the background.

'Lovely day,' said Fudge, casting an eye over the lake. 'Pity ... pity ...'

He sighed deeply and looked down at Harry.

'I'm here on an unpleasant mission, Harry. The Committee for the Disposal of Dangerous Creatures required a witness to the execution of a mad Hippogriff. As I needed to visit Hogwarts to check on the Black

淇淋。星期三下午是草药学考试，在温室里被大太阳烤着，回到公共休息室时脖子后面都晒伤了。大家都向往着明天的这个时候，到那时一切就都结束了。

星期四上午是倒数第二场考试，黑魔法防御术。卢平教授出了他们有生以来考过的最不同寻常的试题，是一种类似于障碍赛的户外考试。必须蹚过一片有格林迪洛的深水塘，穿过一系列满是红帽子的坑洞，咕叽咕叽地走过沼泽地，不能理会一头欣克庞克发出的误导，然后还要爬进一个旧箱子，跟一个新的博格特搏斗。

"很好，哈利，"哈利从箱子里爬出来时，卢平笑眯眯地对他说，"满分。"

哈利兴奋得红了脸，留下来看罗恩和赫敏考试。罗恩一开始很顺利，可是碰到欣克庞克就不行了，被带到齐腰深的沼泽里陷了进去。赫敏前面几项都做得无懈可击，到藏有博格特的箱子时，她进去才一分钟就尖叫着冲了出来。

"赫敏！"卢平吃惊地问，"怎么回事？"

"麦—麦—麦格教授！"赫敏指着箱子气喘吁吁地说，"她—她说我所有的考试都不及格！"

赫敏过了好一会儿才平静下来。当她终于恢复镇定之后，三人一起走回城堡。罗恩还有点想拿赫敏的博格特开玩笑，但台阶顶上的情况使他们避免了一场争吵。

康奈利·福吉站在那儿朝场地上望着，他穿着那件细条纹的斗篷，微微有点儿冒汗。看到哈利，他吃了一惊。

"嘿，哈利！"他说，"刚考完试？快结束了吧？"

"嗯。"哈利说。赫敏和罗恩没有跟魔法部部长说过话，尴尬地站在后面。

"好天气啊，"福吉说着，把目光投向湖面，"可惜……可惜……"

他深深叹了口气，俯视着哈利。

"我此行有一个不愉快的使命，哈利。处置危险生物委员会要求在处决一头发狂的鹰头马身有翼兽时有一名证人在场，我正好要到霍格

situation, I was asked to step in.'

'Does that mean the appeal's already happened?' Ron interrupted, stepping forwards.

'No, no, it's scheduled for this afternoon,' said Fudge, looking curiously at Ron.

'Then you might not have to witness an execution at all!' said Ron stoutly. 'The Hippogriff might get off!'

Before Fudge could answer, two wizards came through the castle doors behind him. One was so ancient he appeared to be withering before their very eyes; the other was tall and strapping, with a thin black moustache. Harry gathered that they were representatives of the Committee for the Disposal of Dangerous Creatures, because the very old wizard squinted towards Hagrid's cabin and said in a feeble voice, 'Dear, dear, I'm getting too old for this ... two o'clock, isn't it, Fudge?'

The black-moustached man was fingering something in his belt; Harry looked and saw that he was running one broad thumb along the blade of a shining axe. Ron opened his mouth to say something, but Hermione nudged him hard in the ribs and jerked her head towards the Entrance Hall.

'Why'd you stop me?' said Ron angrily, as they entered the Great Hall for lunch. 'Did you see them? They've even got the axe ready! This isn't justice!'

'Ron, your dad works for the Ministry. You can't go saying things like that to his boss!' said Hermione, but she, too, looked very upset. 'As long as Hagrid keeps his head this time, and argues his case properly, they can't possibly execute Buckbeak ...'

But Harry could tell Hermione didn't really believe what she was saying. All around them, people were talking excitedly as they ate their lunch, happily anticipating the end of exams that afternoon, but Harry, Ron and Hermione, lost in worry about Hagrid and Buckbeak, didn't join in.

Harry and Ron's last exam was Divination; Hermione's, Muggle Studies. They walked up the marble staircase together. Hermione left them on the first floor and Harry and Ron proceeded all the way up to the seventh, where many of their class were sitting on the spiral staircase to Professor Trelawney's classroom, trying to cram in a bit of last-minute revision.

'She's seeing us all separately,' Neville informed them, as they went to sit down next to him. He had his copy of *Unfogging the Future* open on his lap at the pages devoted to crystal-gazing. 'Have either of you ever seen *anything* in

第16章 特里劳尼教授的预言

沃茨来核查布莱克的情况,就被拉了个差。"

"这么说的意思是上诉早就已经结束了?"罗恩走上前插嘴问道。

"没有,没有,上诉是在今天下午。"福吉惊奇地打量着罗恩说。

"那您可能根本不需要见证处决!"罗恩坚定地说,"那头鹰头马身有翼兽可能获释!"

福吉还没来得及回答,身后的城堡大门里走出来两个巫师,一个衰老得好像正在他们眼前萎缩下去,另一个高大魁梧,留着稀疏的黑髭须。哈利猜想他们是处置危险生物委员会的代表,因为那个老巫师眯眼看着海格的小屋,用颤巍巍的声音说:"哎哟,哎哟,我老啦,干不了这差事啦……两点钟是吧,福吉?"

黑髭须的壮汉摸着腰带里的什么东西,哈利看了一眼,发现他在用粗大的拇指抚摩一柄锃亮的大斧的锋刃。罗恩张嘴想说话,赫敏使劲捅了捅他的肋部,把头朝门厅一摆。

"你干吗要拦着我呢?"罗恩气呼呼地问,他们三人进了礼堂去吃午饭,"你没看到他们吗?他们甚至连斧头都准备好了!这太不公平!"

"罗恩,你爸爸在魔法部工作,你不能那样对他的上司说话!"赫敏说,但她也显得心烦意乱,"只要海格这次保持冷静,好好地陈述理由,他们就不可能处决巴克比克……"

哈利看得出来,赫敏并不真的相信她自己的话。周围的人吃饭时都在热烈交谈,愉快地期待下午考试结束,但是哈利、罗恩和赫敏担心着海格和巴克比克,没有参加聊天。

哈利和罗恩的最后一门考试是占卜,赫敏的是麻瓜研究。三人一起走上大理石楼梯,赫敏在二楼跟他们分手,哈利和罗恩一直爬到八楼,许多同学坐在通往特里劳尼教授那间教室的螺旋楼梯上,还指望在最后再抱抱佛脚呢。

"她一个个地见我们。"纳威说,他们走过去坐在他旁边。纳威腿上摊着那本《拨开迷雾看未来》,翻开在水晶球的章节。"你们在水晶

CHAPTER SIXTEEN   Professor Trelawney's Prediction

a crystal ball?' he asked them unhappily.

'Nope,' said Ron, in an offhand voice. He kept checking his watch; Harry knew that he was counting down the time until Buckbeak's appeal started.

The queue of people outside the classroom shortened very slowly. As each person climbed back down the silver ladder, the rest of the class hissed, 'What did she ask? Was it OK?'

But they all refused to say.

'She says the crystal ball's told her that, if I tell you, I'll have a horrible accident!' squeaked Neville, as he clambered back down the ladder towards Harry and Ron, who had now reached the landing.

'That's convenient,' snorted Ron. 'You know, I'm starting to think Hermione was right about her' (he jabbed his thumb towards the trapdoor overhead), 'she's a right old fraud.'

'Yeah,' said Harry, looking at his own watch. It was now two o'clock. 'Wish she'd hurry up ...'

Parvati came back down the ladder glowing with pride.

'She says I've got all the makings of a true Seer,' she informed Harry and Ron. 'I saw *loads* of stuff ... well, good luck!'

She hurried off down the spiral staircase towards Lavender.

'Ronald Weasley,' said the familiar, misty voice from over their heads. Ron grimaced at Harry, and climbed the silver ladder out of sight. Harry was now the only person left to be tested. He settled himself on the floor with his back against the wall, listening to a fly buzzing in the sunny window, his mind across the grounds with Hagrid.

Finally, after about twenty minutes, Ron's large feet reappeared on the ladder.

'How'd it go?' Harry asked him, standing up.

'Rubbish,' said Ron. 'Couldn't see a thing, so I made some stuff up. Don't think she was convinced, though ...'

'Meet you in the common room,' Harry muttered, as Professor Trelawney's voice called, 'Harry Potter!'

The tower room was hotter than ever before; the curtains were closed, the fire was alight, and the usual sickly scent made Harry cough as he stumbled through the clutter of chairs and tables to where Professor Trelawney sat waiting for him before a large crystal ball.

第16章 特里劳尼教授的预言

球里看到过什么东西吗？"他苦恼地问。

"没有。"罗恩不当回事地说。他不停地看表。哈利知道他是在看巴克比克的上诉还有多久开始。

教室外的队伍缩短得非常慢，每个人从银梯上下来时，其他同学都悄声问："她问了什么？还好吧？"

但他们都不肯说。

"她说水晶球告诉她，我要是说了就会有一场大劫难！"纳威在梯子上对哈利和罗恩尖声说，这时他们俩已经排到了楼梯平台上。

"这倒方便，"罗恩轻蔑地说，"哼，我开始觉得赫敏说她的话有道理，"——他用拇指朝头顶上的活板门一指——"她就是个老骗子。"

"是啊。"哈利也看了看自己的表，已经两点了，"希望她能快点儿……"

帕瓦蒂下来时满脸得意。

"她说我具备了真正先知的全部资质，"她告诉哈利和罗恩，"我看到好多东西……行了，祝你们好运！"

她匆匆跑下螺旋楼梯，迎向拉文德。

"罗恩·韦斯莱！"那熟悉的、梦呓般的声音从头顶上传来。罗恩朝哈利做了个苦脸，登上银梯不见了。现在只有哈利一个人还在等待考试。他背靠墙壁坐在地上，听着一只苍蝇在阳光明媚的窗口嗡嗡地叫，心已越过场地飞到了海格那里。

终于，大约二十分钟之后，罗恩的大脚又出现在梯子上。

"怎么样？"哈利站起来问。

"一塌糊涂。"罗恩说，"什么也看不见，我就胡诌了一些，可是我觉得她没有相信……"

"公共休息室见。"哈利小声说，特里劳尼教授的声音已经在叫道："哈利·波特！"

这个塔楼顶上的房间比任何时候都闷热，窗帘都拉上了，壁炉里生着火，惯常的那种熏人的香味呛得哈利咳嗽起来。他跌跌撞撞地绕过那些横七竖八的桌椅，朝坐在一个大水晶球前的特里劳尼教授走去。

CHAPTER SIXTEEN Professor Trelawney's Prediction

'Good day, my dear,' she said softly. 'If you would kindly gaze into the Orb ... take your time, now ... then tell me what you see within it ...'

Harry bent over the crystal ball and stared, stared as hard as he could, willing it to show him something other than swirling white fog, but nothing happened.

'Well?' Professor Trelawney prompted delicately. 'What do you see?'

The heat was overpowering and his nostrils were stinging with the perfumed smoke wafting from the fire beside them. He thought of what Ron had just said, and decided to pretend.

'Er –,' said Harry, 'a dark shape ... um ...'

'What does it resemble?' whispered Professor Trelawney. 'Think, now ...'

Harry cast his mind around and it landed on Buckbeak.

'A Hippogriff,' he said firmly.

'Indeed!' whispered Professor Trelawney, scribbling keenly on the parchment perched upon her knees. 'My boy, you may well be seeing the outcome of poor Hagrid's trouble with the Ministry of Magic! Look closer ... does the Hippogriff appear to ... have its head?'

'Yes,' said Harry firmly.

'Are you sure?' Professor Trelawney urged him. 'Are you quite sure, dear? You don't see it writhing on the ground, perhaps, and a shadowy figure raising an axe behind it?'

'No!' said Harry, starting to feel slightly sick.

'No blood? No weeping Hagrid?'

'No!' said Harry again, wanting more than ever to leave the room and the heat. 'It looks fine, it's – flying away ...'

Professor Trelawney sighed.

'Well, dear, I think we'll leave it there ... a little disappointing ... but I'm sure you did your best.'

Relieved, Harry got up, picked up his bag and turned to go, but then a loud, harsh voice spoke behind him.

'*It will happen tonight.*'

Harry wheeled around. Professor Trelawney had gone rigid in her armchair; her eyes were unfocused and her mouth sagging.

'S-sorry?' said Harry.

第16章 特里劳尼教授的预言

"你好，亲爱的，"特里劳尼教授轻声说，"请看着这个水晶球……慢慢看……然后跟我讲讲你看到了什么……"

哈利俯身注视水晶球，使劲盯着它，希望它除了旋转的白雾外还能向他显示一些别的，然而什么也没有。

"怎么样？"特里劳尼教授温和地问道，"看到了什么？"

房间里热不可耐，哈利的鼻孔被近旁壁炉中飘出的香味烟雾熏得火辣辣地刺痛，他想起了罗恩的话，决定假装一下。

"呃——"哈利说，"一个黑影……嗯……"

"它像什么？"特里劳尼教授轻声问，"想一想……"

哈利在脑子里搜索了一通，想到了巴克比克。

"鹰头马身有翼兽。"他肯定地说。

"是嘛！"特里劳尼教授喃喃道，热切地在膝头的羊皮纸上记着，"我的孩子，你很可能看到了可怜的海格与魔法部之间那场麻烦的结局！仔细看看……那头鹰头马身有翼兽……有脑袋吗？"

"有。"哈利坚定地说。

"你确定吗？"特里劳尼教授追问道，"你很确定吗，孩子？你没有看到它在地上扭动，后面有个阴影举起了大斧？"

"没有！"哈利说，感到有点想吐了。

"没有鲜血？没有哭泣的海格？"

"没有！"哈利又说，比任何时候更想逃离这个房间和这种闷热，"它看上去挺好的，它——飞走了……"

特里劳尼教授叹了口气。

"好吧，孩子，就到这里吧……我有点失望……但我相信你尽力了。"

哈利松了口气，站起来，拎了书包转身要走，却听到身后响起了一个响亮、刺耳的声音。

"就在今晚。"

哈利急转过身，只见特里劳尼教授直挺挺地坐在扶手椅上，两眼失神，嘴巴张着。

"您—您说什么？"哈利说。

CHAPTER SIXTEEN — Professor Trelawney's Prediction

But Professor Trelawney didn't seem to hear him. Her eyes started to roll. Harry stood there in a panic. She looked as though she was about to have some sort of seizure. He hesitated, thinking of running to the hospital wing – and then Professor Trelawney spoke again, in the same harsh voice, quite unlike her own:

'*The Dark Lord lies alone and friendless, abandoned by his followers. His servant has been chained these twelve years. Tonight, before midnight, the servant will break free and set out to rejoin his master. The Dark Lord will rise again with his servant's aid, greater and more terrible than ever before. Tonight ... before midnight ... the servant ... will set out ... to rejoin ... his master ...*'

Professor Trelawney's head fell forwards onto her chest. She made a grunting sort of noise. Then, quite suddenly, her head snapped up again.

'I'm so sorry, dear boy,' she said dreamily. 'The heat of the day, you know ... I drifted off for a moment ...'

Harry stood there, still staring.

'Is there anything wrong, my dear?'

'You – you just told me that the – the Dark Lord's going to rise again ... that his servant's going to go back to him ...'

Professor Trelawney looked thoroughly startled.

'The Dark Lord? He Who Must Not Be Named? My dear boy, that's hardly something to joke about ... rise again, indeed ...'

'But you just said it! You said the Dark Lord –'

'I think you must have dozed off too, dear!' said Professor Trelawney. 'I would certainly not presume to predict anything quite as far-fetched as *that*!'

Harry climbed back down the ladder and the spiral staircase, wondering ... had he just heard Professor Trelawney make a real prediction? Or had that been her idea of an impressive end to the test?

Five minutes later he was dashing past the security trolls outside the entrance to Gryffindor Tower, Professor Trelawney's words still resounding in his head. People were striding past him in the opposite direction, laughing and joking, heading for the grounds and a bit of long-awaited freedom; by the time he had reached the portrait hole and entered the common room, it was almost deserted. Over in a corner, however, sat Ron and Hermione.

'Professor Trelawney,' Harry panted, 'just told me –'

第16章 特里劳尼教授的预言

但特里劳尼教授似乎没听见,她的眼珠开始转动,哈利惊恐地站在那儿,觉得她好像要发病的样子。他犹豫不决,想着要不要跑到校医院去——这时特里劳尼教授又说话了,还是那种刺耳的声音,跟她本人平常的声音大不一样。

"黑魔头孤零零地躺在那里,没有朋友,被手下遗弃,他的仆人这十二年锁链加身。今晚,午夜之前,这仆人将挣脱锁链,动身去和主人会合。黑魔头将在仆人的帮助下卷土重来,比以前更强大、更可怕。今晚……午夜之前……那仆人……将动身……去和主人……会合……"

特里劳尼教授的脑袋垂到胸前,发出一种呜噜呜噜的声音。然后,很突然地,她的脑袋又抬了起来。

"对不起,亲爱的孩子,"她恍恍惚惚地说,"天气太热,你知道……我打了个盹儿……"

哈利仍呆呆地看着她。

"有什么不对吗,亲爱的?"

"您——您刚才对我说那——那黑魔头要卷土重来……他的仆人要回到他的身边……"

特里劳尼教授显得大为震惊。

"黑魔头?那个连名字都不能提的人?我亲爱的孩子,那可不是开玩笑的……卷土重来,天哪——"

"可这是您刚才说的!您说黑魔头——"

"我想你准是也睡着了,亲爱的!"特里劳尼教授说,"我肯定不可能预言那么离谱的事情!"

哈利爬下梯子和螺旋楼梯,心想……难道他刚才听到特里劳尼教授说了一个真正的预言?还是她觉得这样结束考试令人印象深刻?

五分钟后,哈利从格兰芬多塔楼入口处的保安巨怪面前冲了过去,特里劳尼教授的话音仍在他脑畔回响。人们迎面走来,有说有笑地走向场地,去享受那一点期待已久的自由。哈利来到肖像洞口,爬进公共休息室时,那儿几乎都没人了,但角落里坐着罗恩和赫敏。

"特里劳尼教授,"哈利气喘吁吁地说,"刚才对我说——"

CHAPTER SIXTEEN Professor Trelawney's Prediction

But he stopped abruptly at the sight of their faces.

'Buckbeak lost,' said Ron weakly. 'Hagrid's just sent this.'

Hagrid's note was dry this time, no tears had splattered it, yet his hand seemed to have shaken so much as he wrote that it was hardly legible.

> LOST APPEAL. THEY'RE GOING TO EXECUTE AT SUNSET. NOTHING YOU CAN DO. DON'T COME DOWN. I DON'T WANT YOU TO SEE IT.
> HAGRID

'We've got to go,' said Harry at once. 'He can't just sit there on his own, waiting for the executioner!'

'Sunset, though,' said Ron, who was staring out of the window in a glazed sort of way. 'We'd never be allowed ... specially you, Harry ...'

Harry sank his head into his hands, thinking.

'If we only had the Invisibility Cloak ...'

'Where is it?' said Hermione.

Harry told her about leaving it in the passageway under the one-eyed witch.

'... if Snape sees me anywhere near there again, I'm in serious trouble,' he finished.

'That's true,' said Hermione, getting to her feet. 'If he sees *you* ... how do you open the witch's hump again?'

'You – you tap it and say, "Dissendium",' said Harry. 'But –'

Hermione didn't wait for the rest of his sentence; she strode across the room, pushed the Fat Lady's portrait open and vanished from sight.

'She hasn't gone to get it?' Ron said, staring after her.

She had. Hermione returned a quarter of an hour later with the silvery Cloak folded carefully under her robes.

'Hermione, I don't know what's got into you lately!' said Ron, astounded. 'First you hit Malfoy, then you walk out on Professor Trelawney –'

Hermione looked rather flattered.

They went down to dinner with everybody else, but did not return to Gryffindor Tower afterwards. Harry had the Cloak hidden down the front

第 16 章　特里劳尼教授的预言

他猛然住口，看到了他们俩的脸色。

"巴克比克败诉了，"罗恩无力地说，"海格刚送来的。"

这次海格的字条是干的，没有被泪水打湿，但是他的手好像抖得厉害，字迹难以辨认。

　　败诉了。日落处决。你们帮不了忙，不要过来，我不想让你们看见。

海　格

"我们必须过去，"哈利马上说，"不能让他一个人坐着等行刑官！"

"可是日落的时候，"罗恩目光呆滞地望着窗外说，"不会让我们去的……特别是你，哈利……"

哈利用手捧住脑袋，思索着。

"要是有隐形衣就好了……"

"它在哪儿？"赫敏问。

哈利告诉她隐形衣留在独眼女巫雕像下面的通道里了。

"……如果斯内普再看见我在那附近，我可就惨了。"他最后说。

"是啊，"赫敏站了起来，"如果他看见你……再说一次，要怎么做才能打开那女巫的驼背？"

"你——你敲敲它，说：'左右分离。'"哈利说，"可是——"

赫敏没等他说完，就大步走过房间，推开胖夫人的肖像，消失了。

"她不会去拿隐形衣了吧？"罗恩瞪着她的背影说。

她确实去拿隐形衣了。一刻钟后，赫敏回来了，银色的隐形衣小心地藏在她的袍子里。

"赫敏，我不知道你最近是怎么了！"罗恩震惊地说，"先是打了马尔福，然后又在特里劳尼教授的课上拂袖而去——"

赫敏听了似乎很受用。

他们跟众人一起去吃晚饭，但之后没有再回格兰芬多塔楼。哈利

CHAPTER SIXTEEN — Professor Trelawney's Prediction

of his robes; he had to keep his arms folded to hide the lump. They skulked in an empty chamber off the Entrance Hall, listening, until they were sure it was deserted. They heard a last pair of people hurrying across the Hall, and a door slamming. Hermione poked her head around the door.

'OK,' she whispered, 'no one there – Cloak on –'

Walking very close together so that nobody would see them, they crossed the Hall on tiptoe beneath the Cloak, then walked down the stone front steps into the grounds. The sun was already sinking behind the Forbidden Forest, gilding the top branches of the trees.

They reached Hagrid's cabin and knocked. He was a minute in answering, and when he did, he looked all around for his visitor, pale-faced and trembling.

'It's us,' Harry hissed. 'We're wearing the Invisibility Cloak. Let us in and we can take it off.'

'Yeh shouldn've come!' Hagrid whispered, but he stood back, and they stepped inside. Hagrid shut the door quickly and Harry pulled off the Cloak.

Hagrid was not crying, nor did he throw himself upon their necks. He looked like a man who did not know where he was or what to do. This helplessness was worse to watch than tears.

'Wan' some tea?' he said. His great hands were shaking as he reached for the kettle.

'Where's Buckbeak, Hagrid?' said Hermione hesitantly.

'I – I took him outside,' said Hagrid, spilling milk all over the table as he filled up the jug. 'He's tethered in me pumpkin patch. Thought he oughta see the trees an' – an' smell fresh air – before –'

Hagrid's hand trembled so violently that the milk jug slipped from his grasp and shattered all over the floor.

'I'll do it, Hagrid,' said Hermione quickly, hurrying over and starting to clean up the mess.

'There's another one in the cupboard,' Hagrid said, sitting down and wiping his forehead on his sleeve. Harry glanced at Ron, who looked back hopelessly.

'Isn't there anything anyone can do, Hagrid?' Harry asked fiercely, sitting down next to him. 'Dumbledore –'

'He's tried,' said Hagrid. 'He's got no power ter overrule the Committee.

第 16 章 特里劳尼教授的预言

把隐形衣藏在袍襟里,他必须抱着手臂,遮住那块隆起的鼓包。三人躲在门厅旁的一个空房间里听着动静,直到确定门厅里不再有人。听到最后两个人快步穿过门厅,一扇门砰地关上,赫敏把脑袋从门边探了出去。

"好了,"她小声说,"没有人了——披上隐形衣——"

三人紧挨在一起走,以免被人看见。他们在隐形衣下踮着脚穿过门厅,下了石阶,走到场地上。太阳已经落到禁林后面,余晖把树梢染成了金色。

他们走到海格的小屋前敲门,过了一分钟他才应声,打开门后他四下寻找来者。他脸色苍白,浑身发抖。

"是我们,"哈利悄声说,"穿着隐形衣呢。让我们进去把它脱下来。"

"你们不该来的!"海格小声说,但退后一步,让他们走了进去。海格迅速关上门,哈利扯下了隐形衣。

海格没有哭,也没有扑过来搂住他们的脖子。他好像不知道自己身在何处,该做什么。这种无助比眼泪更令人难受。

"要喝茶吗?"他说,大手颤抖着去拿茶壶。

"巴克比克在哪儿,海格?"赫敏迟疑地问。

"我——我把它带出去了。"海格说,往罐里倒牛奶时洒得满桌都是,"我把它拴在南瓜地里。想让它看看树——呼吸点新鲜的空气——因为——"

海格的手抖得那么厉害,奶罐从手中滑落下来掉到地上,一地碎片。

"我来吧,海格。"赫敏忙说,抢着过去打扫。

"碗柜里还有一个。"海格坐下来,用袖子擦着额头。哈利看看罗恩,罗恩也不知所措地看着他。

"还有什么办法吗,海格?"哈利急切地问,坐到他旁边,"邓布利多——"

"他尽力了,"海格说,"但他无权支配委员会。他告诉他们巴克比

CHAPTER SIXTEEN   Professor Trelawney's Prediction

He told 'em Buckbeak's all right, but they're scared ... yeh know what Lucius Malfoy's like ... threatened 'em, I expect ... an' the executioner, Macnair, he's an old pal o' Malfoy's ... but it'll be quick an' clean ... an' I'll be beside him ...'

Hagrid swallowed. His eyes were darting all over the cabin, as though looking for some shred of hope or comfort.

'Dumbledore's gonna come down while it – while it happens. Wrote me this mornin'. Said he wants ter – ter be with me. Great man, Dumbledore ...'

Hermione, who had been rummaging in Hagrid's cupboard for another milk jug, let out a small, quickly stifled sob. She straightened up with the new jug in her hands, fighting back tears.

'We'll stay with you, too, Hagrid,' she began, but Hagrid shook his shaggy head.

'Yeh're ter go back up ter the castle. I told yeh, I don' wan' yeh watchin'. An' yeh shouldn' be down here anyway ... if Fudge an' Dumbledore catch yeh out without permission, Harry, yeh'll be in big trouble.'

Silent tears were now streaming down Hermione's face, but she hid them from Hagrid, bustling around making tea. Then, as she picked up the milk bottle to pour some into the jug, she let out a shriek.

'Ron! I – I don't believe it – it's *Scabbers*!'

Ron gaped at her.

'What are you talking about?'

Hermione carried the milk jug over to the table and turned it upside-down. With a frantic squeak, and much scrambling to get back inside, Scabbers the rat came sliding out onto the table.

'Scabbers!' said Ron blankly. 'Scabbers, what are you doing here?'

He grabbed the struggling rat and held him up to the light. Scabbers looked dreadful. He was thinner than ever, large tufts of hair had fallen out leaving wide bald patches, and he writhed in Ron's hands as though desperate to free himself.

'It's OK, Scabbers!' said Ron. 'No cats! There's nothing here to hurt you!'

Hagrid suddenly stood up, his eyes fixed on the window. His normally ruddy face had gone the colour of parchment.

'They're comin' ...'

Harry, Ron and Hermione whipped around. A group of men was walking down the distant castle steps. In front was Albus Dumbledore, his silver beard gleaming in the dying sun. Next to him trotted Cornelius Fudge. Behind

第16章 特里劳尼教授的预言

克没有危险，但他们害怕……你们知道卢修斯·马尔福那人……威胁过他们，我想……还有那个行刑官，麦克尼尔，他是马尔福的老朋友……不过会很快，很利落……而且我会陪在它身边……"

海格哽噎了，目光在屋中到处游移，仿佛在寻找一丝希望或安慰。

"邓布利多要过来，来——送送它。今天早上给我写了信，说他想——想陪着我。好人哪，邓布利多……"

在海格碗柜里找奶罐的赫敏发出一声轻轻的抽泣，但她迅速掩饰住了。她手捧新的罐子直起身来，强忍住眼泪。

"我们也会陪着你，海格。"她说，但海格摇了摇蓬乱的脑袋。

"你们得回城堡去。我说过，我不想让你们看见，你们本来就不该来的……如果福吉或邓布利多发现你擅自出来，哈利，你的麻烦可就大了。"

泪水无声地从赫敏的脸颊上流淌下来，但她假装忙着煮茶，没让海格看见。她拿起奶瓶往罐子里倒牛奶时，突然尖叫起来。

"罗恩！我——我不敢相信——是斑斑！"

罗恩愣愣地看着她。

"你说什么？"

赫敏把奶罐端到桌上，把它底朝上翻了过来。老鼠斑斑吱吱惊叫着滑出奶罐，小腿拼命踢蹬着想爬回去。

"斑斑！"罗恩茫然地说，"斑斑，你在这儿干什么？"

他抓住挣扎的老鼠，举到有光线的地方。斑斑的样子很吓人，比以前更瘦了，掉了很多毛，露出大块的秃斑。它在罗恩的手里扭动，好像拚命想挣脱。

"别怕，斑斑！"罗恩说，"没有猫！这儿没有东西会伤害你。"

海格突然站起来，眼睛望着窗外，红红的面孔变成了羊皮纸的颜色。

"他们来了……"

哈利、罗恩和赫敏急忙转过身。一群人远远地从城堡台阶上走下来，前面是阿不思·邓布利多，银白色的胡子在夕阳残照中闪闪发亮。旁边快步跟着康奈利·福吉，后面是那位老态龙钟的委员会成员和行刑

CHAPTER SIXTEEN   Professor Trelawney's Prediction

them came the feeble old Committee member and the executioner, Macnair.

'Yeh gotta go,' said Hagrid. Every inch of him was trembling. 'They mustn' find yeh here ... go on, now ...'

Ron stuffed Scabbers into his pocket and Hermione picked up the Cloak.

'I'll let yeh out the back way,' said Hagrid.

They followed him to the door into his back garden. Harry felt strangely unreal, and even more so when he saw Buckbeak a few yards away, tethered to a tree behind Hagrid's pumpkin patch. Buckbeak seemed to know something was happening. He turned his sharp head from side to side, and pawed the ground nervously.

'It's OK, Beaky,' said Hagrid softly. 'It's OK ...' He turned to Harry, Ron and Hermione. 'Go on,' he said. 'Get goin'.'

But they didn't move.

'Hagrid, we can't –'

'We'll tell them what really happened –'

'They can't kill him –'

'Go!' said Hagrid fiercely. 'It's bad enough without you lot in trouble an' all!'

They had no choice. As Hermione threw the Cloak over Harry and Ron, they heard voices at the front of the cabin. Hagrid looked at the place where they had just vanished from sight.

'Go quick,' he said hoarsely. 'Don' listen ...'

And he strode back into his cabin as someone knocked at the front door.

Slowly, in a kind of horrified trance, Harry, Ron and Hermione set off silently around Hagrid's house. As they reached the other side, the front door closed with a sharp snap.

'Please, let's hurry,' Hermione whispered. 'I can't stand it, I can't bear it ...'

They started up the sloping lawn towards the castle. The sun was sinking fast now; the sky had turned to a clear, purple-tinged grey, but to the west there was a ruby-red glow.

Ron stopped dead.

'Oh, please, Ron,' Hermione began.

'It's Scabbers – he won't – stay put –'

Ron was bent over, trying to keep Scabbers in his pocket, but the rat was

第16章 特里劳尼教授的预言

官麦克尼尔。

"你们快走，"海格说，他浑身都在颤抖，"不能让他们发现你们在这儿……快走……"

罗恩把斑斑塞进口袋，赫敏抓起隐形衣。

"我带你们从后面出去。"海格说。

三人跟他走到通向后园子的门口。哈利有一种奇怪的不真实感，当他看到几米之外的巴克比克时，这种感觉更加明显了。巴克比克拴在海格南瓜地后面的一棵树上，好像知道要发生什么事情似的，尖脑袋转来转去，不安地用爪子刨着地。

"没事，比克，"海格轻声说，"没事……"他又转向哈利、罗恩和赫敏说，"走吧，快走。"

但是他们没有动。

"海格，我们不能——"

"我们要向他们说明真相——"

"他们不能杀它——"

"走！"海格凶巴巴地说，"事情已经够糟的了，不要再搭上你们。"

他们别无选择，赫敏用隐形衣罩住了哈利和罗恩，这时他们已经听到前门传来了说话声。海格看着三人刚刚消失的地方。

"快走，"他嘶哑地说，"不要听……"

他大步走进小屋，这时，前门被敲响了。

哈利、罗恩和赫敏仿佛被吓傻了，默默地从海格的屋后绕过。他们走到前面时，前门啪的一声关上了。

"求求你们，快走吧，"赫敏小声说，"我受不了，受不了……"

三人顺着倾斜的草坪走向城堡。夕阳在迅速下沉，天空变成了澄净的灰紫色，但西天还有一抹红宝石般的光亮。

罗恩突然停了下来。

"哦，求求你，罗恩。"赫敏说。

"是斑斑——它不肯——老实待着——"

罗恩弯下腰，想把斑斑捂在口袋里，可是小老鼠变得躁动不安，

CHAPTER SIXTEEN — Professor Trelawney's Prediction

going berserk; squeaking madly, twisting and flailing, trying to sink his teeth into Ron's hand.

'Scabbers, it's me, you idiot, it's Ron,' Ron hissed.

They heard a door open behind them and men's voices.

'Oh Ron, please let's move, they're going to do it!' Hermione breathed.

'OK – Scabbers, stay *put* –'

They walked forwards; Harry, like Hermione, was trying not to listen to the rumble of voices behind them. Ron stopped again.

'I can't hold him – Scabbers, shut up, everyone'll hear us –'

The rat was squealing wildly, but not loudly enough to cover up the sounds drifting from Hagrid's garden. There was a jumble of indistinct male voices, a silence and then, without warning, the unmistakeable swish and thud of an axe.

Hermione swayed on the spot.

'They did it!' she whispered to Harry. 'I d-don't believe it – they did it!'

疯狂地尖叫着，使劲扭动，想去咬罗恩的手。

"斑斑，是我呀，你这笨蛋，我是罗恩。"罗恩小声说。

他们听到身后传来开门声和说话声。

"哦，罗恩，咱们快走吧，他们要下手了！"赫敏悄声央求。

"好吧——斑斑，老实待着——"

三人继续前行。哈利跟赫敏一样，努力不去听身后的话语声。罗恩又停住了。

"我按不住它——斑斑，闭嘴，人家会听见的——"

老鼠疯狂地尖叫，但盖不过海格后园子里传来的声音。几个男人的说话声混杂在一起，接着是一阵沉默。随后，突然地，他们分明听到了呼的一声和斧子落下的闷响。

赫敏在原地摇晃了一下。

"他们下手了！"她小声对哈利说，"我——不敢相信——他们下手了！"

CHAPTER SEVENTEEN

Cat, Rat and Dog

Harry's mind had gone blank with shock. The three of them stood transfixed with horror under the Invisibility Cloak. The very last rays of the setting sun were casting a bloody light over the long-shadowed grounds. Then, behind them, they heard a wild howling.

'Hagrid,' Harry muttered. Without thinking about what he was doing, he made to turn back, but both Ron and Hermione seized his arms.

'We can't,' said Ron, who was paper white. 'He'll be in worse trouble if they know we've been to see him ...'

Hermione's breathing was shallow and uneven.

'How – could – they?' she choked. 'How *could* they?'

'Come on,' said Ron, whose teeth seemed to be chattering.

They set off back towards the castle, walking slowly to keep themselves hidden under the Cloak. Light was fading fast now. By the time they reached open ground, darkness was settling like a spell around them.

'Scabbers, keep still,' Ron hissed, clamping his hand over his chest. The rat was wriggling madly. Ron came to a sudden halt, trying to force Scabbers deeper into his pocket. 'What's the matter with you, you stupid rat? Stay still – OUCH! He bit me!'

'Ron, be quiet!' Hermione whispered urgently. 'Fudge'll be out here in a minute –'

'He won't – stay – put –'

Scabbers was plainly terrified. He was writhing with all his might, trying to break free of Ron's grip.

'What's the *matter* with him?'

But Harry had just seen – slinking towards them, his body low to the ground, wide yellow eyes glinting eerily in the darkness – Crookshanks.

第 17 章

猫、老鼠和狗

哈利也很震惊，脑子里一片空白。三人恐惧地呆立在隐形衣下。落日最后的余晖给场地涂上了血红的光，投下长长的阴影。然后，他们听到身后传来一声狂嗥。

"海格。"哈利低声说，不假思索地就要转身，但罗恩和赫敏抓住了他的胳膊。

"不行，"罗恩说，脸色苍白如纸，"要是让他们知道我们去看过海格，他会更倒霉的……"

赫敏呼吸急促不匀。

"他们——怎么——能？"她哽咽道，"怎么能？"

"走吧。"罗恩说，他的牙齿好像在打架。

他们继续朝城堡走去，走得很慢，以确保一直能藏在隐形衣下。光线消失得很快，等他们走到场地上时，黑暗像符咒一样罩住了他们。

"斑斑，安静！"罗恩用手紧捂着胸口，小声说。老鼠疯狂地扭动着，罗恩突然停住脚，想把斑斑往口袋里塞得更深一些。"你怎么了，你这只笨老鼠？待着别动——哎哟！它咬我！"

"罗恩，别出声！"赫敏着急地悄声说，"福吉马上就会出来了——"

"它不肯——老实——待着——"

斑斑显然是吓坏了，拼命挣扎着，想从罗恩手中挣脱。

"它是怎么啦？"

但是哈利刚才看见了，克鲁克山悄无声息地向他们走来，身体低低地贴近地面，两只大大的黄眼睛在黑暗中闪着诡异的荧光。哈利不

CHAPTER SEVENTEEN Cat, Rat and Dog

Whether he could see them, or was following the sound of Scabbers's squeaks, Harry couldn't tell.

'Crookshanks!' Hermione moaned. 'No, go away, Crookshanks! Go away!'

But the cat was getting nearer –

'Scabbers – NO!'

Too late – the rat had slipped between Ron's clutching fingers, hit the ground and scampered away. In one bound, Crookshanks sprang after him, and before Harry or Hermione could stop him, Ron had thrown the Invisibility Cloak off himself and pelted away into the darkness.

'*Ron*!' Hermione moaned.

She and Harry looked at each other, then followed at a sprint; it was impossible to run full out under the Cloak; they pulled it off and it streamed behind them like a banner as they hurtled after Ron; they could hear his feet thundering along ahead, and his shouts at Crookshanks.

'Get away from him – get away – Scabbers, come *here* –'

There was a loud thud.

'*Gotcha!* Get off, you stinking cat –'

Harry and Hermione almost fell over Ron; they skidded to a stop right in front of him. He was sprawled on the ground, but Scabbers was back in his pocket; he had both hands held tight over the quivering lump.

'Ron – come on – back under the Cloak –' Hermione panted. 'Dumbledore – the Minister – they'll be coming back out in a minute –'

But before they could cover themselves again, before they could even catch their breath, they heard the soft pounding of gigantic paws. Something was bounding towards them out of the dark – an enormous, pale-eyed, jet-black dog.

Harry reached for his wand, but too late – the dog had made an enormous leap and its front paws hit him on the chest. He keeled over backwards in a whirl of hair; he felt its hot breath, saw inch-long teeth –

But the force of its leap had carried it too far; it rolled off him; dazed, feeling as though his ribs were broken, Harry tried to stand up; he could hear it growling as it skidded around for a new attack.

Ron was on his feet. As the dog sprang back towards them, he pushed Harry aside; the dog's jaws fastened instead around Ron's outstretched arm. Harry lunged at it and seized a handful of the brute's hair, but it was

知道它是看到了他们，还是循着斑斑的叫声过来的。

"克鲁克山！"赫敏叹息道，"别捣乱，走开，克鲁克山！走开！"

但是猫越来越近——

"斑斑——**不要！**"

太晚了——老鼠从罗恩的指缝间钻了出去，掉到地上，飞快地逃走了。克鲁克山一跃而上，紧追不舍。哈利和赫敏没有来得及阻拦，罗恩已经甩开隐形衣，冲入了夜幕中。

"罗恩！"赫敏轻声哀叫。

她和哈利对视一下，拔腿追了上去。披着隐形衣跑不快，他们便把它扯了下来，隐形衣像旗帜一样在身后飘扬，两人全速追赶罗恩，能听到前面咚咚的脚步声，还听到罗恩呵斥克鲁克山的声音。

"走开——走开——斑斑，到这儿来——"

很响的扑通一声。

"抓到了！滚开，你这只臭猫——"

哈利和赫敏差点儿摔到罗恩身上，两人刚好在他跟前刹住脚步。罗恩横在地上，斑斑已回到他的口袋里，他双手紧攥着那团颤抖的东西。

"罗恩——快——回到隐形衣里来——"赫敏气喘吁吁地说，"邓布利多——还有部长——他们马上就要出来了——"

但是他们还没来得及隐身，也没来得及把气喘匀，就听到巨爪轻轻着地的响声……有东西从黑暗中在朝他们奔来——是一条庞大的、灰色眼睛的黑狗。

哈利伸手去拔魔杖，但是太晚了——大狗高高跃起，前爪撞到了他胸口，哈利在一团狗毛中向后倒去，感觉到狗嘴里喷出的热气，看到了那寸把长的尖牙——

大狗扑过来时力气过猛，从他身上滚了过去。哈利觉得自己好像断了几根肋骨，努力想站起来；他听到大狗咆哮着掉转过身，准备再次袭击。

罗恩站了起来，在大狗又扑上来时把哈利推到一边。大狗咬住了罗恩伸出来的胳膊。哈利冲上去揪住那畜生的一撮毛，但它像拖一个

CHAPTER SEVENTEEN — Cat, Rat and Dog

dragging Ron away as easily as if he were a rag-doll –

Then, out of nowhere, something hit Harry so hard across the face he was knocked off his feet again. He heard Hermione shriek with pain and fall, too. Harry groped for his wand, blinking blood out of his eyes –

'*Lumos!*' he whispered.

The wand-light showed him the trunk of a thick tree; they had chased Scabbers into the shadow of the Whomping Willow and its branches were creaking as though in a high wind, whipping backwards and forwards to stop them going nearer.

And there, at the base of the trunk, was the dog, dragging Ron backwards into a large gap in the roots – Ron was fighting furiously, but his head and torso were slipping out of sight –

'Ron!' Harry shouted, trying to follow, but a heavy branch whipped lethally through the air and he was forced backwards again.

All they could see now was one of Ron's legs, which he had hooked around a root in an effort to stop the dog pulling him further underground. Then a horrible crack cut the air like a gunshot; Ron's leg had broken, and next second, his foot had vanished from sight.

'Harry – we've got to go for help –' Hermione cried; she was bleeding, too; the Willow had cut her across the shoulder.

'No! That thing's big enough to eat him, we haven't got time –'

'We're never going to get through without help –'

Another branch whipped down at them, twigs clenched like knuckles.

'If that dog can get in, we can,' Harry panted, darting here and there, trying to find a way through the vicious, swishing branches, but he couldn't get an inch nearer to the tree-roots without being in range of the tree's blows.

'Oh, help, help,' Hermione whispered frantically, dancing uncertainly on the spot, 'please …'

Crookshanks darted forwards. He slithered between the battering branches like a snake and placed his front paws upon a knot on the trunk.

Abruptly, as though the tree had been turned to marble, it stopped moving. Not a leaf twitched or shook.

'Crookshanks!' Hermione whispered uncertainly. She now grasped Harry's arm painfully hard. 'How did he know –?'

'He's friends with that dog,' said Harry grimly. 'I've seen them together.

第17章 猫、老鼠和狗

布娃娃一样毫不费力地把罗恩拖走了。

突然,哈利脸上挨了不知从何而来的重重一击,他又摔倒在地,同时听到赫敏喊痛和倒地的声音。哈利摸到了魔杖,眨了眨眼睛挤掉血水——

"荧光闪烁!"他低声说。

魔杖的荧光照出一棵粗大的树干,原来他们追着斑斑跑到了打人柳的树影里。柳条像在狂风中一样嘎吱作响,鞭子似的来回抽打,不让他们走近。

那大狗就在树干旁边,正在把罗恩倒拖进树根间的一个大洞——罗恩奋力挣扎,但是他的脑袋和上半身正在消失——

"罗恩!"哈利大叫,想要冲过去,可是一根粗树枝凶险地在空中抽打着,逼得他退了回来。

现在他们只能看到罗恩的一条腿了。罗恩用腿钩住了一条树根,希望能阻止大狗把他拖入地下——然而,啪的一声可怕的脆响,像枪声划破夜空,罗恩的腿断了。一眨眼间,他的脚也消失了。

"哈利——我们必须去找人帮忙——"赫敏惊恐地叫着,她也在流血,柳条在她肩上抽了一道口子。

"不行!那畜生大得能把他吃掉,我们来不及——"

"哈利——没有人帮忙,我们不可能钻过去——"

又一根枝条打下来,细枝子像拳头一样攥得紧紧的。

"那条狗能进去,我们也能。"哈利喘着气说,一边左冲右突,试图绕过那些带着恶意嗖嗖摆动的枝条,可怎么也躲不过;他若想再靠近树根一寸,就肯定被打到。

"哦,救命,救命,"赫敏绝望地低喊,在原地团团转,"求求……"

克鲁克山飞奔上前,像蛇一样从舞动的枝条间钻过去,把前爪按在树身的一个节疤上。

那棵树突然不动了,好像化成了石头,连树叶都不再抖动一下。

"克鲁克山!"赫敏惊疑地轻轻叫道,她把哈利的胳膊都攥痛了,"它怎么知道——?"

"它跟那条狗是朋友,"哈利沉着脸说,"我见过它们在一起。走

CHAPTER SEVENTEEN   Cat, Rat and Dog

Come on – and keep your wand out –'

They covered the distance to the trunk in seconds, but before they had reached the gap in the roots, Crookshanks had slid into it with a flick of his bottle-brush tail. Harry went next; he crawled forwards, head first, and slid down an earthy slope to the bottom of a very low tunnel. Crookshanks was a little way along, his eyes flashing in the light from Harry's wand. Seconds later, Hermione slithered down beside him.

'Where's Ron?' she whispered in a terrified voice.

'This way,' said Harry, setting off, bent-backed, after Crookshanks.

'Where does this tunnel come out?' Hermione asked breathlessly from behind him.

'I don't know ... it's marked on the Marauder's Map but Fred and George said no one's ever got into it. It goes off the edge of the map, but it looked like it ends up in Hogsmeade ...'

They moved as fast as they could, bent almost double; ahead of them, Crookshanks's tail bobbed in and out of view. On and on went the passage; it felt at least as long as the one to Honeydukes. All Harry could think of was Ron, and what the enormous dog might be doing to him ... he was drawing breath in sharp, painful gasps, running at a crouch ...

And then the tunnel began to rise; moments later it twisted, and Crookshanks had gone. Instead, Harry could see a patch of dim light through a small opening.

He and Hermione paused, gasping for breath, edging forwards. Both raised their wands to see what lay beyond.

It was a room, a very disordered, dusty room. Paper was peeling from the walls; there were stains all over the floor; every piece of furniture was broken as though somebody had smashed it. The windows were all boarded-up.

Harry glanced at Hermione, who looked very frightened, but nodded.

Harry pulled himself out of the hole, staring around. The room was deserted, but a door to their right stood open, leading to a shadowy hallway. Hermione suddenly grabbed Harry's arm again. Her wide eyes were travelling around the boarded windows.

'Harry,' she whispered. 'I think we're in the Shrieking Shack.'

Harry looked around. His eyes fell on a wooden chair near them. Large chunks had been torn out of it; one of the legs had been ripped off entirely.

第 17 章 猫、老鼠和狗

吧——把魔杖拿在手里——"

几秒钟内,两人就冲到了树干旁,但是还没走到树根间的那个洞口,克鲁克山就已经把毛茸茸的尾巴轻轻一弹,钻进了洞里。哈利跟了进去,头朝前往里面爬,顺着土坡滑入了一条非常低矮的地道底部。克鲁克山在前方不远处,一双猫眼在哈利魔杖的微光中闪烁。几秒钟后,赫敏也滑到了哈利的身边。

"罗恩呢?"她低声问,声音中带着恐惧。

"这边。"哈利说,弯着腰跟上了克鲁克山。

"这条地道通到哪儿?"赫敏在后面屏着气问。

"不知道……活点地图上有这条通道,但弗雷德和乔治说从来没人进来过……它出了地图的边缘,但看上去可能通到霍格莫德……"

两人尽可能地快速前进,腰弯得很低。克鲁克山的尾巴在前面忽隐忽现。地道不断向前延伸,感觉至少跟通到蜂蜜公爵的那条一样长……哈利一心惦记着罗恩,不知道大狗会对他怎么样……他痛苦地用力张口吸气,猫着腰急跑……

地道开始向上倾斜,过了一会儿,拐了个弯,克鲁克山不见了。哈利只看到一片微光,是个小小的出口。

他和赫敏停住脚步,喘着气,慢慢地侧身向前挪动,两人都举着魔杖,想看清前面有什么。

是一个房间,一个乱糟糟、灰蒙蒙的房间。墙纸剥落,满地污渍,家具全是破的,好像被人砸过,窗户都用木板封住了。

哈利看看赫敏,她神色非常恐惧,但点了点头。

哈利从洞口钻了过去,环顾四周。房间里没有人,右边有一扇门开着,通到一个幽暗的门厅。赫敏又一把抓住哈利的胳膊,瞪大眼睛扫视着被封住的窗户。

"哈利,"她小声说,"我想我们是在尖叫棚屋。"

哈利的目光在屋里扫了一圈,落到近处的一把木椅上,它的木板被扯去了一大块,一条腿也不见了。

CHAPTER SEVENTEEN Cat, Rat and Dog

'Ghosts didn't do that,' he said slowly.

At that moment, there was a creak overhead. Something had moved upstairs. Both of them looked up at the ceiling. Hermione's grip on Harry's arm was so tight he was losing feeling in his fingers. He raised his eyebrows at her; she nodded again and let go.

Quietly as they could, they crept out into the hall and up the crumbling staircase. Everything was covered in a thick layer of dust except the floor, where a wide, shiny stripe had been made by something being dragged upstairs.

They reached the dark landing.

'*Nox*,' they whispered together, and the lights at the end of their wands went out. Only one door was open. As they crept towards it, they heard movement from behind it; a low moan, and then a deep, loud purring. They exchanged a last look, a last nod.

Wand held tightly before him, Harry kicked the door wide open.

On a magnificent four-poster bed with dusty hangings, lay Crookshanks, purring loudly at the sight of them. On the floor beside him, clutching his leg, which stuck out at a strange angle, was Ron.

Harry and Hermione dashed across to him.

'Ron – are you OK?'

'Where's the dog?'

'Not a dog,' Ron moaned. His teeth were gritted with pain. 'Harry, it's a trap –'

'What –'

'*He's the dog ... he's an Animagus ...*'

Ron was staring over Harry's shoulder. Harry wheeled around. With a snap, the man in the shadows closed the door behind them.

A mass of filthy, matted hair hung to his elbows. If eyes hadn't been shining out of the deep, dark sockets, he might have been a corpse. The waxy skin was stretched so tightly over the bones of his face, it looked like a skull. His yellow teeth were bared in a grin. It was Sirius Black.

'*Expelliarmus!*' he croaked, pointing Ron's wand at them.

Harry's and Hermione's wands shot out of their hands, high in the air, and Black caught them. Then he took a step closer. His eyes were fixed on Harry.

'I thought you'd come and help your friend,' he said hoarsely. His voice

第 17 章　猫、老鼠和狗

"不是幽灵干的。"哈利缓缓说道。

这时头顶上传来嘎吱一响，楼上有什么东西在动。两人抬头望着天花板。哈利的胳膊被赫敏攥得紧紧的，手指都开始失去知觉了。他对赫敏扬扬眉毛，赫敏点点头，放开了手。

他们尽可能轻手轻脚地来到厅里，踏上那道快要倒塌的楼梯。到处都蒙着厚厚的灰尘，只是地上有一条宽宽的发亮的印子，好像什么东西被拖上楼去了。

两人走到黑暗的楼梯平台上。

"诺克斯。"他们同时小声说，杖头的荧光应声熄灭。只有一扇门开着，他们轻轻走近时，听到门后面有动静，一声低低的呻吟，接着是响亮、深沉的猫叫。两人最后对视了一眼，点了点头。

哈利紧握魔杖，猛地踢开了门。

一张挂着灰扑扑帷帐的四柱大床，克鲁克山伏在床上冲他们喵喵大叫。罗恩坐在床边的地板上，抱着他那条姿势很别扭的伤腿。

哈利和赫敏冲了过去。

"罗恩——你怎么样？"

"大狗呢？"

"没有狗。"罗恩呻吟道，痛得咬紧牙关，"哈利，这是个圈套——"

"什么？"

"他就是那条狗……他是个阿尼马格斯……"

罗恩瞪着哈利身后，哈利迅疾转身，阴影中的那个男子啪地关上了他们身后的房门。

肮脏的乱发垂到胳膊肘，如果不是深陷的黑色眼窝里那双眼睛的亮光，他简直就像一具死尸。蜡白的皮肤紧绷在颧骨上，像个骷髅。他咧嘴狞笑着，露出一口黄牙。是小天狼星布莱克。

"除你武器！"他嘶声叫道，用罗恩的魔杖朝他们一指。

哈利和赫敏的魔杖脱手而出，高高飞到空中，布莱克将它们接住，然后走近一步，眼睛盯着哈利。

"我料到你会来救你的朋友。"他嗓音嘶哑，好像很久不用了，"你

sounded as though he had long ago lost the habit of using it. 'Your father would have done the same for me. Brave of you, not to run for a teacher. I'm grateful ... it will make everything much easier ...'

The taunt about his father rang in Harry's ears as though Black had bellowed it. A boiling hate erupted in Harry's chest, leaving no place for fear. For the first time in his life, he wanted his wand back in his hand, not to defend himself, but to attack ... to kill. Without knowing what he was doing, he started forwards, but there was a sudden movement on either side of him and two pairs of hands grabbed him and held him back. 'No, Harry!' Hermione gasped in a petrified whisper; Ron, however, spoke to Black.

'If you want to kill Harry, you'll have to kill us, too!' he said fiercely, though the effort of standing up had drained him of still more colour, and he swayed slightly as he spoke.

Something flickered in Black's shadowed eyes.

'Lie down,' he said quietly to Ron. 'You will damage that leg even more.'

'Did you hear me?' Ron said weakly, though he was clinging painfully to Harry to stay upright. 'You'll have to kill all three of us!'

'There'll only be one murder here tonight,' said Black, and his grin widened.

'Why's that?' Harry spat, trying to wrench himself free of Ron and Hermione. 'Didn't care last time, did you? Didn't mind slaughtering all those Muggles to get at Pettigrew ... What's the matter, gone soft in Azkaban?'

'Harry!' Hermione whimpered. 'Be quiet!'

'HE KILLED MY MUM AND DAD!' Harry roared, and with a huge effort he broke free of Hermione and Ron's restraint and lunged forwards –

He had forgotten about magic – he had forgotten that he was short and skinny and thirteen, whereas Black was a tall, full-grown man. All Harry knew was that he wanted to hurt Black as badly as he could and that he didn't care how much he got hurt in return ...

Perhaps it was the shock of Harry doing something so stupid, but Black didn't raise the wands in time. One of Harry's hands fastened over Black's wasted wrist, forcing the wandtips away; the knuckles of Harry's other hand collided with the side of Black's head and they fell, backwards, into the wall –

Hermione was screaming; Ron was yelling; there was a blinding flash as the wands in Black's hand sent into the air a jet of sparks which missed

第 17 章 猫、老鼠和狗

父亲也会这样对我的。你们很勇敢,没跑去找老师。我很感激……这样就好办多了……"

哈利耳边回响着对他父亲的嘲讽,仿佛是布莱克大声吼出来的一般。一股憎恨从哈利胸中腾起,把恐惧挤了出去。他希望夺回魔杖,平生第一次不是为了自卫,而是为了攻击……为了杀人。他下意识地冲向前去,但两边都有人扑上来,两双手紧紧拽住了他……"不要,哈利!"赫敏恐惧地小声说。罗恩则冲着布莱克说话了。

"你要杀哈利,就必须把我们也杀掉!"他情绪激烈地说,虽然勉强站起时脸上更是血色全无,身体也在微微摇晃。

布莱克阴郁的眼睛里有什么一闪。

"躺下,"他平静地对罗恩说,"你会把那条腿伤得更重的。"

"你听见了吗?"罗恩虚弱地说,一边忍痛抓住哈利保持站立,"你必须把我们三个全部杀掉!"

"今晚这里只会有一人被杀。"布莱克的嘴咧得更开了。

"为什么?"哈利愤愤地说,试图挣脱罗恩和赫敏的阻拦,"你上次可不在乎,是不是?为了追杀小矮星不惜屠杀那么多的麻瓜……怎么,在阿兹卡班把心肠蹲软了?"

"哈利!"赫敏急叫,"别说了!"

"他杀了我的爸爸妈妈!" 哈利吼道,奋力挣脱了赫敏和罗恩,一个箭步冲了上去。

他忘记了魔法,忘记了自己又瘦又小只有十三岁,而布莱克是个高大的成年人。哈利此刻只想拼足全力重创布莱克,而不顾自己会受多大的伤——

也许是对哈利做出这样愚蠢的举动感到吃惊,布莱克没有及时举起魔杖。哈利一只手抓住了他瘦骨嶙峋的手腕,迫使杖尖指向别处,同时一拳打在布莱克的脑袋侧面,然后两人一起向后摔倒,撞在了墙上——

赫敏尖叫,罗恩大喊,在一阵令人目眩的闪光中,布莱克手中的两根魔杖射出一串火星,险些击中哈利的面部。哈利感到那皱缩的手

CHAPTER SEVENTEEN   Cat, Rat and Dog

Harry's face by inches; Harry felt the shrunken arm under his fingers twisting madly, but he clung on, his other hand punching every part of Black it could find.

But Black's free hand had found Harry's throat –

'No,' he hissed. 'I've waited too long –'

The fingers tightened, Harry choked, his glasses askew.

Then he saw Hermione's foot swing out of nowhere. Black let go of Harry with a grunt of pain. Ron had thrown himself on Black's wand hand and Harry heard a faint clatter –

He fought free of the tangle of bodies and saw his own wand rolling across the floor; he threw himself towards it but –

'Argh!'

Crookshanks had joined the fray; both sets of front claws had sunk themselves deep into Harry's arm; Harry threw him off, but Crookshanks now darted towards Harry's wand –

'NO YOU DON'T!' roared Harry, and he aimed a kick at Crookshanks that made the cat leap aside, spitting; Harry snatched up his wand and turned –

'Get out of the way!' he shouted at Ron and Hermione.

They didn't need telling twice. Hermione, gasping for breath, her lip bleeding, scrambled aside, snatching up her and Ron's wands. Ron crawled to the four-poster and collapsed onto it, panting, his white face now tinged with green, both hands clutching his broken leg.

Black was sprawled at the bottom of the wall. His thin chest rose and fell rapidly as he watched Harry walking slowly nearer, his wand pointing straight at Black's heart.

'Going to kill me, Harry?' he whispered.

Harry stopped right above him, his wand still pointing at Black's chest, looking down at him. A livid bruise was rising around Black's left eye and his nose was bleeding.

'You killed my parents,' said Harry, his voice shaking slightly, but his wand hand quite steady.

Black stared up at him out of those sunken eyes.

'I don't deny it,' he said, very quietly. 'But if you knew the whole story –'

'The whole story?' Harry repeated, a furious pounding in his ears. 'You

第17章 猫、老鼠和狗

臂在他手指下疯狂地挣扎,但他紧紧抓住不放,另一只手猛击布莱克身上他能打到的每一个地方。

可是布莱克的另一只手摸到了哈利的喉咙——

"不,"他嘶声说,"我等得太久了——"

手指卡紧了,哈利呼吸困难,眼镜歪到了一边。

在这危急关头,他看到赫敏的脚凌空飞来。布莱克痛得哼了一声,放开了哈利。罗恩扑向布莱克那只拿着魔杖的手,哈利听到哗啦一声轻响——

他挣扎着从纠缠在一起的人堆中爬出来,看见自己的魔杖滚到地上,连忙扑过去,然而——

"啊!"

克鲁克山来助战了,两只前爪深深扎进哈利的手臂。哈利把它甩掉,但克鲁克山又扑向哈利的魔杖——

"没门儿!"哈利吼道,朝克鲁克山踹了一脚,猫跳到一边,喷着唾沫。哈利抓起魔杖转过身来——

"闪开!"他朝罗恩和赫敏大喊。

他们俩不需要他再说第二遍。赫敏嘴唇流血,大口喘气,迅速爬到一边,拾起她和罗恩的魔杖。罗恩爬向四柱床,气喘吁吁地瘫倒在上面,双手抱着断腿,苍白的面孔有些发青。

布莱克倒在墙根,瘦削的胸部急速起伏,他看着哈利慢慢走近,魔杖直指他的心脏。

"要杀我吗,哈利?"他低声问。

哈利在他跟前停下了,俯视着他,魔杖依然指着他的胸膛。布莱克的左眼周围肿起一块青瘀,鼻子也流血了。

"你杀了我的爸爸妈妈。"哈利说,声音微微颤抖,但握着魔杖的手很坚定。

布莱克用深陷的眼睛盯着他。

"我不否认,"他声音很轻,"但如果你知道全部经过——"

"全部经过?"哈利重复了一遍,感觉耳朵里有热血在撞击,"你

CHAPTER SEVENTEEN Cat, Rat and Dog

sold them to Voldemort, that's all I need to know!'

'You've got to listen to me,' Black said, and there was a note of urgency in his voice now. 'You'll regret it if you don't ... you don't understand ...'

'I understand a lot better than you think,' said Harry, and his voice shook more than ever. 'You never heard her, did you? My mum ... trying to stop Voldemort killing me ... and you did that ... you did it ...'

Before either of them could say another word, something ginger streaked past Harry; Crookshanks leapt onto Black's chest, and settled himself there, right over Black's heart. Black blinked and looked down at the cat.

'Get off,' he murmured, trying to push Crookshanks off him.

But Crookshanks sank his claws into Black's robes and wouldn't shift. He turned his ugly, squashed face to Harry, and looked up at him with those great yellow eyes. To his right, Hermione gave a dry sob.

Harry stared down at Black and Crookshanks, his grip tightening on the wand. So what if he had to kill the cat, too? It was in league with Black ... if it was prepared to die, trying to protect Black, that wasn't Harry's business ... if Black wanted to save it, that only proved he cared more for Crookshanks than Harry's parents ...

Harry raised the wand. Now was the moment to do it. Now was the moment to avenge his mother and father. He was going to kill Black. He had to kill Black. This was his chance ...

The seconds lengthened, and still Harry stood frozen there, wand poised, Black staring up at him, Crookshanks on his chest. Ron's ragged breathing came from the bed; Hermione was quite silent.

And then came a new sound –

Muffled footsteps were echoing up through the floor – someone was moving downstairs.

'WE'RE UP HERE!' Hermione screamed suddenly. 'WE'RE UP HERE – SIRIUS BLACK – QUICK!'

Black made a startled movement that almost dislodged Crookshanks; Harry gripped his wand convulsively – *Do it now!* said a voice in his head – but the footsteps were thundering up the stairs and Harry still hadn't done it.

The door of the room burst open in a shower of red sparks and Harry wheeled around as Professor Lupin came hurtling into the room, his face bloodless, his wand raised and ready. His eyes flickered over Ron, lying on

第17章 猫、老鼠和狗

把他们出卖给了伏地魔。我只需要知道这么多。"

"你必须听我说，"布莱克说，语气有些急迫，"不然你会后悔的……你不知道……"

"我知道的比你想象的多得多。"哈利说，声音颤抖得更厉害了，"你没听过她的恳求，是不是？我的妈妈……她想阻止伏地魔杀我……而你做了那种事……你做了……"

两人还没来得及多说什么，突然，一个姜黄色的东西从哈利身边闪过，克鲁克山跳到布莱克的胸口伏了下来，正好挡住他的心脏。布莱克惊奇地眨眨眼睛，低头看着那只猫。

"下去。"他咕哝着，想把克鲁克山推开。

但是克鲁克山用爪子抠住布莱克的袍子，不肯挪动。它把丑陋的扁脸转向哈利，大大的黄眼睛望着他。在哈利右边，赫敏抽了一下鼻子。

哈利盯着布莱克和克鲁克山，攥紧了魔杖。就算把这只猫也杀了又怎么样？这只猫是布莱克的同盟……如果它为了保护布莱克而自愿送死，那不关哈利的事……如果布莱克想救猫，那只能证明他关心克鲁克山胜于关心哈利的父母……

哈利举起了魔杖。时候到了，为父母报仇的时候到了，他要杀死布莱克，必须杀死布莱克，这是他的机会……

漫长的几秒钟，哈利仍举着魔杖僵立在那里，布莱克盯着哈利，克鲁克山蹲在他胸口。罗恩粗重的呼吸声从床上传来，赫敏沉默不语。

然后传来了一个新的声音——

闷闷的脚步声透过地板缝隙传上来，有人在楼下走动。

"**我们在上面！**"赫敏突然尖叫道，"**我们在上面——小天狼星布莱克——快来呀！**"

布莱克惊得动了一下，几乎把克鲁克山甩下去。哈利的手痉挛地握紧魔杖——快动手！一个声音在他脑子里说，但脚步声已咚咚地上了楼梯，哈利还是没有动手。

门砰地开了，红色的火星四下迸射。哈利急忙转身，卢平教授冲了进来，面无血色，手举魔杖。他的目光掠过躺在地上的罗恩，掠过

497

CHAPTER SEVENTEEN Cat, Rat and Dog

the floor, over Hermione, cowering next to the door, to Harry, standing there with his wand covering Black, and then to Black himself, crumpled and bleeding at Harry's feet.

'*Expelliarmus!*' Lupin shouted.

Harry's wand flew once more out of his hand; so did the two Hermione was holding. Lupin caught them all deftly, then moved into the room, staring at Black, who still had Crookshanks lying protectively across his chest.

Harry stood there, feeling suddenly empty. He hadn't done it. His nerve had failed him. Black was going to be handed back to the Dementors.

Then Lupin spoke, in an odd voice, a voice that shook with some suppressed emotion. 'Where is he, Sirius?'

Harry looked quickly at Lupin. He didn't understand what Lupin meant. Who was Lupin talking about? He turned to look at Black again.

Black's face was quite expressionless. For a few seconds, he didn't move at all. Then, very slowly, he raised his empty hand, and pointed straight at Ron. Mystified, Harry glanced around at Ron, who looked bewildered.

'But then ...' Lupin muttered, staring at Black so intently it seemed he was trying to read his mind, '... why hasn't he shown himself before now? Unless –' Lupin's eyes suddenly widened, as though he was seeing something beyond Black, something none of the rest could see, '– unless *he* was the one ... unless you switched ... without telling me?'

Very slowly, his sunken gaze never leaving Lupin's face, Black nodded.

'Professor Lupin,' Harry interrupted loudly, 'what's going –?'

But he never finished the question, because what he saw made his voice die in his throat. Lupin was lowering his wand. Next moment, he had walked to Black's side, seized his hand, pulled him to his feet so that Crookshanks fell to the floor, and embraced Black like a brother.

Harry felt as though the bottom had dropped out of his stomach.

'I DON'T BELIEVE IT!' Hermione screamed.

Lupin let go of Black and turned to her. She had raised herself off the floor, and was pointing at Lupin, wild-eyed. 'You – you –'

'Hermione –'

'– you and him!'

第 17 章　猫、老鼠和狗

畏缩在门边的赫敏，掠过站在那儿用魔杖指着布莱克的哈利，落到瘫在哈利脚边的流着血的布莱克身上。

"除你武器！"卢平喊道。

哈利的魔杖再次脱手飞出，赫敏拿着的那两根也飞了出去。卢平敏捷地接住它们，然后走到屋子中间，盯着布莱克，克鲁克山仍然趴在布莱克的胸口保护着他。

哈利站在那儿，突然感到极度空虚。他没有报仇，他胆量不够。布莱克将被交给摄魂怪了。

这时卢平说话了，声音很奇怪，因压抑着某种情感而颤抖。"他在哪儿，小天狼星？"

哈利迅速望向卢平，不明白他的意思，说的是谁？他又回头看着布莱克。

布莱克面无表情，几秒钟里，他一动不动。然后，他非常缓慢地举起一只空着的手，直指罗恩。哈利莫名其妙，目光移到罗恩身上，罗恩也一脸迷惑。

"可是……"卢平低声说，目光紧盯着布莱克，仿佛要看穿他的思想，"……他为什么以前一直没有现身？除非——"卢平的眼睛突然瞪大了，仿佛看到了布莱克身后的什么东西，而其他人都看不到，"除非他就是那个……除非你换了……没有告诉我？"

布莱克凹陷的双眼一直盯着卢平的面孔，缓缓地点了点头。

"卢平教授，"哈利大声打断了卢平的话，"这是怎么——？"

但他没有说完，因为眼前的情景使他的声音消失在了嗓子眼里。卢平垂下魔杖，然后走到布莱克身边，抓住他的手，把他拉了起来，克鲁克山落到地上。卢平教授像拥抱兄弟一般拥抱了布莱克。

哈利觉得自己的心重重地往下一沉。

"**我不相信！**"赫敏尖叫。

卢平放开布莱克，朝她转过身。赫敏已经从地上站了起来，指着卢平，眼睛睁得大大的："你——你——"

"赫敏——"

"——你和他！"

CHAPTER SEVENTEEN Cat, Rat and Dog

'Hermione, calm down –'

'I didn't tell anyone!' Hermione shrieked. 'I've been covering up for you –'

'Hermione, listen to me, please!' Lupin shouted. 'I can explain –'

Harry could feel himself shaking, not with fear, but with a fresh wave of fury.

'I trusted you,' he shouted at Lupin, his voice wavering out of control, 'and all the time you've been his friend!'

'You're wrong,' said Lupin. 'I haven't been Sirius' friend for twelve years, but I am now ... let me explain ...'

'NO!' Hermione screamed, 'Harry, don't trust him, he's been helping Black get into the castle, he wants you dead too – *he's a werewolf!*'

There was a ringing silence. Everyone's eyes were now on Lupin, who looked remarkably calm, though rather pale.

'Not at all up to your usual standard, Hermione,' he said. 'Only one out of three, I'm afraid. I have not been helping Sirius get into the castle and I certainly don't want Harry dead ...' An odd shiver passed over his face. 'But I won't deny that I am a werewolf.'

Ron made a valiant effort to get up again, but fell back with a whimper of pain. Lupin made towards him, looking concerned, but Ron gasped, '*Get away from me, werewolf!*'

Lupin stopped dead. Then, with an obvious effort, he turned to Hermione and said, 'How long have you known?'

'Ages,' Hermione whispered. 'Since I did Professor Snape's essay ...'

'He'll be delighted,' said Lupin coolly. 'He set that essay hoping someone would realise what my symptoms meant. Did you check the lunar chart and realise that I was always ill at the full moon? Or did you realise that the Boggart changed into the moon when it saw me?'

'Both,' Hermione said quietly.

Lupin forced a laugh.

'You're the cleverest witch of your age I've ever met, Hermione.'

'I'm not,' Hermione whispered. 'If I'd been a bit cleverer, I'd have told everyone what you are!'

'But they already know,' said Lupin. 'At least, the staff do.'

'Dumbledore hired you when he knew you were a werewolf?' Ron gasped. 'Is he mad?'

第 17 章 猫、老鼠和狗

"赫敏，冷静些——"

"我谁都没有告诉！"赫敏尖声嚷道，"我一直帮你瞒着——"

"赫敏，请你听我说！"卢平喊道，"我会解释——"

哈利感到自己在哆嗦，不是因为恐惧，而是因为新涌上来的愤怒。

"我那么信任你，"他朝卢平吼道，声音失控地颤抖着，"原来你一直是他的朋友！"

"你错了，"卢平说，"我过去十二年并不是小天狼星的朋友，但现在是了——让我解释……"

"不！"赫敏尖叫道，"哈利，别相信他，是他帮布莱克潜入城堡的，他也希望你死——他是狼人！"

一阵压迫耳膜的寂静。现在所有人的目光都盯着卢平，他显得异常镇静，尽管脸色苍白。

"这完全不是你平时的水平，赫敏，"他说，"恐怕只说对了三分之一。我没有帮小天狼星潜入城堡，当然也不希望哈利死……"他的面部肌肉奇怪地哆嗦了一下，"但我不否认我是狼人。"

罗恩奋力想站起来，但痛得哼了一声，又倒了下去。卢平朝他走去，显出关切之色，罗恩却气喘吁吁地说："别碰我，狼人！"

卢平猛然止步，然后转向赫敏，艰难地问道："你知道多久了？"

"好久了，"赫敏小声说，"自从我做了斯内普教授布置的论文……"

"他会很高兴的，"卢平冷冷地说，"他布置那篇论文，就是希望有人想到我的症状意味着什么……你是不是查了月亮盈亏表，发现我总是在满月时发病？或者你发现博格特看到我就变成了月亮？"

"都发现了。"赫敏轻轻地说。

卢平勉强笑了一下。

"你是我见过的你同龄中最聪明的女巫，赫敏。"

"我不是，"赫敏喃喃地说，"如果我聪明一点儿，就会告诉大家你是什么人！"

"可他们已经知道了，"卢平说，"至少教员们都知道。"

"邓布利多知道你是狼人还聘用你？"罗恩吃惊地问，"他疯了吗？"

CHAPTER SEVENTEEN Cat, Rat and Dog

'Some of the staff thought so,' said Lupin. 'He had to work very hard to convince certain teachers that I'm trustworthy –'

'AND HE WAS WRONG!' Harry yelled. 'YOU'VE BEEN HELPING HIM ALL THE TIME!' He was pointing at Black, who had crossed to the four-poster bed and sunk onto it, his face hidden in one shaking hand. Crookshanks leapt up beside him and stepped onto his lap, purring. Ron edged away from both of them, dragging his leg.

'I have *not* been helping Sirius,' said Lupin. 'If you'll give me a chance, I'll explain. Look –'

He separated Harry, Ron and Hermione's wands and threw each back to its owner; Harry caught his, stunned.

'There,' said Lupin, sticking his own wand back into his belt. 'You're armed, we're not. Now will you listen?'

Harry didn't know what to think. Was it a trick?

'If you haven't been helping him,' he said, with a furious glance at Black, 'how did you know he was here?'

'The map,' said Lupin. 'The Marauder's Map. I was in my office examining it –'

'You know how to work it?' Harry said suspiciously.

'Of course I know how to work it,' said Lupin, waving his hand impatiently. 'I helped write it. I'm Moony – that was my friends' nickname for me at school.'

'You *wrote* –?'

'The important thing is, I was watching it carefully this evening, because I had an idea that you, Ron and Hermione might try and sneak out of the castle to visit Hagrid before his Hippogriff was executed. And I was right, wasn't I?'

He had started to pace up and down, looking at them. Little patches of dust rose at his feet.

'You might have been wearing your father's old Cloak, Harry –'

'How d'you know about the Cloak?'

'The number of times I saw James disappearing under it …' said Lupin, waving an impatient hand again. 'The point is, even if you're wearing an Invisibility Cloak you show up on the Marauder's Map. I watched you cross the grounds and enter Hagrid's hut. Twenty minutes later, you left Hagrid, and set off back towards the castle. But you were now accompanied by

第17章 猫、老鼠和狗

"有些教员也认为他疯了,"卢平说,"邓布利多做了很大努力才让一些老师相信我是可靠的——"

"**可是他错了!**"哈利吼道,"**你一直在帮他!**"他指着布莱克,布莱克突然走到四柱床前,倒在床上,用一只颤抖的手捂着脸。克鲁克山也跳上床去,爬到他的膝上,喵喵叫着。罗恩拖着伤腿从他们旁边挪开。

"我并没有帮助小天狼星,"卢平说,"如果你给我机会,我可以解释。看——"

他把哈利、罗恩和赫敏的魔杖分开,分别扔回给他们。哈利接住魔杖,目瞪口呆。

"好了,"卢平把自己的魔杖插回皮带中,"现在你们有武器,我们没有,愿意听我说了吗?"

哈利不知该怎么看待这件事。这是个圈套吗?

"如果你没帮他,"他狂怒地看着布莱克,"怎么会知道他在这儿?"

"地图,"卢平说,"那张活点地图。我刚才在办公室里看地图——"

"你会用?"哈利怀疑地问。

"我当然会用,"卢平说着不耐烦地挥了一下手,"是我参与画的,我就是月亮脸——那是上学时朋友们给我起的绰号。"

"你画的?"

"重要的是,今晚我在仔细查看地图。因为我想,在海格的鹰头马身有翼兽被处死之前,你和罗恩、赫敏可能会设法溜出城堡去看他。我猜对了,是不是?"

他开始踱来踱去,眼睛望着他们,脚边扬起小片尘土。

"你可能穿着你爸爸的隐形衣,哈利——"

"你怎么知道这件隐形衣?"

"我看见詹姆用它隐身过多少回了……"卢平说着,又不耐烦地把手一挥,"关键是,即使你穿着隐形衣,在活点地图上也能显示出来。我看到你们穿过场地,进了海格的小屋。二十分钟后,你们离开海格

CHAPTER SEVENTEEN   Cat, Rat and Dog

somebody else.'

'What?' said Harry. 'No, we weren't!'

'I couldn't believe my eyes,' said Lupin, still pacing, and ignoring Harry's interruption. 'I thought the map must be malfunctioning. How could he be with you?'

'No one was with us!' said Harry.

'And then I saw another dot, moving fast towards you, labelled Sirius Black ... I saw him collide with you, I watched as he pulled two of you into the Whomping Willow –'

'One of us!' Ron said angrily.

'No, Ron,' said Lupin. 'Two of you.'

He had stopped his pacing, his eyes moving over Ron.

'Do you think I could have a look at the rat?' he said evenly.

'What?' said Ron. 'What's Scabbers got to do with it?'

'Everything,' said Lupin. 'Could I see him, please?'

Ron hesitated, then put a hand inside his robes. Scabbers emerged, thrashing desperately; Ron had to seize his long bald tail to stop him escaping. Crookshanks stood up on Black's lap and made a soft hissing noise.

Lupin moved closer to Ron. He seemed to be holding his breath as he gazed intently at Scabbers.

'What?' Ron said again, holding Scabbers close to him, looking scared. 'What's my rat got to do with anything?'

'That's not a rat,' croaked Sirius Black suddenly.

'What d'you mean – of course he's a rat –'

'No, he's not,' said Lupin quietly. 'He's a wizard.'

'An Animagus,' said Black, 'by the name of Peter Pettigrew.'

第17章 猫、老鼠和狗

走回城堡，但旁边多了一个人。"

"什么？"哈利说，"没有啊！"

"我不相信我的眼睛，"卢平说，他继续踱步，没有理会哈利的插话，"我想地图准是出问题了，他怎么会跟你们在一起呢？"

"没有人跟我们在一起！"哈利说。

"然后我又看到一个黑点，在快速地向你们移动，标着小天狼星布莱克……我看到他跟你们撞到一起，把你们中间的两个拖进了打人柳——"

"我们中间的一个！"罗恩恼火地说。

"不，罗恩，"卢平说，"是两个。"

他停止了踱步，目光投向罗恩。

"我可以看看那只老鼠吗？"他平静地问。

"怎么？"罗恩说，"这件事和斑斑有什么关系？"

"大有关系，"卢平说，"请让我看看它，可以吗？"

罗恩犹豫了一下，然后把手伸进袍子里。斑斑被掏了出来，拼命扭个不停。罗恩只好抓住它长长的秃尾巴，才没有让它逃走。克鲁克山站在布莱克的腿上，发出轻轻的嘶嘶声。

卢平走近罗恩，专注地盯着斑斑，似乎屏住了呼吸。

"怎么？"罗恩又问，害怕地搂紧了斑斑，"我的老鼠招谁惹谁了？"

"这不是老鼠。"小天狼星布莱克突然声音嘶哑地说。

"你说什么？它当然是老鼠——"

"不，不是，"卢平平静地说，"他是个巫师。"

"阿尼马格斯，"布莱克说，"名叫小矮星彼得。"

CHAPTER EIGHTEEN

Moony, Wormtail, Padfoot and Prongs

It took a few seconds for the absurdity of this statement to sink in. Then Ron voiced what Harry was thinking.

'You're both mental.'

'Ridiculous!' said Hermione faintly.

'Peter Pettigrew's dead!' said Harry. 'He killed him twelve years ago!'

He pointed at Black, whose face twitched convulsively.

'I meant to,' he growled, his yellow teeth bared, 'but little Peter got the better of me ... not this time, though!'

And Crookshanks was thrown to the floor as Black lunged at Scabbers; Ron yelled with pain as Black's weight fell on his broken leg.

'Sirius, NO!' Lupin yelled, launching himself forwards and dragging Black away from Ron again, 'WAIT! You can't do it just like that – they need to understand – we've got to explain –'

'We can explain afterwards!' snarled Black, trying to throw Lupin off, one hand still clawing the air as it tried to reach Scabbers, who was squealing like a piglet, scratching Ron's face and neck as he tried to escape.

'They've – got – a – right – to – know – everything!' Lupin panted, still trying to restrain Black. 'Ron's kept him as a pet! There are parts of it even I don't understand! And Harry – you owe Harry the truth, Sirius!'

Black stopped struggling, though his hollowed eyes were still fixed on Scabbers, who was clamped tightly under Ron's bitten, scratched and bleeding hands.

'All right, then,' Black said, without taking his eyes off the rat. 'Tell them whatever you like. But make it quick, Remus. I want to commit the murder I was imprisoned for ...'

第18章

月亮脸、虫尾巴、大脚板和尖头叉子

过了几秒钟他们才意识到这话的荒谬,然后罗恩说出了哈利想说的话。

"你们两个都疯了。"

"荒唐!"赫敏轻轻地说。

"小矮星彼得已经死了!"哈利说,"十二年前被他杀死的!"

他指着布莱克,布莱克的面孔在抽搐。

"我确实想杀他,"他吼道,露出了一嘴黄牙,"但是小彼得胜我一筹……这次不会了!"

布莱克朝斑斑扑去,克鲁克山被甩到地上。罗恩痛得大叫一声,布莱克的身体压到了他的断腿上。

"小天狼星,**不要**!"卢平叫道,冲上前把布莱克从罗恩身上拽开,"**等等**!你不能这样做——必须让他们明白——我们必须解释——"

"以后解释也不迟!"布莱克咆哮道,使劲想甩开卢平,一只手还在空中乱抓,想要抓到斑斑。老鼠像小猪一样尖叫,挠着罗恩的面颊和脖子,试图逃脱。

"他们——有——权利——知道——一切!"卢平喘着气说,仍在努力拦着布莱克,"罗恩是把它当宠物养的!何况有些地方连我也不明白!还有哈利——你应该把真相告诉哈利,小天狼星!"

布莱克停止了挣扎,那双凹陷的眼睛仍然盯着斑斑。斑斑被罗恩紧紧地握在手里,罗恩那双手被抓咬得鲜血淋漓。

"好吧。"布莱克说,他的目光没有从斑斑身上移开,"随便你对他们讲什么,但是要快,莱姆斯。我要杀人,就为了这桩命案我被关了……"

CHAPTER EIGHTEEN   Moony, Wormtail, Padfoot and Prongs

'You're nutters, both of you,' said Ron shakily, looking round at Harry and Hermione for support. 'I've had enough of this. I'm off.'

He tried to heave himself up on his good leg, but Lupin raised his wand again, pointing it at Scabbers.

'You're going to hear me out, Ron,' he said quietly. 'Just keep a tight hold on Peter while you listen.'

'HE'S NOT PETER, HE'S SCABBERS!' Ron yelled, trying to force the rat back into his front pocket, but Scabbers was fighting too hard; Ron swayed and overbalanced, and Harry caught him and pushed him back down to the bed. Then, ignoring Black, Harry turned to Lupin.

'There were witnesses who saw Pettigrew die,' he said. 'A whole street full of them ...'

'They didn't see what they thought they saw!' said Black savagely, still watching Scabbers struggling in Ron's hands.

'Everyone thought Sirius killed Peter,' said Lupin, nodding. 'I believed it myself – until I saw the map tonight. Because the Marauder's Map never lies ... Peter's alive. Ron's holding him, Harry.'

Harry looked down at Ron, and as their eyes met they agreed, silently: Black and Lupin were both out of their minds. Their story made no sense whatsoever. How could Scabbers be Peter Pettigrew? Azkaban must have unhinged Black after all – but why was Lupin playing along with him?

Then Hermione spoke, in a trembling, would-be calm sort of voice, as though trying to will Professor Lupin to talk sensibly.

'But Professor Lupin ... Scabbers can't be Pettigrew ... it just can't be true, you know it can't ...'

'Why can't it be true?' Lupin said calmly, as though they were in class, and Hermione had simply spotted a problem in an experiment with Grindylows.

'Because ... because people would know if Peter Pettigrew had been an Animagus. We did Animagi in class with Professor McGonagall. And I looked them up when I did my homework – the Ministry keeps tabs on witches and wizards who can become animals; there's a register showing what animal they become, and their markings and things ... and I went and looked Professor McGonagall up on the register, and there have only been seven Animagi this century, and Pettigrew's name wasn't on the list –'

Harry barely had time to marvel inwardly at the effort Hermione put into her homework, when Lupin started to laugh.

第18章 月亮脸、虫尾巴、大脚板和尖头叉子

"你们是疯子,你们两个都是。"罗恩颤抖地说,把目光投向哈利和赫敏寻找支持,"我听够了,我走了。"

他试图靠那条好腿站起来,但卢平又举起魔杖,指着斑斑。

"你必须听我说完,罗恩,"他平静地说,"听的时候把彼得抓牢。"

"**它不是彼得,它是斑斑!**"罗恩喊道,想把老鼠塞回他胸前的口袋里,但斑斑挣扎得太凶了。罗恩摇晃一下,失去了平衡,哈利扶住他,把他推回到床上。然后,哈利没有理会布莱克,转向卢平。

"小矮星的死是有目击者的,"他说,"整条街的人呢……"

"他们看到的事情并不是他们以为的那样!"布莱克粗暴地说,依然盯着在罗恩手中挣扎的斑斑。

"所有的人都以为小天狼星杀死了彼得,"卢平点头道,"我也信了——直到今晚看到地图,因为活点地图从不说谎……彼得还活着。罗恩正抓着他,哈利。"

哈利低头看看罗恩,两人目光相交,默默达成共识:布莱克和卢平的脑子都出了问题。他们说的话荒诞不稽。斑斑怎么可能是小矮星彼得?想必是阿兹卡班使布莱克精神错乱了——但卢平为什么跟他一唱一和呢?

赫敏开口了,声音颤抖,强作镇静,好像努力想用意念让卢平教授恢复理智。

"可是卢平教授……斑斑不可能是小矮星彼得……这是不可能的,您知道这不可能……"

"为什么不可能?"卢平镇静地问,好像他们是在课堂上,赫敏只是发现了格林迪洛实验中的一个问题。

"因为……因为如果小矮星彼得是阿尼马格斯,人们会知道的。我们在麦格教授的课上学过阿尼马格斯,我做作业时查了资料,魔法部对能变成动物的巫师都有记录,有登记簿显示他们能变成什么动物,还有标记之类的……我在登记簿中查到了麦格教授,本世纪只有七位阿尼马格斯,小矮星彼得的名字不在上面——"

哈利刚来得及暗自惊叹赫敏做功课所下的功夫,卢平笑了起来。

CHAPTER EIGHTEEN   Moony, Wormtail, Padfoot and Prongs

'Right again, Hermione!' he said. 'But the Ministry never knew that there used to be three unregistered Animagi running around Hogwarts.'

'If you're going to tell them the story, get a move on, Remus,' snarled Black, who was still watching Scabbers's every desperate move. 'I've waited twelve years, I'm not going to wait much longer.'

'All right ... but you'll need to help me, Sirius,' said Lupin, 'I only know how it began ...'

Lupin broke off. There had been a loud creak behind him. The bedroom door had opened of its own accord. All five of them stared at it. Then Lupin strode towards it and looked out into the landing.

'No one there ...'

'This place is haunted!' said Ron.

'It's not,' said Lupin, still looking at the door in a puzzled way. 'The Shrieking Shack was never haunted ... the screams and howls the villagers used to hear were made by me.'

He pushed his greying hair out of his eyes, thought for a moment, then said, 'That's where all of this starts – with my becoming a werewolf. None of this could have happened if I hadn't been bitten ... and if I hadn't been so foolhardy ...'

He looked sober and tired. Ron started to interrupt, but Hermione said, 'Shh!' She was watching Lupin very intently.

'I was a very small boy when I received the bite. My parents tried everything, but in those days there was no cure. The Potion that Professor Snape has been making for me is a very recent discovery. It makes me safe, you see. As long as I take it in the week preceding the full moon, I keep my mind when I transform ... I am able to curl up in my office, a harmless wolf, and wait for the moon to wane again.

'Before the Wolfsbane Potion was discovered, however, I became a fully fledged monster once a month. It seemed impossible that I would be able to come to Hogwarts. Other parents weren't likely to want their children exposed to me.

'But then Dumbledore became Headmaster, and he was sympathetic. He said that, as long as we took certain precautions, there was no reason I shouldn't come to school ...' Lupin sighed, and looked directly at Harry. 'I told you, months ago, that the Whomping Willow was planted the year I came to Hogwarts. The truth is that it was planted *because* I had come to

"又说对了，赫敏！"他说，"但魔法部不知道曾有三名未登记的阿尼马格斯在霍格沃茨活动。"

"如果你想把事情告诉他们，就快点讲，莱姆斯！"布莱克咆哮道，仍注视着斑斑每一个绝望的挣扎，"我等了十二年，不想再等了。"

"好吧……但是你得帮我，小天狼星。"卢平说，"我只知道开头……"

卢平停住了，因为后面传来响亮的吱呀一声。卧室的门自动开了。五个人都瞪着门。卢平走过去朝楼梯口张望了一下。

"没人……"

"这地方闹鬼！"罗恩说。

"不。"卢平说，还在疑惑地看着那扇门，"尖叫棚屋从来没闹过鬼……村民们曾经听到的那些尖叫和嗥叫都是我发出来的。"

他把灰白的头发从眼前捋开，沉思片刻，说道："所有的事情都是从这里——从我变成狼人开始的。如果我没有被咬，这些事都不会发生……如果我不是那么鲁莽……"

他看上去严肃而疲惫。罗恩想插话，但是赫敏"嘘——"了一声。她专注地望着卢平。

"我是很小的时候被咬的，我的父母试了各种办法，但那个时候无法治愈。斯内普教授为我制作的药是最近才发明的。它让我变得安全了。我只要在满月前一周喝了这药，就能在变形时保持神志清醒……可以蜷缩在我的办公室里，是一匹无害的狼，等待月缺。

"但是，在狼毒药剂发明之前，我每个月都会变成一头可怕的怪物。我要进霍格沃茨几乎是不可能的，家长们不会愿意让他们的孩子与我接触。

"后来邓布利多当了校长，他很同情我。说只要采取一些预防措施，就没有理由不让我进霍格沃茨……"卢平叹息一声，直视着哈利，"几个月前我对你说过，打人柳是我进霍格沃茨那年栽的。实际上它是因为我进霍格沃茨才栽的。这屋子——"卢平苦涩地打量着这个房间，"以

CHAPTER EIGHTEEN   Moony, Wormtail, Padfoot and Prongs

Hogwarts. This house –' Lupin looked miserably around the room, '– the tunnel that leads to it – they were built for my use. Once a month, I was smuggled out of the castle, into this place, to transform. The tree was placed at the tunnel mouth to stop anyone coming across me while I was dangerous.'

Harry couldn't see where this story was going, but he was listening raptly all the same. The only sound apart from Lupin's voice was Scabbers's frightened squeaking.

'My transformations in those days were – were terrible. It is very painful to turn into a werewolf. I was separated from humans to bite, so I bit and scratched myself instead. The villagers heard the noise and the screaming and thought they were hearing particularly violent spirits. Dumbledore encouraged the rumour ... even now, when the house has been silent for years, the villagers don't dare approach it ...

'But apart from my transformations, I was happier than I had ever been in my life. For the first time ever, I had friends, three great friends. Sirius Black ... Peter Pettigrew ... and, of course, your father, Harry – James Potter.

'Now, my three friends could hardly fail to notice that I disappeared once a month. I made up all sorts of stories. I told them my mother was ill, and that I had to go home to see her ... I was terrified they would desert me the moment they found out what I was. But of course, they, like you, Hermione, worked out the truth ...

'And they didn't desert me at all. Instead they did something for me that would make my transformations not only bearable, but the best times of my life. They became Animagi.'

'My dad, too?' said Harry, astounded.

'Yes, indeed,' said Lupin. 'It took them the best part of three years to work out how to do it. Your father and Sirius here were the cleverest students in the school, and lucky they were, because the Animagus transformation can go horribly wrong – one reason the Ministry keeps a close watch on those attempting to do it. Peter needed all the help he could get from James and Sirius. Finally, in our fifth year, they managed it. They could each turn into a different animal at will.'

'But how did that help you?' said Hermione, sounding puzzled.

'They couldn't keep me company as humans, so they kept me company as animals,' said Lupin. 'A werewolf is only a danger to people. They sneaked out

及通向它的地道——都是为我而修的。每月一次,我被秘密带出城堡,到这个地方来变形。那棵树被栽在地道口,免得有人在我的危险期碰到我。"

哈利看不出这个故事想说明什么,但还是着迷地听着。除了卢平的声音之外,只有斑斑惊恐的尖叫声。

"那些日子我的变形——非常恐怖。变成狼人是很痛苦的。我被迫与人隔离,无法咬人类,于是就咬自己、抓自己。村民们听到那些声音和尖叫,以为自己听到的是特别狂暴的幽灵,邓布利多让这类谣言传开了……即使到了现在,这屋子已经安静好多年了,村民们还是不敢靠近……

"不过,除去变形之外,那段时光是我此生前所未有的快乐时光。我第一次有了朋友,三个极好的朋友。小天狼星布莱克……小矮星彼得……当然啦,哈利,还有你爸爸——詹姆·波特。

"我的三个朋友不会注意不到我每月一次的失踪。我编了各种各样的借口,说我妈妈病了,我必须回家去看她,等等,我怕他们知道了我是狼人就会离开我。但是,当然啦,赫敏,他们像你一样,发现了真相……

"可是他们并没有离开我,而是想出了一个办法,让我的变形期不仅好受一些,而且成了我一生中最美好的时光。他们学成了阿尼马格斯。"

"我爸爸也是?"哈利很吃惊。

"是的,"卢平说,"整整三年,他们一有时间就去练习,最后才学会。你爸爸和小天狼星曾经是全校最聪明的学生,幸好如此,因为阿尼马格斯变形有可能出现可怕的错误——这是魔法部对阿尼马格斯严格控制的原因之一。彼得需要詹姆和小天狼星的全力帮助。最后,在五年级时,他们终于练成了,每个人都能随意变成一种不同的动物。"

"可是这对你有什么帮助呢?"赫敏不解地问。

"他们作为人不能跟我在一起,所以就变成动物来陪我。"卢平说,"狼人只对人有危险,他们每个月披着詹姆的隐形衣溜出城堡。他们变

CHAPTER EIGHTEEN   Moony, Wormtail, Padfoot and Prongs

of the castle every month under James's Invisibility Cloak. They transformed ... Peter, as the smallest, could slip beneath the Willow's attacking branches and touch the knot that freezes it. They would then slip down the tunnel and join me. Under their influence, I became less dangerous. My body was still wolfish, but my mind seemed to become less so while I was with them.'

'Hurry up, Remus,' snarled Black, who was still watching Scabbers with a horrible sort of hunger in his face.

'I'm getting there, Sirius, I'm getting there ... well, highly exciting possibilities were open to us now we could all transform. Soon we were leaving the Shrieking Shack and roaming the school grounds and the village by night. Sirius and James transformed into such large animals, they were able to keep a werewolf in check. I doubt whether any Hogwarts students ever found out more about the Hogwarts grounds and Hogsmeade than we did ... And that's how we came to write the Marauder's Map, and sign it with our nicknames. Sirius is Padfoot. Peter is Wormtail. James was Prongs.'

'What sort of animal –?' Harry began, but Hermione cut across him.

'That was still really dangerous! Running around in the dark with a werewolf! What if you'd given the others the slip, and bitten somebody?'

'A thought that still haunts me,' said Lupin heavily. 'And there were near misses, many of them. We laughed about them afterwards. We were young, thoughtless – carried away with our own cleverness.

'I sometimes felt guilty about betraying Dumbledore's trust, of course ... he had admitted me to Hogwarts when no other Headmaster would have done so, and he had no idea I was breaking the rules he had set down for my own and others' safety. He never knew I had led three fellow students into becoming Animagi illegally. But I always managed to forget my guilty feelings every time we sat down to plan our next month's adventure. And I haven't changed ...'

Lupin's face had hardened, and there was self-disgust in his voice. 'All this year, I have been battling with myself, wondering whether I should tell Dumbledore that Sirius was an Animagus. But I didn't do it. Why? Because I was too cowardly. It would have meant admitting that I'd betrayed his trust while I was at school, admitting that I'd led others along with me ... and Dumbledore's trust has meant everything to me. He let me into Hogwarts as a boy, and he gave me a job, when I have been shunned all my adult life, unable to find paid work because of what I am. And so I convinced

成动物……彼得个子最小，能从打人柳的攻击性枝条下钻过来，按到能让它定住的那个节疤，然后他们滑入地道来找我。在他们的影响下，我变得不那么危险了。我的身体还是狼形，但跟他们在一起时，我的心智好像不那么像狼了。"

"快点儿，莱姆斯！"布莱克吼道，他仍然盯着斑斑，脸上带着一种可怕的饥渴。

"快了，小天狼星，快了……嗯，我们都能变形以后，有多少刺激的事情可以做啊。我们不久便离开了尖叫棚屋，夜间在学校和村子里游荡。小天狼星和詹姆变成了那么大的动物，能够控制住狼人。我认为霍格沃茨没有哪个学生能把学校和霍格莫德摸得比我们更清楚……所以我们就画了那张活点地图，署上了自己的外号。小天狼星是大脚板，彼得是虫尾巴，詹姆是尖头叉子。"

"是什么动物？"哈利问道，但赫敏打断了他。

"那还是挺危险的！在夜里跟一个狼人乱跑！要是你摆脱了同伴，咬到了人怎么办？"

"我现在想想还后怕呢，"卢平沉重地说，"有过险情，很多次。我们过后拿这些事开玩笑。那时我们年少轻狂——陶醉在自己的小聪明里。

"当然，我有时还会为辜负了邓布利多的信任而感到内疚……当初没有一个校长肯收我，邓布利多把我招进了霍格沃茨，而现在他却不知道我在违反他为保护我和他人的安全而制定的规矩，他不知道我引得三个同学变成了非法的阿尼马格斯。但是，每当我们坐下来商量下个月的冒险活动时，我总是把负疚感忘到脑后。我一直没有改变……"

卢平面容凝重起来，话音中流露出对自己的厌恶。"今年我一直在进行思想斗争，考虑要不要去对邓布利多说小天狼星是阿尼马格斯。但我没有去说。为什么？因为我太懦弱。如果说了，就意味着承认我上学时辜负了他的信任，承认我让别人跟我一道……而邓布利多的信任对我意味着一切。我小时候，是他让我进入了霍格沃茨；我长大后，又因为自己的身份一直受排斥，找不到一份有收入的工作，又是邓布

CHAPTER EIGHTEEN   Moony, Wormtail, Padfoot and Prongs

myself that Sirius was getting into the school using Dark Arts he learnt from Voldemort, that being an Animagus had nothing to do with it ... so, in a way, Snape's been right about me all along.'

'Snape?' said Black harshly, taking his eyes off Scabbers for the first time in minutes and looking up at Lupin. 'What's Snape got to do with it?'

'He's here, Sirius,' said Lupin heavily. 'He's teaching here as well.' He looked up at Harry, Ron and Hermione.

'Professor Snape was at school with us. He fought very hard against my appointment to the Defence Against the Dark Arts job. He has been telling Dumbledore all year that I am not to be trusted. He has his reasons ... you see, Sirius here played a trick on him which nearly killed him, a trick which involved me –'

Black made a derisive noise.

'It served him right,' he sneered. 'Sneaking around, trying to find out what we were up to ... hoping he could get us expelled ...'

'Severus was very interested in where I went every month,' Lupin told Harry, Ron and Hermione. 'We were in the same year, you know, and we – er – didn't like each other very much. He especially disliked James. Jealous, I think, of James's talent on the Quidditch pitch ... anyway, Snape had seen me crossing the grounds with Madam Pomfrey one evening as she led me towards the Whomping Willow to transform. Sirius thought it would be – er – amusing, to tell Snape all he had to do was prod the knot on the tree-trunk with a long stick, and he'd be able to get in after me. Well, of course, Snape tried it – if he'd got as far as this house, he'd have met a fully grown werewolf – but your father, who'd heard what Sirius had done, went after Snape and pulled him back, at great risk to his life ... Snape glimpsed me, though, at the end of the tunnel. He was forbidden to tell anybody by Dumbledore, but from that time on he knew what I was ...'

'So that's why Snape doesn't like you,' said Harry slowly, 'because he thought you were in on the joke?'

'That's right,' sneered a cold voice from the wall behind Lupin.

Severus Snape was pulling off the Invisibility Cloak, his wand pointing directly at Lupin.

利多录用了我。所以我就对自己说，小天狼星是用跟伏地魔学来的黑魔法潜入学校的，与阿尼马格斯无关……由此可见，从某种意义上说，斯内普对我的看法是对的。"

"斯内普？"布莱克厉声说，几分钟内第一次把目光从斑斑身上移开，抬头看着卢平，"这跟斯内普有什么关系？"

"斯内普在这儿，小天狼星，"卢平沉重地说，"他也在这儿任教。"他抬眼望着哈利、罗恩和赫敏。

"斯内普教授跟我们是同学。他竭力反对让我教黑魔法防御术。他这一年都在跟邓布利多讲我是多么不值得信任。他是有理由的……小天狼星曾经搞了个恶作剧，差点要了斯内普的命，这恶作剧与我有关——"

布莱克轻蔑地哼了一声。

"他活该，"他嘲讽道，"鬼鬼祟祟地想发现我们在干什么……指望他能让我们被开除……"

"西弗勒斯对我每月去了哪里很感兴趣，"卢平对哈利、赫敏和罗恩说，"我们是同一个年级的，我们——嗯——交情不太好。他特别讨厌詹姆。我想是嫉妒詹姆在魁地奇球场上的才能吧……总之，斯内普有天晚上见到我跟庞弗雷女士一起穿过场地，庞弗雷女士送我到打人柳那里去变形。小天狼星为了寻开心，告诉斯内普说只要用长棍子捣捣树干上的那个节疤，就能跟着我进去。当然，斯内普就这么试了——他要是跟到这屋子里，就会碰到一匹兽性十足的狼——你爸爸听说了小天狼星做的事，冒着生命危险追上斯内普，把他拽了回去……但斯内普看见了我在地道那头。邓布利多不许他告诉别人，然而，从那时起他就知道我是什么了……"

"这就是斯内普不喜欢你的原因？"哈利缓缓地问道，"他认为你也参与了那个恶作剧？"

"没错。"卢平身后的墙上传来一声冷冷的嘲讽。

西弗勒斯·斯内普揭下隐形衣，他的魔杖直指卢平。

CHAPTER NINETEEN

The Servant of Lord Voldemort

Hermione screamed. Black leapt to his feet. Harry jumped as though he'd received a huge electric shock.

'I found this at the base of the Whomping Willow,' said Snape, throwing the Cloak aside, careful to keep his wand pointing directly at Lupin's chest. 'Very useful, Potter, I thank you ...'

Snape was slightly breathless, but his face was full of suppressed triumph. 'You're wondering, perhaps, how I knew you were here?' he said, his eyes glittering. 'I've just been to your office, Lupin. You forgot to take your Potion tonight, so I took a gobletful along. And very lucky I did ... lucky for me, I mean. Lying on your desk was a certain map. One glance at it told me all I needed to know. I saw you running along this passageway and out of sight.'

'Severus –' Lupin began, but Snape overrode him.

'I've told the Headmaster again and again that you've been helping your old friend Black into the castle, Lupin, and here's the proof. Not even I dreamed you would have the nerve to use this old place as your hideout –'

'Severus, you're making a mistake,' said Lupin urgently. 'You haven't heard everything – I can explain – Sirius is not here to kill Harry –'

'Two more for Azkaban tonight,' said Snape, his eyes now gleaming fanatically. 'I shall be interested to see how Dumbledore takes this ... he was quite convinced you were harmless, you know, Lupin ... a *tame* werewolf ...'

'You fool,' said Lupin softly. 'Is a schoolboy grudge worth putting an innocent man back inside Azkaban?'

BANG! Thin, snake-like cords burst from the end of Snape's wand and twisted themselves around Lupin's mouth, wrists and ankles; he overbalanced

第 19 章

伏地魔的仆人

赫敏尖叫起来，布莱克一跃而起，哈利好像突然遭受了强烈的电击一样跳起来。

"我在打人柳底下发现了这个。"斯内普把隐形衣丢到一边，一面仍小心地用魔杖直指卢平的胸膛，"很有用的，波特，我要谢谢你……"

斯内普有点气喘，但一脸抑制不住的得意。"诸位也许在想，我怎么知道你们在这里？"他说，眼睛闪闪发光，"我去了你的办公室，卢平。你今晚忘记喝药了，所以我带了一杯去，很幸运我这么做了……对我来说很幸运。你桌上放着一张地图，一目了然，我看到你沿着这条通道过来，然后就没影了。"

"西弗勒斯——"卢平想说话，但斯内普阻止了他。

"我一再对校长说，你在帮你的老朋友布莱克潜入城堡，卢平，眼前便是证据。连我都没想到你还敢用这个老地方做你的庇护所——"

"西弗勒斯，你误会了，"卢平急切地说，"你没有听全——我可以解释——小天狼星不是来杀哈利的——"

"今晚阿兹卡班又要多两个囚犯了，"斯内普说，眼里放出狂热的光，"我倒想看看邓布利多的反应……他确信你没有危险，卢平……一个驯服的狼人——"

"你这傻瓜，"卢平温和地说，"值得为学生时代的过节将一个无辜的人送到阿兹卡班吗？"

砰！斯内普的魔杖尖射出蛇状的细绳，缠住了卢平的嘴、手腕和脚脖子。卢平失去平衡，摔倒在地，动弹不得。布莱克怒吼一声，冲

CHAPTER NINETEEN   The Servant of Lord Voldemort

and fell to the floor, unable to move. With a roar of rage, Black started towards Snape, but Snape pointed his wand straight between Black's eyes.

'Give me a reason,' he whispered. 'Give me a reason to do it, and I swear I will.'

Black stopped dead. It would have been impossible to say which face showed more hatred.

Harry stood there, paralysed, not knowing what to do or who to believe. He glanced around at Ron and Hermione. Ron looked just as confused as he did, still fighting to keep hold of the struggling Scabbers. Hermione, however, took an uncertain step towards Snape and said, in a very breathless voice, 'Professor Snape – it – it wouldn't hurt to hear what they've got to say, w-would it?'

'Miss Granger, you are already facing suspension from this school,' Snape spat. 'You, Potter and Weasley are out of bounds, in the company of a convicted murderer and a werewolf. For once in your life, *hold your tongue.*'

'But if – if there *was* a mistake –'

'KEEP QUIET, YOU STUPID GIRL!' Snape shouted, looking suddenly quite deranged. 'DON'T TALK ABOUT WHAT YOU DON'T UNDERSTAND!' A few sparks shot out of the end of his wand, which was still pointing at Black's face. Hermione fell silent.

'Vengeance is very sweet,' Snape breathed at Black. 'How I hoped I would be the one to catch you ...'

'The joke's on you again, Severus,' snarled Black. 'As long as this boy brings his rat up to the castle –' he jerked his head at Ron, '– I'll come quietly ...'

'Up to the castle?' said Snape silkily. 'I don't think we need to go that far. All I have to do is call the Dementors once we get out of the Willow. They'll be very pleased to see you, Black ... pleased enough to give you a little kiss, I daresay ...'

What little colour there was in Black's face left it.

'You – you've got to hear me out,' he croaked. 'The rat – look at the rat –'

But there was a mad glint in Snape's eye that Harry had never seen before. He seemed beyond reason.

'Come on, all of you,' he said. He clicked his fingers, and the ends of the cords that bound Lupin flew to his hands. 'I'll drag the werewolf. Perhaps the Dementors will have a kiss for him, too –'

第19章 伏地魔的仆人

向斯内普,但斯内普用魔杖直指布莱克的眉心。

"给我一个理由,"他小声说,"给我一个出手的理由,我发誓我不会手软。"

布莱克猛然停住。此刻很难判断哪张脸上的仇恨更多。

哈利站在那儿,如同瘫痪了一般,不知该做什么,该相信谁。他望望罗恩和赫敏。罗恩看上去和他一样困惑,仍在努力抓着不停挣扎的斑斑。但赫敏怯怯地朝斯内普走了一步,用极其微弱的声音说:"斯内普教授——听——听一下他们有什么话要说也没有害处,是——是不是?"

"格兰杰小姐,你已经面临休学了,"斯内普厉声说道,"你、波特,还有韦斯莱擅自外出,并与杀人犯和狼人混迹一处。你一贯多嘴多舌,还不闭嘴!"

"可是如果——如果有误会——"

"**闭嘴,你这愚蠢的丫头!**"斯内普吼道,突然像发了狂,"**不要议论自己不懂的东西!**"他的魔杖尖射出几个火星,魔杖依然指着布莱克的眉心。赫敏沉默了。

"复仇的滋味多么美妙啊,"斯内普对布莱克轻声说,"我一直巴望着能让我抓到你……"

"这次闹笑话的还是你,西弗勒斯。"布莱克叫道,"只要这男孩把老鼠带回城堡——"他把脑袋朝罗恩一摆,"——我就会悄悄跟去……"

"回城堡?"斯内普油腔滑调地说,"我想用不着走那么远。我只要一走出这棵柳树,就会招来摄魂怪。它们会很高兴看到你的,布莱克……我想,它们会高兴得给你一个小小的吻,布莱克……"

布莱克脸上仅存的那点血色消失了。

"你——你必须听我说,"他声音嘶哑地说,"那只老鼠——看看那只老鼠——"

但斯内普眼里发出哈利从没见过的疯狂光芒,似乎丧失了理智。

"走吧,全部出去。"说着,他打了个响指,绑卢平的绳头就飞到了他手中,"我拖着这个狼人,也许摄魂怪也会给他一个吻——"

CHAPTER NINETEEN — The Servant of Lord Voldemort

Before he knew what he was doing, Harry had crossed the room in three strides, and blocked the door.

'Get out of the way, Potter, you're in enough trouble already,' snarled Snape. 'If I hadn't been here to save your skin –'

'Professor Lupin could have killed me about a hundred times this year,' Harry said. 'I've been alone with him loads of times, having defence lessons against the Dementors. If he was helping Black, why didn't he just finish me off then?'

'Don't ask me to fathom the way a werewolf's mind works,' hissed Snape. 'Get out of the way, Potter.'

'YOU'RE PATHETIC!' Harry yelled. 'JUST BECAUSE THEY MADE A FOOL OF YOU AT SCHOOL YOU WON'T EVEN LISTEN –'

'SILENCE! I WILL NOT BE SPOKEN TO LIKE THAT!' Snape shrieked, looking madder than ever. 'Like father, like son, Potter! I have just saved your neck, you should be thanking me on bended knee! You would have been well served if he'd killed you! You'd have died like your father, too arrogant to believe you might be mistaken in Black – now get out of the way, or I will *make* you. GET OUT OF THE WAY, POTTER!'

Harry made up his mind in a split second. Before Snape could take even one step towards him, he had raised his wand.

'*Expelliarmus!* ' he yelled – except that his wasn't the only voice that shouted. There was a blast that made the door rattle on its hinges; Snape was lifted off his feet and slammed into the wall, then slid down it to the floor, a trickle of blood oozing from under his hair. He had been knocked out.

Harry looked around. Both Ron and Hermione had tried to disarm Snape at exactly the same moment. Snape's wand soared in a high arc and landed on the bed next to Crookshanks.

'You shouldn't have done that,' said Black, looking at Harry. 'You should have left him to me ...'

Harry avoided Black's eyes. He wasn't sure, even now, that he'd done the right thing.

'We attacked a teacher ... we attacked a teacher ...' Hermione whimpered, staring at the lifeless Snape with frightened eyes. 'Oh, we're going to be in so much trouble –'

Lupin was struggling against his bonds. Black bent down quickly and untied him. Lupin straightened up, rubbing his arms where the ropes had cut into them.

第19章 伏地魔的仆人

哈利下意识地三步跨过房间，堵住了门口。

"让开，波特，你的麻烦已经够多了，"斯内普吼道，"要不是我来救你——"

"卢平教授今年有一百次机会可以杀死我，"哈利说，"我好多时间单独跟他在一起，学习抵御摄魂怪的办法，如果他要帮助布莱克，那时候为什么不动手？"

"别要我去揣摩狼人的思维方式。"斯内普鄙夷地说，"让开，波特。"

"**你真可怜！**"哈利嚷道，"**就因为他们当年在学校里捉弄过你，你就连听都不听——**"

"**住口！不许那样对我说话！**"斯内普尖叫道，看上去更加疯狂了，"有其父必有其子，波特！我刚刚救了你的命，你应该跪在地上感谢我！其实你活该让他杀死！死得跟你父亲一样，因为太骄傲，不肯承认自己看错了布莱克——让开，不然我就不客气了，**让开，波特！**"

哈利瞬间下了决心，在斯内普的脚步跨出之前，哈利已经举起了魔杖。

"除你武器！"他喊道——但不只是他一个人的声音。一阵气浪把那扇门震得嘎嘎响，斯内普的身子飞了起来，撞到墙上，然后顺着墙滑到地上，头发里渗出一股鲜血。他昏了过去。

哈利回头一看，是罗恩和赫敏同时想到了解除斯内普的武器。斯内普的魔杖在空中高高地划了一道弧线，然后落到床上的克鲁克山旁边。

"你不该那么做，"布莱克看着哈利说，"应该把他留给我……"

哈利避开了布莱克的目光，他到现在都不能确定自己做的事情对不对。

"我们打了老师……我们打了老师……"赫敏呜咽道，恐惧的眼睛瞪着一动不动的斯内普，"哦，我们要倒霉了——"

卢平努力想挣脱绑绳，布莱克迅速俯身为他解开了。卢平直起身子，揉着被勒痛的胳膊。

CHAPTER NINETEEN   The Servant of Lord Voldemort

'Thank you, Harry,' he said.

'I'm still not saying I believe you,' Harry retorted.

'Then it's time we offered you some proof,' said Black. 'You, boy – give me Peter. Now.'

Ron clutched Scabbers closer to his chest.

'Come off it,' he said weakly. 'Are you trying to say you broke out of Azkaban just to get your hands on *Scabbers*? I mean ...' he looked up at Harry and Hermione for support. 'OK, say Pettigrew could turn into a rat – there are millions of rats – how's he supposed to know which one he's after if he was locked up in Azkaban?'

'You know, Sirius, that's a fair question,' said Lupin, turning to Black and frowning slightly. 'How *did* you find out where he was?'

Black put one of his claw-like hands inside his robes and took out a crumpled piece of paper, which he smoothed flat, and held out to show the others.

It was the photograph of Ron and his family that had appeared in the *Daily Prophet* the previous summer, and there, on Ron's shoulder, was Scabbers.

'How did you get this?' Lupin asked Black, thunderstruck.

'Fudge,' said Black. 'When he came to inspect Azkaban last year, he gave me his paper. And there was Peter, on the front page ... on this boy's shoulder ... I knew him at once ... how many times had I seen him transform? And the caption said the boy would be going back to Hogwarts ... to where Harry was ...'

'My God,' said Lupin softly, staring from Scabbers to the picture in the paper and back again. 'His front paw ...'

'What about it?' said Ron defiantly.

'He's got a toe missing,' said Black.

'Of course,' Lupin breathed, 'so simple ... so *brilliant* ... He cut it off himself?'

'Just before he transformed,' said Black. 'When I cornered him, he yelled for the whole street to hear that I'd betrayed Lily and James. Then, before I could curse him, he blew apart the street with the wand behind his back, killed everyone within twenty feet of himself – and sped down into the sewer with the other rats ...'

第19章 伏地魔的仆人

"谢谢你,哈利。"他说。

"我还没说相信你呢。"哈利回道。

"好吧,我们这就给你一些证明,"卢平说,"你,孩子——把彼得交给我。现在。"

罗恩把斑斑紧搂在胸口。

"得了吧,"他无力地说,"你想说他从阿兹卡班逃出来就是为了抓斑斑?我是说……"他求助地看着哈利和赫敏,"好吧,就算小矮星能变成老鼠——老鼠有成千上万——他关在阿兹卡班,怎么知道要抓哪只?"

"对啊,小天狼星,这问得有些道理,"卢平说着,转向布莱克,微微皱起眉头,"你是怎么知道他在哪儿的?"

布莱克把枯爪般的手伸进袍子里,掏出一张皱巴巴的纸,抹平了举给大家看。

那是去年夏天《预言家日报》上登的罗恩一家的照片,蹲在罗恩肩头的,正是斑斑。

"你怎么弄到的?"卢平震惊地问。

"福吉,"布莱克说,"去年他来阿兹卡班视察,给了我这张报纸。头版就有彼得……在这个男孩的肩上……我立刻认出了他……我看过他变形多少次了。照片下面的文字说这男孩要回霍格沃茨……到哈利那儿去……"

"上帝啊。"卢平来回打量着斑斑和报纸上的照片,轻声叫道,"他的前爪……"

"怎么啦?"罗恩没好气地问。

"少了一根爪子。"布莱克说。

"当然,"卢平喃喃地说,"多么简单……多么聪明……他自己砍掉的?"

"在他变形的前一刻,"布莱克说,"我堵住他之后,他高声大叫,让整条街的人都听到我出卖了莉莉和詹姆。然后,我还没来得及念咒语,他就用藏在背后的魔杖炸开了街道,杀死了周围二十英尺之内的所有人——然后和其他老鼠一起钻进了阴沟里……"

CHAPTER NINETEEN   The Servant of Lord Voldemort

'Didn't you ever hear, Ron?' said Lupin. 'The biggest bit of Peter they found was his finger.'

'Look, Scabbers probably had a fight with another rat or something! He's been in my family for ages, right –'

'Twelve years, in fact,' said Lupin. 'Didn't you ever wonder why he was living so long?'

'We – we've been taking good care of him!' said Ron.

'Not looking too good at the moment, though, is he?' said Lupin. 'I'd guess he's been losing weight ever since he heard Sirius was on the loose again …'

'He's been scared of that mad cat!' said Ron, nodding towards Crookshanks, who was still purring on the bed.

But that wasn't right, Harry thought suddenly … Scabbers had been looking ill before he met Crookshanks … ever since Ron's return from Egypt … since the time when Black had escaped …

'This cat isn't mad,' said Black hoarsely. He reached out a bony hand and stroked Crookshanks's fluffy head. 'He's the most intelligent of his kind I've ever met. He recognised Peter for what he was straight away. And when he met me, he knew I was no dog. It was a while before he trusted me. Finally, I managed to communicate to him what I was after, and he's been helping me …'

'What do you mean?' breathed Hermione.

'He tried to bring Peter to me, but couldn't … so he stole the passwords into Gryffindor Tower for me … As I understand it, he took them from a boy's bedside table …'

Harry's brain seemed to be sagging under the weight of what he was hearing. It was absurd … and yet …

'But Peter got wind of what was going on and ran for it … this cat – Crookshanks, did you call him? – told me Peter had left blood on the sheets … I suppose he bit himself … well, faking his own death had worked once …'

These words jolted Harry to his senses.

'And why did he fake his death?' he said furiously. 'Because he knew you were about to kill him like you killed my parents!'

'No,' said Lupin. 'Harry –'

'And now you've come to finish him off!'

'Yes, I have,' said Black, with an evil look at Scabbers.

'Then I should've let Snape take you!' Harry shouted.

第19章 伏地魔的仆人

"罗恩，你听说没有？"卢平说，"他们找到的彼得的最大一块残骸，就是他的一根手指。"

"哎呀，斑斑可能跟别的老鼠打过一架什么的！它在我家好多年了，对不——"

"十二年了，"卢平说，"你没有奇怪它怎么能活这么长吗？"

"我们——我们照顾得好！"罗恩说。

"但是它现在看上去不太好，对不对？"卢平说，"我猜自从听到小天狼星出来之后，它的体重就一直在下降……"

"它是害怕那只疯猫！"罗恩朝克鲁克山点点头，那猫还在床上叫着。

不对，哈利突然想到……斑斑在遇到克鲁克山之前就病恹恹的了……就是罗恩从埃及回来以后……也就是在布莱克越狱之后……

"这只猫没有疯。"布莱克嘶哑地说，伸出瘦骨嶙峋的手摸了摸克鲁克山毛茸茸的脑袋，"它是我见过的最聪明的猫。它一下子就认出了彼得，见到我时也知道我不是狗。它过了一阵子才信任我……但我终于让它明白了我在找什么，这猫一直在帮我……"

"你是说——？"赫敏小声问。

"它试图把彼得给我带来，可是不行……于是它就偷来了进格兰芬多塔楼的口令……我估计是从哪个男生的床头柜上拿的……"

哈利的大脑似乎不堪重负了，这一切太不可思议……可是……

"但是彼得听到风声，跑了……"布莱克用嘶哑的声音说，"这只猫——克鲁克山，你们是这么叫它的吗？——告诉我彼得在床单上留了血迹……我猜想它是咬伤了自己……哼，毕竟他成功装死过一次……"

这话猛然触动了哈利。

"他干吗要装死？"他气愤地问，"因为他知道你要来杀他？就像当年杀我父母一样？"

"不是的，"卢平说，"哈利——"

"现在你来结果他了！"

"是的。"布莱克恶狠狠地看着斑斑说。

"我应该让斯内普把你抓走的！"哈利喊道。

CHAPTER NINETEEN The Servant of Lord Voldemort

'Harry,' said Lupin hurriedly, 'don't you see? All this time we've thought Sirius betrayed your parents, and Peter tracked him down – but it was the other way around, don't you see? *Peter* betrayed your mother and father – Sirius tracked *Peter* down –'

'THAT'S NOT TRUE!' Harry yelled. 'HE WAS THEIR SECRET KEEPER! HE SAID SO BEFORE YOU TURNED UP, HE SAID HE KILLED THEM!'

He was pointing at Black, who shook his head slowly; the sunken eyes were suddenly over-bright.

'Harry ... I as good as killed them,' he croaked. 'I persuaded Lily and James to change to Peter at the last moment, persuaded them to use him as Secret Keeper instead of me ... I'm to blame, I know it ... the night they died, I'd arranged to check on Peter, make sure he was still safe, but when I arrived at his hiding place, he'd gone. Yet there was no sign of a struggle. It didn't feel right. I was scared. I set out for your parents' house straight away. And when I saw their house, destroyed, and their bodies – I realised what Peter must have done. What I'd done.'

His voice broke. He turned away.

'Enough of this,' said Lupin, and there was a steely note in his voice Harry had never heard before. 'There's one certain way to prove what really happened. Ron, *give me that rat.*'

'What are you going to do with him if I give him to you?' Ron asked Lupin tensely.

'Force him to show himself,' said Lupin. 'If he really is a rat, it won't hurt him.'

Ron hesitated, then at long last held out Scabbers and Lupin took him. Scabbers began to squeak without stopping, twisting and turning, his tiny black eyes bulging in his head.

'Ready, Sirius?' said Lupin.

Black had already retrieved Snape's wand from the bed. He approached Lupin and the struggling rat, and his wet eyes suddenly seemed to be burning in his face.

'Together?' he said quietly.

'I think so,' said Lupin, holding Scabbers tightly in one hand and his wand in the other. 'On the count of three. One – two – THREE!'

A flash of blue-white light erupted from both wands; for a moment, Scabbers

第19章 伏地魔的仆人

"哈利,"卢平急忙说,"你看不出来吗?我们一直以为是小天狼星出卖了你的父母,彼得去追捕他——但事实恰恰相反。你还看不出来吗?是彼得出卖了你的父母——是小天狼星去追捕彼得——"

"这不是真的!"哈利大叫道,"他是他们的保密人!你来之前他都承认了。他说是他杀了他们!"

他指着布莱克,布莱克缓缓地摇了摇头,凹陷的眼睛突然异样地亮了起来。

"哈利……我等于是害了他们,"他嘶哑地说,"我在最后一刻劝莉莉和詹姆改用彼得,让彼得而不是我来当他们的保密人……都怪我,我知道……他们遇难的那天夜里,我去看看彼得是否还安全,可是当我赶到他的藏身之处时,彼得已经不见了,但是那里并没有搏斗的痕迹。我感觉不妙,害怕起来,马上去了你父母家。当我看到他们房子的废墟,看到他们的尸体……我才意识到彼得做了什么……我做了什么……"

布莱克的声音哽咽了,他背过脸去。

"够了,"卢平说,声音中有一种哈利从没感到过的寒气,"有个可靠的办法可以证明事实真相。罗恩,把老鼠给我。"

"如果我把它交给你,你要把它怎么样?"罗恩紧张地问。

"迫使它现出原形,"卢平说,"如果它真是一只老鼠,这不会伤害它。"

罗恩犹豫着,好一会儿才交出斑斑,卢平接了过去。斑斑开始不停地尖叫,扭来扭去,小小的黑眼睛从脑袋上鼓了出来。

"准备好了吗,小天狼星?"卢平问。

布莱克已经从床上捡起斯内普的魔杖。他走向卢平和那只挣扎的老鼠,潮湿的眼睛突然像在脸上燃烧起来一样。

"一起来吗?"他轻声问。

"我想是的,"卢平一手紧抓着斑斑,一手举起了魔杖,"数到三。一——二——三!"

两根魔杖都喷出一道蓝光,一瞬间,斑斑停在半空中,黑色的小

CHAPTER NINETEEN The Servant of Lord Voldemort

was frozen in mid-air, his small black form twisting madly – Ron yelled – the rat fell and hit the floor. There was another blinding flash of light and then –

It was like watching a speeded-up film of a growing tree. A head was shooting upwards from the ground; limbs were sprouting; next moment, a man was standing where Scabbers had been, cringing and wringing his hands. Crookshanks was spitting and snarling on the bed, the hair on his back standing up.

He was a very short man, hardly taller than Harry and Hermione. His thin, colourless hair was unkempt and there was a large bald patch on top. He had the shrunken appearance of a plump man who had lost a lot of weight in a short time. His skin looked grubby, almost like Scabbers's fur, and something of the rat lingered around his pointed nose, his very small, watery eyes. He looked around at them all, his breathing fast and shallow. Harry saw his eyes dart to the door and back again.

'Well, hello, Peter,' said Lupin pleasantly, as though rats frequently erupted into old schoolfriends around him. 'Long time, no see.'

'S-Sirius ... R-Remus ...' Even Pettigrew's voice was squeaky. Again, his eyes darted towards the door. 'My friends ... my old friends ...'

Black's wand arm rose, but Lupin seized him around the wrist, gave him a warning look, then turned again to Pettigrew, his voice light and casual.

'We've been having a little chat, Peter, about what happened the night Lily and James died. You might have missed the finer points while you were squeaking around down there on the bed –'

'Remus,' gasped Pettigrew, and Harry could see beads of sweat breaking out over his pasty face, 'you don't believe him, do you ... He tried to kill me, Remus ...'

'So we've heard,' said Lupin, more coldly. 'I'd like to clear up one or two little matters with you, Peter, if you'd be so –'

'He's come to try and kill me again!' Pettigrew shrieked suddenly, pointing at Black, and Harry saw that he used his middle finger, because his index was missing. 'He killed Lily and James and now he's going to kill me, too ... you've got to help me, Remus ...'

Black's face looked more skull-like than ever as he stared at Pettigrew with his fathomless eyes.

'No one's going to try and kill you until we've sorted a few things out,' said

第19章 伏地魔的仆人

身子疯狂地扭动——罗恩大叫——老鼠落到地上,又一阵炫目的闪光,然后——

就像一棵树成长的快放镜头一样,从地面上急速冒出了一个脑袋,四肢也出来了。片刻之后,一个男子站在斑斑原来的地方,畏畏缩缩,绞着双手。克鲁克山在床上怒吼,吐着唾沫,它背上的毛都竖了起来。

这是个非常矮小的男人,比哈利和赫敏高不了多少。稀疏的、没有光泽的头发乱糟糟的,顶上还秃了一大块。他看上去皱巴巴的,像一个胖子在短时间里掉了很多肉;皮肤很脏,几乎跟斑斑的毛皮一样,尖鼻子和水汪汪的绿豆眼还带着几分老鼠的特征。他扫视着众人,呼吸急促,哈利看到他的眼睛往门那儿瞟来瞟去。

"你好啊,彼得。"卢平愉快地说,好像经常有老鼠在他面前变成老同学似的,"好久不见。"

"小—小天狼星……莱—莱姆斯……"小矮星彼得连声音都很尖细,眼睛又朝门口瞟了瞟,"我的朋友……我的老朋友……"

布莱克举起拿魔杖的胳膊,但是卢平抓住了他的手腕,对布莱克使了一个警告的眼色,然后再次转向小矮星,卢平的语气依然轻松随意。

"我们刚才在聊天,彼得,说到莉莉和詹姆遇难那天夜里的事情,你在床上吱吱乱叫时,可能漏过了一些细节——"

"莱姆斯,"小矮星急促地说,哈利看到他苍白的面孔上冒出了汗珠,"你不会相信他吧……?他想杀死我,莱姆斯……"

"我们听说是这样。"卢平说,声音冷淡了一些,"我想跟你澄清一两个小问题,彼得,如果你愿意——"

"他又来杀我了!"彼得突然尖叫起来,指着布莱克。哈利看到他用的是中指,因为没有食指。"他杀了莉莉和詹姆,现在又来杀我……你要救我,莱姆斯……"

布莱克的脸看上去更像骷髅了,深不可测的眼睛盯着小矮星。

"在我们把一些事情弄清楚之前,没人会杀你的。"卢平说。

CHAPTER NINETEEN The Servant of Lord Voldemort

Lupin.

'Sorted things out?' squealed Pettigrew, looking wildly about him once more, eyes taking in the boarded windows and, again, the only door. 'I knew he'd come after me! I knew he'd be back for me! I've been waiting for this for twelve years!'

'You knew Sirius was going to break out of Azkaban?' said Lupin, his brow furrowed. 'When nobody has ever done it before?'

'He's got Dark powers the rest of us can only dream of!' Pettigrew shouted shrilly. 'How else did he get out of there? I suppose He Who Must Not Be Named taught him a few tricks!'

Black started to laugh, a horrible, mirthless laugh that filled the whole room.

'Voldemort, teach me tricks?' he said.

Pettigrew flinched as though Black had brandished a whip at him.

'What, scared to hear your old master's name?' said Black. 'I don't blame you, Peter. His lot aren't very happy with you, are they?'

'Don't know – what you mean, Sirius –' muttered Pettigrew, his breathing faster than ever. His whole face was shining with sweat now.

'You haven't been hiding from *me* for twelve years,' said Black. 'You've been hiding from Voldemort's old supporters. I heard things in Azkaban, Peter ... they all think you're dead, or you'd have to answer to them ... I've heard them screaming all sorts of things in their sleep. Sounds like they think the double-crosser double-crossed them. Voldemort went to the Potters' on your information ... and Voldemort met his downfall there. And not all Voldemort's supporters ended up in Azkaban, did they? There are still plenty out here, biding their time, pretending they've seen the error of their ways ... If they ever got wind that you were still alive, Peter –'

'Don't know ... what you're talking about ...' said Pettigrew again, more shrilly than ever. He wiped his face on his sleeve and looked up at Lupin. 'You don't believe this – this madness, Remus –'

'I must admit, Peter, I have difficulty in understanding why an innocent man would want to spend twelve years as a rat,' said Lupin evenly.

'Innocent, but scared!' squealed Pettigrew. 'If Voldemort's supporters were after me, it was because I put one of their best men in Azkaban – the spy, Sirius Black!'

第19章 伏地魔的仆人

"弄清楚?"小矮星尖声叫道,又张皇四顾,眼睛瞟到封死的窗户,又瞟到那扇唯一的门,"我知道他会来找我!我知道他会回来找我的!我等了十二年了!"

"你知道小天狼星会从阿兹卡班逃出来吗?"卢平皱眉道,"以前可没人做到过这点。"

"他有我们做梦都想不到的黑魔力!"小矮星尖厉地叫道,"不然他怎么能从那里逃出来?我猜是那个连名字都不能提的人教了他几手!"

布莱克笑了起来,一种可怕的、没有快乐的笑声,充满了整个房间。

"伏地魔?教了我几手?"他说。

小矮星畏缩了一下,好像布莱克朝他抽了一鞭子似的。

"怎么?听到你老主人的名字害怕了?"布莱克说,"情有可原,彼得。他手下的那些人对你可不太满意啊,是不是?"

"不知道——你在说什么,小天狼星?"小矮星嘟哝道,呼吸更加急促,现在已经满脸都是晶亮的汗珠了。

"这十二年你不是在躲我,"布莱克说,"而是在躲伏地魔的老部下。我在阿兹卡班听到了一些事情。彼得……他们都以为你死了,不然就会让你坦白交代……我听到他们在梦里嚷嚷各种话,似乎认为是那个骗子骗了他们。伏地魔按你提供的情报去了波特家……伏地魔在那儿被打垮了。伏地魔的部下并没有全部进入阿兹卡班,是不是?还有好些在外面,等待时机,假装已经改过自新……他们要是得知你还活着,彼得——"

"不知道……你在说什么……"小矮星又说,声音比之前更加尖厉。他用袖子擦了擦脸,抬头看着卢平。"你不相信这——这些疯话吧,莱姆斯?"

"必须承认,彼得,我想不通为什么一个清清白白的人会愿意做十二年老鼠。"卢平公正地说。

"清白是清白的,但是害怕呀!"小矮星尖叫道,"如果伏地魔的部下在找我,那是因为我把他们最得力的干将送进了阿兹卡班——就是这个奸细,小天狼星布莱克!"

CHAPTER NINETEEN — The Servant of Lord Voldemort

Black's face contorted.

'How dare you,' he growled, sounding suddenly like the bear-sized dog he had been. 'I, a spy for Voldemort? When did I ever sneak around people who were stronger and more powerful than myself? But you, Peter – I'll never understand why I didn't see you were the spy from the start. You always liked big friends who'd look after you, didn't you? It used to be us ... me and Remus ... and James ...'

Pettigrew wiped his face again; he was almost panting for breath.

'Me, a spy ... must be out of your mind ... never ... don't know how you can say such a –'

'Lily and James only made you Secret Keeper because I suggested it,' Black hissed, so venomously that Pettigrew took a step backwards. 'I thought it was the perfect plan ... a bluff ... Voldemort would be sure to come after me, would never dream they'd use a weak, talentless thing like you ... it must have been the finest moment of your miserable life, telling Voldemort you could hand him the Potters.'

Pettigrew was muttering distractedly; Harry caught words like 'far-fetched' and 'lunacy', but he couldn't help paying more attention to the ashen colour of Pettigrew's face, and the way his eyes continued to dart towards the windows and door.

'Professor Lupin?' said Hermione timidly. 'Can – can I say something?'

'Certainly, Hermione,' said Lupin courteously.

'Well – Scabbers – I mean, this – this man – he's been sleeping in Harry's dormitory for three years. If he's working for You-know-Who, how come he never tried to hurt Harry before now?'

'There!' said Pettigrew shrilly, pointing at Hermione with his maimed hand. 'Thank you! You see, Remus? I have never hurt a hair of Harry's head! Why should I?'

'I'll tell you why,' said Black. 'Because you never did anything for anyone unless you could see what was in it for you. Voldemort's been in hiding for twelve years, they say he's half-dead. You weren't about to commit murder right under Albus Dumbledore's nose, for a wreck of a wizard who'd lost all his power, were you? You'd want to be quite sure he was the biggest bully in the playground before you went back to him, wouldn't you? Why else did you find a wizard family to take you in? Keeping an ear out for news, weren't

第19章 伏地魔的仆人

布莱克的脸都歪了。

"你怎么敢！"他咆哮道，听起来很像他变的那条熊一般的大狗，"我，伏地魔的奸细？我什么时候巴结过比我强大、有势力的人？而你——我搞不懂自己为什么没有一开始就看出你是奸细。你一向喜欢强大的朋友，好得到他们的关照，是不是？以前是我们……我和莱姆斯……还有詹姆……"

小矮星又擦了擦脸，几乎喘不过气来了。

"我，奸细……你准是疯了……没有的事……不知道你怎么能说出这样——"

"莉莉和詹姆是听了我的建议才让你做保密人的。"布莱克咬牙切齿地说，语气那么激烈，小矮星后退了一步，"我以为那是个好计策……一个调包计……伏地魔一定会来找我，而没有想到他们会用你这样一个软弱无能的东西……你告诉伏地魔，你可以把波特一家献给他，那一定是你卑劣的一生中最得意的时刻。"

小矮星语无伦次地咕哝着，哈利听见了"荒唐""神经病"之类的字眼，但他不能不注意到小矮星那土灰般的脸色，还有那双眼睛又在不断瞟向窗户和门口。

"卢平教授，"赫敏怯生生地问，"我——我可以说一句吗？"

"当然可以，赫敏。"卢平亲切地说。

"嗯——斑斑——我是说，这个——这个人——他在哈利的寝室里睡了三年，如果他是神秘人的帮凶，那他为什么一直没有伤害哈利呢？"

"对啊！"小矮星尖声说，用他残缺的手指着赫敏，"谢谢你！看到了吗，莱姆斯？我没有动过哈利一根头发！凭什么呀？"

"我来告诉你为什么，"布莱克说，"因为你从来都是不见兔子不撒鹰。伏地魔销声匿迹十二年，人家说他已经半死不活。你不会为了一个残废、失势的巫师在阿不思·邓布利多的眼皮底下杀人，是不是？你必须确定他还是最大的霸主，才会回去跟他，是不是？不然你为什么会找一个巫师家庭来收留你呢？因为这样可以竖着耳朵听消息，是不是，彼得？万一你的老庇护人卷土重来，形势安全了，你再回去投

CHAPTER NINETEEN   The Servant of Lord Voldemort

you, Peter? Just in case your old protector regained strength, and it was safe to rejoin him ...'

Pettigrew opened his mouth and closed it several times. He seemed to have lost the ability to talk.

'Er – Mr Black – Sirius?' said Hermione timidly.

Black jumped at being addressed like this and stared at Hermione as though being spoken to politely was something he'd long forgotten.

'If you don't mind me asking, how – how did you get out of Azkaban, if you didn't use Dark Magic?'

'Thank you!' gasped Pettigrew, nodding frantically at her. 'Exactly! Precisely what I –'

But Lupin silenced him with a look. Black was frowning slightly at Hermione, but not as though he was annoyed with her. He seemed to be pondering his answer.

'I don't know how I did it,' he said slowly. 'I think the only reason I never lost my mind is that I knew I was innocent. That wasn't a happy thought, so the Dementors couldn't suck it out of me ... but it kept me sane and knowing who I am ... helped me keep my powers ... so when it all became ... too much ... I could transform in my cell ... become a dog. Dementors can't see, you know ...' He swallowed. 'They feel their way towards people by sensing their emotions ... they could tell that my feelings were less – less human, less complex when I was a dog ... but they thought, of course, that I was losing my mind like everyone else in there, so it didn't trouble them. But I was weak, very weak, and I had no hope of driving them away from me without a wand ...

'But then I saw Peter in that picture ... I realised he was at Hogwarts with Harry ... perfectly positioned to act, if one hint reached his ears that the Dark Side was gathering strength again ...'

Pettigrew was shaking his head, mouthing noiselessly, but staring all the while at Black as though hypnotised.

'... ready to strike the moment he could be sure of allies ... to deliver the last Potter to them. If he gave them Harry, who'd dare say he'd betrayed Lord Voldemort? He'd be welcomed back with honours ...

'So you see, I had to do something. I was the only one who knew Peter was still alive ...'

Harry remembered what Mr Weasley had told Mrs Weasley. 'The guards

靠他……"

小矮星的嘴巴张了几下,似乎失去了说话的能力。

"呃——布莱克先生——小天狼星?"赫敏说。

布莱克听到有人这样称呼自己,惊得一跳,瞪着赫敏,好像很久没有人礼貌地对他说话了。

"希望您不介意我问一下,您——您是怎么逃出阿兹卡班的呢,如果没有用黑魔法?"

"谢谢你!"小矮星叫道,一个劲儿朝她点头,"对啊!这正是我——"

卢平用一个眼神打断了他。布莱克眉头微皱地看着赫敏,但似乎并不是对她感到恼火,而像在考虑怎么回答。

"我也不知道自己是怎么做到的,"他缓缓说道,"我想,我没有失去理智的唯一原因是知道自己是清白的。那不是一个愉快的念头,所以摄魂怪不能把它从我的脑子里吸走……但它让我保持神志清醒,知道自己是谁……也使我能够保存我的法力……所以当情况变得……太难熬的时候……我可以在牢房里变形……变成狗。你们知道,摄魂怪看不见……"他咽了口唾沫,"它们靠感知人的感情向人靠近……我变成了狗的时候,它们可能觉察出我的感情不大——不大像人,也不太复杂……不过,当然啦,它们以为我像其他囚犯一样正在丧失理智,所以没有在意。但是我很虚弱、很虚弱,没有魔杖,没有希望驱逐它们……

"可是后来,当我在那张照片上看到彼得……我意识到他在霍格沃茨,在哈利身边……如果有消息传到他耳朵里,说黑势力在重新抬头,他在霍格沃茨下手最合适不过了……"

小矮星摇着头,无声地动着嘴巴,但好像被催眠了似的一直瞪着布莱克。

"……一旦确定自己有了同盟,他就会采取行动……把波特家的最后一个人献给他们。如果他能献上哈利,谁还敢说他背叛过伏地魔?他会被当成功臣一样受到欢迎……

"所以,我必须做些什么,因为只有我知道彼得还活着……"

哈利想起韦斯莱先生曾对妻子说过:"守卫说他常说梦话……总是

say he's been talking in his sleep ... always the same words ... *"He's at Hogwarts".'*

'It was as if someone had lit a fire in my head, and the Dementors couldn't destroy it ... it wasn't a happy feeling ... it was an obsession ... but it gave me strength, it cleared my mind. So, one night when they opened my door to bring food, I slipped past them as a dog ... it's so much harder for them to sense animal emotions that they were confused ... I was thin, very thin ... thin enough to slip through the bars ... I swam as a dog back to the mainland ... I journeyed north and slipped into the Hogwarts grounds as a dog ... I've been living in the Forest ever since ... except when I come to watch the Quidditch, of course ... you fly as well as your father did, Harry ...'

He looked at Harry, who did not look away.

'Believe me,' croaked Black. 'Believe me. I never betrayed James and Lily. I would have died before I betrayed them.'

And at long last, Harry believed him. Throat too tight to speak, he nodded.

'No!'

Pettigrew had fallen to his knees as though Harry's nod had been his own death sentence. He shuffled forward on his knees, grovelling, his hands clasped in front of him as though praying.

'Sirius – it's me ... it's Peter ... your friend ... you wouldn't ...'

Black kicked out and Pettigrew recoiled.

'There's enough filth on my robes without you touching them,' said Black.

'Remus!' Pettigrew squeaked, turning to Lupin instead, writhing imploringly in front of him. 'You don't believe this ... Wouldn't Sirius have told you they'd changed the plan?'

'Not if he thought I was the spy, Peter,' said Lupin. 'I assume that's why you didn't tell me, Sirius?' he said casually over Pettigrew's head.

'Forgive me, Remus,' said Black.

'Not at all, Padfoot, old friend,' said Lupin, who was now rolling up his sleeves. 'And will you, in turn, forgive me for believing *you* were the spy?'

'Of course,' said Black, and the ghost of a grin flitted across his gaunt face. He, too, began rolling up his sleeves. 'Shall we kill him together?'

'Yes, I think so,' said Lupin grimly.

那一句……'他在霍格沃茨。'"

"好像有人在我脑子里点起了一把火，摄魂怪无法消灭它……那不是一个愉快的念头……那是一种执念……但它给了我力量，让我头脑清醒。所以，一天晚上，当它们开门送饭进来时，我变成狗溜了过去……它们对动物的感情不太敏感，就被弄糊涂了……我很瘦很瘦……瘦得能从铁栅栏之间钻过去……我用狗的身子游回了大陆……然后往北走，以狗的形态溜进了霍格沃茨校园。之后我一直住在禁林里，当然啦，看魁地奇比赛的时候除外。你飞得和你爸爸一样好，哈利……"

他看着哈利，哈利没有转过脸去。

"相信我，"布莱克嘶哑地说，"相信我，哈利。我从来没有出卖过詹姆和莉莉，我宁死也不会出卖他们。"

哈利终于相信了。他嗓子眼发紧，说不出话来，只是点了点头。

"不！"

小矮星跪了下来，好像哈利点头就是对他判了死刑。他跪着爬向前，低声下气，双手紧握在胸口像是在祈祷。

"小天狼星——是我呀……是彼得……你的朋友……你不会……"

布莱克踢了一脚，小矮星畏缩了一下。

"我袍子上的污秽已经够多了，不要你碰。"布莱克说。

"莱姆斯！"小矮星哀叫着转向卢平，在他面前乞怜地扭动着身躯，"你不会相信这些吧……要是他们换了方案，小天狼星不会告诉你吗？"

"不会，如果他以为我是奸细，就不会告诉我，彼得。"卢平说，"我想这就是你没有告诉我的原因吧，小天狼星？"他越过小矮星的头顶不经意地说。

"原谅我，莱姆斯。"布莱克说。

"哪里的话，大脚板，老伙计，"卢平说着，卷起了袖子，"那么你也原谅我曾经以为你是奸细，好吗？"

"当然。"布莱克憔悴的脸上掠过一丝笑意，他也卷起了袖子，"我们俩一起把他干掉？"

"我想可以。"卢平冷峻地说。

CHAPTER NINETEEN — The Servant of Lord Voldemort

'You wouldn't ... you won't ...' gasped Pettigrew. And he scrambled around to Ron.

'Ron ... haven't I been a good friend ... a good pet? You won't let them kill me, Ron, will you ... you're on my side, aren't you?'

But Ron was staring at Pettigrew with the utmost revulsion.

'I let you sleep in my *bed*!' he said.

'Kind boy ... kind master ...' Pettigrew crawled towards Ron, 'you won't let them do it ... I was your rat ... I was a good pet ...'

'If you made a better rat than human, it's not much to boast about, Peter,' said Black harshly. Ron, going still paler with pain, wrenched his broken leg out of Pettigrew's reach. Pettigrew turned on his knees, staggered forwards and seized the hem of Hermione's robes.

'Sweet girl ... clever girl ... you – you won't let them ... help me ...'

Hermione pulled her robes out of Pettigrew's clutching hands and backed away against the wall, looking horrified.

Pettigrew knelt, trembling uncontrollably, and turned his head slowly towards Harry.

'Harry ... Harry ... you look just like your father ... just like him ...'

'HOW DARE YOU SPEAK TO HARRY?' roared Black. 'HOW DARE YOU FACE HIM? HOW DARE YOU TALK ABOUT JAMES IN FRONT OF HIM?'

'*Harry*,' whispered Pettigrew, shuffling towards him, hands outstretched, 'Harry, James wouldn't have wanted me killed ... James would have understood, Harry ... he would have shown me mercy ...'

Both Black and Lupin strode forwards, seized Pettigrew's shoulders and threw him backwards onto the floor. He sat there, twitching with terror, staring up at them.

'You sold Lily and James to Voldemort,' said Black, who was shaking too. 'Do you deny it?'

Pettigrew burst into tears. It was horrible to watch: he looked like an oversized, balding baby, cowering on the floor.

'Sirius, Sirius, what could I have done? The Dark Lord ... you have no idea ... he has weapons you can't imagine ... I was scared, Sirius, I was never brave like you and Remus and James. I never meant it to happen ... He Who Must Not Be Named forced me –'

第19章 伏地魔的仆人

"不……不要……"小矮星惊恐地叫道,慌忙转身爬向罗恩。

"罗恩……我不是你的好朋友……好宠物吗?你不会让他们杀我的,罗恩,对吧……你会站在我一边,是不是?"

但罗恩带着极度的厌恶瞪着小矮星。

"我竟然让你睡在我的床上!"罗恩说。

"好心的孩子……好心的主人……"小矮星朝罗恩爬去,"你不会让他们那么做的……我是你的小老鼠……我是一个好宠物……"

"如果你当老鼠当得比人好一些的话,那也没有什么可夸耀的,彼得。"布莱克尖刻地说。罗恩的脸色因疼痛而显得更加苍白,他把伤腿移开,不让小矮星碰到。小矮星跪在地上转过身,跟踉向前,扯住了赫敏的袍子的下摆。

"可爱的女孩……聪明的女孩……你——你不会让他们……帮帮我……"

赫敏把袍子从小矮星的手里拽了出来,退到墙边,看上去很害怕。

小矮星跪在那儿,控制不住地哆嗦着,慢慢把头转向了哈利。

"哈利……哈利……你长得跟你爸一模一样……一模一样……"

"**你怎么还敢对哈利说话?**"布莱克怒吼,"**你怎么还敢面对他?你怎么还敢在他面前说到詹姆?**"

"哈利,"小矮星低声说,张开双手跪着走向他,"哈利,詹姆不会希望我被杀死的……詹姆会理解的,哈利……他会对我手下留情……"

布莱克和卢平一齐上前抓住了小矮星的肩膀,把他撂倒在地。小矮星坐在那儿,恐惧地抽搐着,仰视着他们。

"你把莉莉和詹姆出卖给了伏地魔,"布莱克说,他的身子也在哆嗦,"你还想抵赖吗?"

小矮星痛哭起来,那样子看着十分恐怖,像一个秃了顶的大婴儿,畏缩地坐在地上。

"小天狼星,小天狼星,我能怎么做呢?黑魔王……你们不知道……他有你们想象不到的武器……我害怕啊,小天狼星,我一向不如你、莱姆斯,还有詹姆那样勇敢。我从来没想这样……是那个连名字都不能提的人逼我——"

CHAPTER NINETEEN The Servant of Lord Voldemort

'DON'T LIE!' bellowed Black. 'YOU'D BEEN PASSING INFORMATION TO HIM FOR A YEAR BEFORE LILY AND JAMES DIED! YOU WERE HIS SPY!'

'He – he was taking over everywhere!' gasped Pettigrew. 'Wh-what was there to be gained by refusing him?'

'What was there to be gained by fighting the most evil wizard who has ever existed?' said Black, with a terrible fury in his face. 'Only innocent lives, Peter!'

'You don't understand!' whined Pettigrew. 'He would have killed me, Sirius!'

'THEN YOU SHOULD HAVE DIED!' roared Black. 'DIED RATHER THAN BETRAY YOUR FRIENDS, AS WE WOULD HAVE DONE FOR YOU!'

Black and Lupin stood shoulder to shoulder, wands raised.

'You should have realised,' said Lupin quietly. 'If Voldemort didn't kill you, we would. Goodbye, Peter.'

Hermione covered her face with her hands and turned to the wall.

'NO!' Harry yelled. He ran forwards, placing himself in front of Pettigrew, facing the wands. 'You can't kill him,' he said breathlessly. 'You can't.'

Black and Lupin both looked staggered.

'Harry, this piece of vermin is the reason you have no parents,' Black snarled. 'This cringing bit of filth would have seen you die, too, without turning a hair. You heard him. His own stinking skin meant more to him than your whole family.'

'I know,' Harry panted. 'We'll take him up to the castle. We'll hand him over to the Dementors. He can go to Azkaban ... just don't kill him.'

'Harry!' gasped Pettigrew, and he flung his arms around Harry's knees. 'You – thank you – it's more than I deserve – thank you –'

'Get off me,' Harry spat, throwing Pettigrew's hands off him in disgust. 'I'm not doing this for you. I'm doing it because I don't reckon my dad would've wanted his best friends to become killers – just for you.'

No one moved or made a sound except Pettigrew, whose breath was coming in wheezes as he clutched his chest. Black and Lupin were looking at each other. Then, with one movement, they lowered their wands.

'You're the only person who has the right to decide, Harry,' said Black. 'But think ... think what he did ...'

第19章 伏地魔的仆人

"别说鬼话！"布莱克吼道，"莉莉和詹姆被杀之前，你就已经给他传了一年的情报了！你就是他的奸细！"

"他——他到处得势！"小矮星叫道，"违抗他有——有什么好处？"

"对抗世上最邪恶的巫师有什么好处？"布莱克一脸可怕的狂怒，"是为了拯救一些无辜的生命啊，彼得！"

"你们不知道！"小矮星哀叫，"他会杀了我的，小天狼星！"

"那你就应该死！"布莱克咆哮道，"**宁死也不能出卖朋友，我们为了你也会这样做的！**"

布莱克和卢平并肩而立，举起了魔杖。

"你应该想到，"卢平轻声说，"伏地魔不杀你，我们也会杀你。永别了，彼得。"

赫敏捂住面孔，身子转向了墙壁。

"不！"哈利喊道，他跑上去，挡在小矮星身前，面对那两根魔杖，"你们不能杀他，"他气喘吁吁地说，"你们不能。"

布莱克和卢平都很吃惊。

"哈利，是这个恶棍害得你父母双亡，"布莱克吼道，"这个卑躬屈膝的垃圾看着你死掉连汗毛都不会动一下。你听到他自己说了，对他来说他这副臭皮囊比你全家的性命都重要。"

"我知道，"哈利喘着气说，"我们把他带到城堡去，交给摄魂怪……他可以进阿兹卡班……但不要杀他。"

"哈利！"小矮星叫道，一把搂住了哈利的膝盖，"你——谢谢你——我不配啊——谢谢你——"

"放开我！"哈利厉声说，厌恶地甩开小矮星的手，"我这么做不是为了你，而是因为——我想我爸爸不会愿意他最好的两个朋友成为杀人犯——为了你这种人。"

没有人动一动，没有人发出声音，只有小矮星紧捂着胸口，艰难地喘息。布莱克和卢平对视了一下，然后一齐垂下了魔杖。

"你是唯一有权做出决定的人，哈利，"布莱克说，"可是想想……想想他做的……"

'He can go to Azkaban,' Harry repeated. 'If anyone deserves that place, he does ...'

Pettigrew was still wheezing behind him.

'Very well,' said Lupin. 'Stand aside, Harry.'

Harry hesitated.

'I'm going to tie him up,' said Lupin. 'That's all, I swear.'

Harry stepped out of the way. Thin cords shot from Lupin's wand this time, and next moment, Pettigrew was wriggling on the floor, bound and gagged.

'But if you transform, Peter,' growled Black, his own wand pointing at Pettigrew, too, 'we *will* kill you. You agree, Harry?'

Harry looked down at the pitiful figure on the floor, and nodded so that Pettigrew could see him.

'Right,' said Lupin, suddenly business-like. 'Ron, I can't mend bones nearly as well as Madam Pomfrey, so I think it's best if we just strap your leg up until we can get you to the hospital wing.'

He hurried over to Ron, bent down, tapped Ron's leg with his wand and muttered, '*Ferula.*' Bandages spun up Ron's leg, strapping it tightly to a splint. Lupin helped him to his feet; Ron put his weight gingerly on the leg and didn't wince.

'That's better,' he said. 'Thanks.'

'What about Professor Snape?' said Hermione in a small voice, looking down at Snape's prone figure.

'There's nothing seriously wrong with him,' said Lupin, bending over Snape and checking his pulse. 'You were just a little – over-enthusiastic. Still out cold. Er – perhaps it will be best if we don't revive him until we're safely back in the castle. We can take him like this ...'

He muttered, '*Mobilicorpus.*' As though invisible strings were tied to Snape's wrists, neck and knees, he was pulled into a standing position, head still lolling unpleasantly, like a grotesque puppet. He hung a few inches above the ground, his limp feet dangling. Lupin picked up the Invisibility Cloak and tucked it safely into his pocket.

'And two of us should be chained to this,' said Black, nudging Pettigrew with his toe. 'Just to make sure.'

'I'll do it,' said Lupin.

'And me,' said Ron savagely, limping forwards.

第19章 伏地魔的仆人

"他可以进阿兹卡班。"哈利又说,"如果有人该进那个地方,那就是他……"

小矮星还在他后面呼哧呼哧地喘气。

"很好,"卢平说,"让开,哈利。"

哈利犹豫着。

"我把他绑起来,"卢平说,"没别的,我发誓。"

哈利站到一边。这次是卢平的魔杖射出了细绳,接着便见小矮星在地上扭动着,被绑得结结实实,嘴巴也被塞住了。

"但是,彼得,你要是敢变形,"布莱克低吼道,他的魔杖也指着小矮星,"我们就马上杀了你。哈利,你同意吗?"

哈利看着地上那个可鄙的家伙,点了点头,使小矮星也能看到。

"好,"卢平说,突然变得高效务实,"罗恩,我接骨头不如庞弗雷女士拿手,所以我想最好先把你的腿扎起来,待会儿送你去校医院。"

他快步走过去,弯腰用魔杖敲了敲罗恩的腿,念道:"夹板紧扎。"绷带一圈圈地绕着,把罗恩的腿紧紧绑到一根薄木条上。卢平扶他站了起来,罗恩轻轻地将身体的重量移到伤腿上,没有皱眉。

"好些了,谢谢。"他说。

"斯内普教授怎么办呢?"赫敏望着趴在地上的斯内普,小声问。

"他没什么大事儿,"卢平说着,俯身摸了摸斯内普的脉搏,"你们只是有点——有点劲头太足了。他还没有知觉。呃——也许最好是回到城堡之后再把他弄醒。可以这样带他走……"

他念了一声:"僵尸飘行。"斯内普的手腕、脖子和膝盖上好像拴了根看不见的绳子,他被拉得站了起来,但脑袋还是难看地耷拉着,像个怪诞的木偶,双脚无力地悬在离地面几英寸的地方。卢平捡起隐形衣,把它妥帖地塞进自己的口袋里。

"应该有两个人跟这个家伙铐在一起,"布莱克用脚趾踢了踢小矮星说,"以防万一。"

"我可以。"卢平说。

"还有我。"罗恩粗声说,跛着腿走上前。

CHAPTER NINETEEN   The Servant of Lord Voldemort

Black conjured heavy manacles from thin air; soon Pettigrew was upright again, left arm chained to Lupin's right, right arm to Ron's left. Ron's face was set. He seemed to have taken Scabbers's true identity as a personal insult. Crookshanks leapt lightly off the bed and led the way out of the room, his bottlebrush tail held jauntily high.

第19章 伏地魔的仆人

布莱克凭空变出沉重的手铐,小矮星很快就被拉了起来,左右胳膊分别铐在卢平的右臂和罗恩的左臂上。罗恩沉着脸,似乎斑斑的真实身份对他的人格构成了侮辱。克鲁克山轻巧地从床上跳下来,领先跑出房间,毛茸茸的尾巴快乐地高高翘起。

CHAPTER TWENTY

The Dementor's Kiss

Harry had never been part of a stranger group. Crookshanks led the way down the stairs; Lupin, Pettigrew and Ron went next, looking like contestants in a six-legged race. Next came Professor Snape, drifting creepily along, his toes hitting each stair as they descended, held up by his own wand, which was being pointed at him by Sirius. Harry and Hermione brought up the rear.

Getting back into the tunnel was difficult. Lupin, Pettigrew and Ron had to turn sideways to manage it; Lupin still had Pettigrew covered with his wand. Harry could see them edging awkwardly along the tunnel in single file. Crookshanks was still in the lead. Harry went right after Sirius, who was still making Snape drift along ahead of them; he kept bumping his lolling head on the low ceiling. Harry had the impression Sirius was making no effort to prevent this.

'You know what this means?' Sirius said abruptly to Harry, as they made their slow progress along the tunnel. 'Turning Pettigrew in?'

'You're free,' said Harry.

'Yes ...' said Sirius. 'But I'm also – I don't know if anyone ever told you – I'm your godfather.'

'Yeah, I knew that,' said Harry.

'Well ... your parents appointed me your guardian,' said Sirius stiffly. 'If anything happened to them ...'

Harry waited. Did Sirius mean what he thought he meant?

'I'll understand, of course, if you want to stay with your aunt and uncle,' said Sirius. 'But ... well ... think about it. Once my name's cleared ... if you wanted a ... a different home ...'

第 20 章

摄魂怪的吻

哈利从没置身于比这更古怪的队伍。克鲁克山领头跑下楼梯，卢平、小矮星和罗恩跟在后面，看上去像三个连体赛跑的运动员。然后是斯内普教授。被自己的魔杖控制着——小天狼星拿着他的魔杖指着他，他令人毛骨悚然地飘下楼去，脚趾碰撞到每一级台阶。哈利和赫敏在后面压阵。

钻回地道里很困难，卢平、小矮星和罗恩必须侧着身子，卢平仍用魔杖提防着小矮星。哈利看到他们三人排成一条直线，笨拙地在地道里往前挪动。克鲁克山依然跑在前面，哈利紧跟着布莱克钻了进去，斯内普仍在他们前面飘着，耷拉的脑袋不时磕到低矮的地道顶部，哈利觉得布莱克故意不去避免。

"把小矮星交出去，"在地道里缓缓前进时，布莱克突然对哈利说，"你知道这意味着什么吗？"

"你自由了。"哈利说。

"对……"小天狼星说，"但我还——我不知道有没有人告诉过你——我是你的教父。"

"嗯，我知道。"哈利说。

"是这样……你的父母指定我做你的监护人，"布莱克不自然地说，"万一他们遭遇不测……"

哈利等待着，布莱克真的会是他想的那个意思吗？

"当然啦，如果你想跟你的姨妈和姨父住在一起，我可以理解，"布莱克说，"但是……嗯……考虑一下吧。一旦我洗刷了罪名……如果你想要一个……一个不一样的家……"

CHAPTER TWENTY   The Dementor's Kiss

Some sort of explosion took place in the pit of Harry's stomach.

'What – live with you?' he said, accidentally cracking his head on a bit of rock protruding from the ceiling. 'Leave the Dursleys?'

'Of course, I thought you wouldn't want to,' said Sirius quickly. 'I understand. I just thought I'd –'

'Are you mad?' said Harry, his voice easily as croaky as Sirius'. 'Of course I want to leave the Dursleys! Have you got a house? When can I move in?'

Sirius turned right around to look at him; Snape's head was scraping the ceiling but Sirius didn't seem to care.

'You want to?' he said. 'You mean it?'

'Yeah, I mean it!' said Harry.

Sirius' gaunt face broke into the first true smile Harry had seen upon it. The difference it made was startling, as though a person ten years younger was shining through the starved mask; for a moment, he was recognisable as the man who had laughed at Harry's parents' wedding.

They did not speak again until they had reached the end of the tunnel. Crookshanks darted up first; he had evidently pressed his paw to the knot on the trunk, because Lupin, Pettigrew and Ron clambered upwards without any sound of savaging branches.

Sirius saw Snape up through the hole, then stood back for Harry and Hermione to pass. At last, all of them were out.

The grounds were very dark now, the only light came from the distant windows of the castle. Without a word, they set off. Pettigrew was still wheezing and occasionally whimpering. Harry's mind was buzzing. He was going to leave the Dursleys. He was going to live with Sirius Black, his parents' best friend ... he felt dazed ... What would happen when he told the Dursleys he was going to live with the convict they'd seen on television?

'One wrong move, Peter,' said Lupin threateningly, ahead. His wand was still pointed sideways at Pettigrew's chest.

Silently they tramped through the grounds, the castle lights growing slowly larger. Snape was still drifting weirdly ahead of Sirius, his chin bumping on his chest. And then –

A cloud shifted. There were suddenly dim shadows on the ground. Their party was bathed in moonlight.

第 20 章　摄魂怪的吻

哈利感觉自己一下子心花怒放。

"什么——跟你一起生活？"他说，一不留神脑袋撞到了地道顶部一块突出的石头上，"离开德思礼家？"

"当然，我想你不会愿意的，"布莱克马上说，"我能理解，我只是觉得我——"

"你糊涂了吗？"哈利说，声音几乎和布莱克的一样嘶哑，"我当然愿意离开德思礼家！你有房子吗？我什么时候可以搬进去？"

小天狼星迅速转身看着他，斯内普的头擦着了地道顶部，但小天狼星似乎毫不在意。

"你愿意？"他问，"真的？"

"是啊，我真的愿意！"哈利说。

布莱克憔悴的脸上第一次绽出真正的笑容，它带来的变化令人吃惊，好像一个比他年轻十岁的人从那枯瘦的面具后面闪露出来。一瞬间，可以看出他就是在哈利父母婚礼上欢笑的那个人了。

他们没再说话，一直走到了地道口。克鲁克山第一个跳了上去，它显然是用爪子按了树干上的节疤，因为卢平、小矮星和罗恩爬上去时，没有听到柳树枝条的抽打声。

布莱克把斯内普送出洞口，然后站到一边，让哈利和赫敏上去。终于，大家全都出来了。

地面上很黑，只有远处城堡的窗户透出微光。他们一言不发地往前走去。小矮星还在呼哧呼哧地喘气，并不时地呜咽两声。哈利脑子里嗡嗡作响，他要离开德思礼家，住到父母最好的朋友小天狼星布莱克那儿去了……他有点晕头转向……如果他对德思礼家的人说自己要去跟电视上的那个逃犯一起生活，他们会怎么样？

"你敢乱动一下，彼得。"卢平在前面威胁地说。他的魔杖仍然斜指着小矮星的胸口。

他们默默地穿过场地，城堡的灯光渐渐亮了起来。斯内普仍在布莱克前面怪异地飘浮着，下巴在胸前一磕一磕。这时——

一片云移开，地上出现了模糊的阴影，几个人沐浴在月光中。

CHAPTER TWENTY   The Dementor's Kiss

Snape collided with Lupin, Pettigrew and Ron, who had stopped abruptly. Sirius froze. He flung out an arm to make Harry and Hermione stop.

Harry could see Lupin's silhouette. He had gone rigid. Then his limbs began to shake.

'Oh my –' Hermione gasped. 'He didn't take his Potion tonight! He's not safe!'

'Run,' Sirius whispered. 'Run! Now!'

But Harry couldn't run. Ron was chained to Pettigrew and Lupin. He leapt forwards but Sirius caught him around the chest and threw him back.

'Leave it to me – RUN!'

There was a terrible snarling noise. Lupin's head was lengthening. So was his body. His shoulders were hunching. Hair was sprouting visibly on his face and hands, which were curling into clawed paws. Crookshanks's fur was on end again, he was backing away –

As the werewolf reared, snapping its long jaws, Sirius disappeared from Harry's side. He had transformed. The enormous, bear-like dog bounded forwards. As the werewolf wrenched itself free of the manacle binding it, the dog seized it about the neck and pulled it backwards, away from Ron and Pettigrew. They were locked, jaw to jaw, claws ripping at each other –

Harry stood, transfixed by the sight; too intent upon the battle to notice anything else. It was Hermione's scream that alerted him –

Pettigrew had dived for Lupin's dropped wand. Ron, unsteady on his bandaged leg, fell. There was a bang, a burst of light – and Ron lay motionless on the ground. Another bang – Crookshanks flew into the air and back to the earth in a heap.

'*Expelliarmus!*' Harry yelled, pointing his own wand at Pettigrew; Lupin's wand flew high into the air and out of sight. 'Stay where you are!' Harry shouted, running forwards.

Too late. Pettigrew had transformed. Harry saw his bald tail whip through the manacle on Ron's outstretched arm, and heard a scurrying through the grass.

There was a howl and a rumbling growl; Harry turned to see the werewolf taking flight; it was galloping into the Forest –

'Sirius, he's gone, Pettigrew transformed!' Harry yelled.

Sirius was bleeding; there were gashes across his muzzle and back, but at Harry's words he scrambled up again, and in an instant, the sound of his paws was fading to silence as he pounded away across the grounds.

第20章 摄魂怪的吻

斯内普撞到了突然停下的卢平、小矮星和罗恩身上。布莱克站住了，伸出胳膊拦住哈利和赫敏。

哈利看到卢平的侧影，卢平好像僵住了，然后四肢开始颤抖起来。

"哦，天哪——"赫敏惊叫道，"他今晚没有喝药！他不安全！"

"跑，"布莱克低声说，"跑，快跑！"

但哈利不能跑，罗恩还跟小矮星和卢平铐在一起呢。他冲上前，但布莱克当胸抱住他，把他扔了回去。

"交给我吧——**快跑！**"

一阵可怕的咆哮声，卢平的脑袋在拉长，身体也变长了。他的肩部弓起，脸上和手上都长出毛来，手指弯成了尖爪。克鲁克山的毛又竖了起来，它在往后退——

狼人后腿立起，长长的嘴巴一张一合。小天狼星在哈利身边消失了，他变形了，变成熊一般的大狗蹿上前去。正当狼人挣脱手铐时，大狗攫住了它的脖子，把它往后拖，让它离开罗恩和小矮星。狼嘴与狗嘴咬在一起，爪子互相撕抓——

哈利站在那儿看呆了，他全神贯注地看着眼前的搏斗，没有注意到别的。是赫敏的尖叫提醒了他——

小矮星扑向卢平丢下的魔杖。罗恩腿上绑着夹板站立不稳，摔倒下去。砰的一声，一道闪光——罗恩一动不动地躺在地上。又是砰的一声——克鲁克山飞到空中，又软绵绵地落到地上。

"除你武器！"哈利高喊，用自己的魔杖指着小矮星。卢平的魔杖高高飞起，消失不见了。"不许动！"哈利吼道，一边跑向前去。

太晚了，小矮星已经变形，哈利看到他的秃尾巴从罗恩张开的胳膊上的手铐里抽了出去，又听到草丛中传出一阵窸窣声。

一声长嗥和一阵低沉的咆哮，哈利转身看到狼人逃走，跑进禁林里去了——

"小天狼星，他不见了，小矮星变形了！"哈利喊道。

小天狼星在流血，嘴部和背上都有深深的伤口，但是听到哈利的话又爬了起来，奋力追去，转瞬间他爪子踏地的声音便消失在寂静中。

CHAPTER TWENTY The Dementor's Kiss

Harry and Hermione dashed over to Ron.

'What did he do to him?' Hermione whispered. Ron's eyes were only half-closed; his mouth hung open. He was definitely alive, they could hear him breathing, but he didn't seem to recognise them.

'I don't know.'

Harry looked desperately around. Black and Lupin both gone ... they had no one but Snape for company, still hanging, unconscious, in mid-air.

'We'd better get them up to the castle and tell someone,' said Harry, pushing his hair out of his eyes, trying to think straight. 'Come –'

But then, out of the darkness, they heard a yelping, a whining; a dog in pain ...

'Sirius,' Harry muttered, staring into the darkness.

He had a moment's indecision, but there was nothing they could do for Ron at the moment, and by the sound of it, Black was in trouble –

Harry set off at a run, Hermione right behind him. The yelping seemed to be coming from near the lake. They pelted towards it, and Harry, running flat out, felt the cold without realising what it must mean –

The yelping stopped abruptly. As they reached the lake's shore they saw why – Sirius had turned back into a man. He was crouched on all fours, his hands over his head.

'*Nooo*,' he moaned. '*Noooo.... please ...*'

And then Harry saw them. Dementors, at least a hundred of them, gliding in a black mass around the lake towards them. He spun around, the familiar, icy cold penetrating his insides, fog starting to obscure his vision; more were appearing out of the darkness on every side; they were encircling them ...

'Hermione, think of something happy!' Harry yelled, raising his wand, blinking furiously to try and clear his vision, shaking his head to rid it of the faint screaming that had started inside it –

I'm going to live with my godfather. I'm leaving the Dursleys.

He forced himself to think of Sirius, and only Sirius, and began to chant: '*Expecto patronum! Expecto patronum!*'

Black gave a shudder, rolled over and lay motionless on the ground, pale as death.

He'll be all right. I'm going to go and live with him.

'*Expecto patronum!* Hermione, help me! *Expecto patronum!*'

第20章 摄魂怪的吻

哈利和赫敏冲到罗恩身边。

"他对他做了什么？"赫敏小声问。罗恩眼睛半闭，嘴巴张着。他无疑还活着，可以听到他在呼吸，但他似乎认不出他们了。

"我不知道……"

哈利焦急地左右张望，布莱克和卢平都不见了……只有斯内普还在旁边，还是没有知觉地悬在半空。

"我们最好把他们带进城堡，然后告诉别人。"哈利说，他把头发从眼前撩开，努力理清思路，"走吧——"

但是就在这时，视野之外传来一声犬吠，一声哀号，一条狗在痛苦地吠叫……

"小天狼星！"哈利叫道，朝黑暗中望去。

他一时犹豫不决，眼下他们对罗恩束手无措，而听声音布莱克遇到了麻烦——

哈利拔腿飞奔，赫敏紧跟在后。犬吠声好像是从湖边传来的，他们冲过去，全速奔跑的哈利感到一股寒气，但没有意识到那是什么——

犬吠声突然停止了，两人跑到湖边，明白了是怎么回事——小天狼星已变回人形。他蜷伏在地上，双手捂着头。

"别——"他呻吟道，"别……请别……"

接着哈利看到了它们，摄魂怪，至少有一百个，黑压压地沿湖边向他们逼来。他迅速转过身，那股寒意透彻肺腑，雾气开始模糊了他的视线。黑暗中，越来越多的摄魂怪从四面八方出现，包围过来……

"赫敏，想想高兴的事！"哈利喊道，举起了魔杖，拼命眨眼想看得更清楚，使劲摇头想甩掉脑子里开始听到的微弱的尖叫——

我要跟教父住在一起了，我要离开德思礼家了。

他强迫自己去想小天狼星，只想小天狼星，并开始高喊："呼神护卫！呼神护卫！"

布莱克浑身一震，打了个滚，躺在地上不动了，苍白得像个死人。

他不会有事的，我会去跟他一起生活。

"呼神护卫！赫敏，快帮我！呼神护卫！"

CHAPTER TWENTY The Dementor's Kiss

'*Expecto –*' Hermione whispered, '*expecto – expecto –*'

But she couldn't do it. The Dementors were closing in, barely ten feet from them. They formed a solid wall around Harry and Hermione, and were getting closer ...

'*EXPECTO PATRONUM!*' Harry yelled, trying to blot the screaming from his ears. '*EXPECTO PATRONUM!*'

A thin wisp of silver escaped his wand and hovered like mist before him. At the same moment, Harry felt Hermione collapse next to him. He was alone ... completely alone ...

'*Expecto – expecto patronum –*'

Harry felt his knees hit the cold grass. Fog was clouding his eyes. With a huge effort, he fought to remember – Sirius was innocent – innocent – *we'll be OK – I'm going to live with him –*

'*Expecto patronum!*' he gasped.

By the feeble light of his formless Patronus, he saw a Dementor halt, very close to him. It couldn't walk through the cloud of silver mist Harry had conjured. A dead, slimy hand slid out from under the cloak. It made a gesture as though to sweep the Patronus aside.

'No – *no* –' Harry gasped. 'He's innocent ... *expecto – expecto patronum –*'

He could feel them watching him, hear their rattling breath like an evil wind around him. The nearest Dementor seemed to be considering him. Then it raised both its rotting hands – and lowered its hood.

Where there should have been eyes, there was only thin, grey, scabbed skin, stretched blankly over empty sockets. But there was a mouth ... a gaping, shapeless hole, sucking the air with the sound of a death-rattle.

A paralysing terror filled Harry so that he couldn't move or speak. His Patronus flickered and died.

White fog was blinding him. He had to fight ... *expecto patronum* ... he couldn't see ... and in the distance, he heard the familiar screaming ... *expecto patronum* ... he groped in the mist for Sirius, and found his arm ... they weren't going to take him ...

But a pair of strong, clammy hands suddenly wrapped themselves around Harry's neck. They were forcing his face upwards ... he could feel its breath ... it was going to get rid of him first ... he could feel its putrid breath ... his mother was screaming in his ears ... she was going to be the last thing he

第20章 摄魂怪的吻

"呼神——"赫敏小声说,"呼神——呼神——"

可是她念不下去了,摄魂怪在逼近,离他们只有十英尺了。它们像一堵墙一样把哈利和赫敏围得严严实实,越来越近……

"**呼神护卫!**"哈利呐喊,竭力让声音盖过耳中的尖叫,"**呼神护卫!**"

一缕银丝从他魔杖上飘出,雾一般地悬在面前。与此同时,哈利感到赫敏在他旁边倒了下去。只有他一个人了……孤军奋战……

"呼神——呼神护卫——"

哈利感到自己跪到了草地上。雾气迷住了眼睛。他拼命回忆——小天狼星是清白的——清白的——我们会没事的——我要去跟他一起生活——

"呼神护卫!"他艰难地说。

借着他那不成形的守护神的微光,哈利看到一个摄魂怪在离他很近的地方停了下来,它无法穿过哈利变出的那团银雾。一只黏糊糊的死人手从斗篷下伸出来,挥了一下,好像要把守护神拨开。

"不——不——"哈利叫道,"他是清白的……呼神——呼神护卫!"

他能感到它们在观察他,听到它们咯咯的呼吸声像恶风一样围绕着他。离得最近的一个摄魂怪似乎在打量他,然后举起腐烂的双手——脱下了它的兜帽。

在应该长眼睛的地方只有结着灰痂的薄皮,蒙在空洞洞的眼窝上。但是有嘴……一个不成形的大洞,吸吮着空气,发出临死的人才发出的那种咯咯的喉音。

恐怖麻痹了哈利的全身,他不能动,也说不出话来。他的守护神闪烁了几下,熄灭了。

白雾模糊了他的视线。他必须反抗……呼神护卫!……他看不见……听到远处有熟悉的呼喊声……呼神护卫……他在迷雾中摸索着小天狼星,摸到了他的胳膊……不能让它们把他带走……

然而,一双有力的、冰冷黏湿的大手突然卡住了哈利的脖子,把他的脸朝上抬起……他能感觉到它的呼吸……它是想先除掉他……哈利感觉到了它腐臭的气息……妈妈在他耳朵里呼喊……这将是他听到

CHAPTER TWENTY   The Dementor's Kiss

ever heard –

And then, through the fog that was drowning him, he thought he saw a silvery light, growing brighter and brighter ... he felt himself fall forwards onto the grass –

Face down, too weak to move, sick and shaking, Harry opened his eyes. The blinding light was illuminating the grass around him ... The screaming had stopped, the cold was ebbing away ...

Something was driving the Dementors back ... it was circling around him and Sirius and Hermione ... the rattling, sucking sounds of the Dementors were fading. They were leaving ... the air was warm again ...

With every ounce of strength he could muster, Harry raised his head a few inches and saw an animal amidst the light, galloping away across the lake. Eyes blurred with sweat, Harry tried to make out what it was ... it was bright as a unicorn. Fighting to stay conscious, Harry watched it canter to a halt as it reached the opposite shore. For a moment, Harry saw, by its brightness, somebody welcoming it back ... raising his hand to pat it ... someone who looked strangely familiar ... but it couldn't be ...

Harry didn't understand. He couldn't think any more. He felt the last of his strength leave him, and his head hit the ground as he fainted.

第 20 章 摄魂怪的吻

的最后的声音——

然后，在将要把他吞没的浓雾中，他好像看到一道银光越来越亮……接着感到自己扑倒在草地上——

哈利脸朝下，没有力气动弹，恶心难受，浑身颤抖。他睁开眼睛，耀眼的银光仍照着他周围的草地……呼喊声停止了，寒气在消退……

什么东西把摄魂怪驱退了……这东西环绕着哈利、小天狼星和赫敏……摄魂怪那吸吮的声音，那咯咯的喉音在慢慢消失。它们在离开……空气又温暖起来……

哈利用尽全部的力气，把头抬起几英寸，看到银光中有一只动物，在湖面上越跑越远……哈利试图辨认那是什么，可是汗水模糊了眼睛……它很明亮，像独角兽一样。哈利竭力保持清醒，看着它跑到对岸停了下来。有那么一刻，借着它的亮光，哈利看到有人在迎接它……举起手拍拍它……那个人看上去好眼熟……但不可能是……

哈利想不明白。他不能再想了。他感到最后一丝力气也离开了自己。哈利的脑袋碰到地上，他昏了过去。

CHAPTER TWENTY-ONE

Hermione's Secret

'Shocking business ... shocking ... miracle none of them died ... never heard the like ... by thunder, it was lucky you were there, Snape ...'

'Thank you, Minister.'

'Order of Merlin, Second Class, I'd say. First Class, if I can wangle it!'

'Thank you very much indeed, Minister.'

'Nasty cut you've got there ... Black's work, I suppose?'

'As a matter of fact, it was Potter, Weasley and Granger, Minister ...'

'*No!*'

'Black had bewitched them, I saw it immediately. A Confundus Charm, to judge by their behaviour. They seemed to think there was a possibility he was innocent. They weren't responsible for their actions. On the other hand, their interference might have permitted Black to escape ... they obviously thought they were going to catch Black single-handed. They've got away with a great deal before now ... I'm afraid it's given them a rather high opinion of themselves ... and of course Potter has always been allowed an extraordinary amount of licence by the Headmaster –'

'Ah, well, Snape ... Harry Potter, you know ... we've all got a bit of a blind spot where he's concerned.'

'And yet – is it good for him to be given so much special treatment? Personally I try to treat him like any other student. And any other student would be suspended – at the very least – for leading his friends into such danger. Consider, Minister: against all school rules – after all the precautions put in place for his protection – out of bounds, at night, consorting with a werewolf and a murderer – and I have reason to believe he has been visiting Hogsmeade illegally, too –'

第21章

赫敏的秘密

"**真**是骇人听闻……骇人听闻……他们一个都没死,真是奇迹……从没听说过这种事……我的天哪,幸亏你在那儿,斯内普……"

"谢谢您,部长。"

"梅林爵士团勋章,二级,我敢保证。一级,如果我能争取到的话!"

"非常感谢您,部长。"

"你这伤口很严重啊……是布莱克干的吧?"

"实际上是波特、韦斯莱和格兰杰,部长……"

"不会吧!"

"布莱克蛊惑了他们,我立刻就看出来了。从这三个人的行为来看,是中了混淆咒。他们似乎认为布莱克有可能是清白的。这不能怪他们,但话又说回来,也许是他们的插手才让布莱克得以逃脱的……他们显然认为凭自己就能把布莱克抓住,以前他们干了多次坏事都没受惩罚……我担心这使他们高估了自己……当然,波特在校长那里总是得到特别的纵容——"

"啊,好吧,斯内普……哈利·波特,你知道……在涉及他的事情上,我们都有盲区。"

"可是——享受这么多特殊待遇对他有好处吗?我个人总是尽量对他与其他学生一视同仁。把朋友带入这么危险的境地,换了其他学生都会被勒令休学——休学是最起码的。您想想吧,部长,在为保护他而采取了那么多防范措施之后,他竟然违反所有的校规,夜间擅自外出,与狼人和杀人犯结交——我有理由相信,他违禁去过霍格莫德——"

CHAPTER TWENTY-ONE — Hermione's Secret

'Well, well ... we shall see, Snape, we shall see ... the boy has undoubtedly been foolish ...'

Harry lay listening with his eyes tight shut. He felt very groggy. The words he was hearing seemed to be travelling very slowly from his ears to his brain, so that it was difficult to understand. His limbs felt like lead; his eyelids too heavy to lift ... he wanted to lie here, on this comfortable bed, for ever ...

'What amazes me most is the behaviour of the Dementors ... you've really no idea what made them retreat, Snape?'

'No, Minister. By the time I had come round they were heading back to their positions at the entrances ...'

'Extraordinary. And yet Black, and Harry, and the girl –'

'All unconscious by the time I reached them. I bound and gagged Black, naturally, conjured stretchers and brought them all straight back to the castle.'

There was a pause. Harry's brain seemed to be moving a little faster, and as it did, a gnawing sensation grew in the pit of his stomach ...

He opened his eyes.

Everything was slightly blurred. Somebody had removed his glasses. He was lying in the dark hospital wing. At the very end of the ward, he could make out Madam Pomfrey with her back to him, bending over a bed. Harry squinted. Ron's red hair was visible beneath Madam Pomfrey's arm.

Harry moved his head over on the pillow. In the bed to his right lay Hermione. Moonlight was falling across her bed. Her eyes were open, too. She looked petrified, and when she saw that Harry was awake, pressed a finger to her lips, then pointed to the hospital-wing door. It was ajar, and the voices of Cornelius Fudge and Snape were coming through it from the corridor outside.

Madam Pomfrey now came walking briskly up the dark ward to Harry's bed. He turned to look at her. She was carrying the largest block of chocolate he had ever seen in his life. It looked like a small boulder.

'Ah, you're awake!' she said briskly. She placed the chocolate on Harry's bedside table and began breaking it apart with a small hammer.

'How's Ron?' said Harry and Hermione together.

'He'll live,' said Madam Pomfrey grimly. 'As for you two ... you'll be staying here until I'm satisfied you're – Potter, what do you think you're doing?'

Harry was sitting up, putting his glasses back on and picking up his wand.

"哦,哦……我们会了解的,斯内普,会了解的……这男孩无疑是干了蠢事……"

哈利紧闭双眼躺在那儿听着,他感到头很晕,声音似乎要过很久才从耳朵传到大脑,因而不太容易听懂……四肢像灌了铅一样,眼皮沉重得抬不起来……他真想永远躺在这儿,躺在这张舒适的床上……

"最令我惊异的是那些摄魂怪的行为……你真的不知道是什么让它们退却的吗,斯内普?"

"不知道,部长……我苏醒时它们正在返回各自把守的入口……"

"真是怪事。而布莱克、哈利和那女生——"

"我过去的时候他们都已昏迷不醒。不用说,我把布莱克绑了起来,堵住了他的嘴,又变出担架,把他们直接送回了城堡。"

片刻的静默。哈利的脑子似乎转得快了一点,与此同时,胃里有一种咬啮的感觉越来越强烈……

他睁开眼睛。

一切都有些模糊,他的眼镜被人拿掉了,他躺在昏暗的校医院里。在病房的另一头,他看出庞弗雷女士背对着他,俯身站在一张病床前。哈利眯起眼睛,罗恩的红头发在庞弗雷女士的胳膊下依稀可见。

哈利在枕头上转过头,右边病床上躺着赫敏。月光照在她的床上。她也睁着眼睛,好像吓呆了。见哈利醒了,她把一根手指按在嘴唇上,然后指了指病房门口。那扇门半掩着,康奈利·福吉和斯内普的声音从外面的走廊里传来。

庞弗雷女士在昏暗中快步朝哈利的病床走来,哈利扭头看着她,见她捧着一块他这辈子见过的最大的巧克力,简直像一块大石头。

"啊,你醒了!"她轻快地说,把巧克力放在哈利的床头柜上,开始用一只小锤子把它砸开。

"罗恩怎么样?"哈利和赫敏一起问。

"他会活下来的,"庞弗雷女士沉着脸说,"你们两个嘛……必须在这儿住到我认为满意为止——波特,你在干什么?"

哈利坐了起来,戴上眼镜,拿起魔杖。

CHAPTER TWENTY-ONE Hermione's Secret

'I need to see the Headmaster,' he said.

'Potter,' said Madam Pomfrey soothingly, 'it's all right. They've got Black. He's locked away upstairs. The Dementors will be performing the Kiss any moment now –'

'WHAT?'

Harry jumped up out of bed; Hermione had done the same. But his shout had been heard in the corridor outside; next second, Cornelius Fudge and Snape had entered the ward.

'Harry, Harry, what's this?' said Fudge, looking agitated. 'You should be in bed – has he had any chocolate?' he asked Madam Pomfrey anxiously.

'Minister, listen!' Harry said. 'Sirius Black's innocent! Peter Pettigrew faked his own death! We saw him tonight! You can't let the Dementors do that thing to Sirius, he's –'

But Fudge was shaking his head with a small smile on his face.

'Harry, Harry, you're very confused, you've been through a dreadful ordeal, lie back down, now, we've got everything under control ...'

'YOU HAVEN'T!' Harry yelled. 'YOU'VE GOT THE WRONG MAN!'

'Minister, listen, please,' Hermione said; she had hurried to Harry's side and was gazing imploringly into Fudge's face. 'I saw him, too. It was Ron's rat, he's an Animagus, Pettigrew, I mean, and –'

'You see, Minister?' said Snape. 'Confunded, both of them ... Black's done a very good job on them ...'

'WE'RE NOT CONFUNDED!' Harry roared.

'Minister! Professor!' said Madam Pomfrey angrily. 'I must insist that you leave. Potter is my patient, and he should not be distressed!'

'I'm not distressed, I'm trying to tell them what happened!' Harry said furiously. 'If they'd just listen –'

But Madam Pomfrey suddenly stuffed a large chunk of chocolate into Harry's mouth. He choked, and she seized the opportunity to force him back onto the bed.

'Now, *please*, Minister, these children need care. Please leave –'

The door opened again. It was Dumbledore. Harry swallowed his mouthful of chocolate with great difficulty, and got up again.

'Professor Dumbledore, Sirius Black –'

"我要去见校长。"他说。

"波特,"庞弗雷女士安慰道,"没事了,布莱克已经被抓到,关在楼上,摄魂怪随时都会给他一吻——"

"什么?"

哈利一骨碌跳下床,赫敏也一样。但哈利的叫声被外面走廊上的人听到了。康奈利·福吉和斯内普立刻走进病房。

"哈利,哈利,怎么回事?"福吉不安地说,"你应该躺在床上——他吃过巧克力了吗?"他焦急地问庞弗雷女士。

"部长,听我说!"哈利说,"小天狼星布莱克是清白的!小矮星彼得当年是装死!我们今晚看到他了!你不能让摄魂怪那样对待小天狼星,他是——"

但是福吉摇了摇头,脸上露出一丝淡淡的微笑。

"哈利,哈利,你现在很糊涂,你刚经历了可怕的折磨,躺下来吧,目前我们已经控制了一切……"

"**你们没有!**"哈利喊道,"**你们抓错人了!**"

"部长,请听我们说,"赫敏急忙跑到哈利身边,恳求地望着福吉,"我也看到他了,是罗恩的老鼠,他是阿尼马格斯,我说的是小矮星,还有——"

"看见了吗,部长?"斯内普说,"中了混淆咒,两人都是……布莱克对他们干得很成功……"

"**我们没中混淆咒!**"哈利吼道。

"部长!教授!"庞弗雷女士恼火地说,"我必须坚持让你们离开。波特是我的病人,不应该让他受刺激!"

"我没有受刺激,我只是想告诉他们真实的情况!"哈利激动地说,"如果他们肯听——"

但是庞弗雷女士突然把一大块巧克力塞进了哈利嘴里,他噎住了,她趁机把他按回到床上。

"现在,请原谅,部长,这些孩子需要接受护理。请离开——"

门又开了,是邓布利多。哈利好不容易咽下满嘴巧克力,又坐了起来。

"邓布利多教授,小天狼星布莱克——"

CHAPTER TWENTY-ONE   Hermione's Secret

'For heaven's sake!' said Madam Pomfrey hysterically. 'Is this a hospital wing or not? Headmaster, I must insist –'

'My apologies, Poppy, but I need a word with Mr Potter and Miss Granger,' said Dumbledore calmly. 'I have just been talking to Sirius Black –'

'I suppose he's told you the same fairy tale he's planted in Potter's mind?' spat Snape. 'Something about a rat, and Pettigrew being alive –'

'That, indeed, is Black's story,' said Dumbledore, surveying Snape closely through his half-moon spectacles.

'And does my evidence count for nothing?' snarled Snape. 'Peter Pettigrew was not in the Shrieking Shack, nor did I see any sign of him in the grounds.'

'That was because you were knocked out, Professor!' said Hermione earnestly. 'You didn't arrive in time to hear –'

'Miss Granger, HOLD YOUR TONGUE!'

'Now, Snape,' said Fudge, startled, 'the young lady is disturbed in her mind, we must make allowances –'

'I would like to speak to Harry and Hermione alone,' said Dumbledore abruptly. 'Cornelius, Severus, Poppy – please leave us.'

'Headmaster!' spluttered Madam Pomfrey. 'They need treatment, they need rest –'

'This cannot wait,' said Dumbledore. 'I must insist.'

Madam Pomfrey pursed her lips and strode away into her office at the end of the ward, slamming the door behind her. Fudge consulted the large gold pocket watch dangling from his waistcoat.

'The Dementors should have arrived by now,' he said. 'I'll go and meet them. Dumbledore, I'll see you upstairs.'

He crossed to the door and held it open for Snape, but Snape hadn't moved.

'You surely don't believe a word of Black's story?' Snape whispered, his eyes fixed on Dumbledore's face.

'I wish to speak to Harry and Hermione alone,' Dumbledore repeated.

Snape took a step towards Dumbledore.

'Sirius Black showed he was capable of murder at the age of sixteen,' he breathed. 'You haven't forgotten that, Headmaster? You haven't forgotten that he once tried to kill *me*?'

第21章 赫敏的秘密

"老天爷啊!"庞弗雷女士歇斯底里地说,"这还是不是医院啊?校长,我必须坚持——"

"抱歉,波比,我需要和波特先生和格兰杰小姐谈谈。"邓布利多平静地说,"我刚刚和小天狼星布莱克聊过——"

"我想他已经对您讲了他塞到波特脑子里的那篇鬼话吧,"斯内普讥讽道,"什么老鼠,什么小矮星还活着——"

"布莱克的确是那么说的。"邓布利多说,眼睛透过半月形的眼镜片端详着斯内普。

"我的证词就不算数吗?"斯内普吼道,"小矮星彼得并不在尖叫棚屋里,我在场地上也没有看到他的踪迹。"

"那是因为您被打昏了,教授!"赫敏急切地说,"您去晚了,没有听到——"

"格兰杰小姐,**闭嘴**!"

"哎,斯内普,"福吉惊道,"这位小姐的脑子被搞乱了,我们对她要宽容些——"

"我想跟哈利和赫敏单独谈谈,"邓布利多突然说,"康奈利,西弗勒斯,波比——请离开一下。"

"校长!"庞弗雷女士急了,"他们需要治疗,需要休息——"

"这事不能等,"邓布利多说,"我必须坚持。"

庞弗雷女士嘟着嘴大步走入病房那头她的办公室,重重地关上了门。福吉看了看他马甲上挂的大金怀表。

"摄魂怪应该到了,"他说,"我要去迎接它们。邓布利多,楼上见。"

他走到门口,开门等斯内普出来,但斯内普没有动。

"您当然不会相信布莱克编的故事吧?"斯内普盯着邓布利多的脸,低声问。

"我想单独跟哈利和赫敏谈谈。"邓布利多又说了一遍。

斯内普朝邓布利多走近了一步。

"小天狼星布莱克十六岁就显示出杀人倾向,"他轻声说,"您没有忘记吧,校长?您没忘记他曾经试图杀死我吧?"

CHAPTER TWENTY-ONE Hermione's Secret

'My memory is as good as it ever was, Severus,' said Dumbledore quietly.

Snape turned on his heel and marched through the door Fudge was still holding. It closed behind them and Dumbledore turned to Harry and Hermione. They both burst into speech at the same time.

'Professor, Black's telling the truth – we *saw* Pettigrew –'

'– he escaped when Professor Lupin turned into a werewolf –'

'– he's a rat –'

'– Pettigrew's front paw, I mean, finger, he cut it off –'

'– Pettigrew attacked Ron, it wasn't Sirius –'

But Dumbledore held up his hand to stem the flood of explanations.

'It is your turn to listen, and I beg you will not interrupt me, because there is very little time,' he said quietly. 'There is not a shred of proof to support Black's story, except your word – and the word of two thirteen-year-old wizards will not convince anybody. A street full of eye-witnesses swore they saw Sirius murder Pettigrew. I myself gave evidence to the Ministry that Sirius had been the Potters' Secret Keeper.'

'Professor Lupin can tell you –' Harry said, unable to stop himself.

'Professor Lupin is currently deep in the Forest, unable to tell anyone anything. By the time he is human again, it will be too late, Sirius will be worse than dead. I might add that werewolves are so mistrusted by most of our kind that his support will count for very little – and the fact that he and Sirius are old friends –'

'But –'

'*Listen to me, Harry*. It is too late, you understand me? You must see that Professor Snape's version of events is far more convincing than yours.'

'He hates Sirius,' Hermione said desperately. 'All because of some stupid trick Sirius played on him –'

'Sirius has not acted like an innocent man. The attack on the Fat Lady – entering Gryffindor Tower with a knife – without Pettigrew, alive or dead, we have no chance of over-turning Sirius' sentence.'

'*But you believe us.*'

'Yes, I do,' said Dumbledore quietly. 'But I have no power to make other men see the truth, or to overrule the Minister for Magic ...'

第21章 赫敏的秘密

"我的记忆力跟从前一样好,西弗勒斯。"邓布利多平静地说。

斯内普转身大步从福吉拉开的门走了出去,门在二人身后关上了。邓布利多转向哈利和赫敏,他们俩同时抢着说话。

"教授,布莱克说的是真的——我们看到小矮星了——"

"后来卢平教授变成狼人,小矮星就逃掉了——"

"他是只老鼠——"

"小矮星的前爪,我是说手指,他砍断了一根手指——"

"是小矮星袭击了罗恩,不是小天狼星——"

但是邓布利多抬手止住了他们连珠炮般的汇报。

"轮到你们听了,我请求你们不要打断我,因为时间很少,"他低声说,"除了你们的话之外,没有丝毫证据可以证实布莱克的故事——而两个十三岁巫师的话不足以说服任何人。整条街的目击者都一口咬定他们看到小天狼星杀死了小矮星。我本人也曾向魔法部作证,说小天狼星曾是波特夫妇的保密人。"

"卢平教授可以告诉您——"哈利忍不住插嘴道。

"卢平教授目前在禁林深处,不能跟人说话。等他变回人形就来不及了,小天狼星将会生不如死。再说,狼人在很多人眼里并不值得信任,他的证词分量很轻——况且他和小天狼星还是老朋友——"

"可是——"

"听我说,哈利。来不及了,你明白吗?你必须看到斯内普教授的证词比你们的有力得多。"

"他恨小天狼星,"赫敏急切地说,"都是因为小天狼星对他搞了个愚蠢的恶作剧——"

"小天狼星的所作所为也不像个无辜的人。袭击胖夫人——携刀潜入格兰芬多塔楼——不论小矮星是死是活,找不到他,我们就没有机会为小天狼星翻案。"

"可是您相信我们。"

"我相信,"邓布利多轻声说,"但我没有能力让其他人看到真相,也不能左右魔法部部长……"

CHAPTER TWENTY-ONE   Hermione's Secret

Harry stared up into the grave face and felt as though the ground beneath him was falling sharply away. He had grown used to the idea that Dumbledore could solve anything. He had expected Dumbledore to pull some amazing solution out of the air. But no ... their last hope was gone.

'What we need,' said Dumbledore slowly, and his light-blue eyes moved from Harry to Hermione, 'is more *time*.'

'But –' Hermione began. And then her eyes became very round. 'OH!'

'Now, pay attention,' said Dumbledore, speaking very low, and very clearly. 'Sirius is locked in Professor Flitwick's office on the seventh floor. Thirteenth window from the right of the West Tower. If all goes well, you will be able to save more than one innocent life tonight. But remember this, both of you. *You must not be seen*. Miss Granger, you know the law – you know what is at stake ... *you – must – not – be – seen*.'

Harry didn't have a clue what was going on. Dumbledore had turned on his heel and looked back as he reached the door.

'I am going to lock you in. It is –' he consulted his watch, 'five minutes to midnight. Miss Granger, three turns should do it. Good luck.'

'Good luck?' Harry repeated, as the door closed behind Dumbledore. 'Three turns? What's he talking about? What are we supposed to do?'

But Hermione was fumbling with the neck of her robes, pulling from beneath them a very long, very fine gold chain.

'Harry, come here,' she said urgently. '*Quick!*'

Harry moved towards her, completely bewildered. She was holding the chain out. He saw a tiny, sparkling hourglass hanging from it.

'Here –'

She had thrown the chain around his neck, too.

'Ready?' she said breathlessly.

'What are we doing?' Harry said, completely lost.

Hermione turned the hourglass over three times.

The dark ward dissolved. Harry had the sensation that he was flying, very fast, backwards. A blur of colours and shapes rushed past him; his ears were pounding. He tried to yell but couldn't hear his own voice –

And then he felt solid ground beneath his feet, and everything came into focus again –

He was standing next to Hermione in the deserted Entrance Hall and

第21章 赫敏的秘密

哈利盯着那张严峻的面孔，感到地面好像塌陷下去。他已经习惯了认为邓布利多能解决一切问题，指望邓布利多会凭空拿出一些妙策，然而没有……他们的最后一丝希望破灭了。

"我们需要的，"邓布利多缓缓地说道，那双浅蓝色的眼睛从哈利转向了赫敏，"是更多时间。"

"可是——"赫敏说，然后她的眼睛瞪圆了，"**哦！**"

"现在，请注意，"邓布利多声音很低，但格外清晰，"小天狼星被关在八楼弗立维教授的办公室里，就是西塔楼右边的第十三个窗户。如果一切顺利，你们今晚能够挽救不止一条无辜的生命。但你们俩都要记住：不能被人看见。格兰杰小姐，你知道规则——应该清楚会有什么危险……千万——不能——被人——看见。"

哈利摸不着头脑。邓布利多转身离开了，走到门口又回过头来。

"我要把你们关起来。现在是——"他看了看表，"差五分就到午夜了。格兰杰小姐，转三下就行。祝你们好运。"

"好运？"房门在邓布利多身后关上了，哈利喃喃地说，"转三下？他在说什么呀？我们要做什么？"

赫敏在袍子的领口里摸索着，抽出了一根细细长长的金链子。

"哈利，过来，"她急迫地说，"快！"

哈利走了过去，完全被搞糊涂了。赫敏举着链子，哈利看到上面挂着一个闪闪发光的小沙漏。

"来——"

她把链子也挂到了哈利的脖子上。

"准备好了吗？"她悄声问。

"这是干吗呀？"哈利莫名其妙。

赫敏把沙漏转了三下。

昏暗的病房隐去了，哈利感到自己在疾速向后飞行。模糊的色彩和形状从旁边闪过，耳膜发胀，他想喊叫，却听不到自己的声音——

然后他感到双脚碰到了坚实的地面，一切重又清晰起来——

他站在赫敏旁边，置身于空荡荡的门厅里，一束金色的阳光从敞

CHAPTER TWENTY-ONE   Hermione's Secret

a stream of golden sunlight was falling across the paved floor from the open front doors. He looked wildly around at Hermione, the chain of the hourglass cutting into his neck.

'Hermione, what –?'

'In here!' Hermione seized Harry's arm and dragged him across the hall to the door of a broom cupboard; she opened it, pushed him inside amongst the buckets and mops, followed him in, then slammed the door behind them.

'What – how – Hermione, what happened?'

'We've gone back in time,' Hermione whispered, lifting the chain off Harry's neck in the darkness. 'Three hours back ...'

Harry found his own leg and gave it a very hard pinch. It hurt a lot, which seemed to rule out the possibility that he was having a very bizarre dream.

'But –'

'Shh! Listen! Someone's coming! I think – I think it might be us!'

Hermione had her ear pressed against the cupboard door.

'Footsteps across the hall ... yes, I think it's us going down to Hagrid's!'

'Are you telling me,' Harry whispered, 'that we're here in this cupboard and we're out there, too?'

'Yes,' said Hermione, her ear still glued to the cupboard door. 'I'm sure it's us ... it doesn't sound like more than three people ... and we're walking slowly because we're under the Invisibility Cloak –'

She broke off, still listening intently.

'We've gone down the front steps ...'

Hermione sat down on an upturned bucket; looking desperately anxious, Harry wanted a few questions answered.

'Where did you *get* that hourglass thing?'

'It's called a Time-Turner,' Hermione whispered, 'and I got it from Professor McGonagall on our first day back. I've been using it all year to get to all my lessons. Professor McGonagall made me swear I wouldn't tell anyone. She had to write all sorts of letters to the Ministry of Magic so I could have one. She had to tell them that I was a model student, and that I'd never, ever use it for anything except my studies ... I've been turning it back so I could do hours over again, that's how I've been doing several lessons at once, see? But ...

'Harry, *I don't understand what Dumbledore wants us to do*. Why did he tell us to

开的前门照在地板上。他急忙扭头去看赫敏，沙漏的链子勒进了他脖子上的皮肤里。

"赫敏，这是——？"

"进来！"赫敏抓住哈利的胳膊，穿过门厅把他拖向一间扫帚柜，打开门把他推了进去，让他躲到水桶和拖把中间，自己也跟了进来，关上了门。

"这——怎么——赫敏，怎么回事啊？"

"我们在时间里倒退了。"赫敏小声说，在黑暗中把链子从哈利的脖子上取了下来，"倒退了三小时……"

哈利摸到自己的大腿，狠狠掐了一把，好疼。这似乎意味着他不是在做一个离奇的梦。

"可是——"

"嘘——听！有人来了！我想——我想可能是我们！"

赫敏把耳朵贴在柜门上。

"脚步声从厅里走过……嗯，我想我们正往海格那儿去！"

"你是说，"哈利悄声问，"我们既在柜里，又在外面？"

"对，"赫敏说，耳朵仍然贴在门上，"我肯定那就是我们，听起来不超过三个人……我们走得很慢，因为躲在隐形衣里——"

她停住了，仍然专心地听着。

"我们走下台阶了……"

赫敏坐到倒扣的水桶上，神情万分紧张，但哈利有几个问题要问。

"你那个沙漏是从哪儿弄来的？"

"它叫时间转换器，"赫敏小声说，"返校的第一天我从麦格教授那儿拿来的，这一年里我就是靠它上了所有的课。麦格教授让我发誓不告诉任何人。她给魔法部写了好多信才为我申请到一个。她必须向他们证明我是个模范学生，而且绝不会把转换器用于学业以外的事情……我把它倒转，就可以重过一段时间，所以能在同一时间上好几堂课，明白了吧？可是……

"哈利，我不知道邓布利多要我们做什么。他为什么叫我们倒转三

CHAPTER TWENTY-ONE   Hermione's Secret

go back three hours? How's that going to help Sirius?'

Harry stared at her shadowy face.

'There must be something that happened around now he wants us to change,' he said slowly. 'What happened? We were walking down to Hagrid's three hours ago ...'

'This *is* three hours ago, and we *are* walking down to Hagrid's,' said Hermione. 'We just heard ourselves leaving ...'

Harry frowned; he felt as though he was screwing up his whole brain in concentration.

'Dumbledore just said – just said we could save more than one innocent life ...' And then it hit him. 'Hermione, we're going to save Buckbeak!'

'But – how will that help Sirius?'

'Dumbledore said – he just told us where the window is – the window of Flitwick's office! Where they've got Sirius locked up! We've got to fly Buckbeak up to the window and rescue Sirius! Sirius can escape on Buckbeak – they can escape together!'

From what Harry could see of Hermione's face, she looked terrified.

'If we manage that without being seen, it'll be a miracle!'

'Well, we've got to try, haven't we?' said Harry. He stood up and pressed his own ear against the door.

'Doesn't sound like anyone's there ... come on, let's go ...'

Harry pushed the cupboard door open. The Entrance Hall was deserted. As quietly and quickly as they could, they darted out of the cupboard and down the stone steps. The shadows were already lengthening, the tops of the trees in the Forbidden Forest gilded once more with gold.

'If anyone's looking out of the window –' Hermione squeaked, looking up at the castle behind them.

'We'll run for it,' said Harry determinedly. 'Straight into the Forest, all right? We'll have to hide behind a tree or something and keep a lookout –'

'OK, but we'll go round by the greenhouses!' said Hermione breathlessly. 'We need to keep out of sight of Hagrid's front door, or we'll see us! We must be nearly at Hagrid's by now!'

Still working out what she meant, Harry set off at a sprint, Hermione behind him. They tore across the vegetable gardens to the greenhouses, paused for a moment behind them, then set off again, fast as they could, skirting around the Whomping Willow, tearing towards the shelter of the Forest ...

第21章 赫敏的秘密

小时？这对小天狼星有什么帮助呢？"

哈利瞪着昏暗中她的面孔。

"一定是在这段时间里发生了什么，他希望我们去改变，"他缓缓地说，"发生了什么呢？三小时前，我们正朝海格那儿走去……"

"现在就是三小时前，我们正在朝海格那儿走去。"赫敏说，"我们刚才听到我们出发了……"

哈利皱起眉头，觉得全部脑细胞都调动起来了。

"邓布利多刚才说——刚才说我们能够挽救不止一条无辜的生命……"他突然悟到了，"赫敏，我们要救巴克比克！"

"可是——那对小天狼星有什么帮助呢？"

"邓布利多说——他说到了那扇窗户——弗立维办公室的窗户！小天狼星就关在那儿！我们必须让巴克比克飞到那个窗口，救出小天狼星！小天狼星可以骑着巴克比克逃走——他们可以一起逃走。"

哈利依稀看到赫敏的脸，她似乎很害怕。

"要是能办成这件事而又不被人发现，那可真是奇迹！"

"但我们必须试试，对不对？"哈利说，站起来把耳朵贴到门上。

"好像没人了……走吧……"

哈利推开柜门，门厅里空无一人。他们尽可能轻手轻脚地冲出扫帚柜，跑下石阶。树影已在拉长，禁林的树梢再次被镀上了金色。

"要是有人朝窗外看——"赫敏抬头看着身后的城堡，紧张地说。

"快跑，"哈利果断地说，"一直跑到林子里，行吗？必须躲在树或别的什么东西后面，观察动静——"

"好吧，但要从温室绕一下！"赫敏气喘吁吁地说，"避开海格的前门，不然我们会看见我们的！现在我们应该在海格的小屋附近了！"

哈利撒腿跑了起来，一边还在想她的话是什么意思。赫敏跟在后面。两人穿过菜园奔向温室，在那后面停了一下，然后又跑了起来，全速绕过打人柳，冲向黑黢黢的禁林……

CHAPTER TWENTY-ONE Hermione's Secret

Safe in the shadows of the trees, Harry turned around; seconds later, Hermione arrived beside him, panting.

'Right,' she gasped, 'we need to sneak over to Hagrid's. Keep out of sight, Harry ...'

They made their way silently through the trees, keeping to the very edge of the Forest. Then, as they glimpsed the front of Hagrid's house, they heard a knock upon his door. They moved quickly behind a wide oak trunk and peered out from either side. Hagrid had appeared in his doorway, shaking and white, looking around to see who had knocked. And Harry heard his own voice.

'It's us. We're wearing the Invisibility Cloak. Let us in and we can take it off.'

'Yeh shouldn've come!' Hagrid whispered. He stood back, then shut the door quickly.

'This is the weirdest thing we've ever done,' Harry said fervently.

'Let's move along a bit,' Hermione whispered. 'We need to get nearer to Buckbeak!'

They crept through the trees until they saw the nervous Hippogriff, tethered to the fence around Hagrid's pumpkin patch.

'Now?' Harry whispered.

'No!' said Hermione. 'If we steal him now, those Committee people will think Hagrid set him free! We've got to wait until they've seen he's tied outside!'

'That's going to give us about sixty seconds,' said Harry. This was starting to seem impossible.

At that moment, there was a crash of breaking china from inside Hagrid's cabin.

'That's Hagrid breaking the milk jug,' Hermione whispered. 'I'm going to find Scabbers in a moment –'

Sure enough, a few minutes later, they heard Hermione's shriek of surprise.

'Hermione,' said Harry suddenly, 'what if we – we just run in there, and grab Pettigrew –'

'No!' said Hermione in a terrified whisper. 'Don't you understand? We're breaking one of the most important wizarding laws! Nobody's supposed to change time, nobody! You heard Dumbledore, if we're seen –'

'We'd only be seen by ourselves and Hagrid!'

'Harry, what do you think you'd do if you saw yourself bursting into Hagrid's house?' said Hermione.

第21章 赫敏的秘密

在树影的掩护下,哈利转过身,几秒钟后,赫敏也气喘吁吁地赶到了。

"好,"她上气不接下气地说,"我们要悄悄跑到海格那儿……注意隐蔽,哈利……"

两人悄悄在树丛中穿行,沿着林子边缘往前走。看见海格的前门时,听到了敲门声。他们迅速闪到一棵大橡树后面,从树干两边探头窥视。海格出现在门口,脸色苍白,浑身发抖,四下寻找敲门的人。哈利听见了自己的声音。

"是我们,穿着隐形衣呢。让我们进去把它脱下来。"

"你们不该来的!"海格小声说,他退后一步,然后迅速关上门。

"这是我们做过的最奇怪的事。"哈利兴奋地说。

"往前挪挪,"赫敏小声说,"我们得离巴克比克近一点!"

两人蹑手蹑脚地穿过树丛,终于看见了那头紧张不安的鹰头马身有翼兽,就拴在海格南瓜地的围篱上。

"现在?"哈利悄声问。

"不!"赫敏说,"如果现在就偷走它,委员会的那些人会认为是海格把它放跑的!必须等他们看到它拴在外面之后!"

"那我们就只有六十秒左右的时间。"哈利说,隐约觉得这是不可能的。

这时,海格的小屋里传出瓷器打碎的声音。

"是海格打碎了奶罐,"赫敏低声说,"我马上就要发现斑斑了——"

果然,几分钟后他们听到了赫敏惊讶的叫声。

"赫敏,"哈利突然说,"如果我们——我们直接跑进去抓住小矮星——"

"不!"赫敏恐惧地小声说,"你不明白吗?我们是在违反一条最重要的魔法规则!没有人可以改变时间,没有人!你听到邓布利多说了,如果我们被人看见——"

"我们只会被我们自己和海格看见!"

"哈利,你想想,如果你看到自己冲进海格屋里,你会怎么样?"

CHAPTER TWENTY-ONE Hermione's Secret

'I'd – I'd think I'd gone mad,' said Harry, 'or I'd think there was some Dark Magic going on –'

'*Exactly!* You wouldn't understand, you might even attack yourself! Don't you see? Professor McGonagall told me what awful things have happened when wizards have meddled with time ... loads of them ended up killing their past or future selves by mistake!'

'OK!' said Harry. 'It was just an idea, I just thought –'

But Hermione nudged him, and pointed towards the castle. Harry moved his head a few inches to get a clear view of the distant front doors. Dumbledore, Fudge, the old Committee member and Macnair the executioner were coming down the steps.

'We're about to come out!' Hermione breathed.

And sure enough, moments later, Hagrid's back door opened, and Harry saw himself, Ron and Hermione walking out of it with Hagrid. It was, without a doubt, the strangest sensation of his life, standing behind the tree, and watching himself in the pumpkin patch.

'It's OK, Beaky, it's OK ...' Hagrid said to Buckbeak. Then he turned to Harry, Ron and Hermione. 'Go on. Get goin'.'

'Hagrid, we can't –'

'We'll tell them what really happened –'

'They can't kill him –'

'Go! It's bad enough without you lot in trouble an' all!'

Harry watched the Hermione in the pumpkin patch throw the Invisibility Cloak over himself and Ron.

'Go quick. Don' listen ...'

There was a knock on Hagrid's front door. The execution party had arrived. Hagrid turned around and headed back into his cabin, leaving the back door ajar. Harry watched the grass flatten in patches all around the cabin and heard three pairs of feet retreating. He, Ron and Hermione had gone ... but the Harry and Hermione hidden in the trees could now hear what was happening inside the cabin through the back door.

'Where is the beast?' came the cold voice of Macnair.

'Out – outside,' Hagrid croaked.

Harry pulled his head out of sight as Macnair's face appeared at Hagrid's window, staring out at Buckbeak. Then they heard Fudge.

第21章 赫敏的秘密

"我——我想我会以为自己疯了,"哈利说,"或者认为是黑魔法在作怪——"

"对啊!你会弄不懂的,甚至可能袭击你自己!你不明白吗?麦格教授跟我讲过巫师篡改时间后发生过的可怕事情……很多人误杀了过去或将来的自己!"

"好吧!"哈利说,"我只是想想而已,我本想——"

但赫敏推了推他,指指城堡。哈利把脑袋凑过去一点,以看清远处的城堡大门。邓布利多、福吉、老委员、行刑官麦克尼尔正在走下台阶。

"我们就要出来了!"赫敏屏着气说。

果然,不一会儿,海格的后门打开了,哈利看到自己、罗恩和赫敏跟着海格走了出来。这无疑是他一生中最奇异的体验:站在树后看到自己在南瓜地里。

"没事,比克,"海格对巴克比克说,"没事……"然后转向哈利、罗恩和赫敏,"走吧,快走。"

"海格,我们不能——"

"我们要向他们说明真相——"

"他们不能杀它——"

"走!事情已经够糟的了,不要再搭上你们。"

哈利看到南瓜地里的赫敏用隐形衣罩住了他和罗恩。

"快走,不要听……"

海格的前门响起敲门声。执行处决的一行人到了。海格转身进了屋,后门虚掩着。哈利看到小屋旁边有一小片一小片的草被压平,听到三双脚渐渐走远。他、罗恩和赫敏离开了……但是躲在树后的哈利和赫敏现在能从后门听到木屋里的动静。

"那畜生在哪儿?"麦克尼尔冷酷的声音传来。

"外——外面。"海格声音嘶哑地说。

哈利把脑袋缩了回去。麦克尼尔的脸出现在海格小屋的窗口,向外望着巴克比克。然后他们听到了福吉的声音。

CHAPTER TWENTY-ONE   Hermione's Secret

'We – er – have to read you the official notice of execution, Hagrid. I'll make it quick. And then you and Macnair need to sign it. Macnair, you're supposed to listen too, that's procedure –'

Macnair's face vanished from the window. It was now or never.

'Wait here,' Harry whispered to Hermione. 'I'll do it.'

As Fudge's voice started again, Harry darted out from behind his tree, vaulted the fence into the pumpkin patch and approached Buckbeak.

'*It is the decision of the Committee for the Disposal of Dangerous Creatures that the Hippogriff Buckbeak, hereafter called the condemned, shall be executed on the sixth of June at sundown* –'

Careful not to blink, Harry stared up into Buckbeak's fierce orange eye once more, and bowed. Buckbeak sank to his scaly knees and then stood up again. Harry began to fumble with the rope tying Buckbeak to the fence.

'*... sentenced to execution by beheading, to be carried out by the Committee's appointed executioner, Walden Macnair ...*'

'Come on, Buckbeak,' Harry murmured, 'come on, we're going to help you. Quietly ... quietly ...'

'*... as witnessed below.* Hagrid, you sign here ...'

Harry threw all his weight onto the rope, but Buckbeak had dug in his front feet.

'Well, let's get this over with,' said the reedy voice of the Committee member from inside Hagrid's cabin. 'Hagrid, perhaps it would be better if you stayed inside –'

'No, I – I wan' ter be with him ... I don' wan' him ter be alone –'

Footsteps echoed from within the cabin.

'*Buckbeak, move!*' Harry hissed.

Harry tugged harder on the rope around Buckbeak's neck. The Hippogriff began to walk, rustling its wings irritably. They were still ten feet away from the Forest, in plain view of Hagrid's back door.

'One moment, please, Macnair,' came Dumbledore's voice. 'You need to sign, too.' The footsteps stopped. Harry heaved on the rope. Buckbeak snapped his beak and walked a little faster.

Hermione's white face was sticking out from behind a tree.

'Harry, hurry!' she mouthed.

Harry could still hear Dumbledore's voice talking from within the cabin.

第21章 赫敏的秘密

"我们——呃——不得不向你宣读正式处决的通知,海格。我会念快一点。然后你和麦克尼尔要签名。麦克尼尔,你也得听着,这是程序——"

麦克尼尔的脸从窗口消失了。机会来了!

"等着,"哈利悄悄对赫敏说,"我去。"

福吉的声音再次响起时,哈利从树后冲了出去,翻越篱笆跳进南瓜地,靠近巴克比克。

"处置危险生物委员会裁定,鹰头马身有翼兽巴克比克,下称罪兽,将于6月6日日落时分被处决——"

哈利努力不眨眼地再次盯着那双凶恶的橘黄色眼睛,并且朝它鞠躬。巴克比克带鳞甲的膝部跪了下去,然后又站了起来。哈利开始摸索着去解把它系在篱笆上的绳索。

"……判处斩首,由委员会指定行刑官沃尔顿·麦克尼尔执行……"

"走吧,巴克比克,"哈利小声说,"走吧,我们是来救你的。别出声……别出声……"

"……见证人:海格,你在这儿签名……"

哈利用尽全身的重量拉着绳子,但巴克比克的前蹄死死抠住地面。

"好,这就办了吧。"海格屋里传来那位委员尖细的声音,"海格,也许你待在屋里好一点——"

"不,我——我要跟它在一起……我不愿意它孤零零的——"

屋里传出脚步声。

"巴克比克,走呀!"哈利小声说。

他更加使劲地拉扯巴克比克脖子上的绳子,鹰头马身有翼兽迈开了步子,一边烦躁地抖动翅膀。他们离禁林还有十英尺远,完全暴露在海格后门的视野内。

"请等一等,麦克尼尔,"邓布利多的声音响起,"你也得签名。"脚步声停下了,哈利猛地一拉绳子,巴克比克张了张鹰嘴,走快了一点。

赫敏苍白的面孔从树后探了出来。

"哈利,快!"她用口型说。

哈利仍能听到邓布利多的说话声从屋内传出,他又用力一扯绳子,

CHAPTER TWENTY-ONE Hermione's Secret

He gave the rope another wrench. Buckbeak broke into a grudging trot. They had reached the trees ...

'Quick! Quick!' Hermione moaned, darting out from behind her tree, seizing the rope too and adding her weight to make Buckbeak move faster. Harry looked over his shoulder; they were now blocked from sight; they couldn't see Hagrid's garden at all.

'Stop!' he whispered to Hermione. 'They might hear us –'

Hagrid's back door had opened with a bang. Harry, Hermione and Buckbeak stood quite still; even the Hippogriff seemed to be listening intently.

Silence ... then –

'Where is it?' said the reedy voice of the Committee member. 'Where is the beast?'

'It was tied here!' said the executioner furiously. 'I saw it! Just here!'

'How extraordinary,' said Dumbledore. There was a note of amusement in his voice.

'Beaky!' said Hagrid huskily.

There was a swishing noise, and the thud of an axe. The executioner seemed to have swung it into the fence in anger. And then came the howling, and this time they could hear Hagrid's words through his sobs.

'Gone! Gone! Bless his little beak, he's *gone*! Musta pulled himself free! Beaky, yeh clever boy!'

Buckbeak started to strain against the rope, trying to get back to Hagrid. Harry and Hermione tightened their grip and dug their heels into the Forest floor to stop him.

'Someone untied him!' the executioner was snarling. 'We should search the grounds, the Forest –'

'Macnair, if Buckbeak has indeed been stolen, do you really think the thief will have led him away on foot?' said Dumbledore, still sounding amused. 'Search the skies, if you will ... Hagrid, I could do with a cup of tea. Or a large brandy.'

'O' – o' course, Professor,' said Hagrid, who sounded weak with happiness. 'Come in, come in ...'

Harry and Hermione listened closely. They heard footsteps, the soft cursing of the executioner, the snap of the door, and then silence once more.

'Now what?' whispered Harry, looking around.

第21章 赫敏的秘密

巴克比克不情愿地小跑起来。他们来到了禁林边……

"快!快!"赫敏叫道,从树后冲了出来,也抓住绳子帮着拽巴克比克,想让巴克比克更快一点儿。哈利回头一看,他们现在已被遮住,海格的园子看不见了。

"停下!"他小声对赫敏说,"他们会听到的——"

海格的后门砰地打开了,哈利、赫敏和巴克比克静悄悄地站着,连那头鹰头马身有翼兽都似乎在专注地聆听。

一阵寂静……然后——

"它在哪儿?"是那位委员尖细的声音,"那怪兽在哪儿?"

"刚才还拴在这儿呢!"行刑官气冲冲地说,"我看到的!就在这儿!"

"真是咄咄怪事。"邓布利多说,声音里有一丝窃喜。

"比克!"海格声音嘶哑地叫道。

呼的一声和斧头落下的闷响。行刑官似乎一气之下把斧头扔进了篱笆。然后是一声狂号,这次他们听见了海格抽抽搭搭的话。

"不见了!不见了!上帝保佑小鹰嘴,它不见了!一定是自己挣脱了!比克,你这机灵的孩子!"

巴克比克开始拽绳子,想回到海格那儿去。哈利和赫敏拉紧绳子,脚跟用力钉在林中的地面上。

"有人解开了绳子!"行刑官咆哮道,"搜查这个地方,还有林子——"

"麦克尼尔,如果巴克比克真是被偷走了,你认为那小偷会牵着它步行吗?"邓布利多说,听起来仍有一丝窃喜,"要搜就得搜天空……海格,我想来一杯茶,或一大杯白兰地。"

"当——当然,教授,"海格好像高兴得声音都发软了,"请进,请进……"

哈利和赫敏仔细听着。他们听到了脚步声,行刑官轻轻的诅咒声,关门声,然后一切又归于寂静。

"现在怎么办?"哈利小声问,看着四周。

CHAPTER TWENTY-ONE   Hermione's Secret

'We'll have to hide in here,' said Hermione, who looked very shaken. 'We need to wait until they've gone back to the castle. Then we wait until it's safe to fly Buckbeak up to Sirius' window. He won't be there for another couple of hours ... oh, this is going to be difficult ...'

She looked nervously over her shoulder into the depths of the Forest. The sun was setting now.

'We're going to have to move,' said Harry, thinking hard. 'We've got to be able to see the Whomping Willow, or we won't know what's going on.'

'OK,' said Hermione, getting a firmer grip on Buckbeak's rope. 'But we've got to keep out of sight, Harry, remember ...'

They moved around the edge of the Forest, darkness falling thickly around them, until they were hidden behind a clump of trees through which they could make out the Willow.

'There's Ron!' said Harry suddenly.

A dark figure was sprinting across the lawn and its shout echoed through the still night air.

'Get away from him – get away – Scabbers, come *here* –'

And then they saw two more figures materialise out of nowhere. Harry watched himself and Hermione chasing after Ron. Then he saw Ron dive.

'*Gotcha!* Get off, you stinking cat –'

'There's Sirius!' said Harry. The great shape of the dog had bounded out from the roots of the Willow. They saw him bowl Harry over, then seize Ron ...

'Looks even worse from here, doesn't it?' said Harry, watching the dog pulling Ron into the roots. 'Ouch – look, I just got walloped by the tree – and so did you – this is *weird* –'

The Whomping Willow was creaking and lashing out with its lower branches; they could see themselves darting here and there, trying to reach the trunk. And then the tree froze.

'That was Crookshanks pressing the knot,' said Hermione.

'And there we go ...' Harry muttered. 'We're in.'

The moment they disappeared, the tree began to move again. Seconds later, they heard footsteps quite close by. Dumbledore, Macnair, Fudge and the old Committee member were making their way up to the castle.

'Right after we'd gone down into the passage!' said Hermione. 'If *only* Dumbledore had come with us ...'

第21章 赫敏的秘密

"我们得藏在这儿。"赫敏说,她看上去惊魂未定,"需要等他们都返回城堡,然后再等到安全了,才能让巴克比克飞到小天狼星的窗口。他还要过两个小时才会在那儿……哦,很难……"

她紧张地回头望了望林子深处,太阳正在沉下去。

"我们得换个地方,"哈利说,努力动着脑筋,"必须能看到打人柳,不然我们不知道事情的进展。"

"好,"赫敏说,抓紧了巴克比克的绳子,"但必须保持隐蔽,哈利,记住……"

黑暗浓重地降临下来,他们在林子边移动,最后藏到了一片树丛后面,透过树丛可以看到打人柳。

"罗恩!"哈利突然说。

一个黑影奔过草坪,叫声在寂静的夜空回荡。

"走开——走开——斑斑,到这儿来——"

然后他们又看到两个人影突然显现。哈利看着他自己和赫敏在追赶罗恩,看到罗恩往前一扑。

"抓到了!滚开,你这只臭猫!"

"小天狼星来了!"哈利说。那条大狗从柳树下一跃而出,他们看到大狗把哈利撞倒,咬住了罗恩……

"从这儿看更可怕,是不是?"哈利说,眼睁睁地看着大狗把罗恩拖进树根之间,"哎哟——看,我被那棵树打到了——你也是——多奇怪啊——"

打人柳吱吱作响,低处的枝条猛烈地抽打着。他们看见自己左躲右闪,试图接近树干。突然,那棵树定住了。

"是克鲁克山按了节疤。"赫敏说。

"瞧……"哈利嘟哝道,"我们进去了。"

他们刚一消失,树又动了起来。片刻之后,他们听到脚步声从近处走过,邓布利多、麦克尼尔、福吉和老委员往城堡去了。

"我们刚进地道!"赫敏说,"要是邓布利多跟我们一起……"

CHAPTER TWENTY-ONE   Hermione's Secret

'Macnair and Fudge would've come, too,' said Harry bitterly. 'I bet you anything Fudge would've told Macnair to murder Sirius on the spot ...'

They watched the four men climb the castle steps and disappear from view. For a few minutes the scene was deserted. Then –

'Here comes Lupin!' said Harry, as they saw another figure sprinting down the stone steps and haring towards the Willow. Harry looked up at the sky. Clouds were obscuring the moon completely.

They watched Lupin seize a broken branch from the ground and prod the knot on the trunk. The tree stopped fighting, and Lupin, too, disappeared into the gap in its roots.

'If he'd only grabbed the Cloak,' said Harry. 'It's just lying there ...'

He turned to Hermione.

'If I just dashed out now and grabbed it, Snape'd never be able to get it and –'

'Harry, *we mustn't be seen*!'

'How can you stand this?' he asked Hermione fiercely. 'Just standing here and watching it happen?' He hesitated. 'I'm going to grab the Cloak!'

'Harry, *no*!'

Hermione seized the back of Harry's robes not a moment too soon. Just then, they heard a burst of song. It was Hagrid, making his way up to the castle, singing at the top of his voice, and weaving slightly as he walked. A large bottle was swinging from his hands.

'*See*?' Hermione whispered. '*See what would have happened?* We've got to keep out of sight! *No, Buckbeak!*'

The Hippogriff was making frantic attempts to get to Hagrid again; Harry seized his rope, too, straining to hold Buckbeak back. They watched Hagrid meander tipsily up to the castle. He was gone. Buckbeak stopped fighting to get away. His head drooped sadly.

Barely two minutes later, the castle doors flew open yet again, and Snape had come charging out of them, running towards the Willow.

Harry's fists clenched as they watched Snape skid to a halt next to the tree, looking around. He grabbed the Cloak and held it up.

'Get your filthy hands off it,' Harry snarled under his breath.

'Shh!'

Snape seized the branch Lupin had used to freeze the tree, prodded the knot, and vanished from view as he put on the Cloak.

第21章 赫敏的秘密

"那样麦克尼尔和福吉也会来的,"哈利恨恨地说,"我打赌福吉会让麦克尼尔把小天狼星就地处死……"

他们看着那四人登上城堡的台阶,消失了。几分钟里,视野内空无一人。然后——

"卢平出来了!"哈利说,只见又一个人影冲下石阶,朝打人柳飞奔过来。哈利抬头看看天空,月亮完全被云遮住了。

他们看着卢平从地上抓起一根断树枝,捅了捅那个节疤,树停止了抽打,卢平也消失在树根间的洞口里。

"要是他捡起那件隐形衣就好了,"哈利说,"它就在那儿……"

他转向赫敏。

"要是我现在冲出去把隐形衣拿走,斯内普就不会看到它,也就——"

"哈利,我们不能被人看见!"

"你怎么忍得下去?"哈利激烈地问,"就站在这儿袖手旁观?"他犹豫了一下,"我要去拿隐形衣!"

"哈利,不行!"

赫敏及时拉住了哈利的袍子后摆,就在这时,他们听到了一阵歌声。是海格,他一边往城堡走,一边放声高歌,步子有点歪歪斜斜,一个大酒瓶在手里晃荡着。

"看见了吗?"赫敏悄声说,"差点出事了吧?我们必须保持隐蔽!不要,巴克比克!"

鹰头马身有翼兽又躁动起来,想要冲向海格。哈利也抓紧了绳子,用力拽住巴克比克。他们一起望着海格摇摇晃晃地朝城堡走去,消失在视线外。巴克比克停止了挣扎,脑袋悲哀地耷拉下来。

两分钟不到,城堡大门又突然打开,斯内普冲了出来,奔向打人柳。

哈利握紧了拳头,只见斯内普在柳树跟前刹住脚步,四下看了看,抓起隐形衣,举到眼前。

"放开你的脏手!"哈利在嗓子眼里怒喝。

"嘘——"

斯内普捡起卢平用过的树枝,捅了捅节疤,披上隐形衣消失了。

CHAPTER TWENTY-ONE Hermione's Secret

'So that's it,' said Hermione quietly. 'We're all down there ... and now we've just got to wait until we come back up again ...'

She took the end of Buckbeak's rope and tied it securely around the nearest tree, then sat down on the dry ground, arms around her knees.

'Harry, there's something I don't understand ... why didn't the Dementors get Sirius? I remember them coming, and then I think I passed out ... there were so many of them ...'

Harry sat down, too. He explained what he'd seen; how, as the nearest Dementor had lowered its mouth to Harry's, a large silver something had come galloping across the lake and forced the Dementors to retreat.

Hermione's mouth was slightly open by the time Harry had finished.

'But what was it?'

'There's only one thing it could have been, to make the Dementors go,' said Harry. 'A real Patronus. A powerful one.'

'But who conjured it?'

Harry didn't say anything. He was thinking back to the person he'd seen on the other bank of the lake. He knew who he thought it had been ... but how *could* it have been?

'Didn't you see what they looked like?' said Hermione eagerly. 'Was it one of the teachers?'

'No,' said Harry. 'He wasn't a teacher.'

'But it must have been a really powerful wizard, to drive all those Dementors away ... If the Patronus was shining so brightly, didn't it light him up? Couldn't you see –?'

'Yeah, I saw him,' said Harry slowly. 'But ... maybe I imagined it ... I wasn't thinking straight ... I passed out right afterwards ...'

'*Who did you think it was?*'

'I think –' Harry swallowed, knowing how strange this was going to sound. 'I think it was my dad.'

Harry glanced up at Hermione and saw that her mouth was fully open now. She was gazing at him with a mixture of alarm and pity.

'Harry, your dad's – well – *dead*,' she said quietly.

'I know that,' said Harry quickly.

'You think you saw his ghost?'

第21章 赫敏的秘密

"原来是这样,"赫敏悄悄地说,"我们都在下面……现在就等我们出来了……"

她把巴克比克的绳子一端牢牢地拴在旁边的树上,然后坐到干的地面上,抱着膝盖。

"哈利,有件事我不明白……摄魂怪为什么没抓走小天狼星?我记得它们围了过来,后来我大概是昏过去了……它们数量那么多……"

哈利也坐下来,讲起了他看到的情景:当最近的那个摄魂怪把嘴凑向哈利时,一个银色的大东西从湖上疾驰过来,驱走了摄魂怪。

哈利说完,赫敏的嘴巴微微张着。

"那是什么呢?"

"能够驱走摄魂怪的,只可能是一样东西,"哈利说,"一个真正的、强大的守护神。"

"但是谁召唤来的呢?"

哈利没有说话,回想起当时看到的湖对岸的那个人。他想到了那个人像谁……可是那怎么可能呢?

"你没看到他什么模样吗?"赫敏热切地说,"是不是哪位老师?"

"不是,"哈利说,"他不是老师。"

"但一定是个本领高强的巫师,能把那些摄魂怪都赶走……守护神那么亮,不会照到他吗?你难道没有看见——?"

"嗯,我看见他了,"哈利缓缓地说,"可是……也许是我的幻觉……我当时脑子不大清楚……之后很快就失去了知觉……"

"你觉得那是谁呢?"

"我觉得——"哈利咽了口唾沫,知道这听上去有多离奇,"我觉得那是我爸爸。"

哈利抬头望着赫敏,看到她这次嘴巴张得大大的,用一种震惊和怜悯交织的眼神瞪着他。

"哈利,你爸爸已经——已经——去世了。"她小声说。

"我知道。"哈利马上说。

"你认为你是看到了他的幽灵吗?"

CHAPTER TWENTY-ONE   Hermione's Secret

'I don't know ... no ... he looked solid ...'

'But then —'

'Maybe I was seeing things,' said Harry. 'But ... from what I could see ... it looked like him ... I've got photos of him ...'

Hermione was still looking at him as though worried about his sanity.

'I know it sounds mad,' said Harry flatly. He turned to look at Buckbeak, who was digging his beak into the ground, apparently searching for worms. But he wasn't really watching Buckbeak.

He was thinking about his father, and about his three oldest friends ... Moony, Wormtail, Padfoot and Prongs ... Had all four of them been out in the grounds tonight? Worm-tail had reappeared this evening when everyone had thought he was dead — was it so impossible his father had done the same? Had he been seeing things across the lake? The figure had been too far away to see distinctly ... yet he had felt sure, for a moment, before he'd lost consciousness ...

The leaves overhead rustled faintly in the breeze. The moon drifted in and out of sight behind the shifting clouds. Hermione sat with her face turned towards the Willow, waiting.

And then, at last, after over an hour ...

'Here we come!' Hermione whispered.

She and Harry got to their feet. Buckbeak raised his head. They saw Lupin, Ron and Pettigrew clambering awkwardly out of the hole in the roots, followed by the unconscious Snape, drifting weirdly upwards. Next came Harry, Hermione and Black. They all began to walk towards the castle.

Harry's heart was starting to beat very fast. He glanced up at the sky. Any moment now, that cloud was going to move aside and show the moon ...

'Harry,' Hermione muttered, as though she knew exactly what he was thinking, 'we've got to stay put. We mustn't be seen. There's nothing we can do ...'

'So we're just going to let Pettigrew escape all over again ...' said Harry quietly.

'How do you expect to find a rat in the dark?' snapped Hermione. 'There's nothing we can do! We came back to help Sirius. We're not supposed to be doing anything else!'

'*All right!*'

The moon slid out from behind its cloud. They saw the tiny figures across

第21章 赫敏的秘密

"我不知道……不……他看上去很真实……"

"可是——"

"也许是我的幻觉，"哈利说，"可是……我当时看到的……确实像他……我有他的照片……"

赫敏还是用异样的表情瞪着他，似乎在担心他的神志是否正常。

"我知道这听起来很怪。"哈利坦率地说，转身看着巴克比克。它正把鹰嘴伸进地里，显然是在找虫子。其实哈利并没有在看巴克比克。

他在想他爸爸和他的三个老朋友……月亮脸、虫尾巴、大脚板和尖头叉子……今晚他们四个都出来了吗？虫尾巴在大家都以为他死了之后又于今晚复出……父亲难道就不可能复出？湖对面的景象是幻觉吗？那个人影太远，看不真切……但他当时有一刻感到很肯定，就在他失去知觉之前……

头顶的树叶在微风中发出沙沙轻响，月亮在飘动的云彩间忽隐忽现，赫敏面朝打人柳坐在那儿，等待着。

终于，一个多小时之后……

"我们出来了！"赫敏小声说。

她和哈利站了起来，巴克比克抬起了脑袋。他们看见卢平、罗恩和小矮星笨拙地从树根间的洞口爬了出来，然后是没有知觉的斯内普，诡异地飘了上来。再后面是哈利、赫敏和布莱克，一群人一起朝城堡走去。

哈利的心剧烈地跳起来，他望望天空，云彩随时可能飘开，月亮会露出来……

"哈利，"赫敏悄悄地说，好像猜准了他在想什么，"我们必须待在原地，不能被人看见。我们做不了什么……"

"那就眼睁睁地让小矮星再次跑掉……"哈利轻轻地说。

"在黑暗中怎么可能抓得到一只老鼠？"赫敏着急地说，"我们做不了什么！我们回来是为了救小天狼星，不能做别的！"

"好吧！"

月亮从云彩后面钻了出来。他们看到场地那边那队小小的人影站

CHAPTER TWENTY-ONE   Hermione's Secret

the grounds stop. Then they saw movement –

'There goes Lupin,' Hermione whispered. 'He's transforming –'

'Hermione!' said Harry suddenly. 'We've got to move!'

'We mustn't, I keep telling you –'

'Not to interfere! But Lupin's going to run into the Forest, right at us!'

Hermione gasped.

'Quick!' she moaned, dashing to untie Buckbeak. 'Quick! Where are we going to go? Where are we going to hide? The Dementors will be coming any moment –'

'Back to Hagrid's!' Harry said. 'It's empty now – come on!'

They ran, fast as they could, Buckbeak cantering along behind them. They could hear the werewolf howling behind them ...

The cabin was in sight. Harry skidded to the door, wrenched it open and Hermione and Buckbeak flashed past him; Harry threw himself in after them and bolted the door. Fang the boarhound barked loudly.

'Shh, Fang, it's us!' said Hermione, hurrying over and scratching his ears to quieten him. 'That was really close!' she said to Harry.

'Yeah ...'

Harry was looking out of the window. It was much harder to see what was going on from here. Buckbeak seemed very happy to find himself back inside Hagrid's house. He lay down in front of the fire, folded his wings contentedly and seemed ready for a good nap.

'I think I'd better go outside again, you know,' said Harry slowly. 'I can't see what's going on – we won't know when it's time –'

Hermione looked up. Her expression was suspicious.

'I'm not going to try and interfere,' said Harry quickly. 'But if we don't see what's going on, how're we going to know when it's time to rescue Sirius?'

'Well ... OK, then ... I'll wait here with Buckbeak ... but Harry, be careful – there's a werewolf out there – and the Dementors –'

Harry stepped outside again and edged around the cabin. He could hear yelping in the distance. That meant the Dementors were closing in on Sirius ... he and Hermione would be running to him any moment ...

Harry stared out towards the lake, his heart doing a kind of drum-roll in his chest. Whoever had sent that Patronus would be appearing at any moment.

住了，然后有了动作——

"是卢平，"赫敏低声说，"他在变形——"

"赫敏！"哈利突然说，"我们得走！"

"不行，我一直跟你说——"

"不是去干预！卢平马上就要冲进禁林，正好来我们这儿！"

赫敏倒吸了一口气。

"快！"她轻叫道，冲过去解开巴克比克，"快！我们去哪儿？往哪儿躲？摄魂怪就要来了——"

"回海格那儿去！"哈利说，"那儿现在没人——快走！"

两人使出全力飞奔，巴克比克稳稳地跑在后面。他们能听到狼人在后面嗥叫……

小屋出现在眼前，哈利冲到门前推开了门，赫敏和巴克比克从他身边闪了进去。哈利冲进屋里，转身插上了门。猎狗牙牙大声狂吠。

"嘘——牙牙，是我们！"赫敏赶忙走过去挠挠它的耳朵，让它安静下来。"好险！"她对哈利说。

"是啊……"

哈利望着窗外，从这里很难看到外边的情形。巴克比克发现自己回到了海格屋里，似乎很高兴。它在壁炉前躺下，满足地收起翅膀，看样子准备好好地打一个盹儿。

"我想我最好还是出去，"哈利缓缓地说，"在这儿看不到事情的进展——我们不知道什么时候——"

赫敏抬起头，表情有些怀疑。

"我不是要去干预，"哈利忙说，"但如果看不到进展，我们怎么知道什么时候该去救小天狼星呢？"

"嗯……那好吧……我跟巴克比克在这儿等着……可是哈利，多加小心——外面有狼人——还有那些摄魂怪——"

哈利走了出去，小心地绕过小屋。他听到远处有犬吠声，这意味着摄魂怪正在围住小天狼星……他和赫敏很快就会跑过去……

哈利朝湖面望去，心脏像在胸膛里打鼓一样……那派出守护神的人随时都会出现……

CHAPTER TWENTY-ONE   Hermione's Secret

For a fraction of a second he stood, irresolute, in front of Hagrid's door. *You must not be seen.* But he didn't want to be seen. He wanted to do the seeing ... he had to know ...

And there were the Dementors. They were emerging out of the darkness from every direction, gliding around the edges of the lake ... they were moving away from where Harry stood, to the opposite bank ... he wouldn't have to get near them ...

Harry began to run. He had no thought in his head except his father ... If it was him ... if it really was him ... he had to know, had to find out ...

The lake was coming nearer and nearer, but there was no sign of anybody. On the opposite bank, he could see tiny glimmers of silver – his own attempts at a Patronus –

There was a bush at the very edge of the water. Harry threw himself behind it, peering desperately through the leaves. On the opposite bank, the glimmers of silver were suddenly extinguished. A terrified excitement shot through him – any moment now –

'Come on!' he muttered, staring about. 'Where are you? Dad, come on –'

But no one came. Harry raised his head to look at the circle of Dementors across the lake. One of them was lowering its hood. It was time for the rescuer to appear – but no one was coming to help this time –

And then it hit him – he understood. He hadn't seen his father – he had seen *himself* –

Harry flung himself out from behind the bush and pulled out his wand.

'EXPECTO PATRONUM!' he yelled.

And out of the end of his wand burst, not a shapeless cloud of mist, but a blinding, dazzling, silver animal. He screwed up his eyes, trying to see what it was. It looked like a horse. It was galloping silently away from him, across the black surface of the lake. He saw it lower its head and charge at the swarming Dementors ... now it was galloping around and around the black shapes on the ground, and the Dementors were falling back, scattering, retreating into the darkness ... they were gone.

The Patronus turned. It was cantering back towards Harry across the still surface of the water. It wasn't a horse. It wasn't a unicorn, either. It was a stag. It was shining brightly as the moon above ... it was coming back to him ...

It stopped on the bank. Its hooves made no mark on the soft ground as it stared at Harry with its large, silver eyes. Slowly, it bowed its antlered head. And Harry realised ...

第21章 赫敏的秘密

一时间,他站在海格的门前犹豫不决。不能让人看见。但他并没想让人看见,他只想看看……他必须知道……

摄魂怪来了,在黑暗中从四面八方显现,沿着湖边飘行……它们正在离开哈利所站的地方,朝对岸飘去……他不用靠近它们……

哈利跑了起来,脑子里只有他的爸爸……如果那个人是他……如果真的是他……他必须知道,必须弄明白……

离湖面越来越近了,但看不到一个人影。他能看到对岸有一点点微弱的银光——是他自己正在召唤守护神——

挨着水边有一丛灌木。哈利扑到它的后面,焦急地透过树叶的缝隙窥视着。对岸的银光突然灭了。恐惧与激动袭上他的心头——就要来了——

"快啊!"他小声呼叫着,四下张望,"你在哪儿?爸爸,快出现啊!"

然而没有人来。哈利抬起头望着湖对岸的那圈摄魂怪,其中一个正在脱下兜帽。那个帮助他的人该出现了——可是这次没有人来。

突然灵光一闪——他明白了。他看到的不是爸爸——而是他自己——

哈利从灌木丛后一跃而出,抽出魔杖。

"呼神护卫!"他喊道。

从他的杖尖挣脱出一个东西,不是不成形的云雾,而是一头灿烂夺目的银色动物。他眯起眼睛想看清它是什么。好像是一匹马,无声地从他身边飞驰而去,奔过黑色的湖面。他看到它俯首冲向那一大群摄魂怪……现在它绕着地面上那几个黑影疾驰,摄魂怪纷纷后退,散开,隐入黑暗中……不见了。

守护神掉转身,越过平静的湖面慢慢地朝哈利跑来,它不是马,也不是独角兽,而是一头牡鹿,像天上的月亮一般皎洁……它在向他跑来……

它在岸边停住,用那双银色的大眼睛注视着哈利,蹄子在松软的地面上并没有留下任何痕迹。它缓缓地低下那一对鹿角。哈利看出来了……

CHAPTER TWENTY-ONE   Hermione's Secret

'*Prongs*,' he whispered.

But as his trembling fingertips stretched towards the creature, it vanished.

Harry stood there, hand still outstretched. Then, with a great leap of his heart, he heard hooves behind him – he whirled around and saw Hermione dashing towards him, dragging Buckbeak behind her.

'*What did you do?*' she said fiercely. 'You said you were only going to keep a lookout!'

'I just saved all our lives ...' said Harry. 'Get behind here – behind this bush – I'll explain.'

Hermione listened to what had just happened with her mouth open yet again.

'Did anyone see you?'

'Yes, haven't you been listening? *I* saw me but I thought I was my dad! It's OK!'

'Harry, I can't believe it – you conjured up a Patronus that drove away all those Dementors! That's very, *very* advanced magic ...'

'I knew I could do it this time,' said Harry, 'because I'd already done it ... Does that make sense?'

'I don't know – Harry, look at Snape!'

Together they peered around the bush at the other bank. Snape had regained consciousness. He was conjuring stretchers and lifting the limp forms of Harry, Hermione and Black onto them. A fourth stretcher, no doubt bearing Ron, was already floating at his side. Then, wand held out in front of him, he moved them away towards the castle.

'Right, it's nearly time,' said Hermione tensely, looking at her watch. 'We've got about forty-five minutes until Dumbledore locks the door to the hospital wing. We've got to rescue Sirius and get back into the ward before anybody realises we're missing ...'

They waited, watching the moving clouds reflected in the lake, while the bush next to them whispered in the breeze. Buckbeak, bored, was ferreting for worms again.

'D'you reckon he's up there yet?' said Harry, checking his watch. He looked up at the castle, and began counting the windows to the right of the West Tower.

'Look!' Hermione whispered. 'Who's that? Someone's coming back out of the castle!'

Harry stared through the darkness. The man was hurrying across the

第21章 赫敏的秘密

"尖头叉子。"他轻声说。

可是当他颤抖的指尖伸向那灵兽时,它却消失了。

哈利站在那儿,手仍然伸着。随后心猛地一跳,听到身后有蹄声——他转过身,看到赫敏拽着巴克比克冲了过来。

"你干了什么?"她气急败坏地问,"你说你只是看看的!"

"我刚才救了我们的命……"哈利说,"到这儿来——躲到灌木丛后面——我给你解释。"

赫敏听了刚才发生的事,嘴巴又张开了。

"有人看见你吗?"

"有,你不是一直在听着吗?我看见我了,但我以为是我爸爸!没关系!"

"哈利,真不敢相信……你召来了守护神,把那些摄魂怪都赶跑了!那可是非常非常高深的魔法……"

"我知道我这次能做到,"哈利说,"因为我已经做过了……这能说得通吗?"

"我不知道——哈利,看斯内普!"

两人一起从灌木后向对岸张望。斯内普醒过来了,正在变出担架,把毫无生气的哈利、赫敏和布莱克搬上去。另一副担架已经悬浮在斯内普的身边,那上面无疑是罗恩了。然后,斯内普把魔杖举在身前,把担架运往城堡。

"好,时间差不多了,"赫敏看看表,紧张地说,"离邓布利多锁上校医院的门还有四十五分钟左右。我们必须救出小天狼星,然后在有人发现我们失踪之前返回病房……"

他们等待着,望着湖中浮云变幻的倒影,身旁的灌木在微风中低语。巴克比克闲得无聊,又找起虫子来。

"你认为他已经在那儿了吗?"哈利看着表问。他抬头望着城堡,开始数西塔楼右边的窗户。

"看!"赫敏低声说,"那是谁?又有人从城堡里出来了!"

哈利朝黑暗中望去,那个人影匆匆穿过场地,走向一个入口,腰

CHAPTER TWENTY-ONE Hermione's Secret

grounds, towards one of the entrances. Something shiny glinted in his belt.

'Macnair!' said Harry. 'The executioner! He's gone to get the Dementors! This is it, Hermione —'

Hermione put her hands on Buckbeak's back and Harry gave her a leg up. Then he placed his foot on one of the lower branches of the bush and climbed up in front of her. He pulled Buckbeak's rope back over his neck and tied it to the other side of his collar like reins.

'Ready?' he whispered to Hermione. 'You'd better hold on to me —'

He nudged Buckbeak's sides with his heels.

Buckbeak soared straight into the dark air. Harry gripped his flanks with his knees, feeling the great wings rising powerfully beneath them. Hermione was holding Harry very tightly around the waist; he could hear her muttering, 'Oh, no — I don't like this — oh, I *really* don't like this —'

Harry urged Buckbeak forwards. They were gliding quietly towards the upper floors of the castle ... Harry pulled hard on the left-hand side of the rope, and Buckbeak turned. Harry was trying to count the windows flashing past —

'Whoa!' he said, pulling backwards as hard as he could.

Buckbeak slowed down and they found themselves at a stop, unless you counted the fact that they kept rising up and down several feet as he beat his wings to remain airborne.

'He's there!' Harry said, spotting Sirius as they rose up beside the window. He reached out, and as Buckbeak's wings fell, was able to tap sharply on the glass.

Black looked up. Harry saw his jaw drop. He leapt from his chair, hurried to the window and tried to open it, but it was locked.

'Stand back!' Hermione called to him, and she took out her wand, still gripping the back of Harry's robes with her left hand.

'*Alohomora!*'

The window sprang open.

'How — *how* —?' said Black weakly, staring at the Hippogriff.

'Get on — there's not much time,' said Harry, gripping Buckbeak firmly on either side of his sleek neck to hold him steady. 'You've got to get out of here — the Dementors are coming. Macnair's gone to get them.'

第21章 赫敏的秘密

间还有什么东西闪着寒光。

"麦克尼尔!"哈利说,"那个行刑官!他去找摄魂怪了!是时候了,赫敏——"

赫敏把双手放在巴克比克背上,哈利扶她骑了上去,然后自己蹬着低处的树枝坐到她前面。他把巴克比克的绳头绕过脖子拉过来,系到它项圈的另一边当缰绳用。

"好了吗?"他小声对赫敏说,"你最好抱着我——"

他用脚跟磕了磕巴克比克的肚子。

巴克比克笔直地升上了夜空。哈利用膝盖夹住它的两肋,感到那一对巨大的翅膀在他们下面强有力地扇动着。赫敏紧紧搂着哈利的腰。他听到她喃喃地说:"哦,不——我不喜欢这感觉——哦,真的不喜欢这感觉——"

哈利催促巴克比克向前飞驰,他们静静地飞向城堡上层……哈利用力一拉左手边的绳子,巴克比克朝左拐去,哈利努力数着快速闪过的窗户——

"吁——"他轻呼,一边用全力把绳子往后拉。

巴克比克减慢速度,他们停住了,只是不断地上下浮动几英尺——鹰头马身有翼兽扇动翅膀以保持凌空。

"他在那儿!"哈利叫道,在他们升过那扇窗户时看到了小天狼星。当巴克比克的翅膀落下时,他伸出手,急促地敲了敲窗玻璃。

布莱克抬起头,哈利看到他的嘴巴张大了。他从椅子上跳了起来,跑到窗口想打开它,可是窗户锁着。

"后退!"赫敏对他说,她抽出魔杖,左手仍揪着哈利的袍子的背后。

"阿拉霍洞开!"

窗户一下子打开了。

"怎——怎么——?"布莱克瞪着鹰头马身有翼兽无力地问。

"上来——时间不多了。"哈利说,紧紧抓着巴克比克光滑的脖子两边把它稳住,"你必须离开这儿——摄魂怪马上就要来了。麦克尼尔去找它们了。"

CHAPTER TWENTY-ONE Hermione's Secret

Black placed a hand on either side of the window-frame and heaved his head and shoulders out of it. It was very lucky he was so thin. In seconds, he had managed to fling one leg over Buckbeak's back, and pull himself onto the Hippogriff behind Hermione.

'OK, Buckbeak, up!' said Harry, shaking the rope. 'Up to the tower – come on!'

The Hippogriff gave one sweep of its mighty wings and they were soaring upwards again, high as the top of the West Tower. Buckbeak landed with a clatter on the battlements and Harry and Hermione slid off him at once.

'Sirius, you'd better go, quick,' Harry panted. 'They'll reach Flitwick's office any moment, they'll find out you've gone.'

Buckbeak pawed the ground, tossing his sharp head.

'What happened to the other boy? Ron?' said Sirius urgently.

'He's going to be OK – he's still out of it, but Madam Pomfrey says she'll be able to make him better. Quick – go!'

But Black was still staring down at Harry.

'How can I ever thank –'

'GO!' Harry and Hermione shouted together.

Black wheeled Buckbeak around, facing the open sky.

'We'll see each other again,' he said. 'You are – truly your father's son, Harry ...'

He squeezed Buckbeak's sides with his heels. Harry and Hermione jumped back as the enormous wings rose once more ... the Hippogriff took off into the air ... he and his rider became smaller and smaller as Harry gazed after them ... then a cloud drifted across the moon ... they were gone.

第21章 赫敏的秘密

布莱克双手撑住窗框,把头和肩膀伸了出来。幸好他很瘦。几秒钟后,他就把一条腿跨到巴克比克背上,骑在了赫敏的后面。

"好了,巴克比克,上去!"哈利扯动绳子说,"上塔顶去——快!"

鹰头马身有翼兽扇动巨大的翅膀,他们又高高升起,到了西塔楼的塔顶。巴克比克嗒嗒地降落在垛墙上,哈利和赫敏迅速从它背上滑了下来。

"小天狼星,你快走吧,"哈利喘着气说,"他们随时可能去弗立维的办公室,会发现你失踪了。"

巴克比克用前蹄刨着地面,扬起尖尖的脑袋。

"那个男孩,罗恩呢?"小天狼星急切地问。

"他不会有事的,现在还昏迷着,但是庞弗雷女士说会把他调养好的。快,快走吧!"

但是布莱克仍低头望着哈利。

"我怎么感谢——"

"**快走!**"哈利和赫敏一起喊道。

布莱克让巴克比克掉过头,对着空旷的夜空。

"后会有期。"他说,"你——真不愧是你父亲的儿子,哈利……"

他脚跟一夹巴克比克的肚子,哈利和赫敏往后跳去,巨大的翅膀再次展开……鹰头马身有翼兽飞了起来……哈利目送它驮着背上的人越飞越小……然后,一片云从月亮前面飘过……他们不见了。

CHAPTER TWENTY-TWO

Owl Post Again

'Harry!' Hermione was tugging at his sleeve, staring at her watch. 'We've got exactly ten minutes to get back down to the hospital wing without anybody seeing us – before Dumbledore locks the door –'

'OK,' said Harry, wrenching his gaze from the sky, 'let's go ...'

They slipped through the doorway behind them and down a tightly spiralling stone staircase. As they reached the bottom of it, they heard voices. They flattened themselves against the wall and listened. It sounded like Fudge and Snape. They were walking quickly along the corridor at the foot of the staircase.

'... only hope Dumbledore's not going to make difficulties,' Snape was saying. 'The kiss will be performed immediately?'

'As soon as Macnair returns with the Dementors. This whole Black affair has been highly embarrassing. I can't tell you how much I'm looking forward to informing the *Daily Prophet* that we've got him at last ... I daresay they'll want to interview you, Snape ... and once young Harry's back in his right mind, I expect he'll want to tell the *Prophet* exactly how you saved him ...'

Harry clenched his teeth. He caught a glimpse of Snape's smirk as he and Fudge passed Harry and Hermione's hiding place. Their footsteps died away. Harry and Hermione waited a few moments to make sure they'd really gone, then started to run in the opposite direction. Down one staircase, then another, along a new corridor – then they heard a cackling ahead.

'*Peeves!*' Harry muttered, grabbing Hermione's wrist. 'In here!'

They tore into a deserted classroom to their left just in time. Peeves seemed to be bouncing along the corridor in tearing spirits, laughing his head off.

'Oh, he's horrible,' whispered Hermione, her ear to the door. 'I bet he's all

第22章

又见猫头鹰传书

"哈利！"赫敏拉拉他的袖子，看着表说："我们还有十分钟可以悄悄溜回校医院——在邓布利多锁门之前——"

"好吧，"哈利说，把视线从天空收了回来，"走……"

两人溜进身后的一条走廊，走下一段狭窄的螺旋形石梯。走到楼梯底部时听见有人在说话，他们把身体贴在墙上聆听，好像是福吉和斯内普，正快步走在楼梯下的过道里。

"……但愿邓布利多不再制造麻烦，"斯内普说，"那个吻很快就会执行了吧？"

"只等麦克尼尔把摄魂怪带回来。布莱克这件事非常棘手。我简直无法告诉你，我多么盼望能通知《预言家日报》我们终于抓到他了……我猜他们会希望采访你的，斯内普……当小哈利神志清楚之后，我想他也会愿意告诉《预言家日报》你是怎样搭救他们的……"

哈利咬牙切齿，那两人走过他和赫敏藏身的地方时，他瞥见斯内普满脸的得意。脚步声远去了。哈利和赫敏又等了一会儿，确定那两人真的走了，才朝相反的方向跑去。下了一道楼梯，再下一道楼梯，跑入一条新走廊——忽然他们听到前面有咯咯的笑声。

"皮皮鬼！"哈利低声说，拉住赫敏的手腕，"快进去！"

他们及时冲进了左边的一间空教室。皮皮鬼好像高兴得过了头，在走廊里又蹦又跳，尖声狂笑。

"哦，他真可怕，"赫敏小声说，"我打赌他是因为摄魂怪要来结果

CHAPTER TWENTY-TWO   Owl Post Again

excited because the Dementors are going to finish Sirius ...' She checked her watch. 'Three minutes, Harry!'

They waited until Peeves's gloating voice had faded into the distance, then slid back out of the room and broke into a run again.

'Hermione – what'll happen – if we don't get back inside – before Dumbledore locks the door?' Harry panted.

'I don't want to think about it!' Hermione moaned, checking her watch again. 'One minute!'

They had reached the end of the corridor with the hospital-wing entrance. 'OK – I can hear Dumbledore,' said Hermione tensely. 'Come on, Harry!'

They crept along the corridor. The door opened. Dumbledore's back appeared.

'I am going to lock you in,' they heard him saying. 'It is five minutes to midnight. Miss Granger, three turns should do it. Good luck.'

Dumbledore backed out of the room, closed the door and took out his wand to magically lock it. Panicking, Harry and Hermione ran forwards. Dumbledore looked up, and a wide smile appeared under the long silver moustache. 'Well?' he said quietly.

'We did it!' said Harry breathlessly. 'Sirius has gone, on Buckbeak ...'

Dumbledore beamed at them.

'Well done. I think –' he listened intently for any sound within the hospital wing. 'Yes, I think you've gone, too. Get inside – I'll lock you in –'

Harry and Hermione slipped back inside the dormitory. It was empty except for Ron, who was still lying motionless in the end bed. As the lock clicked behind them, Harry and Hermione crept back to their own beds, Hermione tucking the Time-Turner back under her robes. Next moment, Madam Pomfrey had come striding back out of her office.

'Did I hear the Headmaster leaving? Am I allowed to look after my patients now?'

She was in a very bad mood. Harry and Hermione thought it best to accept their chocolate quietly. Madam Pomfrey stood over them, making sure they ate it. But Harry could hardly swallow. He and Hermione were waiting, listening, their nerves jangling ... And then, as they both took a fourth piece of chocolate from Madam Pomfrey, they heard a distant roar of fury echoing from somewhere above them ...

第22章 又见猫头鹰传书

小天狼星才这么兴奋的……"她看了看表,"还有三分钟,哈利。"

一直等到皮皮鬼开心的声音在远处消失,他们才溜出教室,又猛跑起来。

"赫敏——如果我们——在邓布利多锁门以前——没赶回去——会怎么样?"哈利气喘吁吁地问。

"我不愿去想!"赫敏呻吟道,又看了看表,"还有一分钟!"

他们已经到了校医院所在的走廊尽头。"好——我听到邓布利多的声音了,"赫敏紧张地说,"快,哈利!"

两人悄悄沿走廊跑去,门开了,露出邓布利多的背影。

"我要把你们关起来。现在是——"他们听到他说,"差五分就到午夜了。格兰杰小姐,转三下就行。祝你们好运。"

邓布利多退了出来,关上门,抽出魔杖要锁门。哈利和赫敏大惊失色,连忙冲过去。邓布利多抬起头,银白色的长胡子后面露出一个大大的笑容。"怎么样?"他轻声问。

"办成了!"哈利上气不接下气地说,"小天狼星逃走了,骑着巴克比克……"

邓布利多微笑地看着他们。

"干得好。我认为——"他仔细听听校医院里有没有声音,"对,我认为你们也逃脱了——进去吧——我要把你们锁在里面——"

哈利和赫敏溜回病房,里面只有罗恩一人,仍然一动不动地躺在最顶头的床上。门锁咔嗒锁上了,哈利和赫敏都爬回自己的床上。赫敏把时间转换器塞回袍子里。片刻之后,庞弗雷女士从她的办公室大步走了出来。

"我是听到校长走了吗?我可以照看我的病人了吗?"

她情绪很坏,哈利和赫敏觉得最好老老实实地吃她给的巧克力。庞弗雷女士站在他们面前看着他们吃下去。但哈利觉得难以下咽。他和赫敏在等待着,聆听着,神经高度紧张……然后,当他们俩吃到庞弗雷女士发的第四块巧克力时,听见上面远远地传来一声雷霆般的怒吼……

CHAPTER TWENTY-TWO Owl Post Again

'What was that?' said Madam Pomfrey in alarm.

Now they could hear angry voices, growing louder and louder. Madam Pomfrey was staring at the door.

'Really – they'll wake everybody up! What do they think they're doing?'

Harry was trying to hear what the voices were saying. They were drawing nearer –

'He must have Disapparated, Severus, we should have left somebody in the room with him. When this gets out –'

'HE DIDN'T DISAPPARATE!' Snape roared, now very close at hand. 'YOU CAN'T APPARATE OR DISAPPARATE INSIDE THIS CASTLE! THIS – HAS – SOMETHING – TO – DO – WITH – POTTER!'

'Severus – be reasonable – Harry has been locked up –'

BAM.

The door of the hospital wing burst open.

Fudge, Snape and Dumbledore came striding into the ward. Dumbledore alone looked calm. Indeed, he looked as though he was quite enjoying himself. Fudge appeared angry. But Snape was beside himself.

'OUT WITH IT, POTTER!' he bellowed. 'WHAT DID YOU DO?'

'Professor Snape!' shrieked Madam Pomfrey. 'Control yourself!'

'See here, Snape, be reasonable,' said Fudge. 'This door's been locked, we just saw –'

'THEY HELPED HIM ESCAPE, I KNOW IT!' Snape howled, pointing at Harry and Hermione. His face was twisted, spit was flying from his mouth.

'Calm down, man!' Fudge barked. 'You're talking nonsense!'

'YOU DON'T KNOW POTTER!' shrieked Snape. 'HE DID IT, I KNOW HE DID IT –'

'That will do, Severus,' said Dumbledore quietly. 'Think about what you are saying. This door has been locked since I left the ward ten minutes ago. Madam Pomfrey, have these students left their beds?'

'Of course not!' said Madam Pomfrey, bristling. 'I've been with them ever since you left!'

'Well, there you have it, Severus,' said Dumbledore calmly. 'Unless you are suggesting that Harry and Hermione are able to be in two places at once, I'm afraid I don't see any point in troubling them further.'

Snape stood there, seething, staring from Fudge, who looked thoroughly

"怎么回事？"庞弗雷女士吃惊地问。

现在他们听到了愤怒的说话声，越来越响，庞弗雷女士瞪着门口。

"真是——他们会把人都吵醒的！搞什么名堂？"

哈利努力想听清那些声音在说什么。声音渐渐近了——

"他一定是幻影移形了，西弗勒斯。我们应该在屋里留个人看着他的。这要是传出去——"

"**他没有幻影移形！**"斯内普咆哮道，他现在已经很近了，"**在城堡里不能幻影显形或幻影移形！这——肯定——又是——波特！**"

"西弗勒斯——理智点——哈利一直被锁在里头——"

咣。

校医院的门被猛地撞开了。

福吉、斯内普和邓布利多大步走进病房。只有邓布利多一人镇定自若，实际上，他看上去好像兴致不错。福吉面带怒容，斯内普则是发狂一般。

"**说，波特！**"他吼道，"**你干了什么？**"

"斯内普教授！"庞弗雷女士尖叫道，"克制一些！"

"听我说，斯内普，理智点，"福吉说，"这门是锁着的，我们刚才看见——"

"**是他们帮他逃走的，我知道！**"斯内普指着哈利和赫敏大吼，他的脸都气歪了，唾沫星子乱溅。

"冷静点，先生！"福吉厉声说，"你是在说胡话呢！"

"你不了解波特！"斯内普尖叫道，"**是他干的，我知道是他干的！**"

"够了，西弗勒斯，"邓布利多轻声说，"想想你在说些什么吧。从我十分钟前离开之后，这扇门一直是锁着的。庞弗雷女士，这些学生离开过病床吗？"

"当然没有！"庞弗雷女士不悦地说，"不然我会听见的！"

"你看，西弗勒斯，"邓布利多平静地说，"除非你是说哈利和赫敏有分身术，否则，我想我们没有理由继续打扰他们。"

斯内普狂怒地站在那儿，瞪眼望望福吉，又望望邓布利多，福吉

CHAPTER TWENTY-TWO Owl Post Again

shocked at his behaviour, to Dumbledore, whose eyes were twinkling behind his glasses. Snape whirled about, robes swishing behind him, and stormed out of the ward.

'Fellow seems quite unbalanced,' said Fudge, staring after him. 'I'd watch out for him, if I were you, Dumbledore.'

'Oh, he's not unbalanced,' said Dumbledore quietly. 'He's just suffered a severe disappointment.'

'He's not the only one!' puffed Fudge. 'The *Daily Prophet's* going to have a field day! We had Black cornered and he slipped through our fingers yet again! All it needs now is for the story of that Hippogriff's escape to get out, and I'll be a laughing stock! Well ... I'd better go and notify the Ministry ...'

'And the Dementors?' said Dumbledore. 'They'll be removed from the school, I trust?'

'Oh, yes, they'll have to go,' said Fudge, running his fingers distractedly through his hair. 'Never dreamed they'd attempt to administer the kiss on an innocent boy ... completely out of control ... No, I'll have them packed off back to Azkaban tonight. Perhaps we should think about dragons at the school entrance ...'

'Hagrid would like that,' said Dumbledore, with a swift smile at Harry and Hermione. As he and Fudge left the dormitory, Madam Pomfrey hurried to the door and locked it again. Muttering angrily to herself, she headed back to her office.

There was a low moan from the other end of the ward. Ron had woken up. They could see him sitting up, rubbing his head, looking around.

'What – what happened?' he groaned. 'Harry? Why are we in here? Where's Sirius? Where's Lupin? What's going on?'

Harry and Hermione looked at each other.

'You explain,' said Harry, helping himself to some more chocolate.

When Harry, Ron and Hermione left the hospital wing at noon next day, it was to find an almost deserted castle. The sweltering heat and the end of the exams meant that everyone was taking full advantage of another Hogsmeade visit. Neither Ron nor Hermione felt like going, however, so they and Harry wandered into the grounds, still talking about the extraordinary events of the previous night and wondering where Sirius and Buckbeak were now. Sitting

第22章 又见猫头鹰传书

似乎对他的表现十分惊愕,邓布利多的眼睛在镜片后面闪烁着。斯内普猛然转身,袍子发出呼呼的声音,大步冲出了病房。

"这人好像有点精神失常,"福吉望着他的背影说,"我要是你,就会盯着他,邓布利多。"

"哦,他不是精神失常,"邓布利多平静地说,"他只是非常失望罢了。"

"不只是他,"福吉气哼哼地说,"《预言家日报》有事干了!我们抓到了布莱克,又让他从手指缝里溜掉了!那头鹰头马身有翼兽逃走的事再一泄漏,我就整个成为笑柄了!唉……我最好现在去通知魔法部……"

"那些摄魂怪呢?"邓布利多问,"它们可以撤出学校了吧?"

"哦,对,它们必须得离开,"福吉心烦意乱地用手指捋了捋头发说,"想不到它们竟会试图去吻一个无辜的男孩……完全不受控制了……不行,我要连夜把它们赶回阿兹卡班……也许应该考虑让火龙来把守校门……"

"海格会喜欢的。"邓布利多说,朝哈利和赫敏笑了笑。他和福吉走出病房,庞弗雷女士快步过去把门重新锁好,恼火地嘟哝着回办公室去了。

病房那头传来一声低低的呻吟,罗恩醒了。他们看到他坐了起来,揉着脑袋环顾四周。

"咦——怎么搞的?"他嘟哝道,"哈利?我们怎么在这儿?小天狼星呢?卢平呢?发生了什么事?"

哈利和赫敏对视了一下。

"你讲吧。"哈利说,伸手又拿起一块巧克力。

第二天中午,哈利、罗恩和赫敏走出校医院时,发现城堡里空荡荡的。天气炎热再加上考试结束,所有的人都到霍格莫德度假去了。但罗恩和赫敏都不想去,所以三人漫步到场地上,一边仍在说着前一天晚上的奇异经历,猜测小天狼星和巴克比克现在到了哪里。他们坐在湖边,看着巨乌贼懒洋洋地在水面摇动着触手,哈利的思绪游离开去。

CHAPTER TWENTY-TWO   Owl Post Again

near the lake, watching the giant squid waving its tentacles lazily above the water, Harry lost the thread of the conversation as he looked across to the opposite bank. The stag had galloped towards him from there just last night ...

A shadow fell across them and they looked up to see a very bleary-eyed Hagrid, mopping his sweaty face with one of his tablecloth-sized handkerchiefs and beaming down at them.

'Know I shouldn' feel happy, after wha' happened las' night,' he said. 'I mean, Black escapin' again, an' everythin' – but guess what?'

'What?' they said, pretending to look curious.

'Beaky! He escaped! He's free! Bin celebratin' all night!'

'That's wonderful!' said Hermione, giving Ron a reproving look because he looked as though he was close to laughing.

'Yeah ... can't've tied him up properly,' said Hagrid, gazing happily out over the grounds. 'I was worried this mornin', mind ... thought he mighta met Professor Lupin in the grounds, but Lupin says he never ate anythin' las' night ...'

'What?' said Harry quickly.

'Blimey, haven' yeh heard?' said Hagrid, his smile fading a little. He lowered his voice, even though there was nobody in sight. 'Er – Snape told all the Slytherins this mornin' ... thought everyone'd know by now ... Professor Lupin's a werewolf, see. An' he was loose in the grounds las' night. He's packin' now, o' course.'

'He's *packing*?' said Harry, alarmed. 'Why?'

'Leavin', isn' he?' said Hagrid, looking surprised that Harry had to ask. 'Resigned firs' thing this mornin'. Says he can' risk it happenin' again.'

Harry scrambled to his feet.

'I'm going to see him,' he said to Ron and Hermione.

'But if he's resigned –'

'– doesn't sound like there's anything we can do –'

'I don't care. I still want to see him. I'll meet you back here.'

Lupin's office door was open. He had already packed most of his things. The Grindylow's empty tank stood next to his battered old suitcase, which was open and nearly full. Lupin was bending over something on his desk, and only looked up when Harry knocked on the door.

他望着对岸，就在昨晚，牡鹿从那边向他奔来……

一个影子落到他们身上，三人抬起头，看到了泪眼模糊的海格。他用那块桌布大的手帕擦着汗津津的面孔，朝他们笑着。

"我知道不应该高兴，昨晚出了那样的事，"他说，"我是说，布莱克又跑掉了，还有别的事情——可是你们猜怎么着？"

"怎么啦？"他们假装好奇地问。

"比克！它逃走了！它自由了！我庆祝了一晚上！"

"太棒了！"赫敏说，同时不满地瞪了罗恩一眼，因为他好像要笑出来了。

"是啊……可能没有拴好，"海格快活地望着场地说，"今天早上我有点担心……怕它会在场地上碰到卢平教授，但卢平说他昨晚什么也没吃……"

"什么？"哈利忙问。

"哎呀，你没有听说吗？"海格的笑容退去了一些，他把声音压得低低的，尽管周围并没有人，"呃——斯内普早上对斯莱特林的全体学生说了……我以为现在人人都知道了……卢平教授是狼人，昨晚跑到了场地上……当然，他现在正在收拾行李呢。"

"他在收拾行李？"哈利吃惊地问，"为什么？"

"走人啊，不是吗？"海格似乎很奇怪哈利会这么问，"今天一大早他就辞职了，说不能再冒这种风险。"

哈利站了起来。

"我要去看他。"他对罗恩和赫敏说。

"可是如果他已经辞职了——"

"我们似乎也无能为力——"

"我不管，我就是想见见他。我回来再来这里找你们。"

卢平办公室的门开着。他已经把大部分东西都收拾好了。格林迪洛的空水箱立在他那只破旧的皮箱旁边，箱子敞着，里面快装满了。卢平趴在桌上看着什么，哈利敲门后他才抬起头来。

CHAPTER TWENTY-TWO Owl Post Again

'I saw you coming,' said Lupin, smiling. He pointed to the parchment he had been poring over. It was the Marauder's Map.

'I just saw Hagrid,' said Harry. 'And he said you'd resigned. It's not true, is it?'

'I'm afraid it is,' said Lupin. He started opening his desk drawers and taking out the contents.

'*Why?*' said Harry. 'The Ministry of Magic don't think you were helping Sirius, do they?'

Lupin crossed to the door and closed it behind Harry.

'No. Professor Dumbledore managed to convince Fudge that I was trying to save your lives.' He sighed. 'That was the final straw for Severus. I think the loss of the Order of Merlin hit him hard. So he – er – *accidentally* let slip that I am a werewolf this morning at breakfast.'

'You're not leaving just because of that!' said Harry.

Lupin smiled wryly.

'This time tomorrow, the owls will start arriving from parents – they will not want a werewolf teaching their children, Harry. And after last night, I see their point. I could have bitten any of you ... that must never happen again.'

'You're the best Defence Against the Dark Arts teacher we've ever had!' said Harry. 'Don't go!'

Lupin shook his head and didn't speak. He carried on emptying his drawers. Then, while Harry was trying to think of a good argument to make him stay, Lupin said, 'From what the Headmaster told me this morning, you saved a lot of lives last night, Harry. If I'm proud of anything, it's how much you've learned. Tell me about your Patronus.'

'How d'you know about that?' said Harry, distracted.

'What else could have driven the Dementors back?'

Harry told Lupin what had happened. When he'd finished, Lupin was smiling again.

'Yes, your father was always a stag when he transformed,' he said. 'You guessed right ... that's why we called him Prongs.'

Lupin threw his last few books into his case, closed the desk drawers and turned to look at Harry.

'Here – I brought this from the Shrieking Shack last night,' he said, handing Harry back the Invisibility Cloak. 'And ...' he hesitated, then held out the Marauder's Map, too. 'I am no longer your teacher, so I don't feel

"我看见你来了。"卢平微笑道,指了指他刚才看的那张羊皮纸,是活点地图。

"我刚才看到海格了,"哈利说,"他说你辞职了,不会是真的吧?"

"恐怕是真的。"卢平说,开始打开桌子的抽屉把里面的东西拿出来。

"为什么?"哈利问,"魔法部没有认为是你帮助了小天狼星吧?"

卢平走到门口,把哈利身后的门关上了。

"没有,邓布利多教授让福吉相信我是去救你们的。"他叹了口气说,"这让西弗勒斯忍无可忍——我想,失去梅林爵士团勋章对他打击很大。所以今天早餐时——呃——他无意中透露了我是狼人。"

"你不是就因为这个要走吧?"哈利说。

卢平苦笑了一下。

"明天这个时候,猫头鹰就会送来家长的信……他们不会愿意让一个狼人教自己孩子的。哈利,经过昨晚的事,我认为他们是对的,我很可能会咬伤你们……这种事绝对不能再发生了。"

"你是我们最好的黑魔法防御术教师,"哈利说,"别走!"

卢平摇了摇头,没有说话,继续清理他的抽屉。哈利正绞尽脑汁考虑怎么劝他留下来时,卢平说:"今天早上听校长说,你昨晚救了好几条命,哈利。如果今年有什么事令我自豪的话,那就是你的长进……跟我讲讲你的守护神吧。"

"你是怎么知道的?"哈利问,感觉有些慌乱。

"还有什么能驱走摄魂怪呢?"

哈利跟卢平讲了当时的情形。他讲完后,卢平又微笑起来。

"是啊,你爸爸总是每次都变成一头牡鹿。"他说,"你猜对了……他的绰号尖头叉子就是这么来的。"

卢平把最后几本书丢进箱子,关上桌子抽屉,转身看着哈利。

"给——我昨晚从尖叫棚屋拿出来的。"他把隐形衣还给了哈利,"还有……"他犹豫了一下,把活点地图也递了过去,"我不再是你的老师了,所以把这个还给你也不会感到内疚。它在我这儿没有用,我猜你和罗恩、

CHAPTER TWENTY-TWO Owl Post Again

guilty about giving you this back as well. It's no use to me, and I daresay you, Ron and Hermione will find uses for it.'

Harry took the map and grinned.

'You told me Moony, Wormtail, Padfoot and Prongs would've wanted to lure me out of school ... you said they'd have thought it was funny.'

'And so we would have done,' said Lupin, now reaching down to close his case. 'I have no hesitation in saying that James would have been highly disappointed if his son had never found any of the secret passages out of the castle.'

There was a knock on the door. Harry hastily stuffed the Marauder's Map and the Invisibility Cloak into his pocket.

It was Professor Dumbledore. He didn't look surprised to see Harry there.

'Your carriage is at the gates, Remus,' he said.

'Thank you, Headmaster.'

Lupin picked up his old suitcase and the empty Grindylow tank.

'Well – goodbye, Harry,' he said, smiling. 'It has been a real pleasure teaching you. I feel sure we'll meet again some time. Headmaster, there is no need to see me to the gates, I can manage ...'

Harry had the impression that Lupin wanted to leave as quickly as possible.

'Goodbye, then, Remus,' said Dumbledore soberly. Lupin shifted the Grindylow tank slightly so that he and Dumbledore could shake hands. Then, with a final nod to Harry, and a swift smile, Lupin left the office.

Harry sat down in his vacated chair, staring glumly at the floor. He heard the door close and looked up. Dumbledore was still there.

'Why so miserable, Harry?' he said quietly. 'You should be very proud of yourself after last night.'

'It didn't make any difference,' said Harry bitterly. 'Pettigrew got away.'

'Didn't make any difference?' said Dumbledore quietly. 'It made all the difference in the world, Harry. You helped uncover the truth. You saved an innocent man from a terrible fate.'

Terrible. Something stirred in Harry's memory. *Greater and more terrible than ever before* ... Professor Trelawney's prediction!

'Professor Dumbledore – yesterday, when I was having my Divination exam, Professor Trelawney went very – very strange.'

'Indeed?' said Dumbledore. 'Er – stranger than usual, you mean?'

第22章 又见猫头鹰传书

赫敏会用得着的。"

哈利接过地图,咧嘴一笑。

"你说过月亮脸、虫尾巴、大脚板和尖头叉子可能想把我引出学校……你说他们会觉得这挺好玩的。"

"确实如此。"卢平说,一边弯腰关上皮箱,"我毫不怀疑地说,如果詹姆看到他儿子从没发现溜出城堡的秘密通道,他会感到非常失望的。"

敲门声响起。哈利赶紧把活点地图和隐形衣塞进口袋。

是邓布利多教授。看到哈利在这儿,他似乎并不惊讶。

"你的马车停在门口,莱姆斯。"他说。

"谢谢你,校长。"

卢平拎起旧皮箱和那个格林迪洛空水箱。

"好了——再见,哈利,"他微笑着说,"教你真的很愉快。我相信我们还会再见的。校长,不用送我到门口,我能行……"

哈利感觉卢平想尽快离开。

"那就再会了,莱姆斯。"邓布利多冷静地说。卢平把格林迪洛水箱稍稍移开一点,和邓布利多握了握手。接着,他最后朝哈利点了一下头,笑了笑,迅速离开了办公室。

哈利坐到了卢平的空椅子上,忧郁地看着地板。他听到关门声,抬起头来。邓布利多还在屋里。

"为什么这么不开心呢,哈利?"他轻声问,"你应该为昨晚做的事情而自豪啊。"

"没什么区别,"哈利痛苦地说,"小矮星逃走了。"

"没什么区别?"邓布利多轻声说,"区别可大了,哈利,你帮助揭开了真相,并让一个无辜的人逃离了可怕的厄运。"

可怕。什么东西唤起了哈利的记忆。比以前更强大、更可怕……特里劳尼教授的预言!

"邓布利多教授——昨天,占卜课考试的时候,特里劳尼教授变得非常——非常奇怪。"

"是吗?"邓布利多说,"呃——你是说比往常还要奇怪?"

CHAPTER TWENTY-TWO Owl Post Again

'Yes ... her voice went all deep and her eyes rolled and she said ... she said Voldemort's servant was going to set out to return to him before midnight ... she said the servant would help him come back to power.' Harry stared up at Dumbledore. 'And then she sort of became normal again, and she couldn't remember anything she'd said. Was it – was she making a real prediction?'

Dumbledore looked mildly impressed.

'Do you know, Harry, I think she might have been,' he said thoughtfully. 'Who'd have thought it? That brings her total of real predictions up to two. I should offer her a pay rise ...'

'But –' Harry looked at him, aghast. How could Dumbledore take this so calmly?

'But – I stopped Sirius and Professor Lupin killing Pettigrew! That makes it my fault, if Voldemort comes back!'

'It does not,' said Dumbledore quietly. 'Hasn't your experience with the Time-Turner taught you anything, Harry? The consequences of our actions are always so complicated, so diverse, that predicting the future is a very difficult business indeed ... Professor Trelawney, bless her, is living proof of that. You did a very noble thing, in saving Pettigrew's life.'

'But if he helps Voldemort back to power –!'

'Pettigrew owes his life to you. You have sent Voldemort a deputy who is in your debt. When one wizard saves another wizard's life, it creates a certain bond between them ... and I'm much mistaken if Voldemort wants his servant in the debt of Harry Potter.'

'I don't want a bond with Pettigrew!' said Harry. 'He betrayed my parents!'

'This is magic at its deepest, its most impenetrable, Harry. But trust me ... the time may come when you will be very glad you saved Pettigrew's life.'

Harry couldn't imagine when that would be. Dumbledore looked as though he knew what Harry was thinking.

'I knew your father very well, both at Hogwarts and later, Harry,' he said gently. 'He would have saved Pettigrew too, I am sure of it.'

Harry looked up at him. Dumbledore wouldn't laugh – he could tell Dumbledore ...

'Last night ... I thought it was my dad who'd conjured my Patronus. I mean, when I saw myself across the lake ... I thought I was seeing him.'

第22章 又见猫头鹰传书

"是的……她声音那么低沉，眼珠转来转去，她说……她说伏地魔的仆人午夜之前要动身去和他会合……还说那仆人将帮助他卷土重来。"哈利抬头望着邓布利多，"然后特里劳尼教授又恢复了正常状态，不记得自己说过这些话。会不会——会不会是她做了一个真正的预言？"

邓布利多显得有点惊奇。

"知道吗，哈利，我认为很有可能。"他若有所思地说，"谁想得到呢？这样她总共就做了两个真正的预言了。我该给她加薪……"

"可是——"哈利诧异地看着邓布利多，他的反应怎能如此平静？

"可是——我阻止了小天狼星和卢平教授杀死小矮星！如果伏地魔卷土重来，那就是我的过错了！"

"不，"邓布利多轻声说，"时间转换器没有让你学到一些东西吗，哈利？我们行为的因果关系总是如此复杂、如此多变，所以预测未来是非常困难的……特里劳尼教授就是一个活的证明，愿上帝保佑她……你饶小矮星一命是非常高尚的行为。"

"可是如果他帮伏地魔卷土重来——"

"小矮星的命是你给的。你给伏地魔送去了一个欠你情分的助手……当一个巫师救了另一个巫师的命，他们两人之间就产生了某种联系……如果我猜得不错，伏地魔是不会喜欢他的仆人欠哈利·波特的情分的。"

"我不想跟小矮星有什么联系！"哈利说，"他出卖了我的父母！"

"那是最深奥、最不可捉摸的魔法联系，哈利。但相信我……有一天你会高兴你这次救了小矮星的命。"

哈利无法想象会有那一天。邓布利多似乎洞悉了他的思想。

"我很了解你父亲，在霍格沃茨和后来都很了解，哈利，"他温和地说，"他也会救小矮星的，我相信。"

哈利抬头看着邓布利多。邓布利多不会笑他的——他可以告诉邓布利多……

"昨天晚上……我以为是我爸爸招来的守护神。我是说，当我看到湖对面的自己时……我以为是看到了他。"

CHAPTER TWENTY-TWO   Owl Post Again

'An easy mistake to make,' said Dumbledore softly. 'I expect you're tired of hearing it, but you do look *extraordinarily* like James. Except for your eyes ... you have your mother's eyes.'

Harry shook his head.

'It was stupid, thinking it was him,' he muttered. 'I mean, I knew he was dead.'

'You think the dead we have loved ever truly leave us? You think that we don't recall them more clearly than ever in times of great trouble? Your father is alive in you, Harry, and shows himself most plainly when you have need of him. How else could you produce that *particular* Patronus? Prongs rode again last night.'

It took a moment for Harry to realise what Dumbledore had said.

'Sirius told me all about how they became Animagi last night,' said Dumbledore, smiling. 'An extraordinary achievement – not least, keeping it quiet from me. And then I remembered the most unusual form your Patronus took, when it charged Mr Malfoy down at your Quidditch match against Ravenclaw. So you did see your father last night, Harry ... you found him inside yourself.'

And Dumbledore left the office, leaving Harry to his very confused thoughts.

*   *   *

Nobody at Hogwarts knew the truth of what had happened the night that Sirius, Buckbeak and Pettigrew had vanished except Harry, Ron, Hermione and Professor Dumbledore. As the end of term approached, Harry heard many different theories about what had really happened, but none of them came close to the truth.

Malfoy was furious about Buckbeak. He was convinced that Hagrid had found a way of smuggling the Hippogriff to safety, and seemed outraged that he and his father had been outwitted by a gamekeeper. Percy Weasley, meanwhile, had much to say on the subject of Sirius' escape.

'If I manage to get into the Ministry, I'll have a lot of proposals to make about Magical Law Enforcement!' he told the only person who would listen – his girlfriend, Penelope.

Though the weather was perfect, though the atmosphere was so cheerful, though he knew they had achieved the near impossible in helping Sirius to

第22章 又见猫头鹰传书

"很容易犯的错误，"邓布利多轻声说，"我猜这个话你已经听厌了，但你确实特别像詹姆，除了眼睛……你的眼睛像你妈妈。"

哈利摇摇头。

"真傻，我还以为那是他，"他喃喃地说，"我是说，我明知道他已经死了。"

"你认为我们爱过的人会真正离开我们吗？你不认为在困难的时候，我们会更清晰地想起他们吗？你父亲活在你的心里，哈利，在你需要他的时候他就会格外清晰地显现出来。否则你怎么会召来那样一个特别的守护神呢？昨晚尖头叉子再度驰骋。"

哈利好一会儿才领会到了邓布利多在说什么。

"昨天夜里小天狼星把他们成为阿尼马格斯的事全告诉了我。"邓布利多微笑着说，"真是了不起的成就——能一直瞒着我就不简单。然后我想起了你的守护神那不寻常的形状，它曾在你们对拉文克劳的魁地奇比赛中朝马尔福冲去。哈利，在某种意义上，你昨晚确实看到了你父亲……你发现他在你的心中。"

邓布利多走出了办公室，留下哈利去清理自己纷乱的思绪。

除了哈利、罗恩、赫敏和邓布利多教授之外，霍格沃茨再没有人知道小天狼星、巴克比克和小矮星消失那个晚上的真相。随着期末的临近，哈利听到了许多不同的说法，都是关于那天到底发生了什么的，但没有一个接近事实。

马尔福对巴克比克的事大为恼火，断定海格用某种手段把那头鹰头马身有翼兽偷偷送走了，他们父子居然被一个猎场看守给耍了，这简直是奇耻大辱。与此同时，珀西·韦斯莱则对小天狼星的逃脱有许多高论。

"我要是进了魔法部，一定会提出很多加强执法的方案！"他告诉唯一一个肯听他说话的人——他的女朋友佩内洛。

尽管天气好极了，气氛又这么愉快，尽管哈利知道救走小天狼星是完成了一件几乎不可能的事情，但在期末前的那段日子里他的情绪

CHAPTER TWENTY-TWO   Owl Post Again

freedom, Harry had never approached the end of a school year in worse spirits.

He certainly wasn't the only one who was sorry to see Professor Lupin go. The whole of Harry's Defence Against the Dark Arts class were miserable about his resignation.

'Wonder what they'll give us next year?' said Seamus Finnigan gloomily.

'Maybe a vampire,' suggested Dean Thomas hopefully.

It wasn't only Professor Lupin's departure that was weighing on Harry's mind. He couldn't help thinking a lot about Professor Trelawney's prediction. He kept wondering where Pettigrew was now, whether he had sought sanctuary with Voldemort yet. But the thing that was lowering Harry's spirits most of all was the prospect of returning to the Dursleys. For maybe half an hour, a glorious half hour, he had believed he would be living with Sirius from now on ... his parents' best friend ... it would have been the next best thing to having his own father back. And while no news of Sirius was definitely good news, because it meant he had successfully gone into hiding, Harry couldn't help feeling miserable when he thought of the home he might have had, and the fact that it was now impossible.

The exam results came out on the last day of term. Harry, Ron and Hermione had passed every subject. Harry was amazed that he had got through Potions. He had a shrewd suspicion that Dumbledore had stepped in to stop Snape failing him on purpose. Snape's behaviour towards Harry over the past week had been quite alarming. Harry wouldn't have thought it possible that Snape's dislike for him could increase, but it certainly had done. A muscle twitched unpleasantly at the corner of Snape's thin mouth every time he looked at Harry, and he was constantly flexing his fingers, as though itching to place them around Harry's throat.

Percy had got his top-grade N.E.W.T.s; Fred and George had scraped a handful of O.W.L.s each. Gryffindor house, meanwhile, largely thanks to their spectacular performance in the Quidditch Cup, had won the House Championship for the third year running. This meant that the end-of-term feast took place amid decorations of scarlet and gold, and that the Gryffindor table was the noisiest of the lot, as everybody celebrated. Even Harry managed to forget about the journey back to the Dursleys next day as he ate, drank, talked and laughed with the rest.

第22章 又见猫头鹰传书

比以往期末前要更加低落。

当然，不只是他一个人为卢平教授的离开而难过，与哈利一起上黑魔法防御术课的同学都因卢平离职而感到沮丧。

"不知道明年会给我们派个什么样的老师！"西莫·斐尼甘郁闷地说。

"也许是个吸血鬼。"迪安·托马斯憧憬道。

让哈利心情沉重的不只是卢平教授的辞职。他无法不去仔细思考特里劳妮教授的预言，他一直在想小矮星现在到了哪里，有没有去投靠伏地魔。然而，最令哈利心情压抑的是想到要回德思礼家。在大约半小时——那美妙的半小时里，他曾以为今后可以跟小天狼星一起生活了……他父母最好的朋友……这件事太棒了，仅次于父亲重新回来。没有小天狼星的消息固然是好事，因为这意味着他隐蔽成功，但是哈利想到他本来可以有的家，现在又成为了泡影，就觉得苦不堪言。

学期的最后一天，考试成绩出来了。哈利、罗恩和赫敏每门功课都通过了。哈利惊奇地发现自己的魔药课也及格了。他敏锐地怀疑是邓布利多进行了干预，使斯内普没能故意给他不及格。过去这一个星期斯内普对哈利的态度令人震惊。哈利想不到斯内普对他的厌恶还可能再增加，但事实就是如此。每次看到哈利，斯内普那薄嘴唇一角的肌肉便难看地抽搐起来，他还不停地屈伸手指，好像巴不得能掐住哈利的喉咙。

珀西拿到了N.E.W.T.（终极巫师考试）的高分，弗雷德和乔治也拿了些O.W.L.（普通巫师等级考试）证书。格兰芬多学院主要靠了在魁地奇杯中的出色表现，第三年蝉联学院杯冠军，这意味着期末宴会是在红金两色的装饰中举行，而且格兰芬多的桌子最热闹，人人都在庆祝。哈利也忘记了明天就要回德思礼家的事，跟大家一起又吃又喝，说说笑笑。

CHAPTER TWENTY-TWO   Owl Post Again

As the Hogwarts Express pulled out of the station next morning, Hermione gave Harry and Ron some surprising news.

'I went to see Professor McGonagall this morning, just before breakfast. I've decided to drop Muggle Studies.'

'But you passed your exam with three hundred and twenty per cent!' said Ron.

'I know,' sighed Hermione, 'but I can't stand another year like this one. That Time-Turner, it was driving me mad. I've handed it in. Without Muggle Studies and Divination, I'll be able to have a normal timetable again.'

'I still can't *believe* you didn't tell us about it,' said Ron grumpily. 'We're supposed to be your *friends*.'

'I promised I wouldn't tell *anyone*,' said Hermione severely. She looked around at Harry, who was watching Hogwarts disappear from view behind a mountain. Two whole months before he'd see it again ...

'Oh, cheer up, Harry!' said Hermione sadly.

'I'm OK,' said Harry quickly. 'Just thinking about the holidays.'

'Yeah, I've been thinking about them, too,' said Ron. 'Harry, you've got to come and stay with us. I'll fix it up with Mum and Dad, then I'll call you. I know how to use a fellytone now –'

'A *telephone*, Ron,' said Hermione. 'Honestly, *you* should take Muggle Studies next year ...'

Ron ignored her.

'It's the Quidditch World Cup this summer! How about it, Harry? Come and stay, and we'll go and see it! Dad can usually get tickets from work.'

This proposal had the effect of cheering Harry up a great deal.

'Yeah ... I bet the Dursleys'd be pleased to let me come ... especially after what I did to Aunt Marge ...'

Feeling considerably more cheerful, Harry joined Ron and Hermione in several games of Exploding Snap, and when the witch with the tea trolley arrived, he bought himself a very large lunch, though nothing with chocolate in it.

But it was late in the afternoon before the thing that made him truly happy turned up ...

'Harry,' said Hermione suddenly, peering over his shoulder. 'What's that thing outside your window?'

第22章 又见猫头鹰传书

第二天上午，霍格沃茨特快列车驶出车站时，赫敏向哈利和罗恩宣布了一个意外的消息。

"我早上去见麦格教授了，就在早餐前。我决定不上麻瓜研究了。"

"可是你考了三百二十分呢！"罗恩说。

"我知道，"赫敏叹了口气说，"但我受不了再来这么一年。那个时间转换器快把我弄疯了。我已经把它交回去了。没有了麻瓜研究和占卜，我就又可以有正常的时间表了。"

"我仍然不能相信你竟然没把时间转换器的事告诉我们，"罗恩气鼓鼓地说，"我们还是你的朋友呢。"

"我保证了不告诉任何人的。"赫敏一本正经地说，扭头看看哈利，哈利正凝神注视着霍格沃茨消失在一座山的后面，他要过整整两个月才能再见到它。

"哦，开心点吧，哈利！"赫敏哀求道。

"我没事，"哈利赶快说，"只是在想假期。"

"是啊，我也在想，"罗恩说，"哈利，你一定要住到我家里来。我会跟爸爸妈妈说好的，到时候通知你。我会打串话了——"

"是电话，罗恩，"赫敏说，"说真的，你明年应该学一学麻瓜研究……"

罗恩没理睬她。

"暑假里有魁地奇世界杯！怎么样，哈利？住过来吧，我们一起去看！爸爸那儿一般会发票的。"

这个提议让哈利振作了很多。

"好啊……我打赌德思礼家会很高兴让我走的……尤其是在我对玛姬姑妈做了那样的事之后……"

哈利心情好多了，跟罗恩和赫敏玩了几局噼啪爆炸，当推餐车的女巫过来时，他给自己买了一份大大的午饭，可惜里面没有带巧克力的东西。

临近傍晚时，让他真正快乐起来的事情出现了……

"哈利，"赫敏突然叫道，盯着他的身后，"你的车窗外面是什么呀？"

CHAPTER TWENTY-TWO   Owl Post Again

Harry turned to look outside. Something very small and grey was bobbing in and out of sight beyond the glass. He stood up for a better look and saw that it was a tiny owl, carrying a letter which was much too big for it. The owl was so small, in fact, that it kept tumbling over in the air, buffeted this way and that in the train's slipstream. Harry quickly pulled down the window, stretched out his arm and caught it. It felt like a very fluffy Snitch. He brought it carefully inside. The owl dropped its letter onto Harry's seat and began zooming around their compartment, apparently very pleased with itself for accomplishing its task. Hedwig clicked her beak with a sort of dignified disapproval. Crookshanks sat up in his seat, following the owl with his great yellow eyes. Ron, noticing this, snatched the owl safely out of harm's way.

Harry picked up the letter. It was addressed to him. He ripped open the letter and shouted, 'It's from Sirius!'

'What?' said Ron and Hermione excitedly. 'Read it aloud!'

> *Dear Harry,*
>
> *I hope this finds you before you reach your aunt and uncle. I don't know whether they're used to owl post.*
>
> *Buckbeak and I are in hiding. I won't tell you where, in case this falls into the wrong hands. I have some doubt about the owl's reliability, but he is the best I could find, and he did seem eager for the job.*
>
> *I believe the Dementors are still searching for me, but they haven't a hope of finding me here. I am planning to allow some Muggles to glimpse me soon, a long way from Hogwarts, so that the security on the castle will be lifted.*
>
> *There is something I never got round to telling you during our brief meeting. It was I who sent you the Firebolt –*

'Ha!' said Hermione triumphantly. 'See! I *told* you it was from him!'

'Yes, but he hadn't jinxed it, had he?' said Ron. 'Ouch!'

The tiny owl, now hooting happily in his hand, had nibbled one of his fingers in what it seemed to think was an affectionate way.

> *Crookshanks took the order to the Owl Office for me. I used your*

第22章 又见猫头鹰传书

哈利扭头望去,一个小小的、灰色的东西在窗玻璃外忽上忽下,忽隐忽现。他站起来定睛细看,发现是一只瘦小的猫头鹰,叼着一封对它来说显得过大的信。这只猫头鹰太小了,在空中不停地翻跟头,被火车气流冲得东倒西歪。哈利急忙拉下车窗,伸出手臂抓住了它,感觉像抓住了一个毛茸茸的飞贼。他小心翼翼地把猫头鹰拿了进来,它把信丢在哈利的座位上,开始在车厢里一圈圈地飞,显然对自己完成了任务感到非常满意。海德薇嘴巴发出咔嗒声,高贵地显示出一种不满。克鲁克山在椅子上坐了起来,黄色的大眼睛追随着那只小猫头鹰。罗恩看到了,把猫头鹰抓到了安全的地方。

哈利拿起信,是寄给他的。他撕开信封,叫了一声:"小天狼星!"
"什么?"罗恩和赫敏兴奋地说,"快念!"

亲爱的哈利:
　　希望这封信能在你见到你姨妈和姨父之前送到。我不知道他们是否习惯猫头鹰信使。
　　我和巴克比克藏起来了。我不告诉你藏在哪儿,怕这只猫头鹰会落到坏人手里。我对它的可靠性有些怀疑,但它是我能找到的最好的一只了,而且它似乎很渴望承担这个任务。
　　我相信摄魂怪还在找我,但它们不可能找到这儿来。再过一阵子,我打算让一些麻瓜在远离霍格沃茨的地方看到我,这样城堡的警戒就可以解除了。
　　上次见面太仓促,有件事一直没能告诉你,火弩箭是我送给你的——

"哈!"赫敏得意地说,"看到了吧!我说过是他送的!"
"没错,但他没有给它加恶咒呀,对不对?"罗恩说,"哎哟!"
正在他手中欢叫的小猫头鹰啄了一下他的手指,它似乎觉得那是一种亲昵的方式。

　　克鲁克山替我把订单送到猫头鹰邮局。我用了你的名字,但

CHAPTER TWENTY-TWO — Owl Post Again

name but told them to take the gold from Gringotts vault number seven hundred and eleven — my own. Please consider it as thirteen birthdays' worth of presents from your godfather.

I would also like to apologise for the fright I think I gave you, that night last year when you left your uncle's house. I had only hoped to get a glimpse of you before starting my journey north, but I think the sight of me alarmed you.

I am enclosing something else for you, which I think will make your next year at Hogwarts more enjoyable.

If ever you need me, send word. Your owl will find me.

I'll write again soon.

Sirius

Harry looked eagerly inside the envelope. There was another piece of parchment in there. He read it through quickly and felt suddenly as warm and contented as though he'd swallowed a bottle of hot Butterbeer in one go.

I, Sirius Black, Harry Potter's godfather, hereby give him permission to visit Hogsmeade at weekends.

'That'll be good enough for Dumbledore!' said Harry happily. He looked back at Sirius' letter.

'Hang on, there's a PS …

I thought your friend Ron might like to keep this owl, as it's my fault he no longer has a rat.

Ron's eyes widened. The minute owl was still hooting excitedly.

'Keep him?' he said uncertainly. He looked closely at the owl for a moment, then, to Harry and Hermione's great surprise, he held him out for Crookshanks to sniff.

'What d'you reckon?' Ron asked the cat. 'Definitely an owl?'

Crookshanks purred.

第22章 又见猫头鹰传书

是让他们从古灵阁的711号金库——我自己的金库里取出了金子。请把它当作教父补偿给你的十三岁的生日礼物。

　　我还想为一件事向你道歉,去年你离开你姨父家时被我吓着了吧,我只是想在我去北方之前看你一眼,但我的样子好像让你感到恐慌了。

　　我附了一样东西给你,我想它会让你下一学期在霍格沃茨的生活更愉快一些。

　　如果需要我,就捎个信。你的猫头鹰能找到我。

　　我很快还会写信给你。

小天狼星

哈利急切地往信封里看,里面还有一张羊皮纸。他迅速扫了一遍,顿时像一口气喝了一瓶热黄油啤酒一样,浑身暖洋洋的,洋溢着心满意足的快乐。

　　本人小天狼星布莱克,哈利·波特的教父,同意他周末去霍格莫德。

"给邓布利多看这个就行了。"哈利高兴地说。他又看了看小天狼星的信。

"哎,这儿还有一句,又及……"

　　我想你的朋友罗恩也许愿意收养这只猫头鹰,是我害得他失去了那只老鼠。

罗恩瞪大了眼睛。小猫头鹰还在兴奋地大叫。

"收养它?"他半信半疑地说,仔细盯着那只猫头鹰看了一会儿,然后,大大出乎哈利和赫敏的意料,他把它递过去让克鲁克山嗅了嗅。

"你说呢?"罗恩问那只大猫,"肯定是猫头鹰吗?"

克鲁克山喵喵叫了两声。

CHAPTER TWENTY-TWO — Owl Post Again

'That's good enough for me,' said Ron happily. 'He's mine.'

Harry read and reread the letter from Sirius all the way back into King's Cross station. It was still clutched tightly in his hand as he, Ron and Hermione stepped back through the barrier of platform nine and three-quarters. Harry spotted Uncle Vernon at once. He was standing a good distance from Mr and Mrs Weasley, eyeing them suspiciously, and when Mrs Weasley hugged Harry in greeting, his worst suspicions about them seemed confirmed.

'I'll call about the World Cup!' Ron yelled after Harry, as Harry bid him and Hermione goodbye, then wheeled the trolley bearing his trunk and Hedwig's cage towards Uncle Vernon, who greeted him in usual fashion.

'What's that?' he snarled, staring at the envelope Harry was still clutching in his hand. 'If it's another form for me to sign, you've got another –'

'It's not,' said Harry cheerfully. 'It's a letter from my godfather.'

'Godfather?' spluttered Uncle Vernon. 'You haven't got a godfather!'

'Yes, I have,' said Harry brightly. 'He was my mum and dad's best friend. He's a convicted murderer, but he's broken out of wizard prison and he's on the run. He likes to keep in touch with me, though ... keep up with my news ... check I'm happy ...'

And grinning broadly at the look of horror on Uncle Vernon's face, Harry set off towards the station exit, Hedwig rattling along in front of him, for what looked like a much better summer than the last.

第22章 又见猫头鹰传书

"对我来说够好的了,"罗恩快活地说,"它归我啦。"

哈利把小天狼星的信读了一遍又一遍,直到列车驶进国王十字车站。他跟罗恩和赫敏穿过 $9\frac{3}{4}$ 站台的隔墙时,仍然把信紧紧攥在手里。哈利一下子就认出了弗农姨父。他站在离韦斯莱夫妇比较远的地方,怀疑地打量着这两个人。当韦斯莱夫人和哈利拥抱问候时,他对他们的怀疑似乎被证实了。

"我会打电话说世界杯的事!"罗恩在哈利身后喊道,哈利跟两位朋友道过别,用手推车推着行李箱和海德薇的笼子朝弗农姨父走去,弗农姨父用一贯的方式迎接了他。

"那是什么?"他瞪着哈利攥在手里的信封吼道,"如果又是要我签字的表格,你必须有——"

"不是,"哈利欣然说道,"是我教父的来信。"

"教父?"弗农姨父疑惑地问,"你没有教父!"

"我有,"哈利神采飞扬地说,"他是我爸爸妈妈最好的朋友,他被判了杀人罪,但他从巫师监狱里逃出来了,现在仍然出逃在外。他愿意跟我保持联系……了解我的情况……看我过得开不开心……"

看到弗农姨父脸上恐惧的表情,哈利开心地笑了。他迈步走向出站口,海德薇在前面发出咔啦啦的轻响,这个暑假看起来会比上一个美好得多。